ORDER OF THE SEERS

BOOK I

CERECE RENNIE MURPHY

This book is dedicated to my mother:

"Every good thing I am, you taught me…You don't have to keep
on paying for what you bought me, just look at me—here I stand. I'm
your girl, your little girl, then and now and always."
– Phoebe Snow

Other Titles by Cerece Rennie Murphy

Order of the Seers — Book I

Order of the Seers: The Red Order — Book II

Order of the Seers: The Last Seer — Book III (Coming Soon!)

Acknowledgements

My deepest love and gratitude to my family and friends. To my first editor and dear friend, Jessica Faulkner, thank you for being the literary "Shaft" who saved this story from all manner of grammatical missteps and plot mayhem. You're one bad…well, you know. To my brother Al, Trice Hickman, Shawna McGerr, Lori McMullin, Danielle Cox, Monica Washington, Kamishia Lee, Ebony Ross, Michael Daugherty, Stephanie Carnes, Kea Taylor, Jessica Tilles, Samiha Dauk, Kenya Johnson, Kareem Murphy, DeWayne Davis, Shon Thomas and so many others who not only read this story, but took the time to tell me that they liked it. Your love, talent, constructive criticism and encouragement made this book possible. To my husband, Sekou, thank you for giving me the best that you've got – every day. I love you.

ORDER OF THE SEERS

BOOK I

CHAPTER 1: THE END

Sunday, June 22, 2008

L iam was losing his patience. "Aw, come on! Are you serious? You can't want to ride this thing again!"

Instead of answering her older brother, Lilli remained in her seat as the Ferris wheel conductor looked on expectantly, hand outstretched and waiting for another two tokens.

The way Lilli's skinny arms hugged her book bag while she stared blankly at the pressed metal floor of their "Fairy Land Caboose" made it hard for Liam to stay angry. The sight of her looking so dejected softened him enough to give the conductor his fifth set of tokens in less than 45 minutes. Liam settled back into his seat just as the lap bar clamped down uncomfortably against his thighs.

"Lilli, say something. Why'd you drag me out here if you were just gonna sulk? I hate the carnival, you know that."

"I know something… okay? Just… trust me. We have to stay here." Her voice was so low he could barely hear her over the wind-up music that was blaring from the overhead speakers.

"Did Mom say something to you?"

Lilli responded to his question with silence and a barely discernable shake of her head back and forth. He tried again.

"Lilli! Did Mom…?"

"Yes," she snapped.

They both fell silent again as Liam took in the latest weird thing of the day. Lilith Knight, or Lilli as she preferred to be called, had always been strange. Even when she was five, she could beat Liam at chess lazily, without even thinking about it. She would find things and give them to you before you asked for them. Before you, or even she, knew why. Up until recently, he thought she was just a freak. *No biggie. All little sisters are like that,* he told himself.

It was only in the past few months that his perception of her began to shift, after her prediction that he would catch his new girlfriend, Krista, kissing his teammate Lance in the locker room after their championship game. At the time, he'd brushed off her premonition as meddling. Krista wasn't even his girlfriend and his team was 1-1 with the whole basketball season ahead of them.

He'd forgotten her warning completely until two months later when he ran back into the locker room after winning the championship to get the jacket he'd left behind and immediately smelled Krista's perfume. When he found them, two thoughts overshadowed the scene unfolding in front of him. The first was that what they were doing wasn't really "kissing," though he could see how a sheltered thirteen-year-old would describe it that way. His second thought was that Lilli was right; she was exactly right. He was so stunned by Lilli's accuracy that he didn't even bother to disturb them, leaving his new ex-girlfriend and her new boyfriend to their business. From that moment, Liam understood that Lilli wasn't *just* a freak, or more accurately, that she wasn't a freak at all. She was special…gifted.

The sound of Lilli's sniffling followed by the trembling of her body as she began to cry uncontrollably broke the long silence that had fallen between them. *What the…,* Liam half-mumbled as his mind swung from irritation to absolute bewilderment. Slowly and deliberately, Liam moved his palms down the front of his face as he fought the urge to shake the truth right out of her and end whatever this was. But he couldn't. *She's so brittle already,* he thought, without any idea as to why. So instead, he reached out to envelop his sister in his arms, trying to soothe her and comfort her from some unknown force.

"Lilli, it's all right. I'm sorry, okay? Don't cry. Just... tell me what's going on. Why are we here?"

He tried to wait patiently, to rein in the confusion and frustration that had been piercing through the calm day he had planned for himself when he woke up that morning, as cool and carefree as any sixteen-year-old boy. It was Lilli who had dragged him out of the house before he could even wolf down his second bowl of Honeycombs. *"Mom said you have to take me to the carnival. NOW!"* She had demanded.

He had started to head upstairs to launch his appeal when his eye caught his mother's note on the refrigerator door. "Take Lilli to the fair. NOW. — Love, Mom," it read. He knew that meant his mother had left the house early; there was no appeal to be made. Begrudgingly, he slipped on his sneakers and grabbed the car keys, all the while wondering if Lilli was still too young to be left at the fair by herself.

His earlier thoughts of abandonment brought him back to his sister's form beside him. Not knowing what else to do, Liam simply held her tight as her convulsing turned to trembling, and finally, back to stillness. At the top of the Ferris wheel, she finally spoke.

"It's over now, we can go home," she whispered. But as impatient for answers and a reprieve from big brother duties as he was, Liam knew that it was not over. The emotionless tone in her voice scared him. It made him want to stay on the Ferris wheel he'd been begging to get off of a few short minutes ago. As the music died down and their feet got closer to the ground, he suddenly felt conflicting urges to stay where he was and to rush home to his mother. As the ride came to a stop, he suddenly realized with profound certainty that this was much more than one of Lilli's "episodes." Something was very, very wrong.

When Liam pulled his father's green 2002 Saab in front of their small brick house, everything seemed as it always did — quiet and predictable in their modest yet comfortable home. They had lived in a much bigger house before his father died, but Liam never minded sharing a bathroom with his mother and sister. All the toys and trinkets that had mattered to him when he was a child were rendered insignificant the moment his mother told him that his father would never come home again. As he got out of the car and began to take the front steps two at a time, he noticed that Lilli had stopped at the tree stump his mother had cut down the week before. Sitting down, her eyes remained on the ground. Just as his mouth formed the shape of a question, she spoke.

"No, you go. I can't see it again."

Liam didn't stop to ask what she meant. Whatever she meant, he was sure it was worse than he thought. He tried to hold back the swell of fear in his chest as he ran to the front door, but his emotions spun out of control the moment he tested the front door knob and found it opened — easily. They never left the front door unlocked.

When he stepped into the house, he actually felt the life, the person he had been, rush past him and out the door as his eyes took in the overturned, splintered remains of their living room. It was a feeling he'd felt only once before, when his father died. But what made it worse, what made it permanent, was lying in the middle of the floor, with its contents thrown everywhere. It was his mother's purse, which had not been there when he left that morning.

"Mom!" he shouted as he raced up the stairs to her room. "Mom. Please!" he shouted again, but no one answered. In every room he looked, it was the same: scattered clothes, broken mirrors, and silence—a deafening silence that rang louder than the sound of his own shallow breathing.

If he took the stairs at lightning speed to make it to the second floor, an age could have passed during his descent. The entire house consisted of three bedrooms, one and a half bathrooms, a kitchen, a living room, and a small open dining area that you could see clearly from the front door. As he walked down the steps, he knew there was only one room left to check. His mind was frozen on what to hope for as his hand reached the end of the banister. If she wasn't in the kitchen, she might have been taken, but at least there was a chance she was still alive. If she was in the kitchen, it was unthinkable.

Lilli's words came to him just as he rounded the doorway to the kitchen.

"No, you go. I can't see it again."

He found his mother sitting with her feet planted on the floor, shoulder width apart, bright eyes open and cast to the ceiling, with a hole blown through the middle of her chest.

Liam braced himself against the door frame as he began to sob, the sounds seemingly emanating from a place far away from where he stood. He could not look away from the horrific image before him, the last image of his mother. He stood there with wide-eyed and tear-stained pain as the last measure of his youth drained from him like blood rushing from an open vein. When it was done, his body slid to the ground.

We are alone, he thought. *There's no one left.*

Ever since his father had died, Liam lived in fear that one day he would lose her. Unable to tear his eyes away from her body, he could hear her vehemently denying that there would ever be a time when she wasn't with them. *"Never,"* she would say.

Never, he thought, *has finally come.*

Though Liam had been staring at her body since he entered the kitchen, he had not seen the gun in her hand until he noticed a fly land on it. Years of training to keep the gun out of Lilli's sight made him jump to his feet until he remembered that Lilli was still outside. He knew the gun well; it was his mother's. She had taught him how to use it and to keep it out of Lilli's reach when she was small.

At first his mind could not decipher the meaning of the scene before him. *Was he meant to believe that she did this to herself? Why would the people who broke into their house ransack the place and then try to make it look like a suicide?* But he couldn't think straight, couldn't figure out the logic or the answer to any of the crazy questions running through his mind. *Why would she kill herself?* He was sure the answers were obvious; he just wasn't making sense. None of this was making any sense.

His confusion caused him to draw closer to her body. Kneeling down beside his mother, Liam took the lifeless hand that dangled at her side, the one that was not holding the gun. Though his eyes were still filled with tears, they were no longer breaking through the barriers of his lower lids. This momentary fortitude allowed him to have the courage to look directly into her face and see her open smile. The sight of it knocked him down and back into the base cabinets. *She was smiling. She was smiling,* he thought. *She had known what was coming, and she was smiling.*

Suddenly, he remembered his mother's constant warning every time they went to the shooting range. *"Don't pick up a gun unless you mean to use it. There can be no hesitation. Do you understand me?"* she would ask him sternly. Liam knew Jill Knight was skilled at using a firearm. If she had a chance to draw her gun, no one could take it from her. The implications made him immediately sick and angry before their full meaning could even register.

As if retching the contents of his stomach into the kitchen sink made room for clarity, he suddenly understood the reason behind her smile. She had killed herself. She had done this to herself, on purpose. He threw up again in a wave of protest at the notion that she would abandon them, even as the resentment of her betrayal took root. When he was done, he didn't want to turn around, didn't want to face her.

How could she do this? She wouldn't do this. She promised.

Holding himself up at the sink, his thoughts turned to Lilli. *Is this what she saw?* he wondered, fighting a new wave of nausea. *No wonder she cried like that. No wonder...* Rather than try to sort out the conflict of thoughts and emotions inside him, he decided to check on Lilli and make sure that she remained outside while he tried to figure out what to do next.

As he peered over his shoulder toward the doorway, his eyes caught the folded cuff of his mother's sweatshirt, which was turquoise save for the blood, and a little corner of white paper that was peeking out. He knew his mother hid things in the cuff of her sleeve all the time; it was one of the many old lady habits Liam enjoyed teasing her about. He stared at the white edge of paper for a long time, warring with his own feelings of anger and grief before simple curiosity forced him to bend down and retrieve it. As his fingers curved around the edge of her sleeve, he could feel something flat and hard inside. When he rolled down her sleeve to get it, the key to his gym locker at school slipped out before he could fully unroll the note. When he did, it unleashed a new avalanche of questions upon heartbreak over questions.

In his mother's tiny cursive handwriting, the note read, *'Go now. Protect her.'* Liam felt a new level of understanding peel back in his mind as he read her note again. He began to see the very real possibility that perhaps his mother had not wanted to do this to herself. Perhaps she was forced by the same people who came into their home. The same people who she wanted him to protect Lilli from now. Liam grabbed the key off the floor before rising to meet his mother's eyes one last time. They looked so different from how they had even two minutes ago and held so much he couldn't understand, couldn't handle right now. He closed his eyes and softly kissed her on her forehead before running out of his home for what he knew would be the last time.

Liam closed the front door behind him and turned to find Lilli sitting exactly where he left her twenty minutes before. He had only two objectives at that point: making sure that she was safe, and getting the hell out of there. As Liam scanned the neighborhood for anything suspicious, he took in the studied quiet of his block. There was no one on the street at 11:23 am on a beautiful Sunday morning. *Where is everyone,* he wondered, suddenly wary of the neighbors with whom he had grown up. *How had no one heard the gunshot? Why didn't anyone call the police?*

The tremor in his neighbors' curtains gave credence to the sensation that they were being watched, but no one would step outside to help them. This realization came over him with a bitterness that cast itself over all the sorrow he held inside. *They had all been witnesses,* he guessed, *but they would no longer be friends.*

Watching Liam as he crossed the small front lawn to reach her, Lilli was struck by how much older her brother looked compared to just a few hours ago. Though his straight black hair hung as sloppy and heavy as it always did over his blue-green eyes, there was none of the playful nonchalance that usually characterized her brother's disposition. His hair was slick, spiked, and jet black with sweat, and it framed the angles of his face in a way that made her easy-going brother look cold and menacing. But it wasn't a surprise, Lilli could see everything Liam felt on his face — anger, sorrow, betrayal, and a ferocity emerging that she did not understand. Seeing her brother so unlike himself made Lilli's face crumple in agony as she trembled under the weight of her own choices.

"I'm sorry, Liam," she begged in between sobs. "I know you're mad at me for not telling you. Mom told me that if I did, they would kill you. She said I had to be strong enough... strong enough to save you."

"Shhh, Lilli. It's all right. We'll talk about this later. Don't cry. Shhh."

Lilli knew Liam meant his response to be soothing, but his words came out cold, devoid of any life or feeling behind them. When she looked up to search his face and understand the hollowness in his voice, she found him scanning the street with the same look of fierceness. Something in the clenched set of his jaw made her finally understand. He was determined to keep her alive, to protect the only family he had left.

"We need to go," he said, as he led her to the car.

"Where?"

"I don't know, Lilli. I don't know."

Chapter 2: Botched Job

It…disturbs me greatly—our failure today…" Miguel Far spoke quietly as he stared out the window of their black SUV. He was not the sort of man who was familiar with failure in anything. The feelings of inadequacy that hovered like fog around the edges of his stoic countenance were foreign and unwelcome. They made him shift in his seat, restlessly, as he tried to shake them off.

Jason Earley merely shrugged his shoulders in response. His only disappointment with the botched capture of Lilith Knight was in the missed opportunity to use his gun, like they had planned.

"The mother knew we were coming. She…anticipated our plan. She waited for us and then killed herself to stop us!" Miguel continued. He felt incredulous even as he tried to put the pieces together. No one stopped them. It was a point of professional pride that whenever he was sent to gather a Seer, he *always* brought his target back. To be empty handed, with neither a hostage to leverage nor a Seer in hand, was almost inconceivable to him.

Exasperated by Miguel's inability to let it go, Jason offered up the only points he felt were worth making. "Look, she was probably born to some hippie woman out in who cares where. I mean, she barely had a birth certificate, remember? There was no way we could have known the mother was a Seer. The Guild will understand. Besides, we still scared the heck out of the neighbors," Jason added with a chuckle. "Did you see the looks on their faces when we told them there was a Seer in their precious little community? If those kids come back, no one will help them. That's for sure."

Miguel met Jason's explanation with a sideways glance that did little to mask his disdain for Jason's half-baked theories. Miguel had worked with Jason for two years, and while Miguel respected Jason's abilities as an enforcer, they were co-workers in Miguel's eyes–not equals, not friends.

"There is more here than we have discovered today," Miguel responded, through gritted teeth. "The entire house didn't have a single picture in it. No paperwork or vital documents. Why? She knew that we knew about the girl, so what else was she hiding? She killed herself so that we would never know. If the mother and the daughter were Seers, do you know what that would *mean*? It's never happened before, and we *lost* them!" Miguel took a long, deep breath to calm himself before continuing. "So, no, this will not be forgiven by the Guild."

Miguel and Jason were silent for the rest of the trip as they each considered the consequences that awaited them when they returned to Chicago. After just under 6 hours of driving, Jason finally pulled over on the service road behind a large, modern house at the end of a *cul de sac*. The atmosphere inside the car shifted palpably as both men prepared for another gathering.

"We'll figure out what happened later," Miguel said, as if they were in mid-conversation. "We need to make sure this goes…" He trailed off as he watched Jason slip his gold Desert Eagle pistol with custom tiger striping into his inside jacket pocket.

"What the hell do you think you're doing?"

"Just in case," Jason smiled sheepishly.

"This is a gas leak, not a burglary. You were sloppy enough back there at the Knights," Miguel snapped, as he leaned over and yanked the gun from Jason's jacket. "Use your damn hands if you have to, but no guns. We need this one to be clean." Jason was about to protest, but then thought better of it as he stared into Miguel's icy blue eyes. Even though Jason was slightly taller than Miguel, Jason knew enough to be intimidated by his partner. If Miguel wanted you dead, that was exactly what would happen. Jason never wanted to be caught on the unforgiving side of Miguel's calculations. Miguel had been with the Guild for a long time–almost ten years. He had earned the right to kill without question.

With the discussion over, Jason pulled on his black baseball cap and grabbed his tool kit before handing Miguel his matching cap and duffel bag. They became single-file shadows as they stepped out of the SUV and headed into the Parsons' backyard. Once they were inside the high fence, they broke formation with Jason moving wordlessly to locate the main gas line while Miguel circled the house to make sure all family members were present.

It was a beautiful, lazy Sunday afternoon, and everyone was where they should be. Mrs. Parsons was in the kitchen making a late afternoon snack while Mr. Parsons and his son lounged on the couch watching TV in the family room. Their daughter, Emma, glanced at the TV occasionally from the desk behind the couch while texting her boyfriend. From the surveillance report that he had received en route to the Parsons, Miguel knew that the neighbors would not be a problem. The Reeses were conveniently away on a surprise sweepstakes vacation, and the Mosleys were busy arguing in the bedroom while their five-year-old daughter watched Barney videos in the kitchen and pretended not to hear them.

Miguel retraced his steps to the back porch just before making final contact with Jason on his wireless earpiece.

"Target confirmed. Take the front. Keep it quiet."

Despite Miguel's reservations about Jason's intelligence and character, he knew Jason was good at what he did. It was the only reason he had let him stick around for longer than the year it took to train an enforcer. Jason was fast and efficient in hand-to-hand combat and exacting and careful most of the time. Miguel guessed that the real reason why Jason was sloppy at the last gathering was because he was pissed off that he didn't get to use his gun. With most Seer gatherings being staged as accidental deaths, Jason rarely got a chance to use his favorite weapon. *He loves that thing*, Miguel thought ruefully as he watched Mrs. Parsons make her way from the stove to the wastebasket closest to Miguel and the back door.

This is just too easy.

Miguel knew he needed to start the gathering by taking Mrs. Parsons first. Cooperation was facilitated best when the strongest in the family felt responsible for protecting the weakest. At 5'3" and already suffering from early-onset osteoporosis, Mrs. Parsons was shorter and frailer than her youngest child. Miguel slipped the spare key that the family left under their doormat into the back door slowly as he watched Mrs. Parsons recycle the popcorn bag and turn toward the living room.

Suburbia, he thought with a smirk as he eased the back door open. The breeze coming from behind him was the only thing that alerted her to his presence, but by the time she turned around to catch the first glimpse of his face, it was already too late. His left-hand grip was deadly around her neck as he quickly closed his right hand over her mouth and began walking her towards the family room. She didn't even have a chance to inhale the breath she needed to scream. No one heard the sound of the plastic mixing bowl as it hit the linoleum, scattering popcorn under their feet.

For Miguel, Jason's entry through the front door was equally satisfying. Timing was an important element of inspiring the cooperation necessary to stage a proper gathering. The stealth of Miguel's entrance–followed by Jason's more dramatic kick-down-the-door approach–helped to elicit the perfect blend of surprise and terror in the hearts of the target family. Each face, no matter how brave, displayed the same mix of emotion every time: surprise, terror and protectiveness at the sudden sight of Miguel, followed quickly by complete and overwhelmed surrender at the subsequent appearance of Jason. No matter how many family members were present, the effect of this synchronized attack left families feeling completely outnumbered.

Miguel had done it for so long that he could track the stages like clockwork. Once they accepted surrender as their only option, each family member entered what Miguel called the scavenger stage, when each person became willing to do whatever it took to simply survive. This was the mindset needed to break a Seer.

"Don't make a sound," Miguel announced calmly as he walked Mrs. Parsons into the family room to stand just in front of the enormous flat screen TV. As he moved, he could feel her tears rolling down and in-between the fingers of his hand. Each tear tickled then cooled under the steady flow from the air conditioner vents.

Good, he thought as he appraised their frozen faces. *This group will be easy, docile.*

He nodded toward Jason, who quickly grabbed Emma from her place behind the couch and held her to him closely.

"Shhh," Jason purred into her ear seductively as she began to cry. From behind her, Jason noticed the way her fear caused her nipples to pebble under the thin cotton of her t-shirt and licked his lips appreciatively. *Emma*, he thought, *I think her name is Emma.*

"Shhh, Emma. I know you have a boyfriend, but you could learn to like me, too," he whispered loud enough for everyone to hear.

Instinctively, her father jumped up from the couch, holding his son tightly behind him. "Oh God, please, no… don't do this. We'll give you anything you want. Just don't do this…" Mr. Parsons begged just as Mrs. Parsons' arms began flailing wildly toward her daughter.

"Enough, Jason!" Miguel roared before tightening his grip on Mrs. Parsons' throat, then turning his attention to Mr. Parsons.

"If you are quiet, no harm will come to your daughter. I promise," Miguel offered, as he willed Mr. Parsons to sit back down with the mere force of his gaze. It worked. It always worked.

They had only been in the house for twenty-two seconds.

Mr. Parsons sat back on the couch, nervously gripping the only child he could reach.

"Good. Very good," Miguel cooed as he set Mrs. Parsons gently down in a nearby arm chair. When he released his hands from her neck and mouth, he knew she would not run or shift from her location. She was nearly catatonic with fear. Only her eyes moved as they roamed the faces of the people she loved most. Trying to remember them laughing for the last time. *She knows*, Miguel thought. *The mother always knows.*

Miguel crouched down beside her and slid the duffel bag he'd been carrying from his shoulder. As he dragged the zipper slowly open, he felt like a magician who had hypnotized the crowd. All eyes watched him as he opened the bag. If there was anything that amused him about his job, that was it, as he tried to imagine pulling a white rabbit from his bag rather than a gas mask.

He nodded again to Jason just before pulling the mask out. At his signal, Jason pulled a syringe filled with tranquilizer from his jacket pocket and stabbed it into Emma's neck. The force of the blow made her knees buckle as she felt a strange tingle, followed by numbness, spreading over her limbs. She could hear her mother and brother's screams and some scuffling sounds as her father yelled, "Please stop!" But she couldn't see them from where she fell. Even though she could no longer move, Emma realized that all her other senses were completely alert as Jason dragged her from behind the couch to lay her on the floor facing her family.

While her body lay listless, she watched as Jason covered her face with a mask, just before Miguel sprayed an aerosol into the air. All around, her family began to scatter. Her father tried to push her brother out of the room, but was immediately yanked back from his efforts by Miguel and thrown to the floor just as he began to gag and choke. She could see blood begin to leak from his eyes and mouth as he convulsed, but she could not blink, could not look away. Her brother went next, making his way only a few feet before stumbling and succumbing to the same fate as her father. While she could not see his face, she could hear the gurgling sounds in his throat become softer and softer as he died. Miraculously, her mother was the only one who remained upright, crying, even in death, with red streaks down her face.

Emma only knew she was crying when her face began to recover its sensation and she could feel the dampness of her hair pressed against her cheek, but she had no need of her muscles now. When she needed them to fight for her family, they had failed her. Now that her family was gone, her only hope was to catch a whiff of whatever had taken them from her. But that was not what Miguel and Jason had planned. She could see the shins of their pants moving around quickly as they arranged her parents' bodies at different locations on the floor. But when it came to her brother, Jason simply turned her brother's body to face her so that she could memorize the pain and sweat and blood on his face.

"We're three minutes thirty-two seconds in. Quit playing with that boy and get the bag. We need to get out of here now to be far enough from the blast."

Just as she heard Miguel say the words, she thought she could smell the gas. Emma screamed in protest, but it came out as a muffled groan behind the mask she still wore as Jason yanked her up from the floor and over his shoulder. She felt him run with her to their SUV and prop her up length-wise in the back seat. Why he took the time to buckle her in she couldn't imagine, but it gave her a perfect view of her house as it blew up in the distance, taking all her family and her sanity with it.

CHAPTER 3: 1 YEAR, 9 MONTHS AND COUNTING...

March 2010

They had traveled from Oregon to Texas to New Mexico to San Francisco, mostly hiding, mostly scared. It had been almost two years since their mom had died, and Liam couldn't stop running, from the sight of his mother's body in the kitchen and the fact that every night since, his mind readily replaced her body with Lilli's. It was an easy reminder of what was at stake if he failed.

After they had walked away from their home, Liam drove around the outskirts of town for hours before he felt safe enough to go back to his school and retrieve whatever his mother had left for him in his locker. As they hid in the Riverside County car impound lot waiting for nightfall, Lilli lay on the backseat, having cried herself to sleep with the burger and fries her brother bought for her uneaten on the floor. He couldn't blame her. *I only saw the aftermath,* Liam thought with a shudder. *She saw it happen.*

He couldn't imagine the gift and the burden she was now carrying. Just the thought of it stamped out any anger he held towards Lilli for keeping him in the dark. He was sorry she had to do it, but his mother had been right. If he'd had even a clue about what was happening, he would have gone back, would have tried to save her, and would have gladly gotten himself killed for the chance.

There among the rusted cars, Liam huddled, red-eyed and shaken, in the driver's seat. Though his facial expression was frozen in a state of shock, inside he was fighting desperately to balance the torrent of grief that threatened to overtake him with the need to come up with a plan—quickly.

Where do we live? What do I do for money? His thoughts raced as he tried to keep his mind from shutting down completely. The only real job he'd ever had was as a summer lifeguard at the local pool, and he was pretty sure that what he made wouldn't even pay for a safe place to sleep. He had some savings bonds in his name, but he wasn't sure if he could even cash them in before he was eighteen. *At least it's summer,* Liam thought with a hint of relief. He wouldn't have to worry about school until the fall.

The thought of figuring out their education brought tears to his eyes as he realized that his mother would not be there to do any of the things she always did. "No, don't go there," he begged aloud as he tried to banish the thought from his mind. *I'll figure this out. We've just got to keep moving,* he told himself as he wiped his eyes with the heels of his hands. His mother had always said he had good instincts, but he'd never really given any thought to if it was true or how it might be applied. Now he needed to trust them, whether she was right or not.

'Go now. Protect her.'

What if I need help? Who can I trust?

It was only after this thought, after hours in the car, that he remembered that he still didn't have his cell phone. *I probably shouldn't call anyone anyway.* As his mind processed the thought, a new, sobering possibility crept in. *Maybe no one is safe.* The recollection of his neighbors' inaction made him rigid with tension as he tried to find a place in his body to manage the overwhelming feeling created by his newfound sense of isolation, but he couldn't. So, the tears began to slip from his eyes like too much water spilling over the rim of a cup. His uncontrolled tears made him feel so small, so unequal to the task his mother had left for him. He sensed, even as he cried, that he didn't have time for his doubts.

I need to figure out what we're going to do, how we're going to live, he pleaded as he tried to get himself back under control. Before he could succumb to the fear and despair he felt, Liam decided to start driving back to Salem. When he pulled into the parking lot behind his school, his only hope was that his mother had left some clue for him as to what he should do next. When he and Lilli finally opened the door to his locker, Liam realized his mother had left them that and more.

On top of a large duffel bag stuffed with clothes for him and Lilli, he found a brand new cell phone and a large manila envelope. He handed Lilli the envelope while he turned on the phone. Once it was on, he saw that one text message was already waiting for him.

[June 22, 2008: 7:54AM] Don't call anyone. They will begin looking for you again tomorrow. You have until then to leave OR. Head to TX. Drive. The videos on this phone will explain more. Love always, Mom

Liam was still staring at the text when he heard Lilli's soft gasp beside him. "Oh my God!"

He looked up to see that Lilli had fanned out at least three dozen $100 bills in her hands. They stared at each other in amazement as they tried to comprehend how their mother had come by more money than they had ever seen in their lives. Jill Knight had always been generous with her love and frugal with her money. While they never wanted for what they needed, extras were few and far between. Liam and Lilli had always assumed it was because her job as an art teacher at their school didn't pay a lot. The crisp bills now in Lilli's hands seemed to suggest something else.

Disoriented by the notion of even a small measure of wealth, they put the money aside and went through the rest of the package. There was a map of Texas with an arrow drawn near Galveston and a post-it with an address for Home Town Bank, N.A,, a new driver's license for Liam, birth certificates, social security cards, a set of new passports, a small silver key inside a plastic bag with a five digit code scribbled on another post-it, two new sets of license plates, a business card for a person named Nigel Smith, and three pictures—one each of Liam and Lilli as babies, and their last family photo when all of them were alive and happy.

Lilli gently took their family photo from Liam when she saw his hands begin to shake.

"I know… I know we need to go, Lilli," he said after a moment. "I just can't move. I already feel like we've been running for so long and we haven't even started yet."

"Liam, you don't have to figure everything out alone. We're a family now. You and me."

They stared at each other for a long time, seeking and finding the strength they needed to face whatever would begin once they left the only life they knew. After gathering the sum total of their belongings, they made their way back to the car. Just before checking the directions his mother had left them for heading to Galveston, Liam turned to Lilli to ask her the question that he both wanted and dreaded to know.

"Lilli… I don't want to push you, but if you can do what I think you can do, it could help us. I need to ask you… if you see anything?"

Lilli sighed heavily. She had been thinking the same thing and beating herself up for not being of more use.

"No, not yet, but… I'm trying," she whispered as she looked down at her hands.

"Ok."

Even though Liam couldn't think of anything else to say, he took comfort in the fact that he wasn't the only one trying to move forward in the dark.

Because Liam knew he couldn't handle seeing his mother's face so soon after her death, they decided that Lilli would watch the videos that their mother left them while he listened as they drove to Galveston.

With the first video, they learned that their mother was a Seer, but had been afraid of it all her life. She hid it from everyone except their father, who was so inspired by her ability that he left his lucrative position at a private medical research company to join a group of international scientists studying paranormal behavior. As she told them these stories, Liam and Lilli could hear the pride mixed with the sadness in her voice.

"*Your father was a brilliant man,*" she began. "*He was among the group of scientists that first discovered the genetic marker for the Seer gift. Willem, Eli, and so many others, only meant to discover and understand the potential in all of us. They had no idea that their work would be used to hurt people.*"

Though Jill tried to keep the trembling from her voice, her children could still hear how haunted she was as she finally told them the truth about their father, Willem Knight's death.

"*When your father discovered what they were going to do, what the Guild would try to do, he tried to stop them. Please forgive me for what I am about to say. I only lied because I didn't want to burden you with this, but there is no way to protect you now. My time is up and you need to know.*"

Liam and Lilli could hear her take a long, deep breath before she continued. As Jill shifted on the gym locker bench where she sat, Lilli could see her mother's whole demeanor change. The confessional, quiet bearing Jill had kept up to this point was replaced with a steely expression that Lilli recognized from less than twenty-four hours ago. It spoke of her anger, her fierceness. As she watched her mother's nostrils flare, Lilli realized how much it reminded her of Liam's face as he'd led her from their home. A strange sense of relief replaced another corner of her fear as she accepted that this part of her mother, a part she had never really seen before, was still with her in Liam.

"Your father didn't die in a car accident like I told you. He was murdered - tortured and murdered - by an organization known as The Guild; the same group that claims to manage and rehabilitate Seers, but that's not what they do. The Seers they use are kidnapped and enslaved for their ability to see the future. The Guild uses that power to control us. All of us."

Her words were clipped, rough, and sure. As soon as Liam heard his mother admit that their father had not died in a car accident, he put on his right-turn signal and began moving toward the shoulder of the highway.

As they pulled to a stop, Lilli hit "pause" on the video screen.

"I just need a minute," he explained in response to Lilli's questioning gaze.

"Do you want me to turn it off?" Lilli offered hesitantly.

"No. Keep going." Liam put the car in park and fixed his unseeing eyes on the dashboard. "Keep going."

Lilli nodded and pushed the "play" button.

"That's why I had to stop them. That's why I had to do what I did today. I had to stop them before they found you. You see, I've been hiding you both from them since your father died."

For the first time since the video started, Jill looked away from the camera. The screen shook slightly as she spoke.

"When they came to the house to tell me your father died, I'd been anxious all day. The night before I had a terrible vision of your father being killed by a man I'd never seen before. I thought it was just a bad dream, but when I woke up, I tried everything I could to convince him not to go to work that day - not to confront the Guild's Oversight panel about their plans for the Seers, but Willem was so stubborn, so sure they would be reasonable.

When I opened the door and they told me your father had been killed in a car accident, I knew immediately that it was a lie. The man they sent to tell me was the same man from my dream the night before. Even though I knew, I couldn't let them know. We went to the funeral just to keep up appearances, but I was just biding my time until I could get the two of you away from them safely. I couldn't risk that they would find out what Willem and I had been hiding.

"You see, once your father discovered the genetic marker, he immediately tested you, Liam, and then Lilli when she was born. When Lilli tested positive, I begged him to hide the results, to switch the samples, and he did. I think that was his one comfort after all the ugliness came to light, that he had listened to me and protected his children from the Guild. I don't know how many ways they hurt him after he was taken, but I know he never told them. If he had, they would have come for us before now." Even though her eyes never met the camera, her chin lifted as she spoke.

"Last Tuesday, the guidance counselor at school mentioned to the principal that Lilli seemed to be a very bright and gifted student. Apparently, that's all it took. When the principal told me that Lilli had been selected for some special testing, I knew that they had found us."

Jill lifted her eyes to the camera to make sure her children understood the seriousness of what she was about to share. *"Once the Guild identifies a Seer, they don't stop—ever. They kill the Seer's immediate family members and kidnap the Seer. They are never seen or heard from again, as far as I know. So I had to do something. We couldn't run together without leaving a trail and I wasn't about to let them take any more of my family from me. That's why I know they are still looking for you. That's why you have to go to Texas now."*

Jill drew in a shaky breath before she continued. This was the part she dreaded most, breaking her promise. *"Liam, I'm so sorry. I know I promised you, but this was the only way… If I hadn't done it, you would be dead, and Lilli…"* Jill let her voice trail off as she shook her head at the horrible image in her mind: her daughter with white eyes, pale and dead to everything but sight. *"But you need to know that I'm still with you, baby. I will always be with you both. I'm your mother,"* she said in a trembling whisper just before the video cut off.

The words of her message hovered and stung like new lashes over fresh, bleeding cuts. Lilli and Liam struggled with shallow breathes as they each tried to absorb the burning, pulsing sensations. *Why is this happening? Who is the Guild? What will happen to us? Will we survive?* When their eyes finally met, it gave them both permission to release the flood of grief and doubt between them. They held each other across the console as they grieved for their mother, their father, and themselves, releasing their sadness and secret fears to each other. Finally, after an hour, and one inquiry from an older man who noticed them on the road, Liam felt stable enough to pull back onto the highway.

As they passed from Idaho into Utah, they listened to and talked about the next two videos that their mother had left them. Because of the limited memory capacity of the phone, each video was no more than four minutes long. In that time she explained as much as she could. By the second video, Jill had wiped away her tears and assumed a more businesslike posture as she informed them that they, in fact, had a lot of money — millions of dollars deposited at different banks all over the country and abroad. With this information, Liam let out a long string of expletives, which, combined with his gawking at Lilli, nearly caused a ten car pile-up during rush hour traffic in Salt Lake City. After their near miss, Lilli had refused to resume the video until Liam displayed what she considered to be an acceptable level of composure. When the video resumed, they learned that their mother had saved all the money from their father's hefty life insurance policy as well as the considerable sum made from the sale of their custom built house and their father's lucrative stock investments. Despite those resources, she had insisted that they live solely on her salary as an art teacher, *"Just in case,"* as she put it.

"The three thousand six hundred dollars in the envelope is not for you to go on a shopping spree," she ordered sternly. *"You will need to buy another car in Denver."*

Her voice softened as she continued. *"I know this will be difficult for you guys, knowing that it's your father's car, but you can't think about that now. The places you're going, no one drives a Saab. You'll stick out like a sore thumb and you can't afford that now. You need to be as invisible as possible.*

"I wish I could tell you more, but I just can't see," she said as she scratched her cheek in frustration. *"You know, all my life I have fought this "gift." From the moment I saw my dad die when I was a child, I have suppressed this, never wanting to know or learn anything about it. Your father tried to encourage me, but I never listened. Now I need it to guide you and I can't. I can't control it. Don't know a damn thing about how this works. I just see flashes of things with no context. I can't even tell you where in Denver you need to go. I just know that you'll go there and some man in a beat-up green baseball cap will give you $5,500 for the Saab and you will need $2,000 more to buy the truck. White… I think. Anyway, this video is almost*

up... I guess…" Jill sighed, closed her eyes, and shook her head before she looked back into the camera lens.

"Lilli, I'm sorry, baby girl," she said, using her favorite nickname from her southern upbringing. *"I wish I could tell you what you're in for, but I just can't."*

The third video was only three minutes long. In it, she explained in images and phrases the small glimpses she could see of their future. She told them that they would eventually need to go to a commune in Iowa, where there was a man named Eli Tanner who had been an old friend of her and their father's since college and would help them. *"I can't tell you when to go, all I know is that you will be alone for a while before it's safe to go there. But when you do, he will help you in any way that he can,"* she said with conviction. Lilli watched her mother fidget with her earring as she said Eli's name and wondered why the mention of this man would make her nervous if she trusted him, but before she could ask Liam about it, the video cut off abruptly.

The last two videos were private messages—one for Liam and one for Lilli. They decided to listen to them later, once they had checked into the Rodeway Inn in Ardmore, Oklahoma, just outside of Texas and had dinner and a shower. With the exception of brief catnaps on the side of the road, they had driven non-stop from Oregon, both wanting to put as much distance between them and whoever would be pursuing them as possible.

To keep Liam awake and alert, they talked about their mother's videos and speculated on their newfound wealth, where they would live, and how their mother had managed to keep her face in the frame through most of the videos she recorded. The chatter made them feel comforted and safe in the confines of their car.

And that was how they had managed to keep each other from falling apart. Once they reached Galveston in their non-descript white Ford pick-up, they retrieved the money Jill had left in the safe deposit box and decided over ice cream sundaes and French fries at the Two Frog's Grill to rent a lake cottage in the town of Hunt and spend the rest of the summer near the place where their mother had grown up. For two months, they spent their time under the Cypress and pecan trees, talking, swimming, fishing, learning to use a gun, and doing whatever else they wanted. Their cottage was deep enough in the woods that they were rarely seen or noticed by the locals. By the looks they received when they went grocery shopping, Liam could tell that everyone assumed that they were a runaway couple in love and Liam did nothing to correct them. When Liam told Lilli about this misperception one afternoon while he was teaching her to fly fish, Lilli gagged in mock disgust.

"Yuck! As if!" she scoffed.

"Hey, I've got more to lose than you do. I'm not getting any play because of you."

"Please!" Lilli exclaimed, looking him over doubtfully. "Don't blame me. Look at you. You're like a Chia pet. You've got hair coming out of everywhere."

Liam laughed as he scratched the beard that he'd let grow far beyond anything his mother would have allowed.

"Whatever," he chuckled. "Being hairy has its benefits. People assume I'm older—*we're* older," he said proudly before adding, "Not many 16-year-olds can grow a beard like this."

"Can or would? There's a difference, you know," Lilli mocked playfully. "If the girls at school could see you now..." Lilli's voice trailed off as she realized she was venturing into territory they both tried to avoid—talking about their former lives. As a mere freshman in high school when they had to leave Oregon, Lilli didn't have much of a social life to miss, but her brother was another matter entirely. Liam Knight was a living legend at Longleaf High. With a 4.5 GPA and celebrated speed and agility on the basketball court and the track, he was revered by both jocks and geeks alike. At a lean and muscular six feet tall with room to grow, Liam was the spitting image of his father–

tall, dark, and handsome, with blue-green eyes that sparkled when he laughed. He had everything and everyone he wanted. Plus, he was nice about it—a gentleman to the ladies (because his mother would have killed him if he was anything less) and a friend to anyone in need.

"Do you miss it?" Lilli asked quietly. "School, I mean, your friends...everything." The shift in Liam's body away from her before he answered did not go unnoticed.

"No. I don't know. Sometimes, maybe, but it feels like that life isn't a part of me anymore. So it's not real. It's not something I can go back to, you know?" Liam took his time baiting his line and casting out, before turning to face Lilli again.

"What about you?" he asked.

"It's different for me. I was never like you," Lilli admitted, looking down at the frayed edges of her denim cut-offs. "I was never popular."

"What do you mean? You had friends. People liked you..."

"Liam," Lilli started, "You know, what I mean. I was never "cool." I always felt different, weird around other people besides you and mom. Now that it's just us, I don't know. It's kind of nice. I feel like I can just be myself."

The broad smile they shared at Lilli's confession made them both laugh out loud before shaking off the sudden seriousness of their mood.

"Besides," Lilli began, picking up their conversation from earlier, "You ought to be glad I'm your girl-filter. There might be another Krista around here," she said with a shudder before another thought occurred to her. "Hey, I thought you hadn't done it yet." Lilli cast her line out wide, just as Liam had shown her. Liam nodded his approval before he answered. There were no secrets between them anymore. The summer had made them more than brother and sister. They had become each other's only confidante, each other's only friend, and it made the bond between them unbreakable.

"No, not technically, but Krista was pretty... experienced, so we did a lot of stuff."

"Wow. I am so glad I never got a vision of that," Lilli said, just as she felt the tug of her third trout that day.

It was on their way home that day that Lilli and Liam got their first glimpse of Miguel and Jason. At the time, Liam and Lilli didn't know who they were, but they were sure who sent them. As they watched the strange men go through their cabin from their hiding place in the trees, Liam was grateful that he listened to his instincts that morning and hid their documents, the pictures his mother had given them, and the majority of their cash in the secret compartment in the floor of their truck. *They won't know to look there,* he thought hopefully.

When the men finally left the cabin, they were so close that Lilli held her breath as she gripped Liam's hand tightly. Beside her, Liam was frozen in place—watching, but ready to pounce. He knew this day would come and he was ready for it. He reached into the backside of his jeans and quietly unlatched the safety on his gun. They were no more than 40 feet away.

"Should we wait here for them?" Jason asked.

"No, the woman at the tackle place said that they were going fly fishing a little farther down the lake. Let's try there. There's only a few more hours of sunlight left. If they're not there, then we can catch them coming home. They obviously didn't take the truck."

Jason nodded his assent as both men got into their black SUV and headed toward the trail Liam and Lilli had just left behind. Liam closed his eyes in relief, realizing that he never expected to be so grateful for Lilli's rigid habit of watching *Clueless* reruns at 5:00 pm every day. If she hadn't been so insistent that they leave the lake in time for her show, they would have stayed at the lake–stayed and died. They were packed up and out of the cabin in five minutes. Lilli left their dead fish on the bed, just so the stench would greet Miguel and Jason when they came back.

From there, they headed to New Mexico. It was a random choice that they made while playing a game. Liam picked a letter and Lilli picked a corresponding state, opened her US map, closed her eyes, and picked a city. When they arrived in Albuquerque, Liam insisted that Lilli enroll in school, noting with some relief that since his fake ID said that he was twenty, he didn't have to.

"What are you going to do?" she pouted as Liam gave the school administrator Lilli's fake transcript.

"I don't know. Maybe get a GED. I had enough credits... maybe I could take some college courses." Liam knew that his parents would never forgive him if he didn't tend to their education. Whatever he did, he planned to stay close to Lilli.

"Mom and Dad may not be here anymore, but we still have a responsibility to make something out of our lives," Liam told Lilli, though he didn't have the first clue as to exactly how he should go about making that happen.

Once she was in school, Liam noticed immediately that Lilli was more focused if he was studying, too. So during the day he prepared for his GED and took any self defense class he could find, becoming adept at a variety of martial arts and street-fighting styles. As his skill level increased, his instructors quietly encouraged him to graduate to more effective and unsanctioned fighting techniques. It was there, in the underground world of unregulated fighting, that Liam learned that if he needed to, he could be as lethal as anyone who came for them. His training also introduced him to a network of weapons smugglers, mercenaries and hardened criminals, connections Liam knew he would need if he was going to sustain their survival over the years. While Liam used his martial arts training to explain away the bruises and scars he would regularly come home with, he kept the unsavory side of his training to himself.

When he picked Lilli up from school each day, he would shift his focus to helping with her homework, cooking them dinner, and trying to make a home of the little house they rented just outside the city limits. Their weekends were spent camping in the Grand Canyon, Colorado, the local reservations, and Las Vegas. And at night, they worked on helping Lilli understand her gift.

After they were almost caught in Hunt, Lilli told Liam that she wanted to try to figure out some way to use her gift to help them. At first she just tried to concentrate, but nothing happened. She tried focusing on objects and people in the mall, but that didn't work either. On a day trip to Santa Fe, they came across a bookstore that claimed to specialize in mystical literature. While scanning through the titles, Liam handed Lilli a book on meditation.

"It says you can unlock the secrets of your mind," he said, half joking.

Lilli purchased it with more enthusiasm than he had expected, and after a few very frustrating weekends sitting cross-legged on cold desert floors, Lilli began to see beyond the places she was in. The first time it happened, she had finished her essay on 18th century English poetry early and was practicing meditation in her bedroom while Liam took a shower. He'd taken to running five miles a day and smelled horrible by the time he picked Lilli up from school. The thought of his stench flickered across her mind for the briefest fraction of an instant as she let the sound of the water from his shower calm her, but it was enough. She suddenly had a vision of a man with withered hands and a shapeless grey pinstriped suit signing Liam's acceptance letter to MIT. She was so excited that she burst into their only bathroom and pulled back the shower curtain without a thought. "Liam, you got into MIT!"

"Lilli... what the hell? Get outta here," he yelled as he snatched the curtain back.

"Liam, it worked! I saw it! You got into MIT!"

"What are you talking about? I haven't even finished the application... Wait. What? It worked? You saw it?" Liam slammed the faucet knob shut and hastily wrapped his towel around his waist before stepping out of the shower with a big smile on his face. "Seriously... what did you do?"

"I don't know. I was just really relaxed and thinking about how much you stink, and then I just saw it."

"Lilli, that's awesome! I can't believe it. Can you do it again?"

"I think so," she grinned.

At the end of her sophomore year, they headed north. While her visions were still mostly scattered and fleeting, Lilli was gradually learning to relax enough to hold onto her visions and get more detail from each image she was able to see. That was how she knew that they needed to wait another week to leave New Mexico because Liam's acceptance letter from MIT would be coming the following Wednesday, and how she determined that as long as they headed north and kept to less-popular camp sites, they would be safe for the summer. After spending July and August camping at Big Bear and Yosemite, they ended up in San Francisco because Lilli said she could see them eating big bowls of noodles and living in an apartment in Chinatown.

As Liam looked around their tiny two-bedroom apartment in Chinatown, he knew that they wouldn't exactly blend in, but figured that the constant congestion around them would mask their presence as well as anything else. *Who would look for us here?* He thought sullenly as he took in the yellowing walls.

"How much is this again?" he asked Lilli in dismay as she showed off her rudimentary Chinese to their landlady, Mrs. Chang, with unwarranted enthusiasm.

"It's $1,900 a month. That's cheap for San Francisco. You should be glad, penny pincher," Lilli snapped as she handed the landlady their security deposit and first month's rent in cash.

"Right," Liam muttered as he swiped at the film of grease on the kitchen wall with his fingers.

Mrs. Chang counted the money slowly before handing Lilli the keys to their apartment and closing the door behind her.

They were more than halfway through her junior year before it happened.

Lilli and Liam had fallen into a new routine quickly, with Lilli enrolled in the closest high school with AP classes while Liam began taking advanced physics courses at San Francisco State University. Though he had applied to MIT, he never had any illusions about going there. He knew his life would never be that settled, that normal, again.

He saw his application and acceptance as a promise kept to his mother, who had always dreamt of him going there, following in his father's footsteps.

After school, Lilli would do her homework in the vending room or on the side of the pool while watching Liam teach swimming lessons to five-year-olds at the local YMCA. On the weekends, they would practice their Chinese and roam around the city, then dance all night at every underground dance club they could find.

It was a Saturday afternoon, and they had gone to get some fabric so that Mrs. Chang could teach Lilli how to make a traditional Chinese dress. Almost as soon as they had arrived in San Francisco, Mrs. Chang had taken to Lilli and her broken Cantonese. Liam knew from the moment he had to help Lilli figure out how to use her first tampon how deeply Lilli missed the care and affection she would have gotten if their mother was still alive, and he welcomed Mrs. Chang's tenderness towards his sister. On the way back from the fabric store, they stopped off at their favorite noodle place. Liam was patiently waiting for Lilli to extract herself from the menu she knew by heart and pick between the plum and oyster sauce noodles when he saw them–the same two men from Hunt—searching the congested streets, looking for them. Just as he was about to get Lilli's attention, Liam's eyes locked with Miguel's through the restaurant's large picture windows. Miguel's face spread into a satisfied sneer as he watched Liam slowly rise from his seat.

Lilli's back snapped straight as soon as she looked up to see the lethal expression on her brother's face.

"Oh, no."

"Lilli, get up slowly. We need to leave now."

CHAPTER 4: RUN

I *can't believe I left my fucking gun at home.* It was all Liam could think as he observed them watching him and Lilli as they tried to move smoothly and quietly out of the crowded restaurant.

It's probably a good thing. Mr. Lam and his customers wouldn't appreciate blood in their noodles if this came to a shootout.

As they cleared the restaurant doorway, Liam took in their familiar surroundings, looking for an escape route. Every corner of Chinatown was dense with colors, people, hot food carts, vendors, and a million other things he'd barely registered when he entered the restaurant twenty minutes ago. Liam and Lilli had come all this way, 4,458 miles total, and the Guild had finally found them. The two men who had come to destroy what was left of the Knight family were less than fifteen feet away.

In his peripheral vision, Liam could see the excitement growing on Jason's face as he and Miguel remained locked in their stare, assessing each other as prey and hunter. Miguel knew enough not to underestimate Liam. Without any real experience, this young man had managed to elude or kill everyone they had sent to find them. In the course of his pursuit, Miguel learned that Liam had become an exceptional marksman, with advanced training in weaponry and hand-to-hand combat. Liam looked at Miguel with all the bravado of a young man ready to be tested and determined not to lose. If Miguel didn't know his own strengths, he might have been intimidated, but the emotion just wasn't in him. Liam was a boy; Miguel was a killer. In Miguel's mind, there was no comparison.

Feeling confident, Miguel finally broke Liam's gaze to assess the girl holding his hand. He noted with appreciation that Lilli had grown-up significantly from the pig-tailed photos he and Jason were able to piece together. Though her body had remained small and somewhat boyish for a girl of fifteen years, she had lost most of the plumpness in her cheeks. Her features had become sharper, but still lovely. Her hazel eyes were lighter than the pictures told. *Wider,* he thought, and hardened from a combination of time and loss. The dye that covered her long, naturally dirty blonde hair in shades of hot pink and pale yellow, along with the multiple rings and cuffs she sported on her hands and wrists suited her, he thought, in a punk-rock kind of way. Though he assumed she was afraid, he noted with curiosity that she was not holding her brother's hand as tightly as he would have expected and that disturbed him. *She's only fifteen. Can she see the outcome?* He wondered as he took in the lack of tension in her face. *She feels safe, even now.*

What they didn't know was that she hadn't seen them coming, couldn't see a damn thing beyond her brother out of the corner of her eye. But she didn't need to see more than him to know that this was the safest place that she could be. Whatever happened to them now, they would be together. They would either escape and survive, or fight and die. She would not be taken away from the only family she had left.

Liam's grip was light and gentle as their fingers intertwined. They had practiced this. As soon as his pinky moved down the inside of her own, she knew what that meant. Run, Lilli. Run left.

"Now!" Liam shouted as he cinched Lilli's hand tightly and sprinted left into the crowd. As they ran into the opening that Liam had been looking for, he could feel Lilli already beginning to lag behind. Though her heart and mind were willing, trying to keep up with him, her feet were slow, her legs incapable of matching his speed. As they cut right into the farmer's market, Liam risked a glance behind him.

Shit!

He could feel panic spreading through his chest as he realized that if they kept their current pace, they would be caught within seconds.

Liam couldn't remember when he grabbed Lilli and moved her onto his back. He only registered the relief he felt that she was still so light and fit so easily around him, like she had when they played piggyback as children. The minute she was securely in place, he could feel his body surge with adrenaline as he pushed himself harder and faster through the crowd. The burn in his lungs and legs felt familiar and comforting, like thirty suicide drills on a hot summer's day. Basketball in the winter, track in the spring–he'd never felt so grateful for the rigorous schedule he used to keep as he made a sharp left and narrowly missed the rice ball stand right in front of them. His combat training compelled him to maintain a zigzag pattern as he ran, just in case they decided to shoot, but he knew it was unlikely.

The Guild hadn't survived this long without being discreet, he thought, as he reminded himself that witnesses were one of the advantages of living in a densely populated area. Their chase was already eliciting looks of surprise, curiosity, and concern from bystanders.

So he ran and they chased him, without any clear plan of where he was going beyond *away*. After twenty seconds of running through the bitter taste of death-so-close in his mouth, the sound of Lilli's voice began to slowly register.

Left here, then straight.

Her voice was like the wind on his face, recharging and cooling him at the same time. As Lilli's voice laid out their route of escape, Liam could feel himself relax into his role as carrier.

Seamlessly, they worked in unison.

Her voice. His legs.

Action-Reaction.

Left - shoulder-pivot

Duck - waist-bend

Second light - eyes shifting upwards.

Her voice seemed to obscure everything but where she wanted him to go—faces blurred, street signs merged and faded.

Behind him, he heard the frustrated shouts of their pursuers.

"She must be helping him. Faster!" Miguel growled, even as the sound of their voices came from farther and farther away.

Through the blue doors on your right, Liam. Stop inside. Liam complied immediately.

The room was dark and dusty. *The storage room to a restaurant,* Liam guessed as he locked the door behind him and turned to see large cardboard boxes with bright red Chinese characters stacked high throughout the room. The walls were covered in corrugated steel with exposed beams along the ceiling. Liam moved to the farthest corner of the small room and faced the door, standing with Lilli still perched on his back.

For the first time since they left Mr. Lam's restaurant, Lilli used her voice.

"You can put me down now. They won't find us here."

Instead of obeying, Liam shook his head and tightened his grip on her legs. When he was sure she would stay in place, he brought out the pocket knife that he always carried in his right front pocket and flicked it open.

They stood there in the dark for over a minute before they heard the roughness of Jason's voice.

"Damn it! This is ridiculous! How do we keep missing one snotty-nosed kid and his sister? We should have just killed…"

"Shut up," Miguel hissed as he fisted his hands in frustration. "Just shut the hell up. We're getting out of here, now! We've already drawn enough attention to ourselves today."

The plan had been to just observe the targets, then obtain the Seer later in the night, when they were asleep. Mrs. Chang's extraordinary resistance to telling them where Liam and Lilli were had been unanticipated. She was immediately suspicious of them, even when they produced pictures of Liam and Lilli as children and told her that their extended family just wanted to find them. When their interrogation methods grew rough, the old woman still wouldn't budge. She just kept shouting and glaring at them as she fought back with feeble hands. "I know who you are! 我知道你是谁！" *You are the devil!*" she screamed. Eventually, Miguel had to stop Jason before he choked her to death.

Her panic suggested to Miguel that perhaps Liam and Lilli were close, so they wandered the streets nearby, hoping to find them inconspicuously, but Liam proved to be too observant, too alert. When Miguel's eyes met Liam's on the street, he had to change his plans. The chase had been a bad idea, he knew it, but he couldn't stop himself. He was not used to failure. He couldn't let them get away again, even though in the end, that was exactly what happened.

"Let's just get out of here before we have to deal with the local police," Miguel grunted as he unknowingly walked away from their prize again.

Lilli and Liam could hear the faint echo of their conversation somewhere just outside the door. As they waited, Lilli held onto her brother as she tried to absorb the growing awareness of what she had done, how she had directed Liam in their escape through the clarity of her thoughts alone. *Did I do that*, she wondered in disbelief. With her back pressed into the grooves of cold metal, she tried to remember what was different about this time, but couldn't recall anything beyond a strange mix of urgency and calm that had taken over the minute Liam lifted her onto his back. All she could remember was feeling viscerally connected to him, but she had not registered before that moment that it could have been anything more than the severity of their circumstances and their shared determination to not be captured.

While Lilli tried to decipher exactly what had just happened, Liam's mind returned, as it often did, to his mother's words from her private message to him.

'*You will know when it is time to go to Iowa.*'

Liam could feel the surge of energy that he'd felt during their chase drain from his body as he slowly released Lilli's legs, bent his knees and lowered her to the ground.

They had been at this for almost two years. *One year, nine months, and fourteen days*, Liam thought ruefully. After Jill's death, they had gotten in their car and never looked back. They had been smart. They had been lucky. They had been alone. Standing in the dark, with Lilli looking up at him curiously, he knew it was time to change that.

"Lilli, we need to leave now."

"What about all our stuff?"

"We have what we need in the locker at the storage place. The rest we won't need - not where we're going."

As he pulled her toward the door, Lilli yanked her hand away.

"What about Mrs. Chang?"

"Yeah... yeah, okay. We'll check on her first, but we need to be careful, Lilli."

"I can see them," she said calmly. "They don't think we'll go back to the apartment. We never have before. So they're heading back... over the bridge, I think. They're afraid of all the attention. We have a couple of hours at least."

Liam stared at his sister in relief and amazement before taking her hand again and heading out the door.

"You go. Go now. Protect her," Mrs. Chang pleaded to Liam as she tried to shoo away the cold ice pack Lilli placed over the gash on her head.

Liam nodded stiffly as he was reminded of his mother's words.

"Ah Yah! Lilli, move, okay? I'm okay. You the one who need worry. They will send others, more soon to find you."

"你怎麽知道的？" *How do you know that*" Lilli whispered in shock.

Mrs. Chang paused for several long seconds as she contemplated how to answer Lilli's question. "Because I had niece like you in China. Very special niece, like you." As she said this, Mrs. Chang took her hand and traced a finger over Lilli's temple.

"They took her from us, men like the ones who were here. Different, but the same. They took her from all of us. My sister, nephew, brother-in-law, all of them dead. When it happened, I did not understand.

"We were very close, Li Kim and I. I loved her very much. Before funeral, I went to open her coffin and give her the doll I made for her so that she could have it in her next life, but the body was not there. I was...umm... 歇斯底里歇斯底里... crazy, I think is how you would say it. I screamed, 她在哪兒 to the cold men watching me."

Taking in Liam's confused expression, Mrs. Chang translated for him.

"It means, 'where is she,'" she smiled before continuing. "My friend told me 'Please On Ki, please. They will hurt you. Don't cause trouble,' so I ran. I was young and afraid, so I came here. When I saw you, spend time with you, I knew."

Mrs. Chang rose to her feet while she waited for Lilli and Liam to recover from their shock.

"Liam, come. I have your bag. The one you gave me before. I kept it for you."

Liam stumbled after her, still reeling from the knowledge that what had happened to his family was happening to others all over the world. He didn't even notice she had stopped until he nearly crashed into her back.

"Ah yah! Be careful! Very old woman here," Mrs. Chang said as she turned and slapped him across the chest playfully.

"Thank you… for protecting us. We haven't had anybody…" Liam's voice was thick with emotion and gratitude. He'd never let himself realize how much she cared for them until that moment.

As she handed him the pouch with a sampling of their fake ids and documents, she patted his cheek lovingly. "It's ok, young man. 你是你需要什麼，你是你需要什麼 *You are what you need to be*. Don't worry, Liam. You will see. Now go," she said as she walked them out to the alley, giving Lilli one last hug before releasing her back into her brother's care.

"Protect each other. Let me know that you are ok when it is safe. I will pray," she whispered as her voice began to tremble. She stepped back inside the doorway just as Lilli began to reach for her, nodded her head once, and then closed the door firmly behind her.

Chapter 5: Destiny

If you touch her again, I'll kill you myself." Miguel didn't even bother to look up from his file as he addressed Jason. "What the hell is wrong with you, anyway? She's barely 17, for Pete's sake."

What a difference a few years makes, Jason thought in amazement.

The last time he had seen Emma, she was all trembling shoulders, tears, and sweat, wrapped in too short shorts and a t-shirt. Not a trace of the composed Seer he saw before him now. Though he missed how responsive she was back then, he could at least appreciate that she wouldn't recoil at his touch. He didn't care for the chalky white film that leeched all the Coppertone goodness from her naturally bronzed complexion, or the way her hair had turned from light brown to ash blonde. But he had seen many Seers before and after the purification process.

He was mostly used to the effects of the drugs the Guild gave them and, at the end of the day, Jason prided himself on being a man of simple tastes. *She's still warm and female,* he thought as he reluctantly removed his hand from her thigh. Though it was his least favorite thing to do, he took a quick glance into the milky fog of her pupils, hoping to find a trace of the girl she had been. If she knew he was there, it never registered. She blinked impassively and stared straight ahead.

"Who says 'for Pete's sake' anymore?" Jason countered as he settled back into his seat. Jason had hoped Miguel would be in a better mood when they got the call to leave California immediately for Dubai. They had been assigned to pick up a high priority Seer at the Purification Center there and bring them to the Guild's Seer Rehabilitation and Training Center in Vancouver. At least, he thought, it was a welcome distraction from their latest debacle in San Francisco.

Even though it was frustrating to keep having the Knights, or "The Wonder Twins" as Jason liked to call them, slip through their grasp, he had to admit that he enjoyed the chase. There was very little chasing in their line of work. Almost everything was a foregone conclusion and he, for one, enjoyed the introduction of a worthy adversary. Of course, Miguel didn't see it that way. Every missed opportunity was an epic tragedy to be turned over and analyzed in excruciating detail. "What a tight ass," Jason recalled remarking on more than one occasion.

Though Jason wasn't particularly looking forward to the twenty-plus hour flight, his spirits had improved considerably when he boarded their private jet and found out that they were going to pick up Emma. Unfortunately, she was not alone. He had seen Alessandra Pino only once before, but he never forgot her. It was his first week on the job, and he was invited to the observation room to witness what was supposed to be a routine visioning session. The Seers were in place, six of them along with Alessandra. He had heard that the drugs the Guild had given each Seer were designed to access images and sounds from their audio and visual cortexes. When all the images were synthesized, they could be projected in a hologram that allowed the observer to feel like he was walking through the collective vision of each Seer. He had expected it to be one of the most incredible experiences of his life, but instead, it was a nightmare.

Things started off easily enough. The group of Seers, or Quorum as it was known within the Guild, was asked to focus on potential political threats to the United World Organization (UWO). Almost immediately, the trainees saw a clear picture of a political protest rally unfold. Soldiers lined the sides of a dirt road, while people in the streets threw rocks at the military tanks that appeared to be standing by. The situation quickly escalated as a soldier's gun misfired, killing a young man who had been videotaping the protest, and the scene quickly spiraled into chaos. Most of the trainees in the group had some mercenary experience, so seeing a war unfold in front of them wasn't a big deal. What, or rather who, turned it into something more, something horrific, was Alessandra.

Luridium, the drug that the Guild administered to the Seers regularly, had several useful side effects, one of the most valued being its ability to suppress emotion. The drug made most Seers extremely passive and easily manageable. No matter what the subject of their vision, Seers usually remained unaffected, appearing indifferent to all displays of pain and suffering. That was the effect it had on every Seer except for Alessandra. Despite the excessive dosage Alessandra received every two weeks, her impulse for empathy was never fully suppressed. In visioning sessions, she appeared completely immune to the effects of Luridium. In fact, her connection to the pain she saw seemed to amplify over time. Through her vision, she was able to focus on the particular pain and experience of several victims at once and project these images to others in gruesome detail. Her emotional response was so intense that it often destabilized the Quorum, causing the other Seers to become disoriented, their visions unfocused - making room for only Alessandra's vision to dominate in all its gory detail.

This was the power Jason experienced during his first visioning observation. Suddenly, the observation room hologram went from depicting a small local insurgence to a blood-drenched massacre that each trainee could witness with surreal and terrifying accuracy. Images of internal organs and blood vessels bursting from the shells of bullets were played out over and over from a dozen different angles in a multitude of victims. The images of tears streaming down the faces of mourners as they draped over their dead loved ones also played out from a first person perspective inside their minds. The projection trembled with the raw intensity of the pain and misery that encased them. The echoes of the victims' screams were deafening.

All around him, Jason could hear his classmates gasp and retch as he stood with his mouth open, sucking down the bile in the air.

After several panicked and failed attempts to refocus the other Seers, a medical team finally rushed into the visioning room to inject Alessandra with a sedative, and all visions ceased. The whole incident took less than twenty seconds, but for the trainees, each moment represented the longest seconds of their lives. No one who was in that room ever forgot what happened.

As Jason watched his colleagues being escorted from the observation room in the hands of medics, his shock dissolved, then hardened into anger.

"Why do you keep her alive? How can you keep someone alive who can do that? How did she do that?" he shouted at the backs of the technicians who were busy recalibrating their machines, appearing to be completely unfazed by the events that had just taken place.

When he finished berating them, the one with the thick-rimmed glasses, Patrick, spun his chair around to face Jason. His eyes were red, with heavy shadows under his puffy lids. It was clear to Jason that he hadn't slept in days. He didn't look like the sort of man who would raise his voice.

"You think that's the worst she can do!?" Patrick yelled. "Have you ever seen a body just - God, never mind!"

With his next syllable, his voice shifted from outrage to helpless, hopeless pleading. "She can't control it. She's completely unstable. They keep her alive because she's the only one who can see that level of detail in an event. They think it's...fascinating, okay? But I have to work here!" he said. "I have to work here," he repeated softly, before rising slowly from his chair and leaving the room. Jason noted with pleasure that Alessandra was still face-down on the ground when he left.

So Jason was less than excited to see her again as she was escorted onto their private plane. Since their first encounter, he had heard many rumors about her, but they all ended with the same conclusion. She was crazy, stark-raving-mad-fuck-bat crazy. She kept getting moved from purification site to purification site. Everyone wanted her. No one could handle her. She could render a whole Quorum ineffective for weeks. Miguel told him that she was being moved to Vancouver for a year-long retraining program in hopes that they could stabilize her before her final move to Chicago. Why Chicago thought they had a chance at controlling her was beyond him.

When Alessandra stepped on board and moved quickly to the back of the plane, far away from him, Jason couldn't have been more pleased. Even though there was no visioning or observation room aboard the plane, the fact that he knew what she could do made him as scared as a little boy, and that made him angry. Until Miguel had interfered, he had been able to regain his good mood by focusing his attention on Emma. After Miguel let him know the price of his distractions, Jason resolved to get some sleep. He was just about to drift off when he heard a sweet and unfamiliar voice.

"I can take her, if you would like?"

The pleasure he took from the sound of her voice was short-lived as he realized that it could have only come from one person.

Jason kept his eyes tightly shut as he listened to Miguel's response. "Sure, ok. We should be landing in a few hours anyway."

Jason could feel his whole body shrink involuntarily at Alessandra's proximity. He waited a full minute after he felt Emma leave her seat to open his eyes. When he did, he was immediately confronted with Miguel's barely-disguised smirk.

"Fuck off!" he hissed, before pulling the in-flight blanket over his head and pretending to go back to sleep.

One year and two months later…

Many years I have waited for you. Many long years. Marcus' expression was controlled, betraying nothing of the elation he felt inside as he watched Alessandra move from the ubiquitous black SUV across the Chicago Purification Center courtyard.

Do not be afraid. You have a friend in me.

Chapter 6: Chicago

May 2011

From what I've heard, Vancouver couldn't do anything with her. So why is she here? You know she's unstable." The low tenor of Andreas Menten's voice barely masked his growing irritation.

"How could you let your...infatuations jeopardize what we are building here? I don't understand you."

"Marcus will control her," was Crane Le Dieu's only reply as his eyes followed Alessandra's procession across the courtyard of their compound. Even with her head down and the awkward coverage of the ugly brown coat she wore, he could still make out the subtle curves of her body as she moved. Andreas' voice was less than a faint echo in Crane's ear as his mind filled with images of Alessandra bound, gagged, and screaming—all for his pleasure. "She would be so... delicate," he mused, as he traced the ridge of his top lip with the pad of his index finger.

"Crane!" Andreas shouted. "For God's sake, get a hold of yourself! I'm not about to let your sick games threaten all the work I've done to create the Quorum we have here. Six of the best Seers anywhere in the world and we have them, despite the Guild's constant monitoring. And why? Because I've been careful! I've been careful while you've been... reckless!" Andreas was irate as he slammed his fist onto the polished surface of his desk before continuing.

"And for what, because you can't find more suitable outlets for your baser instincts? We've already lost one because of you. If that happens again, I'll take those knives you like to play with so much and cut you myself."

Somewhere in the middle of Andreas' rant, Crane managed to tear his eyes away from Alessandra. When the pitch of Andreas' voice finally disrupted the scenarios he had been playing out in his mind, Crane turned from the window toward his colleague and friend of over twenty years and sighed. "Andreas, you've always been so dramatic... and crass. I told you what happened with Natasha was..." Crane hesitated for a moment as he tried to control the smile that threatened to expose him, "...an accident."

Andreas could only scoff at Crane's thinly veiled excuse. "That 'accident' cost us a Seer, and it took more than a little covering up to hide it from the Guild. I'm not going out on a limb for you again."

Before Andreas could continue, they were interrupted by his assistant, Christof, as he entered the library.

"Forgive me, but Marcus is ready for you, sir." As Christof addressed Crane, Andreas stared at each of the two men with a suspended expression of disgust and confusion.

"What the hell is going on here?"

"You see, Andreas," Crane interrupted casually, "despite what you think, I am always prepared. Bring him in, Christof."

Marcus Akida was always a sight to behold whenever he entered a room. Even though he was given the same dose of Luridium every two weeks, like all the other Seers, Marcus was the only one who showed an ability to resist some of its most common side effects. Luridium was developed and used exclusively by the Guild for two main purposes. The first was to establish and maintain the calm and passive demeanor of the Seer. The second was to create a reliable and mobile interface with the cerebral cortex and physiological functioning of each Seer. With the right equipment, the metallic properties of the drug could be used to track everything from heart rate to audiovisual impulses. It also had the added benefit of acting as a built-in tracking device.

These metallic properties also made Luridium highly toxic. The extraordinarily resilient immune systems that were present in all Seers made them able to tolerate the drug that would have killed a normal human in a matter of months. It was this resistance to Luridium's lethal side effects that caused the Seer immune system to expel the drug from their bodies every fourteen days, necessitating the two-week dosing schedule.

Once a Seer had been on the drug for a month, a strong dependency developed, creating severe withdrawal symptoms if a Seer went for more than three weeks without a dose. It was the prolonged and constant exposure to the drug that created the loss of pigmentation in the skin, hair, and eyes, making them hypersensitive to the sun. Their features–the ash blonde hair, the cataract-like film over the eyes, the chalky pallor of the skin, and the long red robes they wore to protect them from the sun–were known throughout the Guild as the mark of a Purified Seer. This was true of everyone except Marcus.

Though he had the typical ash blonde hair and clouded eyes, his skin shone with the same ebony brilliance that it had the day he was captured from his small village in Tanzania. At a lean and muscular 6'4", cloaked in the heavy red robe of the Seers, he was at once angel and demon; beautiful and terrifying.

To the Guild, he was their archangel. Marcus was widely known as one of the most powerful Seers the Guild had ever come across. To

Crane and Andreas, he was the crown jewel in their Quorum–their prized possession.

The two men marveled often at their good fortune and the irony of how hard it had been to break him. Marcus had been one of the oldest Seers ever to be captured. Typically, the Guild gathered a Seer in his or her late teens, at the end of the last human growth spurt. That was when the gift most often began to manifest itself. Seers were generally more pliable at that stage and easier to take through the isolation and purification process. When a Seer was captured later in life, the process of mental reprogramming became much more difficult. Those realities created a small window of opportunity for the Guild to act in ideal conditions.

If a Seer was taken too young, their gift would never be realized, almost as if the gift had an innate defense mechanism against captivity. If a Seer was taken too late, they would resist vehemently throughout the purification process and most likely end up "infractus" or permanently broken and, therefore, terminated. Marcus was the exception.

When he was captured at thirty-two, he was an established teacher, healer, husband, and father in his village. Though his wife was killed in front of him, his child was never definitively identified. His village was torched just to be sure they left no stone unturned. That was the problem with Seers in the developing world. Without convenient access to hospital facilities, babies were constantly born without being properly catalogued and tested for the marker, allowing Seers like Marcus to go undetected, and their gift unharnessed for decades. It was the single largest challenge the Guild faced in its efforts to identify and control any Seer, anywhere. It was why the UWO made universal access to health care its top priority.

When they brought Marcus to the purification center in Johannesburg, he was completely uncontrollable. To even begin the purification process, he had to be sedated most of the time. When he was awake, he vacillated between crippling grief and pure rage. Either way, if he was conscious, he screamed his wife and son's names for much of his first few days with the Guild. The Luridium only seemed to incite his fight response, so after a month of great effort with minimal results, he was placed into the first of what would become an ongoing stream of extended stays in solitary containment.

After a year and a half, he was still too unstable to even be considered for participation in any Quorum. When it was possible to give him heavy sedatives, the Luridium showed that his visions were unparalleled in detail and breadth of subject matter. But any progress made towards the completion of his purification would eventually be wiped out by the reemergence of Marcus' memories of his family and their horrific deaths on the day he was captured. Whenever these images resurfaced during his visioning sessions, Marcus would become consumed with grief, and his retraining process would have to begin all over again.

As a result, Marcus remained alone for most of his first three years with the Guild. With no sustained progress made, the Guild had begun discussing his termination when he suddenly became more compliant and open to participation. Crane and Andreas assumed it was the premonition of his own death that inspired his cooperation.

In reality, Marcus had been waiting for his death, planning and praying for it ever since the day he was captured. He had spent a year and a half in that state before he saw a vision of himself and a girl with long, thick ash blonde hair who would help him find a way to escape. Huddled in the darkness, he became fixated on the vision and how it could be possible.

In his confinement, his gift became his companion, creating windows and possibilities to the world beyond his cell. As he got to know his gift, he began to master it, learning to refine and focus it independently and secretly from the Guild. He learned that he could focus on the future actions of an individual or an entire group and monitor their paths simultaneously, without effort. It allowed him to anticipate the Guild's impatience with him and orchestrate his own integration into Quorum in a way that would buy him as much time as he needed to perfect his gift.

By the time he was finally allowed to quorum with other Seers, he quickly learned how to project certain images and keep others private from the Guild and the other Seers. Marcus had seen from his visions that the dominance of his gift within Quorum would allow him to distort or obstruct the visions of less skilled Seers. For ten years, he perfected the use and manipulation of his sight, waiting for the girl in his vision to arrive. As Marcus watched Alessandra move slowly from the SUV through the front entrance of the compound, he could feel all the tension from his waiting give way.

Now we will find a way to fight them, he thought with deep satisfaction. *We will destroy all that they have created here.*

Though he knew what to expect when he was summoned to the compound library, Marcus kept his thoughts calm and vacant so as not to alert other Seers.

"You called, Crane? How can I be of service?"

"Ah, Marcus," Crane smiled fondly. "You are such a comfort to me, always so willing to help. We have a new Seer who has come to us. She is very…emotional during our visioning process and she needs some help — your help, I think, to control this. My hope is that you will be able to strengthen her focus."

"I will do my best," Marcus answered in his most sincere baritone.

"I know you will."

Crane smiled indulgently at Marcus before turning and waving his hand toward Christof, who immediately disappeared to retrieve his charge. Anticipating Christof's return, Crane walked quickly to the coat closet to retrieve the red cashmere cloak that he had custom-made for Alessandra.

As they waited, Marcus kept his eyes on the patterns of the blue and white Oriental rug beneath his feet. He had seen the robe Crane had commissioned for his new Seer and was already deeply disturbed by the way Crane fingered the seam that connected the robe's hood to the body of the garment. He prayed that this new Seer was as powerful as he had foreseen. They would need to build their bond quickly if she was to escape the plans Crane had for her.

Just as Marcus began to fear he might lose the battle he was waging to keep his growing unease from showing on his face, Christof entered the room behind a demure figure dressed in a dirty brown wool coat that exposed the frayed edges of her denim overalls. Her long, thick hair fell in pale yet lustrous contrast to the drabness of her outfit. Her eyes, like Marcus', stayed fixed on the ground.

"My dear, who has you in such a state? Come. There is no need for a beauty like you to wear such rags," Crane declared as he rushed across the room to stand before her.

He balanced her new robe in his left arm as he reached for the dingy brass buttons of her too-small coat. Marcus glanced up just in time to see Alessandra recoil from Crane's touch.

She knows. She understands already, he thought with approval.

"Don't be afraid, dear. I won't..." Crane smiled then as he thought about the lie he was preparing to tell. He was about to continue when Alessandra's head suddenly snapped up to meet Crane's gaze. Her mouth fell open in what he guessed was either shock or terror.

Moments of silence passed between them as he wondered vaguely which of the plans he'd had for her had caused the trembling of her lips. The movement distracted him, made his smile broaden as he took in the details of her beauty–the way the soft pink flesh on the inside of her mouth hugged her bottom teeth, the cream of her skin hovering just below the film of her outer dermis, and her veins betraying their exact location just under the skin on her neck.

Unconsciously, Crane's hand rose up on its own to wipe the lone tear that was making its descent from the corner of her eye. She was afraid. She was afraid of him, and he was in love with her fear.

"Oh, my love…" Crane murmured.

For Andreas, the sight of Crane moving toward Alessandra as if he was both charm and conjurer dragged his thoughts back to the scene he had witnessed just over a month ago — of Crane basking below a body suspended and ruined by his skilled, brutal hands.

Andreas would never forget the enraptured look on Crane's face as he smoothed the running blood over his cheeks with his eyes closed and his head moving slowly back and forth in ecstasy. Andreas had not feared any man before that moment, before he saw evil revealed to him in the face of a friend. Afterward, he tried to recover his indifference, but it would not return. The nature of what he understood his relationship with Crane to be had shifted from a partnership among ambitious equals to a tenuous arrangement between man and beast.

Andreas' body reacted with violent revulsion as he tried to remain a passive bystander as Crane's fingertips shadowed the curve of Alessandra's cheekbone. *Not again*, he thought as his body gave voice to his rage. For his own self-preservation, he needed to get Alessandra away from Crane. He could not be a witness again.

"Crane! Stop this!" Andreas roared. "Give her to Marcus, now!"

Despite Andreas' words, Crane was still transfixed, imagining all the horrors she must have seen and hoping–hoping that he could recreate the look she'd just had, over and over again, but he managed to nod his head as he handed the robe to Christof.

"This is for you, my dear," Crane whispered as he backed away from Alessandra excitedly. "You are a part of us now."

Furious, Andreas grabbed Crane by the arm and pushed him toward the door.

"Leave them!" Andreas hissed over his shoulder.

At Andreas' instruction, Christof hastily handed the robe to Marcus before exiting the room and closing the door firmly behind him.

Marcus ventured a step closer as he slung the robe over his shoulder, hoping to catch her attention. But Alessandra was still staring into the empty space Crane left behind — trapped in the nightmare of fantasies his presence revealed. Taking the moment to observe her more fully, Marcus noted that she was younger than he had expected, taller too, but he was not deterred. He had learned from his life before the Guild that a world could be found in the most unassuming places.

"What is your name?" Marcus asked in the gentlest tone he could muster.

The familiar sound of his voice finally roused her from her trance.

When their eyes finally met, Marcus registered a guarded but unmistakable look of recognition. There was a long silence before she finally spoke in a surprisingly strong voice.

"Alessandra. My name is Alessandra."

Chapter 7: A Friend

When Marcus heard Alessandra's slight Italian accent, he was relieved. Not only by the strength of her voice, but also by the simple fact that she spoke English. He was genuinely surprised that the need for a common tongue between them had not occurred to him earlier, but he was so used to communicating with other Seers in Prime that he rarely considered language.

In Quorum, Seers understood each other from their thoughts and visions alone through a form of communication known within the Guild as Prime. When using this unspoken language, there was no need for translation, regardless of the Seer's native tongue. Given the bond and the secrecy he and Alessandra needed to create, Marcus knew the convenience of a shared spoken language would be extremely beneficial.

"You know who I am?" he asked Alessandra hopefully.

"Yes."

"Good. My name is Marcus Akida. We will talk more soon, but for now we must blend in. Please... put this on."

The fact that he knew his own last name when she could not remember hers immediately put Alessandra on edge. Her eyes narrowed slightly as she clenched her jaw and took a step back, away from his outstretched hand.

"I thought you were a Seer. How do you know your full name?" Both she and Marcus could hear the growing suspicion in her voice. Alessandra was just glad she sounded more angry than afraid.

"Yes," Marcus answered cautiously as he lowered his hand to create more distance between them. "I am a Seer, but I have been able to keep my memories, my past."

Alessandra's heart raced in her chest as she took in his words. She had no memories of her life before the Guild, and the life she lived now, she spent each day trying to forget.

"That's impossible," Alessandra blurted out in willful disbelief. He was different. She could see that from the sheen of his skin. It looked so natural, so much like normal. Alessandra had assumed from her visions of him that his appearance meant that he was newly assimilated, that the drugs hadn't been administered long enough to release their full effect, but now she sensed there was more, that he had an awareness that had escaped the rest, that had escaped her. She wanted to know why, but she was too scared to ask. She didn't want to appear more vulnerable than she already felt. So she fought against her instinct to trust him a little longer while she tried to clear her head.

Perhaps, she questioned, *it was not kindness I heard in his voice. Remember, you can't trust anything with the stuff they give you,* she reminded herself. *You don't know what's real.*

Alessandra's previous visions of Marcus had been fleeting, with nothing beyond a vague aura of safety that made her feel that she could trust him. And she never trusted her feelings, not anymore.

Sensing that their introduction was headed in the wrong direction, Marcus took a step back from her. Even though she stood in the center of the room, Marcus could tell by the frightened intensity in her gaze that she felt cornered, whether by Crane's vile intentions or his own blunders; he couldn't say. But he was sure of one thing: the anger in her voice was as false a front for her fear as the ignorance that he feigned every day as he walked through these halls.

As this new understanding of her took hold, he held his body still in an attempt to make her understand that he was not a threat. He remembered the pose from when he was a boy in Tanzania, watching his father tend to a gazelle with a badly wounded leg in the Ngorongoro wildlife reserve.

"The animals that have been the most badly wounded are always the most dangerous. They'll use their last breath to bite you," his father had warned him while showing Marcus the scars he'd endured to gain this wisdom.

"Even though you're trying to help them?" A wide-eyed, nine-year old Marcus questioned in growing apprehension as he looked between his father and the frightened animal.

"Sometimes because you try to help them," Marcus' father replied. "Sometimes they don't know the difference."

Replaying his father's words, he realized that he needed to approach Alessandra with the same care that his father had taken with that gazelle all those years ago.

"I understand you're afraid. It's ok. It's hard to trust anything here. I understand that," Marcus began. "Please don't be alarmed. I can explain everything, but not here. Despite what you feel now, you *can* trust me. I promise I will answer everything you want to ask me later, but we don't have time now. Please, you need to put this on." Marcus lifted his arm again, offering her the red robe that was made for her.

Alessandra weighed his words on shaky, shifting feet. Despite her suspicion, she found it hard to resist the sincerity in his eyes. She clenched her hands into fists at her side, trying not to let her acquiescence show.

"You don't need to be brave. I'm not going to hurt you," Marcus assured her. "We just can't speak freely here. It's not safe."

No, it's not safe. It's never safe, Alessandra agreed silently as she temporarily gave up her internal battle and motioned for Marcus to hand her the robe. Marcus averted his eyes as she began unfastening the remaining buttons on her coat. When she was dressed, he noticed how carefully she folded her garments and held them to her like a blanket.

New clothes were supplied to Seers so often that they rarely had a chance to get old, much less frayed. In addition to their red robes, all Seers wore the same basic attire: long sheath dresses in grey for the women, simple black long sleeve t-shirts with matching loose pants for the men. Taking in the type and level of wear and tear of the clothes in her arms, Marcus could only come to one conclusion. *They must have been the clothes she wore when they captured her*, he marveled. *How did she manage to keep them?* He knew the Guild was careful to destroy all remnants of a Seer's past. *Perhaps they are more accommodating at other purification centers.* After departing from the purification center in Johannesburg, Marcus had never left the Chicago compound. *She must have put up a legendary fight to keep them*, he thought with admiration.

"Do you know how long you have been with the Guild?" Marcus asked tentatively.

"No. Many years, I think." The wounded expression on Alessandra's face made him immediately regret asking her.

"Of course," he said quickly. "I'm sorry. I didn't mean to be insensitive." Marcus reminded himself again that most Seers were not like him. Most had lost all sense of time and self.

"I am also sorry to say that I do not believe they will let you keep your clothes here. They are very strict," Marcus added as he gestured toward the bundle in her arms.

Though Alessandra nodded her head in acknowledgment, she did not look concerned.

"I scream a lot if they're not near me, even in my sleep. Everyone tries to take them, but after a while they realize that it's not worth it."

Judging by their poor fit, he didn't think they were hers, but he couldn't be sure. Feeling encouraged by their brief communication, Marcus couldn't resist asking his next question.

"Do you know whose clothes they are... who gave them to you?"

Alessandra frowned in response, feeling her irritation grow — both with Marcus and her own inability to answer even the most basic questions. For the second time in less than ten minutes, she wondered how he could ask her these questions if he had gone through the same purification process that she did, that everyone did.

"I... don't know whose they are. I just know that they're important to me. Why are you asking me these things? I suppose you know how long you've been here, right?" She snapped at him.

Marcus was silent for a moment as he tried to figure out how to regain the small ground he had lost. "I'm sorry," he stammered. "I've waited a long time to meet you. I'm not...I don't mean to irritate you. I'm just trying to understand more about you. It's been 13 years, 8 months, and 10 days since I actually tried to hold a conversation with someone. I guess I'm out of practice..."

Alessandra's mouth fell open in response to his admission, but before Marcus could finish, Andreas abruptly opened the library door.

Standing in the doorway as he held the door open, Andreas glanced nervously down the hall looking for Crane before turning his attention back to Marcus and Alessandra.

"Good, you're still here. Marcus, do not leave her alone, under any circumstances. Do you understand me? I will place a guard outside her door at night, but other than that, she is not to be left alone."

At the faint sound of footsteps, Andreas looked behind him again, craning his neck left and right before continuing.

"You are to report her progress to me—me alone. Am I clear?"

"Yes, Andreas. I understand, but should Crane ask..."

"Leave him to me. Just do as I ask," Andreas replied as his eyes darted back and forth, scanning the hall.

"Of course," Marcus said before brushing past Andreas and ushering Alessandra out of the library toward her new living quarters.

"We will have all the time we need now," Marcus said with a smile.

The progress that Marcus thought they had made in the library was quickly erased by the time he met a resolutely silent Alessandra the next morning. It took more time than Marcus had anticipated to break through to Alessandra. Since most Seers were reticent and reclusive, Marcus was completely unaccustomed to and unprepared for Alessandra's open hostility. At every turn, she seemed to be at war–with herself, with the drugs that invaded her system, with her place in the Guild, and the terrifying nature of her gift. When he tried to ask her questions about herself and how she knew him, she shut down completely, often walking away from him while he was in mid-sentence. Since he could not leave her alone, he spent the first few days just trailing behind her as she periodically turned around to glare at him in an alternating pattern of suspicion and loathing while she tried to figure out what he wanted from her.

Finally, after a week of getting nowhere, he decided to tell her about himself. He shared with her everything he could remember, about his past, his family, how he had come to the Guild, the three years he had spent in isolation, and how he had waited and prepared for her ever since. He knew it was a risk sharing so much with her when she gave him nothing in return, but he had to take the chance. He needed her help. He needed her to trust him.

Everything about Marcus - his patience, his kindness, his almost parental demeanor - contradicted the one truth that Alessandra had distilled from her time with the Guild: Seers were nothing to them. That mantra had become a beacon to her whenever she was momentarily confused by someone's motives or in danger of mistaking them for caring, and it served as a safe place for all her rage and loneliness. The few times she had sought out compassion from anyone, the heat of her desperation was met with a thousand pricks of icy indifference, shattering her hope for anything else. *Cruelty*, she often thought, *might have been better.*

By the time her purification process was complete, Alessandra understood that she was simply an asset, a tool to be used and controlled, regardless of how she begged for reprieve from the drugs and the horror of her visions. The fact that she could not shut down like all the other Seers she had met before Marcus only made her feel more isolated, more out of control. She envied them so much that the bitter longing for any measure of indifference was constant in her heart.

She knew she saw things that no one else did; she knew that was why they kept her alive despite the disasters she caused everywhere she went, but she could not control it. If it didn't always hurt her more, she would have gladly used the visions she saw as vengeance against the Guild and everyone who dared to observe her. But, she couldn't turn away when she saw someone in pain, couldn't stop it from feeling like she was on fire, just like they were. She wanted to be numb, but instead she was always raw and tender, consumed with guarding, tending, and inflicting her own wounds.

As she listened to Marcus talk of his hopes that she would help him escape, she was genuinely surprised by the unfamiliar desire to laugh. *Help you?* She answered him silently. *My only power is to steal peace and create nightmares. They call me Shiva, the destroyer. Didn't anybody tell you that?* She wondered.

She knew he wanted something from her, but he offered something, as well. As he told her about his wife and son, how he had thought of them every day since they had been killed, it occurred to her that Marcus was offering her his trust, his friendship. She had no idea what to do with either. She couldn't even remember ever having a friend. But more than all of those things, she heard the urgency in his voice as he offered her a place with him, in freedom–a chance to break the cold horror of her life and replace it with something else. The notion kept her up several nights as she felt a spark of hope inside her try to find enough air to ignite.

When Marcus met her outside her room as he had done every morning for the past three weeks and observed the well-rested look on her face, he knew that she had finally decided to let him in.

He smiled broadly. "Good Morning, Alessandra. I think we are finally ready to begin. Yes?"

"I think so," she said in a soft voice, as she offered him her first conscious smile in two years.

After breakfast, Marcus led Alessandra outside, along one of the white stone covered walkways that would shield them from the light spring rain. As he motioned for her to sit down on a nearby bench, Marcus shook his head in sympathy at the tense, wary expression on Alessandra's face.

"Not all stimulation is bad, Alessandra. You must learn to be less afraid… to participate in life again."

Alessandra was ashamed to admit that even the sensation of the mist from the falling rain on her bare forearms made her feel vulnerable enough to long for the cloak she'd left lying across her bed.

"I can help you, but you must trust me. Try to open yourself up again," Marcus said.

"I feel too open already. Everything feels like it burns." Her voice was a whisper as she tried to steady her breathing. "I can't control myself. I can't control anything."

"Shhh. Close your eyes, Alessandra. Listen to the rain. Take a deep breath. We will quorum together and I will show you that you are not a monster."

Even though she doubted him, Alessandra closed her eyes.

They let the silence fall and settle between them as they both fell into the meditative state that they had been trained to seek as the precursor to a visioning session. Alessandra had never quorumed with just one person. She hoped Marcus was as strong as he claimed.

Just before they both slipped into a deeper meditation, she could hear Marcus' voice speaking to her in a whisper. "See life with me, Alessandra. See new life coming into being... now."

And then she saw them—

The piercing notes of a blood-curdling scream, then pain, pain and the fear of ripping in two.

Alessandra's stomach heaves just as she sees the mother throw up on the floor. Her husband rushes to cradle her head in his arms. Alessandra feels the wave of trust wash over her as the woman is calmed by his touch.

"It's gonna be all right. You're doing fine. I'm so proud of you. I'm so proud of you."

Alessandra can feel the woman's hot breath, panting, and fear. She wonders if the baby is okay. "God, please let the baby be okay..."

"*You're doing great,*" *the doctor yells excitedly. It's a female doctor. She can't have children. She's so excited for everyone who can. There is no conflict in her heart as it beats, pitter pat, pitter pat, only joy rushing forth from every corner of her mind.*

"*I can see the head,*" *the doctor says.* "*It's good! It's good! I need one more big push. Give me one more! You can do it!*"

"*Oh God! UUUgggghhhhhh.*" *The mother pushes so hard her ears go numb, she is trying…*

Strong for him. Strong for him, *she thinks.* Be okay, little baby. Mommy loves you so much.

And then silence.

And then a quivering little cry gives way to…

Bright, bright lights and tears and strong arms hugging and strong lips kissing and joy, exhausted, drunk big tears of joy as little quivering cries grow louder.

The woman can see her son's blood-stained, scrunched-up face looking mad as hell with the assault of the real world on his delicate senses.

The sight makes them both laugh…with joy

Joy

Joy

As the heat of him seeps into her bare breasts waiting,

And joy, and joy.

"*Oh, sweet boy… oh, sweet baby,*" *she coos.*

And joy as he turns his head toward the familiar sound of his mother's voice.

Even as Alessandra felt Marcus pulling them slowly back from the moment to come, the emotions lingered in each fiber of her being as she opened her eyes to find herself clutching her arms to her chest as if holding her own child. The tears came easily as she saw brand new possibilities inside her.

"You are made for more than what they take from you," Marcus whispered to her as he felt the intensity of her emotion coursing through him.

Marcus kept his eyes closed so that he could give Alessandra a moment of privacy. He could see from her thoughts that she did not recall ever having a positive experience with her ability. And for her sake, he wanted the moment to last, for her to finally see her ability as a gift. He only opened his eyes when she began to speak.

"I never knew what I did to deserve this. Why they would take my life and leave me with nothing but nightmares," Alessandra whispered back through her tears.

"It's because they need us," Marcus replied gently. "They need us to stay in power."

"What do you mean? Who needs us?" Alessandra asked, shifting her body to face Marcus more fully and wipe away her tears.

"You are surely too young to remember this, but I recall as a young man the constant bickering and in-fighting among members of the United Nations whenever there was a serious issue that needed to be dealt with. Even though the world leaders at that time had some good intentions, there was no way to force anyone to do anything. So even though they came together, at the end of the day, each leader did whatever they wanted anyway.

"About 19 years ago, all of that changed. The United Nations was reorganized into a more powerful and cohesive body known as the United World Organization, or UWO. Suddenly, leaders from each country seemed to truly work together. They honored treaties and feared breaking ranks with the whole. It was around the same time that the discovery of the first Seers was announced. At the time, I didn't put the two together, but essentially, they are one and the same. We are the reason why the UWO holds together, why they have the power they have."

"How is that even possible?" Alessandra asked, more confused than ever. "They keep us locked away. No one even knows we're here."

"I know it seems that way, Alessandra, but trust me, it's far from the truth. I don't know everything, but from what I have been able to gather over the years, it seems that there are Seers like us all over the world, but our occurrence is a random anomaly. No one knows where a Seer will be born, so the UWO maintains its cooperation as a way of making sure that no singular country develops a monopoly on Seers. The Guild was created to gather, manage, and distribute us to Centers throughout the world, with the idea that as long as each country leader is cooperative, they will have access to our power. Our visions allow them to rule with the ultimate advantage.

"The structure seems to work pretty well, except for when leaders within the Guild try to vie for control. Whoever has the best Seers—those of us with the greatest breadth and depth of vision—will ultimately have the greatest insight and control over the others. That is what Andreas and Crane are secretly doing—trying to create the best Quorum to increase their power and influence within the Guild and ultimately the UWO. It is why they keep me, and why they wanted you."

They were silent for a while, as Marcus gave Alessandra some time to absorb what he had told her. Though Alessandra was grateful to understand more of the reasons behind the rigid structure and torture of her life, it didn't matter to her as much as she thought it would now that she understood something more important, more sacred about herself.

"I never knew I could do that, that I could see...happiness," she said softly as she stared into the rain, a small smile playing on her face.

"Now you know," Marcus replied. "You can do that and much more. When you are ready, I will show you."

Over the next 3 months, Alessandra learned fast. Marcus knew from his own visions that Alessandra was a strong Seer, but even he had not seen how eager she was to learn, to finally have someone teach her something. As he watched her mind awaken under his instruction, he couldn't help but wonder how young she must have been when she was taken, and whether or not she had been as good of a student in school. Even though Marcus suspected that she was somewhere between 17 and 19 years of age, her demeanor made her seem much younger. Once her defenses were down, she was as honest and open as a child. The teacher in him could not help but speculate. *Before here*, he thought, *she must have been very shy or very sheltered.* The more he grew to appreciate her delicate but determined spirit, the more he tried not to think of all that was stolen from her.

Once Marcus showed her how to control her thoughts, she quickly learned how to hide their plans from the Quorum and the Guild. She practiced this constantly to make sure she was fully in control. Now that she had a chance to escape, she would not risk losing it. Marcus encouraged her to test and learn her own power independent of him or the Guild so that she could understand its strength completely.

"Every Seer I have ever come across has a unique color and tone to their sight that makes their visions distinct from any other," he explained once. "I learned mine because I was alone for so long. When I finally quorumed, I could easily see the difference between my visions and those of the others in my group. Most Seers that come here never get a chance to know the full power of their gift because they only use it in Quorum or under the Guild's strict supervision.

"Lucky for us, you're so crazy that they left you alone with me," Marcus teased. "If they only knew, eh?"

"Don't tease," Alessandra said with a shy smile. "Finish what you were saying. I don't understand."

"Hmmm. Okay, let me try this. Imagine that each vision we share is made up of layers, making the vision sharper and more detailed with every layer that is added. Some layers add only small details. Some layers have so much detail that you can understand what is happening at first glance.

"This is how our gift works. I know what I can see if I am alone versus what is added when each Seer in Quorum contributes to that same vision. The more you know the characteristics of your sight, the more you can distinguish your sight from the others. That is what I meant before. Each Seer's vision is like a layer of color—one layered on top of the other. Some colors are more dominant, others more subtle. The more you understand this, the more you can fill in, obscure, or even block the visions we don't want to share. This is how you will learn to dominate the visions in Quorum, to control them."

"Who are they, the Seers in our Quorum? What are their gifts?"

"There are five others: Mai, Kaido, Lucia, Sonja, and Ammon. Ammon and Sonja are known for their ability to see strong detail in an event–nothing like what you can do, of course, but they are very stable and consistent. They've been with Crane and Andreas the longest. Outside of Quorum, they are shadows. I don't think I've spoken more than a dozen words to them in the thirteen years I've been here.

"Mai can see and hold multiple visions of different futures simultaneously. She is very talented. Lucia has a unique ability to link events' causes and effects, no matter how small. It's a very subtle but useful gift, especially when we get a vision where it is difficult to understand the context. Kaido's gift is still difficult for me to understand. I think he somehow blends our visions together in a more cohesive way, but I'm not sure how it works. I don't speak Japanese and his English is limited, but I have always sensed a quiet spirit from him in Quorum. He and Lucia seem to have developed a closeness, which is strange because we are allowed very limited contact with each other outside of Quorum. You and I are a very special case."

Given the range of talents of the other Seers, maintaining the focus to block their visions proved extremely difficult for Alessandra. However, once she learned to control her emotions during visioning, Alessandra discovered that she could either restrain those feelings, or push them onto other Seers as a way to distract them.

At first, Marcus and Alessandra did this often to mask the full extent of her progress from Crane and Andreas while they worked. Later, Alessandra and Marcus used Crane and Andreas' growing impatience to showcase Alessandra's newfound ability for maximum effect. During a visioning session where the Quorum was tasked with seeing the outcome of an insurgence in Pakistan, Crane and Andreas were stunned as they watched Alessandra withstand the volatility of the vision calmly, without losing any of the staggering detail for which she was known. To their amazement, they were able to see not only how the physical battle would play out, but also how and why each of the principal players would make the decisions that led to the outcome.

Crane and Andreas were stunned by the change in Alessandra's visioning. Combined with the breadth of Marcus' range, her visions allowed unparalleled and limitless insight into the outcomes and the internal motivations behind any number of occurrences. In these two powerful Seers, Crane and Andreas had found the key that would secure their dominance within the Guild.

The change in Alessandra made both men more possessive of her, but for completely different reasons. Andreas knew he could not afford to let anything happen to her. Crane could not keep himself from claiming her as his own any longer.

As their visioning sessions became more and more successful, both Marcus and Alessandra could sense that the time for their escape was drawing near.

"It will be soon," Marcus assured her over breakfast. "I overheard them arguing this morning on my way to your room. Crane wants to reward you with better living quarters, closer to him. Andreas is resisting, but it will not last. Crane is too determined."

Alessandra nodded in understanding as she tried to quiet the urge to give in to her panic. Feeling the dull stabbing pain in her throat as it constricted around her first bite of breakfast, she took a sip of water to force it down and returned her spoon to the tray.

"Why can't we leave now? They're leaving for Nice tomorrow."

"We must wait for the level of Luridium in our blood to be as low as possible; otherwise they will be able to track us. Besides, we are more heavily guarded when Andreas and Crane are away. It will be easier to slip away when they return.

"The shipment of our next Luridium dosage will be late by two days next week. That will be our window. Next Wednesday, we will leave this place."

The next five days were tense as they tried to hide their growing hope for a new life outside the compound walls. Even with the increased guard presence, the compound felt more relaxed with Crane and Andreas away at the three-day UWO health summit. Marcus and Alessandra knew there would be no visioning sessions in their absence.

With the need to keep constant watch over Alessandra temporarily relaxed, Marcus focused his attention on blocking any potential sight into their plans. At the same time, Alessandra tried to regain the calm she'd had a week before when she had almost forgotten the images she'd seen of Crane's plans for her from her first day in Chicago.

On the night before Crane and Andreas' return, she had stayed awake all night, trying desperately to be calm enough to see a pleasant vision of the future, any future. Marcus had taught her that she could not vision clearly in fear. That was part of the reason why — before that day on the bench with Marcus — she had never had a strong vision of anything that wasn't stained with death or sorrow.

As soon as she felt herself dissolve into deep meditation, her vision emerged.

Pale blue-green eyes beaming, staring down into hers.

Her brown eyes looking back at him in awe, in gratitude, in love.

He kisses her softly on her mouth. His full lips curling into a smile. They feel like the very meaning of plush – soft, supple, warm, and sweet. He laughs playfully at the shaking of her knees as he pulls her closer, as she holds him to her. "I love you," he says truthfully, as promises drip from every merry little syllable.

"Uccelino," Little bird, he whispers into her ear. She buries her head in his strong, broad chest and smiles, believing every word.

By the time she jolted awake, it was morning and he was not there. The tears came before she even knew they were there as the emptiness that she'd felt for as long as she could remember became flooded with the pull, the need to find him. She wanted to relive the feeling, the all-over warmth of being so *precious* to someone, even if it was only ever in her dreams.

Sitting on the bed, the importance of what she was about to attempt felt like a storm brewing inside her. When she heard Marcus' light knocking, she leapt toward the door. The simple faith she held that their escape would mean something better was no longer good enough. She suddenly needed to know beyond any doubt exactly how it was going to work, how she was going to get to him.

Marcus was immediately alarmed when the door flew open and he saw her tear-stained face.

"Alessandra, what's happened? Are you all right? Has someone...?"

She quickly pulled him into her room and shut the door before her reply came out in a rush.

"Marcus, I have to leave here. I need to know that this will work. What can I do? What can I do? I need to...I have to find him. He... he said he loved me."

Marcus stood for a long moment, taking the time he needed to decipher the layers of meaning in her words. *Him,* he thought. *She has seen someone in her future; she has seen something very good.*

"You will find someone, Alessandra. I am happy for you. Come, walk with me and I will tell you what I know." Marcus smiled as he watched her throw on her robe and beat him out the door.

"Alessandra, I have been watching and waiting for this for a very long time. While it is not without risk, I believe that this plan will work because you have given Crane and Andreas the confidence they needed to feel invincible. It is their arrogance that will help us escape.

"I have been here for thirteen years and they have never suspected me, even though it's quite obvious that they should. They never questioned why, after three years of resisting them, I would suddenly begin to cooperate.

"They assume that the Luridium will be enough to control us, though it clearly doesn't work on either of us the way it should," he said, motioning toward the skin on his arm. "They depend on the Luridium to track us, but Crane and Andreas are so focused on their newfound omnipotence that they haven't even noticed that the shipment is late and every worker here is too afraid to tell them. Until you, a slip like that would have never happened. They have never even asked the Quorum to see any threats to this facility. They believe in themselves too much."

Alessandra was silent as she took in his words, looking for any flaws that she could address before nightfall. All her senses were tuned and vibrating with a strange new desire to survive — to live long enough to see the man in her vision.

"You are awake now. I can feel it." Marcus nodded in understanding.

Alessandra was too stunned by the sensations she felt to answer, but she knew that he was right.

"Why can't I see any of this myself?" Alessandra wondered aloud in frustration. "I could help us, but I can't. I can't see anything clearly."

"Alessandra," Marcus started in a gentle voice as he wrapped his arm around her shoulder. "You must learn to be patient. Seeing ourselves clearly, seeing our own future, takes practice. You have to see past yourself... to find true objectivity. I have worked on this for many years and I still have blind spots. I can't see everything, but this is how it's supposed to be...not knowing everything. It makes me feel normal, like life can still surprise me.

"But mind your thoughts and your emotions, Alessandra. We leave tonight. We must be careful not to betray ourselves."

"Yes, I will," Alessandra whispered as she tried to rein in all the feelings she wanted to set free. "I have to."

CHAPTER 8: 15 SECONDS

As soon as Alessandra woke up from her nap later that evening, she knew they had failed, had somehow missed the details of what would be their undoing. The soft tinkling of keys outside her door told her that Crane had finally come to claim what he felt had always been his.

Having just seen him push the key in the lock on her door, she was momentarily disoriented as the vision she was now about to live through faded from her mind, fusing her present and future before her eyes. She had fifteen seconds before he unlocked the door, fifteen seconds between life and the beginning of a slow, painful death.

On the other side of the door, what could have been mistaken for hesitation was anything but that. Crane was savoring the anticipation, the rush of adrenaline as his fingers hovered above the doorknob. He had waited so long and planned so carefully; he didn't want to rush a single moment. He excitedly wondered if she'd seen him coming and was trembling inside her room with the fear of all he planned to do to her. He desperately hoped so. *It would be such a fine beginning*, he mused as he waited, feeling the quickening of his own pulse.

In the months since Alessandra first came to Chicago, Crane had kept his distance and did his best to appear indifferent as he watched Alessandra blossom under Marcus' instruction. He could tell from their body language that they had formed a close friendship, and even though he knew this was a necessary bond, the knowledge filled him with jealousy. But, in spite of his envy of Marcus' carefree access to her, Crane maintained his control. He knew he needed to bide his time and let Andreas believe that he had been wrong about the depth of Crane's attraction and the nature of his plans for Alessandra.

The truth was that no matter what Andreas thought, he could not imagine the terrible grip of Crane's obsession. Crane had been there the day Miguel brought her to the Purification Center in Berlin, Germany. He had never witnessed a Seer so fragile, so utterly broken, and still more breakable. She was only 11 at the time. He remembered her hands were covered in blood that he knew immediately was not hers. Miguel was one of their best gatherers. He knew better than to hurt her. *A relative that died during the gathering… perhaps a sister,* he guessed as he looked at the decidedly feminine but too small coat she clung to with all the might her tiny frame could muster. Even Miguel could not wrest it from her.

When the nail of her ring finger ripped off from the sheer force of the tug of war between them, Crane had to excuse himself. She hadn't even screamed. It was there in the bathroom, with Crane jerking himself off like a teenage boy, that he knew he had to have her for himself. Since he was not the Guild leader to bring her in, he did not have rights to her. So he waited and watched as she was passed from Center to Center, until at last no one else wanted her and he finally had his chance.

On the plane ride back from Nice, Crane had put his long-awaited plans for her in motion.

"Andreas, as soon as we get to Chicago, I want to have a visioning session. We need to be ready for our next full meeting with the Guild. Camille has gotten completely out of hand."

"Relax, Crane. You're beginning to sound like me," Andreas chuckled. "We have Marcus and Alessandra with us. We will see everything and prepare. There is nothing to worry about anymore." Andreas had completely surrendered to the softness of his leather recliner. "Besides, it will be evening when we return. Our children need their rest."

"We could just use Marcus and Alessandra. There's no need to bother the others."

"Possibly, but we should consult with Marcus first. Alessandra is doing so well. I don't want to push her just yet," Andreas said.

"Yes, I suppose it would be good to know his thoughts on her progress, to make sure she is stable. I've been so busy, I really haven't followed her progress that closely," Crane responded with a yawn.

"I've noticed," Andreas sighed with relief. He was pleased to see that over the past few months, Crane seemed to understand and respect the importance of Alessandra beyond his personal pleasures. "We'll speak to him together."

Crane did not respond as he pretended to drift off to sleep.

When they arrived in Chicago, Andreas sent Christof to find Marcus while he and Crane waited in the library. As Christof exited the dining hall, he was not surprised to find Marcus faithfully escorting Alessandra to her room. They appeared to be deep in conversation.

"He is coming now. Remember, Alessandra, lock your door. I will come back for you as soon as I can," Marcus whispered in a rush before turning to meet Christof as he approached them.

"I suppose you know why I'm here," Christof said with a grin.

"I do," Marcus replied, returning his smile. Marcus had always wondered how such a well-mannered young man had ended up working for the Guild. He bid Alessandra a solemn good night before leaving her with Christof and heading to the library.

"Marcus!" Crane exclaimed enthusiastically. "It seems like it's been ages. You have been so occupied with our Alessandra."

Marcus was not fooled. Though he could not see every aspect of the scene that was about to unfold, he didn't need to be a Seer to know that Crane was practically shaking with jealousy and lust. He took a deep breath before answering. "Yes, you were very wise to bring her here. She is very talented," Marcus answered in a placating tone.

Sometimes it truly irritated Crane how Marcus never seemed to be intimidated by him. "Yes, well, Andreas and I wanted to inquire about Alessandra's progress. Is she stable enough to be fully integrated into our Quorum?"

Andreas looked up from his phone to speak before becoming distracted by one of the voicemail messages he was scanning through. When he appeared to be getting more engrossed in the message, Crane smiled apologetically at Marcus and motioned for him to answer.

"Yes," Marcus said. "I think she is almost there, a week or two at the most and she will be ready to stand on her own."

"I see," Crane replied as he began to pace around the room. "So you don't feel she is ready now?"

"No, I wouldn't want to push her. She is still… somewhat fragile."

"Yes, I know… I mean, I know you two have grown very close."

Marcus didn't know if it was the tone of his voice or the far-off look in Crane's eyes that sickened him, but he couldn't stand by and fail to challenge the man who meant Alessandra harm.

"She is like a daughter to me. I would not let any harm come to her." Marcus knew he sounded too alert, too sharp, but he couldn't help it and he didn't want to.

Marcus' tone did not surprise Crane. They were both men of some years and Crane knew that Marcus understood exactly what he wanted to do to Alessandra, probably better than he did.

"Of course, Marcus. That's how we all feel."

Marcus kept quiet as he and Crane glanced at Andreas, who was now hissing angrily into his phone. Crane was thoroughly satisfied. By the looks of things, the diversion he had planned for Andreas would be completely unnecessary.

At the appearance of Crane's bodyguard, Damon, Crane's entire demeanor became rushed with a sudden urgency.

"It appears that we will have to continue this conversation some other time. Andreas is obviously engaged in some pressing matter I should probably make myself aware of. Damon will escort you back to your room."

Marcus could only comply distractedly as a future he had not seen began to reveal itself. While he was quickly ushered out of the library and down the long corridor to his room, he could see what was about to happen even though he was powerless to stop it. The syringe in Damon's pocket was meant to put him to sleep—all night, leaving Alessandra completely unprotected.

If he fought, he would be put in solitary containment and would not escape. If he didn't, he would be incapacitated and would not escape. *There really isn't much of a choice either way*, Marcus reasoned. By the time Marcus turned around, prepared to block the hand that held out the syringe just above his shoulder, he was met with Damon's face—frozen in shock at the realization that his hand and the syringe it carried were being forced into his own neck by someone else. Damon's body fell to the ground almost instantly, revealing the equally shocked expression of the most unassuming Seer in their Quorum. Marcus and Kaido stared at Damon's limp body in disbelief for a long moment before turning their attention to each other.

"How?" It was all Marcus could manage to get out as he watched a small smile creep across Kaido's broad face.

"I saw my future," was all Kaido offered before dropping to the floor and patting Damon down for his keys. When he retrieved them, he looked up at Marcus and continued.

"First, I must get Lucia while you collect Alessandra, then we leave."

Marcus nodded slowly as he began to understand that the connection between Kaido and Lucia that he had always assumed was platonic was, in fact, much more.

"We can't just leave him here for them to find. Help me lift him up so I can take him to my room," Marcus said, as he motioned to Damon's sleeping form.

Once they lifted his hulking figure over Marcus' shoulder and agreed on where to meet, they each ran off in different directions as silently as they could.

Approaching the staircase that led to Alessandra's floor, Marcus could sense that he and Kaido had lingered too long. After leaving Damon's body in his room, Marcus didn't bother returning to the library to check on Crane's whereabouts. He was sure that Crane would have left the library as quickly as possible to get to Alessandra. All his assumptions and fears were confirmed as Marcus rounded the corner of the stairwell to see Crane outside Alessandra's door, inserting her room key into the lock.

Without thinking, Marcus took off in a sprint and lunged at him, knocking him to the ground. Crane was so surprised to feel his own body suddenly slammed into the floor that he didn't have time to muster the defenses to fight back. Crane still hadn't figured out that it had been *someone* who knocked him down until he was able to focus his eyes enough to see Marcus crouched over him. It was then that he realized that his head was held roughly between the palms of Marcus' large hands. He had only another brief moment to register the look of sheer rage on Marcus' face before he felt his head rattle and crack against the cold marble floor.

At the sound of the loud commotion, Alessandra ran to the door and opened it to find Marcus hovering over Crane's unconscious body while his key still dangled from her door.

"Is he dead?" she asked, in awe of Marcus and what he had managed to do for her.

"No," Marcus sighed. "After all he's taken from me, I still couldn't do it."

"Oh." Even though Alessandra understood, she didn't try to mask the look of disappointment on her face.

"Quickly, Alessandra. Give me the rope from your robe and tie his feet. I'll get his hands."

"Very good," Kaido said when he walked up behind them with a wide-eyed and quivering Lucia under his arm. Alessandra stared at them in surprise before turning her attention back to Marcus, who was smiling as he finished securing Crane's hands.

After Alessandra and Marcus were finished and Crane was slumped over Marcus' shoulder, they made their way to the private entrance that was reserved for Crane and Andreas' personal use. Because it was biometrically controlled, it was the most secure and least monitored door in the entire complex, which allowed Crane to entertain any number of interests without surveillance. No one ever came here unless they were escorted by Andreas or Crane personally, because only their specific hand imprint could open the doors, in or out. With Crane's hands dangling over the side of Marcus' back, he knew it would not be a problem.

"This is almost poetic," Marcus said as he placed Crane's hand on the scanner. On contact the door slid open, letting in a rush of cool night air. No one in their group but Alessandra had cried about anything in a very long time, but as they felt the brisk air hit their bodies all at once, each of them knew they were in danger of losing that battle tonight.

They deposited Crane's limp body and their robes on the ground just inside the door and turned to look at their captor, the symbol of their oppression, one last time before running deep into the night.

Andreas was livid. The Luridium shipment was late. *Two days late and I had to learn about it in a voicemail from some supply line worker,* he seethed. He called Christof first.

"Get back here now!" Andreas hissed into the phone.

"But, Alessandra…" Christof offered as he shrank away from the anger in Andreas' voice.

"I don't give a damn where you are! Get back here now." Andreas sincerely hoped that Christof didn't know anything about the late shipment, or there would be hell to pay.

Next he needed to call the supplier. It was 10 o'clock at night, but he didn't care. Andreas knew Frank Carter, the supply plant manager, well and planned to call him at home so that Frank would know that Andreas expected him to handle the situation personally. Andreas didn't expect a fight when Frank answered the phone, but he yelled anyway, just to put the fear of God or the devil into him.

By the time he got off the phone, he noticed that both Crane and Marcus were gone. *Did Damon come in?* He wondered absently before pushing the pound button on his phone to hear the next message.

All his senses were heightened when he heard Deidra Pile's angry voice on the recording. Deidra was the administrator for the purification facility in Glasgow and a high-ranking member of the Guild. Years ago, when they had met as young recruits to the UWO, Deidra and Andreas had been fond acquaintances, but their relationship had soured once Andreas decided to consolidate his quest for power with Crane's. He knew Deidra had no love for either of them, so the sound of her voice on the answering service could only mean trouble.

"I don't know what you're up to over there, Andreas, but I warned you about Crane a long time ago. Our Seers have discovered some type of disturbance at your site, something happening soon or maybe even right now. They couldn't see any more than that. All the details were clouded, almost as if they were being obscured on purpose, blocked by someone. I don't even know how that could be possible, but I have a feeling you do. All they could see for sure is that whatever you've got going on over there could affect us all, could bring down all that we have worked for, and I won't let you do this, Andreas. I mean it. This is your last warning before I call the Guild Council."

As he replayed her message again, Andreas felt sick with the slow understanding that he had somehow been blind–blinded and wrong about everything.

Chapter 9: Outside

August, 2011

Awe was the only word Marcus could think of to describe the expression on Alessandra's face as she gazed up at the clear night sky. The sliver of light coming in from the storm drain above them held on to the outline of her features enough for him to make out the whites of her eyes and the curve of her neck as it strained so awkwardly to the right that Marcus thought it might snap.

Even though she needed to stay hidden under the concrete shelter, Alessandra couldn't stop staring out between the spaces of the rusted bars they had crawled through and marveling at how different everything looked now that she was free. Periodically, she would lose her balance, tipping over the narrow ledge that separated her from the stream of sewage and rain just below her feet. When this happened, she ended up dipping her hands into the dirty water to steady herself. She barely noticed. The sights and sounds, even the smells around her, were amazing. She couldn't remember anything in real life ever feeling so good.

But even the thrill of their new freedom couldn't keep away the cold. The wind and the rain were bitter, biting things. The fact that they had only one ugly brown coat between the 4 of them didn't matter one bit. They each took turns passing around Alessandra's coat with huge grins stretched over their chattering teeth. They would have laughed out loud if they didn't need the warmth of their own breath so desperately. No one missed the shelter of their red robes.

Once they left the compound, Marcus estimated that they had two hours before they were missed, so they ran as hard and as fast as their muscles could take them, through the cold until the wind turned to rain. Then they ran some more. They didn't ask Marcus why he led them through the alleys and back roads. Their first unrestrained glimpses of "real" people and billboards reminded them all of what they hadn't thought about in so long, what they had all gotten used to – their appearances. An hour before dawn, they crawled into a storm drain, knowing they could not risk anyone seeing them in the light of day.

"It will rain today, which is good. Fewer people out to notice us," Marcus shared hopefully, huddling as close to Alessandra as her wandering gaze would allow.

Taking in Marcus' words, Kaido's heavy brows creased as he absently pulled Lucia's shaking body closer. "Can you see where we need to go? I only saw… bits…a red barn…angry people telling us to go away."

Marcus nodded his understanding. After all the trust they had placed in him, they needed to know what to expect.

"Just across the road there, we will catch a cargo train carrying auto parts and head to Iowa. There we will find a community of people who are outside of everything – just like us. We are the first of our kind to escape the Guild. They will not be familiar with us, so our appearance will frighten them. They will think we are…devils of some kind, so of course we will not be welcome. But eventually they will take us in.

There is an older man with long gray hair who will help us. Beyond that, it is harder for me to see. "

Marcus chuckled then, amused by his own lack of knowing.

"To be honest, it's only now that I realize that I've spent so much time just trying to escape that I haven't focused my sight on much else. Now that we are here, in the open, I think I am just amazed that after all this time, this dream I have had for so long has finally come true. "

"You have carried this for a long time then?" Kaido asked in surprise.

"Yes. Alessandra and I have been blocking this vision for quite awhile. But the fact that you are here now suggests that I have not been completely successful," Marcus continued with a smile. "I am glad for this."

Before Kaido could ask another question, Marcus rose to his feet, signaling to the group that it was time to head out. "I know you don't understand everything I've said, but I will show you what I mean later, when Lucia is well and we are safe."

"彼女は病気ですか？" Kaido blurted out in alarm, turning his head toward Lucia to smooth the untamed curls on her head away from her ash-brown skin. "Why is she sick?"

Sensing the panic in Kaido's voice, Lucia looked up at him and explained what Marcus did not have the heart to tell them. "Not yet," she said, placing a hand that was just beginning to shake on Kaido's forearm. "But I will be soon. We all will be very soon."

It took them nearly seven days to reach the top of the mound that looked down on the small commune. There was nothing to distinguish the cluster of small cabins, barns, and open air meeting halls as anything other than a random scattering of dwellings, except for a large boulder at the base of the hill marked with the words Fox River Commune written in faded red letters. The tiny hill was an anomaly among the endless plains that had been their only landscape for the past 30 miles. Even in his exhaustion, Marcus could appreciate how the topography obstructed any view of the commune from the road, keeping its inhabitants hidden and safe.

After catching the first of several trains, they had survived the week on a steady but stealthy regimen of petty crimes, including breaking and entering to steal clothes, cash, and food when people weren't home, and grand theft auto of a rusted 1989 Camry that was the bane of its 16 year-old, sick of hand-me-downs owner's existence. It took them, sputtering, from the border of New London, Illinois into Iowa. When Marcus, Lucia, Alessandra, and Kaido pushed the car into Lake Wapello, they all agreed that the car's former owner wouldn't miss it and neither would they. They walked the rest of the way, hidden in tall grass and guided along by Marcus' conviction and vague sense of direction.

As they traveled, Alessandra ignored all but the essential, choosing to be driven forward by *his* face in her mind, setting her pace to the memory of his beating heart.

When they made it to the top of the hill, they were starved and shaken from exertion and the onset of their withdrawal symptoms from the Luridium. Seeing their appearance through the narrowed, deep-set eyes of the man who would spot them first, Marcus knew their disheveled state would do little to allay the crowd's compounding fears as they grew closer and each person in the commune got a good look at them.

From the valley, the four Seers were an ominous assortment of grey, black, and navy blue hoodies, sunglasses, blue jeans, and boots.

Their sweatshirts and glasses hid the starkness of their appearance from onlookers and protected their sensitive skin from the sun. But Marcus knew that the group of two dozen people who were beginning to gather in front of them would not understand. Each Seer had already registered the presence of at least two shot guns trained on them as they advanced.

"We are not afraid, Marcus. No matter what happens now, we have already come farther than we expected to," Kaido said, as they made their way down the hill.

Alessandra could feel the depth of her longing ripple through her as she searched the growing crowd. Yet she was calm and confident, knowing that her destiny — their destinies — each lay in this new place.

From the corner of her eye, she saw Marcus raise his arms in a gesture of surrender and peace.

"Please," he began, "we mean you no harm. We have come seeking your help. Please, we ask you to help us. We will not hurt you." When he finished, he pushed his hood off and slowly removed his sunglasses, revealing himself and what he was to the onlookers. About 50 feet away from the crowd, he stopped, motioning for the others to do the same. Alessandra, Kaido, and Lucia all removed their hoods and stood, unwavering, beside him.

Marcus' words and their collective actions were met with a volatile mixture of soft gasps and utter silence as each person from the commune took in the sight of the four strangers. Some simply shook their heads in disbelief, while others hoisted their guns higher with fingers itching to snuff out that which they did not understand.

Finally, the man who had seen them first flicked the safety off of his M14 semi-automatic rifle and spoke in a voice that was deep and gravelly.

"Who the fuck are you, and how the fuck did you find us?" Marshall Farber barked as he repositioned his gun slightly to the right.

From behind him, Marshall could hear Rachel Nemins' gasp, just before he felt her hand settle lightly on his left shoulder.

"Marshall, wait, they're Seers" she said just loud enough for Marcus and the others to hear. Before this moment, Rachel had only seen pictures of the Seers from her father's pulpit. Though the images on the church projector had been grainy, they conveyed the same haunting strangeness that stood before her now. Reverend Nemins had told the congregation that the Seers were a sign of God's judgment against sinners like her–a sign of the end.

"What?" Marshall asked, as he glanced quickly in her direction. But instead of answering him, Rachel took a step towards Marcus in surrender to the judgment she'd always felt was coming for her.

"Rachel!" Marshall called before shifting his gun back to shot-ready position.

"You better get her, man" Vincent Quinn said to Marshall as he leveled his position with Marshall's right shoulder and held his own semi-automatic high. "This is probably not gonna end well."

Ignoring the banter behind her, Rachel took another tentative step forward. "You're from the Guild. How is that possible?" she questioned, looking solemnly at Marcus before shifting her eyes outward to scan the horizon. "Are you here to kill us? Are there more of you?"

"No!" Marcus replied quickly as he shifted his gaze from Rachel to Marshall and Vincent. "Please don't shoot. We are alone. My name is Marcus Akida and these are my companions — Alessandra, Lucia, and Kaido. We have escaped from the Guild. That is why we need your help. Please, we're not here to hurt anyone."

Marcus and the others did not miss the looks of skepticism that now mixed with the fear on the faces of the onlookers. As words like "devil," "evil," "freak," and "kill them" were volleyed among the crowd at an escalating pitch, each Seer held onto their own sense of calm acceptance as they waited for the shift in their future.

"I don't know what the hell you're talking about," Marshall said as he inched close enough to grab Rachel by the wrist and pull her behind him. "But you need to back the fuck-up and get out of here, now!"

Like everyone else, Marshall had heard the Seer spook stories, but never paid them much attention. He'd certainly never seen one before, but what little he did know of the Guild was enough for him to understand he didn't want any part of whatever this was. Escaped or not, harboring fugitives from the Guild was a mistake that could easily cost you your life. As an ex-army soldier in Iraq, he'd learned the hard way that when it came to the unknown, asking questions first and shooting later most often got you killed.

"I don't know where you come from, but you're not bringing any of your troubles in here," Marshall declared. He then raised his voice to address the crowd behind him. "We either kill them now, or they get us killed later. They could be trying to get at one of us right now." When he heard the sound of several guns cocked in agreement, Marshall prepared to open fire before he heard Eli Tanner shout from the back of the crowd.

"Marshall, you don't know that. Let's not start a panic." Eli could barely believe his eyes as he tried to move his portly frame quickly to the front of the group. "The Guild doesn't send Seers out to gather other Seers," he continued, out of breath.

As the man that Marcus had been waiting for began to part the crowd and cut the rising tension, he slowly released the breath he'd been holding. To his relief, Eli walked straight up to him with his hand extended.

"Forgive us. We don't get newcomers often. We're a little short on hospitality, I guess," Eli apologized as he tilted his head back towards the crowd. "I'm Eli. Eli Tanner. Marshall and Vincent don't mean any harm. We're just…protective of what we have here."

Marcus and Eli shared a moment of comfortable silence as they shook hands, allowing each man time to gather their questions for one another before Marcus finally spoke.

"I am Marcus Akida. It is a pleasure to finally meet you, Eli. You have been in my mind for a long time, but I feared you might not get here in time for us to meet," he joked, shifting his eyes back to the tense crowd before letting out a relaxed chuckle.

"Yes, I can understand your concern," Eli smiled. "But forgive me, I must ask. How are you here? How did you escape with three others? I can't imagine…" Eli trailed off as he scanned the Seers who stood beside Marcus.

Watching the ease and understanding that Eli clearly had with them, Marcus began to suspect that Eli had some knowledge of Seers, but he didn't know how that could be possible. Trusting his instincts, he decided to tell Eli the truth.

"Some of us have developed an ability to block the visions of others. This is how we masked our plans to escape from the Guild," Marcus watched him carefully before continuing, giving Eli the time he needed to recover from the shock he displayed at the news. "You have some experience with Seers, I think. We are not new to you."

Eli took a moment before speaking.

"Yes, a long time ago. I was a member of the group of scientists that first discovered the genetic marker. Our research was… cut short when we refused to cooperate with the Guild, but I have never heard of the ability you describe in any of the Seers we studied. With the Luridium they give you, I can't even imagine how you even had the willpower to formulate a plan on your own…" Eli trailed off, looking from Seer to Seer before he noticed that Kaido's hands were shaking.

"How long has it been since your last dose? When did you escape?"

"Over three weeks now. We left last Wednesday. The withdrawal is becoming… difficult," Marcus explained, trying to ignore his own nausea long enough to plead their case effectively.

Eli nodded his understanding as he took in their symptoms of dehydration and exhaustion before turning to the crowd.

"I'm going to help them. They need our help."

"Eli, you don't have the right to put us all in danger!" Marshall protested, even as the crowd began to shift outward and disperse.

"And it's not your right to order them killed before we've even had a chance to understand what's happening here. They may not look like it to you, but they are human beings. The least we can do is show them some decency after everything they've been through to get here," Eli responded sternly.

Though there was no official hierarchy at Fox River, Eli knew his tenure as one of the founding members of the commune would at least make the other members stop and think before they inflicted any violence against the Seers. As the crowd continued to diminish, Eli nodded in acknowledgement that for the moment, Marshall had been temporarily overruled.

"All right Doc, you can help them out — for now, but *we* decide as a group if they stay or not — tonight, in the meeting hall. We'll discuss this then."

While Marcus and the other Seers followed Eli into the compound, Alessandra remained focused on a mass of thick, black hair that was visible through the crowd. They were both still as the group thinned enough for her to get her first unobstructed view of Liam.

His eyes were squinted and cold, but she was still certain of their color and the warmth they could have, even if it wasn't present now. The enormity of her relief at having found him obscured the fact that he did not return her smile. That he was holding a small girl protectively at his side did not arouse the slightest question in Alessandra's mind as to who she was and the nature of their relationship. He was alive. He was real, and that was all that was important to her in that moment.

Liam dug his boot heels into the forgiving earth, trying to hold himself in place. He could not understand how he could find such a thing so frighteningly beautiful. From the minute he and Lilli entered the clearing after running towards the sound of Marshall's voice, he was inexplicably captivated by her. He knew he should have been repulsed by the sick color of her milky eyes instead of wondering what color they used to be, but he couldn't. Something in the way her jaw held steady even as her body quivered like a small bird mesmerized him and drew his admiration against his will. It unhinged him how quickly all his thoughts flowed toward her like a river, drowning all his studied indifference and futile protest with its weight and power. At least he had an excuse for his presence when the near massacre had taken place. But now, with Lilli looking between them with growing understanding, the real reason Liam was still standing there was undeniably clear.

They said her name was Alessandra, he thought, as he tried in vain not to wonder any more about her. He had to say her name two more times before he finally found the strength to look away.

Chapter 10: Decisions

Marshall's voice resonated with condemnation as he concluded his case against the Seers. "I don't give a shit who they are or what they can do. They are NOT one of us!"

Eli let out a long sigh before slowly leaning forward in his chair and resting his forearms on his khaki-covered thighs. It was better than reclining in defeat, he reasoned, as he looked out onto the commune gathering. The meeting had been going on for over two hours with no decision reached for or against letting the Seers remain at Fox River. He and Marcus had tried to combat ignorance with facts, fear with logic. But it had been useless. Hardly anything could penetrate the natural distrust people had for the Seers after so many years of propaganda.

The fact that Marcus was the only Seer well enough to even be present at the meeting didn't help. They all wanted to come, but Eli finally convinced them that a display of violent tremors and vomiting would do little to impress an already-cautious crowd. Looking over at the seat next to him, Eli could tell that with all the back and forth, Marcus was slowly losing his battle to stay upright as the debating went on.

"It *is* true. We are not one of you. We have been given these... abilities, which make us different. But as I understand it, you are all here because you come from different backgrounds, unconventional ways of living. Can we not be accommodated in such a community as this?" Marcus attempted to reason once more in a soft and shaky voice.

"I don't see what the big deal is anyway," Kyle Shaw asked as he stood up to address the commune. "So they're freaks; we're all freaks! They can't help it anymore than we can."

"We don't know that, Kyle" Rachel said in a low voice that was part shame for believing her father's preachings, and part undeniable fear at the Seer's very proximity. "We don't know what their being here means."

Jean Ellis had been sitting on one of the bales of hay that made up the circular seating of their makeshift meeting hall, trying to watch and listen since the meeting began, but she was finally losing patience. They weren't getting anywhere, and though she was shy, she couldn't keep quiet anymore. She stood up to address Marcus directly for the first time since he arrived.

"Look, I'm sorry," she began in her soft New Orleans accent, "you seem like a nice person and all, but you have to understand that everything we've ever heard about Seers has been bad or worse. I mean, I think we all grew up hearing that you guys were crazy. That you look…" Jean paused briefly to try and come up with an adjective that was less offensive than the ones that had already been thrown around. After a moment, she decided that no description at all would be best before continuing, "…like you do because of some weird genetic disorder.

"As a kid, I remember hearing on the news how you guys killed all the doctors who tried to help you. They said that you were too unstable to even be in real society. They said you guys were like Satan-worshippers; that if we trusted you, you would control our minds and make us kill our own mothers or something. Now you say it's all a lie and, I mean, I believe Eli, but it's just a lot to take in right now. I mean, can't we have some more time to think about it? Why do we have to decide this right now?"

Marcus, who had been feeling the weight of his own withdrawal bearing down on him, was suddenly wide awake and outraged. While he appreciated Jean's candor, the extent of the lies told about him and the other Seers made his mouth fill with bile.

Marcus' voice was deep and low as he struggled to control the hardening anger in his voice.

"I am glad that you can trust Eli, because there is no way for me to express how backwards that story is. The Guild killed my family in front of me. My wife! My only son! Every Seer I know has had the same thing done to them with no mercy, no exception. There was a time when I would have served God or the Devil to have my revenge on them, but that is not the nature of my gift. We didn't ask for this, none of us did or would have. It has robbed us of everything important, everything that matters."

"But how do we know you aren't controlling us with your mind right now?" someone yelled out from the back of the crowd.

"Because you're still an asshole, Tim," Kyle quipped before his older sister, Hanna, inflicted a loud smack to the back of his head.

Marcus smiled at Kyle's youthful spirit, even as his strength to continue the fight waned. "I wish there was some way to prove this to you, my friend. I can only assure you that I am not."

If only, Eli thought ruefully. *We could have been done with this meeting an hour and a half ago.*

Silence fell over the meeting hall as each person in the room tried to see through the impasse that held them in place. Everyone at Fox River knew that Eli would not lie to them. He was one of the oldest and most respected members of the commune, but the rumors, the fear, the look of the Seers who were now among them, and the threat of the Guild's retaliation if they were discovered were all hard things to just accept.

As the silence stretched on, Marcus tried to steady his breathing and visualize how far each of his friends would progress in their healing by morning. Eli rehashed the arguments he and Marcus had laid out and tried to analyze if there was any way to make their statements more clear. Across the room, Rachel and Marshall tried to make their case to those sitting closest to them while others simply stared into the confusion on their colleagues' faces.

At the back of the room, Liam sat with sweaty palms, clutching Lilli's hand like a vice. Each new event of the day was like the rolling out of his worst fears in quick succession. As he listened to the crowd when the Seers arrived that morning and again at the group meeting, all his reasons for keeping Lilli's secret hidden were confirmed. Thanks to Eli, when Liam and Lilli had arrived at the commune a year and a half ago, they were more or less welcomed. Eli had been expecting them ever since he received Jill's letter almost two years before they arrived and was overjoyed to finally get confirmation that they had survived the Guild's pursuit. Liam was just grateful that Eli could be trusted with their secret, though he disagreed with Liam's wish to keep their past hidden from the commune.

Even with Eli's endorsement, Liam and Lilli still experienced some of the commune's natural wariness toward strangers, but Lilli's charm and enthusiasm quickly won everyone over. It also didn't hurt that Liam and Lilli were willing to share their considerable resources with the group, giving the Commune the ability to make long-needed repairs and access supplies they hadn't seen in years. Liam fell into the role of resident fix-it-man and Eli's apprentice, while Lilli taught

Chinese and French to the dozen children that lived at Fox River. Over time, they each fell into their roles within the commune, with Lilli being immediately adored and Liam being respected and generally liked, although he kept mostly to himself.

It's worked so far, Liam thought, as he felt Lilli's hand slowly slipping from his fingers. *We're safe here. Please, don't do this.*

Liam didn't need to look at Lilli or have the aid of any special powers to know what his sister was thinking. They had argued about it enough. Over the last year, all their fights seemed to revolve around Lilli's increasing insistence that she was tired of hiding, and her accusations that Liam was overprotective and paranoid. In response, Liam had shamelessly invoked his duty to protect her as the last wish of their mother who had died to keep them safe. As Lilli struggled to break his grasp, he knew he had gone to the well of her guilt one time too many.

The simple truth was that Lilli had grown up since their mother died. While her body and face were still girlish to him, Liam could not deny that Lilli had matured far beyond the 13-year old girl who collected candy wrappers and boy band CDs three and a half years ago. She had always been smart, he knew this, but over the past few years she had somehow become wise. He didn't know if it was her sight that made her surer of herself, or if it was just the knowledge of all she had survived in her short life, but she was different. He knew it was an insult to her for him to deny it, but he couldn't help it. At sixteen, she was ready to be her own person, to face her own consequences. It was Liam who wasn't prepared to change, to give up his role as her protector. He had been so singularly focused on her safety for so long that he couldn't remember what it was like for his life to be about anything else. While the responsibility had been difficult to accept at first, over the years, it had given his life a defined shape and purpose, a certainty to cling to when he couldn't trust anything else.

Until that morning, nothing had ever diverted his attention from this one truth. Seeing Alessandra staring back at him with a thousand emotions he refused to name was his first call to something else, something other than what he had known. With only the look in her eyes, she had made him feel truly vulnerable for the first time since he found his mother in the kitchen. So he ran from her, clinging to Lilli in hopes that she could shield him from what he knew was emerging inside him.

As Liam felt the last of Lilli's fingers squeeze past his palm, he knew his time had run out. He looked up to see her slowly rising from her place beside him, as he silently pleaded with her one last time.

"It'll be all right, Liam. I have to do this," she whispered to him, patting her brother's hand as she stood to her full height of 5'3" and spoke with a clear voice.

"I am a Seer," she said simply.

Heads jerked toward the voice they knew so well in stunned silence. Shock rippled through the room as she repeated, "I am a Seer."

As Lilli expected, no one knew what to say, so she continued on, encouraged by the small smile playing on Eli's face.

"Since we came here, my brother has been afraid to tell you who and what I really am. He was afraid that you would treat me the way you've treated this man, Marcus, today. But I just can't sit here and listen to everything that's been said today and be silent anymore.

"Do you think that I'm a devil? Have I ever harmed any of you or your children? Do you think I honestly would? My mother was a Seer and she lived her whole life afraid of who she was and what everyone else would do if they found out. I don't want that kind of life.

My brother and I came here and learned to trust you, care for you, and become one of you. Now I'm asking you to trust me. This man and his friends are no more a threat to you than Liam and I are. We didn't ask for this, and we wouldn't—I haven't ever used it to hurt anyone, but it's come to this, so now I need to ask you to give them the same safe place that you offered Liam and I. If you can't, I will accept that, but I won't stay here with you and hide."

Lilli remained standing after she was done speaking, surveying the faces of her neighbors and friends, daring them to look at her and see someone other than the person they had known every day for the past year and a half.

But Lilli knew they wouldn't. She had seen this moment coming from the minute she recognized Marcus that morning. He was thinner than he had been in the vision she had 2 days before he arrived, but she knew him on sight. She always marveled at how she could see the future so clearly and still be so impatient for it. *So young about it,* she chided herself. Still, even though she had been waiting for this moment, and felt like she was ready for it, she was glad to feel the warmth of Liam's hand as he reached up to rub her back, assuring her that he supported her, even if he didn't agree with what she was doing. It immediately calmed the shaking of her knees.

Finally, Rachel broke the heavy silence that had become stifling in the room.

"Lilli… I don't know what to say. I just—I think we just need to leave this alone for now. We...*I* had no idea. You're like family to us, all of us. I don't think any of us could imagine this place without you now." Rachel glanced tentatively at Marcus before she continued. "I think we just need some time to take in everything, like Jean said. It's late. I think we all need to just get some rest, sleep on this, and maybe we can talk about this again… tomorrow."

People filed out quickly after that, as if running from the tension of the evening. Some gave furtive smiles toward Lilli as they left, while others avoided her gaze completely. Within two minutes the hall was cleared, leaving only Lilli, Liam, Marcus, and Eli behind.

CHAPTER 11: WITHDRAWAL

After Lilli's admission, the subject of what to do with the Seers was never formally raised again. Though the instinct to fear the latest additions to the commune lingered for quite some time, no one could reignite the hostility needed to evict the Seers from Fox River while facing Lilli every day. To manage that feat would have been like trying to convince someone that the warmth of the sun was bad for them. It just didn't make any sense, so people tiptoed around the issue until it was no longer a sore subject to mention the Seers' existence among them.

In the first three weeks of their presence, this silent truce was made easier by the obvious severity of the Luridium withdrawal each Seer endured. Their screams and moans echoed clear across the 150-acre commune as they fought off the cravings in their bodies. Eli and Liam tried their best to ease their suffering with the medical supplies they had, but Eli knew that, for the most part, there was nothing he could do but let each body purge itself of the dependence the Luridium was designed to create.

Those commune members, like Rachel, who stopped by to satisfy their curiosity and to see if they could help became witnesses to the contorted and shaken expressions of terror on the Seers' faces as they suffered through horrific hallucinations. By the time the high fever and body tremors returned, the relative peace on their faces and the quiet throughout the Commune seemed like a kindness. As news of their ordeal traveled from person to person, it became easier to simply call each Seer by name than to be rude, and with that slow acceptance, any final questions about their status within the Commune were laid to rest.

With no looming threat of expulsion or mistreatment of the Seers, Eli turned his full attention toward their recuperation and trying to understand what their life had been like under the Guild's control. The unfinished work that he left behind at the UWO had been a lingering source of regret. To be able to speak with four Seers with developed abilities was an opportunity he never thought he would have, and sharing the discovery with the son of his best friend and former partner made the gift even more meaningful. Though Eli noted Liam's tense demeanor whenever he was asked to administer aid directly to the Seers who were most sick, he could tell by Liam's enthusiasm toward Marcus that he was eager to learn and understand everything they had been through.

At first, Eli and Liam spent all their time with Marcus. Though the withdrawal was difficult for Marcus, Eli observed with intense curiosity how Marcus' body was able to tolerate and heal from the symptoms much faster than the others. Eli and Liam exhausted their limited arsenal of tests trying to isolate the cause of his ability to repel the drug's effects so efficiently, but they never found anything conclusive.

"Maybe your body chemistry is just predisposed to resist," Eli suggested to Marcus after the last blood tests failed to produce any new information. "The appearance of your skin would certainly seem to support this."

One by one, as their moans quieted and their fevers broke, Kaido, Lucia, and Alessandra began to share stories of their time with the Guild.

Lucia came through first, but wouldn't talk much until Kaido began to show significant improvement. After that, she spoke from his bedside about how isolated she was before Kaido joined their Quorum.

"I know I speak Japanese and Portuguese, and English, of course, but I can't remember why. I don't remember anything about where I'm from, my family... sometimes I think I remember a place, a smell, but I can never hold it." Stroking Kaido's hand gently, she added quietly, "It feels like the first day of my life all over again."

Eventually, Lucia realized that she had been born in Brazil and was married with two children, twin boys, before her capture. Though she was grateful to have regained this essential piece of her past, it troubled her deeply that, no matter how hard she tried, she could not remember their faces. Within a week of his own recovery, Kaido recalled that he had been a freshman in college and living with his grandparents when he was taken. Slowly, Kaido remembered that it was his grandfather who taught him how to cook and to love his grandmother almost as much as his grandfather had. The crippling sadness he felt as he realized that they were dead—though he could not recall their murder—took him weeks to overcome.

Ten days after Alessandra's fever broke, her memories and her grief came all at once when she finally remembered that the tattered brown coat she'd worn for as long as she'd been with the Guild had belonged to her younger sister, Ana, whom she had loved and admired from the day she was born until the day she was burned to death in front of her.

As the Seers recovered more and more of the lives that were stolen from them, their emotions ran from anguish to depression to rage with every new piece of information. The tasks that they each were assigned within the commune kept them sane as they worked through emotions that seemed to change by the hour. Having had everything decided for them for so long, the Seers' transition back to a more normal life was slow. But all the mundane tasks within the commune — preparing meals, tending to the animals and the garden, the constant repairs to the machinery and housing, even the simple act of building a fire — helped to anchor and teach them what it meant to be part of a world where you were expected to give as well as receive. The constant rotation of duties also gave them the unanticipated pleasure of rediscovering their own preferences and dislikes.

While working with a slowly more amenable Marshall to replenish the supply of firewood, Kaido discovered his love for strenuous manual labor. As he helped Marshall cut the huge logs into smaller and smaller pieces, he found himself relishing the simple precision and repetition of his actions and the smooth, clean surface created by a sharp ax delivered with certainty.

Lucia found that she loved to be outside and seemed to have a natural gift for cultivating plants. What Eli meant as a basic introduction to the clinic's medicinal herb garden quickly turned into Lucia taking over all duties for its maintenance and upkeep in her quiet, determined way. Eli simply woke up one morning to make his rounds in the greenhouse and found that Lucia had beaten him to it. By the end of the week, he had finally gotten the hint.

Marcus was anxious to resume his work as a teacher, but knew that his appearance would be unsettling for some of the younger children. But, to his surprise, the older children had taken a liking to him and his "freaked-out" hair and eyes, which allowed him to tutor the middle school aged children when he wasn't helping Alessandra, Lucia, and Kaido cope with the painful reemergence of their memories.

Besides dealing with the strange mixture of loss and relief she felt at finally remembering some of her past, Alessandra had only one interest that overshadowed all her efforts to integrate into daily life: to be close to Liam. She had noticed from the minute she was brought to the clinic that Liam worked there with Eli at least three days a week. In the beginning, when they were the sickest, Liam had been there every day. Even in the most painful stages of her withdrawal, she knew that he was there. As soon as she was sure she could open her mouth without screaming out in pain, she began to try to speak to him. A simple "thank you" for wiping the sweat from her forehead, a timid "hi" when she would wake to find him watching over her, but he would never respond with more than a nod. Often, he looked disturbed or startled when she spoke. After her fifth attempt to make conversation, he stopped coming to her bedside altogether, unless she spoke to him directly. Even then, he would fulfill her requests wordlessly before retreating from her as quickly as he came.

Once her withdrawal subsided completely, Alessandra could see how differently Liam treated her compared to Marcus, Kaido, and Lucia. What she had assumed was shyness when he was around her seemed to verge on contempt when she compared it to the ease he displayed around everyone else. With all her senses new and raw, Alessandra could only come to one conclusion—Liam didn't like her. Though his actions left little room for interpretation, the presumption still didn't make any sense to her cleared mind. She couldn't imagine that in her three weeks of sweating and tears that she had done anything to warrant discrimination or even differentiation from the other Seers.

"So why? Why is he ignoring me?" she asked Marcus impatiently one afternoon after she had been spying on Liam while he and Marcus talked casually for 10 minutes. *I haven't even spent ten minutes with him,* she thought angrily.

"Alessandra! You are all flushed... what lovely color you have now that the Luridium is fading from you," Marcus replied, genuinely pleased with her progress.

Alessandra's whole body vibrated with tension and the hope of everything she had traveled so far to find. There was so much she wanted to say to Liam, experience with him, so much she wanted to understand about him and the world they shared. With the promise of a new life coming true every day since her escape, Alessandra felt like she was walking on the edge of every possibility. The sensation was utterly overwhelming, causing her to react to everything like a live wire, sending intense sparks of whatever she felt in every direction.

"My what?!? Who gives a damn about my *color*! I've come all this way and he won't even look at me. I want to know why! Has he said anything?"

Marcus couldn't help his grin as he stared down at her in amusement. "My, my... all this fire. I guess the temper is just going to stay with you then, or maybe get worse," he mumbled under his breath. "Do you remember having such a bad temper before?" He asked in a normal voice.

"Marcus," she warned.

"All right, all right... no, he hasn't said a word. We don't talk about you. He mostly asks me about my time with the Guild, how I learned to control and understand my sight, and if I can help his sister, Lilli. She's a nice girl, you should meet her..."

Marcus trailed off when he heard Alessandra suck her teeth. *Oh my,* he thought in amazement. *Definitely no more than 19 years old but high-strung and feisty.* He was sure his wife, Evlyn, would have loved her.

Alessandra dug her hands into the flesh on either side of her hips and slipped unconsciously into a thicker Italian lilt. "Stop looking so amused, eh. I am serious now. I want to know why he hates me. How can he hate me? I haven't done anything! How can he love me when he treats me like this? I thought..."

Alessandra shut her eyes to the Technicolor image of his lips tracing the curve of her shoulder — the same image that had been taunting her all day long. She was lost as she tried to reconcile the present with the visions she had of his hands on her so gently, his words in her ear.

Covering her face to hide the color in her cheeks that had nothing to do with her anger, Alessandra tilted her face upwards and opened her eyes to the sky.

"Help me, Marcus. I don't understand what is happening, what I'm supposed to do." Alessandra exhaled a long breath before plopping down on the front step of the clinic porch. Marcus quickly followed suit, putting his long arm around her thin shoulders. The feel of her folding into him so easily reminded him of just how much of a child she truly was.

"You must learn to wait, Alessandra. That is all there is for now. He is a very nice young man, but he is still a boy in many ways. To protect his sister, he has learned to walk like a man, but I don't think he was ready. And now you..." Marcus paused then to give in to the smile that had been welling up inside him, remembering how much he enjoyed being around young people, how easy it was to rediscover life through their eager eyes.

Reading the naked, gentle joy in his eyes, Alessandra smiled despite herself. "Go on. What's so funny, big man?"

"I'm not laughing at you, Alessandra, I promise. I just forgot how it is to be around people your age. There's so much...fumbling."

Alessandra gave him a sharp jab in his ribs, which made him laugh out loud despite the surprising pain that it caused him. "Ouch! No, no… I didn't mean it that way. It's just, I find it so endearing. I was young once, you know."

As both of their quiet chuckling began to fade, Marcus rubbed her shoulder encouragingly, grateful that she chose to confide in him. Marcus knew that he had come to feel very close to Alessandra, but he had never given much thought to whether or not she felt the same until now. The significance of her choice was suddenly like a weight in his chest. It made him choose his words with great care and thought before he interrupted their comfortable silence.

"Only a man can love a woman, Alessandra. Remember this. I would tell this to my own daughter, that is why I am saying this to you. He will come around. Don't worry. There is so much of yourself you have to find now. You'll see."

CHAPTER 12: AT MIDNIGHT

September, 2011

The night air wrapped around her gently, enticing her toward the river's edge. Digging her toes in the sand, Alessandra's thoughts wandered back to the reason why she was there.

It was Sunday and the entire commune had come down to the river to play, sunbathe, or simply watch everyone else make fools of themselves. As with everything else at Fox River, the activities of the day were an eclectic mix of children's activities, picnics, sports, and unplanned mayhem. With the sun blazing at a hazy and unprecedented 88 degrees in late September, some of the more free-spirited members of the Commune decided it was too hot for clothes. Since most of the commune members had lived together for at least two winters, some nudity during the summer months had come to be expected, so when Tim, Lucia, and Kyle decided to move to a more inconspicuous spot on the river bank, no one was surprised.

Alessandra had watched Liam all day–bare, tanned, and glistening in the sun. She'd watched him as he'd thrown his body haphazardly into the river, chasing after little girls and bigger boys, playing children's games. His blue and white swim trunks hung low on his lean, muscular hips as he swam and flipped and dove, doing all the things she longed to do.

It had been days since his strange compliment to her in the dining hall, and Alessandra still didn't know what to make of the fact that he hadn't spoken or looked at her since. With the mid-day sun blazing through the leaves of the large tree she was huddled under, Alessandra told herself and anyone else who asked that her skin was still too sensitive to be in the sun.

"That's not the reason," Lucia teased. "After everything we've been through, who cares about sunburn?"

Lucia paused for a moment to consider how much of Rachel's suntan cooling lotion she should use to soothe her sunburned bottom. Deciding that she couldn't go wrong with excess, she filled her palm with a large mound of Tropical Cucumber gel before continuing.

"I don't think *he* will mind," she smirked while tilting her chin in Liam's direction.

Though Alessandra had been trying her best to avert her eyes from Lucia's very public display of what Alessandra felt sure was an intimate task, her peripheral vision and Lucia's standing proximity made it hard to miss the precise moment when Lucia stopped lotioning her behind and started on her surprisingly ample breasts, which hung almost level with the top of Alessandra's head.

"I don't even know if I can swim," Alessandra mumbled absently as she shifted her position to give her a better view of Liam and block Lucia from her sight completely.

Alessandra noticed two things just then. The first was Kaido briefly obscuring her line of vision as he moved toward Lucia as if she were a pool of cool water in the dessert. The second was how the beads of water that slid down every sinewy, bronze-dusted inch of Liam's skin seemed to wink at her as they caught the light and threw it back over his broad shoulders and into her face, just because they could.

Alessandra couldn't remember when Lucia and Kaido left after that. All she noticed was how beautiful Liam looked as he laughed the hours away while she hovered in the shade, feeling every bit the ugly duckling staring longingly through the reeds at swan after swan, after swan. Every so often, she would clutch nervously at the back of her newly-shorn head, desperately and impatient for it to grow.

But now it was her turn. The Iowa sky was a blanket of midnight and stars as the breeze caressed the goose bumps that covered her skin. All she needed was the courage to dip her feet into the water.

Go on, Alessandra, she told herself. *You know it's not cold. It can't be more than 4 feet at this end. The water barely reached his...*

Alessandra stopped her train of thought abruptly as she tried to clear her head. She both wanted his ever-presence in her mind and didn't. She needed to believe that she was doing this for herself, a sign that she was coming further out of her shell, more into herself, but, in the end, she knew the truth. As with most things now, she was simply discovering life by following the bread crumbs he left behind. It made her a little sad to know that he was as unaware of this, as he seemed to be about most things regarding her. But it made no difference; everything in this new existence had a reference to him. Liam was the lens through which she saw and understood what it meant to be alive.

Thinking back over the events of the last two months, Alessandra knew she'd learned the structures and landmarks within the commune faster than anyone else just by following him around. When she couldn't follow him with her feet, her eyes burned a trail to the places he went, always searching and eager for his return. To her, he seemed so capable and calm as he moved among them. The way he always kissed Lilli on the forehead whenever he left her made Alessandra remember the deep value that family could hold for someone. Though Alessandra didn't think Liam and Lilli looked anything alike, whenever they were together, she'd come to think of them as twins. The minute they came within 10 feet of each other, she noticed how they seemed to move in unison, with Lilli walking carefree and sure in front, and Liam like a shadow, always close behind and scanning the area for any threats. Every time she watched Liam do this, Alessandra felt that her own instincts to protect were renewed.

At breakfast one morning, when she noticed him rush to fill his bowl with the last of the summer strawberries, she immediately wanted to try them. And when the sweet taste of the berries filled her mouth, she reconnected with some long lost understanding of the simple comfort and pleasure of food.

That same morning, she also learned about lust as her senses were jolted awake by the sight of strawberry juice dripping and then clinging to the curve of his bottom lip. By the time he began alternately sucking or licking the juice away, Alessandra had no choice but to give in to the heat that was rising and spreading through each part of her body. Marcus had laughed heartily at her open-mouthed stare until the sound made Liam look up at her from his seat long enough to catch her wide-eyed gaze. She thought he looked annoyed as he quickly wiped his mouth with the back of his hand and left the dining hall.

Even after that, Alessandra remained unashamed in her worship of him. It never occurred to her to hide it. Though she was legally an adult, when it came to Liam, her mind operated with a child-like simplicity.

Want. Get.

And she wanted him. Every available woman in the Commune did, as far as she could tell, but no one appeared to catch his interest. Though he seemed to have the least tolerance for her, Alessandra noted with relief that Liam never looked overjoyed to see anyone but Lilli. The fact that she could see what others could not—their future together—gave her the confidence to continue to be around him, despite his indifference, hoping to be in the right place when the passion of their future would catch up with the strained avoidance of their present.

For the first month after her withdrawal, they interacted like this, with Alessandra continuing to shadow him and Liam barely acknowledging her presence. At odd intervals, they would be forced to interact, through the rotation of chores or Eli and Marcus' occasional meddling. During those times, Alessandra's hopes that they would finally connect were met with monosyllabic responses and an ever-present undertone of annoyance.

Despite a month with no progress, she was still excited when Marshall assigned her to a week of home repair duties with Liam. Though she could never achieve enough objectivity to see exactly how their future would unfold, Alessandra felt sure that the assignment would finally give them the focused time together that they needed to begin realizing their destiny.

But she had been wrong.

By the end of their second day together, she was beginning to doubt the validity of her own visions. She couldn't understand how she would let someone so rude and callous ever touch her or how he would ever come to want to. To Alessandra, Liam seemed to go out of his way to be dismissive, giving her only the barest of instruction and training on what he was doing while never fully answering her questions. He never touched her or looked at her directly, not even to demonstrate a task or ensure she understood the correct way to do something. Despite his decidedly hands-off instruction style, Alessandra had learned enough that by the fourth day they could work independently within the same cabin. That suited Alessandra just fine since she had discovered in her frustration that she knew quite a few curse words in Italian, and being away from him for most of the day gave her the opportunity to practice them, without restraint, while she worked. When they finished a job, Alessandra would wait by his truck while Liam checked her work before leaving. On the fifth day, with no feedback on her progress or attempts on his part to be the least bit cordial, Alessandra exploded.

They were at their third cabin of the morning and she knew she had done a particularly good job of resealing the caulk in the kitchen. She waited for him to say so, but, of course, he didn't. If she hadn't been so pleased with her work, she might have been able to dismiss it, but she was proud. For her, it was a sign that she could be useful to the world in more than just one way, that she was capable of developing other skills. Over the previous days, she had begun to see the possibility of getting a job one day, leading a normal life, being a normal person. For her, the idea was profound, and she wasn't about to let it go.

"What did you think of my work?" Alessandra asked pointedly, once he'd slid into the driver's side of the truck's large cab and slammed the metal door shut. He didn't answer her until he had turned on the engine and the stereo.

"What? Oh… um… it was fine," Liam replied absently while flipping through radio stations.

"That's all you have to say?" Alessandra asked through clenched teeth.

Liam took his time driving down the dirt road while trying to tune the stereo dial on the old green Ford before finally answering her a full minute later.

"Basically."

"Bastardo!" *You bastard,* Alessandra spat, as she slapped her hand hard against the faded, cracked upholstery underneath her.

Liam's response was instantaneous as he slammed on the brake and came to a full stop, causing their bodies to jerk forward forcefully and then back against the seats. Once Liam had overcome his own momentum, he threw the gear into reverse and turned off the truck with his foot still jammed on the clutch.

"Che diavolo stai facendo!" she yelled, as he stared straight out of the windshield with an expression of complete panic on his face. When he didn't answer, it occurred to her that she had spoken in Italian and that he probably didn't understand what she said.

"I said, 'what the hell are you doing?' We're in the middle of the road!"

"You speak Italian," his voice was a hoarse whisper, as though he was struggling with something caught in his throat. "Jesus Christ," he moaned before banging his head against the steering wheel.

"What? You don't like Italian? Of course you don't like Italian. You don't like anything to do with me." Alessandra's voice was suddenly monotone as her temper fizzled into exhaustion.

Silence hung between them while Liam kept his head buried in the steering wheel and Alessandra stared out at the raindrops gathering on the windshield.

"I never said that."

"Said what, Liam?" Alessandra asked distractedly. "I have no idea what you're talking about."

The sound of her voice so close to him made his body break out with a fine sheen of sweat. He was suddenly sorry he spoke up in the first place, because, despite all his maneuvering and avoidance, he couldn't escape her now. They were confined together by the truck and the weather, and she was barely a foot away from him. Determined to regain control, he swallowed hard, trying to dislodge the lump in his throat.

"I never said that I didn't like anything to do with you."

"Please. Don't be stupid. I can see that you can't stand to be around me. I may not know much about the world, but I'm not blind."

Liam sighed heavily, but did not refute her.

"I just don't understand why I would ever let you touch me," Alessandra wondered aloud. "The way you act... so cold."

Her words jolted Liam back from the precipice of his own panic. His mind was a jumble of prophecies and premonitions as the full meaning of his mother's final words to him from her private video came into focus. He'd detected the faint accent in her voice from the first two syllables she'd ever spoken to him, but until that moment, he'd never heard her say anything in Italian so he assumed—he hoped—she didn't speak the language. He was so lost in the twists and turns of his own denial of his mother's message that he only caught the sounds of Alessandra's words, missing the meaning entirely. They filtered into the fog of his brain as an accusation that he had tried to act inappropriately with her.

"What are you talking about? I've never touched you!" His eyes locked with hers purposefully for the first time since she was in the clinic. When he saw her tears begin to well-up against the hurt that was so openly displayed, he knew immediately that he had misunderstood the intent of her words, though their meaning was still unclear to him.

At the softening of his eyes on her, the very fact that he was looking at her at all, Alessandra felt all the places she had tried to harden against him melt away like the last winter's snow sacrificing itself to the warmth of spring.

"But you will," she whispered. "You will touch me."

Liam's lips opened in protest, before closing again slowly as he was drawn into her. The rain picked up its tempo of gentle pitter patters on the hood of his truck as they sat and stared openly at one another.

I can't stop, he thought, as he surrendered another inch of himself over to her.

That's why I never look at you. Please understand, I can't stop.

While she was used to staring at him all the time, the fact that he was finally looking at her warmed her in places she didn't know were cold. She swore she could almost feel the shift in his eyes on her skin as they moved over her features with an intensity she couldn't distinguish as pleasure or dislike until his expression finally settled into a frown when he met her eyes again.

"Your eyes. They're different. Your left eye is almost brown."

He was so close that she could feel his warm breath on her face as he spoke.

Alessandra blinked in confusion, finally releasing the breath she had been holding inside to keep herself from falling into him.

"What...what do you mean?" she whispered.

"Look." Still unable to break his gaze from her face, Liam reached over her shoulder to flip down the sun visor. "Look."

Facing the mirror, Alessandra caught her first glimpse of what he was referring to, the strange, muddy-grey color of her left eye.

"We should get you to Eli to make sure it's okay. It might be some type of infection on the cornea."

Liam caught the flash of fear that rippled across her face and quickly added, "It's probably nothing, but we should check it out anyway, just to be safe." Liam started the truck, making a U-turn in the middle of the road before speeding back to the clinic to find Eli.

When they arrived, Eli assured them both that she was fine.

"Alessandra, I think your system is just purging the last remnants of the Luridium. I've noticed similar signs in the others. Your skin is showing more color and everyone's eyes seem to be returning to normal, slowly but surely. Lucia even told me that the hair under her arms is starting to grow back brown. She came into the garden this morning very excited," Eli chuckled.

While Alessandra was clearly pleased to hear the news, Liam remained tense for several moments as his mind began to leap to all the conclusions that this might mean.

"Liam," Eli said with a hand on his shoulder. "She'll be fine. I promise." Eli's words of assurance struck Alessandra as odd until she looked up from her own thoughts to take in Liam's expression. He looked so worried that he was almost vulnerable, and he was standing so close to her that she was startled to think how long they had been that way without her noticing.

As if just realizing that he was being observed by both her and Eli, Liam quickly nodded his understanding and then turned away from Alessandra, heading for the door. Once he had his hand firmly on the door knob, he turned around awkwardly, feeling the need to say *something* before he escaped.

"Yeah, ok. That's good then," he stammered, while looking in every direction but where Alessandra stood in front of him. "Listen, maybe you should stay here and get some rest or something. I can finish up what's left of the work myself."

Without waiting for a reply, Liam backed his way through the front door and muttered, "ok, then," somewhere between the four front steps and the short path to the passenger side door, which he closed before hopping in the truck and rushing off.

Eli stared at the door for several moments after Liam left. "Poor guy," he remarked with a smile before patting Alessandra on the back and quietly leaving the room.

Alessandra stayed in place for a long time after Liam left, contemplating all the things that had happened so quickly she didn't even register them.

Did he open the truck door for me as we came in?

Alessandra could feel her mind racing to assimilate all the new information that seemed incongruous with her assumption that he hated her: the look of concern on his face as he listened to Eli's explanation, the almost-possessive way he had hovered over her, the opening of her door... All of these clues felt like missing pieces to a puzzle she had been trying to assemble ever since she got to Fox River. She could see now that the picture she had been building of an unfeeling man no longer fit. The new pieces changed the context and the color of the other shapes entirely until she could see nothing but the new picture that was emerging, that of a man who was concerned for her, perhaps more than he wanted to admit. Slowly, his words from earlier came back to the forefront of her mind.

'I never said that I didn't like anything to do with you.'

Alessandra's chest felt like it would burst open with new possibilities.

He might... He might... She was so overwhelmed with emotion that she couldn't even complete the thought.

After the episode at the clinic, Liam acted as if nothing had happened, but his distance no longer bothered Alessandra. She had seen his indifference melt away in the clinic, if only for the briefest moment. For the first time since she had arrived, she could look at him and see the first stepping stones on the path to the visions she had of him every night.

It was Lucia's idea that all the Seers should shave their heads. "It will be a new start for all of us," she promised cheerfully as she shaved a streak of ash blonde puff curls from her head while Lilli looked on approvingly. At the time, Alessandra was not convinced.

I look like a freak already, she thought as she stared at the last flecks of milky white receding from her dark brown eyes. Alessandra had been cataloguing all the beautiful shades and textures of hair that could be found among the women in the commune since she had arrived and knew she was already too jealous of them to lose what hair she did have on her head. It was only when she began to see the brown roots coming through on her own scalp that she decided to take a chance.

The first day she walked into the dining hall with a bald head, she felt the urge to cry, to run and hide, so strongly, it made her weak. Luckily, she was working the 4:30am-7:30am breakfast shift in the kitchen. Alessandra had observed that Liam never ate breakfast before 8am, and since she planned to be well out of sight before then, she didn't expect to see him all day. When she took a quick break to eat at Marcus' insistence, she deflated rather than sat in her chair before picking at her unwanted breakfast.

"You know, my wife used to wear her hair cut like this, very low. She was the most beautiful woman," Marcus shared encouragingly.

Look who's talking, she thought ruefully. *You look all regal and I look like a shaved dog.*

"She would never let it grow long," he went on, as Alessandra continued to sulk. "She used to say that her head was too beautiful to be covered up with hair." He laughed then at the memory and, as usual, the sound made Alessandra smile.

"Your head is the same shape as hers. You should be proud to show it off."

"Thanks, Marcus," Alessandra said quietly before quickly finishing her plate and carrying it back to the kitchen.

At 6:58 am, she ran into the one person she wanted to avoid. She might have seen him if her eyes hadn't been glued to the tray of eggs she was carrying, trying to avoid the sounds of laughter that she was sure were all directed at her.

"Oh!" It was all she could say through her surprise as she saw the tray of eggs collide with a heather-grey hoodie that she knew by heart.

"Umm, sorry. Here, I can take that," Liam offered.

Alessandra stood frozen in shock while she stared at the bits of egg clinging to his zipper. Normally she would have had to resist looking at him, but not now. She didn't want to see any part of his expression as he took in the peach fuzz on her head. Though she could feel his hands gently tugging on the tray, Alessandra couldn't get herself to relax enough to let go of the one diversion she had. Eventually, when the sweat from her palms allowed Liam to slide the tray right out from under her fingers, Alessandra hung her head and her arms in defeat while her feet remained stuck in place.

Her posture and Liam's height gave him the perfect vantage point from which to examine the deep brown stubble that covered her scalp. Even though her hair stuck straight up like a porcupine, he imagined that it would be as soft as a baby's to the touch. Watching her, he had the sudden urge to run his lips across her scalp and test his theory for himself.

Focus! Lilli is watching. Just get this over with so you can get the hell out of here. Since when are you into bald girls, anyway?

In spite of his best efforts to find *anything* about Alessandra that was less than alluring, he was not put-off when he saw her shuffling toward the buffet table without a single strand of hair on her head. At first sight, the word *adorable* came to his mind. Frowning at his own sappiness, he quickly diverted his eyes before he could discover any new tender emotions, but Lilli had other plans.

"Liiiiaaamm," Lilli began in her signature cajoling tone. "You should go talk to her."

"No," was all he said before filling his mouth with a heap of homemade cinnamon and raisin oatmeal. He knew what was coming but couldn't manage the effort required for a preemptive strike. He sighed as he felt Lilli lean within an inch of his ear and inhale enough air to allow her tirade to flow freely.

"Liam, you better get up and say something to that girl right now or I will go over there and tell her that you call her name in your little wet dreams."

Even though Liam had only been half-listening, he was still pretty sure he heard the words 'her name' and 'wet dreams', both of which did not bode well for him. Trying not to overreact, he decided to seek clarification after looking around to make sure no one was aware of their conversation.

"What?" he hissed.

By then, Lilli was back in an erect posture with a heaping spoonful of Fruity Pebbles hovering a moment away from her lips. She didn't bother to look at him as her lips spread into a satisfied grin.

"Oh, you heard me just fine. And to answer your second question — believe it. I am so not bluffing. In fact, it's why *we* are up so early this morning," she declared before placing the spoon in her mouth. Though Lilli's mouth was full of food, Liam could still make out her smirk as she continued eating and he got up from the table.

Even with Lilli's threat fresh in his mind, Liam was still contemplating his escape as he eased the egg tray from Alessandra. He had managed to turn halfway around before a glimpse of Lilli's narrowing eyes stopped him in his tracks. Thinking twice, he abruptly turned back to Alessandra and blurted out the first thing that came to mind.

"Your haircut shows your eyes. That's…good," he finished, and was gone before she could blink.

Somewhere in the background, Alessandra could hear high pitched laughter and squealing, but she was in too much of a daze to notice who it was.

Each day since his abrupt confession in the dining hall, Alessandra felt her need for him grow more acute. The distance between them, which she used to accept so easily, began to feel like thorns pricking her skin. She needed more from him.

Stepping into the river, she tried to shake off the memories of everything that had happened between them, but as she felt the warm water swirling around her thighs, she understood the real reason why she had come here tonight. The moment she saw him wade into the river that morning, she knew she wanted to bathe in the same water that had caressed his skin. Her desire led her there, waist deep and naked.

She submerged herself slowly, savoring the feeling of sand beneath her feet and the weight of the water gently swaying her body from left to right. Instinctively, Alessandra extended her arms forward and pushed off into a lazy breast stroke, laughing with delight at the knowledge that her body still remembered things about her, even if she didn't.

Floating on the warm swell of the water, she let the sounds of frogs croaking in the distance and water lapping at the river bank calm and distract her from the growing ache she felt to be near him. After a few minutes, Alessandra rolled onto her back and spread her legs out to gaze up at the night sky. Drifting with the gentle current, Alessandra was so relaxed that it took her a moment to even register the feel of hands grazing her shins just before Liam's head burst up from the water between her legs.

Alessandra screamed as she took in the sight of him and pulled her legs up toward her chest, unintentionally kicking him in the face before she could submerge her body fully in the water.

"What are you doing here? I thought you couldn't swim!" Liam yelled, as he rubbed the water from his eyes. He was blinking rapidly, trying to block out the glimpses of her naked body that flashed through his mind.

"I... I... I thought I was alone! Where did you come from?" Alessandra stammered breathlessly. She couldn't imagine that she had missed seeing him dive in.

"I was sitting at the bottom of the river. I do that sometimes...to think."

"Seriously?" Alessandra looked down into the dark water, unable to imagine why in the world he would need to go to such lengths to be alone.

Sensing her skepticism, Liam let out a self-conscious laugh. "Yeah, I know. It's kind of weird, right? Sometimes I come here when I can't sleep..." he trailed off. The fact that the reason he couldn't get to sleep was now floating two feet away from him was not a piece of information he planned to share. Ever since Alessandra swore at him in Italian, he was having a hard time processing the fact that his mother's words were coming true right before his eyes.

"*I think you're going to be really glad you stuck it out with those Italian courses, honey,*" his mother had said excitedly. "*Oh, I can't see much, but*

I know I like her. Try not to fight it so much when it happens. I know you'll be scared, but try. You need a family Liam; it's the way you're made."

I'm not the same person I was, Liam thought, every time he considered his mother's words. *She doesn't know what I've done, who I've had to become to survive.* He wrestled with the notion of being responsible for more than Lilli, of loving anyone as much as Lilli and losing them, and couldn't fathom surviving it. *Plus,* he reasoned, *I can't afford the distraction.* He'd seen what carelessness could produce firsthand. It haunted him almost every day since they left Albuquerque. Nothing was worth losing his focus. He had learned that the hard way.

Looking at her in the moonlight, Liam wanted to move toward her with every ounce of the love he knew he felt, but he backed away.

"Liam..." Alessandra began, as she witnessed his expression turn from surprised and boyish to hardened within seconds.

"Listen, I'm sorry I scared you. I'm leaving, okay?" he said in a voice that was softer than he had ever spoken to her as he walked toward the bank.

"You don't have to," Alessandra offered, even though she knew she had lost him again.

"You'll be safe here. Don't worry," he replied while wondering if he should warn her before stepping out of the water naked. Just as he was about to ask her to turn around, another more important thought occurred to him.

"Unless you're scared... I mean, are you scared? I could stay, if you needed me to."

The words came out before he'd even considered them. All he knew was that the thought of her being afraid of anything now was unacceptable. He couldn't let her be scared.

Alessandra wasn't scared of anything but allowing him to walk away from her.

"Yes, I would like that," Alessandra said, watching him carefully. "I don't want to be alone."

She could see Liam nod in agreement, but somehow she knew he would not turn to look at her.

"If you turn around, I'll just sit by that tree over there. I know you don't have any clothes, so I won't look. I'll just be over there until you're ready to leave.

"Ok," was all Alessandra could say before turning away and letting him walk to where he would stand guard over her. The sensation of being kept safe by him was dreamlike and intoxicating, even though it was completely unnecessary in that moment. She hoped he would watch her, because she knew now, without a doubt, that she lived for it.

"I want you to watch me," she said softly as he moved up the slope behind her.

Her words gave him the permission he secretly wanted to watch her through the reeds as she swam and floated leisurely for hours.

CHAPTER 13: BLIND SPOT

The vision came into focus slowly, as if she was floating into the middle of the room from far away. Even though Lilli couldn't yet make out all the words that were being exchanged, it was obvious that the two men were in the middle of a bitter argument. The tall one with smooth jet-black hair shouted in a voice that could be heard throughout the entire floor. She could see all the people that overheard the confrontation scatter and hide like mice.

"This is absolutely unacceptable," Andreas bellowed at Miguel and Jason. "How is it that we can't find four Seers? It's been over three months and nothing! Nothing!"

Before Miguel could defend himself, Crane snapped.

"Do shut up, Andreas! You've been asking the same stupid questions every day since they left and it hasn't gotten us any closer to finding them. At least come up with some new rant. You're becoming tedious."

At first, Andreas narrowed his eyes at Crane's audacity before settling on a thought that made him smile. "Perhaps next week's visit from Deidra and the other Guild members will inspire you. Maybe you'll feel more engaged when I let you explain why we still have no idea how four of the most valuable Seers in the Guild managed to escape from right under our noses, how they continue to render all our Seers blind to their whereabouts. There is always that to look forward to..."

With nothing biting to say in response, Crane drew his mouth into a tight line and turned his attention toward the driving rain outside the library window.

Sensing his chance, Miguel finally voiced his concerns.

"Sir, without permission to circulate pictures of the missing Seers, our ability to trace their steps is extremely limited...after so much time...our job becomes even harder," Miguel explained calmly.

He was not ruffled by Andreas' anger. Miguel felt a similar sense of indignation; he just didn't have the luxury of expressing it as dramatically as Andreas clearly preferred. Nothing like this had ever happened, or even been conceived of as a possibility. They were completely unprepared.

"I know, Miguel... I know it's not your fault. I just... am not used to being blind-sided anymore. I know you want to use the photos, but we can't risk it. They're all supposed to be dead. If one of the photos made its way to the news, it could cause more trouble than we can afford right now."

As he listened to Andreas and Miguel's exchange, Crane's mind fixed on the simple phrase Andreas had been using over and over again for at least a month. Maybe it was Andreas' pitch, or the fact that he just needed to hear it one more time for it to click, but Crane suddenly saw a new solution to the problem of how the Seers escaped.

"You're right, Andreas. We have been blinded, as if someone has been deliberately covering our eyes so that we can't see." Crane turned back to face Andreas as he worked the idea out for the first time out loud.

"It could be Alessandra creating the blind spots in our vision, but I don't believe so. She was too young in her control. It has to be Marcus. He was the only one who could control the Quorum enough to keep this a secret."

Andreas nodded for Crane to continue, putting all blame aside for a moment to see where this emerging theory would lead.

"I think we've been going about this the wrong way, Andreas. We can't find them. They were the best in the Quorum, in the entire Guild. The Seers we have can't do what we need."

"So what are you saying? We should just give up?" Andreas asked incredulously.

"Not at all. We need to shift our approach. We need 'new blood', if you will," Crane said with a smile. *"Instead of trying to find them with the resources we have, we need to find new Seers who can do what they did. We need to find Seers extraordinary enough to create blind spots in their vision."*

Crane and Andreas stared at each other wordlessly as they let this new idea seep in and take hold.

Lilli jolted out of her meditation with the image of the two Seers the Guild would seek to hunt them burned into her brain. A brother and a sister just like her and Liam. The girl stood tall and deceptively unassuming with stringy brown hair that hung unkempt at her shoulders. Her brother stood beside her with the same color hair running into his thick lashes. Without knowing how, Lilli knew their names were Michael and Nina Grey.

At first, every thought in Lilli's head was silent as she was consumed with processing the shock of what she had seen. But, the questions didn't take long to come rushing to the forefront of her mind.

Who are these new Seers? Could they really break through the shield that Marcus has sustained around us? Where would the Guild find them? And when, when, when would all this happen?

Lilli tried to still her mind enough to go back to the vision and see more detail, but her fear had already taken hold. The thought of her brother in danger again after so much time of relative safety was too much for Lilli to endure calmly. After fifteen minutes of trying, she threw on her shoes and ran out the back door of the small four-room cabin that Liam had built for them.

As soon as Marcus looked through the classroom window and caught his first glimpse of Lilli running toward the schoolhouse where he was teaching, he knew he would not be finishing the last half hour of his tutoring session. Lilli never came to visit him while he was in class and she never ran, if she could help it.

"I think I'm going to do you guys a favor today and let you out a little early," Marcus announced, turning back to his class, "but I have homework for you."

"What? How's that fair? We can't have homework from class AND from tutoring," Kyle protested.

"I keep trying to tell you, Kyle... life isn't fair until you turn 18 and make your own decisions. Until then, we can do whatever we want with you," Marcus teased. "Tomorrow, I want everyone to bring me an example of an organism that uses photosynthesis."

Just as the small group began to grumble, Marcus added, "Now get out of here before I think of some more homework for you to do!" Marcus kept his tone light, but his smile never reached the creases at the corners of his eyes. His threat had its intended effect. By the time Lilli reached the doorway, his classroom was empty.

Marcus didn't wait for her to speak before asking, "Lilli, what's wrong?"

Completely out of breath, Lilli couldn't answer him right way. Instead, she chose to bob her head in response as she slumped down into the first seat she reached.

When she was finally able to stop gasping for breath, she looked Marcus in the eye and managed to push out the words she'd sprinted almost half a mile to tell him.

"I saw the Guild. I saw their plans. They're going to try to find someone more powerful than you, someone who can see past the blind spots you've created..."

Pausing just long enough to draw more air into her lungs, Lilli continued. "I don't know when, but there are two of them...I can't see more," she apologized. "I'm just too scared, I can't be objective." Lilli didn't even realize she was crying until she looked down and saw her own tears hitting the rough wood floor.

Marcus took a seat at the desk directly in front of hers and gently placed his hand on her forearm, waiting for her to finish.

"We've been here for so long," Lilli continued through her tears. "Longer than we've been any other place in years. I just thought... we could stay, be safe for once in our lives..."

Marcus decided to wait until her breathing had returned to normal before he spoke. "I am sorry you had to see that, Lilli, but honestly, I can't say that I'm surprised. I know they have been trying harder to find us. I can feel the resistance...the urgency in their search, but I have been managing," Marcus said, rubbing his shoulder absently.

"I've been spending so much of my time blocking their visions that I really haven't had much time to search. It was careless of me. I just assumed that as long as I focused my efforts on hiding us that we would be safe, at least for awhile."

"Marcus, it's not your fault," Lilli countered. "I don't even know how you're doing all that you're doing. I'm barely in control of my sight." A thought occurred to her then that seemed so obvious, she felt a little stupid for not asking before.

"Why aren't the others helping you? They can all do this better than I can."

Marcus nodded his head in understanding of her exasperated expression.

"It's not that they wouldn't. I haven't asked them. I haven't taught them yet. Being here has been so freeing for them. For most of them, it's the first time that they remember ever feeling normal. They've been doing nothing but visioning for years. I just don't think any of them even has a desire to use their gifts, at least not yet. Living in the present has been such a luxury."

"I can understand that, but Marcus, we don't have time for that now. They're out there. I know it."

"I believe you, Lilli. Have you told your brother yet?"

Lilli shook her head tightly as she tried to blink away the tears that hovered at the rims of her eyes. "No, no…I came here first. Liam has enough to handle without me coming to him like this."

"Well, I think it's time we both stopped carrying this burden ourselves. This affects all of us. We need to let the others know what's going on."

●●···●●

"Exactly how long do we have?" Marshall asked, trying to keep the frustration from his voice. "I know this *thing* you do isn't an exact science, but we need to know how long we've got…"

"I don't know…maybe three months. I don't think I've had a vision of anything that was further away than that," Lilli replied sheepishly.

"All right, that gives us three months to get ourselves together and take these bitches down," Tim declared, jumping up from his seat in the meeting hall. "It's about time we started taking the fight to them."

"It's not that simple," Kaido began. "We can't just march back in there…"

Rachel tried to be patient as she listened to Kaido's response to Tim's comment. But having spent most of her young life sitting quietly in her pew while her father sold fear and lies from the pulpit, she found it almost impossible, as an adult of twenty-four years, to sit through any kind of nonsense. As soon as she heard Tim's voice, she knew she couldn't be silent long enough to let Kaido finish.

"Are you serious? Isn't that, like, from a movie or something?" she scoffed.

Kaido turned to Rachel in confusion, thinking at first that she was addressing him until he traced her angry stare across the room to where Tim was standing, doing his best to not look intimidated.

"Just sit down and shut up!" Rachel continued. "They'd see us coming! That's the point, Tim!"

"Look, we can either sit here and wait for them to find us, or we can strike first, that's all I'm saying," Tim growled before sitting down in a huff.

"Maybe we should just leave," Lucia offered.

Even though it was the obvious choice, no one but Tim had even considered expelling the Seers from the commune. Immediately after Lucia reluctantly made the suggestion, Marshall brushed the idea aside.

"It's too late for that, Lucia. Like it or not, you're one of us now," Marshall said with a smile at the surprised look on Lucia's face. "Besides, if the Guild is good enough to get past Marcus and find you wherever you'd go, then I'm sure they would figure out that you spent some time here and I doubt that we'd escape a visit from them after that."

"Can't you guys just see when they're coming and then we could just run?" Jean asked.

"That's just it," Lilli tried to explain. "If they learn to block our sight, we might not see them coming."

"Then we should get the hell out of here now! All of us," someone else shouted out. The outburst initiated a fresh round of circular arguments and rehashing.

Marcus and Liam hung in the back of the crowd while the conversation went around and around. They watched with growing irritation as people asked questions that were only half answered and made declarations to which there was no response. Sentiment within the group seemed to fluctuate between certainty that everyone should make a run for it and conviction that the Commune members could somehow take down the Guild single-handedly.

Witnessing all the back and forth, Liam was incredulous. "This is so stupid," he muttered under his breath.

"Exactly how would we have 'the element of surprise' on our side with four Seers going up against the entire Guild?" He refused to even count Lilli in Tim's proposed suicide mission.

"I don't think they understand what the Guild can do," Marcus responded, even though he knew that Liam wasn't speaking directly to him. "There's no way we can take them on with so few of us."

Liam nodded in acknowledgement before both men turned their attention back to the group discussion.

Liam listened as Lucia, Kaido, and Lilli offered to keep watch over the Guild and give the commune members as much warning as they could. He also noticed how quietly Alessandra sat beside them. Throughout the entire meeting, he had been trying to keep his mind from focusing on the two women who were everything that mattered to him.

He knew from the moment Alessandra and the others came to Fox River that their very presence made his sister more vulnerable, more exposed to the threats they had been running from for so long. The potential for danger was always there, but now there was more, more than he ever thought he could feel. It made him want to keep Alessandra close to him, even as it jeopardized the one person he fought to protect.

Though he still maintained his outward distance from Alessandra, everything had changed for him that night with her by the river. What he had meant as a simple act of protection turned into a silent vigil, a private surrender to everything he felt for her. He could easily recall the way his eyes had felt that night, burning with the need for rest, but he had refused to stop looking at her as long as she wanted him to, as long as she swam for him to see.

Marshall's right, Liam thought. *It's too late for her to walk away from me now. There has to be another way, a way to at least make it safe to be around her.* As his mind began to search for an answer, a thought came slowly to his mind.

How many Seers would Marcus need to create a better blind spot?

"Marcus, can I talk to you? Outside of all this..." Liam asked, waving his hand toward the group discussion, which had descended into a series of independent shouting matches and side conversations.

"Yes, please. I think this discussion ceased being useful a while ago."

Both men pushed through the back door of the barn and wandered toward the orange, pink, and blue autumn horizon in pensive silence before Marcus stopped at the bench Kaido had built for enjoying sunsets just like the one before them.

"This...this is a beautiful place," Marcus whispered as he took a seat and leaned his body forward. "It is so strange to find things that remind me of my home here, even though I am far away."

Liam watched the last light of day ignite in a deep shade of orange before asking the question that he'd been turning over in his mind since they left the meeting.

"Marcus, can you teach the others to do what you can do?"

"Yes, I don't think we have a choice now. Alessandra knows how already, she has just been focused on... other things," Marcus said, turning his head from Liam to hide his faint smile. "But the others I can teach as well, they just have to learn their own gifts first. I can start soon, Liam, but we will not be enough to hold them off forever."

Liam was silent as Marcus continued.

"Since Alessandra first came to Chicago, I felt that her coming was the beginning of my revenge against the Guild, my chance to finally stand up against what they did to my family, but I have not seen how. With Lilli's vision, I can't help but wonder if I haven't missed some crucial step we were supposed to take..."

Marcus squinted into the setting sun as if the answer to his question could be seen there in the margins between dusk and night.

"What if we try to find these other Seers before the Guild does, if we keep them from acquiring their gifts? Lilli says we have three months. We could use that time to search for them. The Guild doesn't know that we know their plans. They won't be expecting us to interfere. It would at least be more unexpected than just hiding."

Marcus was momentarily stunned by the notion before slowly beginning to see the practical possibilities of Liam's idea.

"Yes, I think you're right," Marcus agreed as he shook his head. "All they are expecting from us now is to hide. It wouldn't even occur to them that we would ever try anything against them. Even now, I'm sure they can hardly believe that we got away."

As silence fell between them, Liam felt like he could almost see Marcus figuring out the specifics of what they would need to do. In the short time that Liam had known Marcus, he knew him to be patient and methodical in everything he did. From the stories Marcus had shared with him, Liam knew he never would have survived within the Guild so long without those traits. They were just a few of the many attributes that Liam admired about him.

"Let me think about this further before we share this idea of yours with the others. We need to divide our efforts so that some of us block while others search. But first Kaido and Lucia need to learn to understand and control their sight apart from us."

Taking in Liam's questioning expression, Marcus added, "Most Seers within the Guild never understand their gift outside of Quorum. I learned what I could do on my own first, but that is very rare. I've never heard of another case like mine within the Guild. I believe it was this understanding of my gift first - before I was ever allowed to quorum - that gave my sight the strength that it has. I have seen it work for Alessandra and I think it will be important for the others. If we are to be successful in this new endeavor, every one of us will need to use the full extent of our power."

"Lilli has never quorumed with anyone," Liam added, wondering what Marcus' own experience might mean for her.

"Yes, I believe this will give her an advantage. I have only begun to help her understand how to control her sight, but she learns very quickly. I think she will become a powerful Seer when she has matured."

Liam was both comforted and unnerved by Marcus' assurances. He had no context for anything that Marcus was saying to him.

"So, when can you start?"

Just then, they heard the shuffling of feet through the prairie grass and turned to find Lilli, Lucia, Alessandra, and Kaido walking toward them.

Marcus returned Lilli's grin as he answered Liam's question.

"Now. I think we start right now."

Chapter 14: First Raid

January, 2012

Liam was so close she could feel the heat from his body as they crouched down with their backs pressed against the rear wall of the Gnarus Medical Storage Facility, but Alessandra's thoughts were a million miles away from the man at her side. Even though the night air was cool, she could feel the sweat pooling at her hairline underneath her black baseball cap. In the back of her mind, she was aware that feeling so unaffected by Liam's proximity was, in itself, a sign of how in danger she was.

"Hanna, can you hear me? We're in position," Eli whispered into the military issue walkie-talkie that connected their makeshift hacking operation in Iowa with the team now attempting their first raid in Haxtun, Colorado.

"Yeah, I hear you, Eli. We're almost in. Hang tight until I give the word. Alessandra said we can only loop the camera footage for about 30 minutes before they verify security through satellite imagery, so make it quick. I'll tell you as soon as the countdown starts."

Even though Eli knew they were huddled so close together that there would be no need to repeat Hanna's words, he still turned back to verify the look of recognition on each of their faces. Alessandra, Liam, and Vincent each gave a quick nod to let him know they understood. Marveling at the determination on their young faces, Eli couldn't help but smile at their blind bravery.

We were brave once, he thought, as he remembered the idealism that led him and his colleagues to the discovery that would unleash a new era of silent oppression into the world. *What did Willem always say?* He wondered before remembering the quote from the plaque that hung over the door to the laboratory that he and Willem Knight had shared.

'Fools rush in where angels fear to tread'.

Yes, that was us. That was always us, Eli thought as he turned away, hoping his face didn't betray any of the remorse he felt. *Now they have to fix our mess.*

The four of them were selected to carry out the Commune's first raid against the Guild as a matter of practicality and necessity. Eli had the best understanding of the records that they were looking for as well as firsthand knowledge of the building layout, having been to the facility many years ago. Even though she still had significant gaps in her sight, Alessandra had the most detailed understanding of how they needed to execute the logistics of their break-in and escape. She was also assigned the task of blocking any unanticipated events from the Guild's Seers. In addition to always being up for an adventure, Vincent had the most hand-to-hand combat and weapons experience aside from Marshall thanks to his continuous education in criminal activity from the age of ten. To round out the team, Liam had simply insisted on coming and was not questioned.

As the muscle in the raid operation, Vincent and Liam's preparations were relatively easy. In the two years that Liam spent on the run with Lilli, he'd learned how to get his hands on any number of weapons. Between Liam's small arsenal and Marshall's connections with friends inside the military weapons supply business, Liam and Vincent were well-equipped for anything they might encounter. But the effort it took for Marcus, Alessandra, Eli, and the others to finally have a chance at pulling this off took every single second of the two months they had used to get themselves where they were now—pressed against rough brick, ready and waiting.

It was an unspoken understanding within the commune that everyone had a past, a reason why they had decided to live on the fringe of society. Though there were a few hippie types at Fox River, it was never a commune in the 'free love' sense. There were just too many seemingly normal people keeping too many secrets for their interests to revolve solely around peace and love. People went out of their way not to tell their stories, and if you didn't offer, no one would ask. Running from something was expected.

Because of this expectation, there was little room for error when it came to conduct and safety within the commune. Strangers who seemed too odd or elicited more than the average level of don't-know-you-yet discomfort were dealt with quickly, either by Marshall or Vincent. Given that no one was particularly interested in determining guilt or innocence, there was very little diplomacy to the process. If they felt unsafe, that was enough. If a parent caught you staring at their child in a way that felt off, you would wake up in the middle of the night with Marshall's shotgun in your mouth and a one-time offer to get the fuck out. It was as simple as that.

Never be a danger to the group, and help out however you can. Those were the only rules you had to abide by at Fox River. The Seers were the only ones ever granted exception.

Even with the studied anonymity, the sheer breadth and range of illegal talents available at the commune still managed to surprise some who were involved in the planning of the raid. Once Eli heard Liam and Marcus' idea, he was all too ready to help them formulate a plan to break into the facility where he knew the Guild kept birth records on all Seers. Alessandra was assigned to focus on the facility and learn as much as she could about its operations. After a week of visioning, she was able to detail how the security worked and where the information they needed on Nina and Michael was located. When Alessandra reported what she'd discovered back to the Commune, Hanna and Kyle immediately volunteered to help bypass the security system.

"From what I could tell, they have a very complicated password system that resets itself every time one of the doors is opened, then closed. There are security cameras everywhere, plus satellite imagery, just in case the cameras fail," Alessandra warned.

"Yeah, don't worry about that," Hanna said with confidence. "Kyle can work the software and I'm pretty sure I can get around anything he can't."

It took Kyle and Hanna a month and a half to develop and test spyware that was stealthy enough to go undetected by the Guild's customized virus protection software, yet reliable enough to allow them consistent access to the ever-changing security protocols of the facility. Once their connection was stable, Hanna spent the rest of her time working with Alessandra to develop a bypass sequence that would work, based on the details Alessandra was able to see in her visions.

"I wish we could just save you the trouble of having to go there by accessing their records from here, but that would take more time than we have. The security protocols only get worse the deeper you go into the system. I've never seen anything like it. We'll keep working on it, but right now I'm guessing it would take us at least another four months and a heck of a lot more of Liam and Lilli's money to crack it," Hanna admitted late one night while she and Alessandra were working.

"I know you do, Hanna," Alessandra replied, offering her a small smile. "I know you're worried about us." Alessandra knew Hanna's concern was genuine, though she couldn't figure out why she was putting so much effort into helping them. Hanna had always been a bit standoffish with the Seers before Lilli first told everyone about her vision of the Guild.

"I know you must be wondering why," Hanna continued, anticipating Alessandra's skepticism. "It's just... I know what you're up against. If you get caught, they'll kill you. It doesn't matter how valuable you are to them."

The certainty in Hanna's voice made Alessandra question whether or not she'd missed something in her visioning.

"How? How do you know that?"

"Because my father... he stole something important from the Department of Defense a long time ago. I don't know why. I think he was going to sell it or something. Money was always so important to him..." Hanna frowned as she tried in vain to fight off memories of pale pink cashmere and white mink. It was her first brand new Easter coat or at least the first one she could remember. Even to her four-year old mind, without any understanding of money, Hanna had known it was a very special coat, which made her feel extra-special, too. "Only the best for my little girl," her father had sung as he twirled her out of the fancy store with gold-trimmed picture windows. Later that night with her parents arguing loudly, it had been harder to hold on to that extra-special feeling as she heard her mother declare that it was a waste to spend $1,500 on a coat for a little girl when they had a baby on the way.

"Hanna? Are you okay?" Alessandra asked gently.

"Ah, yeah," Hanna offered quickly as she tried—for the millionth time—to shake off her mother's poorly chosen words and continue her story. "Anyway, he never got the chance. My mom told him they would never let him get away with it, that they would come after all of us, but he didn't believe her. When they finally did come, my mom hid us in the crawl space under the house, just before they took him and my mother away…

"That's why we're here," she said nonchalantly, as she kept working on installing their brand new terabyte server. "We're still on the most wanted lists, even though we didn't do anything."

Alessandra was stunned, both by Hanna's admission and the fact that she was sharing it with her.

"Hanna… I'm so sorry,"

"Yeah, me too."

While Alessandra, Hanna, and Kyle finalized the plans for getting in, Marcus worked to teach Kaido and Lucia how to use their sight. Up until Lilli's revelation, none of them had given much thought to using their gift again. The mere mention of it still brought up memories and nightmares of their time with the Guild. But hearing the urgency in Lilli's voice and the fear among the people who had given them their first real home in years was enough to make each Seer realize that they could no longer afford to hide from something that could help them and those they had come to care for.

Marcus insisted that Lilli, Kaido, and Lucia vision on their own before they quorumed together. For Kaido and Lucia, it was the first time they had ever attempted to control their gift on their own, and it was thrilling. Lucia realized that her visions were not really pictoral at all, but rather impulses of color and meaning and connection without words or a defined structure. Through her visions, she understood that the struggle they would undertake against the Guild would cause the commune to lose some of its members, but that those who chose to stay would be bound by a common purpose, solidifying the commune as a family. She could also decipher all the motivations of love and jealousy, ideology and fear that would drive each person to stay or leave. Without the Luridium, she could see all these connections more clearly than she ever had before.

The same was true of Kaido, who discovered his own ability inadvertently when Marcus sent each of them off to meditate by themselves. At first, he saw nothing until he felt his mind stretch out of his own body, instinctively in search of other Seers until he could see Lucia, Alessandra, and Lilli's visions simultaneously in his mind. Later, when it was clear that none of them had been aware of his presence, he and Marcus began experimenting with his ability to keep tabs on the Quorums within the Guild to make sure they remained blind to their whereabouts and plans. Maintaining a connection with the Guild's Quorums in Glasgow and Chicago became his primary function in their raid operation, while Lilli and Lucia kept looking for Nina and Michael, and Alessandra and Marcus focused on blocking any intrusions into their plans.

"Eli, get ready. The last satellite image just finished being uploaded to their security surveillance server. We're ready in 5-4-3-2-1. Go!"

Without a word they all sprang up and followed Eli around the corner of the building to the back door. Liam and Vincent fanned out in front of Alessandra and Eli, pointing their semi-automatic weapons out toward the fence that enclosed them as Eli went straight to the LCD keypad that was fixed in the center of the steel door. He began to enter the password that Alessandra retrieved from her vision a week ago.

Alessandra watched Eli as he typed the words *Blood Orange* into the digital keypad.

"Remember the G is uppercase," she reminded him. Anxiously, Eli toggled back and changed the case before hitting "enter." They each held their breath until they heard a series of tumblers releasing the deadbolt locks from the door. There was a three-second delay before they heard the final latch release, and the door slowly rolled open.

Eli and Alessandra slipped inside, followed by Vincent and Liam, who slowly backed their way in while leaving the door slightly ajar.

Eli immediately turned on his flashlight and let out a small sigh of relief that the room was as he remembered it.

"Shit. How are we supposed to find anything in here?" Vincent asked as he aimed his own flashlight around and saw that the room spanned at least half a football field in width and length and was stacked seven feet high in every direction with row after row of black file cabinets.

"This is actually a good thing," Eli assured Vincent. "The files are organized by country, region, and then state, if applicable. What we're looking for is over there. The US is along the front wall, for easier access."

"I thought you were long gone before they started cataloguing people, Eli. How do you know so much about this room anyway?" Vincent asked, as he made his way toward the front of the room.

"Unfortunately, no. They hid their operation from us for quite a few months before we finally figured out what they were doing. They actually took me to this room as a way to convince me of all the 'good' they could do around the world because of our research. After coming here, I knew I couldn't be a part of their plans. A bunch of us tried to leave the UWO science team after that."

"Look, we've got less than 25 minutes left. Let's just scan the files and get out of here."

Liam was growing impatient with all of Vincent's idle questions. *They could be here at any moment*, he thought.

Hearing the tension in Liam's voice, Alessandra chimed in, "Lilli said we should focus on the northern part of the country, places where it would still be snowing in the spring."

"That's fucking Boston, I know that for sure," Vincent offered with a snort. When he didn't get the laugh he thought he would, he joined the others in producing their pocket scanners and heading toward the back wall.

"I've got Massachusetts and New York," Eli called out.

In response, the others shouted out the northern states they were responsible for scanning and got to work.

"Am I supposed to be looking for siblings in each state or what...?" Vincent asked.

"God, were you completely asleep for the briefing?" Liam yelled from the "V" section of the files.

"No, son," Eli answered more patiently. "Just scan everything. We'll comb through it once we get back home."

They scanned furiously and in silence for the next fifteen minutes before Vincent couldn't resist another complaint.

"Hell, you'd think that with all this technology, they would have ditched the paper by now."

"Actually, I'm sure they have, Vincent, but most hospitals still record their test results on paper and the Guild keeps those records for redundancy," Eli offered.

"Besides," Alessandra added, "we're trying to stay under the radar. If we got caught trying to hack their electronic files, I think that would be a bit..."

Alessandra whipped her head around at the sound of chain links rattling from the barbed wire fence outside.

Wait... oh God. Someone is coming.

In a panic, Alessandra looked down the wall of files to find Liam absorbed in his scanning, seemingly unfazed. Alessandra turned to find Eli and Vincent similarly engaged and realized with increasing alarm that she was hearing the sound in a vision, a vision that was folding quickly into now.

Liam looked up then to find Alessandra frozen and staring at the door.

"What is it? Alessandra, what is it?"

"They—someone is coming. Here. They're looking for us. They know we're here."

"Shit! Everyone out, right now! Get behind me!" Liam hissed.

Liam was off the small ladder he'd been using to get to the top files and over to Alessandra in seconds. With her hand firmly in his right hand and his semi-automatic hanging securely from his left shoulder, Liam reached for the handgun he always kept tucked into the back of his jeans before he and Vincent led the way back to the front door.

"Are you sure, Alessandra?" Eli asked while he turned off his flashlight and followed Vincent's lead. "I didn't hear anything."

"How long do we have?" Liam asked as he raised his gun toward the narrow corridor that led to the front door, and inched forward.

"No... I mean, I can't tell how long... I'm sorry." The vision was still coming. She could see their faces, but she didn't know who they were and how they knew where to find them. She could only sense their excitement at having found them after searching for so long.

Before anyone could ask another question, Liam, Alessandra, Vincent, and Eli froze in unison as they finally heard what Alessandra had been seeing—the rattling of the fence and 3 pairs of feet hitting the dirt outside the back wall where they had just come in only 26 minutes ago.

CHAPTER 15: OTHERS

D o you think they know we're here?" Jared asked, as he peeked inside the open reinforced steel door, waiting for the others to join him.

"I doubt it," Tess mumbled distractedly while fingering the brand new rip in her favorite jean jacket. "Damn barbed wire," she swore before turning her full attention back to Jared's question. "Hell, I barely know why we're here."

"Babe, you okay?"

Before Tess could answer, Eric closed the distance between them and took her arm carefully into his large hand, inspecting it to make sure the barbed wire hadn't broken her skin. When he was satisfied that she was ok, he took a deep breath to slow his breathing from the quick sprint he ran around the perimeter of the building to make sure no one followed them.

"I thought you said we were going to meet some other Seers here?" Eric asked as he threw his arm around Tess's shoulder and walked toward Jared. "Where are they?"

"I don't know. I mean, yeah, I think that's why we're here, but who knows. I just couldn't get this place out of my mind." Tess looked around with a frown as she tried to pinpoint exactly what it was that drew her there.

"Maybe they're inside already, but we're never going to find out if we sit here talking about it," Jared said, with his foot jammed against the inside of the door.

"Alright, man. You first, since you got your panties all in a bunch," Eric joked.

Once inside the door, they were completely enclosed by darkness.

"Jared," Eric whispered, "you got the…"

"Nope…forgot it in the car. I can't see a thing."

"No shit, Sherlock. That's why you were supposed to bring the flashlight."

They inched along the corridor, trying to feel for a door, the side walls, anything that would let them know where they were going.

As they continued into darkness, Eric could feel his curiosity quickly giving way to caution.

If we're supposed to be meeting people, where the hell are they?

The fact that Tess was still moving forward beside him kept him calm for another three steps before he felt compelled to voice his concern.

"Look, guys, maybe we should just…"

"Aaaahhhh!"

The sound of Jared's high-pitched scream froze Eric and Tess in mid-step.

Four seconds went by before Eric could force himself to blink. The effort to completely override his fear took even longer, but once he was sure he could move, he whipped Tess's body behind him and called out for his friend.

"Jared!"

Nothing but silence echoed back at him.

"Jared! Answer me!" Eric yelled, but there wasn't even a rustle of sound to orient them in the dark.

Eric slowly began to back out of the corridor even though he knew they would be at a disadvantage. The small backlight from the open door behind them would soon pinpoint their position to whomever or whatever had taken Jared.

"I didn't see this. I didn't see this," Tess whispered in a voice so frightened and small that only Eric could hear it.

"Jared!" Eric tried one last time.

"Don't move."

For a second, Tess imagined that the command came from the darkness itself. The tone of the masculine voice reeked of death — cold and final. But the sound of a gun being cocked brought her fears back down to earth. It was not a force of nature. It was a man with a gun who wanted to kill them.

Tess could feel the muscles in Eric's back tense and pulse. The infinitesimal shift forward in his body let her know what he was thinking, and she bunched his t-shirt in her hands, telling him silently that she didn't want him to do what he was thinking — to throw himself into the darkness to save her. When she felt his body move back against her, she slowly lowered her forehead to his spine in relief.

"Do exactly as I say. Turn around and face the door. Put your hands up where I can see them. Both of you."

Slowly, Eric and Tess turned toward the door and stretched their hands above their shoulders.

When they were securely faced away from him, Liam risked a glance down at his watch.

2:12 seconds until satellite verification.

Shit.

"Vincent."

As soon as Liam called Vincent's name, he could hear Alessandra and Eli shuffle behind him while Vincent remained at his side with his hand firmly over Jared's mouth.

"Move forward, open the door, and step outside. Don't run or I'll blow the backs of your heads off. Understand? Now move."

As those in front of and behind him followed Liam's instructions with equal obedience, Alessandra noted that if she ever thought that Liam was cold to her, she had been wrong.

This – him now – this is cold, she thought.

Hearing his voice devoid of even the slightest emotion, calm as a still ocean, ten thousand feet deep and deadly, she was overcome with gratitude to be the one he was protecting.

"Motherfucker!" Eric hissed under his breath as he reluctantly complied with the man who was hidden in the dark while he ordered them around. *If Tess weren't here, I'd pistol whip you with that gun.*

As soon as they got outside, Liam motioned for Alessandra and Eli to head to the car, but with 1 minute and 39 seconds to go before they were all discovered, no one moved.

Liam kept his distance from the large man in front of him. Liam could tell he could handle himself and didn't want to risk getting into a scuffle where his gun might go off accidentally with Alessandra around. Liam knew he didn't have a lot of time to make the decision of whether or not to kill them, but he needed to know. If they weren't from the Guild, he'd have to come up with another plan.

"Who are you?" he asked with his gun trained on the back of Eric's head.

"We're not from the Guild," Tess offered in a rush. "We came here looking for you. Please. We're Seers, Jared and I, like you. We just wanted to talk."

"Fifty-two seconds man, let's plug 'em and get out of here," Vincent said, while tightening his grip on Jared.

"Liam, I don't think they're from the Guild. They're not armed. They're kids, Liam. Look at them!" Eli pleaded.

Taking in their clothes, their demeanor, and how unprepared they seemed, Liam had to agree. With less than 30 seconds to escape, Liam put his gun down.

"To the back wall, now! Let's go!"

They made it out of satellite range with five seconds to spare. When they reached the cover of the wall, Eric grabbed Tess and turned to face the people who held them at gunpoint with a murderous stare.

Understanding the need to protect, Liam could respect Eric's anger, but he still didn't take his finger off the trigger of his gun.

"Vincent, release him."

Vincent released his hold on Jared's mouth and throat immediately and shoved him toward Tess and Eric. Once free, Jared stumbled across to his friends, gagging and rubbing his neck gingerly.

No one spoke for several moments as Alessandra, Eli, Vincent, and Liam stood just out of camera-range at one side of the back wall. Eric, Tess and Jared stood at the other.

It was Eli who finally decided to break the silence.

"Look, I think it's fair to say that you startled us. How did you know we were here?"

Tess looked hesitantly to Eric, whose face was etched in angry stone as his green eyes darted from Liam to Alessandra, Eli, and Vincent. She knew he was mad that they were outnumbered.

"I told you," she started, trying not to sound as scared as she was. *How could I have known to come here and not have seen this?*

"We're Seers like you. I can't really explain it, 'cause I just started having visions about a year ago and they're never as detailed as my vision for coming here was, but I just knew we had to come here.

"I didn't know who we would meet here. I just knew there would be Seers. I mean, it's not like I was expecting guns or anything," she

166 | Cerece Rennie Murphy

continued, risking a glance at Liam and Vincent. "I just knew this is where we needed to be."

"We're sorry we scared you. It's — we have to be so careful. I didn't see you coming," Alessandra added with a frown. "None of us saw you."

"How many of you are there?" Tess asked with timid excitement. "I've never met another Seer besides Jared, and that was, like, totally random."

"Look, can we talk about this later? Right now we need to get off the Guild's property before our luck runs out," Liam interjected. "We need to decide if we're taking them with us or not."

"Who says we want to go anywhere with you, gunslinger?" Eric asked.

"You're welcome to stay here and get caught by the Guild if you want, but you'll be doing that by yourself. We're leaving now." Liam made his way toward the back fence, grabbing Alessandra's hand as he went. Alessandra was so disturbed by the fact that she hadn't seen the girl and her two male companions before that she let Liam's momentum carry her forward while her mind was occupied.

"I'm sorry, but he's right. We need to move," Eli agreed as he turned away from them, preparing to head for the fence. "You're welcome to join us, but we need to leave now." Eli and Vincent headed over the fence then, leaving Eric, Jared, and Tess stunned and staring at the others as they made their exit.

"Tess, we don't even know their names," Eric began, even though he knew it was useless. He could see the longing in Tess's eyes, the blind desire to find others like herself and to understand for sure that she wasn't crazy.

"Look what they did to Jared…." Eric looked over to Jared, expecting corroboration, but instead all he found was Jared staring forward with the same longing toward the fence.

"Tess…" Eric tried again.

He wasn't sure if it was the sound of her name or the fact that the last of the other group had cleared the fence and was heading off into the distance that finally pulled her out of her daze.

"I need to…" She began, looking up at him with pure desperation. "I have to know."

Letting out a sigh of resignation, Eric grabbed Tess's hand and ran with Jared to catch up with the others.

Once Eli noticed that they were being followed, he called for his party to wait. No one said a thing as Tess, Jared, and Eric piled into the black Suburban that Liam rented for the trip.

Once the doors were closed, Liam started the ignition and turned around to address the latest additions to the commune.

"Look, I know I was an ass back there. I would say I'm sorry, but that's just how I am when things get… uncertain. If you decide to stay, it won't happen again. I'm Liam," he said, extending his hand to the large man who was clearly the leader of their group.

Given that he was acutely aware that Liam still had all the guns, Eric wasn't fully reassured by Liam's explanation, even though he appreciated the gesture.

"Eric Kirmse," he said finally. "And this is Jared Miller and Tess Wyler."

Eli, Alessandra, and Vincent chimed in with their introductions before Vincent reminded them that they needed to check in with Hanna.

"Hanna, we made it out. We're headed back, with a few new additions to the clan," Eli said, smiling back at Jared.

"Eli! It's about time! I was just about to break down and call you!"

"Sorry to worry you. We ran into some unanticipated distractions."

"Yeah, I gathered that much. So you have some new additions, huh? Let me guess. Seers."

Everyone stared at the black walkie-talkie in shock as Hanna continued.

"Yeah, well, there's more where they came from. We've got a few new additions here, too. They just showed up. Lilli is pretty excited, even though no one saw them coming. Come back as soon as you can. Lilli and Marcus are trying to keep everyone calm, but... yeah, just hurry back. We've got a lot to sort out here."

Liam drove all night, with the trip back to Iowa taking every bit of the 10 hours that the rental car's GPS system said it would. Everyone's nerves were on edge as they watched Liam struggle not to go over the speed limit. By the time they returned the rental, piled into Eli's minivan, and made it back to the commune, the atmosphere had settled into an uneasy calm. Vincent, Liam, Eli, and Alessandra walked quickly toward the meeting hall with Eric, Tess, and Jared trailing behind them as they tried to make out their surroundings in the faint light of dawn.

"Where the hell are we?" Eric wondered aloud while drawing Tess closer to him. He made a mental note to keep Jared in his line of sight. No one answered him as Liam and Vincent slid open the door to the large red barn and came upon the most strained commune gathering Eli had ever witnessed.

Though Rachel's expression was animated as she paced back and forth, she was strangely quiet as she exchanged worried glances with Marshall. The others who were present were scattered in varying positions around the barn, some standing with their backs pressed up against the wall, others with their hands between their knees as they sat on the bushels of hay that were barely arranged in any type of pattern. Some had even sunk to the ground like rag dolls, as if waiting for the worst to come and overtake them. Looking around, Eli noted that the barn was only three-fourths full, and he couldn't help but wonder where all the others were.

Despite the varying postures and degrees of tension around the room, all those present had one thing in common; with regular intervals, each pair of eyes migrated towards the pair of women standing in the middle of the room. Though they were each beautiful in their own subtle way, they could not have been more different in look and demeanor. The tall blond woman looked wounded by each pair of eyes that settled on her. As the stares continued, her head bent lower and lower in her attempt to use her long, tangled hair as a cloak to shield her from the crowd's suspicions. Her clothes were a combination of tattered wools and worn leather paired with black combat boots and leggings that had been patched too many times. Though her skin was ruddy and her lips chapped, she wore a thick layer of black kohl liner around her deep blue eyes.

The woman standing next to her was only slightly shorter with browned-butter skin and long dreadlocks that extended down her shoulders like thick ropes. She wore no make-up to accompany what looked like a brand new outfit straight out of a Gap winter catalog, complete with a fuchsia fleece hoodie under her down vest with matching gloves and hat. To Eli, she appeared either completely oblivious or unfazed by all the attention she was getting as she met each pair of questioning eyes head-on. Her focus seemed to be on making eye contact with each person in the room and studying them for a moment before turning to seek out another face.

The only ones who looked at ease were the Seers, who sat on the bales of hay to the left of the women in the center of the room. Liam noticed how Lilli seemed to be literally vibrating with enthusiasm while Kaido, Lucia, and Marcus sat beside her with more subdued looks of anticipation.

Once they understood that no one seemed to be in danger, Liam and the others focused their attention on trying to make sense of what was taking place before them. When their presence wasn't acknowledged by anyone but Lilli, who gave a slight wave to her brother, Eli began to worry.

"Hey guys, what's going on here?"

The sound of Eli's voice got Marshall to finally look up from his seated position.

"You tell us, Eli. No one seems to know. And these two," he said, throwing his hand in the direction of the women in the center of the room, "don't seem to know anything, either. And even if they did, it wouldn't make a damn bit of difference, 'cause it doesn't seem like either of them speaks English, which, of course, begs the question—if they can't speak a word of English, how in the heck did they end up here?"

CHAPTER 16: LINES DRAWN

H er name is Katia," Lilli spoke quietly while gently stroking the girl's back as if she were a frightened kitten. "I think she's been alone...for a while before coming here."

With a little probing and an encouraging smile, Lilli was able to determine that both women spoke some English, though Katia was only willing to speak in French.

"How did she know where to find us?" Eli asked, trying to mimic Lilli's soothing tone as he turned to address Katia directly. "How did you find us?"

Eli glanced between the two women as he waited patiently for Lilli to translate his question into the French she spoke so beautifully and interpret Katia's response for the group.

"She says she doesn't know. She was living in...I guess you could call it a rooming house for girls - until a week ago. That's when she got a vision of us that showed her everything she needed to find us–where to go, how to get the money to come here, everything, almost as if she was receiving instructions..."

Lilli could feel the tension in the room gather new weight as it wrapped around her words. Her gaze hadn't made it halfway around the barn before she began to see the evidence that those in the room understood, as she did, how easy it had been for Katia to find them.

Turning toward the other woman, Lilli asked, "Was it like that for you, too, Maura?"

"Yes, almost the same," she nodded, in her thick Cape Verdian accent.

"Me, too," Tess added, amazed by the fact that each of them had been drawn there, unwittingly.

"Who could be orchestrating this?" Marcus interjected from his place outside the loose circle that Lilli, Eli, Alessandra, and Marshall had created around the newcomers. "And for what purpose?"

"It can't be the Guild," Eli whispered, addressing so many unspoken fears. "If they knew where we were, we'd either be captured or dead by now."

"But who, then?" Alessandra asked in frustration. "Who could block all of us from seeing while leading them here? And for what? Why would anyone do this for any other reason but to hurt us?"

Alessandra's questions seared the silence that hung over the room into a sharp awareness that a new, unseen presence was somehow engaged in their lives, without their knowledge or permission.

Sitting in his makeshift seat, baffled by the implication of the night's events, Marcus' eyes began roaming the room, touching on each of the faces in front of him, until he realized that the number of Seers among them had nearly doubled in one evening.

What are the chances of that? He wondered. *Why these Seers? Why now, when we have decided to come out of hiding, only to find them waiting for us—seeking us out?*

The answers to his questions felt too far away as he rose from his seat beside Liam and walked into the center of the circle to stand in front of the young woman who called herself Maura.

"Do you know what your gift is? What you see?" Marcus asked her without explanation or pretext. To be honest, he wasn't even sure what he was asking or why. Though he felt compelled to act, he still couldn't grasp the seed of understanding that he felt pressing at the back of his skull, struggling to untangle itself from his confusion.

Maura's smile as she answered was kind and patient, as if she had already anticipated what Marcus was going to ask and had been waiting for him to figure it out on his own.

"I can see who you are... inside," she said as she pressed her long, slim hand lightly into the middle of his chest. "I know if you are a good man or a bad man by your light. I know if someone is happy or sad. You are both, I think, but you will not hurt me," she finished before returning her hand to her side.

Perplexed and slightly taken off-guard by her answer, Marcus wondered if perhaps she had not understood his choice of words.

"You see these things in the future?" he asked slowly in his calm, low voice, trying to clarify her meaning in the context of his first questions.

"Nooo," Maura answered, trying to mimic the slower pace of his words. Taking in the confusion that pinched his smooth features, she began to wonder if her English had somehow failed to convey her true meaning. She tried to choose her next words very carefully as she continued.

"I see this now, in you, in everyone," she said, shifting her eyes toward the people she had been silently assessing earlier in the evening, when she needed to know whether or not she was safe. "The future I see only when I am at rest, in my mind."

Marcus was stunned. He had never heard of a Seer having any abilities in addition to their visions. He didn't know what to think as he turned to Lucia, hoping that she would ask his questions again in Portuguese to make sure that she had understood him and, if so, that he truly understood her.

"Lucia, please, I do not understand."

They all waited as Lucia repeated Marcus' question in the language that she and Maura shared, and listened in growing curiosity as the two women giggled at the looks of pure disbelief on the faces around them.

"It is as she said, Marcus. While we have been watching her, she has been learning us, discovering if she and Katia were safe. She says that all the people who were... weak have left, and that those of us who remain are, in her words, very good, strong, like family," Lucia finished her translation proudly, grateful to be of use and hopeful that the news would ease some of the tension in the room.

"So that's why you've had that smile on your face for the past hour?" Marshall asked, addressing Maura directly for only the second time that night.

"Yes," Maura said. "It was not safe to speak before. Some of the people here when I arrived did not have good spirits. They could not be trusted."

"Yes, I'm sure you're right," Eli added pensively. Glancing across all the new and old faces he had come to care for, he wondered what those who left might do with all the information they had.

"Eli, have you ever heard of the ability Maura describes?" Marcus asked, still trying to make sense of what he was hearing.

"No, I've never heard of anything like that... I don't even know what to say..." Eli trailed off.

"I might have," Lilli said in a small voice.

All eyes turned to Lilli, waiting for her to continue.

"I mean, it's not the same exactly," she began, looking sheepishly in her brother's direction to find him leaning forward and watching her intently.

"It was years ago, when Liam and I were still on the run. Liam was carrying me on his back and we were trying to get away from these men who were after us. I don't know how, but I felt like suddenly I was in Liam's head telling him what to do.

"I wasn't visioning, but all of a sudden I knew where we needed to turn, how we needed to escape, like instinct, but I knew it wasn't. It was more than that." Closing her eyes, Lilli tried to bring herself back to that day in Chinatown.

"It was like, for that moment, while we were trying to get away, Liam and I were one person. Like I was his brain and he was my legs. I thought and he reacted. I know it sounds crazy, but it was in…"

"Instantaneous," Liam and Lilli finished in unison. Liam's face held a small smile as he watched his sister with new admiration.

"I remember, Lilli. All this time, I thought I was just hearing your voice, I didn't know…"

"Me, neither," Lilli interrupted. "It was only later, in the storage room when I finally *did* speak, that I realized what had happened, but I didn't know how. I still don't."

No one knew what to say after that. There was too much newness, so much left unexplained. As the moments ticked on, the silence began to rustle with impatience as most people in the barn had reached the limits of their capacity for the strange and unexpected.

"That shit is wild," Kyle murmured through the silence.

Amid a ripple of soft laughter, Marshall shook his head and stood up from the seat he had taken next to Liam half-way through Lucia's conversation with Maura.

"My thoughts exactly," Marshall chuckled as he stretched his long arms up over his head. "I think I'm done for tonight. Eli, can the newbies sleep in the clinic until we get some shut-eye? We'll figure out who's left and assign new quarters tomorrow."

"That sounds like a good plan to me."

Marshall was almost to the barn door before he realized Rachel was not beside him. Turning back, he found her frozen in place, still standing near the haystack he had just vacated.

"Rach, you coming?" he asked, as he followed her gaze from Lilli to Katia to Maura to Tess and back again.

"No, you go ahead," she answered without looking in his direction. He could barely grasp the dozens of questions he suspected were running through her mind. Knowing her as he did, he also knew that she wouldn't leave any of them alone until she was satisfied. He turned away without another word and headed toward the warmth of his bed.

"Can she do that?" Rachel asked to no one in particular as she pointed toward Katia.

"What do you mean, Rachel? Do what?" Lilli asked patiently.

"Can Katia do the same thing as Maura? Can she see… inside us?"

Happy to have all eyes off her for the moment, Lilli quickly translated Rachel's question for Katia.

"She says she doesn't know," Lilli translated. "That she always tries not to see anything. She just couldn't stop the visions that led her here."

Katia kept her eyes to the floor as she wrapped her arms around herself, looking even more distraught than when she came in.

"Ugh! We don't know anything!" Alessandra blurted out suddenly. "We don't know who blocked our sight. We don't know why they are here. We don't know who sent them. Hell, THEY don't even know who sent them! We don't know anything more than when this crazy night began!"

Marcus watched as Alessandra's rage receded as quickly as it came.

"I'm sorry," she exhaled, feeling defeated as she took Marshall's seat on the bale of hay next to Liam. "I just don't like feeling so helpless."

Marcus smiled at Alessandra encouragingly before turning his attention toward the others that remained in the barn. "There is a reason we were all brought here," he began. "I don't yet know the reason, but I have a feeling that if we see this through, we will find out."

CHAPTER 17: JUST THE BEGINNING

Early the next morning, Marcus and Alessandra saw that they would be too late to find Michael and Nina. Before they would even have a chance to finish combing through the data they'd gathered, Nina and Michael would be captured and well into the purification process. Though the vision of their failure worried Alessandra, none of the other Seers seemed particularly concerned, given the myriad of new developments occupying their time. Instead of mourning the lost opportunity, they decided to focus their efforts on training the newest Seers to build their own protection against the Guild's latest acquisitions.

The first two weeks after Tess and the others arrived were almost a blur. Between the rush to prepare accommodations for the commune's five newest members and all the frenzy that went into integrating them into commune life, it seemed like everyone was going in ten different directions. The lack of hands to do all the work that was required didn't help, either. All and all, the commune lost eleven members the night the new Seers arrived. Even though everyone tried their best to pick up the slack, those who knew how seamlessly the commune usually ran could still feel the difference.

Some who left had been with the commune for several years, and Eli was genuinely disappointed to discover how thin their attachment had been when tested. Still, he understood the reasons why not everyone was up for the journey they were now taking. Without ever formally deciding, they had become a haven for the Guild's most sought-after possessions. To keep them hidden and to aid in their escape was, in itself, an act of treason against the UWO that sanctioned and funded the Guild's entire operation. But at least these actions could be considered a crime of pity. The raids and harboring of the latest Seers were acts of willful obstruction, punishable by death. Despite this reality, Lucia and Maura had been right—everyone who stayed at the commune had somehow come to terms with this risk in their own mind and were now committed to this new act of defiance.

Marcus spent all of his time with the new Seers, helping them understand and control their visions. With the exception of Maura, most had negative experiences with their sight, which clouded their access to and understanding of what they could do. Maura was lucky enough to have been abandoned by her drug-addicted mother at birth and left with her maternal grandmother, who raised her with love and little else in the slums of Praia, Cape Verde. By the time she was three, Maura understood what the colors she saw inside the people around her meant. This skill enabled her to steer clear of many of the dangers that thrived in her neighborhood and create a cocoon of people around her with whom she could be safe. Until she saw her vision of the Commune, she had never ventured more than ten miles from her one room apartment.

In contrast, Tess, Jared, and Katia had either fled or been forced out of their homes when their gift first began to manifest, fearing that they were either going crazy or destined to become the evil that they had heard about from the Guild. Tess had run away from home when she was fifteen and met Eric while trying to convince the local gas station owner that she was old enough to be hired as their new full-time cashier. As a regular customer, Eric pulled the owner aside and convinced him to give her the job. Tess finally agreed to go out with Eric after a month of him buying more gum than he could ever chew in a lifetime.

Even though Eric was not a Seer, overtime Tess realized that he was someone who believed in her even when she didn't believe in herself. Several weeks before Tess's first vision of Alessandra and Marcus, they met Jared, who had just run away from home, at a youth hostel in Chicago. They had hung together out of simple relief to find in each other someone with whom to share their secrets safely.

Katia had the worst experience, being cast out by her family at the age of nine for being a 'devil' child. From then on, she had drifted from place to place as her hatred of herself grew. By age ten, to control her visions, she had begun a steady regimen of punishment that could be traced along the thin lines of scars on her arms and thighs that marked whenever a vision would come to her. As she grew older and her visions became more frequent, some of her wounds had little time to heal before new ones were required. In the first few days of her arrival, Eli, Marcus, and Alessandra spent a great deal of time treating her infected cuts and trying to convince her that she was not, in fact, evil. Though Alessandra had never taken her self-loathing to the extreme that Katia had, Alessandra understood her struggle and tried to be the mentor to Katia that Marcus had been to her. Until the first time they quorumed together, Katia remained skeptical.

It took Marcus three weeks from the time the newest Seers arrived to be fully comfortable with each Seer's ability to come into and out of visioning reliably. Since Tess, Katia, Maura, and Jared had never quorumed before, Marcus spent extra time with them to make sure they were able to access and maintain the meditative state required to remain calm and focused during the process. While Marcus worked with the Seers, Eli began sharing with the commune some of the knowledge he had gathered during the years he studied paranormal behavior with the International Science Team.

"The brain activity that each Seer displays while visioning operates in a pattern not found in any other humans," Eli explained the morning that the first Quorum with all the new Seers was scheduled. "We used to refer to it as a language, but it isn't really in the traditional sense. It was most often described by Seers as a kind of shared understanding. I don't think it is or can be spoken. If anything, it might be more accurate to describe it as a language of thought.

"That's actually why we called the language Prime, theorizing that it might be the first language, perhaps something that was used by our ancestors to communicate with each other or even with God, before spoken language was developed." Eli smiled as he saw the expressions of disbelief flash over the faces of commune members and Seers. He had expected as much. As a scientist, he knew the idea itself sounded far-fetched, but he was also aware that if they had seen all the things he had witnessed, they might not be so skeptical.

"We observed that when we put two or more Seers together, they were able to share visions through Prime, regardless of their spoken language, and without any prompting from us. We thought proximity was all that was necessary to facilitate this sharing of visions or what the Guild calls Quorums, but we never got into Phase II testing to verify it. From some of the abilities that the Seers here have already displayed, I would say familiarity with the focus of a vision is probably more important than proximity.

"Keep in mind that none of the Seers we tested had ever had any training or cultivation of their gift. None were able to sustain a vision for more than a few minutes. Their skill levels were nowhere near what you guys are able to do. Anyway, once we realized that Seers were capable of sharing visions, we began testing whether or not these visions could be amplified by the number of Seers participating. This is how the initial drugs for monitoring visions were created. We knew continuous exposure to the drugs was extremely dangerous, so they were never intended for prolonged use..." Eli trailed off as he reflected on how much of his work had been perverted and twisted beyond its intended purpose.

"Of course, the Guild had other plans by then. But we were able to measure changes in the intensity and complexity of audiovisual impulses that the brain processed when visioning, and we noticed immediately that these factors seemed to increase with each Seer that was added to a visioning group, up to seven members. After that, the intensity and complexity of visions seemed to plateau. I assume this is why, as Kaido had informed me, the Guild's typical Quorum is made up of no more than seven members."

"But there are nine of us," Lucia interrupted. "Will that be harmful in some way?"

"I don't think so, Lucia. We never saw any evidence of harm in our trials, even with as many as ten Seers. There is no reason to believe that, but my research was never completed, so I can't answer your question with absolute certainty."

Lucia tried to take comfort in the steadiness of Eli's gaze rather than the uncertainty of his words.

"Look, at least some of us have done this before," Marcus began as he stood up from the crowd. "And if we are ever going to discover why we were brought here together, I think we must take the risk. I am willing to take the risk," he finished, before turning to leave the meeting hall and make his way to the clearing. Following his lead, everyone made their way outside to find Marcus breathing deeply, already into his meditation.

Having never quorumed before, Marcus and the others understood that the newest Seers would be anxious. To help comfort and support them through the experience, Lilli suggested that they all hold hands for their first Quorum together. One by one, they linked hands in a circle and began their breathing techniques as they had been trained to do, until each mind could sense the presence of the other. Marcus had asked that they all focus on trying to vision other Seers who might be looking for them, hoping that the subject would be less volatile than attempting to see whatever the Guild had planned.

Slowly, a common vision came into focus as each Seer began to view images of women, men and some children walking toward them from in front and behind, above and below them. Though they had expected to see the future, the vision that came felt very much in progress, both present and future together. Maura's ability allowed the Quorum to see the light she described to them in each of the new Seers in their collective vision and to understand their emotional state as they moved closer to the commune. Alessandra provided extraordinary detail on the families and histories of each of the Seers they witnessed. Though Lucia's vision added a clear understanding of how each Seer was led to them, no one could see who was motivating them to seek the commune in the first place.

As the vision played out, Marcus searched to find the source. For him, it was like chasing a shadow. Having quorumed with each Seer individually, Marcus recognized the unique tint to each Seer's vision and knew unmistakably that the presence he sensed was unfamiliar. The only evidence that the presence existed at all was the inexplicable feeling of certainty that Marcus could not shake deep down in his bones.

In the vision, as each coming Seer made their way into the circle, they appeared to align themselves with different members of the Quorum, until each member had at least three or four Seers at his or her side, with the exception of Lilli, who stood alone. Despite having never considered the idea before, it struck each of the Quorum members as fitting that Lilli should be set apart.

Though Marcus had felt some anxiety from the group when visioning began, he was pleased to see how quickly they became tranquil and more deeply connected than he'd ever felt before. Even Jared and Katia, the most timid members of the Quorum, maintained their composure and participated fully. By the time Marcus began to pull back from the vision, signaling the end of the session, they each felt a heightened sense of belonging and rightness in coming together. They also knew that Marcus was proud of them and what they had accomplished.

For these reasons, no one registered the sound of Liam shouting Alessandra and Lilli's names until he broke through the circle at the point where Tess and Alessandra's hands were joined. They watched in shock as Liam grabbed Alessandra's arm and drew Lilli's whole body into his right side in one motion. Eric was silent as he barreled in behind Liam and encased Tess in his shaking frame.

Slowly, each Seer peered outward to take in the sudden chaos of their surroundings. The bales of hay that had been set up as seating for the commune members who wanted to witness the Quorum were blistered and thrown hundreds of feet away from their original position. With the exception of Eli, Liam, and Eric, the commune members who were once gathered close by were now only barely visible, as they peeked out from behind trees, the inside of the barn, and the old red pumper truck that was brought out only in case of fire. Sensing the end of whatever had just occurred, each of the members slowly came forward from their temporary shelters with shock, fear, and amazement frozen on their wide-eyed expressions.

Lilli was the last to open her eyes.

●•··•●

"Eli? What happened here?"

As hard as he tried, Marcus could not connect the chaos of the environment around him with any part of the tranquility he had just experienced in Quorum. The look on Eli's face told him that what happened in Quorum and the tempered fear on the faces of his colleagues were intertwined in some sort of cause-effect relationship, but to his mind, nothing seemed farther from reality. He had been a part of a Quorum for more than a decade and nothing like that had ever happened.

It took Eli several moments to answer. The dry wind and impenetrable heat that had encased and emanated from the Quorum less than a minute before was nowhere to be found, as if it never happened. In its place were still trees and unsinged grass.

I didn't imagine this. All of us could not have imagined this, he assured himself as his eyes scanned his surroundings for traces of what they had just witnessed.

"I have no idea," Eli replied in a rush, as he threw down the water hose he had been holding, just in case anything or anyone caught on fire. Out of breath and more than a little frayed, he continued, "I have never seen anything like it, ever! There was some sort of event. About two minutes after Quorum started, the wind picked up. At first we thought it was the weather, but then you all started to get blurry. There was this ring of light that started to surround the Quorum, but it wasn't static; it was moving around you in streaks and flashes. That's when we got worried. Liam and Eric tried to run toward the group, to interrupt the Quorum and make sure you were safe, but by then the wind had become too strong. The longer you quorumed, the stronger the winds got. We started to feel this intense heat coming from the group. Liam and Eric tried, but between the wind and the heat, they were thrown back. We literally could not get close to you.

"At one point, we thought that the trees would catch fire, but we couldn't warn you, no matter how loudly we yelled and screamed. It was like there was an impenetrable force field of some kind around the Quorum! I can't begin to explain…"

Marcus turned back to the Seers, who remained frozen in place. Their initial feelings of accomplishment were replaced with horror at the notion that they could have hurt any one of the commune members without ever being conscious of it.

Turning from Eli to the others, who were slowly growing brave enough to come out of hiding, Marcus' own feelings of shock were quickly overtaken by guilt.

"I'm… Eli… Everyone, I don't know what to say. I don't know how this happened…"

Taking in the defeated look of the man who had become his friend, Eli recovered enough of himself to put his hand on Marcus' shoulder in a gesture of reassurance.

"Marcus, we all know this isn't your fault. We know you wouldn't do anything to hurt us." Despite Marcus' look of dismay, he continued. "Let's think this through. Did you feel anything different? I mean, could you sense anything unusual in your Quorum?"

"Eli, nothing…nothing to suggest what was happening for you here. I would have stopped immediately. You know this! I would never –"

"I know. We all know this, Marcus, but something different happened. Can you think of anything that was different?"

"I just remember a feeling of strong cohesion and peace. To me, we were all of one mind in a way I have never felt before. Even though there were more of us than usual, it seemed we were more together. I know that probably doesn't make any sense, but… I can't describe it any other way."

"Marcus, I felt it too," Alessandra said, as she slowly extricated herself from Liam's grasp to put her arm around Marcus' waist. "I know we all did. It was like we belonged together, all of us visioning together. I felt freer to extend my vision and myself further than I ever had. It felt boundless."

Jared cleared his throat behind them before addressing Marcus directly in his soft, clear voice. "I trusted you enough to allow myself to see without fear. Maybe I shouldn't have, but it felt…safe, good, for the first time…like this is what I was meant for, who I was meant to be. That's never happened to me before."

"Me, too," Tess offered, from the shelter of Eric's arm. "I can't stop shaking. It was like, as soon as we came together, everything I am was just released into the group, but more. It felt even stronger because we were all together."

"It was powerful, freeing–like we could see everything all at once in that moment. Like there were no limits," Lilli added in a quiet voice as she held on closely to her brother.

"But there was a…presence that I felt also," Marcus added, "as if someone else was with us in Quorum. I could not see it, but I felt it. Did anyone else?"

188 | Cerece Rennie Murphy

The Seers were silent in response to his question.

"It sounds like there was a lot that was different about this session." Eli was quiet again before he added cautiously. "I know this sounds crazy, but I think the only way to know for sure is to try to isolate the variables and see if we can't repeat this...experience again."

"Eli, I can't see how..." Marcus interjected.

"No way," Liam agreed.

"I know, I know. We have to be careful, maybe move Quorum to a location a bit farther from the commune, but I think we need some answers here, and this is the only way we're going to get them. I just don't understand why we never saw this reaction before. I mean, if it has to do with expanding the group, then we should have seen some evidence of this before..."

"I think maybe we have," Kyle offered, as he hovered just outside the group of Seers with his video camera in hand. "I know you guys said you wanted privacy when you Quorum, so I guess this was wrong, but I've been videotaping you," Kyle paused, waiting for the reprimand that he had been expecting. When it didn't come, he continued.

"I started noticing that my playback kept getting worse and worse after your first Quorum. Maybe what we saw is part of the reason why. I mean, for the last couple of sessions, I could barely make out anything on the tape, even before the new Seers got here."

"So this could be just the beginning," Hanna added from behind Kyle.

"The beginning of what?" Alessandra asked warily.

Hanna's smile was small, but her eyes glinted with excitement. "The beginning of discovering what you guys can really do."

After Quorum and the ensuing discussion, Lilli returned to her room as quickly as she could without raising suspicion. Given how needless she knew it was, Liam's worry had been almost annoying, but she couldn't blame him.

How else could he interpret me clinging to him like a frightened child?

The truth was that as everyone else rehashed the mayhem that their Quorum today had caused, she struggled to summon even the smallest ounce of concern once she confirmed everyone was okay.

Under the circumstances, Lilli could not explain her betrayal. She should have told them, especially Marcus, but she knew she wouldn't. She would never give him up, never tell another soul what she felt— arms wrapping around her from behind in the gentlest embrace as he whispered in her ear so softly her thoughts went blank just before she disconnected from the Quorum. In that same instance, she felt him take over her mind and her place in the Quorum so that she alone could hear the words he whispered in her ear.

Only you, Lilli.

I was meant to stand with only you.

Only you will know who I am.

Only you can find me.

Find me, Lilli.

Find me.

Chapter 18: Heat and Expansion

March, 2012

Making his way carefully up the incline that marked the southern-most border of the commune, Kyle found himself humming along with the pick-up's diesel engine as he recounted for the umpteenth time all the amazing benefits that came out of his unsanctioned videotaping of the Seers.

1) He finally got that top of the line Sony digital camcorder that he had his eye on for the past 6 months that Hanna refused to even consider. In addition to getting better footage of the Seers, Kyle couldn't wait until the Iowa winter broke so he could use his new acquisition to catch Tess, Katia, or Maura sunbathing in the nude as soon as possible;

2) The tool shed behind the clinic was turned into what Kyle liked to call the Super Geek's Paranormal Emporium, with state-of-the-art Geiger counters, spectroscopes, infrared cameras, and other stuff that he knew nothing about. But he got to play with all of it and that's what mattered;

3) Marshall let him drive the pick-up truck on a regular basis;

4) Due to the almost-constant testing that Eli did on the Seers these days, Kyle, his technical assistant, was excused from all other Commune chores, and

5) Thanks to Liam and Lilli, he didn't have to drop a dime for his all-access pass to all the electronic wizardry that a growing boy could ever want.

Coming down the other side of the incline, he could see Eli waiting for him, already getting set up for a visioning session. Since the first 'event,' as Eli liked to call it, they had moved all Seer visioning activities out to the commune's southern border to keep things a safe distance from the population. Today, they were preparing to observe three of the less experienced Seers in the group.

As usual, Eli launched right into his pre-testing orientation the minute Kyle jumped out of the pick-up truck and started unloading the portable spectroscope. "The goal today is to try to get comparison readings on Seers in varying stages of their visioning development. Yesterday we did Marcus, Alessandra, and Kaido. Today, if my theory holds, there should be a distinct difference in the amount of electromagnetic energy this group emits as compared to yesterday's group."

"Yeah, ok," Kyle mumbled, as he continued unloading the rest of their equipment. In truth, he was just happy to have a good excuse to watch Maura, Katia, and Tess in action.

It had been like this for months, ever since the 'event' — testing each Seer, getting physiological data before and after visioning, and observing abnormal occurrences with small groups to develop a catalog of effects that could occur before all the Seers quorumed together again.

Some of the results were mundane. For example, Seer body temperature was not significantly affected by the visioning process or the heat that was generated with increasing intensity during the sessions, especially among Seers with advanced abilities. Other results, like the fact that the speed of electromagnetic waves seemed to increase once visioning began, despite no reduction in the mass of the Quorum, defied basic laws of physics and seemed to suggest that when visioning, the basic molecular composition of each Seer was somehow altered or reduced temporarily. To make matters more complex, the extent to which this occurred varied according to the talent and experience of the Seer.

And Lilli was a complete anomaly. Though she was technically one of the least experienced Seers, her heat emission and electromagnetic wave readings rivaled those of Alessandra, or even Marcus at times. For these inconsistencies, as with so many discoveries over the past few months, Eli had yet to come up with any explanation.

Between daily life and duties within the commune, regular testing of the Seers, and the continued raids that were carried out against the Guild, fall had quickly passed into winter, with everyone in the commune in a constant state of motion.

In addition to training Tess, Jared, Katia, and Maura, Marcus, Lilli, and Alessandra continued the search for new Seers who would become a part of their group. From these visions, it became clear that they needed to continue to run more raids against the Guild. Without help, they could see that not everyone who belonged with them would escape the Guild's pursuit. Some would need to be warned and others rescued from the Guild's constant gathering practices. For this to happen, they would need to re-enter the world outside their commune and go after this group of Seers, one by one.

Lilli and Alessandra coordinated with Hanna to plan each aspect of the raids, while Marcus, Kaido, and Lucia worked with the others Seers individually to develop and hone their ability to block the group's plans and control their thoughts when they were not actively blocking. To break up the monotony of their near-constant training, Lucia created a blocking game that the Seers played amongst each other, with one group responsible for visioning, while the other group tried to block their sight. As the groups alternated, each Seer was able to understand and strengthen their abilities. Though they each got better, no one was ever able to match or surpass Marcus or Katia, whose years of practice in blocking her own visions translated into a powerful gift for suppressing that ability in others.

The game also helped Tess discover her ability to project her visions onto others. After two hours of a particularly long and competitive blocking game, Tess knew she was losing her struggle to resist Jared's efforts to block her vision as she sat quietly by the river. Suddenly, Tess felt a stream of ice cold water pouring down her back. Just before she let out a yelp into the frigid air, Tess sought out the only other Seer who was still connected to the game and placed her vision safely in Lucia's mind before losing her concentration and running after the sound of Eric cackling away only ten feet behind her. Later, after exacting her revenge on Eric, she was able to explore her ability with Lucia and others until she was able to reliably project images from her mind or other Seers' visions into the minds of Seers and non-Seers alike.

The combination of Katia's blocking and Tess's projection capacity with Maura's ability to see the character and intentions of each person they approached proved extremely effective in executing their raids despite the risk of exposure. Once Alessandra and Lilli were able to determine where each of their Seers was located and the timeframe in which they would be targeted by the Guild, a team that almost always included Alessandra and Tess traveled to those locations.

With each trip to rescue a family, Tess's ability gave the Seers a powerful way to show Seers they approached and their families the tragedy that had befallen other Seers who were captured by the Guild, as well as their own fate if they did not heed the warning they were given. Some chose to come with them, others chose to run on their own, but everyone got the message.

Despite the risk of being discovered or reported by the families they approached, there was never a shortage of raid volunteers. Each Seer was eager to do what they could to stop what had or could have been done to them. This was especially true of Alessandra, who made sure she went on every raid.

"Alessandra, you don't have to do this," Marcus insisted, when she signed up for her third raid in a row. "I know the memories are still painful for you."

"I know I don't have to, Marcus. I know that. But...I need to," she said quietly. "For every Seer we save, there are so many others who will lose their families, lose everything because of the Guild. With what Tess can do—I know when they see what happened to us, to me, they won't doubt us. They might not come with us, but at least they will know. They will have the chance that I didn't have—that none of us had."

Marcus stared at her as she made the circuit between her small bed to the dresser and back again, packing her duffel bag for the next day's raid. She had grown so much in the time since they had arrived at the commune almost seven months ago.

When we came here, she was just frail bones and wide eyes. Now, look at her, all quiet strength and steady determination. She does not need me anymore, he thought, with a heavy dose of pride and sadness.

"Do you have them back now, all your memories?" Marcus asked.

"No, but I get a little bit more every day. Every day they become more real; *I* become more real." Looking into the mirror above her dresser, Alessandra ran her fingers through the layered, chin-length mass of soft brown curls that framed the oval face that was so much like her father's. "So don't ask me not to go."

After that, Marcus never did. If he didn't need to stay with Katia and Lilli and focus on blocking the complexity of their plans, he would have done the same thing.

Being outside in the open had special significance for Marcus, Alessandra, Kaido, and Lucia. The first time they walked out of the commune and into a crowded area without having to hide behind a cloak or hoodie and shades was a revelation. It was, they realized at that moment, their first true taste of freedom. Even with the risk of recapture, they had lingered that first day outside of the local shopping mall as they waited for their rental car, just to watch in quiet bliss as people passed them by without giving them the slightest glance.

In two months, they had brought five new Seers into their group, while warning another four families with younger teens about the Guild and convincing them to go into hiding. Two of these families eventually made their way to the commune. All this was in addition to the three new Seers who simply showed up, telling a familiar tale of a powerful vision coming to them out of nowhere with specific details and a driving compulsion to find the commune.

Keeping up with the expansion at Fox River was an on-going challenge, with Marshall and Rachel constantly working to redistribute, organize, and orient the new and old commune members to make sure all the necessary work was completed. As head of the construction teams, Liam, Kaido, Eric, and Caleb, the father of one of the commune's youngest Seers, were always two steps behind as they tried to juggle regular maintenance and build new cabins. Even with these duties and despite Marshall having taken over raid security, Liam, Kaido, and Eric still insisted on going to the raids in which Alessandra, Lilli, Lucia, or Tess were a part of the field team.

To Alessandra, it was a frustrating dichotomy. On one hand, she and Liam worked more closely together now than ever before. He accompanied her on every raid, watched over her at every turn, but he was still hard-pressed to carry on even the most basic conversation with her. From time to time, she would catch him looking at her, sometimes with just the hint of a smile, but he never engaged, and he never got closer. Except at night, where in her dreams his touch was ever present and his laugh so easy, it made her cry.

During their last raid, in reaction to her careless attempt to reach their target Seer without checking to make sure that only the family was at home, Liam had pulled her flush against him with his arm firmly secured around her waist. It was the most physical contact they'd ever shared, with so much of her touching so much of him. She felt dizzy with the warmth of his chest, broad and strong, against her back. Though the sensation was more than anything she had felt in her visions, the glorious feeling of belonging was the same as she recalled from her dreams when she saw them napping lazily on a bed that was unlike any at the commune, with his arms and legs draped deliciously heavy across her body.

After that night, when he had released her from his grasp almost as quickly as he'd taken her into it, Alessandra decided that she couldn't stand it any longer. She needed to figure out a way to shake her visions loose and make them real. The next day she had gone to Lucia, but before she could knock on her door, she heard the soft sounds of Lucia and Kaido gasping and whispering in tones that she knew well from her own dreams.

Determined, Alessandra turned to Rachel. Though they were not particularly close, Alessandra noticed that ever since the night when the first new Seers arrived, Rachel seemed happier, more friendly and embracing of the close knit family the commune had become. But more than that, Rachel was beautiful, feminine and desired. Alessandra had seen the way Marshall and many of the men at the commune looked at her when they thought she wasn't aware. Though Alessandra had noted with relief that Liam didn't seem particularly enamored with Rachel, she hoped that Rachel would at least impart some insight into how she might go about making herself more alluring.

At 2pm on a Saturday, with Marshall, Liam, and Eric on a supply run, Alessandra knew exactly where Rachel would be. Alessandra crossed the snow-covered expanse from her two-room cabin to the commune's main kitchen with uneasy but focused steps. As she walked, Alessandra was happy to note that the snow had melted significantly since the morning, thanks to an ample amount of sun and a temperature of 41 degrees. Even though it was much warmer than it had been, Alessandra was still surprised to find the backdoor to the kitchen wide open.

Anyone could hear the high whistle and hum of the song she played from halfway across the compound, but you would have to be standing pretty close to hear Rachel's soft voice as she sang the sad and soulful lyrics.

As a jarring guitar kicked in with the chorus, Rachel wiped her forehead with the back of her hand, mixing flour with sweat before returning to her labor. With her right hand around the handle of her rolling pin, Rachel's body leaned heavily into the counter as she folded and pounded butter into dough for her second batch of chocolate raspberry croissants.

Watching her, Alessandra could understand why Rachel was clad in nothing more than jeans and a thin white tank under her faded blue apron. The heat from the ovens was oppressive, making Rachel's arms glisten with perspiration. Most of her wavy hair was secured on top of her head in a messy ponytail, save for a few pale blonde strands that stuck to the sides of her face and neck as she worked. Her full cheeks wore a rosy blush from the heat and exertion, and her long lashes fluttered frequently over her clear green eyes to keep the baking powder away.

To Alessandra, Rachel was everything a woman was supposed to look like—with soft curves and valleys that reminded Alessandra why skinny was a bad thing. Even now, in her disheveled state, Rachel's chest was a testament to the essential relationship between breasts and tank tops, and why it was a minor tragedy for women like Alessandra to have one without the other.

Though her coloring had been darker, Alessandra suddenly realized how much Rachel reminded her of her own mother, who had been the epitome of womanhood to her as a child. Alessandra remembered well how her mother never had to convince a man to come after her. Standing behind yet another example of all she was not, Alessandra felt steeped in a familiar feeling of inadequacy. In self-defense, Alessandra crossed her legs where she stood, trying in vain to hide at least one of her knobby knees.

"Did you want something?" Rachel asked once the music had begun to fade. "They won't be ready until tomorrow." When Rachel finally looked up and took in Alessandra's shocked expression, she smiled affectionately at what she thought was a look of deep disappointment. "I made some cookies, though. They'll be out of the oven in a minute."

In reality, Alessandra was just embarrassed for having been caught staring.

"Uhmm, no, thank you. I really just wanted to ask you something... about men."

"Men?" Rachel said in surprise as she wrapped the dough in cellophane and put it in the large refrigerator. "What makes you think I know anything about men?"

"You're with Marshall," Alessandra answered, not bothering to hide the confusion in her voice. "I've seen the way he's always around you, touching you." As Alessandra said the words, she realized that although she'd seen Marshall exhibit this behavior constantly, she rarely saw Rachel reciprocate. "Other men — they look at you the same way," Alessandra continued. "I thought…"

"What — that I was sleeping with them? That I'm a slut? It's not my fault, you know. I don't *ask* for their attention." Rachel snapped.

"No!" Alessandra hurried to explain. "It's just…you're so beautiful. I thought maybe you could show me how to be like that."

Rachel could feel the heat from her body chill at even the mention of the word.

"Where I come from that's blasphemy — to be beautiful, to be too beautiful." Rachel said in a haunted tone.

"But it's true. You are," Alessandra replied.

"Marshall was the first person to ever say that to me and not mean it as a curse."

Alessandra was at a loss for words as she stared back into Rachel's sad eyes.

"I'm sorry. I didn't mean to upset you." Alessandra finally said as she turned to leave.

"Wait, it's not your fault. I didn't mean to snap. I'm just so used to…never mind. What do you need help with?" Rachel asked kindly. "Is this about Liam?"

●••●●

'Now you go in there, and don't take no for an answer,' Rachel had instructed before leaving her cabin Saturday night.

On Sunday, Alessandra woke up earlier than she ever would have otherwise to begin the regimen that Rachel had painstakingly outlined for her. She had washed her hair, dried and brushed it using the techniques that Rachel indicated for proper volume and shine, then shaved her legs with care and precision before moisturizing her body with scented oils and lotions that smelled like freesia and lilacs. Finally, Alessandra pressed the outfit Rachel had insisted looked best, or at least better than the loose thrift store jeans and oversized sweaters she usually wore. As Alessandrahung the outfit up on her bedroom door, she recalled Rachel's dismay at her limited wardrobe.

"A girl needs at least five different outfits that she can mix and match," Rachel announced excitedly as she thumbed through Alessandra's limited selection.

"Wow. How do you know all this?" Alessandra asked in amazement as she tried on a pair of Rachel's stretch jeans. "Who told you?"

"Cosmo," Rachel answered earnestly. "Since I left home, I've been reading it a lot."

As a temporary solution to what Rachel referred to as a larger "style problem", she loaned Alessandra one of her microfiber long john shirts that she said had "a little cling to it".

"Wear the jeans – no, wait… the leggings. They give you more of a butt," Rachel had insisted.

Alessandra gave herself the once-over before she headed toward where she knew Liam could always be found on Sunday–the Red Workshop, the one farthest from anything in the commune.

Recalling her reflection in the full length mirror Rachel had lent her, Alessandra didn't think she looked that much different or better as she walked through the commune grounds toward her target. She only hoped that somewhere in the litany of mandates and advice she'd received was the key to holding Liam's attention. Unlike the day before, Alessandra barely felt the cold as she shuffled through the newly fallen snow from last night, absently chewing off the majority of Rachel's lip gloss before she'd even made it halfway there.

Even from 200 feet away, she could sense the aura of tranquility that surrounded the place where Liam worked. With each step closer, Alessandra could smell the cedar from the wood burning stove that Liam had installed shortly after he arrived. It gave the whole area surrounding the small barn a sweet, smoky smell that calmed her. As soon as she opened the front door, she could hear the music–a soft guitar playing to the sound of hands clapping.

The door closed quietly behind her as she stepped inside. She had never been in his workshop before, and she was surprised to find that the front door did not lead straight into the work area. Instead, she found herself in a small room with a drain in the middle of the concrete floor. Along the wall, Liam had placed a small wooden bench and several hooks were you could hang your coat. She placed her blue parka next to Liam's before following the opening in the small room into the main work area. The moment she stepped inside the room, she was hit with the heat from the fire. The room was warm. *Too warm*, she thought as she stood at the doorway, once again unnoticed by Liam as he worked.

She stood behind him, watching him crouched down, burning intricate designs into a desk that he was making. As the music changed, he stood up and reached behind his neck to pull his sweater from his body, revealing the bottom half of his white t-shirt and torso as the sweater swept over his shoulders. At the sight of a small trail of sweat running down the smooth crevice of his backbone, Alessandra licked what was left of her lip gloss clean off.

So beautiful, she thought, right before he began to move.

Slowly, as he inspected his work with the wood-burning iron still in his hand, his hips, shoulders, and legs began to move in one slow, continuous motion to the music. She had never heard the song that was playing, had no idea even what style of music it was, but she could tell by the way he moved that Liam knew the song well. Though he never strayed from his place on the floor, his hips rolled back and forth with the most subtle, sensual movement she had ever seen.

It took almost half the song before Liam heard the sound of her shaky breath behind him. Alarmed, he turned around quickly with his wood-burning iron raised in his hand to find Alessandra, eyes lowered and staring at his hips.

"Alessandra? What are you doing here? How long have you been here?"

It took her a minute to pry her eyes away from his hips and meet his questioning gaze. All the plans she had when she entered the workshop were gone. She couldn't even remember what Rachel had told her she was supposed to do.

Something about being sexy, maybe, she thought as she watched him wait for her to answer. But now she knew—she couldn't be sexy because she couldn't do what he just did. She hadn't even known what sexy was until she saw him dancing just now.

"Alessandra?" Liam said again, softer this time, as he felt her presence drawing him in.

"I…I want to dance…like that. The way you did."

When he didn't answer, she became more insistent. More direct.

"Now. I want to learn to dance like that now."

"You want me to teach you how to dance? That's why you came all the way down here in the cold?" Feeling the familiar warmth run through him as it always did when she was near, Liam was quickly starting not to care why she was there at all. But he still tried to resist the impulse to let it show.

"No... I didn't... I just..." How could she explain without giving into the urge to pour herself out all over him? She couldn't. The thin veil of her restraint was annoying. She didn't care anymore about being coy and "not taking no for an answer". She wasn't coy; she was in love with him. She wanted him to dance with her, so she opened her mouth and said the only thing she could as she stepped toward him.

"I've been watching you dance. You look so beautiful. I want to move like that...like you did. Show me."

Liam was frozen as she came to stand right underneath him before looking up into his face with all her sincerest desires there for him to see. With her full lips just inches from his, Liam could feel the tight grip he kept on his own feelings for her slowly giving way.

"You just have to feel it. No one can really teach you how to dance," he whispered into the softness of her face, holding her gaze helplessly.

The music changed again just as she lowered her head, staring straight ahead as she spoke her words into his heart. "Please."

Liam backed away from her slowly, catching her gaze as he bent down to shut off the wood-burning iron to let her know that he would do what she asked. He would always do what she asked.

Rising to his feet again, he caught her frown as she looked toward the speakers.

"What is it?" he asked.

"Not this song. The slow one from before. I want that one."

He couldn't help his smile as he nodded and grabbed his iPod to rewind the song and set it to repeat. His mother had loved Wolves

(*Song of the Shepherd's Dog*) by Iron and Wine. *How fitting*, he thought as he turned back to Alessandra.

Without a word, he brought his hands up to the back of Alessandra's arms and brought her close enough so that their bodies just touched. Sliding his hands down her arms to her hips slower than he really needed to, he let out a shaky breath as he lowered his lips to her ear.

"Just try to follow me. I'm going to lead you, okay? Just relax, listen to the music, and try to feel it."

He waited to feel her head nod where it hovered and tickled his breastbone.

Then he pulled her closer and let himself fully register her body against his for the first time.

So soft and warm...

Softer than he thought she would be for someone so thin, warmer than she should have been for someone so small, and his dreams were nothing—nothing compared to the reality of her. He pulled her hips closer to his as he began to sway gently to the side. As soon as Alessandra began moving with him, he could feel their bodies shudder with what he knew was the pure pleasure of their shared touch. *I feel it, too. I feel it, too*, he thought before fully giving in to the sensation.

Fuck,

...Fuck.

She's moving...

God, she's moving against me...

...she...

...feels...sooo good...

The air in the shed was heavy and thick with sweat and the scent of them together. Alessandra moved back from him only for the moment it took for her to unzip the fleece jacket that she wore and throw it on the floor. As she folded back into his arms, her thoughts poured out.

I want you...so much... God, I swear I'll move slow...so slow for you. Just show me...

Liam could feel the muscles in her hips tense with determination to follow him.

That's right, love, move with me, Alessandra... Feel me... Don't stop...

Without any other thought besides the craving to feel her stretched out against him, he wrapped his fingers around her wrists where they hung at his waist and raised her arms above her head slowly. The sweat from his palms made her feel slick, made him feel thirsty and frayed with the desire to lick, lick, lick at the creases of her elbow.

Liam wanted to drench her in him–his sweat, his body, everything he had.

Alessandra's arms hung where he moved them, slightly bent and suspended as he inched his grasp up her palms to lace their fingers together while their hip bones brushed against each other in restrained insistence to the rhythm.

left to right

right to left

and then it clicked.

Somewhere along the way, she stopped needing to mimic his movements. Feeling the music through his skin, his body, she finally understood the patterns of the rhythm for herself, felt it in her chest, quivering at the base of her spine.

And in that instant, they both felt the shift–the moment their impulse to move aligned and they gasped quietly as they sank deeper into the air between them.

Liam slid one hand down her left arm and pressed his palm to her back, bringing her firmly into his chest.

Closer. I need you closer.

Alessandra's eyes fell closed at the sensation of his heat all around her.

Feel me. Feel me falling into you, she thought as she pressed her forehead into his chest with her mouth opened and panting out the dizziness of her desire.

Liam wasn't sure how he was standing without being overpowered by the emotion coursing through him, but he hadn't stopped moving, and she hadn't stopped moving, so he kept her right hand in his as he brought it around his neck.

Alessandra immediately moved her left arm up to join her right. The feeling of her fingers intertwined at the base of his skull inexplicably aroused and calmed him at the same time. He had the dual urge to cradle her in his arms forever and ravage her right where they stood.

The softness of her arm against his jaw distracted him from a decision he wasn't ready to make.

So soft…so soft, he mused.

I love you. Did you know that? I've loved you from the minute I saw you. I just…let me just…

He didn't have time to finish the thought as his head turned instinctively toward her and his lips sought out the soft flesh of her arm.

"I just…let me," he murmured to her arm just before exhaling slowly over her skin.

The tickle of his breath on her sent a shiver through Alessandra's entire body as she opened her eyes and looked up to find Liam's lips so close to her skin.

The sight was dream-like, déjà vu, but different. She had seen this moment before, but realized that the premonition of it was false and hollow compared to the smooth fullness of his lips, open and only inches from hers, the pinkness of his tongue as it hovered in the dark cavern of his mouth.

The trembling anticipation, the wonder she felt now had all been watered down and spread so far apart that there was barely any resemblance between her muted vision and the epiphany of his mouth finally touching her skin.

His lips moved slowly back and forth over her forearms, moments before his tongue came out slowly to taste the sweat on her body.

Her soft sigh sounded so much like relief that it made Liam look down to find tears shining in her eyes.

Has she been waiting for this? Wanting me to do this all this time?

The answer came in the parting of her lips as she held his gaze, waiting for him to cross the line and make it real.

At the sound of Lilli's urgent call and her footsteps bursting through the door, Alessandra knew she would not get what she came for, and she let her face fall to his chest as her tears rolled to the floor.

CHAPTER 19: A SECRET

As soon as Lilli rounded the corner to the workshop from the mud room, she immediately regretted the impulse that led her there without anything but her own needs, her own revelation, on her mind. And she hated herself for it, just a little.

Damn it! Why didn't I think to look for him? Make sure it was okay to come here?

She was never more aware of all her brother had lost, all he had sacrificed just to keep her safe, than she was at that moment.

He hasn't thought about himself in so long. What he wants. What he needs...

She knew pulling away from Alessandra was the last thing he wanted to do. It was a miracle in itself that he had even let himself be that close to her. *And I ruined it,* she thought in self-disgust as she swallowed hard to catch her breath from the sprint she'd run to get to him.

"I'm sorry. I should have knocked. I didn't think..."

Neither Alessandra nor Liam made a move to alter their position, their closeness to each other, but Lilli could see the resignation in the hung down sadness of Alessandra's shoulders and the way Liam's strong right hand seemed so gentle as he stroked Alessandra's hair just before kissing her temple and finally stepping away.

"Are you all right, Lilli?" her brother asked in a voice so bemused she barely recognized it. "You ran here."

Of course, she thought. *Even in a lover's haze, he would worry about my safety first.*

"Yes, I'm fine. We can talk later," Lilli stammered. "I shouldn't have come."

"Lilli. Tell me what happened."

The change in his voice from lover to brother to protector was so heartbreaking. From the stiffening of Alessandra's back, Lilli could tell she heard it, too. They watched as Alessandra turned from Liam without a word, grabbed her jacket off the floor, and headed for the door without making eye contact with either of them. Before she could brush past Lilli in the doorway, Liam called out to her.

"Alessandra…"

His voice stopped her movement, though she did not turn around to face him. Lilli could see Alessandra's bottom lip quiver with the effort it took not to shed the tears that deserved to break free.

"There's a place I like to go…fishing sometimes. Will you come with me… tomorrow night around 9 o'clock?"

Only Lilli could see the beautiful smile that crept across Alessandra's face as her tears turned from despair to hope in the time it took for them to roll down her face. Alessandra's nod was subtle but unmistakable. Lilli could hear Liam exhale his relief from across the room.

After Alessandra had closed the door behind her, Lilli walked over to her brother, who was still rooted to the spot where she had found him with his arms wrapped around the woman he loved.

"Liam, I'm so sorry. I didn't see that the two of you would be together. I should have checked…"

"It's all right, Lilli," he began, as he made his way over to collect the etching tools that he'd forgotten on the ground the moment he saw Alessandra standing behind him. "It's probably for the best, anyway."

Lilli groaned at his efforts to shield her from her own insensitivity. "God, you're such a bad liar, Liam," she huffed in exasperation.

"Only with you, Lilli. Only with you."

"Liam, stop it. You're a good-"

Before she could get all her words out, Liam was waving her off. But she wouldn't let him dismiss her, not this time. She needed to get his attention.

"I know you've kept things from me before," she began. "Things you didn't want me to know, to protect me."

The sudden twitch in Liam's hand made him lose his grip on the chisel he was trying to put back in his carving tool pouch. Liam only had one secret that he kept from Lilli. The tone in her voice told him that somehow she'd discovered what it was, but he didn't know how that was possible. No one at the commune had been in New Mexico at the time to witness what he'd done. The only people who knew anything about it were dead or shared his interest in keeping the whole thing hidden.

Turning toward her, Liam's face was tight as he struggled not to give anything away. But Lilli's smile was full of sympathy, understanding, and no small amount of pity.

"Lilli, I don't know what you're talking about…" he began, but it was Lilli's turn to silence him with the one piece of proof he couldn't deny.

"I know why we left Albuquerque before you got your letter from MIT," Lilli spoke as softly as she could. She didn't want to hurt him with the memory, the unnecessary shame she knew he carried because of her. She'd seen the look on his face as he buried them, one by one, by the lake. As she extended the bloodstained acceptance letter that he'd missed in his haste to clean up the mess, dispose of the bodies, and pack before he had to pick her up from school, she watched Liam recoil in guilt and disbelief.

Liam couldn't miss the distinct combination of fuchsia and yellow that made up the MIT emblem. He knew immediately what it had to be; he just couldn't believe it.

"What is that?" he growled. "Where did you get that?" His angry tone did not surprise Lilli. She had expected the letter to rouse his defenses. He'd spent a long time burying the truth inside himself. Slowly, she walked toward him and placed the letter on the unfinished desk beside him.

"I got it from our house in New Mexico."

"Lilli, that's impossible. I was telling the truth. I never got the letter, and what do you mean you got it from our house? I saw you this morning."

It was all logical, his train of thought. All the calculations he had made so quickly in his head of time and distance were right and true; they just didn't apply to her. Not anymore. His reaction made Lilli remember the first time she had broken all those barriers, how disbelieving she was, for days, even though she had been there, had seen the ash on her feet. The impossibility of what she was about to explain made her throat go dry as she prepared to tell him what she could do–what she was capable of.

"I was there, Liam, less than an hour ago. You didn't notice the letter because they had gone through our mail by the time you got home. When you hit the small one over the head with the trash can cover, he knocked the front table over and the letter slid under the rug.

I was able to get it before you burned it with all the other rugs in the backyard."

Lilli could see Liam's façade break wide open as he listened to her recount the things he had done to hide the evidence of the murders that had taken place at his hands. She didn't know if it was the memory of that sunny mid-morning or the fact that she knew about it that precipitated the pained look on his face. But she knew he had only just begun to understand the meaning of what she'd said and all that was left to say. Lilli was silent while she waited for Liam to absorb the implications behind her words. After a few moments, Liam's voice came out as a choked whisper as he asked her the question she'd been waiting for.

"What are you saying, Lilli?"

"I'm trying to tell you that I've—when I vision…something's changed since I first started seeing things. I can see more now, not just the future, but the past, too. And sometimes, if I want to, I can travel to the places I see."

Liam moved in silence as he placed his tool pouch down quietly on the desk, then propped himself up against it. He tried to take her words in as slowly and deeply as his breathing, to take what she was telling him one breath at a time. *What can I say to that*, he thought, as he took in his sister's expectant expression. *There isn't a damn thing I can say to that.*

Even though he was silent, Lilli felt relieved that she could finally tell him most of the secrets she'd been hiding for months, ever since the day in Quorum when she first heard *him* call to her, when she decided to find *him*.

●•··•●

Though Lilli's goal had been clear, how to go about achieving it proved much more difficult, since she lacked a name or face upon which to focus. After several fruitless attempts to conjure an image of him that would help her, Lilli finally decided to try a different approach. Rather than seeking a specific target in her thoughts, she resolved to simply try to open her mind.

I was open to him that day, more open than I've ever been in visioning. Maybe if I can get my mind to that place, he will see me looking for him and find me, she reasoned that first night.

Lilli wasn't sure how long she'd been meditating before she suddenly felt a hot wind blow across her face. When she opened her eyes again, she was not in her bedroom.

Though she was sure her first instinct should have been panic, the depth of her meditative state was such that it allowed her to somehow step out of her own emotions and take in her surroundings without fear. She could see that she was standing in the corner of a room within a thatched-roof, dirt floor structure that was burning. Though she stood only inches from where the fire seemed to originate and spread, and she could feel its heat along the entire left side of her body, she knew that she would not be burned. When the flames did touch her skin, they seemed to pass through her, as if she was more air than solid.

Seeing clearly through the smoke, Lilli noticed two small desks, a long table covered with a thin mattress, and a medicine cabinet with shelves that were overflowing with see-through bags and jars filled with roots, powders, herbs, pastes, some brightly colored charms, and small statues. *People were treated here for their ailments,* she heard her mind conclude before she was even aware that she was processing the thought. As she continued to take in the room, her eye caught movement on the floor among a loose pile of jackets that had been thrown and left there by the open doorway.

It was then that she heard the sound of a small child crying softly to himself for his Mama and Baba. Though he spoke in Swahili, a language she had never heard and did not know, she understood him perfectly.

"Inuka mama! tafadhali inuka! nitakuwa mtoto mzuri, sitacheza mbali tena."

Get up, Mommy! Please get up! I will be a good boy. I won't play too far away anymore.

The sound of his small voice pleading seized her whole being. Her feet were drawn to him, seeking him out to soothe and understand. As she walked up behind him, Lilli could just make out the outline of his body underneath the pile of clothes.

"Usimuumize baba yangu. msimchukue tafadhali, msimchukue na baba yangu pia."

Don't hurt my father. Please. Please don't take him away. Don't take my father, too.

Lilli could see a small opening in the clothes where his head was lifted slightly above the rest of his body, and she followed his gaze outside the doorway of their burning hut to see an entire village ablaze.

But the focus of this little boy's attention was not on the flaming rooftops or the heavy smell of burning flesh in the air. It was on the scene taking place less than three feet away from him. On the ground were the charred remains of a woman whose arms were black-coal ridged as they reached above her body, frozen in her final defense.

Only a foot away from her was a clawing, rabid, red-eyed Marcus. Two men struggled to grab hold of his lower body as he dangled upside down. Tears, mucus, and saliva poured from every orifice on his face as he screamed and dragged his bloody nails across the dirt, trying to get back to his wife and a small figure of a child whose foot lay charred and still at the edge of Lilli's line of sight.

"Joel! Joel! Evlyn!"

"Baba niko hapa, angalia baba usilie, niko hapa hawa kunichukua baba. Hawa kunichukua."

Father, I'm here. Father look, don't cry. I'm here. They didn't get me, Father. They didn't get me, the little boy cried, but nothing could be heard over the bottomless agony in Marcus' screams. As the men finally gained enough leverage to drag Marcus away and put him into the black SUV that had been waiting for them, his calls for his son and wife dissolved into guttural screams that made Lilli's throat sore just to hear them.

Lilli forced her gaze away from Marcus as he was taken away to give her full attention to the sobbing, shaking boy at her feet. In that same instant, she heard the sound of the roof supports finally giving way. Before she could even move to shield him, the boy shot out from underneath his hiding place and bolted through the doorway just before the building collapsed around her. The embers passed right through her where she stood, but Lilli was unfazed and barely aware of anything but the form of the little boy and his skinny legs flying behind him as he disappeared into the smoke.

"I've found you, Joel. I've found you," she whispered, just as she began to feel the coolness of her own pillow underneath her head.

With each following night, Lilli had learned more about Joel's journey from a frightened boy to the man he had become, and why she needed to keep him a secret for as long as she could. The more she learned about him and her new ability, the more their secrets intertwined, making it more difficult for her to expose her gift to others without prompting the inevitable questions that would lead to Joel's discovery. So she guarded her gifts as she guarded him.

"How long have you been doing this, Lilli?" Though his bewilderment was still apparent, Liam's voice was calm, his breathing measured and even.

"A couple months now," she answered softly. Lilli knew her answer would sting. She hadn't kept anything from him since their mother died. When she saw the hurt look on his face, she moved closer, hoping to find a way for him to understand that her life was about more now, and that her silence had nothing to do with her trust in him.

As Liam watched his sister move closer to him, his regret that she had not confided in him was pushed aside by a more important possibility. When he looked up, the urgency in his eyes stopped Lilli were she stood.

"Wait... When you go back, can you see Mom? Can you change what happened?"

Understanding his intensity and the hope that shone in his eyes, Lilli closed the distance between them and let her hand rest gently on his arm as she let out her own sigh of remorse. "No, I can't. It doesn't work that way. The things we see are certain. In the past, just like in the future, I can only be a witness."

Lilli paused briefly, averting her eyes from his penetrating gaze before continuing. "But the truth is, I've never gone back to the day Mom died. I learned...earlier that I can't affect the outcome of the things I see, because I tried it with Dad."

"You saw him?!" Liam whispered in shock.

"Yeah... I don't know why I started with him. I guess I thought that if I could stop them from killing him, then maybe they wouldn't have gotten to Mom, and that we could have been together as a family. I was so young when he died. I never really got to know him."

"How did you find him? I mean, what did you do?"

"I just tried to concentrate on the details that Mom left us from the videos until I could find my way back to the day he died. I was in the car with him when he left for work that day, after Mom begged him not to go. But he was so focused on what he was planning to do that he didn't even sense me in the car with him. No matter how much I yelled and tried to make myself seen, he wouldn't...he couldn't. I was so *desperate* to reach him that I even managed to knock over the coffee on his desk, right before he went in to make his presentation to the Oversight Committee, but he just dismissed it as his own clumsiness. He never even stopped to clean it up. There was nothing I could do."

Several long moments passed between them as Lilli watched Liam try to wrap his mind around all the things she'd said. His face was a cauldron of emotion, moving too fast for her to predict which thought or feeling would become dominant. When he finally spoke, she had been expecting anything but an apology.

"Lilli, I'm sorry. Why didn't you tell me?"

"Liam, it's not because I don't..."

"I knew you were growing distant. I could feel it. You've been so quiet lately, but I just thought..." Liam paused a moment before exhaling a long breath. "Lilli, I know I've been distracted these past few months. I'm sorry. I've just been trying to do too much. You're my priority and I shouldn't have..."

"Liam, stop it. I wanted to do this alone. I needed to." Lilli reached her arms up to cup Liam's rough cheeks gently in her small hands. "Look at me."

She had to nudge him with the heels of her palms to get him to finally lift his eyes toward hers. When he finally met her gaze, it hurt her heart to see what she found there.

Failure. Shame.

So much shame. So much needless shame, she thought as she fought back tears.

"Lilli, you're my responsibility. I should have been..."

"Liam, I'm not your responsibility."

"What do you mean? How can you even say that?" His voice broke and crumbled over his question. Her words had the power to cut him from the only thing he was sure of — the only thing that had made sense since the day they left Oregon. *Protect Her.* If he didn't have that, he didn't know who he was or what the point of anything was at all.

"Your life has to be about more than me now. More than keeping me safe. I am learning to do that for myself. I'm old enough now, Liam. You deserve more than this."

Liam closed his eyes in silent response. *There is nothing else, Lilli. I don't have anything else.*

Refusing to let him retreat from her, Lilli followed him, without effort, into his hiding place.

Yes, you do, Liam. You did what you had to do in New Mexico. You saved us. You know that. If you hadn't done it, we wouldn't be here.

Liam's eyes shot open in surprise. He could hear her clearly in his mind, as if she were a part of his own thoughts.

Lilli? How...

We will always be this close. The distance between us does not exist. I know that now. Don't be afraid, Liam. You will never lose me and I will always have you, just as you are. I love you, but it's time now for you to have something for yourself.

Lilli could feel the void of his own thoughts as he struggled to process what was happening, even as she could feel his acceptance from some primal part of his brain.

I am in awe of what you did that day, Liam. Watching you has taught me what it really means to protect what you love. I always took for granted that I was safe with you. I never thought about — never knew — what it cost you until today. But I'm learning now what it means to protect, rather than to always be protected. I'm going to learn how to protect you now, and I know that when I'm ready, you will be as proud of me as I am of you.

Knowing he couldn't — he wouldn't say anything else, Lilli reached up to kiss her brother on his forehead before finally releasing his stubble-covered jaw from her grasp and leaving him alone with his thoughts once more.

Chapter 20: Night of Desirable Objects

The night air was colder than Liam expected as he helped Alessandra onto the small fishing boat he and Kaido had made. Normally, the chill felt like company on his solitary trips, but tonight he was worried about her. As soon as she was situated, he grabbed the blanket he'd brought from his duffel bag and draped it over her shoulders.

He could see the shy smile of thanks she offered him even in the dark. *Beautiful*, he thought.

"There's hot chocolate if you want it, or you can just hold the flask to keep your hands warm."

Looking at him in the dim, starlit night, Alessandra knew the real reason her insides trembled. The blanket around her smelled like him. Thinking of all the ways it might have been wrapped around his body made her tighten her grip on the fabric as she tried to pull it closer to her.

She watched in silence as he paddled them out on the lake. He didn't speak much, except to ask her periodically if she was warm enough. He had apparently brought a small battery-operated space heater, just in case.

It was the same silence that they shared on the ride out to the boat. When Liam came to pick her up, he was greeted by a very excited Lucia as she opened the door to Alessandra's cabin. He smiled at them both then, a small smile that said that while he was happy to see her, his mind was miles away. When he'd asked her to come with him, Alessandra had thought that maybe, *maybe* he was finally ready to give in to what she knew he felt for her. But as they drove to the dock, with the same silent treatment as always, she found herself wondering why he'd bothered to invite her if he was not going to speak.

But she felt patient tonight. He had asked her to be there and that was at least something. She watched as he anchored the boat and brought out their fishing rods, showing her with care and occasional touches the right way to select and hook the bait, how far to lean back before casting out, and how to tell if a fish was biting. All of it she found fascinating, but none of it was more than what she wanted from him.

After a half hour of silence, she leaned forward as she licked her lips and passed the flask of hot chocolate they were sharing. As soon as he met her gaze without offering a word, she realized she would have to take matters into her own hands.

"Why are you afraid of me?" she asked.

Liam was silent as he took the flask from her hands and tipped his head back, taking a large gulp of their now-lukewarm beverage. She noticed how his lips lingered on the edges of the container, where her mouth had been.

I know you are savoring me, she thought. *You can't hide that from me. I do the same thing.*

When a minute had passed and he still hadn't answered, she decided to continue, even if it would only be a one-way conversation.

"You are so strange," she began, as she shook her head and kept her gaze out towards the lake. "I mean, *I* like to talk. I think every human being in the world likes to talk but you. Were you always like this?"

Liam had to laugh then.

"God, you're blunt," he blurted out through his laughter before passing the flask back to her. "Everything you think comes out of your mouth."

"Marcus says it's because I'm immature, because they took me so young that I didn't have time to develop a 'social filter'." Alessandra finished the last of the hot chocolate before shrugging unapologetically. "I don't know. If I don't say what I'm thinking, what else is there to say?"

Liam nodded his understanding before preparing to answer the question he was more comfortable with.

"No, I wasn't always like this. I used to talk a lot, believe it or not. I was always cracking jokes and fooling around."

"Really? I can't imagine you like that."

Liam smiled sadly as he absorbed her unintended insult.

"My teammates used to call me 'Easy', because I was always laid back, joking around. School, sports, friends, they all came so easily." Liam paused as he realized he was talking about a person he barely knew or remembered. "I guess there isn't a lot that's funny these days."

"That's not true. You just close yourself off from everything. For me, everything is new. Wonderful. I have a future... That's something I didn't think would ever be possible. Before I came here, my whole life was darkness. But you walk around like you're waiting to die."

The accuracy of her words shocked him. *That's exactly how I feel,* he thought as he looked over to her. *How did she know that?*

Alessandra thought he looked both surprised and pleased as he stared back at her. She had worried that her last comments were too candid, but she couldn't help herself. He was actually talking to her, and she couldn't stop.

"Don't you see a future, some possibility of happiness for yourself?" Of everything she'd said to him, he looked the most disturbed by this simple question.

Liam turned from her and thought carefully as he prepared to answer her first question. His voice was calm as he described a life that had died to him a long time ago.

"You know what I thought my life would be like three or four years ago? What I wanted?" He didn't wait for her to reply before he continued. "I thought I would graduate from high school, go to MIT, and be an engineer or something that would allow me to have my own business so I could work when I wanted and come home when I wanted. My dad didn't have a job like that, and I missed him a lot as a kid. I figured when I grew up, I was going to be the cool dad — coaching all the teams, hosting all the cool parties. I always thought I would get married young, find a girl who wanted a lot of kids like I did. We'd get a big house and just live in it and be happy. I never questioned it. I just knew that was how it was going to be. And that's what I thought right up until I found my mother dead in our kitchen.

"Now, I live in a world where people see the future and use that power for their own agenda, no matter how much it costs the rest of us, where Lilli and I have to be ready to fight, run, or die every single second of our lives. I live in a world where what I do every day, just protecting the only family I have, is considered treason. Where we are hunted as if we've done something wrong, and she hasn't. She hasn't done anything to deserve this!"

Somewhere in the telling, Liam felt his tone slip from calm to angry to cold, but he didn't care. *This is who I am and she needs to know it. She needs to understand why the way she looks at me and the way I feel for her doesn't matter.*

"But we're safe now. Here, we're safe," Alessandra promised, with the first of her tears pricking at the corners of her eyes.

To Liam, the notion was ludicrous, completely out of sync with the day-to-day reality of their lives. Liam spun around to face her so quickly that the sides of the boat nearly met the water as it rocked back and forth.

"You can think that if you want, but I *know* the consequences of believing that it's like that." Liam swallowed hard as he watched Alessandra closely, making sure he had her full attention.

"I've killed three people, two with my bare hands, because I let down my guard just for a second, lingered too long in a place I stupidly thought was safe instead of facing the fucked-up world we live in. I dream of them every night, the blood on their faces, the way a neck sounds when I snap it, the feel of flesh under my fingers as I force a man to choke to death on his own blood."

"And you know the worst part, what lets me know that I am nothing like the boy I used to be? The worst part is how *easy* it was for me to do it. I didn't even hesitate. When I finished with the two in our house and I saw the woman who had come on to me at the track three miles from where we lived suddenly sitting in a running car outside my front door, I *felt* she was with them, but I didn't bother to ask. I just put a bullet in her head and dragged her ass to the trunk of the car with the rest of them. So I don't know what kind of future is out there for someone who could do the things I've done. But no, I don't think about it. I can't afford to."

When he was finished, Alessandra could see him searching her face, her body language, waiting for the horror and disgust that he felt for himself to be reflected in her. When he didn't find it, she could tell that he was at a loss. But the thought of them being any farther apart than they already were hurt her more than the story he had just shared. To Alessandra, his admission explained only why he was hurting, not the reason he refused to accept the absolution, the love she offered him.

"Why are you looking at me like that? Like you're expecting me to hate you? I came here for you. I didn't know anything about you, but I came here for you. Don't you know that? Why do you think what you've done would matter now?"

"Because it should, Alessandra. I don't have anything to offer you. I can't risk...*feeling* more for you than I already do. I can't imagine anything in the world that we live in. I just can't function like that. I've tried, but I'm sorry. I can't."

Though Alessandra didn't believe his words for a second, she knew he did and for the first time she could recall, she was speechless.

When Liam dropped her back at her home, Alessandra was thankful that Lucia had not stayed to see how their 'first date' went. Though her eyes were finally dry, she knew her face would tell too much. Alessandra threw her clothes on the floor as she crawled into bed, naked and alone. For the first time since the night before she left the Guild, she didn't dream of Liam.

Chapter 21: What if

Nearly every day for the past month, the commune had received at least one new Seer. Between those they rescued in the raids and those who just showed up, the commune was stretched to the boundaries of its capacity with a total of forty-three Seers and thirty-two commune members. Alessandra threw herself into her roles as teacher, mentor, friend, trainer, and student, trying to be grateful for the life she had, for the chance to be useful. There was so much to do that most days, it almost worked.

In the daylight she worked hard, training herself and the newest Seers to master their visioning and harness the energy that was generated by their ability. It was a role that she, Kaido, Lucia, Lilli, and Marcus all played, working to mentor Seers who had similar abilities to their own.

Once Lilli decided that the timing was right, she began to share the abilities that she had developed in secret with the group. For several weeks, Lilli had been teaching them how to channel the energy they generated in their visioning like a current moving outward from within. During their first training sessions, Lilli explained that, "Once you become fully aware of this energy, you can begin to mold it, shape it, give it purpose, and project it out from your body onto anything or anyone. As you get used to it, it will become an extension of you."

Though her words were simple enough, it was difficult for the Seers to comprehend what she meant. It was still a novelty that Maura and Tess had any ability outside of visioning, so no one was prepared for Lilli's demonstration. To watch Lilli lift Liam and Eli into the air or move a dozen heavy wooden tables or Marshall's truck with the slightest wave of her hand was astonishing. By using her energy to manipulate the light around her, Lilli had even found a way to become invisible to the human eye. As the awe wore off, Lilli was inundated with questions about how and when she had discovered these gifts. In answering, Lilli was as specific as possible and vague when necessary, explaining that she had discovered her abilities mainly during her own private visioning sessions and wanted to make sure she could control them safely before exposing them to others. But when all the questions had died down, people seemed genuinely excited that in between Eli's constant testing, Lilli was now patiently and carefully opening up a new world to them.

Though no Seer came close to displaying Lilli's control and versatility in these new abilities, they all worked hard to understand their individual potential and how to use that ability in Quorum. The new training was difficult and exciting, but most of all, for Alessandra, it was a distraction. The only time she had to see *him* was during a raid, but that wasn't nearly as difficult as she had anticipated after their fishing trip. Liam rarely spoke to her before, so the only difference now was that she pretended not to have anything to say, either. Any spare time she didn't spend with the Seers or on a raid was used to help out with duties around the commune. She poured all her energy into these tasks, so that at night she only needed the slightest effort not to dream of Liam. Exhausted, her body would drift off into a deep slumber, too worn out and spent to hope.

The sight of him and all that didn't exist between them was the hardest to avoid during the commune's increasingly frequent social gatherings. Before Katia and Maura arrived, organized socials within the commune were sporadic at best–pleasant and fun, but never intimate. Though there had been fewer people in the commune before, it never felt like a family. But with the arrival of so many Seers, a new tradition had emerged. What started as a type of confessional meeting, where everyone finally revealed the true reasons why they came to the commune, had quickly evolved into a social gathering where people brought their favorite dishes, games, jokes, and stories, and shared them with anyone willing to take part. Most Fridays, everyone was there. From Jean frying up her uncle's secret *beignet* recipe, to Marcus, Eli, Lilli, and Rachel debating the mysteries of the universe, to all night chess matches that always included Eric, Kaido, Marshall, Liam, and a host of other men and women hovering over half a dozen chess sets with large carafes of homemade sake or moonshine — sometimes both.

By the end of the evening, all the losers were convinced they'd actually won, and Liam, though always sober, would occasionally crack a smile. Maura had taken to sharing bedtime stories that her grandmother used to tell her to the children within the commune while Katia sat cross-legged among them, drinking in the innocence of those around her as she rediscovered her own. Kyle and Jared usually sat close to Maura and Katia, hoping to be noticed. In between and within these groups were a dozen different side conversations and activities that kept the lights on and the room overflowing with warmth until the early morning.

On those nights, Alessandra usually floated among the different groups, getting to know new Seers and hearing new stories from old friends. There were enough people that it was possible to avoid making direct eye contact with Liam most of the time. On the rare occasion when she faltered, it was always too painful to bear and she would end up leaving early.

Such was the case a week before, when she had caught his eye as they both turned at the sound of Tess, Lilli, and Laura, one of the new Seers, screaming with laughter as they tried to recreate the *Thriller* dance sequence for an enthusiastic crowd. Alessandra had left immediately after.

Once out of the meeting hall, she had wandered around the Commune before noticing a light on in the clinic and deciding to visit Eli, who had been uncharacteristically absent from their Friday gathering.

She was all the way inside before she heard them–whispers in Japanese and Portuguese followed by soft gasps and sounds of pleasure that could only be expressed in low moans and wet kisses. She knew she should leave; she knew with certainty that Eli was not there, but her loneliness made her stay, made her want to see love being made rather than denied. As she tiptoed past the clinic's front room to peek behind the curtain, she could not feel any of the shame she knew she should feel at violating Lucia and Kaido's privacy. All she felt was longing and a thirst to see what real love looked like, even if she could not feel it for herself.

What she saw behind the curtain took her breath away. The sole candle that lit the room made their bodies look like sculpture come to life, with Lucia's legs wrapped around Kaido's strong back and hips as she straddled him on the narrow hospital bed. Alessandra could see the muscles of Kaido's back pulse with tension and release as he held Lucia close to him. Even from her hidden place, Alessandra could not mistake the reverent abandon in Kaido's profile as he pressed his left cheek against Lucia's breast.

In his arms, Lucia moved slowly, matching the languid upward thrust of his hips. Her arms held him to her chest with her head thrown back and mouth open. To Alessandra, they looked like one being, and the thought made her ache so deeply she had to cover her mouth to stifle the sob that threatened to escape.

Alessandra braced herself against the wall as she heard them murmur words that she had heard them say before in laughter and smiles. In those moments, she had thought of them only as lovely terms of endearment. But now, in candlelit whispers, she recognized their true power as sacred things, the naming of one soul by another.

Meu amor

My Love

Tenshi

Angel

At the sound of their true names, their bodies seemed to grow more excited, more desperate to become completely unseparated. Alessandra trembled at the urgency in the way Kaido reached up behind Lucia's back to anchor her shoulders in his large hands, to bring her further down, closer to him as he took advantage of the arch in her back to suck her right nipple into his mouth. In response, Lucia fisted her hands in his thick black hair as her head began to move back and forth and her moans became louder. He anchored her right hip to him then, bending his back so that he could curl into her more deeply.

Alessandra could hear the gasp just before Lucia's head seemed to crash forward into Kaido's shoulder. Her arms went limp around him, but he didn't loosen his grip as he continued to move inside her, for the both of them. Lucia cried softly as he moved, whispering her sacred name until her arms came back to life and cradled his head against her chest once more, kissing him gently on his temple over and over again.

Nothing could be heard then except for the sound of Kaido's ragged breathing, as Lucia began to move above him again. They were so quiet that Alessandra had not expected his sudden shudder or the strangled cry that came from some finally free place deep inside as Kaido clung to Lucia and trembled more than the shadows on the wall. Through all of this, Lucia never let go, never stopped kissing his face as she whispered words too soft and precious for Alessandra to hear.

Alessandra had enough sense to hope that they had not heard her as she ran from the clinic with the sight of their passionate embrace seared into her mind. When she reached her own front door, she nearly crumpled at the ache in her chest that seemed to have ripped open and caught fire in the cool air. She knew she was not nearly tired enough to escape what was coming. All her senses were too aware to ignore Liam's absence. As she crawled onto her bed, Alessandra let her cries turn to wailing as every vision of her and Liam together came flooding back.

Though the reasons were different, Alessandra was not the only one for whom it had been a difficult month. The more Seers came and the more raids they planned, the greater the need was to block any sight from the Guild. Marcus remained the lynchpin for this effort, with Katia, Jared, Kaido, and ten others working around the clock to make sure their plans remained hidden. But the effort was not made more difficult by their increase in activity alone. Through the Seers' constant efforts to monitor the Guild's attempts to find them, they learned that Crane and Andreas had formed an alliance with seven other Purification Centers across the globe.

In response to the commune's success with the home raids, the partnership was formed for the sole purpose of finding and eliminating the Seers who escaped. Kaido was also able to see that Michael and Nina were progressing quickly in their visioning capacity, so that when combined with the other Quorum members in the alliance, they would have sight capabilities that would rival the best of them—Marcus, Lilli, and Alessandra.

With every step forward, the effort it took to block the Guild's visioning powers became more physically and mentally exhausting. Though the others rotated duties regularly to refresh themselves, Marcus was always engaged. Even when they didn't know it, he was able to use some part of his mind to actively block intrusions from the Guild. And as with most physical stress, Marcus seemed almost immune to the physical toll that blocking took on other Seers.

So when his headaches and cold symptoms began, he didn't think much of it beyond the need for an occasional painkiller. Though he couldn't remember ever being sick a day in his life, he understood that he was getting older, a man of 45 years in a climate that was conducive to the common cold. When he began to see blood on his pillow in the morning, he immediately dismissed it as a nosebleed. *How many times has Eli refused to visit my home because he says I keep it "like a sauna" in here? Claiming it would be so hot it would give him a nosebleed?* He chuckled to himself as he added another log to his fire. This is how, with more than a little amusement, Marcus dismissed his symptoms without the first notion of anything being seriously wrong.

By the time his coughing began and he finally realized that the blood on his pillow was from his mouth, not his nose, it was too late.

Hanna, Alessandra, Tess, and Lucia had been planning the raid that was to take place that night for over two months, carefully deciphering when and how they needed to approach this particular family. The Seer was their youngest so far, a nine-year-old boy who was already showing strong visioning ability. His parents were scheduled to take him in for what they believed was a psychiatric evaluation at 8 o'clock the next morning. What they did not know was that the psychiatrist they planned to see was hired by the Guild to assess Seer potential in children. The family was slated to be killed in a car accident on their way home from the appointment, unless they were rescued. The raid team, which included Alessandra, Lucia, Tess, Eric, Marshall, Liam, Kaido, and Maura, was already packed to leave in the afternoon for the three and a half hour drive to Kansas City when Marcus collapsed during a blocking Quorum with Jared, Katia, Lilli, and five of their newest Seers.

Lilli and the other Seers stayed with Marcus while Katia ran to find Eli, who had taken a rare moment off from monitoring the Seers' every move to take a nap. By the time Eli, Marshall, and Kyle carried Marcus into the clinic, he was conscious enough to be coughing up blood at an alarming rate. The fever, the shortness of breath, and the duration of symptoms led Eli to the diagnosis that Marcus had contracted pneumonia. The extent of his illness let Eli know that it had gone ignored and untreated for some time.

Looking around his medicine cabinet, Eli could see that he was missing some of the medicine he would need to treat Marcus aggressively. Confused by the change in his medical supplies, Eli began to tear through his supply closet until he remembered Lucia's red-faced apology at the accidental loss of some of his medical supplies while she was 'cleaning' his office the week before. He had ordered new supplies, but they would not arrive until the following week. *He'll be dead by next week if we can't get him started on antibiotics by tonight,*

Eli realized as he headed back to Marcus' side, scanning the room for Liam. He found him crowded around Marcus' bed with so many others who cared about him.

"Liam, I can't leave Marcus like this, and I don't have the medical supplies I need to treat him properly. I need you to go get them from my contact in Des Moines."

Liam didn't look up from where Marcus lay as he gave his reply. "Of course. You don't even have to ask, Eli. I can call Dr. Barrett if you want."

"I need you to go tonight, Liam. It can't wait."

Eli knew what he was asking of him, knew the reason Liam never missed a raid when Alessandra was involved. He had seen the love in Liam's eyes from the day Liam had brought Alessandra into his office to examine the changing color of her eyes. And Eli had watched with growing concern as Liam denied his love for her every day since then. It was a tragedy with which Eli was acutely familiar; having procrastinated and chickened out from telling the one woman he had ever loved how he felt until it was too late, until she had accepted his best friend instead, so that the first and last time he had ever danced with her was at her wedding to someone else.

In their time together, Eli tried in subtle ways to warn Liam about his romantic resistance and to coax him into a more *carpe diem* frame of mind. The fact that Eli's own story revolved around his love for Liam's mother and his deep envy of his life-long colleague and friend who also happened to be Liam's father made the story difficult and too complicated to be helpful to a young man struggling with his own demons.

But none of that could be helped now. Marcus was dying and Liam was the only other person who had ever had contact with the ethically compromised but reliable Dr. Barrett. As Eli's medical apprentice of sorts, Liam was also the only one who had enough knowledge to pass as a medical student, which was the only other kind of person aside from a *bona fide* medical doctor to whom Dr. Barrett would smuggle drugs.

"Liam, I wouldn't ask if it wasn't…"

"I know, I know. Just let me…um… I need to talk… I mean, I'll be right back," Liam stammered as he backed out of the clinic.

"Hurry, Liam," Eli called. "The drive is at least two hours. Everything will be ready by the time you get back."

Liam knew she would be at the meeting hall, waiting like the others for word on Marcus before they left. He could barely get the barn door open before Kaido, Lucia, and Alessandra jumped up in unison.

"How is he?"

"Is he all right?"

"What happened?" they asked all at once.

"He has pneumonia. Eli says it's bad, but he's going to treat him as best he can," Liam replied.

"He's not going to…?" Alessandra asked in a shaky voice.

"No," Liam said forcefully, cutting her fear and her worry off. "Eli wouldn't let that happen. He needs some medicine. We're arranging to get it now."

In that moment, they were all grateful for the resolve, the hard certainty in Liam's voice. While waiting for news, they had tried to vision, to see what would happen to Marcus, but they couldn't focus. There was too much fear among them to be objective, especially for the man who had led all of them to freedom.

"Alessandra," Liam began hesitantly. "Can I talk to you outside, just for a minute?"

His posture, his voice, everything about him was suddenly tense and unsure as he looked at her, waiting for her reply.

Alessandra was slightly disappointed to hear herself agree before she had even decided, but he took her hand and guided her outdoors quickly, before she had a chance to rethink it.

They stopped just outside the barn before he turned around to face her, still holding her hand.

"Alessandra, I can't come with you. Don't go. Please. I won't be there to protect you..."

The cool night air helped to clear her mind enough to absorb the urgent pleading in his voice. The fact that he never pleaded with her about anything was not lost on her, but it still didn't have the effect she thought it would, the effect she knew it would have had a few weeks before. Her instinct to give him anything, everything he asked for was finally becoming tempered with her own needs, her own desire to be to him what he was to her.

Alessandra searched his face as she let the images of Kaido and Lucia making love replay in her mind along with all the other visions of her and Liam together that had never come true. Instead of the usual longing and excitement that accompanied those scenes, all she could feel was exhaustion at the weight of all her stored up hope and disappointment.

She was tired of being haunted by their future. *No, I need more now,* she thought. *Tell me something more.*

"Am I yours to protect?"

Her question took him completely by surprise.

Of course, he thought. *Doesn't she know? How can she not understand that?*

Looking at the shroud of questions straining against her clear gaze, he could see that she didn't know the first thing about what he felt for her. *I never told her. She wants me to tell her.*

The words, the certainty he felt, stuck in his throat, even as he tried to pry them free. But his desire to say them was not nearly enough to make the action possible. He wondered how he had not seen the necessity of this moment, the words he needed to say. *I would do anything for her. Why can't I do this?* He wondered in frustration. His indecision surprised him enough that he didn't feel gravity pulling her hand slowly from his; he wasn't even aware of the loss until he saw her turn and walk away.

He didn't have time to linger on his mistake; he had to go and get Marcus' medicine. But he didn't have to worry. The sting of his failure burned all the way to Des Moines, as he berated himself over how he could have let her look of despair linger and deepen the lines on her face.

What the hell is wrong with me? What the hell is it going to take?

The answer came to his mind without hesitation. *A better world than this.*

A better world than this? That's never going to happen, he thought. *Never.*

Will you risk it? Losing her while you wait?

What if I lose her?

You are losing her now, with no one to blame but yourself.

What if I lose her?

What if I lose her?

What if I lose her?

His mind was stuck on this thought as he picked up the antibiotics and painkillers from Dr. Barrett and headed back to Fox River in a haze. He was halfway home before he heard Lilli's voice become a part of his thoughts.

Liam, come home. Oh God, Liam, I can't see them. I can't see anything! Liam, I know you can hear me. I can feel your thoughts. Come home now!

Lilli left him then. He knew it because he felt nothing but pitch-black darkness around him as he barreled through the night with his foot pressed down on the accelerator. His question was now being answered with a hollow-deep collapse growing out from within his chest. He needed to make it back to her before he fell in and was all consumed.

What if I lose her?

What if I lose her?

Clutching his chest and gasping for air as he tried to slow the spread of emptiness inside him, he realized, *This. This is what happens if I lose her.*

CHAPTER 22: TRUTH

L iam, it's crazy to drive all the way there now. Liam! Are you listening to me? There is no way you could make it in time. They're there already. You know that! Think of Lilli..."

Eli had asked Kyle to keep watch over Marcus while he tried to talk some sense into the crazed man Liam had become. When he made the trip back from Des Moines in just under an hour and twenty minutes, Eli was alarmed. Liam didn't say a word as he burst through the clinic's front door, cutting through the crowd of caregivers and children that had begun to take up every corner of the three-room interior to kneel beside Lilli as he placed the small brown box full of medicine into her hands. His strong eyebrows twitched with the depth of his emotion as he looked into Lilli's face, waiting for her to say something, anything that would pull him back from the edge of his worst fears.

"I don't know what to do, Liam. It's like a black fog inside my head. I can barely feel myself connecting," she whispered as the tears welled in her eyes.

Absolute hopelessness flashed across Liam's mind for only the briefest moment before he beat it into submission with the brute force of his anger. His silence continued as he rose from beside Lilli, turned and left the clinic, but Eli knew where he was going... after them.

Jumping into Marshall's truck, Eli followed the cloud of dust that led to the workshop that Liam had claimed, unofficially, for himself. By the time he made his way through the doorway to the main room, Liam was halfway packed with a duffel bag full of ammunition. Liam all but ignored Eli as he tossed hand grenades and tear gas into his bag with a carelessness that bordered on suicidal. When Eli saw him pull out a rocket launcher from a hidden compartment beneath the floor boards, he knew nothing would reach Liam but the threat of harm to Lilli.

At the mention of his sister's name, the mere question of her safety, Liam stilled. He knew what the emergency procedures were as well as Eli and everyone else in the commune. Children and teenagers to the clinic, with designated caregivers, at least one parent per family. Everyone else had their assigned posts, with Seers and non-Seers alike taking up arms to defend their home. While Liam was among their best-trained fighters, he was by no means the only one.

Lilli will be safe until I get back. I just need to find her, he told himself.

But Eli's insinuation caught him off guard, made him second guess his assumptions. Putting down the handgun he had taken from the back of his jeans to reload, Liam finally met Eli's pleading eyes with a look of pure hate.

"What do you expect me to do?" he spat in a low, ragged voice made hoarse by his efforts not to give into the feeling of mourning that was slowly squeezing the air from his chest.

"I expect you to wait, Liam. Wait, like the rest of us who can't see the future."

As the hours ticked on with the stars high in the black ink sky, Liam sat below them, cold and wanting so many things that seemed as far away as the heavens.

With his back pressed against a tree and his vision cast out on the river bank, he recounted the time. Liam knew the raid team's timetable, the plan that had been carefully laid out, by heart — leave by 3 pm, arrive by 6:30 pm. Check the front and back of the house. The whole family would be home for dinner. Alessandra would knock and introduce herself. *"My name is Alessandra Pino. We, my friends and I, need a moment to talk with you about something very important regarding your son."*

He'd heard her use the introduction more times than he wanted to think about now. Tess would come up next with her big, deep blue eyes that would remind the boy's father of his own mother's gaze in their wide-open sincerity. *"Please,"* Tess would say, *"We know your son is in danger. It's important that we speak with you now."* Maura would give the signal that the team was safe before the father would hesitantly step aside and let them in. Marshall, Kaido, and Eric would conceal their weapons.

Alessandra told them the conversation would take two hours, seventeen minutes, and thirty-one seconds, then another fifty-six minutes for the family to pack. The family would not come with them, but they would run and be safe. The thought of Alessandra's absolute precision made Liam smile. *It's amazing what you can do. I never told you, but I'm in awe of you.*

Sitting by the river where he first watched her swim, he looked at his watch. *12:48 am. If they made it out alive, they should be here in less than half an hour, especially if Eric drives.*

After Eli helped Liam retrieve some of his sanity, they went to the meeting hall to join the planning that they knew was already underway. With what appeared to be the deliberate sabotaging of the Seers, no one in the commune was taking chances. As soon as Eli arrived, he and Vincent began running the briefings in two separate groups simultaneously–one for defense, one for offense. Liam joined the offensive briefing.

"You get the medicine ok?" Vincent asked before Liam could sit down.

"Yeah, it's being administered now."

"Good." Vincent said as everyone in the group relaxed a little with relief.

"Alright, all the kids are in place at the clinic. Lilli will be stationed with them, just in case she can reconnect with her sight. We're hoping she can be a strong defensive asset if things go south."

Liam couldn't argue. Lilli was in the safest place in the commune with the best chance of survival. It would be the offensive team's job to make sure no one breached the commune's perimeter and the defensive team's job to catch anyone who did.

"Remember, short-range walkies only," Vincent continued. "We can't use the military issue anymore. They have built-in trackers that can't be disabled without destroying the whole thing. Liam, we've got three posts left - river, south block east, or south block west. Do you have a preference?"

"River. I'll take the river."

He had chosen that spot for his look-out post because it was the only place that was theirs. It was the first place he had ever allowed anything intimate to pass between them. The thought that there were only two places like that in the world forced a tear out of the corner of his eye. He wiped it away quickly.

You don't deserve to cry, he told himself. *This is your fucking fault. If you lose her tonight without ever loving her, ever being with her, it's your fucking fault.*

He wasn't trying to be strong. He had his flare gun, rocket launcher, M-16 semi-automatic, hand grenades, and back-up FN-Five-seven handgun for that. Though he'd set up his post as well as any other across the Commune's perimeter, prepared for whatever might come, he'd never felt so defenseless in his life. He knew the weapons would do what they were designed to do and, if it came down to it, his body would respond in the way it was trained — to keep anything and everything away from those he loved.

But now, looking out over the river, he understood in the deepest part of himself just how shortsighted his focus had been. *How do you forget to cherish what you protect? How can you protect what you don't allow yourself to love?* The realization was like acid in his stomach, churning over all the time he had wasted.

Tonight, they may have stolen her body, but I could have had the rest of her, to protect, to keep from them, if I'd only reached out and grabbed the chance - any of the dozens of times she offered herself to me.

The hot tears ran down his frozen cheeks like razors, but he didn't move to wipe them away this time.

But tonight she turned away from me. She let go of my hand, he thought before admitting the truth. *She let go because you didn't hold on. She needed you to hold on.*

And that's what he'd decided to do in their place. It was his first stance made in hope, his first act of faith since his mother had died. To defend what they had, the life they might have, in the first place they'd ever truly been together. Understanding for the first time his own true powerlessness to stop any of the madness around them, he decided finally to do the one thing she had ever asked of him — to hold on to her for as long as he could.

The sound of Eli's minivan was unmistakable as it coughed and hissed under Eric's insistence. When Rachel saw the van barrel down the incline that led to the commune's front entrance with no signs of stopping, she knew that whatever had stopped the Seers from visioning was not a fluke. As Eric cleared the entrance, Rachel could see his frantic motions to roll down the manually-operated window. She got close enough to the car to register the ash on his face just before Eric stuck his head out of the window and yelled, "Marshall's been shot! He's shot! Meet us at the clinic!" Since Marshall was rapidly losing blood in the back of the car, Eric didn't wait for confirmation as he sped ahead, leaving Rachel shaken and those who were able running toward the sound of Marshall's screams.

Eli had heard Tess's desperate call from the walkie-talkie as soon as they were in range and was prepared for their arrival. The children and their parents were moved to the greenhouse behind the clinic while any remaining adults gathered in tents. With the exception of Marcus and those assigned to help Eli, the clinic had been cleared out and rearranged as a trauma unit. Eli and Kyle followed the cloud of dust that signaled Eric's approach and watched Rachel and a few others run behind the truck, hoping to help.

Eric had barely put the van in park in front of the clinic before all the doors seemed to open at once, with Eric and Tess jumping out of the front seats and Maura throwing the side door open from the back. From what Eli could tell, they were all covered in blood, debris, and ash. The knuckles on Eric's right hand were raw as he met Tess at the side door. Maura jumped out next with her face nearly covered in soot and her beautiful brown eyes bloodshot from ash and crying.

"They attacked us as we were leaving. The family got away but..." Maura's trembling voice faded away as Eli rushed into the van to find

Alessandra hovering over Marshall with her hands pressed down on his right thigh with so much force her arms shook. Eli tried to move in closer to assess the damage, but Alessandra would not move.

"He was shot in the leg right as we were about to leave," Eric explained. "We had no idea, Eli — no idea they were coming. The whole damn house must have been wired. I mean, we were almost out and it just exploded. We couldn't stop it, Eli. They were in the doorway, but it was too late. It was too late."

Eric's words barely registered over Marshall's screams, but he got the gist enough to know what he was dealing with. Anxious to get started, Eli placed his hand on Alessandra's arm, ready to gently nudge her out of the way when Marshall stopped screaming long enough for him to hear Alessandra softly chanting to herself.

"No blood. No more blood. Just keep the pressure. Keep the pressure."

Realizing that he would have to work around her for the moment, he began removing the belt from his pants as he called for Kyle.

"Morphine. I need the morphine, Kyle."

Kyle placed the syringe in his hand just as Eli reached for it. He was glad that Alessandra and Eli were blocking his view. He could see the blood soaked carpet underneath Marshall's leg from where he stood outside the van and that was enough for him.

"Alessandra," Eli began. "I'm going to need you to keep putting pressure on his leg just like you're doing until I can get this belt around his leg. Okay?"

Alessandra's eyes darted to him as if registering his presence for the first time. "We can't move him!" she shouted. "The blood! We have to stop the blood!"

"Alessandra," Eli tried again, "if we're going to help him, you need to help me. Do you understand?"

She blinked a few times before she recognized the man in front of her as Eli. When she did, she gave him a slow nod as the tears finally began welling in her eyes. *I'm home*, she thought with overwhelming relief. *I made it home.*

When the belt was secured in place and Marshall was knocked out from the respite the morphine allowed, Marshall and Kyle moved him carefully onto the gurney and into the clinic. The sudden lull in commotion gave Eli the mental space he needed to finally connect Eric's words with the sense of absence he felt as soon as he had crawled into the van. Turning back from the clinic, Eli looked into the van to see Alessandra still kneeling on the floor with her head turned toward the two vacant seats at the back of the van.

"Alessandra, where are Lucia and Kaido?"

"They didn't make it home," Alessandra said in a quiet voice that was just barely her own.

From the moment Liam sensed the commotion, he started toward the clinic. Like everyone else, he'd heard the screams, and though it made his stomach twist to think that Eric, Marshall, or Kaido might be hurt, it meant more to him that the screams were not female, not Alessandra's.

His stride was long, but he did not run as he made his progression. He'd left all his weapons at his post when he called for relief and gladly passed his handgun to Caleb before heading on. Where he was going, what he sought to find, no weapons would be necessary. All he needed was the strength to face his mistake, if he didn't get a second chance. If he did, no strength was required. He would finally surrender.

When he reached the clinic door, there was an air of mourning that made him stumble before his hand settled on the front door handle.

Someone died. Someone didn't make it back. As soon as he stepped inside, he knew it wasn't Alessandra. Too many eyes met his searching gaze. If she hadn't made it, he knew that would not have been the case.

She's here. She's alive, he thought.

His feet turned in her direction instinctively. He knew how much Marcus meant to her and how much she would have needed to see him alive after the loss she had most likely witnessed. *It was just the four of them, her first new family,* he thought as he realized with deep sadness that everyone but Kaido and Lucia were there. Pushing aside the curtain that separated Marcus' makeshift room from the rest of the clinic, Liam found her where he knew she would be, kneeling on the floor beside Marcus' bed as she grasped his knee and buried her face in the side of his mattress.

I know you think he's all you have left, but it's not true, Alessandra. I'm ready now. I'm here.

Lilli smiled up at her brother from the small metal chair that she had not vacated since Marcus had fallen sick.

As Liam walked up behind Alessandra quietly, he was surprised to see Marcus wide awake with his hand placed gently over Alessandra's at his knee. When Marcus saw Liam come to stand behind her, he smiled at the resolve, the submission he noted in Liam's eyes.

Finally, he thought, as he closed his eyes briefly and thanked God that something good had come out of such a horrible night.

When Marcus opened his eyes again and looked at him, Liam's chest swelled with the meaning behind Marcus' faint smile, the tear rolling down his cheek, and the reason why Marcus nodded toward Liam just as he lifted his hand from Alessandra's, allowing Liam's to take his place.

Placing his large calloused hand over her small bloodied one, Liam could feel her jump just before he called her name.

"Alessandra."

Alessandra swung out of her curled-up position so fast that it took him by surprise. He didn't anticipate the force with which she would crash into him, but he still didn't stumble. Instead, he lifted her to him as her arms clung around his neck, trembling like the little bird she always reminded him of.

He turned then and carried her out of the clinic, walking the distance to his workshop where he planned to keep her safe and warm.

She didn't say a word as he walked and she cried, but he didn't need her to say anything. Liam kept her in his arms until he reached the inside of his workshop and passed through the hidden door that led to a small bath and bedroom that he'd made for himself for when he wanted to be alone. He sat her gently on the bed as he turned on the small lamp beside it and went to start the fire. When he returned, she had not moved. It was what he expected. So he continued to work around her, pulling some extra clothes from his storage bin under the bed before starting the hot water for her shower. When it was warm enough, he lit a candle in the bathroom and returned to find that her tears had stopped but her trembling continued.

Slowly, he knelt down before her and began to remove her shoes and socks. Her face was impassive as she watched him, but she did not turn away.

It's the shock, he thought. *She hasn't seen anything like that in so long. She just needs to warm up.*

After removing her jacket and sweater, he kicked off his own shoes and socks before carrying her to the bathroom. She watched him as he brought them both under the water fully clothed before he began peeling away the rest of her layers. He undressed her quickly, refusing to linger as he revealed her skin. He didn't want to touch her that way until he had her permission, until she was fully herself again.

But he needed no permission to care for her. As he reached for the washcloth and soap, he kept his hands gentle, only using the pressure that was necessary to wash the blood from her hands and legs and the ash that was caked onto her face and neck. He had to wash her hair three times to untangle all the wood and glass debris that was trapped there. *Some type of fire or explosion,* he surmised, but he refused to ask, to force her to relive memories from which she was still struggling to break free.

After he'd finished washing the front of her, he began to slowly turn her around to wash her back. When her feet stumbled over his in the small space of his shower, he held her tightly with one arm while bracing his other hand in front of them against the shower wall. The shudder she made was the first sound he'd heard from her since she'd stopped crying.

She's coming back to me, he thought.

"I've got you now. Don't worry, Alessandra. I'm here."

As he continued washing her back, he could hear her breathing begin to deepen. He had just finished when he felt her hand slide up over his on the wall. Slowly, he moved his hand to rest on her hip as he stood behind her with the water washing over them, waiting for her to turn around and face him. When she didn't move, he dropped the washcloth, shifted his hand to the side of her face, and gently turned her head enough to see her profile.

"Are you okay?" he asked softly.

Alessandra nodded as she placed her hand over his on her cheek and turned to face him. She felt like she had just woken up from a bad dream to find herself standing naked in a warm shower with him. She lifted her other hand, the one that had been pressed directly against Marshall's wound, and looked at it in amazement.

"You washed it all away," she whispered, as she placed her hand gently against the drenched t-shirt that clung to him.

"Yes," was all Liam could manage to say. He had never been much good with words when he was this close to her. In a shower, with her completely bare, 'yes' was all he could manage.

"Thank you," she said softly, as she pulled his hand from her face and let them hang together at her side.

Liam carried her from the shower to the bedroom, where he knew the heat from the wood burning fire would keep them warm. She made no move to help or distract him as he patted the towel over her shoulders and back, between her breasts and down her stomach. She even parted her legs slightly as he knelt to dry her feet, then moved the towel back up to pass over her calves and thighs.

After helping her dress in his high school sweatshirt and long johns, he left her sitting on the bed while he undressed in front of the fire in the other room and laid their wet clothes out to dry.

As she sat on the bed, wrapped in his oversized clothes, all Alessandra could think was that even though he was just in the other room, the distance between them felt too great. *We've wasted so much time already,* she thought, as she rose from the bed and pulled out the waist band of his long johns, letting them drop to the floor. The fact that he had come for her, without hesitation, told her that he was finally ready to stop fighting and accept what she had to give. *I've never liked sleeping with clothes,* she thought, as she pulled his sweatshirt off over her head. Tonight, if he planned to sleep beside her, she didn't want anything between them.

Stepping from the bedroom to seek him out, she found him crouched down and naked in front of the stove, staring into the flames. At the sound of her footsteps, Liam turned and froze at the sight of her bathed in saffron light.

"Do you love me, Liam?" she asked, as she moved toward him slowly, tracing her fingers over the place in her belly that fluttered and tightened whenever he was near.

He shook his head as he watched her approach. Instead of standing up to meet her, he found himself kneeling on the ground in front of the fire, watching her move.

"More. It's more than that," he whispered.

Reaching the space where he kneeled before her, she extended her arms out to bring him to her and feel his skin against hers. The minute she laced her fingers through his still-damp hair, he pulled her toward him, burying his nose in her belly while he encased her hips and bottom in his arms.

"Tell me. Tell me how much," she whispered back as her body began to hum with need.

She could feel him tracing the roughness of his cheeks back and forth across her stomach. Without seeing him, she knew his eyes were closed as he let out a soft sigh and pulled her body closer to his. Gently, she tugged on his hair so that he would meet her eyes and tell her what she had waited so long to hear.

The fire made his eyes look like polished glass as he stared at her. He was naked and in love and so certain he belonged there with her.

"I adore you," he whispered. "I adore you, Alessandra."

The tears welling in her eyes made him finally rise from the cold ground. As he took her face in his hands, Alessandra noticed how his expression had changed to one of complete seriousness. He stared at her for several long moments before breathing in and exhaling the words.

"Be with me, Alessandra. For whatever is left of our lives, I want you to be with me."

Leaning down to finally put his lips to hers, he knew it was what she wanted, what he should have said from the minute he saw her. It was the reason she had come to find him.

Their first kiss was soft, the most gentle pressing-together of their lips. He held her face in his hand as he watched her eyes flutter closed before tilting her head up toward him and pressing his mouth more fully onto hers. Their lips parted at the same instant. The sensation felt like a tremor running straight through the center of her body as Liam grazed his tongue over her bottom lip.

Following his lead, Alessandra met the tip of his tongue just before their lips pressed together more fully, bringing him into her mouth. As they continued, their kisses became less focused as Liam trailed his lips over the corner of her mouth, her cheeks, her hair, and back to her jaw, never letting go of her face to guide her where and how he wanted her. She was overwhelmed with so much contact all at once, the unimaginable softness of his lips on her face contrasting sharply with the gentle roughness of his hands and the firmness of his body. She could feel him harden on her stomach where they had been pressing together in unconscious movement. Without realizing it, her hand moved from behind his neck to reach for him, smooth and rigid between them.

The minute Liam felt her touch, he froze, trying to suppress his shudder at the feel of her small hand around him. They both looked down to where he stood between them, leaking and tight and so hungry for home. Liam didn't miss the way her tongue darted out at the sight of him, and it made him groan into her hair while pushing further into her hand. Pressing his forehead heavily against the top of her head, Liam's voice was strained as he tried to calm his desire.

"Are you sure?"

Alessandra answered him by lifting her head up to kiss him fiercely, crushing her body to his until he finally lifted her up and carried her back to his room. She was still kissing him, still clinging to his body as he lowered her to the bed and then settled himself between her legs.

She was so soft beneath him that his whole body ached with conflicting needs. He wanted to see her, touch her, kiss her everywhere and take his time, while in the same moment wanting only to be inside her.

"I love you," Liam whispered as Alessandra wrapped her arms and legs tighter around him, bringing his full weight onto her as they began to move together.

"Aaahhh," she cried out as she began to rub herself against him right where he lay, so heavy and warm at the center of where her body ached for him.

He looked up from sucking gently on her neck to find her eyes shut tight and her body beginning to glisten with sweat. She looked like she was hovering at the edge of pain and pleasure as she rubbed herself against him with her legs locking him in place. The sight of her so lost in the way his body made her feel released the last threads of caution he held onto as he rose up onto his elbows and slid back against her grinding motions with his own.

Having repositioned his body, he could feel exactly what was happening, how he slid right over the center of her folds and pressed against her clit.

She's so wet. God, she's so wet.

He saw her face relax as he moved with her, so that when she opened her eyes to find him, there was only pleasure.

"Liam, I love you… I love you," she breathed, as she stroked the side of his face.

His body shuddered with the intensity of how her words made him feel, and the realization of how much he'd needed to hear them. The weight of her finally belonging to him caused him to break his rhythm as he bent down to kiss her softly.

"You're everything, Alessandra. You're everything now."

Liam watched as she closed her eyes just before reaching for one of his hands to press up against her lips, releasing her gasps and moans into the palm of his hand.

He took in everything he could from his position above her—the pure ecstasy on her face, the way her breasts moved softly up and down in time with their movement, and the change in her moans from low to higher and higher pitches. As he watched and savored her, his own body began to tremble, letting him know that he was fast approaching his release. He had the sudden urge to see it when she came and when he came on her. As gently as he could manage, he pried her left leg from his hip and slid his hand down the inside of her thigh, flattening her leg against the mattress.

"I want to see you, Alessandra. I want to see it when you come." Her right leg fell from him then, hitting the bed as he anchored himself to her with one hand around her waist and the other one planted in the space beside her.

His words, the feeling of being spread so wide-open for him, made her frantic. She grabbed his sides as best she could, tilting her hips upward as they rode each other, eyes held together and lost in the beauty of their pleasure. She was becoming so wet that he could feel himself slipping lower toward her opening and higher up over her clit. As her eyes closed once more, Liam looked down to see himself nestled between her, leaking, weeping for her insides so bad he couldn't tell and didn't care how they mixed together as he strained to watch himself move faster and faster over her.

His mind was fixed on the look of them together and the feeling she brought him until he heard her scream. He looked up from where her hips were grinding against him with hard and broken strokes to find her entire torso bowed and lifted off the bed with her head thrown back and both her hands pressed against the headboard of his bed. It was in that moment that he felt himself suddenly surrounded by warmth as he slipped then pushed inside her.

Liam had had sex before, twice while he was in Albuquerque. Both times had been so quick and random there had been little to savor. So there was nothing in his past that would have prepared him for what it was like to make love. His mind struggled to comprehend the feeling, the tightness and heat that suddenly encased him, and his body collapsed on top of her from the overload of sensation and emotion he felt.

I'm inside. I'm inside her, he thought in amazement.

Underneath him, Alessandra was overcome, still in the middle of her orgasm when she felt him push into her as if he had always belonged there. The feeling was delicious - sudden sharp pain, followed by warmth, pleasure, and fullness, and finally total possession as his body covered her from without and within. Even in their surprise at coming together, the urge to move was all consuming and she held onto him tightly, experiencing the aftershocks of her orgasm as she heard him gasping into her neck.

"It's so good," she heard him say, as she felt his fingers dig into the sheets beside her head.

"I know, I know…"

"I can't… I can't hold it… You feel so good."

"Don't…Don't. I want to hear you," Alessandra whispered into his ear.

Liam could barely keep his eyes open as he turned to look at her. "I didn't know... I didn't know it would be like this..." he said before pressing his forehead to hers.

"Liam," Alessandra whispered, as she watched his eyes shut tight from the strain she didn't want him to bear. "Liam, look at me." It took a while for him to gather the focus needed to do what she asked, but when he did, he saw the desperate love he felt in the movement of his hips mirrored in her eyes.

"Show me. Show me how good it feels..."

He took over then, driving into her with a force he didn't know he still had in him until he found a spot so deep inside her that he knew he was safe. He didn't bury his face in her neck like he wanted to, choosing instead to show her–through the broken syllables of his words and the slackening of his jaw as he threw his head back and moaned deep and low–everything she wanted to see, just how good it was for him.

The sight of him being so lost in her was almost as intoxicating as her own release, except for the fact that she was able to focus, able to think and keep her eyes open. When Liam finally lowered his body to hers, they showered each other with soft, reverent kisses, holding each other just as they were. They made no move to untangle themselves, and fell asleep quickly, still joined together, until dawn.

Chapter 23: Recoil

"Well, I must say, Miguel, I am pleased by this news. You've done well."

Crane's unqualified praise took Miguel by surprise.

What is he talking about? Miguel wondered. *We lost Jason and Renoir last night. Two of our best men, with nothing to show for it.*

Crane's response made Miguel feel the need to repeat himself, if only to make sure he understood the extent of Crane's disregard for his employees.

"But, as I said, we didn't recover any lost Seers. Jason and Renoir arrived too late. By the time they reached the house, the family was already packed and preparing to flee. With the exception of our men, only two were killed at the Isaac's house. The others got away."

The small gathering of Guild members shifted uncomfortably in their plush leather chairs as they watched the dawn break from the refined comfort of the Chicago Purification Center's executive conference room. Though it had been a long and tense night, Andreas knew that fact alone did not account for the somber mood that hung in the air. Looking around the table, it was obvious to him how each of the eight members of their shaky alliance were trying to mask their rapt attention to Miguel's every word. The distracted looks on their faces did little to hide the hurried calculations he knew they were making about what the night's events meant for them, the effectiveness of their Seers, and their standing within the Guild.

He couldn't blame them. Andreas was busy with more than a few calculations of his own. Their Seers had been, at best, both right and wrong. Even with Nina and Michael's blocking abilities combined with those of the Alliance focused on finding Marcus, Alessandra, Lucia, and Kaido, they had missed vital details, like the precise time the 'lost Seers', as they'd come to be known within the Guild, would arrive at the Isaac's home, and exactly who and how many of them would be there. Most importantly, the Alliance had hoped to finally discover where the lost Seers had been hiding out. Their failure to obtain any of that information called into question the Alliance's fundamental ability to perform its mission to eliminate any threats to the Guild's claim on all Seers.

The Alliance knew that the number of lost Seers had grown. Anyone could have surmised as much from their increasing success at stealing new recruits from the Guild. But when Michael told them last week that he believed their numbers had grown beyond the 12 Seers the Alliance had estimated, they had put together their most concerted effort yet to stop the lost Seers from chipping away at any more of the Guild's operations. By Andreas' estimate, the plan had been a monumental failure, with the benefit of hindsight as their only gain. Of course, Crane saw things differently.

"Come now, Miguel. You mustn't be so hard on yourself," Crane's tone was almost patronizing, as if soothing a child who dropped his ice cream cone. "We all know how delicate an operation like this is to coordinate, with a dozen potential targets under surveillance in the last 24 hours alone. We were fortunate enough to get the last minute break that finally showed us which Seer they would target. A few casualties… could not be helped."

"I'm glad you're so encouraged, Crane," Camille snapped, "because this looks nothing like progress to me. While we were able to narrow down the targets, all we seemed to have accomplished tonight is tipping our hand to the lost Seers, who will no doubt redouble their efforts to hide from us. We also diminished our ranks by two men. If I'm missing some silver lining here, please enlighten me."

Crane always bristled whenever Camille Bordeaux of the European delegation spoke. To him, hearing her voice was like listening to broken glass being crushed into gravel. It alternated between high pitched screeching and dull rumbling tones, sometimes within the same sentence. Even in French, her native tongue and his favorite language, Crane marveled at how ugly it sounded coming from her thin slit of a mouth. While imagining widening her smile with the tip of his shaving razor, Crane's own smirk broadened as he turned from Miguel to face her.

"Camille," Crane sighed, "your pessimism is so difficult to overcome. We managed to catch them off guard, to surprise them for once. This is surely a sign of progress, even to your narrow mind."

"Don't you dare insult me, you skunk! We wouldn't even *be* in this position if it wasn't for your carelessness!"

"Enough!" Deidra interjected. "For all your salesmanship, Crane, Camille is right. To have risked so much and gained so little hardly seems cause for celebration. At this point, we don't even know who the dead ones are. If they are civilians, this whole exercise will have been a complete loss. We have to report to the Council in one hour. Let's focus on figuring out something to say that doesn't make us sound completely incapable of handling this situation."

As one of the most respected members of the Guild, Deidra's opinion held the power to momentarily silence even Crane. In a show of begrudging solidarity, Andreas spoke up in Crane's defense.

260 | Cerece Rennie Murphy

"We tell them that we have found a way to block their visions, though the ability is still limited and in development. We can also report that we were able to gain a brief window into their plans. Though our timing was obviously flawed, it does suggest that there are potential weaknesses in their group that could be exploited as we learn more. Miguel, when will we have confirmation on the bodies?"

"In less than 30 minutes."

"Good. That will be all for now."

Andreas dismissed Miguel with a wave of his hand before continuing to address the group. "If the IDs are positive, we'll be in an even better position. Though it's not what we hoped for, this is the closest we've ever gotten. No one has achieved more than this. They will not be pleased, but our actions were not without some value."

"Fine," Deidra conceded, after watching her colleagues nod in silent agreement. "We'll wait and hope for good news from the examiner, then report what we have. Our Quorum continues to see a great threat coming from this group of Seers, though we still cannot obtain any specific information on the nature of the threat."

She hesitated for a moment before bringing her own personal fears to light.

"Has anyone considered that if we find out the two bodies were Seers, this could trigger some sort of retaliation from them?"

At the alarmed looks she received in response to her question, Deidra felt even more concerned by the fact that she was the only one to whom this thought had occurred. In contrast, the ominous silence in the room caused Crane to squint in disbelief at the anxiety he could see growing around the oblong table.

"I can't believe there is even one among us who would seriously consider this!" he scoffed. "They've done nothing but hide from us from the moment they left, coming out only to pick off, what… maybe a dozen other Seers? If they wanted to expose us, they could have easily tried it before now. With the public's fear of them as it is, I doubt they would find any sympathy.

"If we managed to kill two of their own, the logical reaction, given their past behavior, would be for them to retreat. Marcus, more than any one of them, knows our capacities. Even if Michael is right and their numbers have grown beyond our current estimates, we have thousands of Seers and the world's resources at our disposal. As part of the UWO, we have the power to make our own rules without interference from the outside. There *is* no retaliation against us."

Before Camille could pounce, Deidra silenced her with a hand held midway between them.

Listening to Crane, Deidra always found it hard to remember that he was considered a pioneer within the Guild for his work in perfecting the Luridium formula that they all used and, until recently, he was well-known for his ability to break the most difficult Seers. She tried hard to recall these facts any time she had to address him directly.

"Crane, even now, you amaze me. Listening to you, it's as if none of this ever occurred. Though we like to fool ourselves by calling them lost Seers, we here cannot afford to lose sight of the truth. They escaped, Crane, right under all of our noses, and continue to do so, despite all our advantages!" She was quickly losing her patience with his arrogance, and she struggled to control the pitch of her voice as the sun came up.

"They go out now and manage to convince complete strangers to let them into their homes. Have you not wondered how they are able to do this with their appearance? Clearly, they have learned to adapt in some way."

Crane sat back in his chair and relaxed as he watched Deidra's nostrils flare. Even though her agitation amused him, he tried to project an air of professionalism for the sake of the group as he responded to her.

"Deidra, of course I've considered this, but you mentioned retaliation. I think convincing a handful of people to let you into their homes by choice or force is a completely different matter than taking on the entire Guild. Marcus would never be that stupid."

"You have underestimated them before, Crane," Deidra said as she gathered her files and prepared to leave the conference room for the library where she would give her report directly to the Guild Chair. Though she tried to ignore it, the sound of Crane's assuredness frightened her, as if it held within it the very reason they would fail. She hadn't planned to look back as Christof opened the conference room door and stepped aside to let her pass. But as she reached the doorway, she turned again to look directly into Crane's cold grey eyes and added, "To the detriment of us all, Crane. To the detriment of us all."

Liam woke to the feeling of something soft brushing against his face. When his attempts to wriggle free from the distraction were met with a throaty giggle, his eyes opened slowly to find Alessandra nose to nose with him, smiling the widest smile he could ever remember seeing on her face.

He knew his smile matched hers when his cheeks started to hurt, but he couldn't stop it, even if he tried. They lay in bed like that until the sky turned from pale gray to watercolor blue. It looked like the first day of spring.

Occasionally, they would trade teasing nose brushes, feather-light kisses, and the gentlest of fingertip touches to bare skin. To Liam, Alessandra's presence felt magical. Though he knew it didn't make sense, he found himself almost scared to speak for fear his voice would make the image of her dissolve right in front of his eyes. The thought was so frivolous, so silly, that it made him smile even harder, until he could barely see the shoulder he was caressing.

"I like the crinkles at the corners of your eyes when you smile like that..." Alessandra whispered, as she snuggled closer to him and traced the object of her affection.

He didn't answer right away, choosing instead to take a moment to just listen to the echo of her voice in his head before he closed his eyes completely and whispered, "I love you," into the palm of the hand that was still stroking the side of his face.

When he heard her sigh, he opened his eyes. It was then that he noticed the bruise that was beginning to turn purple at the right corner of her hairline. Though he knew last night's events were responsible for finally bringing them together, everything beyond their cocoon seemed a world away to him. The bruise on her face was a reminder of how far away his feeling was from the truth that you couldn't have one without the other.

"Are you okay?" he asked, as he fingered her hair just above the bruise line. Alessandra's flinch was slight, but he noticed.

"No," she answered honestly. "I don't ever want to be okay with losing people I loved so much, but I will survive it. I have you now. I can do anything."

Liam wrapped his arms and leg around her and pulled her deeper into his embrace. She was so still curled up against him, but he knew without looking that she was crying.

"You do have me. No matter what, you will always have me."

"I know, Liam. I know."

They lingered in the bed only a few moments more before they showered together and dressed in Liam's clothes after Alessandra decided to burn everything she had worn the day before. After stopping off at her cabin to change, they walked hand-in-hand into the dining hall where they knew everyone would still be gathered, though breakfast had stopped being served over an hour before.

As soon as she saw them, Lilli slid over on the bench she'd reserved for them near the back of the room. As they made their way toward her, no one stopped talking, though Liam and Alessandra noticed several small congratulatory nods as others noticed that they were finally together. When her brother was in reach, Lilli stretched out her arms to take him and Alessandra into her embrace. "I'm so happy for you both," she whispered before they sat down quietly and turned their attention to the conversation. Looking toward the front of the room, Liam and Alessandra were surprised to see Marcus sitting quietly beside Eli with an IV stand stationed beside his chair.

"Basically, we survived last night, but we don't know what that means anymore. I don't think we can afford to just wait here until they find us," Hanna continued. "This is my home, too, but you know our situation. I can't wait around for that."

Kyle sat beside his sister in complete silence. He knew she was only sharing her thoughts for the benefit of the group. He had heard her start packing their things early that morning while she thought he was still asleep. Unless someone could convince her of their safety, they would be gone by the end of the night.

"Look," Marshall said, leaning forward gingerly in his chair, "I'm sorry. I hear you, but they killed two of us last night. They weren't just commune members to me. They became my friends, my family. I want to know what we're going to do about that. I refuse to believe that there isn't a damn thing we can do about that."

As Marshall spoke, Rachel stroked his shoulders gently, exhausted from having been up all night worrying about him.

Touched by Marshall's sentiment but weary of putting anyone else in unnecessary danger, Marcus spoke next. "I don't know what we can do, Marshall. I think my falling ill must have had something to do with their ability to block us. Until I am fully recovered, I don't know what our options are. Perhaps it's best that you get away from us. We have put you all in enough danger."

"If that's all we're here for, then none of this makes any sense," Tess interrupted. "There are 40 of us! Forty people who can see the fucking future, for Christ's sake!" Looking at Lilli, she continued. "Some of us can do a lot more than that. Why are we here if all we're going to do is hide? You said it yourself, Marcus. There must be a reason why we're all here."

"Tess's got a point," Eric added. "I mean, last night, we almost got away. They seemed really surprised when they got out of their car to see us on our way out. If we had left just a little sooner, who knows, maybe Lucia and Kaido would be with us right now.

"Regardless, they definitely weren't expecting the ass-kicking we gave them. Kaido took down that big guy like he was nothing. All he had to do was look like he was going to go after Lucia and it was over. When Marshall got shot, I took out the other guy pretty quick. My point is that we didn't quit, not even when we were blindsided. Kaido and Lucia were walking out the front door when the house exploded. I knew Kaido well enough to know that he wouldn't want that to be his legacy. I don't think Lucia would have wanted that, either."

At the turn of the conversation, Tenzen, one of the newest Seers to have found his way to the commune, spoke up in his soft Tibetan accent.

"I know I have been here for only a couple of weeks now, but I must say, I am surprised by the tone of these discussions. I have never seen a more powerful, self-sufficient group of people, and yet you act as if you are half of what you are. We are not the only ones hiding. The Guild also hides–what they do, what their true intentions are for people like us... Yes, we have weaknesses, but so do they. Perhaps we should..."

Listening to Tenzen speak, Alessandra could feel her spine tingle. She suddenly realized that coming out of hiding would be the worst thing possible for the Guild. All this time, they had been facilitating the lies that the Guild told, keeping them true in their own lives as they hid away like the pariahs everyone believed them to be. But now, they could -they *would* turn the tables.

Alessandra let go of Liam's hand as she and Lilli rose at the same time.

"Exposure," Alessandra blurted out before Tenzen could finish his thought. "Their weakness is our ability to expose to the world who we are and what they have done to us."

"Tenzen's right," Lilli continued. "We have been blind to the power of our own stories. Marcus and Alessandra, you are now the only ones who have ever escaped from the Guild. What if we sent a message, telling the world exactly what they did to you, the both of you? We could do that without exposing our location, and the backlash would keep them busy while you recuperate and we figure out our next move."

Marcus and Eli held the same stunned expressions as they tried to wrap their minds around going against the Guild. Though the idea was pure insanity, Marcus knew that it would be the last thing the Guild would expect them to do. The idea made him smile as he remembered a fleeting vision he had more than 12 years ago of a girl who would help him do what no other Seer had ever accomplished. It had been a foolish idea, right up until the moment when he Alessandra, Lucia and Kaido escaped.

Marcus rose carefully from his chair, intending to go back to his cabin and get the rest he needed to expedite his recovery.

"Marcus?" Alessandra called, as she saw him rise from his chair and prepare to leave.

He looked over the crowd at their eager, brilliant faces. *Powerful, indeed,* he thought in amazement.

"If I'm going to play my part, I need to rest so I can be of maximum use when the time comes. I will tell my story and do whatever you decide, but start with Kaido and Lucia's story. They would like that very much, I think." And with that, Marcus left the others to plan their work.

In the end, the plan was as simple as it was effective. Kyle would videotape each Seer's story as well as interview several commune members to testify that the Seers weren't a danger, as the world had been led to believe. The videos would then be sent to news outlets and posted on YouTube from public libraries and cafe servers all across the globe using Hanna and Kyle's superior hacking capabilities.

For safety reasons, the plan necessitated that the commune would need to formally disband, though they would continue to live and work together in smaller groups. Lilli insisted that those with legal issues work with her and Liam's various contacts to get new passports and leave the US before the first video was ever sent or posted. That meant that within a week after the videos were finalized, Hanna and Kyle would be working out of a two-bedroom apartment in Florence, Italy, where they would begin video distribution.

Those who could afford to stay would be a part of the second phase of their plan, an attack on the Chicago Purification Center. With the execution of each phase, they planned to send an unequivocal message to the Guild that they were done hiding.

It took less than an hour after Hanna had pushed the send button for Deidra to see the first of what would be an endless loop of breaking news stories on 'Seers in Captivity' on her private plane back to Scotland. The moment she saw Marcus and Alessandra on her TV screen, healthy and very much alive and without a trace of the Luridium effects that the Guild had assumed were permanent, she collapsed into her in-flight lounge chair. Her eyes locked on the news anchor in horror as he paraphrased and narrated every detail of what Marcus and Alessandra had suffered at the Guild's hands, and what they knew would happen to others like them if the Guild was not stopped.

She received the call she'd been expecting from the Guild Chairman within five minutes of the first story, which was slated for a full exposé with "even more revealing videos" at 8 pm that evening. Her head was spinning so fiercely that she could barely make out any of the Chair's foul language as she let the drink her assistant made for her fall from her fingers.

"This is just the beginning, Chairman," she interjected somewhere in the middle of his tirade.

"This is only the beginning."

Chapter 24: Final Raid

June, 2012

In the end, only fifty-two people remained. Between the Seers who were too young to fight and the others who would risk incarceration or worse if they were caught, the commune felt almost empty. Those who could not stay were split up into small groups so that no one would be alone and everyone would have the resources they needed to stay connected. Once each group reached their new location, either in the US or abroad, they were instructed to make contact with Hanna and Kyle to let them know they arrived safely and report any trouble they experienced.

Even though the Commune was eerily quiet without all the daily sounds of children playing and the constant commotion that they'd become accustomed to, the relative silence didn't make a single person sad. As those who remained worked to clean up any evidence of their friends that could possibly serve as a trail to follow, the common feeling among them was one of peace—peace that they had done the right thing for those they cared about and confidence in the knowledge that they were still all together in spirit, if not yet in person.

Until they could all reunite again in Prague, there would be no direct contact between groups. Any communications related to the commune were to be conveyed through Hanna and Kyle, who were the only ones who knew the location of each member of their group. Together with Eli, who would join them soon, Hanna and Kyle would act as the central information hub for the group. Besides Eli, Marcus and Lilli were the only ones who knew Hanna and Kyle's location.

Phase One of their plan kept the Guild in the news and on the defense every minute of the two weeks since Hanna and Kyle sent the first videos out. Those who were left in Iowa worked on Phase Two—their final raid. Watching the public react with shock and anger to their stories and growing skepticism toward the Guild's denials gave the Seers reason to hope that their plans would eventually bring down the institution that hunted them.

Unlike the first part of their plan, Phase Two required a great deal more external resources and preparation for it to work. Before Caleb left with his family and two other Commune members for Vancouver, he used his connections in the construction industry to obtain a copy of the original architectural designs for Chicago's Purification Center. That information gave the ground assault team, which included Liam, Marshall, and Eric, invaluable insight into how to map out their attack.

If they were successful, the thirty-two Seers who remained would keep the Guild blind to their plans until they arrived in Chicago. From there, the strategy was to engage their security forces as a diversion from their ultimate goal–freeing the Seers inside, and if possible, capturing Crane and Andreas. When Marshall asked how they planned to deal with calls for back up from local authorities, Eli reminded him of the Guild's unique status around the world.

"Remember, they don't operate on the same plane as the rest of us. Purification Centers are given sovereignty wherever they are located. Local authorities, national governments—even international laws have no jurisdiction in these places. It's what allows them to torture Seers and use them with complete impunity.

"It's also the reason why they won't call the local police for help. They don't want to open their doors to scrutiny from the outside. They even have the authority to treat any intrusion by local authorities as a declaration of war by the country they occupy. Trust me, that will be the least of our worries."

While Kyle completed video distribution, Hanna worked around the clock to hack into the Chicago's Purification Center's servers and find out everything from their security protocol and daily staff presence to who was scheduled to visit the Purification Center and when. Normally, Alessandra would have been able to see many of these details herself, but as each Seer became more involved and invested in the planning, their ability to use their visions to see details and outcomes surrounding their plans began to diminish. They simply lost their ability to be objective about the future and their role in it.

As a result, the planning for their attack was determined by a combination of their visions and what Hanna and Kyle were able to patch together from inside the Center's security systems. With Marcus making a full recovery in just under a week after falling ill, they were able to resume full Quorums with the confidence that their plans would remain hidden. As Kaido's apprentice, Jared stepped into Kaido's role as silent participant in several of the Guild's Quorums to monitor their visions and make sure none of the commune's plans were seen.

During one of their first Quorums after Lucia and Kaido's deaths, Jared was able to detect the Glasgow Quorum's reoccurring premonition of the threat the 'lost Seers' would be to the Guild. But after several days of monitoring, Jared could tell they were still unable to see any details about their plans.

Ironically, the one to expose them did so without any conscious effort on her part. During one of Chicago's routine training Quorums, this Seer suddenly had a vision of being comforted by a young woman with curly chin length hair and warm brown eyes. Despite the change in her appearance, Crane and Andreas knew her well. The young Seer's name was Emma, and other than her plane ride from Dubai to Chicago, Crane and Andreas knew she would have no reason to know Alessandra or feel any connection to her. To Crane, Andreas, and the Alliance partners with whom they shared this information, the clarity of the vision could only mean one thing–Alessandra would be coming to Chicago.

But no matter how many Seer resources the Guild used to focus on and draw out Emma's initial vision, the Guild could not see past the increased blocking efforts of the commune's Seers. The future was completely opaque in the same way it had been when the lost Seers escaped. When the details of Emma's vision were reported to the Guild, the Alliance partners were ordered to bring their most resourceful Seers and security teams to support and secure the Guild's Chicago facility. All reinforcements were scheduled to be in place by the end of the month. In order to maximize their potential success while minimizing casualties on their side, the commune decided to execute their raid before the Center's reinforcements arrived. That gave the commune two and a half weeks to finalize their plans and act.

During those weeks, everyone worked harder than they ever had. The energy that appeared during that first 'event' in Quorum was magnified by the determination and focus of each Seer. But instead of the raw, unharnessed force they witnessed the first time they quorumed together, the Seers had learned to shape and control the electromagnetic field around them, drawing the power in when they wanted and sending it outward to disrupt their environment if necessary. Within the field, they could move freely while being completely protected due to the deflective properties of the energy that surrounded them. Utilizing its protective qualities, the Quorum planned to act as a frontal shield for the non-Seers in their group.

But the Seers' plans weren't limited to visioning and blocking alone. Driven by Tess's success in mastering her ability to project visions, she and Alessandra came up with a way to turn their joint abilities into an offensive weapon. At first, Tess practiced on non-Seers in the Commune, sharing the Seers' visions in Quorum with increasingly larger groups, so that by the time Marcus was up and well, she could include or exclude sub-sets or the entire group of non-Seers.

For Alessandra, the plan would require more sacrifice. Since she had arrived at the commune, Alessandra had purposefully avoided focusing on anything painful in her visions, nothing that had the potential to remind her of her darkest days with the Guild. Alessandra remembered well the reputation she had earned there and the impact she had on anyone unlucky enough to see what she saw. She knew that if she could go to that place in her mind again, with Tess's help, the images would debilitate anyone who came within their sphere of sight. To Alessandra, the advantage of protecting everyone she loved by using her gift was worth more than what it cost her.

With a wide and varied supply of agony brought on by the Guild, Alessandra held onto that simple fact whenever the visions that she and Tess shared became almost too much to bear. And at night, when her nightmares returned, Liam shared and soothed her fears until she was calm and whole again.

From behind the front line of Seers, Liam and Marshall would lead the others in a ground assault that would rely heavily on projectile missiles until the real fighting started. With only twenty of them, they needed to keep the fighting long-distance for as long as possible. As well thought-out as it was, Marshall often remarked how the whole endeavor would be little more than a long shot, a suicide mission, had it not been for their secret weapon–Lilli.

Rather than participating as a Quorum member, Lilli knew she needed to operate independently to be of maximum use. Though Liam hated the fact of it, it was Lilli who made it even possible to get into the facility to attempt to rescue the Seers there. Her ability to manipulate light made her appear invisible to the naked eye and all but infrared cameras. She could literally walk into the facility undetected. And once inside, she could do more than that. Out of everyone in the group, Lilli also had the greatest ability to defend herself against anything she might encounter, but that didn't give Liam any comfort.

"This feels so wrong, like exactly backwards. Instead of being out in front, I'm hiding behind my girlfriend while my little sister runs into the one place we've been trying to avoid – alone," Liam complained to Lilli after a long night of finalizing their plans to leave for Chicago in two days.

"Please tell me how this makes sense," he finished, as he opened the front door to their small cabin.

Lilli didn't answer him as she passed through the doorway and headed straight to her room. She was tired and didn't have the energy to calm her overprotective brother. Once inside, he followed Lilli to her bedroom, only to find her spread out on her bed, fully clothed with her eyes shut.

"So… What? You're just going to ignore me?"

"Yes," Lilli finally replied with a half-hearted sigh. "Yes, I am, Liam."

"I'm just worried about you, Lilli. You're my little sister. I know what you can do, but still."

Lilli turned her head to Liam then, and she stared at the lines on his forehead as his eyebrows drew together with worry. Even though he was still overprotective, he had lost the dogmatic edge that used to drive her crazy. His 'pleases' sounded more like requests, and his 'don'ts' were now open to discussion. Though she knew he loved her as much as he ever had, she was glad to see that he had surrendered to the fact that he didn't and *couldn't* have control over everything. The humility in his eyes suited him.

"You know I love you, right?" she began, looking at him with tired but clear eyes.

"Of course I know that, Lilli. Why are you..."

"Because you have to let me go, Liam. No matter how this turns out, worrying about me can't be your full-time job anymore. In two days, all of our lives will change forever. You have to let me go."

The subtle urgency in her voice scared him so much he had to jam his hands in his pockets to keep them from shaking.

"What are you saying? Have you seen something? Is something going to happen?"

"Yes, but it's not what you think. I don't see myself dying," Lilli paused for a moment then, looking up at the ceiling as she let out a little chuckle. "I mean, I hope I don't die. That would really suck." Her laugh got louder until she noticed the ashen look on Liam's face.

"Liam, don't. I just mean things will be different. We'll need to... separate for a while."

"Lilli, you, me, and Alessandra are going to Mexico after this is all over. I won't leave without you," Liam answered in a shaky voice. "I won't," he whispered.

"Liam, it's not like that. I know you would never leave me behind. I…I can't explain. Just know that it's time and it's okay. I'll be seventeen next week, you know."

"What does your birthday have to do with anything? What are we even talking about?"

Lilli closed her eyes, too tired to regret the fact that she probably shouldn't have said anything to Liam about all the things she knew were coming. *I want to tell you. I just don't know how*, she thought. Letting out a sigh, she opened her eyes again and turned to him.

"Liam, please don't worry. That's the last thing I want you to do. Please, I'm just really tired. It's been a long day. You should go. Alessandra is waiting for you."

"She's just going through a few things with Tess. I told her I would walk you home before I came back for her."

"I love to see you with her," Lilli smiled sleepily. "Go on, I'm sure she's finished by now and is just as tired as I am."

Liam knew that was true. He could see the fatigue in Alessandra's eyes when he kissed her goodbye before he left the barn with Lilli. But he felt so conflicted, *so warned*, by her words that he felt frozen in place, unable to understand the meaning behind what she was trying to tell him.

He stood there for so long, staring at his workmanship in the floorboards, wondering what to do, that when he finally looked up, Lilli was fast asleep. Resigned to postpone his search for answers until morning, Liam quickly covered his sister with her blanket before locking the front door behind him and heading back to the barn for Alessandra.

●●··●●

The bonfire potluck to celebrate their last night at the commune had been Rachel and Marshall's idea, though to everyone's surprise, Eli took care of most of the cooking. With all the preparations checked and rechecked the night before, the day was filled with private pursuits as each person took the time they needed to say goodbye to the place they called home and to be with those who mattered most.

For Liam and Alessandra, it meant rising before the sun to make official what was already real in every other sense. When the sun broke through the horizon, Liam slipped his mother's wedding band onto Alessandra's hand in a ceremony that only included his sister to give him away and Marcus to walk Alessandra down the path from her quarters to the river. Afterwards, they shared a simple breakfast in Marcus' overheated cabin while listening and laughing as he told stories about his courtship with his wife, Evlyn, and how she made him wait three years before finally agreeing to marry him.

"You see, Alessandra, you are blessed. This one could have been like that!" Marcus laughed, pointing toward Liam as he ducked his head behind Alessandra's hair and shook his head in embarrassment. "But I knew God could only make one person as stubborn as my Evlyn. Praise God for that!"

When everyone had a chance to dry their tears of laughter, Marcus continued.

"When our son was born, I wanted to name him Ismail, after my grandfather, but Evlyn wouldn't hear of it. She wanted to name him Joel. Who even knows how she came up with that name, but she insisted. She just looked at me and said '*Marcus, when you carry the babies, you can name them.*' It was very much against tradition, but what could I say?"

"You know, you never talk about him, your son," Lilli began in a voice she hoped sounded a lot more casual than she felt. "What was he like as a child?" Listening to Marcus, Lilli realized that, though she knew a lot about Joel after his mother's death, she'd never seen what he was like as a carefree little boy.

"He was a wonderful child. Always laughing, always into mischief, but if you pulled him aside and talked to him, he would listen to what you had to say. Even as a baby, he was like that—watching you as if he understood every word you said.

"People used to say that I spoiled him because if he wasn't playing with his friends, he was with me, asking questions and getting in my way." Marcus paused for a moment, trying to control the overwhelming grief he always felt whenever he allowed himself to speak of his son.

"We used to eat from the same plate. No one could get him to eat a single piece of food if I didn't feed it to him... I miss him," he finished, "more than it is possible to say." Lilli fidgeted with her earring nervously as she kept her eyes on the small plate of grapes in front of her, trying to resist the urge to ease Marcus' pain with a truth he would not yet understand.

"I'm sorry, Marcus, I didn't mean to upset you," Lilli whispered as she got up from her seat at the small table to give him a hug. Liam had never heard Marcus speak of his son before that moment, and as he took in his struggle to keep the tears from rolling down his face, it was obvious why.

"No, no. I'm the one who is sorry," he said, patting Lilli gently on the back. "I didn't mean to tarnish this joyous occasion. I have a daughter to celebrate and a new son. Come, I want to make a toast. To the Bride and Groom - may nothing separate you from each other!" After raising his glass of orange juice, Liam took Alessandra's face into his hands and kissed her as if sealing the toast to make it true.

By the time Liam and Alessandra joined everyone for the bonfire, the sun had just set. Though the night would stay a cool 50 degrees, the heat from the fire reminded everyone of some of the commune's best summer night cook-outs. The laughter and stories came easily as food and drinks were passed and consumed at a leisurely pace. No one was in a hurry to rush what was already ending.

But as the night went on, the enormity of the task before them loomed like an unseen burden that weighed down each of their thoughts. Maura could see it happening as the hours passed, and she watched each of their lights grow dimmer with the crowding of heavy, muted colors.

"I can see your sadness," she finally admitted to the group. "Our sadness is growing the more we all try to hold it in. Please, if this is our last night together, let us be honest with each other one last time," she pleaded. When no one spoke, Maura grew frustrated, then bold as she stood up and continued.

"I am terrified something will happen to one of you tomorrow, and I'll never get the chance to say goodbye. I'm too afraid to do it now, but I am scared that if I don't, I won't get the chance. I never got to say goodbye to Kaido and Lucia and it hurts me to know this and not be able to stop myself from making the same mistake again with one of you." She sat down then, watching her friends nod and smile at her courage to admit at least some of what they were all feeling.

Tenzen spoke up next, though from what Maura could tell, he was the least affected of the group.

"I wouldn't say I'm sad, exactly. I guess I'm more anxious to know what will happen. Since I arrived here, I've learned to see so much. To not know the outcome of something so important is very…unsettling, I guess." Before speaking again, he looked over the fire to focus his attention on the non-Seers among them, with his attention finally settling on Marshall.

"But I would like to know something before we go. I'd like to know why all of the non-Seers, if you will, are doing this?" When the look of surprise on Marshall's face quickly turned to offense, Tenzen continued hurriedly.

"Wait, please, I don't mean to offend you. I mean, Eli, Liam, Eric, I understand, but the rest of you, you could just walk away. You don't have to put yourselves in danger for us. So, I would like to know, why would you do such a selfless thing for us?"

Having given Tenzen the chance to finish his question, Marshall understood how out of place their level of commitment must have seemed, especially given his initial reaction to the Seers. There really was no reason beyond loyalty and friendship that could explain his actions, but those happened to be the only two reasons that mattered to him.

"When the first of you showed up," Marshall began, "Well, as many of you know, I was a little less than welcoming."

The air began to rumble with laughter as Rachel rolled her eyes at the understatement.

"All right, I'll admit, I was an ass–okay?" All the Seers erupted in applause then, prompting Marshall to raise his cup in a toast before continuing. "At the time, I didn't know you. Didn't understand what you were or what you'd been through. Since you arrived, you've all given so much to this place. I've always been a soldier and I always will be, but it's been a long time since I felt like there was something to really fight for in this world. A cause that I could be sure I was on the right side of. Seeing you all, getting to know you like I do now, you've given that back to me. I finally know where I'm supposed to be.

As Tenzen looked around the bonfire, he could see that the sentiment Marshall expressed resonated deeply with each of the people there in spite of their diverse backgrounds. When he turned back to Marshall, his voice almost faltered with gratitude for their willingness to accept him, someone they barely knew, but Tenzen made himself heard, "Then it is truly my honor to stand with you tomorrow."

Marshall didn't respond as he drew Rachel into his embrace and enjoyed the sight of his friends and family smiling and laughing with each other one last time.

They headed out at midnight, in groups of three or four to a car, bound for Chicago. Liam had mapped out five different routes to the Purification Center that would keep their journey conspicuous while allowing them all to arrive at roughly the same time, with no more than three cars traveling any one route. Only Eli and Jean took the train in order to send last minute details and information to Hanna and Kyle while en route.

Once in Chicago, they would all make their way to a warehouse that had been recently abandoned by a failed shipping supply company. Marshall and Liam arranged to rent the place for a month for that specific day and purpose. In addition to being a large open space that allowed them to hide and switch their vehicles for the raid, the facility was situated less than one mile away from the Purification Center and was at an ideal location for crossing into the facility's southern border.

Liam, Alessandra, Lilli, and Marcus were the first to arrive and helped everyone else get into the flak jackets, weapons carriers, and other equipment they would need. By 6:58am they had all loaded into the five armored white vans that Marshall had procured for them and were inches from crossing into the Purification Center.

"Are you ready for this?" Liam asked Alessandra quietly as he took her hand in his. They watched in silence through the windshield as Eric and Jared used their mirrored deflectors to disarm a small section of the electronic fence that guarded their side of the perimeter.

"As ready as I'm ever going to be to return to this place."

Liam turned to her and nodded in silent understanding while they waited for Eric and Jared to come back into the van.

"All right then, here we go," Liam said a little louder as he put his foot on the gas and passed from neutral territory right into a trap.

CHAPTER 25: SURRENDER

"The tall, lanky boy is attractive," Crane mumbled absently as he watched the South Wing monitor from Andreas' antique blue velvet loveseat.

Crane's comment disturbed Andreas' concentration enough to warrant only the briefest sideways glance, just enough to register his disgust before turning back to the monitor. He immediately resumed counting the number of people that were coming from the five white vans that their intruders parked along the tree line that divided the courtyard from the wooded areas. Sweat covered his brow as he realized that he had no idea how many of the fifty-one people he counted were Seers.

"They're well-armed," Andreas whispered into the tense air of his office as he watched them unload several hundred pounds of guns, projectiles, and ammunition from their trucks. No person, it seemed, was left without a weapon.

"Yes, well, so are we," Crane replied curtly, as he reached over the couch armrest to pick up the phone and give the order for the Guild's Toronto Security Force to strike.

The confidence Crane displayed at that moment was in sharp contrast to the terror he felt eight days before when he woke up clutching his face in panic from a dream in which he saw the face of a young girl with dirty blond hair, appearing to him in his office while he worked late. In the dream, her form was like a mirage drawing closer. Looking into her piercing hazel eyes, he was instantly afraid. Somehow, she knew who he was and had come for no other purpose than to destroy him. As she blew her ice-cold breath over his face, he felt his skin begin to burn and peel away, leaving only charred bone and agony in her wake. Before he could ask who she was and how she knew him, she was gone, leaving him shaken and sweaty in his bed.

Unaccustomed to being on the receiving end of fear, the morning after his dream, Crane called for the closest Purification Center to send reinforcements immediately, without giving an explanation to Andreas or anyone else. He'd also requested that the search to find Marcus and the others be extended to more of the Guild's Purification Centers, effectively doubling the number of Seers that had ever been focused on this task alone. Though it seemed paranoid at the time, each Purification Center honored his request out of loyalty and acknowledgement of his many past accomplishments as a leader within the Guild. After his request, Toronto's reinforcements had come quickly, but Crane's confidence was not fully restored until he verified that the girl from his dream had not come out of one of the vans.

"Not yet," Andreas rasped, trying to work his voice around the dryness in his throat. "Don't call them yet. Our security should be able to handle it if this is all of them. If not, then we'll have more reinforcements."

"Andreas, you can't possibly be afraid of this little band of children..." Crane chided as the nervousness he thought he'd left behind crept back up his spine. *If this is all of them...*

Andreas shifted his condescending gaze across his desk and would have smirked at the twitch he saw in Crane's brow if he felt he had the time. Instead, he turned his attention back to the monitor before he spoke. "I've known you a long time, Crane. I'm nervous for the same reason you are. Nothing like this has ever happened before. We don't know what…"

Before Andreas could finish his sentence, the visual feed on the monitor went completely black.

Crane reached the phone first, dialing the security station in such a rush he didn't wait for someone to pick up before he started shouting.

"What the hell is going on? Why aren't the monitors working?"

"I'm sorry, sir," the security technician sputtered. "We've lost the link to our cameras. They seem to be operating fine, but something is jamming our signal. We can't get anything down here, either."

Having launched himself from behind his desk, Andreas grabbed the phone from Crane and put the technician on speakerphone. After having the technician repeat his explanation, Andreas was silent for a moment as he tried to process how the technician's description of events could even be possible.

"That doesn't make sense. You're more than 30 feet below ground. They didn't unload anything that could have carried the electromagnetic pulse necessary to jam us."

"I know. I know, sir. We can't locate the jamming signal; there's nothing around for miles that could have done this."

Crane and Andreas stared at each other in silence then, listening to the frantic background noise in the security room as people scrambled to bring their cameras back online. Andreas was the first to release himself from their silent exchange. From the frozen expression on Crane's face, Andreas could tell that Crane could no longer see him. It was as if his colleague had suddenly been stricken with the fear of something far beyond Andreas' reach. For the first time in all the years that Andreas had known him, he realized that Crane would be of no use.

"Call us back when you have a solution. Until then, tell all of our security to engage them in the courtyard. Now. Keep the Toronto guard on standby, watching the Seers until I give the order."

"They're almost here," Marcus said to Liam just before the Seers began to quorum. Unlike the early days when several minutes were required to achieve the meditative state they needed, the connection between them now was so strong that visioning was almost instant.

Liam didn't have time to give him the thumbs up before he could see the first glimmer of their shield coming into place. The wind and the heat it generated — though greatly diminished from the first time they experienced it — still necessitated a safe distance from anyone who was not inside the Quorum. From where he stood almost 50 feet away from the Quorum, Liam turned behind him to check the positions of each person in their group before speaking into his earpiece.

"Lilli is inside. She's making her way through the underground levels now. She jammed their cameras so they should be coming out soon, just like Marcus said. She'll let me know when she has the Seers."

"How do you even know that, man? I thought Lilli wasn't on our link," Marshall whispered into his earpiece as he crouched down beside Rachel.

"I just hear her. In my head. I can't explain it any better than that," Liam sighed.

"She's full of surprises, isn't she?"

Liam didn't answer as he looked out toward the Quorum again to see if he could make out Alessandra's form inside the glow from their force field. If he squinted really hard, he thought he could just make out her body's outline at the center of the line, holding hands with Tess, but he couldn't be sure.

No one can touch her there. No one, he reminded himself, as he extended his focus out to the large white limestone building in front of them. It had been Lilli's idea to jump out of the van as soon as Eric and Jared breeched the fence. To him, the edifice looked like an art museum, someplace that valued and nurtured beautiful things. Under normal circumstances, it would never be a place that would make him fear for his sister's life. He barely had time to consider the irony before he noticed the first troops advancing from behind the glass doors and on top of the roof.

"Marshall's team, you take the roof. We'll get the ground level. Go!"

As soon as he gave the order, the sound of gunfire and rockets launching was deafening. But they only had time to fire the first round of their assault before Liam saw the first troops crumple in pain. Some dropped their guns and staggered around holding their heads while others clung to their guns in defiance, firing aimlessly as they tried to kill what was invading their minds. But Liam knew their bullets would be useless. He could see the sparks as their ammunition ricocheted off the line of Seers.

Alessandra, he thought. *She's showing them.*

He had offered many times, while she and Tess practiced, to be their test subject, but each time Alessandra had refused. *"You don't want to see what I've seen,"* she had said softly as she walked away from him the way she often needed to after one of their practice sessions. Looking at the agony on the men's and women's faces as they clawed off their clothes and exposed themselves, frantically trying to rid themselves of the nightmares that were invading their minds, Liam finally believed her.

"What will you show them?" Liam had asked Alessandra the first night her nightmares came back.

"Consequences. I will show them the consequences of their actions."

●•···•●

From their window, Crane and Andreas could not escape how utterly outmatched they were.

We are defenseless, Crane shuddered, as he began to step away from the sight in front of him: Seers wrapped in light, deflecting bullets, safely inside an impenetrable space as they crippled their entire security force. As soon as he saw the anguish on the guard's faces, he knew who was to blame, though he could not fathom how she had managed to push her private horrors into the minds of the soldiers, without aid, without Luridium, with only the people around her.

She must have known it would be more painful for us to stand by helplessly, he thought, as he tried to understand why he and Andreas had not been afflicted. *Can she control it, or is it the group together that holds this power?*

Everything Crane thought he knew about Seers and the limits of their gifts was being negated before him. But even in his fear, Crane found a place in his mind to envy the man he knew was among them and marvel at how Marcus had managed to unleash the wealth of power he had been so content to sample in tea cups.

In his daze, Crane felt Andreas rush past him toward the phone and heard him order the use of the Toronto guard, all the while thinking that the effort was in vain. His feet moved faster than he thought capable as he retreated to his office, in terror of what was to come. He didn't look back to see why Andreas had returned to the window and was now shouting his name. Instead, he barricaded himself in his seldom-used office, huddling as he lit the fire to keep him from a chill that he'd never felt before.

But from down the long hallway that separated Crane's office from Andreas', it seemed as if the tide was turning. Andreas watched in some unstable mix of disbelief and elation as he saw the light that had surrounded the large Quorum begin to break apart until he could make out the image of Marcus stumbling, then collapsing to the ground, as Alessandra ran toward him. The other Seers looked completely shocked as their eyes moved from Marcus to the small army standing less than twenty feet away from them, recovering from their torture and slowly reaching for their weapons.

●●··●●

"Marcus! Oh God, please. Marcus!"

It all happened so fast.

We were fine. We were fine! Alessandra thought, as she tried to make sense of why Marcus was lying on the ground, struggling to breathe. *And then I could feel it–the instant his coughing turned to choking and his mucus turned to blood, and I couldn't stop it. I couldn't stop it.*

The moment Alessandra sensed Marcus' pain, her vision was drawn to it, becoming more detailed, more acute, until it shook her and Tess apart, breaking the barrier that had kept the Quorum from seeing what Alessandra and Tess unleashed onto their enemies. Without this barrier and focus, Alessandra's insight into Marcus' suffering was poured out into the Quorum. The combination of their understanding of Marcus' pain and his own inability to remain connected to the group caused their focus to falter and their Quorum to dissolve until they were completely exposed and under attack.

Once their shield was down, the ground assault team sprang into action. Taking advantage of the momentary disorientation of the Guild's troops, they ran to pull each Seer into the shelter of their makeshift barricades while Liam and Alessandra carried Marcus to safety.

They'd barely reached Liam's post before the shooting resumed. As Alessandra shielded Marcus' body with her own, Liam and the others fired everything they had at the guard in front of them. Though they had chosen their positions carefully, they were outnumbered by more than 20. The rocket launchers and grenades would keep the Guild's troops at bay, but only for so long.

As Alessandra waited for Eli to make his way to them, she hovered over Marcus, tilting his head to the side in an effort to let some of the blood pour from his mouth. When Eli arrived, he struggled to open his medic's kit without getting burned from the exhaust every time Liam fired a rocket. He barely had time to position his scalpel for the tracheotomy he'd planned before Alessandra stilled his hand. Looking up at her in confusion, Eli quickly found the reason behind her gesture as he followed her eyes toward the tanks that were rolling toward them from behind.

"Liam!" Eli shouted as he caught hold of the leg of his pants. "We're not going to make it."

Liam's first thought was of Lilli, still inside, as he turned from the building he was facing to see a row of tanks advancing just before they became obscured behind a blazing wall of fire that advanced from left to right beside a man who was running with his head turned back and his right arm stretched out toward the flames. Behind him was a group of fifteen others Liam had never seen before. Men and women with their hands extended out in every direction. Their movements were effortlessly synchronized with the sounds of tanks exploding, people screaming and glass shattering behind them. Every member of the commune was dumb-struck as they watched their group become encased and protected behind three walls of fire. The only route that was not burning was the route to their vans, the route to their escape.

Once safely surrounded, seven within the group broke off and began to form a new line where the Quorum once stood. It was only then that one of the members of the newly-arrived group turned to face the others. A small, stout woman with light brown eyes situated in a round, dark face looked directly at Katia as she spoke in a calm but urgent voice: "Please, we are not safe. They will see if we do not Quorum. Join us." Though no one knew them, the intent and meaning of her words were immediately understood and the Seers hurried to their feet to join them.

Through all the commotion, Liam did not take his eyes off the man he was sure had started this. The man he *knew* had somehow led this group of strangers who came out of nowhere to help them. The man he watched did not turn around until Liam heard the last of the five tanks explode. When he did, Liam knew immediately who he was, who he had to be, running toward them again with a face and form so much like his father.

By now Lilli could feel him near. It made it hard for her to stay focused in the way she needed to, in the way he'd taught her was most important. Passing through the underground levels undetected had been easier than she thought. There was so much frenzy over what was happening outside that she had slipped past without a single soul even sensing her presence.

But once she reached the fourth floor, she knew things would be different. The 4th floor was primarily residential, where the Seers private quarters were situated. Given the designated purpose of the floor and the quiet isolation Lilli knew the Guild's Seers lived in, she had expected a more subdued atmosphere. But when she reached the stairwell door leading to the fourth floor hallway, she was surprised to hear a series of pounding noises calling her forward. As she peeked around the corner from the stairwell, she could see that the wide hallway was clear, with eight guards quietly sweating through their stoic facades. The pounding noises grew louder as she stepped further into the hallway. Standing there, hidden in light, Lilli could make out the sounds of flesh pounding, slapping and banging against heavy oak, trapped on the inside, trying desperately to come to what was calling them. She felt their pull like a magnet, just as she knew they felt hers. The closer she got to them, the more she realized that the attraction between herself and the Seers was centered around the energy radiating from her body.

It's the Luridium, she thought. *It's the metal in the Luridium that's moving them toward me.* Standing in the middle of the corridor with four guards behind and four in front, she decided to make her presence known. She could only imagine the pain the Seers would be in as all their veins pulsed violently against the tender barrier of their skin, blood rushing forward, wanting out.

She appeared to the guards literally out of thin air, as the light around her waxed and waned until she was three-dimensional and real. Before they could recover from their shock, Lilli had already lifted all eight men into the air and hurled their bodies down the hall, zigzagging them back and forth against the corridor walls as they flew, rendering them unconscious before they each hit the other end of the hall and collapsed, piled high on the floor.

Once she was sure they would not get up, she focused on the sounds of pounding hands and scratching nails as she rolled back the locks on their doors. Lilli was silent as she offered a small smile of comfort, acknowledging the relief she saw on their faces as they came out one-by-one and surrounded her. There were no words needed or spoken as she walked through the small crowd of Seers and prepared to head to the sixth floor, where she knew Crane and Andreas would be.

Just as she reached the intersection to the corridor that would take them left and up the internal stairwell, Lilli felt Joel's presence near, as if he was standing right next to her. The feeling made her tremble as it always did whenever he was so close. Even though she could barely afford to, she couldn't help but close her eyes for a moment and imagine she could hear the soft intake of breath he would make just before he spoke directly to her thoughts.

Love, we've run out of time. You need to take the others and leave now.

But I'm almost there, Joel. I have them now. I can do this. Wait for me.

I know you can. I know you can, but they have seen what we can do. They are retreating; they will destroy the building, the evidence. They've already begun. There won't be enough time for you to go after them and come out safely. It doesn't happen this way. Please, trust me. You must come now.

Lilli opened her eyes in defeat as she nodded her head in understanding. She could see his vision in their shared thoughts. She knew he was right, but the thought of leaving things so unfinished made her inexplicably angry. From where she stood frozen in place, she was suddenly keenly aware of Crane and Andreas' presence, with one awash in gratitude for his pending escape and the other cowering in his office paralyzed by an image — an image of her.

Lilli acted without a thought. Though she'd done it many times in visioning, she'd never thought to project herself out in the present, but the act came as naturally to her as her anger as she sought out the one whom Maura had told her was worse than all the others.

He knew she was coming. Though he had not seen her and could not verify her presence there or anywhere else, he knew she was real as he sat at his desk, bug-eyed and staring at the door, waiting for her to come in.

"Crane, I'm coming to get you in two minutes. We have to go! Did you hear me? We have to leave now! Why the hell aren't you here, anyway? We can't get in touch with any of the Guards who were watching the Seers. Thank God you sent Michael and Nina to Deidra for safe-keeping. I think we've lost the others."

Andreas' voice over the intercom was like a lifeline of control over a rushing water of panic. Though Crane appreciated the solace Andreas was trying to offer him, he could not be reached from where he sat as the air began to shimmer in front of his desk just before his angel of death appeared.

"Have mercy," he whispered with trembling lips, as he fell out of his chair and onto his knees. Frantically, he scurried under his desk in a feeble attempt to hide. But the image of her face went straight through the desk where he huddled, and came to hover at his side in condemnation.

"I know who you are. We will come back for you. We will come back for you," she whispered in a voice so soft and certain that the words made the tip of his left ear feel on fire.

Then she was gone.

He screamed as he covered his ears and tried to shut out the ice-cold fear he felt at hearing her words and the taste of the bitter judgment he knew was coming.

●●···●●

Even though she was deep inside the building, Joel Akida could feel her drawing nearer and nearer as she ran to him. He would have smiled at what she'd done, the warning she could not resist sending, but his father lay dying in his arms. Outside of her safety, he could think of nothing else.

Marcus had refused the tracheotomy as soon as he'd seen the figure of his son appear over his body. Though Marcus was grateful for this vision of Joel all grown up, he was sure it meant the end had come and his son was now an angel coming to take him back to his wife, finally home again. The warm touch of Joel's hand startled Marcus back into his own body, choking as he grasped and clutched for his son's hands. Marcus could only mouth the words 'how,' as the tears fell down his face.

"It was my friend Kweku. They didn't get me, Baba. I tried to tell you, but you were screaming so loud. They never got me. I'm here."

The pain in his lungs was completely inconsequential as Marcus struggled to sit up, to reach his son's face and wipe the tears he saw there.

My son! My son!

He tried to turn his head slightly to spit out the blood that was coming too fast, so that he could call out to his son one last time, but the effort proved beyond him as his body convulsed in pain.

"Wait, Baba. I can do it now. I can lift you. Here. Here," Joel said in his soft British accent as he lifted his father, bracing Marcus' back against his bent knee while he brought his father's hand to his cheek. The blood-stained smile that appeared on Marcus' face when he covered his father's hand with his own made Joel's body feel like it would break apart with the overwhelming regret he felt.

As Eli moved towards Marcus to attempt the tracheotomy once more, Joel met his eyes and shook his head before returning back to his father's gaze.

"It's too late for that now. It's not just his lungs. All the soft tissue in his body is deteriorating," Joel explained as his voice trembled around the words.

"How do you kn-" Eli began.

"Because this is how it happens. This is the vision I woke to when I was nine, and I knew I needed to find him, to help make sure his sacrifice was worth it." Bringing his father's face closer to him, he spoke to Marcus in desperate whispers as he stroked the lines that covered the face that he knew so well.

"You have saved us, Baba. You have. I love you, Baba. I love you," he sobbed as he crushed Marcus' dying body to his chest.

Though Joel had seen this exact moment in his mind countless times, he knew by now the vision of things was nothing like the experience. Even after ten years of carrying it, Joel was still so unprepared to let his father go only moments after he'd found him.

As he heard his father's coughing and sputtering increase, Joel could feel the energy his father was expending unconsciously to heal himself for the last time. Carefully, he loosened his grip on Marcus and propped him up again against his knee.

This is it, Joel thought in agony, just as he felt the one person who could possibly help him survive the moment slide her small hands across his back as she knelt down beside him.

Marcus' eyes grew wide with understanding as he saw Lilli draw his son to her side. Though Joel's broad shoulders should have overpowered her, Marcus marveled at how exactly right they were together.

As Marcus watched them, the explosives meant to destroy any evidence of the Guild's activities detonated. The sky overhead lit up with orange and red flames and flying debris that did not descend as the complex began to crumble around them. The sound of the explosion roared at a level that was frightening, but still too low to make sense given their proximity to the building that was quickly being reduced to ash and black smoke.

Inside the cocoon that protected them, while all the commune members looked up and around in amazement at the burning debris suspended forty feet over their heads, those that came with Joel knew how they were being protected and looked at him with quiet gratitude as he said goodbye to his father.

"Joel. My son," Marcus sighed as he returned his gaze from the burning orange turned black-grey sky to the eyes that held his most sacred wish come true. Feeling the last bit of life drain from him, Marcus felt immeasurable peace as he closed his eyes and surrendered the only struggle he never thought he'd win.

Chapter 26: Goodbye...for now

They needed to move. Everyone knew it; Joel knew it, but he couldn't bring himself to release the lifeless man he held so tightly in his arms. And so the others worked around him, as quietly as they could to gather their weapons and return to their vehicles before the smoke cleared and revealed their position. In the end, the trio that hovered over Marcus' body was the last to leave the inferno after Eli reluctantly approached Joel and placed his hand gently on Marcus' head.

"I'm sorry, but we need to go. We can't wait any longer."

Joel nodded his understanding and moved to his feet, lifting his father in his arms. While the Seers that came with Joel left to retrieve their cars, Eli guided him to the nearest van where Liam helped to get Marcus' body in and secured along the rubber corrugated floor.

"I'm sorry," Liam said, as he watched Joel climb into the van. "He was...an amazing person."

Joel met Liam's sincere eyes briefly in an effort to acknowledge his condolences, but he couldn't speak the gratitude he felt for Liam's sympathy. Knowing they would want to be with Marcus, Liam held the door open as Lilli, Alessandra, Maura, and Katia climbed in after Joel.

Leaving behind the burning remains of the Purification Center, the fact that they had won a great victory was barely a thought amongst them as the vans rambled back to the warehouse. The elation they should have felt in escaping with their lives was completely overshadowed by the heavy cloak of sorrow, grief, and quiet tears that could be seen on every face that knew Marcus.

"How could this have happened? He was fine. He was fine," Alessandra whispered to herself, trying to make sense of what she felt just before Marcus collapsed.

Seeing her anguish, Joel swallowed hard, trying to loosen the ache in his throat enough to answer the girl who obviously cared so deeply for his father.

"To block so many, to absorb all the energy that he did in order to keep our plans secret… He didn't know how to channel it, to release it. He just held it in until his body couldn't heal fast enough. He would never have lasted this long if he didn't have this gift… but he couldn't sustain it, not with so many trying to get in."

"But there were over thirty of us," Alessandra pleaded. "He wasn't alone."

"Yes, but he always took on more of his share than he ever let on. No one could block like him. He knew that. If he didn't keep up the constant blocking that he did, you all would have been found by now. He would never have let that happen while his body could withstand it."

"Withstand what? I don't understand? What did this to him?"

"The same energy that protects us allows us to do all the things we do. We're not the only ones who have it. The Guild Seers have it, too, but it's muted because of the drugs. They are never fully engaged, but when they vision, they tap into the same energy that we do. When we block them, we absorb that energy. If you don't know how to channel it outward, it can be too much for our bodies. You get tired. You need to rest. All of you have experienced this.

"My father's ability to heal made his recovery almost instantaneous, so much so that he could take the burden off other Seers who could not withstand it otherwise. But today they had more than 140 Seers all focused on destroying us and they would have, but he made sure they only took him."

"I should have done more," Katia blurted out through her own sobs as Maura tried to comfort her. "I let him die. He was so good to us and I let him die!" she moaned before her tears kept her from speaking.

"No!" Joel said as forcefully as he could. "You mustn't think that. There was nothing any of you could have done."

The words came out of Alessandra's mouth before she had time to consider them.

"But you knew..."

By the time she caught herself, it was too late. Joel looked away from Alessandra in shame, even as Lilli tried to pull him closer.

"It's okay," he began. "You can say it. Why didn't I do anything about it? Why didn't I come to him, or at least warn him?"

His soft brown eyes bore witness to the conflict he'd felt inside ever since he was barely more than a boy.

"I'm sorry. I know he was your father. I just…" Alessandra tried to push the feeling out of her mind that somehow things could have been different, but she couldn't. Even as she realized that though she could see it, she never could change the future.

Looking up at Joel with fresh tears, she suddenly understood why all his insight didn't make a damn bit of difference.

"You couldn't change it, could you? Even though you knew?"

Lilli finished what she knew Joel couldn't say, what she knew would never fully be reconciled in his heart.

"None of us would be here if he had tried. If Marcus had even the slightest idea that Joel was still alive, he would have been consumed with trying to find him. What Marcus did, what Marcus started in all of us, none of it would have happened.

"When Joel first found out his father was alive, he tried to reach him, but nothing worked. Everything got in his way until he was old enough to realize that the purpose of his sight was not to change the future, but to figure out his role in it—to help his father fulfill his destiny."

For Joel, listening to Lilli's words, so succinct and perfect as they described what had taken him almost all his nineteen years to come to, was a strange kind of relief. It all sounded so simple coming out of his beloved's mouth. He almost believed it but for the pain that never left him—the helplessness he felt even now that it was over.

In order to accommodate Marcus' body and give Joel some privacy, the other vans were overcrowded with everyone else from the commune and the new Seers they had rescued. As they pulled into the warehouse, they were only slightly surprised to see the same Seers that had arrived with Joel waiting for them. By the time they all poured out of the vehicles, their legs were cramped and their minds were overflowing with questions about the Seers who had saved them and how any of what they had witnessed was possible.

The silence as they watched each other was awkward and thick with cautious fascination. The only presence of fear came from the Guild's Seers who huddled together as they looked around, both grateful and frightened to be someplace new. Seeing the tension from where she sat in the van, Lilli leaned closer to whisper in Joel's ear.

"Joel..."

The warmth of her breath on his skin got his attention immediately and he looked up from his father into her steady eyes before following them out of their now open van to see the tense gathering before him. Understanding what needed to be done, he kissed his father on the head softly, covered Marcus with his jacket, and then took Lilli's hand before stepping out into the crowd.

"I believe some introductions are needed. I am Joel Akida, Marcus' son, and these are my friends, other Seers like some of you who I've found over the last three years. They are here to help you, just as I am… to join my father's cause."

Joel was encouraged to see how his explanation seemed to ease some of the group members' hesitation, as their eyes darted from him to those who had come with him.

"Thank you for your help today," Eli said as he approached Joel, extending his hand. "I don't know how we would have gotten out of there in one piece if you all hadn't shown up!"

"It was our purpose to arrive in time," Joel said softly as he shook Eli's hand.

As if on cue, the Seers he'd come with began to move forward, extending their hands and introducing themselves to the others.

Nodding his approval at their groups coming together, Eli turned from the introductions back to Joel.

"How did you find us? No one saw you…"

Eli's voice trailed off as he noticed that Joel's other hand was clasped together with Lilli's as they stood with their arms pressed against each other. *Maybe some of us did,* he thought, as he took in Lilli's shy smile.

"She kept my secret. It was…necessary," Joel offered apologetically.

Having ridden in the van with Marshall, Eli didn't understand what Joel meant, but he also knew that it was not the time to press. *His father just died,* he reminded himself. He trusted that there would be a time and place for his questions to be answered.

"Your father was a great man. I am so sorry for your loss," Eli added sincerely.

"Thank you," Joel whispered as he averted his eyes. The pain was far too close for the comfort of condolences.

"Oh!" Joel said, grateful for the sudden distraction. "Before I forget, you'll need this to help with the recovery of the Guild's Seers. This should expedite the purging of the Luridium from their bodies." Eli watched as Joel gathered a thin tan cord from around his neck and drew it up until he pulled a small pouch from inside his shirt and handed it to him.

"It will be…more painful at first, but it will accelerate their recovery and disable their tracking signal within a few days, but it must be administered as soon as possible."

Eli stared back at Joel for a few seconds before unzipping the pouch and removing one of the thin vials of brown liquid. He held it up to the light briefly before looking back at Joel with more questions that needed to be answered.

"Where did you get this?"

Joel took a moment to draw in a deep breath, willing himself to override the natural distrust he had in everyone and everything. *I can trust him,* he reminded himself. *These people are safe.*

"Dr. Chandra and Dr. Assad made it. They have been helping me… prepare for this day."

Eli was stunned. The last time he saw Neva Chandra and Hasaam Assad was the night after their friend, Willem Knight, was murdered. They'd met in the alley behind their alma mater and exchanged what little they knew of the fate of others on their team before parting. Eli had not seen or heard from them since. He had assumed they were either dead or captured, like so many others.

"Neva and Hasaam are alive?"

"Very much so. They have continued the work that you began together. They're based in London now. I found them about 5 years ago. When I told them what my father would do, they began working on this treatment so that when others escaped, we could help them."

Eli's mind was spinning. There was so much he wanted to say, so many competing curiosities and questions, but he tried to focus on the most pressing issues as he formed his next sentence.

"But we shouldn't need this. Hanna was deleting their tracking frequencies while we were on our way here… unless she wasn't successful."

"No. No," Joel explained. "She's already finished, but any changes to their database are backed up during the night. In a last minute decision, Andreas ordered last night's files to be sent to the Guild's main headquarters when he initiated the evacuation. Although many of their files were corrupted thanks to Lilli, it will take them less than a week to recover the data. The Luridium will need to be out of their bodies by then."

"I see," was all Eli could manage. His movements were slowed by all the questions that raced through his mind as he replaced the vial in its pouch and put it around his neck.

"I know you have many questions, too many for me to answer now, but when the week is up, the Seers will be well enough to travel. I have arranged a plane for you. It will meet you in Iowa and take you and the Seers to London. Neva and Hasaam will meet you there and explain more," Joel continued.

"But what about their appearance?" Eli asked, pointing to the group of frightened Seers. "It will take months to clear and we don't have papers for them..."

"These things have all been arranged. It's a private plane, Eli. They will not ask any questions."

"I see," Eli said again as he walked away, lost in his own thoughts.

Even though he knew they were nowhere near the end of the day, Joel felt exhausted as he drew Lilli closer to him, letting the edges of her blunt bangs tickle his neck just like he dreamt they would.

Marshall waited as long as he could, trying to be sensitive and patient as he helped unload the vans while working hard not to stare. After Eli and Joel finished their conversation and he broke away from Lilli's embrace, Joel joined the bustling around the warehouse as everyone helped to unload weapons from the vans and put them back into the cars they'd driven from Iowa before changing clothes and finalizing plans for their escape. Though some would be returning to the commune to help the Guild's Seers through the worst of their withdrawal from the Luridium, most would not.

With every heavy gun he unloaded, Marshall could see Joel's face relax into the exertion of his work. It made him feel a little better about what he knew he couldn't keep himself from doing. At the first chance Marshall had to get close enough for eye-to-eye contact with Joel, all his questions came spilling out.

"How did you do all that? I mean, you came out of nowhere like...I don't even know..." Marshall could barely get his thoughts together to comprehend what he'd just witnessed.

"What I did was nothing more than you would have done if you'd known you could do it," Joel replied quietly.

Marshall thought he had been prepared to hear anything in response to his question, but he hadn't been prepared for something so simple and utterly absurd.

"What? Last I checked I couldn't incinerate a whole line of tanks with my bare hands!"

"You can...and if you give yourself half the chance, you will."

Joel busied himself with packing up the last of their ammunition while he waited for Marshall's next question. When the silence stretched on longer than he expected, he looked up to find a bewildered Marshall, too stunned to speak. Joel nodded his head in understanding before heading back to his work.

"The Seers," Joel began, "we're only the first to show these abilities, but there is nothing special about us. Our bodies, our minds are just the first to return to a more original state, to re-establish a connection that never should have been broken."

Handing the last crate to Tenzen, Joel turned to face Marshall before he continued.

"You, me, we all must learn to reestablish that connection to everything that is our birthright."

While Marshall was still speechless, Eli, who had been eavesdropping on their conversation since it began, spoke up as he made a path to where Joel stood.

"What are you saying, Joel? We never found any evidence to suggest that any other people have the ability to do what you can do."

"Yes, I know, but remember, your research was interrupted before you had time to truly understand what you were seeing. Neva and Hasaam have been able to continue the work you started in secret, since the time your team was disbanded. They can explain it more scientifically than I can. I just know what I feel. But what you think of as a genetic marker is not actually unique to us. Every human has it; it's just that for us, those chromosomes are active, while in others they remain dormant. We all have this potential." Joel shook his head in sympathy as he saw people gather around, looking more and more perplexed with every word he spoke.

I wish we had more time for this. They need to know so much. It just can't happen here. Not now. Trusting in what he knew would come, Joel turned his attention back to Eli.

"When you go to London and speak with Neva and the others, you'll understand much more."

"But what do you mean 'birthright'? What birthright?" Jared asked apprehensively. Thinking of Marcus, cold and lifeless, it was hard to view their gift as anything more than a curse, even if it *had* saved most of them.

"Have you never wondered about the source of our gift? Where it comes from? Why we have it? Our birthright is our ability to connect with the God that created us, the source and power that gave us life — the one thing that makes everything else possible.

"Our whole beings are designed for this connection and yet we have lost it. The Seers are the first to have that connection restored, but we won't be the last."

The look of skepticism that cinched Jared's smooth features was almost immediate. Joel knew the expression well from countless other conversations he'd had with people who struggled to reconcile his words with traditional notions of what God and whose God he might be referring to. In the interest of time, Joel decided to answer Jared's silent question aloud.

"What you call Him does not matter," Joel answered. "It's the connection that is important."

"But…" Rachel began before Vincent interrupted.

"Look, that's all well and good, but we don't have time for God right now. We need to get the hell out of here while we still can," Vincent announced with more than a little impatience in his voice. Turning to Joel, he asked, "How are you guys planning to get out of here?"

"We'll drive our own cars. Alma, Henry, and I will return to the commune with you, if that's all right."

"Of course it is," Lilli urged as she took Joel's hand. "I'll come with you."

Before Liam could express the anxiety she knew he would feel watching his kid sister walk off with a total stranger, she turned to her brother and added, "We'll follow you, Liam. We'll meet you at Fox River."

As soon as the declaration was made, all around him Liam could hear the hurried sounds of quick goodbyes and car doors slamming as the members of the only family he had prepared to scatter in every direction. Liam could only return the nod Lilli and Joel gave him before they turned and walked out of the warehouse, with Lilli tucked securely under Joel's arm. They didn't speak a word from what Liam could tell as they walked away, but Liam caught the look they shared when they turned their heads toward each other. Liam wasn't sure how, but he understood then that Lilli knew this man he had never seen before — she knew him well enough to love him. From the way Joel held her close, Liam could also see that Joel felt the same.

With only four cars headed back to the commune, Liam felt like the drive took half the time it did when they all headed to Chicago. Along the way, he consciously replayed all his favorite memories of him and Lilli together, trying to stamp down the fear that they would all be somehow taken from him the moment they crossed over into Iowa. In between his reminiscing, Liam told himself that he kept checking the rearview to make sure they weren't being followed, but Alessandra knew otherwise.

"They're right behind us, Liam, just like she promised. You know Lilli would never leave without saying goodbye. She loves you just as much as you love her."

Liam couldn't speak, so he kept his eyes on the road as he squeezed Alessandra's hand in his lap.

When they finally arrived at the commune, everyone helped Eli administer the serum Joel brought for the Seers before getting them changed into hospital gowns that could be easily discarded when the inevitable vomiting, fever, night sweats, and diarrhea took hold.

After they were sedated and as comfortable as possible, Alessandra looked around to find that Liam and Lilli had slipped out of the clinic. Heading toward the front door, her face broke into a sad smile as she watched her husband try to put forth a brave face as his little sister prepared to move on without him.

"Joel and I need to go away for a while. We'll be returning to Tanzania to bury Marcus," Lilli began softly, as she stood in front of her brother.

Returning? He wondered. *Has she been there with him already? Maybe in the past…*

"I know," Liam said as he nodded stiffly. "You'll need to leave soon to preserve the body for the trip."

Liam's efforts to be strong, to not cry, broke Lilli's heart and made her own tears fall.

"Are you sure about him, Lilli? I mean, how long have you known him?"

"All my life, it seems. I can't explain it. We're a part of each other."

Watching Lilli and Joel move about the clinic as he had done for the last hour made it hard for him to disagree with her. Seeing how they moved together in an unconscious dance, Liam had the strange notion that Joel had somehow always been with Lilli, almost as if he was a shadow in Lilli's life that Liam was somehow just noticing for the first time.

"I know. I think…I can see that. It's just…hard for me, Lilli. I don't even know him and you want me to just…"

When Lilli put her arms around Liam to comfort him, his whole body vibrated with the intensity of their connection, their love for each other.

"But you *will* know him and you'll see. He loves me, Liam, the way you would want him to love me. I promise, you'll see."

Lilli felt him nod against the top of her head, trying to hold himself together.

"He better love you, Lilli, or I don't give a damn what he can do. I'll come after him. You know I will."

Lilli couldn't help but laugh through her tears at Liam's overprotectiveness.

"You're so stupid," she smiled.

"I mean it," he said forcefully, holding her tightly against him. "I mean it."

I know you do, she said to him silently as she lifted her head to look into his eyes. *I know you do. I'll see you in one month. Okay? I'll see you in Italy in one month.*

But we're going to Mexico, Liam thought, as he watched Lilli's smile grow. *At least I thought we were going to Mexico.*

Mmmm. At first, but then you'll change your mind. Like I said, Italy in one month.

What?

Never mind, Liam. Never mind, she thought, as she brought her cheek to his chest again and listened to the strong beat of his heart.

By the time Lilli and Liam released each other from their embrace, Joel had joined Alessandra by the clinic front door. They stood there, watching their other halves through the screened door in comfortable silence for several moments before Joel spoke.

"I know you have a lot of questions that I haven't answered. Later, when Lilli and I have returned, we will talk. I promise."

Alessandra smiled in acknowledgement, not taking her eyes from Liam's pained expression. She knew it was hard for him to accept that he was no longer responsible for Lilli, that his role in her life had changed forever. He looked so lost as he walked toward Alessandra, with his sister's hand in his.

As if drawn to her, Joel opened the front door to match Lilli's progression toward him. They met at the bottom of the steps.

Slowly, Liam moved to place Lilli's hand in Joel's waiting ones. Liam watched Joel intently, searching for any sign that he wasn't ready — wasn't *worthy* of the gift he was bestowing. But Joel barely noticed Liam's scrutiny. From the moment Lilli turned from Liam toward Joel, their gazes were locked together.

I guess that's how it should be, Liam thought. It was too early for him to feel relief, even though he could sense that the two of them were right together.

"Take care of her," he said, gaining Joel's attention. Liam had meant for his voice to sound demanding, authoritative, but was deeply disappointed when his words came out as more of a plea.

"I will," Joel replied earnestly, turning to look at Liam, hoping he could see the truth of his love for Lilli in his eyes. "Thank you."

It was the thank you that broke through Liam's apprehension, allowing him to feel the calm he knew was there below the surface.

He knows what I'm letting go of, Liam thought with relief. *He knows how precious she is.*

And with this new understanding, Liam let the barest of smiles hover on his lips as he finally - *finally* let go of Lilli's hand.

OOTS Part II: The Red Order—PREVIEW

"Ladies and Gentleman of the Guild, I know we have suffered a crushing defeat, but it is my sincere belief that we can not only recover from this setback, but that we can regain our control over the Seers and stop Marcus' son...this Joel, from following through with his plans to destroy us.

"With your permission, I would like to use the painful lessons we have learned from these lost Seers to create a new caliber of Seer that is capable of all the things we witnessed six months ago. They will be set-apart from our current stock in that they will join our cause of their own free will, thereby eliminating the need for the high doses of Luridium that clearly diminish the full realization of their potential. This new generation of Seers would be known to us as the Red Order."

The looks around the room as Crane finished his speech were everything he expected: surprise muted by the reticent skepticism that he knew was ever-present in less imaginative minds.

"Can this be done?" Yusef asked. Even though the man was old and frail, Crane was encouraged by the flicker of hope he saw in his otherwise subdued posture. "How can we be sure of their loyalty without the Luridium to control them?"

"My dear friend," Crane began with a satisfied smile, "It has already begun."

Cerece Rennie Murphy lives and writes just outside of her hometown of Washington, DC. In addition to completing the *Order of the Seers* trilogy, Ms. Murphy is also developing a children's book series titled *Enchanted: 5 Tales of Magic in the Everyday* and a book on understanding marriage/relationship advice for single women entitled *More than the Ring*. To learn more about the author and her upcoming projects, visit her website at www.crmurphybooks.com.

www.ingramcontent.com/pod-product-compliance
Lightning Source LLC
Chambersburg PA
CBHW031201020726
47499CB00002B/445

our full potential.

Very true. Ishta said Hathors brought the Moon here, if we kill them what will become of the moon will it crash into the Earth? Destroying all life forever?

Don't be such a pessimist, but we do need some help with this, to work out some answers.

Who, The Octo, or Dad's geeks and scientists, Shiny?

That's it, Shiny is very old, she must know a lot about our universe and how things work, but is she animal or sentient machine or both, we need to ask her, talk to her. We need to talk to Conner, get him here again, and show him Shiny. Tell him when and what we saw regarding the hit and assure him we will return. Oh, yeah and maybe tell him we are still going to go through with our wedding regardless of the apocalypse as it is important to Taxi's coherence as a survivalist society. What do you think?

Perfect I think I love you. We sat and watched the sun slowly set over the mountains, as shadows grew longer, a dingo howled and Curlews cried out to far off partners. Dark shadows of Flying Foxes headed off on their dusk patrol in search of fruit for their supper as we sipped bourbon by the crackling fire light and considered what lay ahead. This was daunting and very scary and Bett turned to the only comfort she knew and trusted, me. Her hand still resting on my thigh became more active, slowly getting closer, touching me, poking me and scratching me. She giggled as she kissed me, enticing me to become more aroused. I obliged, slowly lifting, expanding, hardening, as I kissed her longingly and passionately. She felt my passion deep inside her as I moved my hands over and into her sweet body. She shuddered all over and grabbed me tightly.

I need this; I want this inside me, can I? But she already knew the answer. She suddenly and expertly swung her body onto mine in one perfect maneuver. Betty sensually slid down onto me, taking me all in, groaning loudly with pleasure.

Hmm, Daniel, yes! She moved like a magician gradually bringing me there. I could not hold back my intense feelings, suddenly letting go in ecstasy with Betty screaming out in joy at the same instant. We rocked together as one in pure bliss with the campfire glowing on our bodies warmly. We held on tightly to each other kissing madly. Betty slowed and grabbed my face in both her hands.

I trust you completely, I Love you and you make me so happy. Do you mind if we go to bed now, to sleep?

No, I'm tired too. Betty effortlessly lifted each of us off the couch and we floated into the tent and she laid us gently down on the soft mattress. I was still firmly wedged inside her, and she was still on me, gently squeezing me rhythmically, smiling and sweetly kissing my neck. Her weary head lay on my shoulder and she felt so amazing as she slowly pulled the warm rug up. I closed my eyes and fell into a deep sleep in seconds.

* * *

I suddenly opened my eyes, but I was still asleep. Where am I? This is the Earth, I am sure, but it is long ago, thirteen thousand years ago. I remember it I had been in this place before. I was laying on exotic furs in a beautiful tent, full of rich smelling incense, lush plants and colorful bowls of fruit. I sat up disturbing an animal next to me, it was large and its tawny coat was covered with black spots. It stretched out and slowly rolled over and started to quietly purr when it saw I was awake, it was a Cheetah, it snuggled into me. I patted it and scratched it under the chin. It yawned widely baring its razor sharp teeth and stretched out like a kitten. It clearly knows me, thank goodness.

I stood up slowly, I was totally naked and covered in strange tattoos from head to toe. My skin was slightly golden and seemed to swirl around. I had an ornate gold sash around my waist. I touched my face, same nose, but I had a full thick beard. I looked down at myself, yep that is me. I walked to the tent flap and pulled it open. There were large tents everywhere, all stunningly beautiful. Tall palm trees swayed in the breeze, there were people everywhere, all naked and covered in tattoos. Off in the distance I could see a huge ornate temple or structure, unlike anything I had ever seen. People were flying around in the sky holding hands and I could see many orbs like Shiny, lined up at the shore of the ocean and some were zipping through the sky.

Someone tapped me on the shoulder.

Hey, you, are you trying to sneak away?

Bett is that you? I turned, it was Betty, covered in tattoos, golden skin, and golden braided hair down past her waist she had a crown of flowers on her head. She looked stunning as always.

Danny, where are we? You have a big black beard! She exclaimed, touching it. *This is so strange, everyone has tattoos, all the men have beards, and everyone is like us, fully awake.*

Bett this is a version of us, from our past, long ago, just before a reset, I can feel it, it is a few days away. Is Shiny here too? We called her and an orb zipped down in front of us.

Hi Old Ones, hop in. We entered Shiny and she shivered with pleasure as we gulped the jelly water, slightly gagging.

Old ones, you are different, you are both here, four of you, two from our future and two from now, how are you doing this?

Shiny our dreams have led us here.

Come future Old Ones, all of you, let's fly. We held hands and laid horizontally as Shiny zipped straight up and stopped at a thousand feet. She then flew out over the ocean, it was so stunning. Up ahead a huge city loomed up out of the water. It appeared as if it was floating in the ocean, sparkling beautifully like it was covered in jewels and made of crystals. Magical boats sailed majestically into its harbors.

What place is this?

This is the place you know as Atlantis.

Shiny, you know what is about to happen?

Yes, Old One, it is forbidden for any off-world species to interfere.

Who forbids it?

You know the answer, it is the mighty Hathors, they rule this system from their huge and powerful starship that is in orbit, you call it the Moon.'

Can we see it?

I will show you from space, but it is forbidden to get close. We lifted into space and zipped around the earth and there it was, with no dirt on it, an off-white metallic sphere. A third of it appeared to be covered with soil. We were still a long way off but Shiny would go no closer.

Shiny what are they?

They are the Grays ships they work for the Hathors, they are harvesting humans, taking DNA and they ship dirt from the Earth and other asteroids to slowly cover their craft from those who wish to find them, but I know not who that is.

Shiny you understand it is wrong, what they are doing to humans?

Yes, very wrong, but we are helpless, they are very powerful, they see everything.

Well, they can't see you Shiny, that makes you stronger than them, understand?

Yes, thank you Old One you are very wise.

Shiny we are from the distant future, and we are still your friends, thousands of years from now, we are your friends for eternity.

I am grateful for knowing you both. You bring joy to this world and to me, thank you. I can feel you are leaving now goodbye future Old Ones. Welcome back to consciousness' present Old Ones, you will never guess who had control of your bodies.

2

Friday, three days before
the end of the world.

A nd just like that we woke up. I was still inside my beautiful girl.
"Wow, these dreams are wild." Betty said, I smiled at her and she squeezed me.

"Oh Bett, I don't even know if that was a dream, we were asleep here but it felt as if we were conscious there in those versions of us. Shiny said it too, there were four of us."

"Okay, but that could be part of the dream too."

"Very true, we can ask Shiny if she remembers carrying four of us in two bodies thirteen thousand years ago..." We both laughed.

"Good luck! I can't remember what happened yesterday, except the part where I fell asleep inside you, sorry."

"Ha, sorry, as if. You are still loving me right now; I can feel you."

"Betty please don't move, just stay as we are, you feel amazing whenever you do this to me, that didn't sound right, because you always feel amazing, but this, this is off this world level of greatness and comfort, and you are everything, you are my home. You will always be my home." Betty suddenly started to shiver, shake and moan, uncontrollably, holding me tightly, clenching and releasing as wave after wave of orgasm ran through her gorgeous body.

"Sorry!" she squealed out between loud moans.

That was it, I exploded pushing Betty up into the air, she gasped as she flew us out of the tent again. Up we went as I kept pushing upwards into her still climaxing. Betty was controlling me carefully, just enough, then one big last squeeze and scream as she let go of me and flew up and away. She was spinning like a ballerina, arms outstretched in pure bliss. I cried out in joy and slowly stopped as I just happened to look down at the lake, it was pulsing with light, changing color and heaving. Shiny was now in our heads crying out joyfully in bliss. Pulsing in time with us and humming loudly. I took a breath and calmed myself.

"Whew! Wow, Bett, er what was that?"

"Danny, you told me not to move and then you said that I was home; what did you expect was going to happen? I lost my shit, uncontrolled multiple orgasms, utter eroticism and now I am near the stratosphere, I'm coming down now, calming myself, oh man!"

"Bett, I think Shiny, lost it too baby."

"Shiny too, what?

"I think she is part of us now, baby, she feels everything we do."

"Swim Danny?" Betty zipped past in a blur I heard the splash as she went in. I swooped down, Betty was swimming on her back watching my approach, so I slowed down and floated a few feet above her admiring her body, she smiled up at me, admiring my body.

Your bodies are both perfect, your coupling is incredible, and you fill Shiny with love and bliss, I had a huge orgasm too, I couldn't shut you out it was beautiful. Sorry I am so loud. I will try for more control, but it has been so long between waves. I love you and leave you in peace, thank you for my bliss.

Shiny you are so humble and sweet, we honestly love everything about you, we want you to feel us if we give you love and bliss. I had dived in next to Betty.

How do you describe yourself are you animal or machine, you seem neither?

I am both Danny, and more, a bio-engineered entity grown with multiple different DNA, including human. All Orbs share similar combined water molecules attached to our DNA similar to Taxi's special water. We don't age, but we can die through severe injury or trauma. The Octo gave us life, but I am slightly different to their Orbs as I share both of your DNA in my being, this is how I am so in tune with you, I am made of you two.

This is the only way Octo could give me to you. I cannot carry others only you and your family, those who share our DNA.

Shiny, that makes you even more special to us as you are part of our family; this makes us proud and very happy to have you with us. When we are inside you, how do we go to the toilet in space?

When you are inside me, I absorb all your bodily fluids and waste before it leaves your bodies. I continually recycle everything and feed you all the nutrients you require, and I am perfectly hygienic. Unfortunately, I do have a side effect, the longer you ride in me the more golden your skin will swirl with my jelly. I am a part of you now as you are a part of me.

Wow, and what if we need to exit you in space or some hostile environment?

When I sense that, I can create a protective layer around you, my jelly stays in your lungs so you can still breathe, it is like a biological spacesuit, it will last for three hours.

That is amazing and good to know. Shiny we want you to meet Betty's father, Conner, he needs to understand why we cannot enter his bunker immediately as you need to show us our planet as it gets destroyed. Can you take us all into space just to show him the beauty of this planet?

I am honored, it will be my pleasure, he is my family. Bring him to me I will welcome him with love.

Danny, you want to fly naked in space with my naked dad holding my hand? Are you serious or just crazy? He is my dad. That is so awkward. I can't do this.

Betty, I can blur all your bits and you too Danny, he will see you are naked but not see everything I can blur him from you too, Bett even with you outside of me, I understand your feelings, I've got you.

Shiny you are even taking on our speech mannerisms, but that will be awesome thank you. I have one more question Shiny, do you remember future Old Ones in present Old Ones in your past, travelling to look at the moon before it became hidden? Shiny shivered.

Was that you? I can't tell, but inside me it feels like you.

We do not know, tell us of your experience, what you remember, please Shiny.

You called to me, I came, you entered me, but I felt a difference, yes, *future you, was that you? This is unreal, I have waited so long, it was you, thank you my beautiful friends, you are my friends for eternity.* Shiny had repeated my exact words after thirteen thousand years, we looked at each other as we floated in the lake.

Our consciences had travelled back in time thirteen thousand years, *this was incredible, how could we use this against The Hathors?*

Okay, thank you Shiny that was us, rest now, sleep. Shiny happily fell asleep. We finished washing ourselves and left the lake.

Bett, please contact Conner, get him out here as soon as possible, tell him we have something fantastic and something terrifying to tell him, but it must be in person today and as soon as possible, we need to see him for a couple of hours and come alone.

That will draw him in. Let's get dressed, have a bite to eat and wait for his reply. Betty sent her text. He replied in a few seconds.

'*I will be there in fifteen minutes.*'

"Excellent Bett, we need to move."

"Danny?"

"I got this Bett, trust me, okay?"

I so trust you, just come here quickly and give me a freaking kiss, please. I obliged willingly.

I love you Baby.

I know Danny, it is legend, past and present. I looked at her, she nodded.

True Danny, check the history books. We are there. She winked at me.

We were dressed casually sitting on our couch by the lake, the fire raging, sipping bourbon. The 65 Lincoln soon roared in, surrounded in dust, he pulled up nearby. We had a Jack Daniels floating in front of him as he jumped out. He grabbed it.

"You have my attention guys, what is going on?"

"Conner, sit first please, have a big drink, the time is near, the rock will be here on Monday, this Monday, we have seen it up close, it is terrifying and followed by hundreds of smaller rocks that are all massive. This is the end of life as we currently know it. We know you and Taxi are all safe in The House of *Ra*, but we cannot join you, not initially. We need to be off world." Conner skolled his drink, the bottle of Sinatra sailed over and immediately refilled his glass.

"What do you mean, off world? The news has reports of a meteor, but it will miss us completely."

"Okay, yeah no, it will hit. Conner you are aware of our abilities, you have seen our tricks, but there is a lot more to us than you realise, and it is fantastic." He looked at Betty in bewilderment.

"Daddy, listen, Danny is right, this is fantastic. We have something to show you."

"Conner, we have some new friends, and they don't live on this planet, they have been trying to aid us, to stop this from happening. Together we have done our best but still it comes, so our only option is for us to aid the Earth in space while you and Taxi lock up below ground in The House of *Ra* but we need to be up there for a short while." I pointed straight up.

"What do you mean Daniel? Up there, how? You don't have a rocket, do you?"

"We would like you to meet an old friend her name is Shiny. Do not be afraid. We will help your mind so you can hear her. She is telepathic like us, are you ready for one of the wildest hot-rod rides in your life, drink up, we are heading into space. I will call her when you are ready." Betty patted Conner on his knee.

"You got this Daddy; this is one hell of a ride. You won't be disappointed." I looked at Conner, he nodded okay and drank his JD, and I said to him,

"Conner, please say hello to Shiny." We looked at the lake together, Conner followed our gaze. Shiny went into theatre mode trying to be dramatic. The lake started glowing and changing colors, a low hum and the water pulsed and we could feel Conner's apprehension. Shiny lifted slowly out of the water, glowing brightly still changing colors, rising to ten yards, slowly spinning around, then dropping back to one, slowly coming over and stopping two yards from the shore. Conner gasped with exasperation.

"Conner, this is Shiny, she is our Starship, a gift from an alien race who have known us for thousands of years, but that is a whole other story." Conner's eyes were wide in awe and bewilderment.

"Please take all your clothes off." Conner looked at me as if I was crazy and skolled his drink in silence as Betty and I slowly undressed in front of him.

"Come on Daddy you won't see anything, but to enter Shiny you must be naked." Betty encouraged him.

"This is your only chance to fly in space, get it off now." Danny demanded. Conner slowly pulled off his clothes and stood with his hands covering himself. I motioned him forward.

"Take our hands, we must drink the jelly inside, it is uncomfortable at first, and you will feel as if you are drowning. You will gag but you will breathe her water, it is full of oxygen, we've got you okay?" Conner was like a scared child, but he could not go back, he loved a challenge, and this, this was the ultimate challenge. We floated in. Shiny shivered as we entered, Conner's enthusiasm was overwhelming. He gulped the jelly and gagged; eyes wide.

Please relax, Conner I am Shiny, I am so very pleased to have you inside me it is an honor, let me show you the beauty of your world, hold their hands and fly with us. We held hands and lay prone. Conner looked around in awe as he became aware of Shiny's transparency as she rose off the lake. We lifted slowly to five hundred feet and flew over Taxi leisurely; Conner was ecstatic and happy. Then Shiny lifted straight up as Taxi shrunk away.

Floor it Shiny! She squealed with joy; Conner grinned widely as we launched into space and we could feel his exhilaration. Blue to black as stars emerged, Conners' hands were gripping us tightly with a slight fear and amazement, he had so many mixed feelings as his eyes darted around. Ultimately, he loved it. We zoomed past the Moon and soon zipped past Mars. Then weaved our way through the tumbling asteroid belt at high speed.

We will only have time for Jupiter if you wish to be back in two Earth hours.

It is okay Shiny, take us close to Jupiter and show us her beautiful moons then back, a couple of orbits around Mars and the moon then home.

Okay Danny, will do, Conner do you like this? I can feel a lot of emotion coming from you, but you are hard to read. Conner looked around at us then back out to space and said in his mind to us all.

This is so hard to comprehend, my mind struggles to take it all in, I feel so blessed to be with you all. There is so much more to life than I know, now I understand your decisions and know they are difficult for you; Shiny you are so beautiful too. She shivered with his admiration. He felt her and was amazed with her. Conner gasped as Jupiter filled the sky above our heads. The gigantic red storm raged less than a mile from us. We looked on in utter awe. The massive angry giant sat above us silently. Its clouds full of lightning and fury. It was a spectacle that no human had seen this close and we stared at it unable to turn away from its terrifying beauty. A short time later we zipped back towards home and flew low around Mars, Conner's eyes were wide with bewilderment. We then flew quickly to the Moon and finally on to Earth. Shiny took us around the globe a few times slowly. Conner's eyes shone wide, locked on the Earths beauty.

Wow! He said, sounding somewhat astounded and yet dumbfounded. We slowed over Queensland and came up the coast, above The Great Barrier Reef, headed inland and stopped above Taxi. Conner's eyes were wide taking it all in, analyzing weaknesses in mere seconds. Then we flew out to the lake and dropped down.

Thank you Shiny that was great, Conner?

Shiny, that was amazing, thank you, you are extraordinary, thank you, I loved every second. That was incredible, thank you Shiny.

Thank you, Conner I am happy, to have taken you for a ride. Goodbye my family. The circle opened, and we floated out holding hands and threw up the foreign contents of our lungs together. Shiny went back out and slowly sank down into the lake. We were hanging naked together above the lake we dropped Conner in gently and dived in. We made sure he was okay but he was a good swimmer. We swam around briefly, and eventually walked onto shore and moved away from him as all our towels came flying out to us, we left to allow him to dress with dignity. We waited on the couches with a glass of Jack Daniels floating, waiting for him. Conner soon arrived and took his glass and skolled it. It was immediately refilled.

"Thank you. I don't know where to start, that was life changing. I truly thank you both. Amazing, incredible, awesome, every adjective possible, my whole body is trembling. What exactly is Shiny?"

"Dad, she is difficult to explain. She is a Bio-engineered entity using a mix of DNA including ours, she is thirteen thousand years old, and has been our friend for all that time. Betty looked at him.

"Betty, you are thirty-two years old, not thirteen thousand years old, what on earth are you talking about?"

"Dad, seriously, after what we just showed you, please listen. Hang on this is wild, the enormity of what I'm about to tell you will be hard to take. Daniel and I are called The Old Ones. We are reborn eternal souls, we have known each other through an eternity, we always end up together. We have no memories of our past until we re-awaken. Dad please, remember what we just showed you. "We did this with you today because we still need to marry tomorrow, Daddy we will tell Taxi of the imminent apocalypse at the reception, but we will make it joyous, something to embrace as we know Taxi will survive thanks to you. They all need us to be optimistic so they can follow our lead as a survivalist community. We will need to ignore the huge loss of life to survive with positivity. Dad, get all the livestock ready, today, finalize everything with *Ra*. Get Elouise here as early as you can. Go for a flight on Sunday with her as far as you can, if possible. See this country for the last time Daddy." Bett was sobbing now, the finality of what was about to happen hitting her hard.

"My Bett, thank you my sweet. You and Daniel are amazing, I never imagined anything like this, let Shiny protect you, but stay in touch if you can, I need to know you are safe. Come back to Taxi as soon as you can, do what is needed for humanity sweetheart." "Yes Daddy, I promise with all my heart."

"See you both on Saturday." Conner hugged us both warmly.

"Daddy is it alright to bring Shiny to the reception, she would love to come, the times are changing, and all of Taxi needs to know about her?"

"Betty sweetheart you can do whatever you like, it is your wedding, and I would love to have Shiny there too. I must go now, I'm sorry, thank you, Bye." He practically ran to his car and roared off; he had a lot to do.

"Danny, can we go into Taxi? I would like to see how Rita is getting on with all the preparations for tomorrow. We can have a schnitzel at The

Dermy and a tap beer and take Osiris for a spin too."

"That sounds great I'll bring the beast over to Horus and come in and brush my teeth and hair, babe I think I might grow a beard."

"Ha, and get some tattoos?" Betty laughed, "How about waiting until after the wedding?"

"Okay, deal." I ran off to get the new Hummer that Conner had gifted us, this would be only our second drive in it. I started the black beast of a car and it roared like a hungry lion. I took it out of the tent and did a couple of doughnuts in the dirt before pulling in next to Horus our Maui van. Betty had changed into a long hippy dress.

"How do I look baby?

"Gorgeous darling." She blew me a kiss and took me in her mouth with her mind.

"Whoa, don't start what you can't finish." I started brushing my teeth as my groin started to harden.

"Bett, I thought we had to go?" She released her grip on me and kissed my cheek.

"Maybe later then." She gave me a sexy wink and squeezed my bum. I gently slipped in and then out of her with my mind. She squealed and smacked my bum.

"Ratbag!" I threw on some fresh clothes and sprayed some smelly stuff on me and we jumped in Osiris and headed into Taxi, Betty in charge of the music put on REM, 'End of the World as we know it,' very loud. I shook my head despondently. That finished, she put on The Doors. 'This is the End.'

"Bett now you are just depressing me." She changed it to Kiss, 'I Was Made for Loving You,' and sang on the top of her lungs to me, but she could sing, she was pitch perfect. '*I love you*' I mouthed to her. She was rocking it, shaking her head in time, playing air guitar, I could not stop smiling. That finished and 'Shout it Out Loud' by Kiss, came on. She knew all the words of this too and joined in gloriously loud. We pulled up at Gertie's, there were trucks everywhere with workers unloading chairs and tables. Rita was standing there giving directions stoically and saw us getting out of the truck and she ran over with arms wide.

"Hello, to the most beautiful about to be married couple in the whole world!" She wrapped her arms around both of us squeezing tight and kissing us on our cheeks.

"Hello Rita, what a nice welcome." We said this in unison and kissed her back. She laughed and stood back, looking Betty up and down.

"You look fabulous, sweet pea. So glowing and alive, can I?" She placed her hand softly on Betty's stomach and moved her hand around gently, "Hello, you two lucky ones." She grinned lovingly and turned to me looking me up and down. "And you, you are as handsome as ever, too bad Betty got to you first, or you would be all mine." She winked at both of us. We all laughed.

"Rita are you all set for Maid of Honor tomorrow?"

"Yes, Bett, thank you, just don't call me *maid* and we will have a blast. Come around the back and have a look, we still have a way to go, our goal is to be all done by ten tomorrow morning. Guys, your cake is amazing and *OMG* the food, good lord you would think King Charles himself was coming." We all laughed again.

"Oh, Rita it all looks fantastic, I love the archway." Betty said looking around.

"Yes, that still has more flowers to go on it yet."

"This is the Bridal table, with these stunning leather chairs and the dance floor here for all the drunken dances. The Taxi Cabs are setting up their gear over here, they are great, I heard them at the Dermy a while back. The DJ will be here, and all these long tables are for all of Taxi. Sorry I'm talking your ears off, I'll let you look around by yourselves, but better if you stay outside, it is chaos in there, which is where I'm headed. See you both tomorrow." She hugged us both and kissed us again and raced off.

"Whew." I looked at Betty smiling.

"Yes, like a whirlwind sometimes, but she is an excellent caterer and chef, I trust her and love her completely."

"Bett where can Shiny sit? I think we should wait a while before calling her in, she can watch from above for a bit."

"Danny, she can sit here above the pond, so no one can touch her, she might get overwhelmed with hands all over her."

"Good point, this will be great, just out of reach, perfect, we should tell her when we get back to camp."

"Oh yes, she will be over the moon with joy."

"Dermy time yeah?"

"Absolutely, Dermy time Bett." We jumped in Osiris and took off for the hotel. We pulled in and jumped out, walked hand in hand into Taxi's Dermy Hotel.

"Hey welcome royalty, good to see you!" Davo shouted from the other end of the bar. He was chatting to Robbo, one of the Taxidermist's a regular at the Dermy. Delores, Billie and Rose were behind the bar chatting. They waved hello and smiled broadly.

"Hey Davo, hey Robbo, how you doing?" We replied in unison. He roared with laughter; Robbo joined in.

"Ha, you guys crack me up, two beers, one non-alcoholic?"

"Yes thanks, can we order two schnitty's as well please."

"No worries, here's your beers, this is yours Betty. I'll get started on your schnitzels, see you in a minute." He went into the kitchen and started preparing our lunch. Betty looked at me and smiled.

"Danny, can I drink alcohol at our wedding? I'll shield the twins completely, but I'm not sure I can block all of Taxi from noticing, maybe we can block half each?"

"I have never even tried that, Bett."

"Do it to Davo, and Robbo and the girls, order us two cocktails, Whisky sours and make them forget about the twins. Easy."

"Okay, then." Davo soon emerged from the kitchen.

"Hey Daniel, Conner lent me a suit for my spot as best man, it is a dam fine suit and fits like a glove, but do you mind if I wear my flip-flops?" He winked at Betty, we laughed. "Just kidding. He gave some shoes too, perfect fit. Thanks for asking me, I've never been anyone's Best Man, what time does the Bucks Show start, are all the strippers organized?" He slapped the bar and howled at his own humor. "There isn't a stripper in a thousand miles from this place!" His laughter was infectious, we joined in.

"Hey Davo, can we get two Whisky Sours, make 'em nice and strong too, thanks mate."

"No sweat, I just need to check in the kitchen first, be right back." he raced off.

"Oh, Danny no Bucks Show? At least you can get a strip show a little later," she ran her foot up my leg under the table. I looked at her sideways, she giggled.

"Thanks baby, I tip good, really good."

"I know you will when you see what is under this dress." Another wicked wink, her hand slid under the table and squeezed me hard. I sat up straight.

"Ahh, being a little naughty, are we?" I slapped her bottom with my mind, now she sat up.

"Wow! I like it," she giggled. Now her hand was going up and down the length of me. I opened my eyes wide and shivered.

"Betty, stop." I put my hand on hers and lifted it off just as Davo came in with the cocktails.

"Here you go folks, don't light any matches nearby. Your food is nearly ready, five minutes."

"Thanks, Davo cheers." We raised our glasses, clinked them, and had a sip.

"Delicious mate." We said together. He laughed and gave us the thumbs up and went back to the kitchen. The drinks were really strong but nice.

"Well, I did it, he didn't say a thing."

"Yes, it worked; tomorrow you do all the men, and I will do the women, men are easier because they pay less attention to things like this."

"I guess you're right, men only think of things like this."

I held her face and kissed her while I entered her gently with my mind, lingered and slipped out, she moaned in pleasure while I kissed her.

"Again?" she whispered, so I did it again, slower, she trembled and shook as a tiny orgasm took her briefly, but she controlled herself.

"Hey, get a room you two, tomorrow night after you get married." Davo came bustling in with two huge schnitzels that filled the plates smiling broadly. Betty was blushing, barely in control.

"I love the cocktail; can we get two more big ones? This looks fantastic Davo." Betty let out in a flurry of words. He grinned widely,

"Thank you Betty, sure can." He left us again and we started to eat.

"Oops sorry, Danny, control, none of this at the wedding, okay? I mean it."

"Okay, baby, not at the wedding." *Imagine, while taking our vows with Father John.*

Definitely not!

What about during the Bridal Dance?

No. Danny. No. None of that or you won't have me after the reception.

I will behave, I promise. The schnitzels were delicious, chips perfect as always. Davo soon returned with the cocktails.

"How's it all going you two love birds?"

"Davo, this is the best schnitty ever, hands down." We said together.

He burst out laughing so hard, he caught his breath and spoke.

"Do you guys practice this shit? You should do stand-up; you would be awesome." We looked at each other at the same time.

"We would, wouldn't we!" He lost it; he totally lost it with hysterical laughter and continued laughing as he walked off. The food was delicious as usual, and the cocktails were strong enough to make us slightly tipsy as we finished the second one. Davo came out with two amazing looking Margaritas.

"One for the road, just drive carefully, okay?"

"Deal, thank you." We said together with deadpan faces. He shook his head in disbelief and lost it again, laughing as he went back chatting to Robbo.

We finished our meal and sat back, very content and satisfied. Betty snuggled up to me on the seat and we chatted and slowly finished off our drinks.

"See, you tomorrow Davo, Robbo, ladies!" We called out.

"Yep, see you at the church!" They waved to us enthusiastically. We jumped into Osiris and sped back to camp. Betty had Fleetwood Mac playing loudly on the stereo. We pulled up and went to the couches by the firepit. I lit it and sent in a few more logs.

Betty had two bourbons waiting, and put Dreams on by Fleetwood Mac. She swayed her arms and started dancing around and singing along, I sat back on the couch watching her, mesmerized, she locked her eyes on me and lifted her arms, her dress slowly lifted off her, revealing her new sexy lingerie. *Yes Bett, I approve, you look gorgeous.* She smiled and gave me a wink and started to dance again, slowly gyrating coming closer. *Very sexy baby*, she loved my attention.

She pointed at me, and my clothes literally fell apart and flew onto the ground. *Oh, okay then Bett.* Her new bra started to slowly come apart and flew into the fire; she was right in front of me. The fire making her beautiful breasts glow golden. Jack Daniels in one hand gyrating and drinking. Her other arm was in the air swirling around. She sent her glass to the table and lifted off the ground, spinning slowly, just out of my reach, her sexy knickers slowly falling off her. She stopped spinning and had her hands on her hips staring at my fully erect cock.

She pulled me up in the air in front of her and gently wrapped one hand around me and took me in her mouth, slowly kissing and sucking, she felt my pleasure and let go of me, rising up and wrapping her legs around me, slowly guiding me inside her. We were slowly turning around floating by the fire as she moved around on me, she was being careful trying to prolong her pre orgasmic bliss and it was working beautifully. Holding my face and kissing me tenderly, gyrating, squeezing and lifting all at once. Her kisses slowly started to become more passionate as her pace increased with her heartbeat; I could barely stop myself as she was close.

The first orgasm hit us hard, we trembled and shook in unison, crying out loudly in bliss. Betty held me tightly as she continued gyrating and moaning loudly as another wave hit her. She was squeezing and lifting as we were turning in the air. Betty cried out again and then whispered; *look, it's Shiny.* Betty moaned again. I looked to the lake, and Shiny was just above the water spinning in time with us, pulsing brightly all colors of the rainbow.

Betty carried us over to Shiny and gently sat us down on top of her, Shiny trembled with joy making Betty cry out in ecstasy as another wave hit. *Oh, Danny*, Shiny glowed brightly in time with Betty, she started sending fine vibrations through us and the whole lake started shimmering in time with us, Betty held me tighter and squeezed down hard making me come again. *Oh Danny*, she moaned again and then gently lifted off of me. We laid back on Shiny in each other's arms; totally exhausted.

Shiny stopped vibrating and slowly dimmed, her colors changing in time with our breathing.

Are you okay Shiny?

Oh yes, oh yes, Danny, thank you both for coming over to me and sharing yourselves, oh, your love is so strong it makes me stronger, faster, lighter and brighter, I am so happy and so alive, that was exciting and intoxicating, your bodies are buzzing with eroticism and joy.

Betty grabbed my hand and squeezed tightly, I looked into her eyes and she was crying, glistening tears streaming down her face.

Bett, are you okay?

Yes, I'm in heaven with you, and Shiny thank you for your beautiful words, I feel just the same as you do. Thank you, Danny you are incredible, you took me to the highest mountain, I feel absolutely exhilarated, I can still feel you and you are amazing. She was still sobbing and rolled over on her side facing me, one leg over my groin, her breasts heaving on the side of my chest, she turned and held my head and gave me a very wet kiss and laid her head on my shoulder.

I patted Shiny. *Hey Shiny, would you like to come to our wedding reception tomorrow? You will be our special guest.* Shiny shook and trembled with excitement.

Really? Yes, I would love to come along, but where do I hide? She trembled in excitement again.

You won't need to hide, you will be our Guest of Honor, we want all of Taxi's people to meet you. They are all going in the caves very soon, this will be something extremely special to everyone, you can sit above the small pond out the back of Gerties, so no one can touch you, what do you think Shiny?

Thank you yes, I would love to be there, listening to everything. Is there music too?

Yes, we have live music, a band called Taxi Cabs, and some people will dance. But at the start of the reception, you must hide in the air above until we call you, then you come down slowly, shimmering in all colors, making a grand entrance. Some people will be scared but the three of us can help them, so they are not afraid, alright?

Oh Danny, I like a grand entrance. This is great, thank you very much

Old Ones. Can we fly together now, a quick joy flight, we can go to the ocean and down into it, underwater. I want to show you something truly wonderful.

A joy flight, you say, Betty, you up for a joy flight?

Sure, why not? Let's go.

We floated up and Shiny opened the circle, we floated in, gulping and gagging. Shiny shivered as we entered her.

Okay Shiny, floor it!

Whoopee! She shrieked in glee. We flew up five hundred feet as Bett and I held hands and lay prone. Then Shiny zoomed out towards the coast arriving in minutes. She skimmed low across the Coral Sea, lifting high as we approached the Great Barrier Reef, which looked stunning as we flew naked along it. Shiny then went low and slow so we could see beautiful brightly colored fish and playful dolphins.

We heard the whales in our heads before we saw them, they sang their sweet songs to us. We told them to stay deep when the rock hits within forty-eight hours. They told us they would know where it would hit about ten hours before hand, and that they would tell us. We thanked them and told them to stay safe. They said thank you and they would warn the dolphins and octopi. Shiny lifted and took us out further.

Hold your breath. She said and then suddenly dived under the water at speed. Shiny giggled, we were going fast It was the weirdest sensation, but hard to see anything, she slowed down and took us to the ocean bed and started glowing brightly outside so we could see.

Shiny this is amazing! We exclaimed together in utter awe.

Old Ones, there is another race who lives down here, you need to meet them.

What? Where, can you show us?

They are very shy and never venture from their realm, but we can go briefly they know you; we have been here together before. You need to warn them, they can take precautions, they are more advanced than humans. I have informed them of our imminent arrival and they are joyous.

We looked at each other, eyes wide. Shiny came to a spot on the ocean floor that just looked like a sandy seabed, she went straight down into it, it was a thick layer of floating sand. We emerged one hundred feet deeper, it was like a submerged ocean a huge endless cave that was illuminated with bioluminescence. Below us was a brightly lit city, full of crystal domed buildings. There were a few small craft buzzing around. Shiny went down to a landing pad, and we had no idea at all what to expect. A dome closed over us and the water drained out.

It is safe to exit now, they are kind little amphibians, do not stress, they remember you. We floated out and threw up the jelly from our lungs, wiping the jelly off each other with our hands. We stood on the pad waiting. The whole pad started to go down, like a big elevator. We could hear a fanfare of exotic music getting louder and louder and thousands of voices cheering. Suddenly before us were a thousand tiny frog like fish men, all in fancy clothes.

We felt awkwardly big and naked. They were all looking up at a giant dick and balls hanging in front of them. *Betty let's sit down.*

Good idea Danny, we sat gently. They all moved forward, it was slightly intimidating, but they were only about fourteen inches high. Most were fully dressed in ornate bright clothes and gold, but some were naked, allowing us to see what they looked like. It was a fascinating com-bination of frog, fish and human. They had webbed feet and hands like frogs. Luminescent scales covered their bodies and there were pointed fins on their arms, legs and back. Their heads were oddly human in ap-pearance, except for the big, bulging eyes and being covered in scales. It was very hard to tell their sex but some females had make-up on and wore fancy dresses.

Ω

"*Welcome, Old Ones, I am Sir Gibblish Fish, we have legends about you, how you saved our people thousands of years ago, you are the uniters, the bringers of good health, prosperity and love, we cherish your ways. Do the land people still fight and kill each other all the time? Do they still destroy their habitat, and fill it with pollution and rubbish? Why have you returned to us?*"

"Hello all, we are happy to meet with you again. This time we come as Daniel and this is Betty, yes, they still fight, destroy and pollute. But in two sunrises a huge rock from space will collide with this planet once again, and you must prepare to defend yourselves, should the rock hit the ocean above you. Your beautiful city may be destroyed."

"*Thank you, Old One Daniel we have a force-field that we can deploy at the barrier to the ocean above ours. Should the water above be vaporized our city will be safe, we are glad you gave us this warning. We understand your time is short so we held a lottery, step forward Jillyish Fish our winner, she is ready to leave with you, she will be of great assistance, she is honored to join your team.*

Team?

"Yes, sir I am." The little Jillyish jumped up on my knee and held out her hand for me to shake. I poked my index finger at her; she grabbed it and shook it hard.

"Hello, Old One Daniel," she somersaulted sideways across onto Betty's knee and did the same, Betty shook her tiny, boney hand.

"Hello, Old One Betty. Let us go now, time is short for you surface people."

"Hello, little one, wait, Shiny might not be able to take you."

"Yes, she can, we share your DNA too. All of us do. I will explain the legend later." Betty and I looked at each other and shrugged as we closed our minds to them. *Looks like we must babysit this little fish for a while, who knows? She might be useful.*

"I need to bring this, it is biological and has been coded with our DNA too. It is my tools, okay?"

Again, we shrugged. The fanfare started back up, tiny streamers filled the air as a thousand or more little fish people cheered us as we looked on in amazement. Jillyish jumped up onto Betty's shoulder and sat down, her little suckers on her hands and feet gripping on tightly. We stood up carefully. Betty collected Jillyish's tools off the ground and gave it to her, she stuck it on her back, and it melded with her body.

"Goodbye friends stay safe," we called and waved, thousands of tiny hands waved back. Jillyish was waving frantically too.

We lifted off the ground and floated to Shiny's circle.

"Have you done this before?' Betty asked Jillyish.

"No, but I understand the science and know what to expect, I'll be fine." *Unbelievable!* We headed in, all gulping and gagging together. Shiny shivered.

Hello, Jillyish, nice to have you inside me, welcome aboard.

"Hello Shiny, I can't wait to fully understand your essence, you feel incredible." The landing pad lurched upwards and came to a stop, water filled the dome, and it slid back silently. Shiny glided through the water effortlessly, little Jillyish was shrieking with joy but covering one eye. Up through the barrier then swiftly up to the surface. We broke through the surface and up into the vast sky and then space. Jillyish had her eyes wide open in shock and awe.

"I have read about this place, none of my people alive now have seen it, it is like an endless ocean without water."

How old are you Jillyish? You sound like a very smart child. Shiny asked.

"I am a child I am only eighty earth years. We live to around five or six hundred, our technology has enabled our lengthy lives."

"You are older than both of us put together, but we only live to about eighty." I said.

"Shiny is about thirteen thousand years old. But she is very young at heart, like all of us." Shiny took us back into the atmosphere over New York City. We sped up the coast and headed east, coming to England then France, Jillyish was wide eyed, taking it all in. We zipped across to Europe then Asia and down to Far North Queensland, until finally our little lake was below us. We zoomed down.

"This is our home for now Jillyish." Betty told her.

"Is that freshwater?" She asked.

"Yes, not sure if you like that, be careful, okay?"

"I breathe oxygen, the air, but here it might be too dirty, I can get oxygen from water, it just slows me down a bit." She answered.

Shiny pulled up above the lake, we floated out and threw up the contents of our lungs, Jillyish jumped into the water and took off at speed. We dove in and swam around; Betty summoned the gel as Shiny dropped into the lake.

"Danny, I hate to say this but no sex until after the reception tomorrow, okay? Seriously, okay? This will make our consummation special; I love you so much and want you all the time, but this is slightly weird I can't control my urges and get carried away, so if we hold off until then it will make our wedding so much more special, agreed?"

"Okay, yes Bett, I agree, you are very special, and I want our wedding to be perfect, I will do whatever you want, seriously. I love you."

"Danny, I know, thank you baby."

Where is Jillyish? Suddenly she popped up with a fish head hanging from her mouth.

"I'm here, eating all your fish, they are nice and very different to my fish down at home. Please carry on, my eating is nearly done. I will return soon." Her head disappeared below the surface. We finished washing ourselves and left the lake. Our towels flew over to us, as I restocked the firepit. We sat by the fire and Bett sent out a bourbon for me and a bottle of water for her.

"Steak Danny?"

"Sure, can I help?"

"No need Danny, I got this."

Most of her magic happened in Horus. A short time later, the scotch fillet steaks came out on a tray and landed on the hotplate. With a sizzle, they soon flipped, and she had the tossed salad ready. The chips were nearly done. The juicy steaks soon rested on a plate and then were sliced thick. Bett speedily sent our plates out to us. I looked down at my generous plate of food.

"This is amazing, thank you babe." We ate quietly as Jillyish came out of the water and jumped up onto the side table and sat down, she seemed fascinated by the flames.

"I have never seen fire; I have read all about it, seen drawings and how dangerous it can be. It is beautiful and mesmerizing. It is too hot to touch, isn't it?"

"Oh, yes Jillyish it will burn your skin off stay away from it, the closer you get the hotter it becomes, okay?"

"Yes, I understand, why do you use tools to eat, you have big hands and feet and big mouths you could just gobble it up without wasting time."

"You are correct Jilly, we could gobble it up, but we choose not to, because we eat for pleasure too, not just nourishment, we enjoy eating slowly, it allows us to appreciate the flavors and textures of the food." Betty explained. Jillyish tilted her head.

"Why did you just call me Jilly when my name is Jillyish?"

"It is common for us to shorten names amongst friends, he is Daniel, I call him Danny, he is my close friend. I am Betty, he calls me Bett I am his close friend. Do you mind us calling you Jilly?"

"Do you consider me a close friend?"

"You are part of our team now, you are our friend and yes, I believe you will become a close friend."

"Okay. You can call me Jilly or Jillyish Fish."

"Thank you, Jilly, we are glad you are with us."

"Can I call you Bett, Old One Betty?'

"Of course, you can, and call him Danny please".

"Okay Bett and Danny, thank you friends. What do you drink? It smells disgusting, is that, Rum?"

"No, it is not rum it is a similar drink, with a different taste, it is a bourbon called Jack Daniels, how do you know Rum?"

"Many years ago, a wooden sailing ship sank in a bad storm and went down through our barrier, there were no sailors on board but many barrels of Rum. Some drank it, and liked its taste and effect, so we analyzed it and make it ourselves now. Can I try your bourbon, called Jack Daniels?"

We looked at each other, unsure if it was a good idea, Betty nodded, and flew a shot glass out and raised her hand to catch it, is this glass too heavy? She passed it to Jillyish, it looked massive in her tiny hands.

"This is good, I am stronger than I look thank you for the glass but it is empty."

"Please hold it up, and I will pour some in. Betty floated the bottle to Jillyish and poured in a little. Wait for us Jilly, we will have a toast." Betty poured some more in our glasses and put the bottle down. Jilly watched us closely as we all raised our glasses in the air. "Here's to new friends!"

"Okay, here's to new friends." We all took a big sip, we watched Jillyish's face and she grinned widely and then skolled the rest, we did the same.

"This is good bourbon, called Jack Daniels, can we have another toast?" We laughed as the bottle lifted and refilled our glasses.

"Jilly you can shorten the name of this drink to JD, and we don't need to have a toast each drink we can just drink it, slowly to enjoy it, not fast to get drunk." Jilly took a little sip and then waited, then another little sip and waited.

"Do we call this JD because it is a close friend?" We laughed, she is so cute, we drank along with her.

"Yes, I suppose it is a good friend, would you like to hear some of our music?"

"Yes, please Bett."

Jillyish couldn't take her eyes off the fire. Betty put on Dreams by Fleetwood Mac and stood up and slowly danced and sang along by the fire totally naked and beautiful, now I was mesmerized with her.

Jillyish stood up on the table and moved exactly like Betty, copying her every movement perfectly, Betty squealed in delight and so did Jillyish. Betty raised her drink and took a good swig, so did Jilly. Betty lifted her arms and swirled around; Jilly copied her exactly. Betty said to Jilly.

"Trust me Jilly." Betty lifted Jilly in the air and herself, she put both glasses down. Jilly watched closely; 'Run Through the Jungle,' by Credence came on. Betty started dancing in the air to the beat of the song Jilly joined in with a crazy swim dance, copying Betty, she was full of joy. They both were, Betty's arms in the air, her beautiful breasts moving in time with the song. Betty was smiling broadly at me; she knew exactly what I was thinking. *Not tonight baby*, but I was slowly hardening. Betty could sense my discomfort, and pointed at me, it instantly went soft. *Oh, really?*

Yes, sorry Baby, now you can enjoy me without that hardening.

"I'm fine baby. I just love watching you."

"I know Danny." I couldn't take my eyes off her, I was still fully excited but with no hard on. My whole body prickled and tingled in delight.

Jilly flew over and had another drink and she looked at me up and down,

"Danny, you don't dance? Why not? You should, it feels very good, just copy Bett, she is a good dancer, and your music has a great beat." Jilly skolled her drink and flew off with Betty's help, Betty beckoned me to dance.

Come on Danny, please, for me. I lifted off and floated over to Betty and took her hand and swirled her around. She grinned widely. I put one hand behind her back, held her other hand and started to swing her around back and forth, shoulders swinging in and out. 'The Boys are Back in Town' came on, and I picked up our pace. Betty was shaking her head in disbelief.

"You can dance Danny! And you dance so well."

"Well, I never said I couldn't, I had lessons a few years ago, thought I might find a new partner, but they all just wanted to take me to bed for a night or two."

"Oh, really, all of them?" I winked at her as Jilly danced around us blissfully. 'Dancing in the Moonlight' by Thin Lizzy came on and I pulled Betty in close and I rocked her in my arms sensually, sliding my hand up and down her back, shoulders going back and forth as we slowly went around. Our naked bodies were pressed against each other with my flaccid cock squished against her leg and groin.

Now it was Betty's turn to get excited, she caught her breath and bit her lip.

Oh, Danny this feels too nice, how are you doing this?

I'm just dancing baby. I kissed her on the neck, she tensed and gasped. Too late, she started to shake in my arms as an orgasm took over her body and I pulled her in tight.

"Oh Danny," she moaned and shook.

"It's okay Bett, just let go." She cried out again as another wave hit. Jilly stopped dancing and watched in wonder, and suddenly realized Betty was overtaken with pleasure. She smiled and did back flips and cartwheels.

"Oh, I'm sorry Danny," she moaned again. "I made you make a promise and then I broke it."

"Not true Bett, we didn't do anything wrong we were dancing, and you were enjoying yourself and your body reacted, no promises were broken, it's fine baby."

"Oh Danny, it is a dumb promise anyway, I don't even know why I said it."

"No baby, not dumb, forget it." I took Betty to the couch and gently lowered her.

"Is Bett alright? She was taken over with joy, it made me feel good to feel her."

"You can feel her?"

"Oh yes, and you, when you started to stiffen. I am tired I am going to sleep now, in the lake, okay?"

"Will you be safe there?" I answered

"Oh yes, no problems. Thank you for the JD and dancing, goodnight." She hopped away, to the placid, dark lake,

"Goodnight, Jilly," we called.

Danny, can I satisfy you without breaking the promise too?

You don't have to do anything to me, I'm fine, really. I sat next to her and reached for my drink. She put her hand on my knee and squeezed gently.

Danny, I suppressed you before, that was not fair, I will never do that again. Danny, sit back, relax, please, I want to, I won't touch you and I won't get carried away, please Baby. She begged in my mind.

"Okay Bett you know I won't mind." She filled my glass, I took a sip and sat back, Betty sat with her legs folded up under her off to the side, one arm up behind my head. *I felt my dick tingling, I looked down, there were ripples travelling down the length of it, slowly hardening, growing in length and lifting off my lap. Bett's eyes were closed so I closed mine. I've got you in my mouth,* immediately I felt her sucking, kissing licking all over, she felt incredible. *Now I am on you squeezing you with my muscle,* slowly she built up her speed and intensity as I felt every part of her body on me, slowly bringing me to the edge of ecstasy.

Do it Danny, I got you. I groaned loudly as I let go, my cum flying into the fire, Bett's aim was perfect.

Oh, yes Danny, do it baby, I was heaving in bliss, back fully arched my bum had lifted off the seat, every muscle on my body taut. I slowly opened my eyes and Betty was watching my body in joy. She was shaking too having her own orgasm, she slowed down and just held me gently with her mind, the last few drips flew into the fire. She came forward and gave me a long, wet passionate kiss, moved back a little and smiled at me. Then she erotically came forward and kissed me intensely again.

She released me with her mind, and took hold of me in her hand, just holding me tenderly as my cock slowly subsided and kissed me with her beautiful lips.

"Danny your body is beautiful when you climax, your whole body with all your muscles rippling and your cock gets huge when you blow, it throbs and quivers, your head flares out amazingly, you are a beautiful man." She kissed me again. "Come on Mister Starr, bedtime."

"Okay babe." We lifted off the couch and floated into the tent, dropping onto the super soft mattress. We fell asleep instantly.

3

Saturday, Our Wedding

I woke up with Jillyish, jumping up and down on me.

"Wake up sleepy heads." She somersaulted onto Betty landing on her soft breast and wobbling around Betty was awake instantly.

"Hey Jilly, wow, can you please get off my boob," but she had sat down and bounced around laughing.

"Oh, this so soft and bouncy, I like this." Betty grabbed her and lifted her gently off placing her on the mattress.

"Jilly, you shouldn't wake us like that, a five-year-old behaves like that, not an eighty-year-old, okay?"

"Yes, sorry baby." We sat up and shook our heads at each other.

"Jilly, you can't call Bett, baby, it sounds a little weird."

"But you do, you are in love with Bett and so am I. It is an affectionate term to show her I care." We frowned at each other.

"Your turn Bett, I give up." I smiled at Betty as she spoke to Jilly.

"Come here little one, sit here with me," Betty patted the mattress next to her, but Jilly flipped up landing gently on Betty's leg and sat with crossed legs looking up at her.

"Okay, Jilly, that is nice, but that term is only for us to use, it is nice that you love me, but love takes time to build up."

"How long do you need Bett; I will wait for you to love me."

"Thank you, Jilly, give me a few days. Today is a very special day for Danny and me. We are getting married today, do you know what that means?"

"Yes, I have read books; you make promises of love and give little rings to each other, kiss, eat lots of food and drink JD and then play with each other's bodies until little babies come out of there. She pointed at Betty's vagina.

"Oh, right, very good that happens today at three thirty in the afternoon."

"All of it? Babies too?'

"Jilly, babies take a while, nine months to grow in here, put your hand here and feel them." Jilly leant forward and placed her hand on Betty's womb, her eyes widened in amazement.

"Oh, you have little babies, they will be too big in nine months to come out of there, are you getting married again, babies should not be in there yet, they come after the wedding not before, you are very confusing to me."

"Sorry Jilly, we are a confusing species, let's leave it at that, unfortunately you cannot attend, someone might want to eat you by mistake with all the lobster and prawns that will be there, alright?" I grimaced.

Too far Bett.

No Danny, trust me, she cannot attend, it would be a disaster.

"You have live lobster and prawns there?'

"No Jilly, we cook them in boiling water first."

"Eww, I'm absolutely not coming, that is gross, would they put me in boiling water?"

"I honestly don't think so, but I cannot rule it out, you are better off staying here and eating fish, we will return later with Shiny."

"Oh, you take Shiny but not me."

"They can't eat Shiny, but who knows with you. You will be safer here."

"Okay I listen now I will stay and eat all your fish. Thank you for being wise."

"I will bring you back some raw fish if they have any."

"Yes, good but no frogs, I don't eat raw frogs, I go now, you make me hungry for fish, I will go on adventure in your lake and river, have a good wedding goodbye."

"Bye, Jilly, please be careful, see you later at night."

I looked at Betty and shrugged.

"What a handful she is." I spoke.

"Oh, yeah and then some; quite frustrating at times. But she is very intelligent, just very different and funny too. We are worlds apart but somehow familiar."

"I think eventually we will find common ground; we are close but not quite there."

"I agree, I like her, she is fun. Once she fully understands us, she will be a blast."

"Today is huge, what is the agenda again?"

"I need to go into Taxi by one pm for my hair and makeup with Dianne and Rita will be with me. You will meet up with Davo and the other lads at two pm for drinks at the Dermy. Not too many please, you should be at the church by three so all of Taxi can meet you and see how handsome you are. Just be yourself you will be fine, I will arrive at the church by three twenty-five and our ceremony starts at three thirty. You got this my man, I can't wait babe."

"I'm so looking forward to all of this. Do you remember your vows?"

"I have been practicing, I hope you remember."

"I got it, trust me."

"I do my love we will be right, even if we stuff up it won't matter, our love rules this planet."

"Yes, it does, how about a run and swim Bett?" Keeping it all grounded, "We won't get many chances for this for a long while."

"Yes, come on then." We threw on some clothes and our joggers. "Thirty miles Danny, jogs and sprints and push-ups halfway, okay?"

"Let's do this."

"Two-mile jog, one mile sprint, all the way, you can do this Danny. Go!' Betty took off and I chased after her. Jog, sprint, jog, sprint, jog, sprint, we arrived at the halfway point.

"Give me seventy Danny," I hit the dirt and powered through seventy push-ups, easily. Betty hit the dirt and did seventy easily as well. We headed back, sprinting and jogging all the way. We reached the lake panting and took our time to regain our breath.

"Swim?"

"Of course, Bett," I had my clothes off before her for the first time.

I ran in and powered ahead.

Shit! Well done. After three crossings she caught up with me. "Danny, well done, you are great, such an improvement. Good on you Danny."

"Thanks, Bett, this is all because of you, I feel so much stronger. You girl, have done this to me, thank you my darling." We did another ten crossings, before coming to a stop. Bett called the gel over and we swam to the shallows I grabbed the gel and started to wash Bett.

"Danny please don't, please wait for tonight." I stopped but I so wanted to continue.

"Okay Bett, sorry," I finished up washing myself and left the lake. Betty was right behind me; we dried with our towels and sat by the fire. It was nine thirty in the morning.

Bett had eggs and bacon with toast, fried tomato and mushroom, ready for us as we sat by the fire. We ate quietly, I watched her closely and she seemed troubled.

"Are you right?"

"Danny today will be perfect, but Monday is the end of everything, everyone's dreams and futures, so many will not survive, how do we help those that do? This will be the darkest time of our lives."

"I want you to think that it is not the end but the beginning, the start of our future together, we will oversee the rebirth of humanity once again. It will be tough, and sure many will die, but our job is to give hope to the survivors. We need to be strong and not show sorrow for those who do not make it, only give hope to those who are with us. This will be the brightest we can shine for everyone left, okay? Together we can do this." Betty went into Horus and had a quick shower and gathered her bags, then we sat at the kitchen table with some hot coffee.

Bett close your mind to Hathors again.

Done Danny, what's up?

When you first showed me your powers, the first thing you showed me was that you swirled the fire up into a vortex.

Yes, I remember Danny that was easy. What are you thinking?

I have been thinking hard about all this since The Hathors ruined our first attempt to redirect the meteor. If we can't stop it, maybe we can reduce its impact by removing some of the debris in the atmosphere straight after impact with a vortex. A huge vortex, you and I and the infinite mirror and Shiny, possibly the Octo too. Pulling everything out into space, rather than allowing it to fall back into our atmosphere. We need to prevent or decrease the following extended ice age, with our atmosphere full of dirt and debris for hundreds of years, speeding up the recovery of humanity.

We will have to be above the impact and create the vortex immediately. Pulling up everything, all debris, dirt and smoke and fire and send it deep into space, so it cannot fall back. It will not stop the huge Tidal waves or destruction from the super-heated air that will surround the planet. The vortex might be able to pull some of the heat out into space too, reducing the fires that will engulf the planet but ultimately, hopefully, we can reduce the ice age that will follow. Dramatically increasing humanities chances for survival.

Danny, what? How did you come up with this? And now? Just before our wedding, I need to leave in twenty minutes for my hair, and you want to create a vortex above the impact to slow the coming ice age?

Yes Bett, that's the plan I first thought of using it for something when you intensified the fire of the pig hunters. What do you think?

I think you are crazy enough to make a difference Danny. And how about we aim the vortex at the Hathors lair on the moon and direct a few small rocks through their life supports or brains, that may be enough to send them running.

Good idea Bett, we got this, let's get married first. Come here and give us a kiss my love. We have totally got this.

I could hear the roar of a powerful V8 coming up the track. *Betty your ride is here, I love you darling and can't wait to be your husband, give me another kiss please.* We kissed passionately and hugged tightly. *See you soon,* we said in unison. *She collected her things and climbed into Elenor; she left me in a cloud of dust. I stood looking at the taillights as they disappeared down the road. Jilly came sauntering up to me, out of nowhere.*

"So, that's it, Bett has left you all alone, but you will meet up and give rings later? Why are you still here?"

"Betty needs to prepare; she wishes to surprise me with her looks, to make me happy. She will be beautiful I know. I will have a shower soon, and dress in a fine suit and will be picked up in an hour from now."

"You are crazy about her, aren't you? Your heart races, thinking of her getting ready to marry you."

"Oh yes Jilly, I can't wait, Bett means everything to me, she is my world, my home."

"Danny, you are sweet and smart, I feel your love, you two will make a difference in the new world."

"Thank you, Jilly, you show a lot of compassion, how did your kind end up with our DNA in you?"

"Can we sit by the fire and have a JD while I tell you?"

"Okay but I can't stay too long." We walked over to the fire pit, it was still alight and we sat in the couch and two JDs came to us. Jilly took a few sips staring at the fire.

"About two thousand years ago Shiny found us, she had you, The Old Ones inside her. Our civilization was dying, we had become sterile and could not reproduce and there were only two thousand of us remaining. We were too scared to leave our city to find hope and then you came and gave us hope. Shiny has your DNA too, it is special and it was modified by The Hathors tens of thousands of years ago. You suggested to us that we take some cells from each of you to make a serum that we could bio-engineer and incorporate into us to stop our sterility, and it worked. We even took on personality traits and other mannerisms of you both as a side effect. But you also made us more confident and smarter. Our technology blossomed after you left and so did our population, we always give birth to twins too, just like you, and we love to share our bodies with each other in multi relationships. We have statues of you both in our cities. We call ourselves The Saved Ones. Cheers to you Danny, half of The Old Ones.'

"Cheers Jilly, fascinating story, Bett will love it, I'm glad we saved you and your kind are beautiful. Do you have a partner?"

"Oh, no, I am a bit too young to be in a permanent relationship, but I have shared myself secretly with a few fish. Thank you for the JD, please have some good fun at your wedding I must go and eat now, bye."

"Thank you, Jilly, and I must go and get ready," we parted ways, I kind of wished Jilly could have attended our wedding, but it would be very awkward for everyone.

I showered and shaved, put on some smelly stuff and dressed in my new suit. I had opted for a nineteen twenties style pinstripe suit with braces, baggy pants with pleats and spats, very gangster; I just hoped it would go with Betty's dress. I could hear a car; it blew its horn. I stepped out, it was Pete in the silver Aston Martin DB5. I checked my pocket, yes, the rings were there, good. I jumped in.

"Hi Pete, how are you going?"

"Wow, would you look at this, you look great, you just need a cigar."

"Oh shit, hang on a second," I ran back to Horus and took the whole box of cigars.

"Thanks Pete, these will go down a treat at the reception."

"Okay, let's do this." Pete smiled and floored it; the DB5 took off roaring.

"A few lads are joining us at the Dermy for a few pre-wedding drinks. You guys have the whole town buzzing you know, Conner has gone all out for this. I been told to tell you the photographer will arrive in half an hour to get some shots of you drinking at the Dermy."

"Yep, okay I was expecting that."

"What on earth?" There were about thirty cars outside the Dermy, Pete laughed.

"Everyone wants to meet you before the wedding Daniel; I'll look after you, no shots, okay?"

"Yes mate." We walked inside as a loud cheer rang out through the Dermy. There were about thirty women and about fifty men all with drinks. Davo came straight over and handed me a pint.

"Here you go champ; you look damn fine, like Al Capone, very fancy. I have a spot at the bar for you, I've told everyone to relax and not surround you."

"Thanks mate that is awesome, cheers." Every person in the Dermy yelled out CHEERS and raised their glasses in time with me. Davo roared with laughter,

"Danny that is tradition here, whenever anyone says that we all say it, and have a drink, we can get quite rowdy on a Friday night. Cheers!"

'CHEERS!'

"Ha, I bet." I paced myself carefully, but I was way too busy talking to everyone anyway. Gradually I met every person there, and they were delightful, extremely nice and friendly. Heaps of comments about my groovy suit, everyone loved it. Even Bart from the service station had a suit and a big smile as he shook my hand.

"I told you. Yes sir, I said you were a stayer!"

All the girls from the bar were smiling and staring at me. They came over and surrounded me. Billie, Delores, Kitty, Rose, Lola, Candice and Penny.

"Oh, Danny you look fabulous, Betty is so lucky. Can we get a kiss and a hug before you get married? Please..." Lola fluttered her eyes at me; they were all smiling and nodding. They had me trapped.

"Okay then ladies, cheeks only." I kissed each of them and gave them a quick squeeze. I could feel some of their hearts pick up pace. Rose was last, she turned her head at the last second so my lips met hers. She kissed me back and squeezed me tightly. My heart skipped a beat. "Hey, not fair, but thank you all. I hope you enjoy the reception; I must keep going bye." I stepped back as they went into a huddle giggling like teenagers. They were all very sweet.

The photographer arrived and introduced himself, Bob, a local too. He looked me up and down and shook his head.

"You look great, it's uncanny."

"What? What is uncanny?" I asked him.

"Oh, nothing but you will look good next to Betty, you are a beautiful couple. Now I need a few shots of you at the bar with a beer and a few with these Taxi folk behind you. Then it will be just about time to get going to the church."

It was soon time to leave for the church. Pete, Davo and I piled into the DB5 and drove the two minutes to the Church most of Taxi was already there apart from a few stragglers still at the pub. Conner and Elouise came straight over. They took a step back in admiration.

"Wow, Daniel, you look fabulous, come here and give us a hug." The three of us embraced warmly. Elouise kissed me then wiped the lipstick from my cheek with a tissue.

"Oops, sorry Danny, you look amazing." I pulled open the coat and showed the details; the braces, the belt, the deep pleats in the trousers and my spats. Conner whistled,

"Straight off Bonny and Clyde, too cool." Bob came over with his camera.

"Hey guys, snap time, smile." I was in the middle, and they stood with their arms around me, smiling proudly.

The Father came over and introduced himself. We shook hands, he seemed nice and jovial.

"How are your nerves, Daniel?"

"I am fine Father."

"Okey dokey then, that is good, all of Taxi is here today full house. I will say my bit, all the religious stuff, but not too heavy just the usual, I will ask for the rings and give you Betty's. Then I will ask you to give your vow to Betty. Holding hands and talking clearly. I have a microphone so everyone will hear you at the back, just speak clearly. When you have finished, it will be Betty's turn. Then once the rings are on, I will announce that you are Bride and Groom and then you may kiss. Everybody will cheer and clap and soon after we will all go and feast and be merry at Gertie's. All good, Daniel?"

"Yes, thanks Father, I will follow your lead, Thank you."

"It is time for us to go inside and wait for the bride, you, David and Peter on the right, Betty, Rita and Dianne on the left, got it?"

"Yes, got it."

"Davo, Pete, get over here. Here are the rings Dave, please when Father John asks for the rings, step forward and hand them to him, okay?"

"No problems Danny."

"Thanks mate." We went into the church and stood in a row; the old church had big ceiling fans which helped but the suits were hot for up here in the tropics even in the winter.

The people of Taxi filled the church, they murmured quietly, and a few had to stand up at the back. We all looked at the altar solemnly; I looked up at Jesus hanging on the cross and suddenly felt the weight of the world on my shoulders. Oh shit, don't think about Monday, think about Bett, the woman you can't get out of your head. She will be here any minute. The crowd started to stir a little, something was up. Hushed whispers.

The organ player started up the Bridal march and we all turned to the doors. They swung open. Betty was brought in by Conner. They took a few steps in and paused so everyone could take in her beauty. Betty had on a knee length white Great Gatsby Flapper, wedding dress with a long string of pearls around her neck. Her hair was nineteen twenties styled with a thick band of diamonds placed around her head. Bright red lipstick and perfect face. I nearly fell as I gasped, taking her in. '*Oh Bett, my beautiful babe.*' She could feel every bit of my emotions.

'*I love you Danny, you look amazing.*' We both had tears in our eyes, a few rolled down our faces. We couldn't help it we were both so happy. When some of the women realized what was going on between us, they started to cry with joy too.

Bett and I could feel the love of all of Taxi and it was nearly overwhelming us.

Whew, Danny, stay in control, it is very hard with all this love around us.

Breathe darling.

Whew, I didn't expect this Bett, huh, control. You match me perfectly.

Yes. We talked as she walked forward with Conner.

Stunning Betty.

I feel so much love coming from you and them, this is unreal. Danny, I feel the same, this is going to be harder than I thought. They were right in front of me; Conner handed over his daughter to me and patted me on the shoulder.

"You got this." He said softly. A tear rolled down my face.

I'm sorry Bett. But she smiled at me and wiped that tear away with her finger,

"I got you." she said. It was picked up by the microphone. All of Taxi shivered as one.

I stood holding both Betty's hands, looking into her eyes, as Father John spoke about God's love for his children and the sanctity of marriage.

I can't wait to fuck you tonight. Bett smiled at me innocently.

Oh, you ratbag, not fair. I started to smile at her too. Father John was looking at me,

"I now request the rings," Father John held out his hand. We waited, and waited then suddenly Dave stepped forward and passed the rings to Father John. He took them and examined them. "Here is Betty's ring, Daniel."

"Daniel you may say your vows to Betty now." I stood up straight and looked out at everyone and then back to Betty, I held the ring at the tip of Bett's finger.

"Thank you, Father. Bett, darling, our paths crossing was always meant to be, from the moment we sat, and we finished a whole bottle of Jack Daniels together in Gertie's on the second night; I knew you were very special." The crowd chuckled, knowing Betty. "In just a few weeks you have grabbed hold of my heart and not let go, you have taken my past pain and shown me light and so much love. The road ahead is never going to be easy but together we rule, we have the power of our love to get through the biggest of obstacles. We will never stop, never give up on each other and use our love to help all others in despair. Bett, take my ring and wear it with pride, I will always be here for you and do my best to keep you happy, whatever comes our way. Family means everything. I love you baby. Accept this with all my heart and all my joy." I pushed her ring on all the way. Betty winked at me.

Beautiful Danny.

Father John looked to Betty.

"Thank you, Daniel, beautiful words, and now Betty, your ring for Daniel and your vows to Daniel."

"My Danny, you entered my life unexpectedly, I had no idea you were the missing piece that makes me whole and that I was missing so much in my life. You opened your heart to me graciously and I fell deeply in love with you, you made loving you so easy, and when you dropped on your knee to ask me, I could not wait to say yes. I will stand by all your decisions and back you up one hundred percent, I love you man. I will love you until the end of time. We have got this together and we are stronger than anyone knows. Our love unites everything. Take this ring and take me as your wife. I love you." She pushed it on my finger.

Oh, Bett, you are so beautiful, Father John stood forward.

"Thank you, Betty, lovely words, should anyone present know of any reason that this couple should not be joined in holy matrimony, speak now or forever hold your peace." The congregation stood silent, holding their breath, looking around.

"I now would like to say, these rockstars are married. Daniel you may kiss your beautiful bride, Mrs. Starr."

Father John stepped back and gave us some space. I pulled her in, but she pulled me equally, we embraced and kissed passionately in front of everyone and they all felt us, we felt them. It was beautiful. Betty hugged me so tight.

"Thank you, my husband."

"Oh, Bett, you are everything. Thank you, my wife." Taxi erupted in joy, cheering and whistling. And that was our wedding done.

Everyone exited the Church as Elvis played loudly 'Can't Help falling in Love' We had a photo shoot with Champagne and the bridal party by the Torrens River. It was soon time to head for Gerties and our reception. Dad had organized the new Bently for us. We had our champagne and drove around Taxi for a while kissing and laughing. We were quite tipsy and having a ball. We finally rocked up at Gertie's. We were the stars of this unbelievable show.

"Bett here we go, keep it all together, this is fantastic. Come baby."

We stepped out as cameras went crazy. We walked confidently out the back of Gertie's as the music started up loudly, 'Celebration', by Cool and The Gang, we looked at each other and started moving with the music as we walked into the back gardens. Taxi went crazy, cheering us and whistling whoop, whoop! The DJ suddenly announced us.

"And here they are 'Mr. and Mrs. Starr!" So, then we danced into the crowded reception, loving the attention. The whole town clapping in unison as we went to our table. Conner had organized fireworks that went off in time with the music. We sat down and thought that was it, but the DJ started telling a story about us, our meeting and whirlwind romance and our musical choices. Taxi listened enthralled with our magical story.

Later as 'All along the Watchtower' by Jimi Hendrix played loudly, one of my all-time favorites, the food started coming out, and it was amazing, layer upon layer of flavor and diversity. Bett requested a mix of raw seafood be put aside and given to us as we leave. She kept looking at me, I could feel her love, and I felt totally in love. The Taxi-Cabs started up and played a lot of Australian songs by some very cool Aussie bands. Bett and I looked up together, we could feel Shiny up there, we so wanted her down here with us, but we could not do it just yet.

Be patient Shiny, soon.

I understand Danny. I still like it.

Shiny, you are so good, be ready to shield their minds, so they feel no fear of the future and you.

I am ready for my show, come on Danny I want to join you.

"Okay, hang on Shiny." All the main meals were done with and the band was on a break. I stood up and tapped the mike, "Can you please put 'Child in Time' by Deep Purple on in the background thank you. You have all become aware of the extra activity in Taxi, everything has gone into overdrive, many of you are aware of The House of Ra but are not aware of the significance of it. Conner Rage has basically built a bunker for all the residents of Taxi to survive a holocaust. Bett and I and Conner, need all of you to enter this place tomorrow night at the latest, as the huge meteor they said will miss, will hit us and hit hard. Our Bunker will protect all of Taxi's people. Conner was blessed with a vision to save you all. And he will. We know that this is huge news but there is more." People were frowning, some gasping. *What is this?* They thought together.

"Relax everyone, and have a drink, breathe, we have you. We will keep you safe, Taxi will survive this. We have no idea how long we will need to stay in there, Conner is well prepared. Have no fear about Monday but it is inevitable it will hit, and many cities will be destroyed. There will be tidal waves and firestorms, anyone out in the open will most likely not survive." We could hear a few people crying and Father John was crossing himself repeatedly and praying.

"Please listen and do not be sad, be joyful tonight. Party, drink and eat more food. We have an incredibly special guest to introduce you to. She is our Guest of Honor; you have never met anyone quite like Shiny. She is our protector, and she is from up there, outer space. She is here to help us all; she is our Starship. Please welcome Shiny." I started the applause off and everyone joined in. Some people looked confused and many were frowning and craning their necks. We all seemed to look up at the same time. Betty stood and held my hand. Shiny started to vibrate and we still could not see her yet, but we could all feel her. Slowly a point of light became brighter as the vibrations continued, the clapping died down as everyone stared in awe, Shiny descended slowly, going through all her colors pulsing and brightening in waves.

Excellent show Shiny. Stop just above Betty and I so we can touch you.

Okay Danny, these people are full of love, only one or two are scared but I am helping them. Betty and I raised our hands and Shiny came to a stop. As we touched her, all vibrations stopped and she was shimmering, glowing softly, her slightly golden glistening surface swirling around. The crowd looked on in silence and awe.

"Please say hello to everyone Shiny," I held the microphone against her body. She used her vibrations to form perfect words and spoke aloud for the first time.

"*Hello Taxi people, I am Shiny, and I am so happy to join in the celebrations of Betty and Danny's wedding it fills me with extreme joy. Please trust Conner, Bett, and Danny, they will look after you. I will too, I am joined with these two beautiful souls below me, to help humanity. Together Taxi will survive, can I hear some loud ACDC now, please and thank you.*

The DJ put on 'Thunderstruck' by ACDC, everyone clapped. She lifted twenty feet and spun like a top. Lighting up the whole town in all her beautiful colors all at once, perfectly in time with the music. The crowd roared in amazement, clapping boisterously. Shiny zipped straight up, then back down, then in a circle. She was so fast it looked as if a giant ring was sitting above Gertie's, changing colors in time with the music. Everyone was cheering enthusiastically, all phones and cameras pointed up at Shiny. She zoomed left then right so quickly and then sat there pulsing in time.

Shiny slowed and dropped down flying low and slow so anyone could reach up and touch her, she made their fingers tingle. As the song finished, Shiny stopped above the pond and dropped to three feet, and quietly sat there shimmering. All of Taxi was buzzing with talk. I nodded to the DJ.

"And now we ask the Bride and Groom to take to the dance floor and kick off the dancing." I took off my coat and led Betty to the floor, Shiny silently lifted above the dancefloor and turned into a giant multi colored mirror ball and the floor swirled as if it was alive.

We danced to 'Wake Up' by The Skeggs, one of our Aussie favorites and danced a rocking waltz, spinning around the floor, Betty followed my lead perfectly. Shiny's light was perfectly in time with the music. As the song finished all of Taxi cheered, whistled and clapped. 'LSD' by Skeggs was next, and Conner and Elouise joined us with about thirty others. We sat down exhausted after that song finished. Bett and I looked up at Shiny.

Thank you Shiny, you are perfect, thank you for coming.

I love this; I loved your dance with Bett, it was perfect, can I do this all night? We laughed. '*Yes of course Shiny if you wish to.*'

I do wish to.

Conner and Elouise came to the table, hugged us and sat down.

"You did very well Daniel, better than I could have ever done, everyone will come, everything is ready in *Ra*. The news reports are almost non-existent regarding the meteor. The US and China are dominating all major news with the threat of war looming. I am sure it is on purpose, to take attention away from it and to give the elite time to run and hide." Conner said.

Excuse me Danny, I can detect it up in the night sky; you can see it with your own eyes, look towards Orion's belt.

Thanks, Shiny.

"Shiny just told me to look towards Orion's belt," we all looked up expectantly.

"There it is!" We gasped; a glowing smudge of light surrounded by a storm of angry smaller lights. It looked like an arrowhead and it was pointed straight at us. It seemed close, too close.

"Oh my god." Conner whispered. "Hey, we should stop looking up at it, we might freak everyone out if they all see it, the mood is incredibly good right now I would hate to spoil it." We all nodded and grabbed our drinks and skolled them, even Elouise.

"Dad, I need to tell you something," Betty looked at me. *The Ishta*. I nodded.

"Medi-Corp belongs to an alien race; they are wearing your skins to survive."

"What, really? No! What? Aliens? No wonder they need so many. No way. How do you know this?" He looked to me almost astonished; I took over.

"We have met four of them two are called Ishta, and two are Lloyds. They are always in twos and wear dark glasses at night to cover their true eyes, but they are energy beings with no true form. Their planet is dying; they can only survive on their new planet by wearing the skins. They can only talk telepathically."

"*Wow! That is incredible*, thank you for telling me that. We have one huge shipment leaving tomorrow, it will be the last one before we shut down everything at midday. Aliens, really? I am glad if it is helping them. I had no idea. That is totally crazy. I'm sorry but please excuse us as I must do my speech now." Conner and Elouise stood and left.

The music stopped and the DJ announced it was time for speeches. Shiny lifted silently and stopped her lights and lowered to within three feet of the pond. Conner stood up at his table with a mike in his hand,

"Thank you all for coming today; it has been a fantastic wedding thanks to all of you. Betty and Daniel make the perfect Bride and Groom don't they." He motioned towards us, and everyone cheered and clapped. "Betty looks fabulous today nothing like the grubby, snotty nose five-year-old who used to roll around in the mud playing with stuffed animals." Everyone roared with laughter. "Betty looks like her grandmother did in these beautiful clothes, she could pass as her twin. She wore a dress remarkably similar when she was married to my father."

"Betty has always strived hard to achieve top marks at school and college; she can sing and dance and play the piano beautifully. Betty is a top marksman, and she is a top chef and honestly an all-round nice person. Her new occupation as astronaut and helper to humanity is a tough gig too; but I know she will do her best and that will be enough, thanks to this man here Daniel. Daniel has set Betty on fire with his love and a passion for the outdoors and they even did a thirty-mile run this morning followed by a three-mile swim. He has put a light in Betty's eyes that I have not seen in a long while and I thank you for that. You have made Betty incredibly happy and together into this new future you will soar."

"Let me tell you all what I did the other day with them." He pointed at us and then to Shiny. "Daniel asked me to come on a flight with them in Shiny. The thing is, to fly inside Shiny you must first be totally naked and once you enter you must drown in a jelly like liquid that supports you. So, there we were laying naked, face down holding hands flying through space. The cool thing is when you are inside Shiny, her hull is totally invisible, it was the most incredible thing I have ever done. She flew us at amazing speeds all the way to Jupiter and back in four hours; the whole time it was like we were flying though space on our own. Thank you, Shiny, Betty and Daniel. Together the three of them will help all survivors get through this travesty. Please show them some love." Everyone stood up and cheered and clapped. "Now, please fill your glasses. To the Bride and Groom."

"To the Bride and Groom!" They all repeated and toasted us. The DJ stood up.

"Thanks Conner, unreal experience you shared. Now, can we get a few words from our stars, Betty and Daniel." We calmly stood and looked around at everybody and spoke together.

"Thank you all so much for making this day so very special. We are blessed to all be together, we just wanted to share our love with you and you have given us so much love back. We can feel it and thank you. This will be a party to remember but sadly the last party out here at the back of Gertie's for a while. We need to tell you, that we are not joining you in The House of Ra. We have been instructed to be in Shiny up in space to do whatever we can to aid humanity. Believe us, we will try our best to reduce damage, but this event is going to change the planet. How can we help, you might be asking, well we can do things with our minds, both of us," we said in unison.

Then I looked at Betty,

"Bett, can I have a drink please." She raised her hand for theatrics as my glass lifted and flew over and then the bottle of Sinatra Century came over and filled my glass. I took a drink. Necks were craning. Now it was my turn.

"Danny, can you spin the chair?"

"Sure Bett." I raised my hand towards my chair, it lifted into the air and started spinning fast. I lifted it quickly to one hundred feet and back down on to the dance floor where it sat motionless just off the floor. Slowly it started turning around before returning to its original spot. The crowd was absolutely incredulous.

"As you can see, we have gained a few special abilities. But now as our gift to you, we would like you all to join us for another dance, a dance with a difference." I took Betty's hand and we lifted into the air effortlessly. The crowd gasped loudly. "A dance above the dance floor please come you will love it." Shiny rose higher this time. "DJ please cue Savage Garden, 'To the Moon and Back,' loud." The music started and I happily swirled Betty around above the floor with ease. Taxi was in stunned silence; phones came out and started recording. People were gasping and pointing. Conner and Elouise and about a dozen brave people ventured onto the floor and immediately lifted into the air, about four feet up. All of Taxi was mesmerized.

Some dancers were experimenting with their newfound floating skills, spinning sideways and doing flips in the air in time with the music. It was the most magical dance I had ever taken part in. Conner and Elouise were ecstatic, their faces full of delight. As the song finished, we floated off to the side of the dance floor watching the fun above the floor. More people joined in, as 'Truly, Madly, Deeply' came on. Our glasses floated over to us. We looked up at Shiny, she was in utter bliss her body shimmering and shivering in delight.

Thanks, Shiny!

Oh, Danny and Bett, this is the best night ever, I love it. The song finished and the DJ put on 'Cry to Me' by Simon Burke. Bett pulled me in and we were back above the floor, we let go of our drinks and they just hung there. Bett was into Dirty Dancing the movie and knew this dance and so did I. We danced sensually and beautifully, above the dancefloor, it opened up as they all started pulling back, watching us.

When it finished, everyone cheered us. We thanked them and I pulled Betty away as I could feel her tensions rising, she was very close.

"Whew, thank you Danny, I was so close."

"I know baby, let's drink and graze the food and take your mind off of where it was going." We sat at our table and drank some Sinatra.

"Danny, it is so cool, everyone knows it is the end of the world soon but tonight is a true party; no one cares, they are all enjoying themselves. And you, you are in for a huge session my dear. I can't wait to be naked in your arms. Tonight has been perfect, thank you husband."

"My darling, this is perfection; thank you gorgeous just look at you, you are my wife now, I can't get my head around it. I am so happy and so in love and ready to fight for all humanity."

"Watch out baby I am coming for you tonight, well probably tomorrow early morning by the time we leave. Here is a preview." I used my mind and slipped in, then out of her slowly. She gasped and leaned forward and kissed me passionately.

"Yes Danny, again, please." This time I licked her clit and then I did it again, slower, lingering and gently thrusting deep, before I pulled away with my mind, I felt her as much as she felt me. She moaned in my ear in pure ecstasy. I was starting to get a very stiff erection.

"Oh, Danny you beautiful man, stop now or I will lose it completely." She held my face and kissed me erotically. Above the dance floor was full of Taxi townsfolk having a ball. 'Honky Tonk Man' by Dwight Yoakam was playing loudly. Shiny was throbbing intensely with her light show. Taxi felt so alive. And love was everywhere, it was all around us. Conner and Elouise came over and sat down.

"Hey guys, we need to get married tonight; we apologize but we feel our time is now, you may not be with us in two weeks and everyone is here. Do you mind? Sorry to drop this bomb on you both we do not want to steal your thunder." We looked at each other and back to them. I said to them.

"No way, this is perfect, please do, Father John is over there, get him organized before he has too many wines."

"You know there may be others too, that feel like you. Last chance before it comes."

"You are right Danny; we should open it up for anyone, okay Elouise?"

"Absolutely Conner, I am with you, tonight is the night." She nodded. So I went over to the DJ and had a chat with him. He looked at me solemnly.

"Yes just wait for my cue." I told him.

"Okay." he said. Conner was talking with Father John whose head was nodding constantly. We came back to the table and had a drink.

"Okay, Conner?"

"Yes, all set." 'Conner I will ask everyone, okay?"

"Yes Daniel, let's do this."

The DJ stopped the music and Shiny settled.

"Attention Taxi, Daniel would like to ask you all a serious question. We will give you a brief time to think about it and then answer. But please remember tonight is your night, to shine... Danny!" Everyone cheered.

"Hey Taxi, thank you for a fantastic night, Bett and I have had a ball the whole night through. But now for those of you who are ready; you have the opportunity to marry now with Conner and Elouise. Think about it, if you are considering getting married, just do it tonight... Now. Because tonight will be perfect, we are all here to help you celebrate. I will give you a few minutes to think about it."

After the three minutes, three couples stood up, somewhat reluctantly but ambitious. Father John stepped up. "These are different times; I thank you for your honesty, four couples who are willing to open up and share their love; Conner Rage you have instigated this. Your love for family has opened other hearts. Please embrace each other on this very special occasion." Shiny went up above the dance floor and put a focused spotlight on the four couples as Father John started his sermon. There was a hushed silence throughout the congregation; this really was a unique night. When he got to the vows, each couple said a few words about each other's love, then they were handed glasses of sparkling champagne. They crossed their arms and shared with each other, rather than give rings. Father John stepped back and announced,

"I now pronounce you all husband-and-wife congratulations; you may kiss your bride." As they kissed, the crowd went wild, cheering and clapping. Many people ran forward and hugged the couples and shook hands. The waiters came out and passed around more glasses of champagne to those who desired it, others took shots of Sinatra, the celebrations just lifted to the next level. The DJ put on 'I Gotta Feeling' by The Black Eyed Peas loudly. Shiny spun up and around and put on an amazing light show as everyone on the dance floor slowly lifted into the air and started dancing, hugging and kissing. 'Love is in the Air' by John Paul Young came on and all of Taxi squeezed in above the floor and joined in the fun. Bett and I could not have been happier, what a fantastic night. We sat after that dance and shared a quiet kiss.

"Oh babe, how perfect is tonight?"

"Yes, Bett it is perfect, perfection." We could see Conner and Elouise making their way over to us. We stood up and ran to them and hugged them tightly. Kissing them we could feel their absolute happiness. We all sat down and I poured out four glasses of Sinatra, and we all raised our glasses together.

"Congratulations to the Bride and Groom!" I announced and we all drank. I raised my glass again. "And here's to Taxi!" We all smiled, raised our glasses and drank again. The waiters came out and put down trays of little hot dogs and fancy sliders and little burgers with beef or chicken on them. They all looked divine. We all took one and they were delicious. The DJ put on 'What a Night' by Elvis.

"Come on you two, let's dance. Conner, you take Bett for a father daughter dance and Elouise, you're stuck with me."

"Great idea Danny," Conner said as he jumped up grabbing Betty's hand. I took Elouise's hand and led her onto the dance floor and we all lifted into the air. I danced rock and roll with Elouise, and she could dance pretty well. Conner and Bett were having a great time together. 'Moon River' by Frank Sinatra came on and I looked over at Bett, but Conner had pulled her in close and was talking to her as they danced, so I did the same with Elouise dancing a slow waltz.

"How are you doing this Danny? Lifting everyone off the floor?" Elouise whispered into my ear. I could smell her sweet perfume; she smelt lovely. Her hand slid down the middle of my back like a feather and her leg slipped between my legs pushing against me sensually.

"Bett and I are doing it together; we just imagine that everyone above the dance floor is lighter than air and we hold that thought continuously." She smiled at me.

"It is amazing, your gift. Was it embarrassing flying naked with Conner?" She grinned widely.

"Ha, only a little. Shiny made all our bits blurry so Conner could see we were naked but could not make out anything. Same with him, it was just a blur." She shook her head in wonder.

"Look after yourselves up there; stay out of danger, okay?"

"Sure, thank you, you are perfect for Conner; we can feel your love, both of you."

"You can feel me?" She squeezed my waist, pulling me closer, her heart rate lifted as her pelvis squished against my groin, involuntarily.

"Well, yes, your emotions, you radiate joy and love, it flows out of you." She leant in and kissed me lightly on the cheek; smiled and shivered, her heart rate rose again.

"Bett is very lucky to have you, and you to have her. Take care of each other." She chewed her lip.

"Thank you, Elouise." I said as Bett and Conner danced over; we swapped partners.

"Thanks for the dance, Danny, have a nice night." Elouise went into Conners arms and kissed him passionately. We left the dance floor. Bett glanced sideways at me then in my head. *I think you just aroused her; she is definitely not far off; do you have that effect on all women?*

"Bett all I did was dance and told her she is perfect for Conner and that she radiates joy and love."

"That she does, well it was enough anyhow, now you can arouse me, okay?" With her mind she started squeezing me. "Follow me, husband," she led me in the side door past the toilets and into her bedroom.

I forgot she had lived here. She shut the door and locked it.

"Just a quickie, okay?" She pushed me back onto her bed undid my fly and belt and pulled me out, "Ah there you are my man; I want you inside me." She slid her knickers off and lifted her dress so I could see her and then she climbed on and slowly took me in. Gasping with pleasure and smiling gorgeously at me we slowly moved in time.

Bett started to tremble instantly and moaned loudly as she suddenly climaxed, throwing her head back in ecstasy. She was squeezing on my cock and gripping it tight, bringing me there too. Bett fell forward and started kissing me to muffle her moans as I thrust up into her.

"Uh." she pushed me down firmly clenching me with her muscles. Bett grabbed the bedspread and shoved it in her mouth and screamed in erotic ecstasy as the second wave took her. She released me, easing her grip and slowed me down. I pulled the bedspread from her mouth and kissed her sexy lips.

"Are you good?" I asked panting heavily.

"Oh, so fucking good. Yes, darling, fuck I needed that ugh, thank you. We should get back; it is time for a cigar."

"Good idea." She lifted off me, washed me with a damp flannel and wiped me with her towel and then kissed and sucked my cock briefly. "Later my love," she said and went to the toilet taking her knickers with her. I stood up and tucked everything in and went to the mirror and brushed my hair. Bett came out and we quietly snuck out. We sat and lit a huge cigar, sipping our Sinatra watching everyone having a good time. We looked at each other and smiled. Betty ran her hand up my leg and gave it a quick squeeze then letting go, she grinned wickedly and kissed me. "That was a perfect first time as a married couple fuck, do you agree?"

"Yes Bett, perfect, my body is buzzing from that," my cock was still semi-hard, hungry for more.

So is mine, I could barely control myself, it was perfect. Shiny admitted in our minds.

Oops, sorry Shiny we should have warned you.

It is okay I was expecting you to sneak away; you did it at the same time as Conner and Elouise. We looked at each other, they hadn't returned yet.

Shiny that is too much information.

Can I tell you that all the couples that got married tonight also did it at the same time, some are still hard at it, down by the river.

Okay stop, Shiny, that is enough, how do you know this, do you feel them too?

When you were together, you sent out a vibration that set the others off, they couldn't help themselves. I don't understand why just them, to me I thought everyone felt it and there was going to be a massive orgy, but it was just the ten of you. I think some of the bar girls orgasmed involuntarily too.

Okay that is plain weird, are you still enjoying yourself Shiny?

Yes, Danny, thank you again for inviting me, I have had a blast.'

That is fantastic Shiny, we are glad you came tonight. I need to talk to you tomorrow, okay?

Sure Danny.

Betty looked over at Conners table; they sat down and kissed passionately.

"Danny what is the time? I have no idea." I looked at my watch

"It's eleven o'clock. Are you tired?"

"No baby, just horny." She winked at me and flashed her wicked smile. "How long do we stay here tonight?"

"Well, we can only stay an hour tonight and then it will be tomorrow."

"Oh, okay smarty bum, you know what I mean."

"Are you still enjoying yourself, Betty?"

"Of course, you know I am,"

"Okay, why would you want to go, there will never be another night like this, possibly ever."

"Yes, that is very true, I want to dance slow can you have a word to the DJ?"

"Last time we danced slow you nearly lost it."

"I know, I want that, I will hide it if it happens."

"Oh, sure, you'll hide it, maybe if I help you. Okay then, and if anyone notices who cares?" I stood and went over to the DJ; he was fine with it, after the next song he would do a whole set.

Shiny, can you do really dim, sexy lights.

Are you sure, sexy lights. It might be too much.

When the slow songs start it will be okay. After the next song.

Okay then sexy lights it is, I can't wait for this.

Thanks, dim and low and slow.

Yes Danny, I got you.

The DJ put on the last fast song. Bett and I lit another cigar and sipped our Sinatra. We stood up and moved towards the dance floor still drinking and chuffing on our cigar and Conner did the same with Elouise. The DJ queued 'The First Time Ever I Saw Your Face' by Roberta Flack; I had requested that as the first. As the fast song finished, we moved slowly forward and floated out, our glasses and cigar went back to our table. Shiny dimmed her lights, but the light felt slightly different, warm and fuzzy, sensual. We felt it immediately.

I pulled Betty in close and shut my eyes. She was in my head already.

Oh Danny, I love you so much, just take me away. We swirled around slowly with my hand sliding down her bare back. Bett moaned quietly.

"Yes baby," she trembled. I pulled her close and gripped her tightly as the first of many orgasms went through her. I glanced around to see if anyone had noticed and I was astonished. It appeared as if every woman above the dance floor was having a quiet orgasm in the arms of their partners, even the older ladies. The partners of all realized what was happening to them, some were kissing and some women had grabbed their men in the pants. One or two had their hands inside the men's trousers already. The people off the dance floor had no idea what was happening, Shiny was fuzzing us out.

Shiny! Are you doing this?

Danny it is you and Bett, but the lights are also affecting the women. I looked over; Elouise had her head back in ecstasy, her hand firmly gripping his crotch. Conner was non-plussed holding her tight, just whispering in her ear. She looked at me and smiled and I could hear her clearly, in my head.

Oh, you did this, oh, to me Danny, oh, thank you, oh.' Shit. Oops. She is my mother-in-law.

Shiny please stop the sexy lights now, but keep the fuzz on us all on the dance floor, at least until the women calm down. And can you please stop the two couples that are about to have intercourse.

Yes Danny, sorry, I should have explained sexy lights, it includes pheromones of attraction and sexual frequencies.

Bett was still carrying on in bliss unaware, as all women were. She suddenly grabbed the back of my head and planted the wettest kiss on my mouth.

Oh Man, you are fantastic Danny, you are my universe, I fought hard to keep my feelings of lust down. My cock wanted to burst out of my pants and fuck Betty on the dance floor. It was pushing hard against the inside of my pants trying to escape. All the women on the dance floor shivered uncontrollably with Betty.

Bett, we need to get off the dance floor.

Oh no, Danny, I want to dance some more. She grabbed my crutch feeling my stiff cock and squeezed gently.

Bett we are affecting all the women here on the dance floor.

Well, good Danny, I hope they are enjoying it as much as I am, can I pull it out? Your huge cock is rock hard, poor man.

Bett they are all enjoying it, but these men have no idea what is going on, including Conner. Betty opened her eyes and looked around.

Oh, shit really?' She heaved again as another orgasm hit; she was rubbing my cock fast.

Uh, stop, Betty, please; look they are all in time with you. Look! She could see them, all shaking in time with her. Elouise was going off, staring at me, rubbing Conners' cock.

Okay Danny, take me off slowly.

Yes, just wait. Shiny can you fuzz us as we leave and calm the women, please. I will do my best, but it is you two. We should probably all go back to camp now.

Shiny can you make these people forget?

No Danny, that is beyond my capabilities. Just move away from the dance floor now, they will be alright.' I held Betty tight, and we slowly moved away from the dance floor and settled on the ground. We casually walked out the front of Gertie's. Bett suddenly pulled me into some dark bushes and swiftly pulled my cock out of my trousers and went down on me, sucking furiously. We both came almost immediately as she took some and pulled away quickly. My cum kept pumping out, shooting into the bushes as she tugged on me. She wiped her mouth and kissed me passionately as I kept coming; moaning in her mouth, until she finally slowed and so did I. She just held my cock softly now as she relaxed in my arms. She went back down on me and licked me clean. Then tucked me back into my pants and did up my fly.

They are all calming down now, they are full of love, and I think they will be leaving this party for their own party with their partners. This night will go down in history, as these women open up to each other later, sharing their experiences on the dance floor. For some it was Betty, who set them off, for others it was you Danny, but the result was the same. All women had multiple uncontrolled orgasms, almost all the way through that first song. My light intensified their feelings and enhanced the experience. Danny this is not a bad thing, it is something that will help unite Taxi through the next few tough years.

Bett called our drinks and cigar to us, she sat with the cigar in her mouth her drink raised to her lips, staring at me, in a daze.

"Danny, my body is in shock. I am vibrating I think, I don't even know what came over me. I was lost, like when the Hathors had me. I was in bliss on the dance floor but felt no control. I think one of them was in me again. Using me, overpowering the others for her own gratification, absorbing all our emotions but I'm glad I got to suck you off I must admit."

Ω

Yes, now I can see her, the one that is separated. She is fat and gloating on her success and the others can't see what she did, she hides it from them.

Bett that one must go as a lesson to the others. Yes just that one, she is self-centered and ruthless. She keeps taking you over and using you despite their warnings to her. They can't control her; we need to stop her from doing this to you. We should do it when the strike occurs, we can target their base, and target her with one small meteor that will be enough. They are weak now.'

Yes Danny, I agree, and then we can enjoy each other in peace without losing control.

What is happening now Shiny?

All the women have stopped climaxing and calmed down. Most are sitting down and some have left. Others have come onto the dancefloor and are unaffected, just dancing around. You're safe to return if you wish. Perhaps not on the dancefloor.

We do need to come back in and say goodbye to everyone. See you in a minute. We stood up and went out the back of Gertie's then back to our table. It was now near midnight and Conner and Elouise were sitting at their table.

"Bett I will tell the DJ we are leaving soon, okay?"

"Yes baby, this has been a crazy, beautiful night we should go and thank dad and Elouise for everything too; after all, he organized everything." We both stood and went to the DJ, he agreed after a few more songs he would ask everyone to form an archway for us to leave through.

We proceeded to Conners table and sat down, he poured us two Sinatra Century's and handed them to us.

"Cheers Bett and Danny, here's to a fabulous wedding."

"Cheers." We all replied and took a swig. I looked at Conner.

"Thank you dad, for everything, tonight has been fantastic. The food incredible and the service, the music, fireworks, and everything thank you both."

"Danny, I'm so glad Shiny came along tonight, she is amazing. Her lights are very special, and everyone here is so close now thanks to you, Betty and Shiny. The shit will hit the fan on Monday, but tonight will be remembered as the night Taxi felt pure joy and love. And then there was that slow song, The First Time Ever I Saw Your Face, I don't know what came over all you women, but it sure seems as if you all shared something very special." Elouise was smiling, staring at me and slowly nodding. She was highly aroused. Betty piped up,

"Daddy, thank you for everything, we are leaving after the next song as we have a big day tomorrow. Okay?"

"Of course, sweetheart, thank you for a lovely night." We all stood and hugged each other Elouise sighed softly, her heart was pounding in her chest as I hugged her.

"Thank you for everything Danny, tonight was exceptional." She whispered as she pecked me on the cheek. Then she hugged Betty and said, "Bett you are amazing, your love is felt everywhere."

We headed back to our table and Betty asked a waiter to get the tray of raw fish and put it in the Bentley and to inform our driver we were leaving in a few minutes. The DJ put on our last song 'Unchained Melody' by the Righteous Brothers.

"Come on Betty, one last dance."

"Sure, baby," we floated up joining the dancers already there. We looked up at Shiny, who was still providing lights for the dancers.

Thank you Shiny, you have made our wedding very special for everyone, you are amazing. We will be leaving after this song.

Thank you, Danny and Bett, you are the perfect couple, you always have been. This world needs more like you. Have fun at camp tonight, I will

stay here until the end of the dancing and put on a big show as everyone leaves.

Thank you so much Shiny, have fun. The song soon finished, and the DJ announced our departure asking everyone to form up into a tunnel. The DJ put on 'Be My Baby' by The Ronettes as we went through the living tunnel of joyous Taxi townsfolk. Each of us were getting a playful slap on our butts by some and others dropping their arms and kissing us on the cheeks. There was so much love here we could feel it radiating from them all. We ran to the Bentley our cigars and fish for Jilly sat in the front, the driver opened the door for us and two glasses of champagne sat there waiting for us. We climbed in and raised our glasses,

"Here's to you, my wife."

"And here's to you my husband," we toasted each other and shared another sweet kiss as we headed back to camp. I was already putting logs in the fire pit and getting it lit, I poured two whiskeys and two champagnes and told Jilly telepathically to hide from the headlights and stay off the road. Betty was excited to be going back to camp and honestly, I couldn't wait to get these stuffy clothes off. We pulled up in camp and the doors opened automatically, with the driver announcing;

"Here we are, Mr. and Mrs. Starr, home sweet home, thank you both for a great night, congratulations." We thanked him and took our cigars and tray for Jilly and watched as he sped off. We lovingly walked hand in hand to the fire pit. The tray of fish and cigars floated in the air following our steps. Jilly popped up onto the side table and smiled at us.

"Hi Bett and Danny, did you have a good wedding?"

"We sure did we had a great night, look here this is for you," Betty lowered the tray down on the table next to Jilly and lifted the lid.

"Oh, yum oysters, tuna, prawns, a lobster tail and what are these?"

"They are Morton Bay bugs, much like lobster."

"Oh, yum, mussels and even some whitebait and two more big fillets of fish. Wow you have spoilt me. I can only eat half of this now." Bett sent a plate to Jilly who immediately started loading it up.

"We will put the rest in the fridge in the tent, okay?"

"Yes, yes, thank you for thinking of me you must have been busy, I do appreciate this, I will go now and eat this by the lake. I like your lake. I will eat this slow like you, to take in all the tastes. Thank you, go now and play with each other, I know you want to, I will not look." Jilly hopped and skipped away, delighted with her bounty.

Bett lifted her arms as her dress slowly lifted into the air. She stood with hands on her hips, looking at me lustfully. She had the most beautiful underwear on that I had ever seen, encrusted with diamantes. She left her pearl necklace on and diamond headband, and summoned the Jack I had ready. A cigar slowly floated to her mouth and lit. Suddenly I lifted off the ground and my shoes and socks fell off. Next was my coat, followed by my braces and tie. A Jack sailed over and another cigar for me. 'Rocket Man' started up on the stereo. Then my pants dropped and my boxers. Lastly my shirt slowly unbuttoned. Bett was watching with eyes wide enjoying her slow strip of me. My shirt slipped off me as I floated in the air in front of her, my cock standing erect. She was grinning gorgeously.

Bett stepped forward and grabbed me and took me in her mouth again, sucking wildly. Her eyes locked on mine, bringing me to climax instantly. I let go as she took me away, taking it all. When I stopped, she skolled her Jack and floated up to me. Her glass refilled and she took a drag of her cigar and another swig. She lifted her arms and her sexy bra flew off and her knickers slid down. She slowly floated forward sensually, her erect nipples at mouth level, so I kissed and bit her. She shivered and slowly wrapped her stunning legs around me guiding me inside her and she gasped in pleasure. I was so hard and excited; I couldn't wait to be inside her and make her delirious.

She slowly started gyrating around on me in bliss, watching me closely. She was still smoking her cigar and swigging her Jack and I smiled at her tenacity. She loved it and took her time as we floated four feet up in the air. She leaned into me and kissed me wetly, "I love you my husband and I am oh so close to screaming, oh, you should block your oh, ears. Oh," she let go of her bourbon and it just hung in the air.

"This is big babe, oh." Betty's body started shaking and vibrating as she looked at me, nodded and threw her head back and cried out in orgasmic bliss. 'Tiny Dancer' blared out the speakers. She clamped down on me, making me climax with her. I buried myself in her beautiful breasts, grunting and howling like a wild beast. Her euphoric orgasm kept going as did mine. Shiny lit the whole sky up suddenly. Betty came forward and kissed me before releasing her grip and slowing down and I eased too and stopped. She slipped off of me and flew away briefly, but soon returned with the cigar still going and the Jack in her hand. Her pearls and diamonds were still on.

"Danny, that was perfect again, every fuckin time you take me, fuck I love you, my man."

"Bett, you are simply amazing do not give me all the credit, we are tuned to each other so closely." I leant forward and kissed her again. She quivered with lust.

"Oh baby, thank you for tonight." I hugged her tightly and she came again in my tender embrace. We sat on the couch staring at the glowing smoldering fire. It was now two thirty in the morning and we did not care less. Shiny zipped in and sat half a dozen yards from us glowing softly.

Hey guys that was incredible I nearly lit up all of Queensland when we climaxed together. It felt amazing to me, what a night. I feel so alive this has been my best night ever, Thank you Bett and Danny. You know four couples conceived tonight, thanks to you.'

"Wait, what? Shiny, who conceived tonight?"

Pete and Pearl, Bob and Sue, and Davo and Lauren, Conner and Elouise. They all have twins coming. Goodnight, I sleep now.

"Shit Bett, you have brothers or sisters coming in nine months."

"*Oh,* wow, I never expected this, and I bet my dad never expected it, either. We have a lot to do tomorrow, Danny."

"Baby tomorrow is the last day for humanity, their last day to make peace with themselves."

"Yes, but right now it is you and me and that is all that matters in our world. We got this baby. Yes, I have you Danny, take me away again baby. I slipped down her body and took her in my mouth. She gasped as I lovingly took her. She heaved up as I used my tongue, she felt so alive. Betty's hands on the back of my head slowly moving around in ecstasy, my face was buried in her love. She didn't last very long, she threw her head back and cried my name out in ecstasy as she climaxed. I moved back up her body and penetrated her pussy with my stiff cock, thrusting in slow and deep. Betty cried out again in erotic joy, her body trembling all over. She clutched my bum cheeks and pulled me in tightly tightening down on me as I suddenly climaxed in her.

Keep going Baby, your cock feels amazing. I kept pumping into her, my hands gripped her hips tight as I pulled her to me, over and over. Our orgasm lasting for ages until finally we slowed and I fell off her onto the ground on my back exhausted.

Betty looked down at me and smiled; "Now that was one hell of a fuck! You and your big cock are incredible. We should go in the tent for some sleep now, okay?"

"Yes Bett, I'm done." Betty lifted us both and floated us into the tent and laid us next to each other.

"Goodnight wife." She took a firm hold of my warm cock with her hand and snuggled up to me closing her exhausted eyes. "Goodnight husband." We fell into a deep sleep instantly.

4

Sunday, The Last Day of the Old World

Betty stirred first and squeezed me firmly. I opened my eyes to her gorgeous face smiling at me.

"Hello, my darling," she squeezed me again as I slowly hardened in her grip. She let go of me and took me with her beautiful mind as she started kissing me. She clamped down on me as she mounted my manhood in my mind. I moaned with extreme pleasure.

I got you Danny, she moaned loudly feeling me, feeling my pleasure as she opened her eyes to watch me climax. My back arched, and all my muscles went tight as I exploded. She cried out as she climaxed too, never taking her eyes off my muscular body. She held my cum in a bubble a few inches away until I had finally finished and then sent it flying away. She cradled my clammy face in her hands and kissed me passionately. Bett then moved down and licked the last remaining drops and kissed my head wetly, smacking her lips loudly as she winked at me.

Thank you, Danny.

Oh, Bett, what a way to wake me up. Love you B. Swim?

Sure baby.

A low mist hung over our lake making it look mystical. We ran to the water naked and dived into the fresh cool water. Jilly suddenly popped her head up.

"Oh, good morning lovers, you have finished playing with each other now?"

"Yes Jilly, for now, anyways. Did you enjoy your feast last night?"

"Oh, yes, it was delicious and very fresh thank you. I will eat the rest for my lunch, okay?"

"Yes, of course Jilly." Bett hailed the shower gel, and it came flying over. Jilly swam off leisurely.

"I go while you wash, I don't like that bubble water."

"Oh, sorry Jilly". We soaped each other up sensually for the first time in ages. Betty climaxed immediately and then concentrated on me. I let go loudly soon after with my cum flying out of me and away. I fell on my back and let it all out while Betty was watching me and moaning loudly too as another wave took her. We slowed down and finally quietened.

"Whew, that was nice." Betty said as she kissed me. We finished washing ourselves and went back out to the fire pit drying up as we went.

Shiny, can we talk now?

Oh yes Danny, do you want me to come out or stay here?

You can stay there, block your thoughts.

Okay they cannot hear me, only you and Bett.

Shiny can you make a vortex? To draw stuff away?

Yes Danny, that is easy, it depends how big you want it.

Very big and powerful when the meteor strikes. Will the electromagnetic pulse (EMP) affect you?

Not if we are high enough, we should ask for Octo's help and Ishta. The Octo have many craft like me on Europa, they have a vast base there.

Shiny do you have any weapons, like lasers?

Who would I shoot? No, I don't have weapons.

Shiny, if we wished to stop one of the Hathors from controlling Bett, would you mind if we wished to kill her, well one of them?

No, I don't mind, it is for your conscience, not mine she is the evil sister and it is not nice what she does to both of you, especially you Bett. And you Danny, harvesting DNA to clone you without permission, is totally wrong. They are ancient beings and that one has lived long enough; her whole life was used to torture innocent people for her own gratification. You need to do what is necessary. I understand and have no judgement.

Okay, thank you Shiny. We will kill her; we warned her, many times. There is no other way to stop her. I will contact The Octo now too. And the Ishta and Lloyds.

– 71 –

Danny, can I listen too?

Of course, Shiny. Bett had summoned the communicator and pushed it for The Octo and I called to The Ishta.

Ishta, Lloyds can you please come for a conference now with the Octo.

Yes Daniel, we were expecting you today and were waiting we will be there shortly.

Danny, we the Octo are on our way. We felt the vibration of the Ishta and Lloyds first, but The Octo craft slipped straight in stopping three feet above the lake.

Hello, Shiny, Bett and Danny.

Hello, Octo, please close off to Hathors, you too Ishta and Lloyds. They walked quickly into the clearing as The Octo splashed into the water and swam over. Jilly came out and stood next to us proudly. The Octo lifted out of the water and waved their long tentacles at us.

What a gathering, Bett and I felt under dressed standing next to the fully clothed Ishta and Lloyds, but we looked at each other and shrugged it off. The Ishta and Lloyds greeted us stiffly as usual.

The rock approaches us quickly, Conner has provided all the skins he can, which has saved more than we could have imagined and we are so grateful.

Ishta, Lloyds why don't you thank him in person, we told him you and Medi-Corps are not from this world. We told him you are wearing his skins for survival and he is happy to have helped you, if you thank him today, we can mediate so he hears you. They glanced at each other and nodded.

We agree to meet him and thank him in person, it is the least we can do, let us know when. How can we help you Bettdanny? We looked across to The Octo and back to them.

We need some help tomorrow from all of you. We want to make a vortex above the main impact to draw heat, flames and ejecta out of the atmosphere. This will then reduce the effects of the after storms and reduce the ice age. Then we can try and save a few lives, if possible. Is there any way either of you can deflect any of the rocks away and do you have more craft that could assist. We wish to help save all universes with your help and our infinite mirror. But there is something more, this is not revenge it is justice. We intend to kill the tortuous Hathor the one who constantly torments us. She has stolen DNA, taken over Bett's body and half of Taxi and fed on us for far too long. We have the means to destroy her, and do not forget, it is they who send this rock to kill our people so they can feed. Billions will die tomorrow thanks to them. This is a warning, a show of force to relent and for them to leave us alone. Bett and I have the power to remove them all from existence, but we don't want that either, they are part of humanity whether we like it or not. They are the reason we are here.' The Octo spoke first with their warbling tones.

Bett and Danny, we are with you, Hathors have ruled your people for far too long, and we agree now is the time to strike. She is weak now. In the past we would never consent to this, but she can be stopped now. Across the universes we join you. We have over a thousand craft to assist; we can deflect many smaller rocks and assist with your vortex.

We the Ishta and Lloyds agree, we cannot stop this, but we can aid you with the vortex and deflection. We have thirty craft and we will do all we can to support your endeavors. Trust us as you have helped our people.

"This is good, isn't it?" Jilly asked us.

"Yes Jilly, this is very good. They will all assist us to help humanity. Thank you, Ishta and Lloyds; we will contact you when Conner is available. Our whales will tell us of the strike, and we will join with you later today, okay?"

Yes, thank you Bettdanny. 'The Ishta and Lloyds walked off, and the Octo's soulful eye stalks followed us precisely.

You are concerned Bett and Danny; tomorrow is terrifying for all of humanity, this is your defining moment as a species. We will help you because you are worthy as a race. We love your kind Bett and Danny. We love you two, your emotions unite our kind and others. We believe in you and trust in us to help you. We will leave you now, so we can prepare for what lies ahead. There is much to organize, a thousand craft. We thank you both for being you. The Octo swam around briefly and jumped up into their stunning craft, waving frantically as they left. Their craft swiftly rose and disappeared into our atmosphere.

Bett, Jilly and I stood on the shore of our lake staring ahead as one.

"Jilly when Conner comes you will need to hide, okay?"

"Yes okay, bye."

"We need to tell Conner what we know is going to happen as soon as possible and that is huge. This is important for humanity going forward."

"I'll call him." Bett replied.

"Yes, do it now please." She called Conner, and he answered immediately,

"Hi Betty how is married life?"

"Hi, Daddy it's great. But you need to come now, we want you to meet the alien race that owns Medi-Corps. They wish to thank you, please come now."

"Bett please tell them I will be right there, in seven minutes." Conner was ecstatic as he had hoped for this moment since he learned of the owners of Medi-Corps. He hung up. I called to Ishta and told them seven minutes. Bett and I threw some clothes on as the Ishta and The Lloyds arrived soon after. Then Conner pulled up in his Lincoln. He climbed out and walked briskly over to us. The Ishta and Lloyds just stood there, innocently. He looked at them, the Ishta, a man in his twenties and a girl in her teens. The Lloyds, two middle aged women in their late fifties. These were the skins they had chosen to wear. We introduced them to Conner and they stepped forward.

Connerelle, we all thank you for saving us, your skins have protected so many of our kind, please accept our sincere thanks. You have been our society's savior. You will go down in our history as legend. You are epic Connerelle; tens of thousands of us now wear your skins to survive. We would like to invite you to our world to see what you have achieved at some stage, maybe after your world has settled and you have time to come. We now have a means to transport you in a new craft that we have been working on, similar to Shiny. Conner would you like to come? I relayed their words and invitation to Conner.

"Danny please tell them I would be honored to join them for a visit to their world as soon as it is safe here on Earth." I told the Ishta of Conner's reply.

That is good, please pass on that we will do whatever we can tomorrow to aid you and we wish him a safe passage in his House of Ra. Next time we see him, we will have a means to communicate directly. Would you like to see our true form? It is a sign of our respect for you. I told Conner, who nodded.

"I would admire and appreciate the honor." Conner answered. There was a bright flash, as the skins and sunglasses fell to the ground. There were four human shaped balls of glowing energy shimmering in front of us. They bowed their forms. Conner bowed back. There was another brilliant flash and they were back in their skins replacing their glasses. They bowed once more and turned away and waved as they silently walked off. The vibration of their craft grew and then subsided. Then they were gone. Conner looked stunned and amazed.

"Wow Conner, they are going to take you for a spin to their planet."

"Yes, that was unreal Danny; that would be interesting and totally frightening. Our last shipment of skins to them leaves shortly so I must get back to Taxi-plus, sorry for my haste."

"No, that's fine, we do understand completely." He hugged us both then jumped into his Lincoln and roared off down the road in a cloud of dust.

You all need to come for a ride and relax, how about around the earth a few times slowly and maybe Venus and Mercury too. Shiny was right, a relaxing pleasure trip to see our planet one last time. Jilly popped out of the water.

"I will stay and eat the fish you have in the fridge."

Of course, Jilly. Bett flew the tray out and put it on the side table. We removed our clothes as Shiny lifted out of the water and floated over to us. We held hands and lightly kissed and lifted into the air and entered Shiny, she shivered with glee. We gulped her jelly and gagged as usual.

Thank you for coming, let's go. We lay prone, arm in arm looking forward and down. Our lake disappeared below as we lifted.

Shiny, take us over Taxi first please.

Will do Danny. Shiny was about three hundred feet up and cruising slowly invisible to the world. We looked down and the clean-up at Gerties was in full swing, chairs and tables being stacked up. Life went on regardless of what tomorrow would bring.

We headed up towards the air strip, skirting around it and spotted four jets ready to leave.

Shiny can you be picked up by radar?

No Danny, I absorb radar, but I can be seen by infra- red cameras, like on military jets, but they must catch me first. I can easily zoom away.

That is good to know, can we go into low orbit now please?

Okay, going up to the edge of space. The land suddenly dropped away, and the sky went dark. We should have been freezing but Shiny was nice and warm. Betty cozily snuggled into me. Below us was the Queensland coast; the curve of the horizon was absolutely stunning.

Betty's hand slowly moved down to my shaft and took a firm hold of me. I looked at her and she was smiling sweetly.

Can we, please baby. She moved under me and wrapped her legs around me, gliding onto me effortlessly. Shiny shivered in bliss and so did Bett. She gave me a big wet jelly kiss as she slowly moved on me and started to groan and vibrate as I started to climax. She moved quicker and held me tightly as I explosively let go moaning in the jelly. Betty's head tilted backwards and her back arched in ecstasy.

Oh fuck! She moaned in my head. Shiny was glowing brightly, throbbing in time with Betty. She started to calm and then another orgasm hit her, *oh*, she shook wildly and clamped down on me making me come again before slowly relaxing her grip and muscles. She would not release me. Betty just rode me as we hurtled through space. Venus loomed ahead, her clouds swirling in the glow of the sun. The whole atmosphere seemed to be one big storm raging around the planet similar to our steamy, sexual tryst. Shiny lifted away swiftly to Mercury. The small rocky planet was only slightly bigger than our moon that loomed ahead. It looked very inhospitable as we went around to the far side of Mercury; a large ring that appeared floating motionless in orbit.

This is the gateway for a wormhole that the Ishta use, it leads to the area of the galaxy where they live. It has always been here hidden from Earth by Mercury. The Martians built it a million years ago, before they destroyed themselves.

Right, so now you casually tell us there were Martians and this ring here is a million years old, that is incredible.

I thought you might like this. Bett you are amazing and that felt amazing. Your love making makes me fly so fast' Shiny shivered and vibrated.

Shiny that was both of us you know, well it felt like it was all three of us. Bett said silently.

It was all three of us, don't forget you are inside me; I feel everything you do, like what you are doing as we speak while gently squeezing Danny. We are all very close to climaxing again. Bett looked at me and tensed, her eyes wide with pleasure. She suddenly shuddered and held onto me tightly as she had another delicious orgasm, her moans and spasms bringing me immediately to climax as Shiny trembled with ecstasy.

Betty buried her head in my neck trembling in bliss.

Oh, Danny another one is coming,' she said in my head, as her whole body quivered and shook as the next wave washed over her. Shiny was pulsing with Betty. I wasn't quite done either, I slowly started pumping into Betty as she grabbed my bum cheeks and squeezed me tightly.

Come Baby, fuck me honey. I pushed harder and deeper and she moaned loudly rocking with me, until finally I let go in a rush grunting and moaning deeply. Betty lost it again shaking madly. Finally, we both calmed down relaxing in Shiny. She was looking up at me grinning widely. Betty pulled my face to hers and kissed me passionately in Shiny's jelly.

Whew, that was extremely intense, I love you both very much. You make me feel beautiful and you make me feel alive and sexy and very fast. That was unbelievable. Shall we go back to Earth now?

Yes, please Shiny. Bett's eyes were locked onto mine, she felt amazing and my penis was still hard inside her. She just stared and smiled; she looked so sexy. I couldn't turn away from her and she knew she had my full attention.

Please excuse my interruption, the rock is near us now if you wish to see it. Betty winked at me and looked outside and started gripping me again slowly inside her. I looked too. She stopped when she saw it.

Oh my God! This was the closest we had ever been to it and it was colossal, slowly tumbling and rolling. There was ice and gases' coming from it and it was surrounded by hundreds of substantial rocks as big as busses or houses, some were even much bigger. *Oh Shit!* Shiny flew within twenty miles of it before speeding away towards Earth, we couldn't speak. Bett had started again.

I looked back to her; there she was temptingly smiling and playfully squeezing me. She started erotically twitching on me that felt like tiny little squeeze and release shudders. I was as hard as ever as I made myself throb inside her once; her sexy eyes widened in curiosity. I did it again and she pouted and blew me a sultry kiss. I began throbbing continuously and she started vigorously vibrating on me and Shiny's jelly was vibrating in harmony too. Betty's crazed eyes locked on mine as she started to orgasm; she convulsed erotically with pure pleasure and pulled me to her as I started briskly pumping her. She was rocking wildly back and forth making me come in an instant. We rolled around in the jelly faster and faster and Bett climaxed again quickly. Shiny was vibrating fast as I let go a second time, this one lasting until Bett came a third time. Shiny's jelly had never felt so invigorating, we were all buzzing with her energy. I knew we all felt comfortable and extremely satisfied as we arrived in orbit above the Earth.

Shiny, Bett and I were totally euphoric; unable to speak as we all felt the same. I pulled out of Betty very slowly; she sighed and lovingly kissed me. We lay in each other's arms watching the planet slowly pass underneath us. It was saddening; we all felt it, knowing tomorrow it would be all gone.

Take us home please Shiny floor it!' Shiny zipped off towards Australia. Stopping above our lake and dropping down she opened. 'Thank you Shiny.'

'Bett and Danny, thank you too, very much, when you do that in me, I fly very fast. Shiny will rest now after all that action; I have absorbed so much of your DNA today. Danny your sex and attraction pheromones are off the charts.

We floated out and threw up the jelly from our lungs as Shiny closed and sank into the water. We dived into the cool lake and swam around briefly.

"Bett, she absorbs our DNA too."

"Of course, Danny, she takes all our waste as well. Each time we did it in her, she took everything into her jelly and we absorbed her jelly. Just look at our skin it is taking on a faint golden hue." The shower gel flew out and we washed ourselves. Betty had started preparing lunch in Horus. Streaky bacon and scrambled eggs, toast, herbed mushrooms and juicy tomatoes. We left the lake as our towels flew over. I flew some logs into the pit and lit it. We sat down on the lounge as Betty's phone pinged, it was Conner.

Bett read it out; '*Hi guys, I will send some men out to pick up Horus and Osiris tomorrow morning when you give me the green light to do so. They will be a lot safer in the hangar under the hill. You might be able to use them after, who knows. I wish to seal the hangar by 10.00am depending on the arrival time. The Americans, Chinese and Russian, are sending rockets today filled with nuclear weapons to try and blow it out of the sky and are advising everyone to stay inside and not go to work or school tomorrow. But the panic buying at the shops in the cities has already started. Roads and highways are starting to jam with a mass of cars with nowhere to go. We will go into Stealth Mode in Taxi at seven pm today. Gates closed. We must seal The House of Ra at least a few hours before impact tomorrow. Stay safe. Please come for last drinks at The Dermy at four this afternoon if you have time, bye for now.*' Bett text him back immediately. "Thanks Daddy, we should be able to make it, see you then." This could be our last chance before the strike.

Two trays flew out of Horus and came to us on the couch as we sat there in our towels. We were absolutely starving so we got stuck into our food eagerly.

"Bett, we need to find some whales and see if they can give us location and time yet." "Yes, Danny we can have one last flight by ourselves after lunch, out over The Coral Sea and swim naked with the Humpbacks."

"That will be nice." I looked at Bett sitting there with the towel wrapped around her slim waist, her beautifully tanned, slightly golden breasts plump and firm and her slightly muscular arms and sexy shoulders. 'What? Husband, are you having sexy thoughts about me?"

"Oh, Bett I am lost in admiration of you."

"I can feel it, thank you my darling. I love you too, every single inch of you, I can't get over our love making Danny, it is next level and it is boss level. Today was interstellar, inter planetary bliss!"

"Hah, yes it was, wasn't it and I never thought we would be having a threesome with a living spaceship. She is amazing, she makes us whole too."

"Oh, Danny she sure does, she is a beautiful soul. I'm sure she is innocently making us horny when we enter her, she can't help it and is unaware she is even doing it."

"I agree, and she does share our combined DNA, she feels our love for each other intensely." We finished up our lunch, drank some more red wine and shared another stogie then sat back quietly. Jilly jumped up on the side table and sat down.

'You two are buzzing from sex and Shiny, what have you been up to this morning?'

"Never mind Jilly, do you understand whale talk?"

'I sure do, they come through our barrier sometimes to say hello, we get along pretty good they are very intelligent, most humans have no idea.'

"Would you like to come with us flying through the sky to The Coral Sea to talk with the whales?"

'Yes, but my big sensitive eyes in the sky might be hurt by the wind.'

"Jilly, we shield our eyes when we fly fast, we can shield you and your eyes too okay?"

'Yes okay, I would like to swim in The Coral Sea.'

"Come on then let's go."

We lifted off the ground still naked and rose two hundred feet into the air as Jilly sat suckered onto Bett's shoulder. We sped forward together as one, slipping silently over the hills and valleys avoiding built up areas and lifting higher near the coast. We were two naked people and a little amphibian, soaring through the sky, nothing to see here. We crossed the coast and headed out; the crystal-clear azure ocean was stunning below us and full of life. We dropped down lower and headed for The Great Barrier Reef staying away from the tourist areas. There were a few fishing boats around and if they saw us good luck to them it would make no difference tomorrow there would be no Instagram posts of a naked couple or news film clips. We became aware of whale song; they were singing to us. We slowed down and dropped to ten feet just below us where a pod of three Humpbacks started breeching. One was Migaloo, the famous all white albino humpback whale.

'Hello Old Ones, come and swim with us. Hello Jillyish, good to see a Saved One out in the open.' We dove into the beautiful blue sea next to them. Betty went over to Migaloo and placed her hands on him embracing him and he cried out in joyful song. I placed my hands on another. Our heads and ears were full of their glorious singing and clicks.

Sadly, there is less than twenty-four hours. After the midday sun in the afternoon tomorrow, the northern hemisphere will bear the full force, all the northern continent. We head south now but we are too slow to get far enough, many are down there now, but our kind always travel north this time of the year to seed. We head south early and will go deep, but many will not survive. Like your kind, you will be devastated. We wish you all the best; we know you have always been protectors of this world. You are part of our legends passed down in song through generations. We too have off world friends, they are like us, they teach us and they know you too. All throughout the galaxy know you two. Your loving happiness fills all and we feel your love. Stay safe little Jilly, your kind are strong.' Jilly spoke up.

"If you feel you can't get far enough away, please go below our barrier so we can protect you with our force shield."

Thank you, Jilly, your kind have always taken us in, we will remember this goodwill.

Migaloo, you are too kind; we thank you for your knowledge and friendship and hope we can speak with you sometime soon. We swam closer to them and held them, our arms outstretched on their smooth bodies; they lay motionless singing with so much compassion. They could feel our love for them. *Until next time our friends, thank you and be safe.* They whistled and whooped with glee.

Stay safe Old Ones and Jilly. They dived down deep into the cool Coral Sea and disappeared into the darkness.

We all lifted into the air. Jilly climbed up on Bett's shoulder and suckered tight and we flew back to camp swiftly and settled on the ground next to the fire pit. Jilly animatedly jumped down and went over to the flickering fire.

"We have an hour and a half before The Dermy." I said to Bett.

"You know they have probably already started drinking there."

"Okay, so where is my drink, we can start right here." I replied as a full glass of Sinatra Century floated in front of my face. Bett took hers and took a big swig.

"Oh, okay, like that are we?" She looked at me,

"Danny, it is the end of the world tomorrow." Jilly swigged from her glass too and looked up at us,

"Cheers!" I took a swig as a cigar came over. "Why not?" I chuffed on it looking down at Jilly.

"That was nice of you with the whales, I know they appreciated it and likely they will go down into your realm, to be saved. Cheers Jilly." I raised my glass to her.

Cheers Jilly. Bett raised her glass to Jilly too.

'Cheers!' We clinked glasses and skolled. Our glasses filled immediately. We need to advise Conner now and the Octo, Ishta and Lloyds. Betty raised her hand for her phone and sent a text; '*Just before two o'clock tomorrow afternoon; North America, Europe, Russia, and Asia, will be hit.*' His reply was; '*Okay, this really is the end.*' We knew exactly what he meant, with those countries gone the whole world would collapse. Devastation would cover the globe. I informed The Octo, Ishta and Lloyds of the whale's information. They thanked me and told me they would meet with us at ten above Mars for our strike.

"Cheers." Jilly looked up at us.

"*Cheers, Jilly.*" We said in unison and clinked our glasses again.

"My tools, I have in my pack on my back; I will save this lake and your camp. I can cover it in a bubble of safety for as long as needed, protect us from whatever comes this way, it is not much but it is something I can do for you. It will be our haven, our home. Shiny can enter but nothing else can, unless we agree. Even the water will be clean and safe. It is the same technology as our barrier above our city. This is my gift to you."

"Oh, Jilly really? This is an incredible gift we had no idea you were capable of this. Thank you, a haven, a home will mean everything to us all including Shiny. There will be months or years of trouble and turmoil on this planet, please tell us if you desire to return to your home and we will take you."

"I am meant to be with you until you retire from this life or pass and only then can I return to find my own partner. This is my duty so I can relay the legend of these days to all who follow; I am with you for future generations of my kind." She said this smiling up at me.

"Jilly, you don't need to record us; you have your own life to live."

"Oh, but I do, this is my society this is how we became strong and smart by being with you; I love being with you, every second is joyous. The JD and your playfulness with your bodies, you are a pleasure to be around so please do not deny me or our race from learning about your love. It is so fulfilling, for all races. You still are innocent of your love for each other but when you are together you awaken the world and any races that are within your reach. Even now as your desires for each other arise, humanity feels it and feels much comfort. The pain of tomorrow eases; they forget and embrace each other. Just do what you want to. Cheers!" We looked at Jilly in a whole new light, there is so much more to this beautiful little fish. She is so intelligent and with it.

Jilly, you are amazing, thank you for everything you said about us, we love you little fish. She knew we meant it and she could feel our love; she skipped off and splashed into the lake and swam away contented.

Bett?

Yes Dan, we have half an hour before going to the Dermy.

We could go for a run.

Just stop it and come here my man. I sat next to Bett and chuffed on the cigar.

That is very sexy Danny.

What is Bett? Her hand landed on my cock and she clasped me firmly while her other hand took the cigar from me and she took a chuff.

"It's not over until the fat lady sings." She squeezed me snug as I quickly hardened; she swiftly jumped on top of me, guiding my hardness inside her sweet velvet. She slipped down onto me and slowly rose back up, "I got you, babe." She fucked me hard and fast, bringing us sensually together. I loved it and she clearly did. She came within minutes and I soon followed howling loudly.

"Oh Bett," I cried out, in ecstasy.

"Now that's exactly what I'm talking about Danny, she sang beautifully" as she whispered in my ear between moans.

She stopped and just sat on me, kissing me, and chewing on my ear. I held her breasts with my thumbs on her luscious hard nipples, slowly massaging them. She was doing her own sensual massaging on me and she felt amazing. She floated a whiskey over for us and the cigar and we sat there drinking, smoking and massaging each other for the next half hour. Gently I held her hips as she started to gyrate on me, lifting and falling, kissing and squeezing until I could hold on no more. I thrust up as I climaxed and she cried out in pure ecstasy as she came too.

'*Yes, uh Danny!*'

Bett sped up and pushed down hard on me grinding, gyrating as I thrust into her. She rose up on me until I was barely inside her and she pulled my head into her breasts and moaned loudly before pushing back down. She did it again and clamped my cock as she rose, instantly bringing us both to climax once more. *Ugg oh. Fuck!* She relaxed and slowed right down and stopped. She looked at me and winked.

"Well, that was fucking awesome." She said seductively. I shook my head at her.

"Ratbag." She smiled and hugged me tightly. She gently lifted off my stiff penis and ran to the water.

"Come on, we need to go to The Dermy." I ran after her awkwardly and dived in. We swam around casually enjoying the refreshing water. Bett called for the gel and it sailed into her hand. She washed herself and then called me to her.

"Stand up Danny." I stood up as she looked at me,

"I thought so, poor man, does it hurt being that stiff?"

"No babe." She covered my body with gel then pulled me down in front of her and gently started pulling on it slowly and firmly, kissing me and whispering in my ear.

"Your cock is beautiful, it is so big and hard and you make me so happy with this," she squeezed me and grabbed hold of my balls massaging them as I slowly started to climax. She felt my tension rising and went down on me with her warm, wet mouth, slowly sucking my crown as I erupted. I moaned loudly holding the back of her head and pulling her in closer. She kept arousing me until I was totally spent. Bett screamed out in ecstasy as an orgasmic explosion rocked her gorgeous, golden body. I fell backwards into the water exhausted. My huge engorged cock slowly going down. Betty kissed my soft manhood and seductively swam away with a massive smile on her face.

"Whew." What a woman. '*Thank you Bett, I love you my sweetheart.* *Danny, I love you baby and that was totally my pleasure.*

"Come on, we need to throw some clothes on and get to the Dermy."

"Hey Bett we can fly there, they all know we can fly, so it doesn't matter."

"Great idea Danny and what an entrance, where did I leave my cape?" We dried ourselves and ran up to Horus. Bett dressed in one of her lovely long hippy dresses and I threw on some baggy linen pants no boxers and a cheesecloth shirt. We didn't worry with shoes we both looked very boho. We went outside and lifted into the air, flying swiftly to the Dermi, only slowing as we arrived.

There were heaps of people outside that suddenly saw us and cheered. People came out of the pub and looked up at us, raising their glasses. As soon as we touched the ground many hands patted our backs and pints of frothy cold beer were thrust into our hands. I lifted my full glass and Bett lifted hers.

"CHEERS!" We said in unison.

"CHEERS!" All the townsfolk replied. "Skoll." They chanted, so we skolled the first one. They were all whooping and cheering us. Someone handed us two fresh glasses. Conner and Elouise pushed through the rowdy crowd to join us.

"Hey Rockstars, glad you could make it, we thought the ruckus was your doing. We heard you flew here, that is so amazing."

"Yes, it is, we love it Daddy."

"Well, this is it, our last few beers at the Dermy for a while, cheers everyone!" He raised his glass.

"CHEERS!" Everyone replied together. Elouise gave her beer to Conner and pulled us both in hugging us very tightly and we lovingly hugged her back. She took a step backwards. "Please stay safe you two and come into *Ra* as soon as you can, for Taxi's sake as well as ours, we need your energy. This place lifted when you both arrived just now, everyone is buzzing with your joyous energy." Conner gave the beers to Elouise and pulled us in for a big bear-hug too. He stepped back, "Elouise is right, your presence is powerful and everyone just became a whole lot louder and joyfully happy."

"Thank you, Daddy we can feel their happiness too." Someone suddenly called out;

"Cheers!"

"CHEERS!" We all replied and took another swig.

"Danny and Bett, no one is scared or concerned about tomorrow, everyone has moved all their personal things into *Ra* and all are committed to make it work. Not sure if you heard, the missiles they sent did nothing. Authorities are telling everyone to find shelter underground, there is pandemonium in the cities already. When do you want us to get your cars?"

"Er, you don't have to worry about the cars or our camp; it will be protected by a bubble and our lake too. One of our friends Jillyish Fish is taking safe care of it." Conner shook his head. "You have some amazing friends, I hope I can meet some more of them."

"Conner you will, she is from a race that live under the ocean and she is only this big." I showed them with my hands. "Also helping us is The Octo who have a base on Europa. They made Shiny. The Octo almost look like big octopi but with huge hands as well as very long tentacles. Their purple bulging eyes are on stalks like snails." Conner and Elouise were both shaking their heads.

"We have also met The Hathors, yes Hathors from Egyptian mythology. Seven beings that take on various forms of beautiful women combined with cows; they have been here for a millennium, influencing humanity. Sometimes good sometimes not so good."

"I would like to meet them too."

"No sorry daddy, not a good idea, we don't even like it when we talk to her and that is only in visions, never in person."

"CHEERS!" Someone shouted.

"CHEERS!" We all replied.

"What are you doing tomorrow?"

"Sorry Conner we will tell you after, no need to worry you with details. Shiny will look after us, please just be confident that we will do our best as that is all we can do anyway."

"Sure, Danny I understand and trust you both." He slipped his arm around Betty and held her tight. Elouise came over to me and did the same, pulling me in close.

"Tomorrow will be hard to watch from space, don't you think?"

"Oh yes Elouise, it will be extremely hard but we will be terribly busy too, hopefully that will take our minds off what we are seeing."

"Well, our hearts will be with you tomorrow as you fly around naked in space." Elouise squeezed me and her heart rate climbed.

You are doing it again to Elouise, Danny.

I am not trying to Bett.

I know Danny, I can try to calm her. I could feel Elouise, her breathing was getting faster, her heart beating like a drum and she was grabbing my waist tighter.

"Yes, that's right we will be thinking of you." Conner said.

Hurry Bett, this could get awkward fast. Elouise took a gulp of her beer and gave me a quick sideways glance and bit her lip. Letting out a quiet gasp she trembled all over lightly, her leg pushing erotically against me. *Bett moaned in my head;*

I took it from her but only just received it, and now I am losing it.

If you go, they all go Bett; I made her numb with my mind, blocking her from letting go.

Whew, thanks Danny. Elouise was watching me closely, shivering ever so slightly against my leg. "Cheers!" I raised my glass to break the silence around us.

"CHEERS!" Bett and I finished our beers together.

"Shall we all go to the bar for some tequila shots?" I asked.

"Great idea" Conner replied. Elouise squeezed my waist and released me letting her hand slide down to my bum, before taking Conner's hand. I grabbed Betty and carefully parted the people in front of us so we could walk freely to the bar. I made space for us before we arrived and placed eight shot glasses, a bowl of sliced lemon and a saltshaker. Two bottles of Padre Azul Blanco flew over as we arrived and I swiftly poured out the eight shots.

"Okay, salt, shot, then lemon. Lick, skoll, suck.' Somehow Elouise ended up next to me. She squirmed sexually when I said suck and made sure that from her hips down she was in close contact with my body.

"Again?"

"Absolutely, keep them coming." Conner said. So, as we had the second the third one was being poured, and so on. By the fourth we stopped with the salt and lemon and simply swigged them.

As we took the fifth round, Elouise casually brushed the palm of her hand against me, pushing her hip against her hand. Feeling the full length of my post sex member, her hand lingered there and pushed against me firmly. Her eyes widened and she caught her breath when she realized how big I was under her hand. Her fingers stealthily feeling the rim of my stiffening crown as she slid her hand sensually down my shaft. I pulled away carefully. *Betty!*

Yes, Danny I felt that too. We can slowly swap places, okay?

Yes good, how about now? Bett and I embraced and had a long passionate kiss. Bett ended up next to Elouise who was breathing hard and moaning softly to herself. With tiny tremors vibrating inside her; her mind was racing around in circles.

"Cheers!" Conner raised his shot in the air.

"CHEERS!" Everyone replied, we skolled the sixth and seventh one and were all feeling the effects of the alcohol.

Now it was Betty's turn to feel me, standing in front of me her hand slid inside my pants and squeezed me firmly, holding on tight. As I looked over, Elouise was doing the same to Conner but looking at me. I quickly looked around the room and most of the women were secretly holding or rubbing their men.

Bett stop! Hathor is here again, making you affect all the women. I blocked myself from ejaculating. Bett, stop! I yelled in her head. I took hold of her hands and said it in her mind. *Look around.* Betty looked and gasped and Elouise's hand was in Conner's pants still rubbing him as they lustfully kissed. I blocked him too. *Shit, now what.*

Hathor hear me now your evil sister will pay for what she is doing, you hear us. You will be sorry. Now block them from our minds, thoughts and emotions. I filled everyone's glasses.

"CHEERS, here's to TAXI!" I yelled on the top of my lungs. Everyone started cheering and clapping.

"CHEERS, to TAXI!" They all shouted. That did it, we broke the spell Hathor had on the women. Conner just sat there with an innocent, satisfied smile on his face and Elouise was flushed like a beetroot and smiling coyly, and breathing hard. I could sense she was picturing it was my cock in her hand. Bett and I hugged tightly. We were very happy, all of Taxi was happy too and slightly drunk and some were off the Richter scales. We stayed for another hour or so.

"We are leaving now, otherwise I won't be able to drive home," Conner said to us.

"Yes, we are leaving too." We walked outside together and did a loving group hug. Betty lifting the four of us off the ground as we spun around slowly.

"Farewell and see you soon." We somberly said this together. We gently released Conner and Elouise and they slowly dropped to the ground. We shot straight up to a thousand feet and sped home. We stopped high above our camp and Betty made my pants fall off and then my shirt. Her sexy knickers and her dress flew quickly away. Finally, her black lacy bra slowly floated to the ground and we hung there suspended by threads of thought, turning slowly for eons just holding hands in front of each other, admiring each other's heavenly bodies.

"Come here my man." Bett pulled me in close and sexually hugged me, running her hands all over my taut back, tight buttocks and hips. She made me shiver all over and then she tantalizingly kissed me, taking hold of my big flaccid cock as I gently cupped her voluptuous breasts. Betty moaned with pleasure in my ear as I let my roaming fingers glide down between her legs to her inviting velvet underground. She erotically squeezed me as I hardened.

Moaning louder now, I moved closer as she guided me inside her warm, moist region. Her powerful muscles were contracting on me as I penetrated her. Bett's body shuddered endlessly as she was consumed in multiple orgasms. Betty was screaming my name lustfully as we climaxed together. She planted a lusciously wet kiss on my mouth with her sweet tongue entwining mine. I started to pull out of her but she grabbed my bum cheeks roughly and pulled me in full hilt and gasped. When I pulled back she drew me in harder to herself. She was grunting and moaning, loving me hard and I was loving her.

I suddenly came again, and we flew up twenty feet. She cried out in bliss as she was once again consumed. We were spinning around gently; I kept pumping her moist tight sweet spot intimately as she moaned in my ear, nearly making me deaf. Another erotic orgasm took hold of her. Bett slid off me but was still in my arms shaking like a leaf, grasping my cock tightly, squeezing and pulling on me until I came again. I let out a primal, guttural moan as I was shooting my cum all over her. It was spraying everywhere, but Bett had no cares, she was still shaking profusely and pulling on me in ecstasy. She tried in vain to kiss me in between moans. Cum was all over both of us and kept pumping out of me. I could not stop while she kept going, but I was moaning loudly too in utter bliss, unaware of the extent of the mess I had made. She slowed down her frenetic pace, and I finally finished climaxing. She reluctantly let go of my penis and wrapped both arms around me, hugging me lovingly. She then kissed me passionately. Betty moved back, and burst out laughing as she was looking at me. I could see her; her body was covered in my juices. She lifted her arms and it was slowly dripping off her, she looked down at herself, still laughing.

"Oh my god Danny, how much? How do you even do that? Oh, I wish I had my camera;" she was still laughing to herself as she hailed her phone to come from below. "Danny, you are not human."

"Oh thanks, right that does it, no more sex for you." She made a crying face and scrubbed her eyes, forgetting about her hand that was also covered. Now it was all over her beautiful face too. Her phone arrived but I was quick to grab it and immediately took three snaps of her. Then I turned away and took a selfie of my face smiling winking and with my hand giving the thumbs up. Bett was pictured floating in the background covered in my cum. I gave her the phone and she looked at the shots and nearly pissed herself laughing. She quickly took some snaps of me. She came closer for a full shot of my dripping semi-hard penis. I shook my head at her. She let go of her phone and it sailed home slowly. "Err, swim or not Bett?"

"Nah, I'm right."

But she was gone, quick as a flash straight down to the water diving in. I flew down fast and dived in too. Bett had the shower gel already and was washing her hair.

"Danny how did you do that, keep going like that?"

I think when Hathor was harvesting me, enlarging me, she did something so she could get more of my DNA, maybe she made my balls super productive, but I am just guessing.

"That does make sense, but you have only done that a few times."

"Yes, I think my subconscious self is stopping me most of the time, and sometimes it just happens."

"Danny, can I take more photos of you and that too, please when we get out of the water."

"Bett this water shrinks me back to normal size almost."

"Do not worry I will make you big again and then take it."

"What? The photo or my cock? Bett what if someone sees these photos?"

"Both Danny, the photo and your cock, do not worry I will hide them in a folder called Danny's huge cock."

"Oh, okay then, that sounds safe. I do not even care honestly if I can get some of you."

"Of course, baby." We finished washing ourselves and walked to the warm crackling fire. Jilly sat there with a whiskey cradled in her small arms.

"JD and I are close friends, you know our lake is full of your DNA now, Danny. Shiny and I are full of it and so is Bett. I poured you both some JD, I spilt a little, sorry." I frowned at her. We looked over at Jilly. She had constructed a complicated pully system to lift and pour the bottle while we were at The Dermy. We looked at each other and smiled.

Jilly that is amazing, thank you; the bottle sat in a cradle made of vines with hundreds of tiny ropes attached all leading to homemade pulleys on an A-frame.

"Can you show us how it works?" Jilly raised her hand, a fine nearly invisible line was attached. She pointed and lifted her hand and the bottle poured into the glass underneath.

"See, just like you. Here is your drink and here is the other one. It only has a little in it as I cannot lift it, I had to push it out the way."

"Jilly, fantastic, thank you so much you are a Gem."

"What am I, a Gem?"

"Yes, Jilly a jewel something worth a lot, sparkling, priceless, that is you."

"Oh, I am humbled; you are so nice to me. That is the nicest thing anyone has ever said to me."

"Jilly you are the humble one. We love having you around. Thank you, Gem. Cheers Jilly."

"Cheers friends." Bett looked lovingly at her.

"Jilly tomorrow is the day the rock hits. Are you coming into space in Shiny with us?"

"Oh, no, I must stay here in camp to protect it; I can only protect our home if I am here. This is my duty, please let me do it, I will only get in the way up there. I like Shiny very much but her jelly is hard on me. I am strong and I will not be scared, my bubble will hold and save home camp. I will help the Earth to recover with you, it is my duty, my life and so be it. I will herd food into our lake for me but I can survive for months without food if need be. I will ration and hibernate. You will return to me I know. I will not drink all your JD, okay? Perhaps Jilly will later go into The House of Ra too.'

"Jilly, we have spoken to Conner about you already, so Ra is also your haven, your home. He wishes to meet you whenever it is possible."

"I protect our haven first then after the storm settles I will say hello to Conner, okay?'

"Yes Jilly, that is your duty and we acknowledge it. We are glad and grateful that you have this responsibility for you are totally awesome in our eyes."

"Thank you, Bett and Danny, I do love you lots, your DNA makes me stronger every day. As does your love for each other. Tonight is the last night for most of humanity and this makes Jilly sad. I understand your sadness, I can feel the pain behind your love but you will save humanity with your love because you two are very special. I am happy I was chosen to be with you, my stories of you will last forever. I will leave you now and herd fish into our lake tonight for my survival. Please love and play with each other and enjoy your last night on Earth as it is now. You both deserve every second together tonight. I go now, we meet again after the strike. This is fact, I got you." Jilly hopped and skipped away and splashed into our lake and then she was gone before we could even say goodbye, but that was a good thing. This was not goodbye and she knew it, and we knew it.

"Hungry Danny?"

"Not really Bett."

"Me, Danny?"

"Always insatiable for you, my girl." She leant into me and kissed me tenderly.

"Thirsty Danny? Stogie?"

"Yes Bett," both of these things sat in front of my face before I could blink. The sun was slowly setting behind our hills as we watched with great sadness. It was so hard to be upbeat tonight, knowing what lay ahead of us. The long dark shadows stretched out, becoming longer and longer. The Curlews were calling out across the lake and Kookaburras laughed as the evening drew close. Flying Foxes flew overhead in search of their dinner of whatever fruit they could find. A dingo howled and a cow moo'ed. I leant closer into Bett. We sat on our comfortable couch as the sun went down on the Earth for the last time before the long darkness. Many Taxi- folk had already entered The House of *Ra* and settled into life in a bunker like no other. Bett wrapped her arms around me and started to softly cry.

"Oh baby, please don't cry,"

"But most don't know tonight is their last night."

"No baby, they don't, but that is a good thing, isn't it? To most it will be the same as any other night, doing what they do. Loving, hating, kissing, fighting, praying or getting high. Tomorrow night everyone alive will be thankful for just making it through the day. That will be humanities only thought. Bett, we got this, we can help, can't we?"

"Danny, be sure of yourself; we will help, we got this, we can do it."

"Yes, you are right. We got this." We held onto each other tightly never wanting to let go. Tonight, would be our longest night ever.

∞

Look at them they are weak, we the Hathors rule strong once again. Our destruction of this planet again will save us and we will feast on their anguish and pain and the death of billions, it has been too long, far too long. We need to feed on them and we will tomorrow. Look at them cry. Our sister Pleione broke the rules, but these are mere pathetic children, so who cares. Our time to feed is now, nothing will stop us.

5

The Long, Last Night.

Betty held me close.

"Danny, I'm making some hotdogs; I am a little hungry."

"Sure, that will be nice." The sky darkened as night came and the brilliant stars started to come out. I looked up towards Orion and there it was, as bright as the moon. A luminescent arrowhead smudge across the heavens and it was heading straight towards the Earth.

"Look there Bett, here it comes." She looked up at the unbridled object and gasped.

"Oh, wow. It is way closer now. Our hotdogs are ready." Betty silently poured two more JDs as the tray gently floated out of Horus. The dogs were loaded with smoky bacon and caramelized onions smothered in a hot chili sauce. I took my first bite.

"Yum, thank you. Uh."

"Yum, yes, my pleasure Danny."

We finished our hotdogs and sat back sipping our drinks and smoking quietly, when suddenly Bett jumped up. "I nearly forgot; I do want some more photos. Okay? Please." She grabbed her phone and took one of me sipping my drink. "Can you stand up by the fire baby, side on, yes like that," she was moving around me and took a few close ups of my face and flaccid cock. "Can I make you stiff?"

"Go on then," she squatted and took me in her sensual mouth, nibbling, licking and sucking. I was rock hard almost instantly. "There we go!" She stepped back grinning broadly at her handywork and took a few close ups and side-on shots. "Danny that really is the biggest most wonderful cock I have ever seen, it even looks powerful."

"Thank you, I guess. Now it is my turn." I pulled my phone to me. "Bett, stand by the fire with your hands on your hips, head to one side like you do, yes, perfect." I slowly moved around her. "Now sitting with your stunning legs up like that, yes, now pose sexy like, oh, perfect. One close-up, beautiful. Thank you, my darling. You are very sexy." My shaft was still pretty hard as I admired her beautiful naked body.

We sat down and looked at our photos, they were very good, Bett was laughing and then was looking at my cock photos and enlarging them, fully zooming in on my head. "I like this one, look at the fine detail."

"Really Betty." She put her phone down and reached down and took hold of me. "Yes really, that is how I see you when I am this close." She moved around so my manhood was right in front of her face. She stared at it, smiling and seductively kissed my throbbing tip and licked the length of me. Very slowly she took my head in her mouth, darting her warm, wet tongue all over it while her hand magically moved up and down my huge shaft.

She winked at me, lightly nibbling on my head. Then widely grinning as I started to tense. She expertly jumped up onto me in mere seconds. As I quickly entered her; she immediately climaxed, crying out my name. I followed with my intense climax, pushing hard up into her. My body rigid and shaking. She held on to me fiercely with her fingernails digging deeply into my back as she let herself go again, grunting and heaving with pure ecstasy. Our lake was glowing brightly; the vibrations in the air were so extreme, taking us to another level of eroticism.

The lake had a surge of waves in it that were changing to different colors, it was throbbing in time with me. I lasted another minute finally slowing down and stopping. Bett sighed deeply and lifted off panting next to me. She just held me softly and tenderly kissed me.

"Wow." I took a deep breath and sighed loudly.

"Danny, you are amazing. I love you baby."

"I love you Betty, with all my heart."

"*And I love you both, you are so intense these days I can hardly keep up with you, I am still buzzing all over. Goodnight.*"

We saw you Shiny, we felt you and we love you too. Goodnight Shiny.

Our bottles of much needed water sailed over to us and we gulped them down. Then our bourbons flew over to us and we both took a light swig. We sat together quietly for another hour. Betty was sleeping with my now soft penis still in her warm hand. She was an absolute picture of beauty as she slept. The fire was bouncing little shadows and highlights across her immaculate body. I could not sleep there was too much adrenalin surging through my body from today and expectancy of what would happen tomorrow. I sent some more logs to the slowly dying fire and watched as the embers flew up into the starry night. *What will we see tomorrow? The horror of destruction of our planet? All those poor souls that we can't save, this is terrible. I should not be taking her up into that. It is not her fight.* Betty suddenly tightened her grip on my cock. Without moving anything else but her sweet head on my shoulder, she squeezed me tighter.

You bet it is my fight too! You need me and don't you forget it. WE need to do this together! Danny stay focused. Betty lifted her head and tilted it back with eyes still closed and her mouth expectantly open, desperately searching for a kiss. I leant in and kissed her luscious lips as she thrust her wet tongue against mine and let out a soft moan. I was rock hard in her grip. She suddenly released me and swiftly maneuvered herself onto my stiff rod allowing me to slide all the way in. Still kissing me passionately she said softly in my mind, I *fucking love you. You are everything to me and more as well as being my gorgeous husband. We are in this together until the end.* But she was losing control as she sat on me motionless. I could feel her muscles contracting on me like a vice. My tongue entwined in hers, her heart racing wildly. She pulled back, her eyes wide as she started shuddering with uncontrolled orgasmic spasms shaking her to her core. She screamed out as I climaxed dramatically lifting us off the couch. I kissed her neck as I heaved into her, roaring with carnal desire. Blood was oozing from her grip on my bum cheeks. We couldn't breathe; we were gasping for air as we finished. Gradually we slowed and stopped moving. Bett grinned at me. *See! Together until the end.* I was shaking my head at her as Bett pulled away and floated to the lake where she dropped into the cool water and quickly washed herself as

I did the same. We came back to the fire with our towels wrapped around us and sat down.

"What now, a game of Scrabble?" I looked at Bett, drying her long hair. She stopped and grinned.

"Yeah right, you're not tired, are you?"

"Nope, neither are you?"

"No, it is all the adrenaline kicking in thinking about tomorrow, isn't it?"

"That's right, are you sore? Down there?" I pointed at her sweet pussy.

"I should be red raw by now, considering your size and frequency. But nope, I am buzzing inside. I am tingling and the twins are happy too. I think the buzzing is making me come instantly and you of course, I just can't hold back. Our sex is fantastic every single time."

"So basically, what you're saying is that we should just fuck all night long." I winked at her.

"Maybe," she winked back. "What about you, is that sore?" She pointed at my flaccid member. I lifted it, inspecting it and dropped it.

"No, he's fine, he's tingling too. My balls are tingling as well and they feel full and heavy again."

"Can I feel their weight? Stand up for a second." I stood in front of her and she lifted my penis out the way and cupped my heavy balls in her other hand gently lifting them.

"Oh, wow. I see what you mean. You are slightly golden now." She let go, smiling at it. I filled two glasses and lit a cigar and sat down next to Betty. She threw away her towel and snuggled up to me as we sat drinking and chatting until we finished the cigar.

I was looking at her, shaking my head in disbelief, "Bett, nobody does this so many times in a day." She looked up at me, and smiled.

"Danny, we do, and that is all that matters. What do you think Conner and Elouise and most of Taxi are doing right now, definitely not playing Scrabble and we are newlyweds!" Two bottles of water and two more glasses of JD came to us, but we were far from drunk and barely tipsy, apparently Shiny's jelly was absorbing some of the alcohol.

"Another cigar, same routine, FRDSFA (Fuck, Rest, Drink, Smoke, Fuck Again)" Bett said and then, "Good, next comes Fuck again." I laughed my head off.

"Really Bett? More?"

"What else is there to do on our last night, we got married yesterday and we are on our honeymoon. Honeymooners fuck all the time; we have JD, a fire, a beautiful lake and soft cushions. The end of the world is looming and ta-dah! I have that deliciously massive cock right in front of me." She held her hands as if my groin was a toaster in a commercial on TV.

"Okay, Bett, I get your point. You know tomorrow is going to be full on and each day after that for a long time?"

"Exactly my point, tonight is a turning point for all humanity, including us, there will possibly never be another night quite like tonight, but if you don't want to fuck me again soon..."

"Bett we are still in the Rest mode, okay? Rest goes through the next two, right?"

"Yes right. Rest my darling and conserve your energy for me."

"Babe, what time is it, anyway?" I pulled my phone to me.

"It is eight o'clock."

"What?" she turned to me and saw my face. She dug her elbow into my ribs. "Ratbag, what time is it?"

"It is eleven thirty."

"That's more like it, okay, I have a request, music and I want you inside me at midnight, after that bed, okay? Hopefully we can sleep, if not, look out."

"Deal Betty, drink up." We skolled and poured another one.

Betty turned on the stereo and put on some Chris Stapleton; 'Tennessee Whisky', quietly. We moved into the tent and the Sinatra followed us. Bett was very deliberate with her movements walking slowly in front of me; my eyes were fixed on her sweet bum.

Nice ass.

Ha, I got you!

It's a trap!

Oh, yes, it is Danny, follow me. So, I did.

We entered the tent and she walked out on the mattress and laid on her side facing me. Her head was propped on her hand leaning on her elbow in the cushions. One knee was bent and raised exposing her vagina. Her breasts and absolutely everything looked perfect as she patted the mattress next to her.

"Oh, Bett, you are perfection, and you are scaring me now."

"Ha Danny just come here and relax my honeymoon husband." I was already aroused some and she could tell. "Oh, Danny, happy to see me? I am happy to be looking at you and I am aroused too baby." I walked over and slowly sat next to her; she pushed me back against the pillows gently and adjusted them for me, so I was almost sitting up. "Comfy baby?"

"Perfect Bett."

"Here's to the start of the new World." Betty said and I raised my glass to her, "The new world." We skolled our drinks and our glasses filled again. "And here's to us."

"Yes, here's to us." We swigged again and she sneakily stroked my penis.

"Oh Danny, what a crazy day. Mind sex for breakfast, water sex straight after. Fucking in Mercury's orbit and Earths, talking with every alien we know in conference. Getting erotic in the Dermy and doing it up there all messy like and I don't know how many times this evening. Thank you, Danny for loving me."

Now she was holding my fully erect penis, staring at it. "Bett, before anything else, I want you to know how happy you make me feel. Regardless of this love-rod, you are so beautiful, just look at yourself you are stunning, every inch of you." I touched her nipple and ran my finger around her areola, she was rock hard too. She drew in a deep breath and shivered. We were at a standoff, not wanting to rush anything.

"Thank you, baby, you are so sweet with your admiration, but I feel your love, totally and intimately every single time we share ourselves and that makes every time special. It's way more than just sex. I have never felt like we are having sex, honest, I just want to make you happy, because Danny, you make me so very happy. I love, love, love you my sweet." I was dripping cum on Bett's hand.

She looked and smiled. "Oh, darling, I can see how much you want me." I was throbbing hard in her hand.

"Bett, you mesmerize me, everything you do, like now, casually talking to me while holding my hard-on like an ice cream cone that is slowly melting.' She laughed loudly and licked my crown like it was a melting ice cream, I shivered.

"Yum! Oh, Danny, I Love you."

She rolled onto her back stuffing some pillows under her bum and spread her legs. "Come over here baby." As I moved closer, she raised her legs straight up high in the air and spread them wide. "Take me my love, fuck me honey." I entered her slowly as she rested her ankles on my shoulders. She trembled as I slowly started pumping into her tenderly as she moaned loudly.

"Oh Danny." I felt like I was going too deep like this, but she was in ecstasy. She suddenly climaxed and called out "Yes!" She was rocking in time with me as I climaxed pushing in hard. She groaned in pleasure and pain, but still pulled me in. I thrust in firmly hitting her g-spot, over and over but I was holding back in fear of hurting her. She knew I was, so she swung her legs down off my shoulders and pushed me over until she was on top of me, now she could control me, lifting and falling and taking as much of me as she desired. She was moaning loudly, as wave after wave flowed over her. She clamped down on me tight making me climax again, her eyes fixed on mine. She smiled, sensing my extreme pleasure. I could feel her erotic bliss and it was way off the charts.

"Oh, Bett. Uh."

"Shh, Danny, just enjoy me." Her muscles took over her body again, squeezing and pushing down on me hard in the throes of an intense orgasm. "Uh, oh Danny." We were so lost in each other as midnight came and went. Betty was continuously moaning as wave after wave of orgasms overtook her, but she kept going until I came a third time. She slowed and stopped, leaning forward and kissed me passionately. She collapsed on my heaving chest with her head on my shoulder and before I realized, she was sleeping deeply. I gently pulled out and closed my eyes. I was exhausted, and fell asleep within minutes. It was a deep restful sleep.

As always, Bett stirred first. I opened my eyes, her beautiful deep emerald eyes were right in front of me, staring into my soul as she smiled at me.

"Good morning, Gorgeous," I whispered as her arms squeezed me tight.

"Hey you, good morning my love. How are you feeling?

"Oh Bett, I am so fucking good, I slept like a baby in your warm sweet embrace."

"Swim Babe?"

"Yes, my love, let's go." We stood up and sprinted to the lake, full of energy and life. I chased her sweet body into the lake. We dived in our strokes synchronized as we powered across the lake, perfectly in time with each other. We swam back and forth fifteen times before we slowed and floated on our backs, panting again. Betty said,

"I feel so alive right now."

"Me too Bett." She swam over and held me close, kissing me tenderly.

"We need a good last meal, don't we? Steak is good for breakfast and last rights."

"Sounds great, with eggs, chips and fried tomatoes."

"Perfect Bett."

"Yes, I have already started." We kissed with passion and then walked out of our lake, drying our cool bodies with our towels and sat on the soft couch. Bett dried her hair as the trays came out to us. Betty's delicious thick rib-eye steaks were perfect. We ate in silence, famished; this meal was perfect for today. We finished our protein and sat back. She looked at me and started sobbing quietly. I put my arms around my girl.

"No Bett, please don't be sad. This is beyond our control. If we can save some people or reduce the ice age, that will be something worthy. Humanity needs our optimism right now, please keep that in mind all the time. We will help them. Okay?"

"Yes Danny, okay." Bett we can fly over to your dad and say see you soon if you want, he may be busy but even five minutes is better than nothing."

"Yes, I agree, okay, I will text him now." She did and he said; 'yes, come now we are sealing the doors in two hours.'

We threw some loose clothes on and flew to The House of Ra. His goons told us to enter as they relayed our arrival to him. There was a buzz all around us as people were entering. People were getting their Id's checked and luggage cleared. This was the last of Taxi as most were inside now. We walked into the airlock, the doors closed behind us and shortly the doors in front opened. Conner and Elouise were waiting for us; they ran forward and embraced us both warmly.

"Thank you both for coming."

"Our pleasure Dad, we have some time to spend with you before we must go and Daddy I needed to see you." Betty grabbed Conner and squeezed him tightly.

"Oh, my little girl, I love you so much I am so proud of you and Daniel, you two are amazing, beyond measure. Thank you for coming." We walked to their luxurious quarters. Taxi townsfolk were everywhere but it was not crowded at all, they all acknowledged us as we passed them. Some people were on bikes and electric scooters and a couple of golf buggies. We could easily settle here. "Jacks anyone?"

"Thanks Conner." We sat down with them in their spacious bar. I started,

"Today will be tough as we will leave in two hours for space, like I said have no fears for your daughter, Shiny and I will look after her. We have no idea how long we will be out there and it is tricky with what we are attempting but with the help of the others we should be able to achieve something. I am sorry for being so vague, but we are being watched, that is all I can tell you until later, okay?"

"Okay, Danny I understand. How do you eat up there in that jelly?"

"Shiny, will provide us with all the nourishment we require and absorb any of our waste or by products. She recycles everything, removing it internally somehow, she is incredible."

"That she is, did you say she shares your DNA?"

"Yes, both of us, when she was bio-engineered thirteen thousand years ago they combined our DNA and a few other species and now she takes more each time we fly in her. She is very in-tune with our thoughts and so easy to fly in. She took us to a hidden ocean under our oceans. This is where we met Jillyish and her civilization, there is a whole city down there and it is amazing. Earlier versions of us saved their kind from dying out thousands of years ago; by giving them our DNA, we are thought of as saviors, it is crazy."

"Unreal, that is fantastic, we cannot wait to hear some of the stories you will come back with. And you, Bett, are you scared at all?"

"No daddy it is exciting what we will be trying, I think we will be too busy to be scared. The destruction will be terrible, and the next few days will be horrific on the surface. There will be massive tidal waves, firestorms and severe floods and it will rain meteors for days. You will be safe in here, this is perfect, it doesn't even feel like we are in a bunker at all."

"Thanks" Bett, I'm glad I could do this and I am happy I can save Taxi's townsfolk."

"I am happy too." Elouise chimed in and we all smiled at her. "Do you think the wave will get this far?"

"Good question Elle. The Great Barrier Reef will slow it down I think. But if the first big impact is North America, that is straight across The Pacific slightly north, that first wave could be two miles high or more. Taxi is nearly three hundred miles from the coast. That wave will wipeout Townsville first and then Charters Towers. We are higher up here and in the hills, I'll put a fifty down that it doesn't reach here." I fished in my pocket and put a fifty dollar note on his table.

"You're on." Conner smiled and put a fifty dollar note on top of mine.

"Really you two?" Betty scoffed at us, smiling.

"After the ice caps melt, Taxi will likely be sitting on the new coast." I spoke.

"I didn't even think of that, you're right Danny, the world will be very different in a few hours, it is hard to comprehend. I have set up a few wireless cameras in Faraday Cages so we can hopefully see what is happening outside. I will give you a fob for the front door, but you Betty can just say 'Open Ra', we should probably test it when you leave. We also have an old-fashioned tube you can talk into, hidden in a box by the front door with a doorbell." Conner refilled our glasses. Elouise leaned forward to Betty,

"You can fly." Bett smiled.

"Yes Elouise, and it is a wonderful, grand feeling. We can go super-fast if we want. Yesterday we flew out over The Coral Sea butt naked with Jilly and swam and talked with Migaloo and two of his mates." They both had their mouths open staring at us stupendously.

"No way."

"Yes way, daddy, they call us The Old Ones too, our stories have been passed down through generations of whales; it was they who told us where and when the rock will hit."

"What? Now that is crazy, how do they know that?"

"Well, they are super intelligent and they have interstellar friends too, they even know when we make love and so does just about fucking everyone else." Bett smiled at her own swearing in front of her dad. Elouise let out a giggle.

I shook my head at that, and Conner skolled his drink and lit a cigar. "Cigar anyone?" he said nonchalantly. We both took one. Then Conner spoke up, "Okay, so you know a lot of aliens and hidden species on earth and you talk whale. You fly naked in our skies and in space, you have a fantastic starship and everyone knows when you are doing it."

"Yep, that's about it but not everyone dad I hope you don't, but it seems many species feel our joy as well as humans. But humans don't know it is us."

"Was that you causing that, on the dance floor at your wedding and at The Dermy. You that made that all happen?" Elouise leaned forward, she wanted to say something else, but held back. She wanted to say *I know when you're doing it.*

"Err, yes, we are afraid so, this has only just started, we will figure it out. We had no idea this would be a side effect of our love for each other."

"Oh Bett, it is a beautiful gift." Elouise said. "Our last few days together have been so crazy. Conner and I, we feel energized and we can't get enough. If it is you two affecting us, we thank you."

"Hush Elle, way too much info, yes Bett what you and Danny have is a gift, something beautiful. Nothing to be afraid of or ashamed. Embrace your love, if your love making is influencing Taxi, like I think it is, that is stupendous and you must embrace it." Bett said in my head; *I want to tell them about the twins they have.*

Whatever you think is right Bett, I trust you.

"Thank you, dad, there is more though, I am unsure if I should speak out as this is personal for you two."

"You have our attention now, spit it out Betty."

"Shiny told us something fantastic when she came home from the wedding. She said four couples conceived on that night at the wedding, Pete and Jan, Bob and Sue, Dave and Lauren and you two. You are all having twins." Conner blushed and Elouise sat up straight and gulped her drink.

"Seriously, or are you m-messing with us," Conner stammered.

"It's true daddy, congratulations you two and I have siblings on the way." Bett and I stood up as did they but they were both stunned. Betty rushed over to Conner and hugged him so hard. I embraced Elouise and hugged her tightly,

"Oh, thank you Danny." I kissed her and let go and raced to Conner as Bett hugged Elouise. Then Conner took Elouise and hugged and kissed her. "Oh, darling this is fantastic."

"Yes, it is my love." Elouise was genuinely happy. Betty and I hugged too.

Well-done Bett that was nice. They took it well.

"Cheers Mum and Dad." I raised my glass and they all lifted their glasses. Elouise looked at me as if almost offended that I had called her mum.

"Cheers." We all sat back down. Bett spoke up.

"I couldn't help myself; I am so happy for you both, I just had to let you know before this afternoon."

"Oh, Bett I'm so glad you did; we still have time to get more supplies, baby supplies and toys."

"Daddy we are so happy for you both, I feel blessed that I could be the one to tell you."

"Bett, I feel you and Danny influenced this in some way, how is it we are all having twins?"

"Yeah, dad we have no idea that is beyond us, we are in awe too."

"Dad, I know you have stuff to do; I feel how anxious you are, we will go now but we will not say goodbye. See you soon is more appropriate because that is what we all want."

"Yes, Bett you are wise beyond your years, our next meeting will be very different, but I can't wait."

"You got that right," we said in unison. Conner and Elouise laughed.

"Come on, let's test your voice commands. Bett close this door."

"Close door three" Betty said. The door slid out silently.

"Okay that worked." Conner said. We made our way slowly to the surface saying goodbye to whoever we ran into.

We finally walked into the sunlight. Conner closed the door. "Betty please say it."

"Open Ra." Bett commanded. The huge door slid open.

"Excellent Bett, at least we know you guys can get back in." Conner stated. We all looked at each other, holding hands. I said to them.

"This is not goodbye, this is see you soon and we will, before you know it. We love you both: I promise to take care of Betty and I will never let her come to any harm, I would sacrifice myself for her. It will not come to that, trust in Shiny and me. We can do this." Tears were rolling down Elouise's cheeks and even Conner's eyes were swollen and wet.

"We trust you Daniel, we know you can do this good luck today. God Speed my family." We all embraced each other refusing to let go. Betty was crying too, we all had tears flowing. Bett and I stepped back. Holding hands we lifted slowly into the air, waved at them and zipped away in a blur.

We arrived back at camp in a minute and before we landed, our clothes flew off, and went into Horus. We would not need clothes for a while.

Bett, can you do a count down on your watch until we need to leave?

What watch? And when is that? Shiny, good morning, when should we go?

Good morning, Danny and Bett, to be at rendezvous by ten am we need to leave at nine fifty exactly.

Thank you Shiny, see you at nine fifty. That gives us about fifty minutes Bett, please set your watch.

I threw my watch away baby; time will soon be irrelevant. Danny, I set my mind. What do we do for fifty minutes?

I know what you want Bett, but maybe we should wait a while as today will be full on. A whiskey floated in front of me, 'Bett it is only about nine in the morning.'

Danny we are still on our honeymoon and I am focusing on our day. Have a drink, relax and focus.

Thanks, Bett, you're right. Cheers baby.

Cheers Danny. We skolled and our glasses refilled and we called for the cigars and took one each. We sat back and chuffed and drank and Bett put on 'The End of the World as we know it' by REM again. It was so fitting for the moment. We looked at each other and knew the enormity of our future. The hours ahead would be very traumatic and desperate for humanity. Above all, we knew it was about us, we held the key somehow. Bett and I could help. We could not stop this now but we knew we could make a big difference together.

Bett, take my hand, the only way we can do this is to be totally together, are you with me Baby?

Yes Danny.

Are you with me Bett?

Yes, Daniel I am, are you with me?

Yes, Betty, we are one, yes, I am with you. We have got this, we can do this we are one and together we are strong.

Danny?

Okay Bett lets be as one before all this happens. Betty kissed me and took my erect penis in her hand as my hand went down in between her legs. She moaned as I touched her.

Oh Danny, yes baby, she kissed me tenderly and moved onto me. Bett lifted and slowly took me completely inside her. She was soothingly warm and tight on me; she gave me a squeeze and I moaned in pleasure.

Oh, Betty.

We are one Danny, this is our power baby, she lifted and moaned and I thrust up slow, she groaned deeply.

Feel me, Bett.

I do baby, you are part of me now, oof oh, Dan...

Oh Babe.

Bett climaxed quietly. She was so totally focused on me and was so sublime I let go as she kissed me and moaned in her mouth as she kissed. She took me to another universe slowly and quietly. This was the most intense love we had ever shared. I couldn't hold back; we erupted in harmonic ecstasy a second time. She rose and fell so smoothly, every movement joyful. Our universe felt our love, and humanity sighed. What will be will be. The rock loomed close. Bett climbed off me panting. It was nearly time to leave.

"How you going Bett? Are you ready?"

"Fuck yes, Danny, you make me feel amazing, seriously amazing."

"Betty that was you."

"Oh, no Danny, that was all you. Look at you, you are perfect."

"No Betty look at yourself, you are perfect darling."

I can settle this; we are all perfect, okay? Get inside me; we need to go you lovebirds. Shiny had the last word.

6

IMPACT!

We looked up and Shiny was sitting in front of us. Our love had been that intense we hadn't even noticed.

Are we together now? I thought you were that lost in each other that you were on planet nine. Jump in please. Shiny opened for us and we floated up and in. Gulping her jelly and gagging as we did, we held hands and lay prone. Shiny lifted silently into the morning sky. This is it. The blue turned to black as we flew to Mars and waited. The Ishta and Lloyds craft zoomed in; it was a huge triangular craft and thirty more arrived soon after, each one a hundred yards across. The Octo zipped in and behind them flew a thousand craft identical to theirs all lined up. The Hathors were oblivious to our super impressive armada.

Hey guys we said in unison, *block them.*

Done, they all said. Only then did I tell them my plan.

Our time is now. As it approaches, we will divert a few tiny meteors to the moon, we will then distract them and take out evil Hathor before the strike. This will steal their thunder and weaken them even more and they will be devastated before the event. They will not be able to consume humanities emotions. Once she is dead, any rocks that can be deflected must be done immediately and as the strike occurs. We will initiate our vortex pulling up as much ejecta as we can.

The heat and moisture of vaporized water and the wall of flames and the ten to twenty square miles of rock will be displaced by the initial impact. We will need to pull all that from the atmosphere and send it away into deep space. *This will lessen the many secondary impacts on the earth. If any of you can deflect the smaller meteors away that will also help. We will engage our infinite mirror to destroy the threat across the universes at the same time. Are you all in agreeance with our plan?*

This is a good plan we hope our efforts will aid your people. The Octo said.

"We, The Ishta and Lloyds agree. It is a worthy plan we can deflect some rocks and aid in your vortex."

Thank you, our friends, you are worthy. How long do we have?

There are less than thirty minutes before the first impact, please join as one. Bett and Danny, your coupling empowers us all. Bett had quietly been making me hard. She silently mounted me and we moaned in unison.

Shiny, it is time to act, Lets go. Bett, open your mind to the infinite mirror. We looked left and right and saw that thousands of us were all in jelly. We were united in our mission, all coupled and ready to act. Shiny moved us closer to Hathors lair.

We selected one small meteor to send to her.

You okay Bett?

Let's do this Dan. I'm with you, we are one.

We sent the tiny meteor spinning into Hathors lair and it penetrated the moon at a thousand miles an hour. It went through the evil Hathor sister a thousand times over and her life saving machine too. She was finally dead. All that was left of her was a mess of torn flesh, oozing all over the floor. All the other Hathors howled in utter despair.

∞

Oh. No. No, what has happened, how have they done this? They have taken our sister. No, you can't do this, you are our children. No, this is devastating to us. You will pay for this. The Hathors must survive but now without the seven we are weak as six. We cannot harvest humanities pain without her. We are lost. We will remain weak for eons. This is not possible. No. No. No.

Hear us Hathors! You did not listen, you did not fear us, now you will listen and fear us. If you do anything else, we will kill you off one by one. We can do this for we are the strong Old Ones. You have bought this destruction on our planet. Shame on you. We never want to feel your presence again, this is the very last of your resets, clear? Are we clear?'

Clear, Daniel, go and do what you feel you must, it will be pointless. Your world is lost, you pathetic children. Suffer and die!

Good riddance Hathors, go morn your holy sister, scrape up her bloody mess off the floor and walls. Beware the Old Ones!

Shiny please take us to the rendezvous.

Danny and Bett, can you please intensify your love it will make me stronger and faster, you will understand. Betty looked up at me smiling.

Perfect Danny let's do this. She kissed me and I was already starting to throb inside her as she swiftly rocked on me clamping down on my shaft tightly. *Oh Danny.* I held her hips and started pumping slowly.

Here we go. Shiny was vibrating fast. We all reached orgasm as one.

Ω

Shiny sped up and we looked around as a thousand Octo craft and about twenty Ishta craft joined us. Betty was moaning loudly as I kept steadily pumping into her, holding her waist firmly as the terrifying meteor flew past us. Many of the Ishta craft were all around it pulling meteoroids away with beams of light as we went faster and faster in a huge circle. The massive rock smashed tumultuously into the Earth below us. In a blinding flash, it shattered into three huge separate pieces that skipped across the globe in an instant.

The impact was brighter than the sun and Shiny's hull dimmed just in time. We heard the almighty unearthly roar from the impact as Bett orgasmed again loudly and clamped down hard on me. Bringing me to climax again I moaned deeply as our planet was going up in flames. The first impact was near Dallas. Everything was flattened for thousands of miles. It was a massive strike with the brightest of flames, cloud and millions of tons of rock flying up towards us. We were hurtling so fast we looked like a solid spinning tube hundreds of miles high. The vortex inside our tube was intense. We could see it was working; billowing smoke, huge broken rocks, loose dirt, fire and water vapor were all getting pulled up and away from the earth. Everything was happening all at once. We climaxed again and then our pace slowed down.

The bottom of the crater was molten and at least twenty miles wide and a mile deep. Everything for two thousand miles around it was burning. Dallas flattened and there was not a building left standing. We had caught a huge amount of rock and sent it hurtling into deep space with the water vapor freezing and becoming a huge solid ice cloud around the rock. A terrific wind caused by the impact spiraled at a thousand miles an hour and ripped across our poor planet. We stayed above in our spinning vortex for many hours.

Shiny tell the others to move our tube to the next impact zone to see if we can do anything there.' The tube moved as one. The second impact was over Europe hitting on the German and French border. This meteor blast had destroyed most of Europe. Our tube settled over the crater and still pulled a multitude of debris into space. The smoke and fine dust was sent out into deep space. All of Europe was burning. The five-mile-high tidal waves were destroying every coastal city on the planet, and the EMP blast had wiped out all electronics. The atmosphere was gradually filling with thick black smoke and dust; we stayed here for hours.

We can't stop it like this. Shiny take us all to the next impact. We moved as one to a strike near New Deli in India; it was very bad here too. The air was filled with heavy, sooty vapor and walls of dirt. We stayed for a while and cleared a lot of debris, but all of India was on fire that would likely burn for weeks and weeks.

How many more impacts Shiny?

One big one in China and there are hundreds of smaller impacts. Russia has most of those.

Okay head to China first. We moved around the planet sucking up as much ejecta as we could. Betty started groping me again.

Hello Bett. I very slowly moved in and out of her as she moaned with pleasure, 'Bett, look into the mirror again. We looked at thousands of us doing the same thing at the same time. They all moaned loudly and dramatically and we all climaxed together. The spinning tube suddenly lit up like a light globe and shone brightly in space. The whole universe was throbbing in time with us.

Uh. Oh! Are you guys seeing this? Every single craft is climaxing with us.

Oh. Shiny exclaimed. We looked around us; every orb and even the Ishta and Lloyd's ships glowed in our rhythm. All across, all the universes, the tube sped up faster and faster, and removed more and more.

Wait, stop, Shiny, we must stop, at this rate we will remove too much oxygen from the atmosphere, we must lift away from the Earth. Every ship in the tube immediately lifted and kept glowing brightly and throbbing, I slowed down and stopped. Betty shuddered as one final orgasm washed over her. She kissed me with a beautiful jelly kiss.

Oh, Danny. The tube slowed and dimmed. All the craft came slowly to a stop. I gently pulled out of Betty. The Octo spoke first;

Betty and Daniel what you did was amazing, all of it. The joy you share when you are coupled together, is incredible. We have achieved much and the other Ishta craft are still stopping meteors. The planet will still be in darkness for many months and we estimate about fifteen percent of humanity has survived the initial blast. Wait, something else is happening, uh-oh, look down there.

Oh no, that is Yellowstone Caldera blowing its top. It was a huge blast. The massive shock wave could be seen clearly from space. *Shit can we do anything? Maybe another Tube?*

No Danny if we take any more oxygen, we will unbalance the atmosphere and I fear more volcanoes are about to erupt. The Earth is super heated from the impacts and that has upset the Magma below the crust.

What about a small vortex around each volcano, or we could stack vortex above vortex until we get it into space? That will leave the oxygen in the atmosphere.

That is worth trying, we will leave some craft in space to catch anything and send it away. Shiny can have four others, hurry now.'

Shiny whooped with glee as we zipped down into the atmosphere.

I'm going to need your help again, to speed up, please. Betty grasped me by the penis and started kissing me passionately and had me hard in mere seconds. She slipped onto me and gyrated rapidly. Shiny sped up and moaned with Bett and we all climaxed intensely as Shiny went into overdrive around Yellowstone. Five Orbs were flying so fast they looked like rings stacked on top of each other. We looked up and could see two others above us doing the same. The other two were too high to see clearly. We started funneling ash and smoke high into the atmosphere. This vortex was filled with sulphur, debris, smoke and lightning; flashing brightly as it went up. We stopped it from spreading as the last craft in the atmosphere sent it into space. Another two stacked craft pushed it away from the Earth harmlessly. We looked out at a spinning tube of muck. With rock, smoke, ash and dust lifting into space away from our atmosphere. We had no sensation of movement except our own bodies on each other. The tube sat on our left rising into space. Below, Yellowstone Caldera was a horrifying turbulent mass of hot glowing lava and fire. There was lightening everywhere but we were above that fortunately.

Danny it is working beautifully. Keep it up Bett you are both helping humanity; you both feel amazing. The impact and volcanoes are causing massive earthquakes all over the globe, every building is crumbling. More passion, please, if you can. Betty needed very little encouragement; she sped up and clamped down on me bringing us to climax once more. We all moaned and gasped loudly. I just watched mesmerized by her amazing body moving on me erotically with her beautiful breasts gently swaying in the glistening jelly, both in time with her movement. I held her rounded hips tightly; she felt like heaven. Shiny's jelly was giving all of us strength. She was watching me, watching her, smiling at my orgasmic rapture.

We are helping humanity Danny; she said in my mind between moans. She slowed down and just sat there looking at me, *did I tell you; your cock is amazing?*

Yes Bett, you did.

Can I try something with your cock, Danny?

Well, that depends, you're not getting kinky with it are you?

No Baby, I just want to see what happens when you cum in the jelly.

You know that sounds kinky right?

Bett laughed and slid off me.

Just give me a minute.

Sure baby. So, she kissed me instead. We looked out at our column of smoke and ash rising into space next to us. It was full of lightning that bounced off our golden bodies and the inside of Shiny's hull. It made her jelly sparkle magically and our bodies glow and shimmer with each flash.

Betty looked amazingly beautiful as she grinned up at me wickedly.

Now Danny?

Okay, Bett. She moved further down to get a better view and held my balls squeezing them gently as her hand took hold of me firmly and slowly started sliding her hand up and down my shaft sensually. Her thumb rubbed my head each time as she ran her tongue sensually around my crown. Before long I started moaning and arching my back. All my muscles went taut as I climaxed and we both stared closely at it throbbing. I was in ecstasy, but nothing was coming out of me Betty raised her eyebrows and put her jelly filled mouth on me and sucked harder. She looked at me and went cross eyed smiling with a mouth full of cock. She removed her mouth and opened it, only jelly, no cum but I felt like it was pumping out of me.

Bett kept going and I was still ejaculating. She could tell by how my penis looked, I reached down and tickled her clitoris and went in. Her eyes widened and she shuddered instantly, pulling harder and faster on me intensifying my continuous orgasm. I went deep inside her and she gasped and climaxed again dramatically. I pulled out and concentrated on her clitoris. She started shaking wildly as she kissed me. Shiny was totally going off, faster than ever.

I put my hand on her hand that was around me. She slowly stopped moving and let go. I sped up and she cried out in bliss and Shiny glowed brightly. I slowed my pace and stopped, kissing her tenderly.

Oh, my darling Danny, you do everything right, you make me feel so loved. I love you so fucking much. She smiled at me.

Oh, hey sorry for interrupting guys, but before the strike there were forty-seven active volcanoes around the world. Right now, there are fifty-two erupting volcanoes; we are controlling all of them by preventing their ash and smoke from filling the atmosphere.

This is great news Shiny.

You two just blew me away with your playfulness and fun. You are looking for Danny's cum, but I have already absorbed it. You give me DNA I give you my jelly. You throw it up when you leave but I am a part of you now, you have absorbed me. We go both ways. You carry my jelly always; it protects you and can save you from injury. My jelly will keep you at this age for a very long time and if you don't eat it will sustain you until you can. When you are inside me our jelly connects, and I absorb as much cum as you wish to make. It is very simple. You can stay coupled for weeks if you wish, without pain or discomfort. You can both absorb your own waste now too if you wish but you can still do what you always do too. Your strength and stamina has doubled and your skin is alive and starting to swirl with my golden patterns. We are as one.

Wow Shiny, that is amazing, no wonder we are so connected and so full of energy. Shiny are you slowing down?

Danny, can you do something soon with Bett? Please it is the only way I can keep that speed up. I looked at Bett and shrugged. She grinned and reached out.

Oh, come here mister. She took me in her arms and kissed me passionately, a big fat jelly kiss. It is so hard to describe but better than a normal kiss. She wrapped her sexy, smooth legs around me and waited for me to harden before guiding me in and I slowly started pumping in and out of her.

Bett moo'ed and I stopped and looked at her and she cracked up hysterically.

I'm messing with you my man, keep doing that. It feels great. So I sped up. Bett was right with me going for it, my hands held her slim waist firmly as I surged into her. Suddenly she threw her head back in euphoria; every part of her trembling and contracting on me as I exploded inside her. She cried out in utter ecstasy. Her long fingernails were digging deep into my shoulders. Shiny was flying faster than ever drawing the ash and smoke away from Yellowstone.

∞

The Earth was a total mess, fifty- two volcanoes were still erupting. We were controlling their output but the fires around the globe still raged. The ground shook constantly and was too hot to walk on. Earth's only survivors were those who took shelter underground. Some of those shelters had collapsed and many had flooded. In Sydney families had camped in the tunnels under Sydney Harbour but the oceans rushed in either end. This had happened when the tidal wave hit, and they just didn't stand a chance. This was also the same with the basements in the city. Those who chose to stay in their apartment blocks were shredded by flying shards of glass from the impact and some were tragically burned alive from the heat as the temperature rose to four hundred and fifty degrees over the following days. Other resilient survivors of the initial impact were later crushed by collapsing buildings.

The ice caps melted quickly and flooded over the lands. The water level rose to three hundred feet in some areas. Many islands all over the globe disappeared under the waves. Millions of people drowned. The oceans cooled with the ice and gloomy darkness ruled. There had been no sunlight since the impact and this would continue indefinitely. All vegetation had already started to die from the scorching heat and acid rain that was full of pale-yellow Sulphur, dust and volcanic ash. The animal kingdom had been devastated with many species wiped from existence. Birds and insects disappeared but they would survive, some of them anyway. Crocodiles and Cockroaches made it through another reset. Migaloo and a hundred others took shelter in the safety of Jilly's realm.

Our Blue Marble was now a dirty brown and it would stay like that for years. The ice age would still come but would not last as long thanks to our efforts. New York, Hong Kong, Japan, Hawaii, Perth, Darwin, Sydney, Adelaide, Melbourne, Los Angeles and all the east and west coasts of America, Holland and England were all destroyed. All totally wiped out. What an absolute disaster. The Ross Ice Shelf was a million icebergs slowly drifting north and melting.

Ω

Bett sat back on me, watching me; she had calmed down and was allowing me to relax a bit. I smiled up at her. My cock still firmly joined us together.

You Bett are everything. I said to her mind, she smiled and winked.

Danny you're the best. Shiny was zooming around Yellowstone. The transmission of thick smoke and ash rose high above us into space. As we looked up we could see rings were forming around the Earth, almost like Saturn's rings on the same plane as the Moon. They were full of impact ejecta and ice that glistened in the Sun magically. Oh my God, look at that Danny the Earth has rings too now!

We need to keep going for a while longer; I am sorry if you are tired, this is an exceptional situation. The longer we do this, the better off the Earth will be. You two are just incredible and my jelly is helping you both to recover and carry on. You cannot hurt each other. Your strength is continuously replenished while you have my jelly. I thank you and your planet thanks you. We together are unstoppable; we are a force to be reckoned with. Betty shrugged, and squeezed me, smiling.

How long have we been at it Shiny?

You and Danny have been coupled for nearly nineteen hours with a few breaks in between. That must be a record for you. Unaided humans would not be able to achieve that. Betty was beaming.

Nineteen hours, I had no idea, feels like only a couple of hours. I didn't even know it was nighttime; it has been pitch black since the impact. Thank you for giving us your jelly Shiny, I know how terrible this all is, my only hope is that we really are making a difference.

Yes Bett, I'm sure we are, at least we caught these volcanoes in time. I reassured her.

We are absolutely making a difference. Danny both of your ideas worked out great, you two will be hailed heroes. Shiny complimented.

I doubt anyone will ever learn of what we did. The tiny pockets of life will be isolated for years to come and anyway that is not important, Bett and I did this because we could, no one else had the opportunity.

Oh Danny, you are so humble, can you get excited one more time. The ash is slowing down and another hour should just about do it. Bett was touching me, making me hard again. I pulled her down to me and kissed her jelly filled mouth and she moaned and grabbed my ass, pulling me in full hilt. She pressed down hard and brought all of us to climax again within seconds. Shiny sped up and hummed along fast and the other Octo orbs did the same. This one lasted for ages for all of us and Shiny's speed had doubled. The eruption below us had subsided. Yellowstone caldera had collapsed and a new volcanic mountain had formed around it made of lava and sedimentary rock. The caldera of deep red lava was at least twenty miles across and still boiling furiously, spitting lava high in the air. The sight below us was unbelievable. We kept at it for another full hour. Our vortex had cooled the lava somewhat, calming it down. We all settled down and sighed deeply, including Shiny. Bett shuddered several times before she stopped climaxing. She fell onto my chest exhausted closing her eyes.

Okay our work here is done. Most of the other Volcanoes have become dormant or at least slowed down, dramatically. Some Octo orbs are returning to Europa; your Octo friends are waiting for us up there, shall we go? I gently pulled out of Betty and she shivered as I did.

Thank you Beautiful, that has been the utter best and most tragic twenty hours of my life, what a crazy honeymoon...

Danny. I can't wait to tell Dad. At least we have a good excuse and maybe we should not say it in front of Elouise she'll likely let go on the spot. We laughed at the thought of it. We arrived at the other Octo Orb. They spoke with their warbled voices.

Welcome back, Daniel and Betty, you have commanded your fleet exceptionally well, every maneuver you have carried out beautifully, even those with Betty. Your gift allowed us all to speed up when needed and we have made a huge difference even though the planet is a mess. Its recovery has been sped up by hundreds if not thousands of years. There are hard times ahead for all the courageous survivors that is for certain. Much of the plant life is dead or dying, a long cold winter lies ahead of you and the atmosphere is filled with sulphur, dust and ash. None of the survivors will be able to venture outside for weeks. We thank you for inspiring all of us to achieve what we did and invite you to come to Europa. We will have a seafood feast planned in your honor. We have a large base on the ocean floor, where you can walk freely in oxygen. First you must look to understand the devastation around your globe. We have seen to it that little Jillyish has abundant fish to eat. She is fine and happy in her bubble. You can visit her; take your time as there is no hurry for our feast. We will leave you now.'

Thank you, friends, we could not have done it without you. We can't wait to thank all who helped us at the feast and it will be our honor to join you, thank you for the invitation. Bye for now. Their Orb zipped away followed by the remainder of their fleet. Ishta, Lloyds are you nearby? Their huge magnificent ships all suddenly flashed to a stop surrounding us; *Thank you our friends, your help today has been invaluable, what you and your kind did helped our cause immensely. You will forever have our gratitude and that of the entire planet.*

"Bettdanny, you are too kind, thank you for your words; your love and joy for each other has driven this whole operation and excited us beyond expectation. Your planning and ideas made this work. You are a natural leader for humanities survival. We too offer an invitation to our new planet; we don't eat food but we can prepare some delights for you. We know what you eat and would be honored to show you our world. You could come when Connerelle comes or you could bring them in Shiny if you like. We don't mind either way. We are building furiously. So, by the time you are all ready, we will be too. One ship will stay in your orbit for a week, in case you need our help with anything."

Thank you, again Ishta and Lloyds, it will be an honor to visit your new planet. What have you named it?

'Why, Connerelle Rage, of course.' We looked at each other and smiled. Conner and Elle have a planet named after them, unreal.

Ishta, Lloyds can we have your blessing to tell him of this honor?

Yes Bettdanny, we thought you would ask this.

Can he bring his wife she is with twins inside, like Bettdanny?

"Yes, of course, you tell us when you are ready, goodbye for now."

"*Yes, we thank you immensely and all who helped us, goodbye.*" Their ships simply disappeared as they moved that fast. One remained and moved into low orbit. *Shiny, please take us down, low and slow. We need to do this and when we have seen it all then straight back to camp and Jilly for some sleep, okay?*

Yes Danny, low and slow, let me know if you wish to stop anywhere or speed up.

Shiny what time is it?

Well, that depends on where we are on the planet.

Taxi time, please.

It is seven forty-five am.

Why aren't we tired?

That is my jelly, this is the longest you have been inside me; you will feel a little tired now the love making has stopped but you will recover quickly, as if you have slept for days in about an hour. Your bodies are golden and glistening now, sorry but that is a side effect. This journey around the planet will take about a week and sadly it will virtually be in total darkness. There may be some breaks in the cloud cover. I will shine down a broad beam of light, but I may need your help later as my light dims, you got me?

Okay Shiny, we got you.

I like us being shiny gold. Bett said smiling and looking down at our glistening bodies.

7

The House of Ra,
twenty-nine hours ago.

Conner and Elouise watched as Betty and Daniel flew off, they were unnerved by seeing the uncanny, something so unbelievable. They shook their heads in disbelief and entered Ra for the last time. "They are amazing, aren't they," Elouise said to Conner

"Yes, they are truly amazing Elle but still so down to earth and so likeable, I love them both."

"Me too Conner, what is next?"

"We need to get to the control room and make sure everyone is inside. We must check the manifest; all heads need accounting for, you with me?"

"Yes, my love, I've got you." Elouise kissed Conner with a passion he had grown to love. He struggled to believe how lucky he was; never imagining anyone else could capture his heart like this. They walked hand in hand to the control room. Pete, sat at a desk monitoring all Taxi's security cameras and John was monitoring arrivals and the huge countdown clock hung on the wall, ominously. It sat at precisely four hours and thirty minutes. The outer gates were locked; The House of Ra was to be sealed in half an hour. "Hey guys please tell me everything is good."

"Everyone is inside but Rita, I think she is trying to get away; I have only just realized but I can't find her on the cameras."

"I'll go after her, we still have four hours plus," Conner said.

"Can't someone else go, Conner?" Elouise pleaded.

"No, I've got this, I must be the one. She will listen to me. I'm taking Eleanor, she is fast. Pete as soon as you see her you let me know, okay?"

"Conner you might be better off with one of the armored four-wheel drives as she has likely gone bush; I will put on our new bush feeds and see if I can spot her, get going."

"Come here." Conner embraced Elouise. "Don't worry darling, I'll be right back with Rita." Conner raced to the hangar and was soon in one of the big armored off roaders. The huge door swung open and Conner headed out with wheels spinning. "Pete, anything yet, I need a direction."

"Head east along Poison Valley Road; she will probably head east towards the coast, not inland as there is nothing out there."

"Okay, please hurry." Conner's adrenaline had kicked in. He must save everyone, that was his promise.

"Conner, there are fresh tire tracks leading off to the left about three hundred and fifty yards ahead. I have Bob onboard with his fastest drone on the way to your location ETA two minutes, he will find her. Your turn off is in two minutes."

"Thanks Pete you have done well." Conner's heart was racing, *why Rita, where are you going? Don't try and run away, you are family and I still have feelings for you.*

"Fifty yards Conner, on the left slow down, just over there." Pete was on it. Conner turned and saw the drone cut the corner and was now ahead of him.

"Where is she?" The drone lifted up higher, searching.

"We have her, Conner, she is cutting her way through the fence, she is nearly through, maybe two hundred yards away follow her tracks. Be very careful we think she is armed we can see something tucked in the back of her jeans and she will not expect it to be you."

"I see her." Conner screeched to a halt. Rita turned and quickly pulled out her Tactical Glock 19 and fired straight at Conner before realizing it was him. The drone had caught it all. Elouise gasped.

"Send back up immediately please Pete. Oh my God!" Elouise screamed. Conner hit the ground from the impact, he was alive and in shock and barely conscious. He had not expected Rita to open fire. Rita gasped when she realized it was Conner.

"Oh why, why did it have to be you that came after me? You should have let me go." She was in severe shock with what she had done. Rita never meant to hurt anyone; she dropped the Glock and ran to Conner. His shoulder had taken the hit and he was in agony but still alive. He couldn't keep his eyes open. "I'm so sorry, Conner I never meant to fire the gun. I'm so scared; the end of the world is not for me. Are, are you okay?" Conner was coughing in agony but the bullet had passed straight through him. He was bleeding badly from both wounds, and time was running out for everyone. "Oh, Conner stay with me, protect me. I know that is what you want, please forgive me. I know you love Elouise now and it was over for us ages ago. I have Charlie now but I still have strong feelings for you. I am so confused."

"It is okay Rita, I understand your..." He coughed again in agony, "your, your pain, I'll be okay." Rita leaned down and kissed Conner lightly on his lips.

"Don't you die Conner. I'm so sorry, stay with me." She pleaded. Elouise was watching all this action from the drone. His white T-shirt was turning red quickly.

"Please hurry he's dying, hurry." She yelled up at the drone; she was beside herself as the countdown continued. There were still three hours to go. The doctor and a team of medics headed out for Conner. It had been twenty minutes since he had been shot and he kept losing consciousness but Rita had his clammy head in her lap with her hand firmly pressed on his shoulder. She was unaware he was also bleeding out the back.

"Stay with me Conner that drone is watching us and help is on the way. I am so sorry; I didn't want this." A Taxi-plus van swiftly arrived. The doc jumped out with two paramedics racing over to the bloody scene. Conner was losing consciousness, slipping in and out.

"Thank you, Rita. Please give us some space," they said to her and she hesitantly moved back as another vehicle arrived. "Come on Rita; let's go home to The House of Ra."

"Okay, I am so sorry I never meant for this." She looked down at her faded blue jeans that were full of Conners blood.

"Are you hurt?" One of the paramedics asked.

"No this is Conner's blood on me, shit, will he live?"

"A wound like this, likely yes, but he has lost a lot of blood so he may need a transfusion." They quickly loaded him into the van and raced him back to *Ra*. Rita sat in front, bawling her eyes out.

Back at The House of *Ra*, all the medical staff were ready. Elouise waited at the hangar for their arrival trembling in anticipation. The van roared in and screeched to a halt. The paramedics piled out and Rita fell to the ground in shock with what she had done to Conner. A paramedic sat down next to her and consoled Rita as best he could as Conner was being pulled from the van on a stretcher.

Elouise raced over and he smiled at her weakly, "I'll be okay." He whispered and coughed.

"Oh darling, please..." She couldn't finish her sentence as tears overwhelmed her. Conner was rushed to surgery in the hospital. The doctors removed his shirt and stood back in astonished shock. The bullet wound was right there, bright red and crusty with blood but it had completely healed. They gently turned him over and it was the same on the other side.

"How is this possible?" They whispered looking at each other nonplussed. Conner stirred.

"What is going on?" Conner asked drowsily.

"Your, your wound, it, it has completely healed." The doctor stammered in shock. They quickly took a sample of Conners blood for analysis. The results were confusing as he had other unknown cells in his blood and he was full of it. They were jelly like and a totally different DNA. The doctors told Conner of their findings. "Jelly like, you say, that must be Shiny, she is inside me now, her jelly is protecting me."

"How do you feel Conner?" The doc asked.

"I am very sore from the impact of the bullet but otherwise I feel good, ready to go back to the control room. I would like just a few pain killers please." The doctors conferred with each other and nodded; he was good to go. They gave him some meds for the pain and put him in a wheelchair for good measure and wheeled him out to Elouise. She stood and ran to him and crouched down.

"What is going on, that was quick, you look good considering you have just been shot?" She leant forward and kissed Conners cheek.

"I'm fine, Shiny has left a gift inside me, her jelly that I breathed whilst inside her is still in me and it repaired my wound completely." He pulled back the gown and showed off his scar. "I don't need this silly wheelchair either." He went to stand up but Elouise gently held him down.

"Stay there darling; let me push you around for a while."

"Okay just until we get to the control room. Poor Rita, so confused that woman, we need to find her a steady man to settle her down. I'm not sure if Charlie is right for her, she can be such a handful sometimes and quite unpredictable. Make sure she gets some meds to keep her nice and calm."

"Will do babe. How is your pain?"

"Feels like Mike Tyson slammed me in the shoulder with his fist but I am pretty numb from the pain killers." As they entered the control room the countdown clock sat at one hour. Conner looked over to the TV news screens. There were ten of them showing news from all over the world. There was pandemonium in every city around the globe; people had waited too long to get out or find shelter. Not that there would ever be enough safe places anyway. The elite were safely tucked away and the billionaires. When this was all over they would be obsolete. Their money would be useless and they would all need to become hunters and gatherers or they would die of starvation. Every man for himself. People were looting soon to be obsolete TVs and stereo systems. Shooting each other over useless possessions. All of the highways were blocked with cars and they too were shooting at each other. The world had gone completely mad. Some screens showed the approaching meteor. There were only one or two TV presenters still on the job as all others had run off to hide and find shelter.

"Are we all locked up; doors sealed?"

"Yes sir, everything is sealed, and all of Taxi accounted for. Geothermal generators are all set to fire up after the EMP and all Faraday Cage rooms are sealed. Everything is ship-shape sir and we are glad you are okay. You really gave us a scare you know."

"Thanks Pete, and thanks for looking after the shop whilst I was gone." Elouise patted Conner lovingly on the knee and kissed him.

"Danny and Bett will be up there now." She pointed up towards the endless sky.

"I trust them, Danny and Shiny, they would never endanger Bett and she is smart enough to keep out of danger."

"Thirty minutes sir." John informed them.

"Thank you, John, if you would like to be with your wife you may go; we can handle this, go to her. Pete, please get Dawn in here to be with you."

"Thank you, sir, I appreciate it, she is very scared too." Pete replied and called her on his phone. John stood, shook Conners hand and left.

"Pete, you good?"

"Yes, sir I would like to stay here with you and watch. Taxi looks like a ghost town but everywhere else is still full of people and there is only fifteen minutes to go until impact. What are they doing?"

"Pete, they just don't understand the enormity of what is coming; most have no idea as media did not tell the truth. They will all die; it is so sad."

"Conner, check this out they are shooting civilians out the front of the Whitehouse and the President is not even there, hundreds are dead."

"Pete everyone above ground will be dead very soon. In ten minutes to be exact."

It was so hard to watch the final minutes. The footage was brutal, not in Taxi but all around the globe. The screens showed people looking up in horror; seeing the meteor above them, ready to strike. Conner took Elouise's hand. "This is it my love," one minute to go. They sat staring at the foreboding screens. Five, four, three, two, one, they sat in silence and waited and waited. The screens started to turn off. Twenty long agonizing minutes had passed before they felt an impact. A deep ominous shudder went through the earth like a long rumbling earthquake as if a huge beast had suddenly awoken beneath the ground. Fine dust fell from the ceiling as Conner glanced up nervously. The whole of Ra creaked and moaned as everything rattled violently. Then another impact equal to the first hit; followed by another slightly lesser than the second and then another. It went on and on like a deep deafening rolling thunder. More dust fell all around them.

Slowly, all the TV programs shut down as the EMP travelled around the devastated globe. All the lights went off until the thermal generators kicked in. "Pete are all the doors and hangar secure?"

"Yes sir, all good sir." All the outside screens went blank, except for the Faraday cameras, they kept going. One camera was pointed down River Road towards Taxiplus where it showed hundreds of thousands of birds of all description headed inland. Another deep loud thump and everything shook.

"Oh wow, look at that!" Elouise exclaimed. The camera shuddered violently as a pressure wave hit it from one of the deadly blasts. The sky gradually changed color to pink and orange as the sun was filtered by particles of dust and smoke. Slowly it filled with clouds made up of vaporized water and dirt. The road to Taxiplus filled with kangaroos, emu, dingoes, possums, wombats, rats, goanna and snakes all headed inland. Thousands of small meteors rained down as well as rocks ejected from the strikes crashing into the buildings and scrub, starting massive bush fires all over the hills. All of Taxi's houses appeared to be on fire. It was hell on earth, a tumultuous inferno. Some of the animals had caught on fire it was a tragic scene. Elouise buried her head against Conners other shoulder and wept.

"Oh my god! Those poor creatures." This hell went on and on for hours and hours. It felt like a barrage of thousands of bombs hitting Taxi. Then a terrifying wind hit at a thousand miles an hour. It was full of glass, rock and steel fragments that shredded everything in its path. *Ra* shook to its very core. It started raining black mud and everything turned a dark muddy grey, absolutely everything. The buildings in town were smashed, burning furiously and turning grey. The screen went dark. Pete had rigged a tiny armored hose to squirt the lens clean. It worked beautifully.

Ω

The tidal wave that hit the east coast did not reach Taxi, thank goodness. Townsville was wiped out completely and half of Charters Towers, but the wave had miraculously stopped there. The sky gradually became ominously black and it was darker than a moonless night. Suddenly there was a loud sonic boom that shook the walls.

"*Shit what was that?* Conner it is ninety degrees outside right now and climbing rapidly." Pete said. The screen was jet black; they could not see anything except the glow of wildfires and thousands of smaller meteors still streaking in. It was five pm. The main barrage was nearly over but a few more heavy thumps could still be felt.

"Anything at all on the Ham Radio Pete?" He had been listening intently. "No Conner just background static. Anyone with a Ham Radio would also need a Faraday cage to protect their electronics, like us."

"Ah, well, looks like we are on our own, all we have is Bett, Danny and Shiny, up in space trying to help us."

"God bless them." Pete said.

"Yes, Pete and God speed my family." Conner said.

"Amen," said Elouise.

"Are you okay here for a while Pete and Dawn? We need to see how everyone is coping out there." Conner stood up from the wheelchair. "Come Elle, let's walk and talk with the Taxi folk." Elouise took his hand proudly.

"Oh, darling, it is working."

"What's that, what is?"

"The House of *Ra*, it is saving us all from the horrors outside Thank you my husband, this is going to be one hell of a honeymoon. I will look after you." She reached down and firmly pressed against Conners' manhood. He turned and kissed her, gently squeezing her lovely breast. No one had this effect on him in twenty years, and Elouise felt the same way about him. They were horny as anything and madly in love. They walked for a while chatting to townsfolk. Everyone was calm and peaceful and enjoying the comfort and safety of Ra. They were all curious about outside but Conner had no answers on that. Everyone's thoughts and concern were for Betty and Daniel's safety.

8

Year Zero, Hathor's arrival

The Pleiades star cluster, one hundred and twenty thousand years ago. Alcyone, the brightest star in the cluster, has a planet called Lust, where Atlas and Pleione rule. They gave birth to seven sisters who later became The Hathors Society. They became mighty beings over ten feet tall. Killing their parents, they soon ruled all of the thousand planets in the cluster. The sisters dominated their male counterparts as they were only half their size. They grew fat on the pain of others including emotions like wrath, lust, greed, envy, anguish, horror, but also pride, joy, bliss and satisfaction. They played with their subjects manipulating them, modifying them for their own gratification. They were never happy with the results as they were shapeshifters who could control what they looked like to fool other species into submission.

They could control other females taking over their bodies to satisfy their own hunger. They had no remorse as they conquered planet after planet. The Hathors were insatiable in their lust. The Hathors Society never needed permanent companions as they were way too busy modifying males and consuming their lustful encounters. A rule like this could never last and eventually there was a rebellion. What ensued was a mighty battle between the enslaved and the free willed throughout the Pleiades Cluster. War, unfortunately seemed universal. The Hathors had gone too far and spread too wide and lost control of some sectors. These former subjects soon joined the attacking force.

After a three-thousand-year rule, The Hathors had met their match;

they were round up one by one. But one Hathor put up a huge fight trying to escape and was permanently disabled, forever to live on a bed on life support. Pleione would become the evil one, bitter with everything that life had dealt her. The rebellion created a moon sized prison, one Hathors would never escape from, to live an eternity entombed alone with no pity and no hope. All their die-hard followers were also entombed and frozen in suspended animation. They sent the prison to the outer reaches of the galaxy an area where there was no civilization. About four hundred and forty-four light years away, our Earth sat inexplicably in their path. Hathors were smart, they learned how to hotwire their prison so they could control it. They could not escape but they could alter its course. After all, they had eighty thousand years to learn how to do this and many other things. The third planet lay in their path and this was perfect for them, Hathors would make this their home. They adjusted the course of their prison and slowed down its approach, taking careful measurements, lining up a perfect orbit in relation to the prisons size. The settling of the orbit would take centuries until a stable orbit was obtained. The turmoil and destruction below caused by their arrival did not concern them. Hathors started recruiting helpers outside their prison, looking for races that could assist them. The Gray's were so easy to manipulate and soon became permanent helpers.

They looked to this planet; the natives were basic, nothing special, humanoids in early development. *We can use this to our advantage; build a race of humanoids who will suit us perfectly. We will be able to feed for a millennium. We can manipulate them easily. This prison is pathetic, our minds cannot be contained, only our physical bodies, and that is not enough to stop us. The Hathors Society will rule once more.*

Send the Gray's to harvest DNA so we can modify them, improve them. We need to find our perfect specimens, ones that can aid our feed throughout our eternal existence. A couple for eternity who will survive our resets and satisfy our lust. They will be super, and be able to adapt and they will be reborn repeatedly to ensure our satisfaction. This is no prison; it is the control of a species. We will start to hide this moon under dirt. The Rebellion will never find us, and we will flourish and live in the minds of those below us. Free and sexy. We are The Hathors. Find us, two, who we can feed on forever, young and free. Two we can modify to perfection. Much earlier versions of Betty and Daniel were chosen by the Gray's. They were injected and probed and all manner of treatments applied and modified, until the Hathors were satisfied. *These two children are perfection, their love is genuine and eternal we feel it. They will be generous as we have filled them with insatiable needs.* And they were, their love beautiful and joyous, insatiable, erotic and sensual. Love down through the ages shared. They inflicted so much pain on these two, so they could feed generously. Each and every death filled their gut but each encounter with The Hathors their children learnt more about their manipulators. They soon became known as The Old Ones to the rebellion.

Until finally thirteen thousand years ago, part of the Hathor Rebellion caught up with The Hathors, The Octo race. They did everything possible to secretly aid The Old Ones, designing a craft for them; something unique just for them and Shiny was born. Engineered using both their DNA and The Octo's. The Hathors could not see her, she was completely invisible to them. Time after time The Old Ones used her to aid them to escape the Hathors clutches. Hathors became perplexed and lost strength. Gradually becoming smaller with no supporters, there was nothing to feed on. They used the resets to regain some strength.

They had relied on this coming reset. The Old Ones had become stronger than them. After a millennia, and had taken their sister's life, this was unheard of. Hathors don't die but there she was all over the floor, the walls and the bed. Hathors were still in shock, never expecting power like this from their children. Their children, who had been abused by them for tens of thousands of years. *We will make them pay, regardless of their threats*, the remaining sisters thought.

9

New York, Sydney and other ruins.

'*New York is ahead guys, I will light up.*' We looked ahead as Shiny came down out of the atmosphere. Ruined buildings were everywhere, most were merely piles of shattered rubble. Shiny flew in between them deathlessly. It was an eerie feeling with no lights on in this huge city where there were only fires and the occasional meteorite. There was fifteen feet of water through Lower Manhattan and the buildings were already crumbling into the Hudson River. Central Park was awash with water and tons of debris and tens of thousands of lifeless bodies. It was hard to watch as we flew silently over; we knew this was going to be extremely hard. Bett grasped my arm tightly and shuddered.

Oh Danny, how awful, so many bodies.

Yes, Bett this is shocking. Look there a cargo ship sitting on Broadway just up from Fifth Avenue, everything feels so surreal in Shiny's light. Take us higher please Shiny. As we looked down, there were so many fires. *Shiny what is the temperature down there?*

It is about three hundred and fifty-degrees Fahrenheit right now. The heat can't escape because of the cloud cover. The planet will cool rapidly due to no sunlight and will slowly start to freeze over the next few weeks. The Magnetic Poles have just shifted too. They have reversed and the North Magnetic Pole is off the West Australian Coast and the South Pole is now in Northern Russia. But I think it will shift back in a few weeks. This planet is very upset right now.'

Can you detect any life anywhere Shiny, in bunkers?

Oh yes Bett, but some will not survive. There are small shelters in back yards but all the 'preppers' are not prepped for this; they will surely die from the cold and running out of power. Others underground are with very little food; they only have a few weeks or months of supplies. They have no chance of survival with probably another thirty five percent likely to die.

Is there anything we can do for these people?

Bett even taking a few to The House of Ra could be devastating to the local Taxi folk and cause civil unrest. We can't help them. Not yet anyway.

We flew back over the initial hit in Dallas, Texas, it was totally unrecognizable. The main crater appeared to be near the airport but the whole city was gone completely. The crater was a cauldron of boiling molten rock. Destruction and desolation was widespread covering thousands of miles.

To Asia Shiny, floor it. Shiny lifted away and before long we came up on the remains of Japan. All that remained was one small island that was Mt Fuji; that had blown its top and was continually spewing out black ash and molten lava. The rest of the islands were underwater. Asia's coastline had changed dramatically too. Hong Kong had disappeared under the waves including Hanoi, and Taipan. Everything was unrecognizable.

Take us south please Shiny; we need to see if Jilly is okay.

Will do Danny. Shiny slipped south. Indonesia, and The Philippine' Islands were underwater.

We should be over Far North Queensland, but it is all oceans. Here are The Atherton Tablelands and this is where Australia starts. We are coming up on Taxi now, what a tragic mess.

Shiny glowed bright so we could see the utter devastation. Taxi was still there but most of the houses and buildings were destroyed by the ferocious impacts and fires. There was no glass in any windows, and everything was covered in thick black soot. Betty's throat tightened and she started to cry when we slowly hovered over Gerties.

Oh. There is nothing left Danny.

Oh, come here baby, this is so terrible what has happened. Fly down to our lake please Shiny.

Yes Danny. Even Shiny was sad. As we came over the hills we came to our little valley. A clear massive bubble covered in ash and dust sat over camp; it glowed softly in the darkness.

Jilly we are back. Shiny announced.

"Yippee! Fly straight in Shiny. Thank you for coming back." Shiny flew though the bubble and came down above the lake, then opened for us to exit.

Oh, thank you Shiny, you were amazing please go and rest now and we will too; see you in twelve hours. What is Taxi time?

It would have been midnight Wednesday, nine days after impact, good night my beautiful friends.

Good night and rest well we still have a lot to do and see. We slowly floated out of her and threw up. We dived into our dark but familiar lake where the water was so cool and refreshing after being in the jelly for so long. The gel flew out and we washed up and waved to Jilly who was watching us from the shore, smiling and waving. We ran out to greet her, she immediately jumped up into Betty's arms and hugged her with her little arms. She was between Betty's full breasts, her hands only reaching just past Bett's nipples, hugging her madly. Bett hugged her back.

"I am so happy you are safe; you are both so pretty now, all golden and glistening. You look almost luminous like Shiny. Come here Danny and give us all a hug." I joined them in a group hug, being careful not to squash little Jilly. Tiny sparks flew off Jilly as we hugged. "Come let us sit and drink JD and talk of your mighty adventures. If you wish to light the fire you may as the bubble will take the smoke away."

We lit the fire and poured out some bourbon. Jilly was snuggled up cozily to Bett on the couch.

"Jilly can you briefly explain your bubble, it is breathtaking, it shimmers as if it is not quite there and yet it is."

"My backpack is generating it from my mind; as long as I am here and safe, it will stay there."

"But what is powering it?"

"I am, of course, that is why I am eating so many fish! We power our barrier at home the same way."

"We were totally baffled but also amazed. Cheers Jilly, thank you for your miraculous bubble."

"Cheers!"

"Have you been awake the whole time we were gone?"

"No, I hibernate to conserve my energy and my food supply, but I have plenty. The Octo dumped tons of fish in the lake. Did you make a difference to the earth?" Bett piped up.

"Oh, Jilly we certainly hope so, we killed the evil Hathor sister. Then a thousand like Shiny joined us to make a huge vortex above the strikes to remove all the debris from the air. The Octo said we did a lot to help the planet recover. But the Earth is upset and the magma angry. Fifty volcanoes erupted soon after the strikes, so we made mini vortices for all of them too; we all worked together as one big team. Were you frightened when it all happened?"

"I was worried for the animals, they were terrified, I allowed a few in and some birds, otherwise they would have died. I only let in as many as the camp could support. There was a huge fire that was scary as it was all around here."

"Jilly the fires are all around the whole Earth."

"Oh, how sad."

"Yes, it is, and it is too hot for any of us outside of your bubble except Shiny. Every city has been affected by this; some were destroyed by the huge tidal waves that raced across the planet, others by the deadly impacts or searing fires. It is a shambles everywhere, but not here thanks to you.

"I will leave you now, you need to play and sleep I can feel your needs. Thank you for coming back so soon, it means a lot to me. Goodnight, babes." We laughed at Jilly.

"Jilly we are so happy you are our friend, goodnight, babe." Jilly smiled broadly and skipped away humming, 'Run through the Jungle.' Bett smiled and sighed and lay over on my lap and looked up at me.

"She is naturally hilarious, I am glad we came back now, before seeing the rest."

"Bett you are gold, even your hair has gold highlights and don't get me started on how good these look. I said motioning at her beautiful golden breasts."

"Now Danny we have just made love for what? Two hundred and sixteen hours straight and you are already talking about my tits." She lifted her head and kissed me without jelly, and it felt nice, real nice. Betty shook her hair in my bare lap knowing it would arouse me. She pushed her mouth firmly onto my penis and flicked her hair around pushing down again. I seductively grinned down at her.

"You are the insatiable one Mrs. Starr. I walked my fingers ever so slowly down her body, like a spider, she squealed in delight and shivered. She moved her head down near my knees, as my golden member slowly rose. Bett was wide-eyed and smiling gorgeously.

Good God man, look at it now, all golden, it reminds me of something I wanted to buy in a sex-shop once. She said this in my mind and winked at me. *This is way bigger than that though and being glistening gold it seems to swirl just under the skin, way more erotic. I am so close to climaxing just looking at it right here.* But Bett just watched me and my golden thing, throbbing away, and she was enjoying every second. Smoothly I slipped her a finger and she went cross-eyed, grinning and tensed her body and started to quiver. Betty lifted her head and wrapped her lips around my crown. Her hand was around my stiff rod as she cried out and nearly bit my tip off. My fingers were moving fast as she moaned again, her mouth lips and tongue quickly bringing me to orgasm. Her emerald eyes were wide and glistening as she watched my muscles twitch and tense and we both groaned in utter pleasure.

I wanted to give her more than my fingers and she knew it. She lifted us off the couch and quickly pulled her mouth away and spun around in the air as I was still coming. Betty deftly mounted me in one swift motion. She took off like a rocket, twerking, rocking and gyrating all at once. We were both in utter ecstasy, and so was Shiny. The lake shivered and shook in harmony with us in our world of utter bliss. Bett took us out over the lake and lowered us into the cool water above Shiny, who slowly rose to meet us. She was within reach, but she stopped there, glowing, shimmering and vibrating with her lights throbbing. We all heaved up and slowed down and came to a complete finish. Bett released me and quickly swam off, returning a few moments later as Shiny slowly sunk back down, moaning quietly to herself. Bett kissed me warmly and took my hand. We swam to shore, and lay there for a moment. This was our bubble world in harmony. The red glow of fires and falling ejecta flickered through the dome. She exhaled deeply and smiled.

Hey, you, amazing man, you wanna' go to bed?

Yes gorgeous I totally do. Bett lifted us out of the lake as our towels met us in the air and moved swiftly around us drying us completely before entering the tent. Bett gently dropped us on the mattress and pulled up the soft rug. We closed our eyes and slept like newborn babies for a solid nine hours.

We awoke together. *Good morning baby is it even morning?*

Betty, I think it is around mid-morning on Thursday. Not sure ten or twelve. It doesn't really matter until we can see our sun. Are you okay or still tired?

No Danny, I feel great, like I'm ready for a swim and run. Danny how can we let dad and Elouise know we are okay, they will be worried about us?

Bett it is still too hot and toxic to enter Ra. But maybe we can send a message. They have the Faraday cameras. We can use them somehow, with Shiny. She glows brightly so they will see her. I know Morse code. I know it. What do you want to say?

How about, 'We did what we could, we are safe and nearby and we will leave again soon. The planet is in chaos, but it will recover. Stay safe, we will too, talk soon. We love you all.'

That is great Bett, I will work it out; all the dots and dashes.

"Hey babe's, what's up?" Jilly waltzed in.

"We are writing a message for Conner, Jilly, it is very important."

"Okay Jilly is silent now quietly sipping your JD." She poured herself a glass of JD and sat back on the couch. She was looking at us intently.

"Oh, Jilly relax, this is something we need to do for all the people locked in Ra. You were relieved when we returned. We wish those in the caves called Ra to feel like you did when we returned. Okay?"

"Yes, yes I am sorry; I do understand the importance of this communication with Ra. Your Dad will be very worried about you Bett as will all of Taxi. You need to let them know; you are both okay. That is very important."

"Jilly drinking in the morning is frowned upon." I winked at her.

"Is it morning now? I am very confused there is no sun to decide the time."

"Very true Jilly and really time does not matter right now. We can all do what we want. Danny right now I would like a steak, please?"

"Yes, I can do that."

"Never mind Danny, I have already started, ETA five minutes. Bett pulled some fresh fish from the lake for Jilly and she was ecstatic.

"Thank you, Bett, very thoughtful of you, this is nice for me. They are still jumping, yum." Jilly tucked in and when our steaks arrived in sandwiches so did we. They were delicious. "Jilly, we need to go now and deliver our message to Dad and Taxi and then focus our attention at the rest of the destruction of the Earth. This is very important to us."

"Okay, Jilly understands, glad you came here now. Jilly will see you soon. We are babe's now. See you soon." Jilly jumped up and ran off to the lake and dived in.

Shiny? You awake?

Yes Danny, I'm coming. Our Shiny arose from the lake majestically. Every single time we saw her we were enthralled with her beauty. We lifted into the air and floated over to her. Shiny opened. We entered her and gagged again and she shivered as we came inside.

Shiny please take us to one of Conner's Faraday Cameras.

Will do Danny. We soon arrived in Main Street.

Shiny listen. Dot shine bright short, dash shine bright long, okay Shiny?

Yes, Danny go ahead, I got this. Danny had memorized the message and relayed it to Shiny as she flashed brightly with each command. Hopefully someone in Ra would notice. They repeated it ten times before leaving.

We will return tomorrow and try again. Let's go to Sydney's remains. The clouds were slightly broken over Sydney and we could see without Shiny's lights. The Sydney Harbour Bridge was all but gone. It had been taken out by a cruise ship in the harbor and had ended up in Pitt St. The Opera House was ripped in half and unrecognizable with water flowing through it. Sydney Tower lay on its side, the lower streets awash with sea water fifteen feet deep. Fires were burning all over. There was not a soul to be seen. The temperature outside was sitting at around six hundred and fifty degrees Fahrenheit but the entire planet was cooling rapidly with no sunlight compensating for the heat contained by the clouds over the last few days.

Look Danny, Bondi is totally gone, underwater, it all looks so different now.

To Melbourne Shiny, please.

Yes, Danny will do.

Melbourne is under water it is below us now, only the highest buildings can be seen with waves crashing over their top floors. Look. Over five million, two hundred and forty thousand souls lived here yesterday and today less than a hundred thousand. In a few weeks probably zero.

Okay Shiny head west, Adelaide then Perth and after that across to South America, Brazil. We soon arrived in Adelaide. Its city had mostly crumbled into piles of rugged cement but it was also awash with seawater as far as the foothills. By the time we reached Western Australia, Shiny needed a top up as her lights started to dim.

Bett and Danny are you able to join up, I realise this is sad times but if you want to see through the darkness, I need some help please. I looked to Bett and held her close; I gave her a jelly kiss and sensually whispered in her ear. I squeezed her soft nipples, but she was numb from what we had seen.

Bett forget what is lost, praise what we can save, and there are still many to save. Come to me my love. She kissed me, and her hand slid down my length and held me tight.

Oh, Danny this is so terrible. She held on to me tenderly.

Baby, come here, make love to me, we need this. She slowly made me hard and guided me into her. She squeezed me tight delicately rising and falling on me.

Oh Danny. She whispered as her tensions rose; she came in minutes bringing me with her. Our climax was so beautiful, quiet and intense. With tears in her eyes Bett smiled up at me.

You are the best. Our sexual pleasure lit Shiny so brightly. Bett stayed on me now, like before, riding me in space and now in our atmosphere. She gently held my muscle with her muscle ever so softly twitching around my shaft. Enjoying me as did Shiny whose light shone on the desolation of our world below us.

Perth was awash with waves too; many high-rise buildings were on their side or wiped out completely from the impact of the tidal waves and earthquakes and whole suburbs were demolished. We could see the zoo was gone and St Mary's Cathedral completely flattened.

Okay Shiny, we get the picture, can we go down to Antarctica first?

Sure thing! Shiny zipped along just above the waves, suddenly lifting and slowing and lighting up brightly. The ocean below filled with floating icebergs as far as we could see. It was surreal. I wished we could go higher with no cloud cover as this looked incredible. *I suppose once these icebergs drift north and melt, the oceans around the globe will cool.*

Will that make the water levels rise even more? Bett asked.

No Bett, they already have displaced the water. Imagine filling a glass with ice and topping it up with water to the very top. What happens when the ice melts, will it overflow? No, it doesn't, its volume stays the same once it is in the water. Water levels will rise when all the ice and snow on land melts.

Here is Antarctica. A lot of land is now exposed, look! Shiny was flying about half a mile up and below us was a barren landscape with water flowing fast from the remaining ice. Some of the ice is still a couple of miles thick but melting very fast. We came to some ancient Temples and buildings that were now exposed by the melting ice. They were perfectly preserved, thanks to the ice. Megalithic constructions that were built using massive rocks that somehow fit together perfectly but they did not look like human construction at all.

Shiny what is this place?

This is very old. It was built eons before me. I am unaware of its purpose as we came here once before, to visit someone you knew. They lived here but did not know who built it either but that was when we went back in time, twenty million years. I estimate it to be at least one hundred million years old.

What? That's crazy! Bett exclaimed.

Yes, it is, and these are probably the best-looking buildings on the planet right now.

There are many more still covered Danny and pyramids.

Wait. What did you say? I just realized what Shiny said. You just said; back in time twenty million years, is that what you said? How the fuck did we do that?

We used the wormhole next to Mercury; we used it to speed up, twenty three times the speed of light. You had to make love superfast together and it nearly broke you.

Who could I possibly know that long ago?

The answer to that will be sometime in the future I believe.

Shiny that is incredible if we can go back in time, we can stop all this destruction from happening.

No Danny, we can't do that, we can't go back and change anything. Our trip back affected nothing. That is the only time we can do it. You will understand later.

I get it; I've seen movies about this. Like, 'The Butterfly Effect.'

Yes, that theory is correct. Look here, the ice is gone completely there is a massive lake below us and the oceans are rising worldwide and cooling the planet. South America?

Yes Please. Shiny sped up into the murky skies and every so often there was a break in the clouds and suddenly bright sunlight beamed down onto the ocean, but that was very rare.

We just crossed the coast at Cape Horn, coming up on Santiago, Chile, first. The highest hotel in Santiago was, 'The Sky Costanera' at sixty-two floors; it was laying across the city in ruins. There had been a few mighty impacts of larger meteors throughout the city and many blazing fires all over, but it was mostly intact. The buildings were crumbled by the earthquakes and were unsafe. *Their underground shelters are full to over-capacity they do not have enough food to last them a week. Things are going to turn nasty quite quickly and they will start killing each other to survive. There is nothing we can do here. I will now fly to Buenos Aires.*

Thanks, Shiny. Will we find any good news anywhere?

Unfortunately, that is highly unlikely Danny.

≤≥

The tidal wave had decimated Buenos Aires arriving at five hundred miles an hour, at nearly two miles high funneled in by the bay called Rio de la Plata. The wave flattened all the buildings, trees and all fauna.

Buenos Aires was completely wiped from existence. We moved up the coast to Rio de Janeiro. The geography saved some of Rio with the narrow opening of Guanabara Bay only just over three miles wide. This would have diffused the wave. But the fires that followed decimated the Favela. It was burnt to the ground; thirteen million eight hundred thousand people had lived there. I could feel that less than seven thousand had survived, who most likely would not survive either, beyond a few weeks maybe. Christ the Redeemer lay smashed at the bottom of Corcovado Mountain; hit by a random meteor.

Okay, Shiny this is dreadful, north to Panama, Costa Rica, Havana and Cuba.

Yes, Danny, Bett my lights are dimming... Bett squeezed tightly and lifted her body and I nearly slipped out, but she slammed back down swiftly and did that again and again. The tenth time bringing us to a dramatic climax that lasted for ages. Bett pulled me close, kissing my ears and whispering.

Magic Danny, baby, you are unreal. Meanwhile Shiny sped up and shook us inside her, vibrating wildly.

Oh, err, Panama, oh, should be below but it is deep under water and so is Havana and all of Cuba by the look of it. Jamaica has vanished too. North and South America are now separated, by nearly five hundred and sixty miles. Florida is just north of us, it should be underneath us now. Key Largo, The Everglades and Miami are all submerged. Orlando is now a set of islands; I will head straight over to New Orleans in Louisianna, but I think that will be undersea too. We are hovering over it now; please tear your eyes away from each other for a second and look here. The coastline is one hundred and five miles inland now. It was becoming a blur to us now; we looked down not knowing what we should be seeing instead of what we were seeing.

Shiny can you take us back to Yellowstone? I wish to see the extent of the lava flow. Then we need to see Europe. Step on it.

Whoopee! Shiny raced away at high speed. *We are coming up on Yellowstone now.* Bett and I were still wrapped in each other's arms and legs. Bett keeping me solid inside her, keeping us both excited and Shiny strong. The glow coming from the lava below us illuminated the cloud cover, everything was lava red. Bett's skin glowed and sparkled red and we instantly felt warmer even though the temperature in the jelly remained the same. The flows of lava had spread one hundred and thirty miles in every direction. The cone around the caldera was over thirteen hundred feet high and twenty-five miles wide. It was now the biggest active volcano on the planet. But it had calmed down considerably.

Good god, have a look at that! Thanks, Shiny, Europe, go flat out. Shiny loved that. She shrieked with delight and raced away. Bett snuggled up to me and gave me a very wet jelly kiss, clamping down on me tightly and squirming around on me beautifully. I moaned.

Oh Bett, I grabbed her slender waist and pulled her against me as she gasped and dug her fingernails into my shoulders.

Oh, yes Danny, I pumped into her and she started moaning loud in my head.

Do me Danny. I was doing her, and speeding up and Bett loved every minute of it. We came within seconds of each other, which was so heightened.

Oh, Baby, we both moaned at the same time shuddering intensely.

Oh! We are coming up on the English coastline in a minute. You two are way more intense than any before you and that is what is making you so strong and me. I love you both. You make me feel so fulfilled. The Bristol Channel is below us and it goes all the way to London, splitting England in two. London is here and you will not see this on any postcard. Oh! So many landmarks were destroyed. The River Thames had burst its banks and water was throughout the city with every building barely standing and on fire. The London Eye was lying immersed in the Thames. We looked on in hopelessness and dismay. Heading over to the Netherlands their dykes could not stop the mass destruction that occurred. The whole country lost, collapsed under stormy seas. We arrived at the second strike. The impact crater was nearly fifty miles across and still a boiling mass of molten rock at its base. Two thousand miles around was demolished and beyond that all was burnt to a crisp. All of Europe was in disarray and decimated. Fires in the Black Forests were still burning out of control in the heated atmosphere. It was very dark above Europe.

Russia, please Shiny.

Will do Danny. Heading into Russia, fires were still raging. This was the only place we did not get to with our vortex, and we could tell the difference. Russia was pitch black and everything was covered in soot or burning profusely. Moscow had a direct hit from a large secondary meteor wiping out the whole city.

The huge bunker here has collapsed trapping those few thousand that remain alive; there is no way to rescue them.

Oh, no, that is tragic. Shiny take us over Africa now please. I asked.

Okay, Africa it is. We arrived in a few minutes. The Mediterranean Sea had expanded into Libya, Algeria, Chad and Tunisa. Most of the Sahara Desert was under water. Cairo was awash with water lapping at the Giza Plateau. Flying south, The Democratic Republic of Congo was blazing with fires throughout the country. The one hundred and eight million residents didn't stand a chance to survive the catastrophic impacts as with most of Africa. Their infrastructure was not prepared for an event like this. People had nowhere to go.

We have so much ahead of us, and I am pregnant, how can we possibly save humanity, her muscle spasmed on me involuntarily.

Baby, my Bett, we have each other; we will work it out, as we have already. We got this. And I have you. Okay? This will be a long process.

Oh Danny, you are my hero, you really make me feel safe. Thank you, my darling. I am totally in love with you. She squeezed me again without trying to.

Betty. Baby.

Sorry, I can't help it, Danny.'

Oh no, keep doing it my love, you feel great Bett.

So do you Danny, when you are inside me like this, I am always on the edge. You fill me and it is pure beauty. I feel your love and so much more, like we really are perfection.

Oh, but you are both amazing, sorry to interrupt but you are perfect. This incarnation of you is different and way more intense than anything I have experienced in my past with you. Honestly you two are the sum of all others before you. This is why you are the first to kill a Hathor. I love your loving, it is beautiful, intense, erotic and so satisfying we are whole when you are together. You make me feel so very happy. Thank you, my loves.'

Bett squeezed me again without trying too.

Oh, Danny oh. Thank you Shiny you are beautiful. Oh, you are both beautiful, oh, oh! She lost it, her contractions on me were so intense that I climaxed immediately as did Shiny. We all cried out together in orgasmic bliss, unaware of the mass destruction beneath us. We were all locked in a harmonious stupor for the next few minutes. Shiny's vibrations were moving us to the next level of eroticism. She flew us slowly back to Australia as we were completely locked on each other.

Shiny knew and let us be as one as she flew on. We had our eyes locked, and Bett gave the occasional twitch-squeeze, smiling widely and close to my face. She kissed me again, a jelly kiss, but it was sweet and beautiful and I slowly became hard in her once again.

Oh Danny, push into me please, my baby. I held her hips, and pushed in deeply. Bett groaned and grabbed my bum cheeks tightly.

Ugh, Oh Danny, I pulled back and pushed in again, Bett bit her lip, trying to stay in control. The third slow push did it and we both let go in a rush. Bett wrapped her arms around me and held me tightly as she shook with passion. I kept pumping into her in utter ecstasy and Shiny was shining radiantly, beating in time with us. We kissed and slowed down, trembling in each other's arms, coming to a stop. Bett was still contracting on me, and I was throbbing hard inside her. Bett smiled wickedly and winked at me.

You feel insane inside of me Danny, oh, so good and that, that was perfect baby.

I love you, Bett.

Coming up on Queensland, lovers. Shiny announced.

Thanks, Shiny, when we get to Taxi, head to the River Road faraday camera, we'll try that one.

My light will be much brighter this time because you are coupled and I am sure someone will notice. We have been gone three days; it would be seven in the morning. Taxi is ahead of us ETA one minute. Here we are. It is still two hundred degrees outside and very dark. I will start the message now. Shiny had memorized it and began the message.

∞

Inside The House of *Ra*, the townsfolk were starting their day with group exercises and breakfast. Conner had just entered the control room with Elouise and was being debriefed by Pete on the status of everything. Pete suddenly caught the River Road screen out the corner of his eye.

"Conner look!" Shiny sat four feet off the road and was flashing ever so brightly. They could only see her when she flashed. "What is she doing, trying to warn us or is something wrong?" Pete said in a rush.

"Give me a pen and paper please Pete, I think it is the old Morse code, yes, it is. They are so clever." Conner started scribbling down dots and dashes, and before long he realized it was being repeated so he stopped writing.

"Can you pull up Morse code on the computer please and type this into the translator. Thanks." Pete started typing and before long they had Betty's message in front of them. '*We did what we could, we are safe and nearby we leave again soon. The planet is a mess, but it will recover. Stay safe, we will too, talk soon. We love you all.*' "That's my girl, perfect. Can we do something so they know we have seen them?"

"The camera has a red light on the front when it is on, we can turn it off and on, so it blinks like Morse code."

"Okay, quick type in "*Thanks, stay safe. Our love to you all.*" Pete got the code and started sending the message. Shiny saw it immediately.

Look, they are replying 'Okay, thanks, stay safe. Our love to you all.' I'll spin around brightly and bob up and down, okay?

Yes Shiny, that will do. Inside Ra they saw Shiny spinning and bobbing and they all cheered "Say, see you please Pete." He did, and Shiny shone brightly as she lifted and flew to camp.

Jilly, we are back!

"Whoopee! Come straight in Shiny." She swooped in and stopped three and a half feet above our lake.

Home folks, safe and sound.

Thanks, Shiny, get some rest, next stop Europa. Leave in about twelve hours, okay?

I can't wait, that is my birthplace. See you then. Shiny opened, we floated out and threw up our jelly and dived into the lake. Shiny slowly sank and disappeared under the water.

"Oh, this feels so good. So different to the jelly." Bett was happy. She raised an arm for the gel as we stood in the shallows soaping ourselves with luxurious bubbles. Jilly watched from shore smiling as we went out deeper and dived in. Betty grabbed me and pulled me in for a hug. We immediately went under and she quickly lifted us out of the water, as we sputtered. Then we had a long, sweet kiss, without jelly.

"Oh Danny, my dear Danny, let's go and get dry for the first time in five days."

"Great idea sweetheart."

"*Hello my babe's, did you see everything you had too?*"

"We did Jilly, we saw too much destruction. Did you miss us?"

"*Yes, but to me hibernating has no sense of time passing, so it feels like I saw you only minutes ago. How long were you gone?*"

"Five days, flying all over the world."

"*Danny were you inside Betty the whole time?*"

"Oh, Jilly, really? Why do you ask?"

"*I can tell, just by looking at that.*" She pointed at my cock. I must admit it was still fully engorged, but it was soft and it looked huge.

"*It is still flooded with blood; how do you do that for five days? Are you Super Dick, like Superman?*" We looked at each and laughed.

"Jilly, you say the funniest things. Okay, yes, I was inside Bett the whole time. Shiny's jelly is the answer and it is still inside us even now. It helps us last and makes us horny."

"*Horny? You grow horns too?*"

"No Jilly horny is the same as feeling aroused, feeling sexy."

"*Oh... I need to fly in that jelly too, I want to be horny.*"

"Jilly with who, where is your partner?"

"*Jilly can please herself too, you know.*"

"Uh, yes, then, but if you leave here the bubble will collapse."

"*Oh yes, mmm, maybe I can sleep in her tonight. I will go and ask her now. See you later.*" Jilly skipped off before we could say anything. Bett smiled.

Look Danny it is probably not a bad thing if she has some of Shiny inside her. But within a few minutes Shiny started to vibrate. We looked out and she was pulsing quickly and we could feel their excitement.

Oh shit. That didn't take long; I wonder what is going on inside her? I asked looking at Bett but she was staring at my penis which was suddenly somehow fully erect She was moaning and gently rubbing herself quietly down there.

She ran to me and launched herself onto me, wrapping her legs around me and lifted me into the air, gliding onto me, swiftly clenching as she suddenly bought us both to climax. Her hot mouth on mine, trying to kiss me while her orgasm was racking her body and mine. We shook and trembled in harmony. The lake below us was a bright purple and then it became yellow pulsing. I was pumping into Betty rapidly and still coming as we all were. I had Betty's sweet breasts in my hands squeezing them tenderly, her nipples were rock hard. Her tongue was dancing around in my mouth, and she was gasping for air as we started spinning slowly above the lake. Shiny's vibrations were going through our bodies as we all kept moving rhythmically. Bett's arms were around me with her long-pointed fingernails digging deeply into my shoulders.

After a full five minutes of solid orgasms, we finally slowed to a stop. Bett and I were panting, trying to catch our breath. She opened her eyes wide smiled and winked, squeezing my cock tight. Betty whispered in my ear.

"That was fantastic, mmm, Captain Super Dick. Uh, that was wild, and our little Jilly started that all off somehow." We dropped into the lake and washed ourselves and then lifted high above and held each other tight.

Ω

Unknown to us, almost all of *Ra* residents had climaxed too. Many in the privacy of their bedrooms together but some in pools and lakes and others behind bookshelves, in cupboards or their kitchens. If they didn't have partners, they pleasured themselves. For Conner and Elouise, they didn't make it to the bedroom and made passionate love on the lounge room floor. They lay on their backs now holding hands naked, smiling at each other, panting and totally exhausted. Her ample breasts were heaving.

This is one way to heal the planet and encourage population growth, Elouise thought. She had always been a little psychic and she felt Bett and Danny had just done something really wild that had affected her and Conner. She would ask around if anyone else had played around this morning. *She was looking at Conner's manhood and smiling but she saw Danny and his huge cock lying there. Lucky Bett!*

Ω

Bett was thinking how lucky she was too; her man was incredible. She jumped off him and floated in front of him, watching his huge cock slowly fall and admiring his delicious golden body. He was full of muscle now and he hadn't shaved in over a week. A sexy beard was forming and his dark hair was unruly and growing long. He looked rugged and strong with his piercing blue eyes that seemed even bluer now against his golden skin that glistened and swirled under the bubble. *Oh god, and that big beautiful cock of his. He knows exactly how to use it without ever hurting me. God, I love him to bits.* She thought.

God, I love her to bits. Just look at her in front of me, she is stunningly beautiful. Her golden glistening body to me is perfect. Muscular and strong too. Her curves are perfection, not too big and not too small. Her golden skin is soft and supple. Large soft but firm golden breasts with huge dark pink nipples and areola. Her belly has a slight baby mound in it now, making her even sexier. Her shaved hairless crotch and beautiful hips. Sculpted legs and petite feet. Slowly my eyes travelled back up to hers, I knew she was assessing me the same way. Her eyes were the greenest of green and becoming greener by the day. They were bottomless, and If I stared too long, I would fall in.

We had been staring at each other in admiration for a full ten minutes. Bett suddenly flew forwards and spun me around hugging me madly. "Oh, my beautiful man, thank you for absolutely everything, you make me so happy so full of life and so gratified. I do love you baby. You are perfection personified; I am aroused just looking at you. You were made for loving me and I was made for fucking you and loving you madly." She winked and kissed me lightly.

"Thank you, my Betty looking at you just now I feel I am the lucky guy, your body is so beautiful and when I look into your eyes all I see is your love for me and that to me makes me so happy. I am so proud that you are mine, you make me feel sexy and I love you with all my heart."

Betty hugged me warmly and gave me a long passionate kiss. "Let's lie down and rest for a while, even though I'm not really tired, but we need to be fully charged for our next flight." Bett pulled me to the tent. We landed softly on the mattresses and our whiskeys came floating over. We clinked glasses and drank. Soon our glasses floated away and we comfortably stretched out. I was on my back and Bett on her side snuggled up to me, her hand resting on my pubic hair with her silky soft leg draped over my thigh, she kissed my cheek and we closed our eyes and fell asleep.

∞

We opened our eyes, a fresh zephyr blew over us, the sun was high with the bluest of skies above us and we were lying in a field of lush green grass. We looked across at each other, our skin golden and sparkling in the sunlight. Nearby there were groves of mangoes, oranges, lemons and limes and off to our left were all manner of crops. We sat up and curiously looked around. A house made of melted rock and glass sat up on the hill. It looked like an ancient construction but was of very modern design. It felt somehow familiar. Danny it's our house, we made it, together. Yes, I remember it now but is this the past or our future, how could we have future memories? Danny it is beautiful, like you, come here my darling. She rolled onto me and kissed me sweetly.

I opened my eyes; Bett was kissing me sweetly.

"Good morning my love, where were we, or when?"

"I don't know baby, our dreams never give answers, only questions, but if we made that house that means we can melt or mold stone and glass somehow." Jilly suddenly started clapping.

"Good morning, babes did you enjoy our light show last night?" She had been sitting there waiting for us to wake up.

"Jilly, you know we did, what went on in Shiny, Jilly?"

"Bett, I did what comes naturally, free love for all. Thanks to me, Shiny allowed me to share it and your DNA played a part in that too. And look at me, all golden and shiny just like you." Jilly was turning gold too.

"Jilly whatever you did was wild we have never experienced that before."

"Jillyish, feels alive, happy and joyful, glad to share. I see why you like flying in her she is very special like you two. JD for breakfast, here." Three shot glasses sat next to Jilly's ingenious pouring contraption.

"I found some more little glasses that Jilly can lift. Cheers!" She raised her glass. "Cheers Jilly, thank you." Betty called her phone. Thanks to the bubble it still worked but no reception or internet. "Danny it is ten o'clock, two hours before we leave for Europa. Are you hungry? We should eat something. How about some more hot dogs? Simple and filling."

"Bett that sounds perfect."

"I have started them already Danny, chili?"

"Oh, yes Babe, thank you." Jilly sat watching us. The dogs soon came out on plates.

"I'm sorry, but that is gross how can you eat that? That thing looks like skinny dick with blood beans and wheat pussy."

"Jilly! Stop. That is not right, don't say that."

"Oops, sorry, but you know that is not good for your guts, all that processed stuff. Once you run out, that is it, back to basics. Fish and, and whatever you can kill."

"So true Jilly we understand, but right now let us just enjoy our hotdogs in peace please."

"I am sorry I will go and leave you in peace."

"Jilly, you don't have to go..."

"I know that but I will anyway, all good, I will eat some fish. Jilly will return later." She hopped and skipped away whistling. I got stuck into my hotdog as did Bett, they were delicious. After spending so much time in Shiny we hadn't been eating much at all, her jelly was keeping us sustained, nourished and satisfied and we felt stronger and fitter than ever before. We finished our scrumptious dogs and sat back on the couch sipping our bourbon.

"We are so lucky to have Jilly. We wouldn't be sitting like this on the only spot on Earth untouched by the impacts. It is amazing isn't it?"

"It is Bett, it's incredible. Jilly is naturally funny and sometimes quite inappropriate but still I'm glad she is with us. Seriously you are the best cook ever, and the best lover I have ever had, the four of us make quite a crazy team."

∞

It was the fifteenth morning inside Ra, and everyone was going about their daily routines Conner and Elouise were in the control room with Pete and John. John spoke first.

"Good morning, folks, day fifteen in the new world. Temperatures outside have finally started to drop. Three days ago, it reached a maximum of seven hundred degrees, yesterday three hundred degrees and today we are at two fifty. The AI model predicts world temperatures to steadily drop over the next week or two to forty degrees, before settling at around two degrees Celsius globally. That will be cold enough to refreeze the vaporized water in the atmosphere, causing weeks of snowstorms, with hail as big as basketballs. Most likely the Artic Circle will freeze over completely first, with the northern hemisphere covered in thick sheet ice as far south as The Tropic of Cancer within five to ten years."

"Okay, wow, any good news?" Conner asked. Pete piped up.

"Maisy, one of our horses gave birth to Daisy this morning, they are both doing well."

"That is good news; we'll go and check on them later. Anything else?"

"The generators are all nominal, waste processing is nominal, oxygen levels perfect and all doors are sealed tight sir." Pete finished.

"Okay, thank you gentlemen, we'll see you a little later."

"Conner, do you mind if I catch up with Rita, see how she is doing?" Elouise asked.

"Sure Elouise, I'll be in the library if you need me." Conner kissed her and they parted.

Elouise headed straight to Rita's quarters. She gently knocked. "Hello Rita, are you there?" Rita opened the door.

"Hello, lovely, I'm just on my way to the Tavern to help behind the bar and with lunches. Come along we can talk and walk together. How is

Conner? I heard a rumor about his wound."

"Conner is good, really good and the rumor is fact. Shiny's jelly is in his lungs and body and had healed the wound by the time he arrived back here. He holds no grudges and thought you were a good shot to hit him in the shoulder from that distance."

"Oh, Elle, I didn't mean to even hit him, it was supposed to be a warning shot and I was aiming for that bloody huge tank he was driving." They both laughed. "Don't tell him that please Elle."

"Don't fret Rita that can be our secret. Hey Rita, last night, anything out of the ordinary?" Elouise grinned and winked at Rita. She stopped and grabbed Elouise's arm.

"What you too? That was amazing, it was like at the wedding on the dance floor, and at The Dermy, my orgasm was so intense."

"Yes, yes mine too, almost out of control." They arrived at the Tavern. Elouise sat at the bar and Rita went behind the bar and said hello to the other three girls.

"What would you like to drink Elle?"

"Just a glass of white wine thanks a Pinot Gris." The tavern was very casual, and the girls used it as release and a way to socialize."

Rita bought the others over and introduced them. "Elle, this is Lola, Candice and Rose." They all smiled and nodded to each other.

"Congratulations on your wedding Elle." Lola said.

"Yes, congratulations," they all said together. Candice poured out four glasses of Pinot Gris. "Cheers!"

"CHEERS!"

"You can call me Candy." Candice said.

"Hey girls, Elle and I were just talking about that dance at the wedding and then Sunday at the Dermy and then last night." Rita stopped; all the girls looked at each other and started giggling and laughing.

"What? This is getting crazy, all of you? What time was it, nine thirty?" Lola giggled.

"Yep, same for me." Rose and Candy said and laughed together.

"Intense?" Candy asked.

"*Hell, yes*, mine lasted for ages." Rose admitted. They all nodded.

"Did any of you think of Bett and Danny straight after or before or during?" Elouise asked expecting nothing.

"Danny." Rose said.

"Danny" said Lola.

"Bett," Rita blushed.

"Danny," Elouise said.

"Shiny and Danny." Candy was shaking her head. They all looked at her.

"Shiny too?'

"Yes. Something about her throbbing lights turns me on." They all laughed.

"Why Danny, Candy?" Elouise asked.

"His dick?" She kept imagining he had a huge cock. It all started at the wedding, She had never even seen him before that. "I'm sure it's enormous and I certainly haven't seen his dick!" Candy blurted out. They all laughed, but they were all nodding.

"Me too." Rita nodded. "I keep imagining him, naked in front of me as if I am seeing him through Bett's eyes. Feeling his cock inside me, fucking me hard. I will always be faithful to Chuck, even though we are only friends. But it arouses me every time it happens." Rita admitted. They all skolled their wine as Lola poured another for all of them.

"Why Danny, Lola?" Elouise asked.

"I imagine I am Betty too, being fucked by Danny and what that must feel like," Lola admitted.

"I felt his penis, and it was massive." Elouise didn't mean to say that aloud. "Oh, shit, forget that, please that can't get out, that I just said that. It was a mistake." She skolled her second glass and Lola poured another.

"Elle come on now, spit it out, *how? When?*"

"I sort of got pushed into him at the bar and my open hand pressed against him. It was nearly an inch longer than my hand." She held up her long slender hand, and they all gasped.

"Was it hard or soft at that length?" Rose asked.

"*Soft*, he wasn't having an erection at the bar but I am sure he was becoming stiff from my touch as he pulled away. He didn't have any boxers on and only thin linen trousers, I felt it perfectly. His girth and circumcised head are *huge, but not too big...* And just before that, he

– 156 –

had his arm around me and I became aroused and I nearly came in my undies. I was so close. Girls, this stays with the five of us, okay? Cheers!"

They raised their glasses and clicked them together. Rose kept holding her hand up and staring at it, trying to picture Danny's cock laying across it, from end to end.

"If Conner finds out I said any of this, he would be very upset and honestly, I don't want Danny. I love Conner, but something weird is going on when they are all around. It is affecting all the women of *Ra*, and that is a good thing. I have never felt more alive, blissful and horny." They all agreed that this circle of girls would meet regularly and have their secret women's talks about their experiences and never divulge their knowledge of Danny's big cock to anyone. Betty was staring at Danny's big cock; he was standing innocently in front of her warming his butt by the fire, sipping his Jack and puffing on a cigar. She desperately wanted to hold and caress it.

Ω

"What Bett, my eyes are up here?" She smiled and squeezed me with her mind, so I tickled her clitoris with mine. Her eyes went wide. I looked down and my shaft was rippling along its length. I closed my eyes and she had me in her mouth with her mind as I entered her gently and withdrew. I opened my eyes and she was floating in front of me like an alluring goddess.

She held out her hand and I took it and we lifted slowly into the air. She took hold of me and spread her magnificent legs guiding me and pulling me in close, her legs entwined around mine. I shuddered as she felt so good on me she was in total control; slowly moving on me, so very slow, squeezing me gently. I kissed her as she started to climax immensely and I moaned as I exploded inside her. This was as intense as the night before and Shiny was lighting up the lake, vibrating forcefully. We climaxed in unison.

∞

The five girls were all holding hands at the bar saying goodbye to Elouise when they all started to shake and *orgasm* in unison. They held on tightly to each other and let it flow over them, all feeling amazing, gasping loudly and moaning deeply. Rose shrieked and Lola doubled over heaving, this went on for another five minutes before they could relax. It was extremely lucky that the tavern was empty. Their faces were aglow with joyful post orgasmic bliss as they smiled and hugged each other. They couldn't speak for a few minutes.

"I felt as if I was floating in the air naked, with him inside me." Candy whispered.

"That was more intense than yesterday. When my eyes were closed, I felt the same thing, floating, with that huge cock throbbing inside me. Lola said.

"I was controlling him; squeezing him, making him come and he felt so incredible inside me." Rita said shaking her head.

"My body is buzzing, how did we share that, what is going on? I have never had an orgasm like that, imagining someone was doing that to me while I'm standing at a bar." Rose admitted.

"I hate to say it, but I loved it, that felt so beautiful and sexually sat-isfying. Not just sex but love coming from him." Elouise admitted. They all agreed. "Conner is in for a good time shortly, see you girls later, I love you all." She left. Rita looked stunned at the others.

"Shall we close the Tavern for a bit and go and find our men?"

"Great idea Rita, come on, half an hour, okay?" They closed the front door and left in a hurry. Their men were in for a big surprise, poor Rose was the only one with no partner. She hurried home, locked the door and filled her bath tub. Happy and horny and just a little lonely she stripped off and slid into her own euphoria. All she had to do was think of Daniel.

≥≤≥≤

Betty and I had floated out into the lake and were enjoying a swim. She motioned for the shower gel. We swam to the shallows, and I slowly lathered Bett. She was truly loving my hands all over her, and quickly climaxed in my arms as I kissed her passionately. Betty was still shaking as she started on me and by the time she reached my stiff erection, she cried out as another orgasm took her.

She pulled me down and I floated on my back in front of her. She started pulling on my slippery rod, kissing me and watching my muscles twitch as she felt me tense. She sped up and her hand was a blur. I cried out as I let go in ecstasy. Bett let my cum fly away about ten feet and kept pulling on me fast, very fast. Her eyes were fixed on my throbbing cock as she came again. I was shaking wildly, she slowed and stopped and eventually so did I. She took my cock in her wet mouth, running her hot tongue over it like crazy, it was so sensitive. I was squirming around with her head in my hands as she went cross eyed and winked at me and then released me. We kissed for an eternity. After that, we sensuously held each other in the shallows, as she wouldn't let go of my throbbing stiff cock. "I love you Dan."

"I love you Bett."

∞

At the same time we were in the lake orgasming, four couples and Rose in Ra were going for it too. The men had no idea what had come over their women, but it was great, erotic and very sexy. The women were in total control, and the men respected their lady's needs. Rose was totally exhausted but extremely satisfied with herself.

10

Europa

*H*ello Shiny, have you seen Jilly?
    She is here, with me. Shiny lifted from the water and came over near the shore, she opened and little golden Jilly jumped out throwing up jelly before hitting the water. Jilly swam furiously to shore; she was smiling from ear hole to ear hole.

"Hello babes, Shiny and I have been together the whole time, we loved what you did twice before, you are so virulent Danny, I love that. I will take more of your DNA from the lake. We are so proud to broadcast your love to everyone."

"Wait Jilly, what are you broadcasting? To whom, and how?"

"Bett and Danny, when you are together you send out a vibration, if I am in Shiny at the same time, we can amplify it together and share it around the globe. Everyone feels it and loves it. They are going off."

"Jilly what do you mean they are going off?"

"They start doing it too, making love and having big orgasms like us. They love it. They forget about the destruction and are happy. There is joy everywhere; men respect the power of their women, thanks to you Bett. This new world will be very different to the last, if we can keep broadcasting, do you get it?"

"Wow, Jilly, Shiny are you in on this, is it as good as Jilly says?"

Danny, Jilly is right, when we broadcast it is like a radar and we receive feedback from their love and that is making everything more intense. It's like a loop. The more we broadcast you, the happier everyone is and the higher the world's population will become and that is a good thing.

"They don't actually see us, do they?" Jilly squirmed a little.

"Only a few maybe, but we are not sure, they don't see you but are aware that it may be your influence. Danny it is a good influence, please believe us. This whole planet is better off now."

"Shiny, can Hathors see or feel any of this?"

Danny no, I am invisible to them so they cannot see or feel anything from you while I am near and my jelly is a part of you both now.

"Thank you Shiny and Jilly, Bett and I will need to think about this while we are on Europa. We should leave soon Shiny."

We can go right now, if you like.

"Yes, good Shiny, let's go. Jilly thank you for your insights, we will consider this. Stay safe little babe. See you soon."

"Bye babes." Jilly skipped into the water humming 'Fortunate Son.' We lifted into the air and entered Shiny. We gulped her jelly, and gagged again, like usual. Shiny quivered as we entered her. We took up our flight positions, holding hands lying prone as the lake shrunk beneath us. As soon as we left the bubble we noticed the difference, the sky was dark and murky from the cloud cover, rising swiftly through the clouds. The sun burst through nearly blinding us with aureate light as we closed our eyes as Shiny adjusted her opaqueness. The few moments of blue sky were swiftly followed by the darkness of space. The stars were opening above us into a glistening vista. Shiny zipped up swiftly past the moon silently invisible to the remaining Hathors. The Earth was no longer a blue and green color. It was now a dirty grey brown globe.

This trip will take three Earth hours. So please feel free to join at any time, you will aid in expediting our trip, and will make Shiny very happy. Bett looked over at me and grinned wickedly, she moved closer to me and took my penis in her warm hand.

Oh, Danny, I love you babe, what a crazy life this is, she gave me a sweet jelly kiss and squished herself against me, her firm breasts felt so beautiful. *Come here my man.* I was now stiff as she moved onto me and guided me in. She immediately moaned as I entered her, I thrust in deep and she smiled and held me tight. *Oh, yes, my Danny, love me my darling,* so I loved her, I thrust again firmly and Bett moaned deeply over and over. I quickened my pace. She slyly winked at me and stayed with my tempo, *Come on Danny!* She moaned and then lifted her pace. *I'm with you, faster, baby.* I sped up. Shiny was flying so fast. Suddenly Bett screamed in the jelly, and her body heaved in ecstasy, her fingernails tearing into my clammy back. She clamped down on me hard and I came immediately. Thrusting deeper into her, she moaned and shuddered and kept coming, her face filled with sexual arousal. I pushed harder, she looked into my eyes and euphorically smiled. *Oh, you Ratbag! Oh!* She cried and faster we went. Uh. *Give it to me!* I kept pumping into her then Bett whispered in my ear, *Now Danny.* I orgasmed again on her command, and it was just incredible. Betty climaxed at the same time, as did Shiny. Her vibrations intensifying all our sensations.

We hurtled through the solar system, Mars slipped past, we sailed through the asteroid belt as the remarkable Jupiter slowly filled our view with all her magnificent moons spread out on either side it was such an extraordinary sight. Shiny started to slow as we approached, I slowed down and stopped. Bett smiled and winked and squeezed me and she whispered in my mind.

You are fucking breathtaking Daniel. I could only kiss her. I was so lost in her.

Shiny does not swear, but Holy shit, that was incredible, you two are amazing. Europa is the sixth closest of the ninety-five moons of Jupiter, straight ahead of us. The outer crust is solid ice, six and a half miles thick; we enter though through a large vent. There look, in front of us, hang on this could be rough. Shiny flew into the vent, out gassing of water vapor causing buffeting against Shiny's hull. Betty clamped down on me tightly and involuntarily.

Oh fuck, I nearly lost it again if not for the violence of our entry.

Hang on, nearly through. Now. We smoothed out and glided through the oceans of Europa. Outside gradually grew brighter and lighter, bio luminescent creatures big and small lit the oceans brightly. *This here is my birthplace, we are expected.*

Below us a brightly lit crystal city of domes of all shapes and sizes, of towers high and mighty, as far as we could perceive. The hundred-mile-deep ocean above us glowing with abundant fluorescent life. Bett squeezed me again in fear, I think.

Bett, I should pull out now, or I will be out there with them with a hard on.

Oh, sorry Danny, yes of course. I pulled out gently but I was still pretty hard.

We are here, the Octo you know are here. You may exit now. Shiny was open. We exited her and threw up as we floated down. In front of us two thousand Octo crying out in joy as we stood in front of them, my penis was still falling but semi-erect. Our friends came silently forward.

Look at him, he is glorious, look how big and impressive his manhood is. These are the Old Ones that helped save the Earth. These two are the heroes, with their Shiny. The masses erupted with jubilation; twelve thousand tentacles waved at us frantically, our minds were full of their gratification. They were all looking at my massive cock.

Oh my god Betty.

Stand proud Daniel they are all impressed by you, they have very small, thin genitals, you are a god to them. Betty raised her finger and my penis stood fully erect, pointing at them.

Look at him! Wow, it stands to attention! Look at it, it is beautiful. They all said. They all cheered with excitement and delight; their tentacles went crazy. I stood with my hands on my hips, fully erect and throbbing with a massive group of eight-foot-high octopi, surrounding us.

This is so weird Betty.

You got this Danny.

Come, oh mighty impressive ones; view our splendid city. Please wash your jelly off here. We welcome your love into our midst, Shiny will be taken care of and loved by her kind, she is home. They will look after her. The Rebellion against The Hathors welcomes you. Hathor killers, The Old Ones, come to our feast in your honor. We followed them, each path had a channel full of water next to it, sometimes they walked next to us other times they swam alongside us. Their long purple eye stalks following our every move. Their grand underwater city was wondrous, full of amazing architecture. We walked on in stunned silence and awe. Some of their buildings were alive like Shiny, their surfaces were shimmering, moving and glistening.

Please sit at our feast table Old Ones. We have a selection of Europa's finest foods that we have carefully selected so that all are totally compatible with your physiology. Please enjoy the meal our friends.

Danny, be confident make your selections and eat, that is what they expect. We turned our attention to the plates; some foods were still alive. *Grab it Danny and eat.* I picked up a big fat worm that squirmed and inched around dropping it into my mouth. I crunched down on it. It tasted just like strawberries and passionfruit. There was a bowl of small crustaceans trying to get away and The Octo swiftly took them one by one and devoured them. I grabbed the slippery sucker and crunched down hard. It moved in my mouth briefly. It was so full of luscious flavors that I immediately popped another in my mouth, they were highly addictive.

Bett, their food is incredible.

Yes, it is I'm loving this. The food kept coming out. Their seaweed was fried and delightful, their jellyfish were treated with enzymes that made them melt in your mouth delicious. We ate and laughed with the Octo. They had a wine made from seaweed grapes that soon had us all very drunk.

Bett are you okay dory?

Not sure if I can stand Dan-Ney. Dis is full-on Babs.

Yus, da sea, weed stuff is mess in wad me. I pod my arm around ma Bitty, I lob ya. The Octo too were falling backwards and many were asleep. This must be quite normal for them. A massive high after a meal, then a siesta. We collapsed where we were and slept. The Octo on the smooth stone floor and Bett and I, arm in arm with our faces in our plates with our food crawling all over us.

I awoke about an hour later to a small crab chewing on my ear. I brushed it off, and shook Betty awake. She sat straight up and tried to tidy her tousled hair but to no avail. She looked at me and burst out laughing.

Come here Danny, your hair is full of worms and crabs.

I suppose that is why The Octo don't fall asleep at the table. My head was numb, I looked down at myself and there was a small purple jellyfish sucking on the head of my fully erect cock. Betty squealed in delight and pulled it gently off me and popped it in her mouth. My golden head had turned bright purple like a plum. Bett rubbed at it and the purple mucus came off in her hand, she licked it off.

Hmm, they are delicious little suckers.

The Octo were all still heavily sleeping. Bett looked around slyly and leant down and then stealthily took my still stiff, slightly purple cock in her mouth and sucked on me until I ejaculated. Right there at the feast table with a thousand sleeping Octo surrounding us. I climaxed as silently as I could, moaning deeply with one hand on Bett's head as she watched me blow and the other covering my mouth. She shook and moaned as an orgasm went through her too. She smiled up at me as I finished, and then gave me a sexy wink. She sat up next to me and I gave her a glass of seaweed grape wine. She skolled it and rinsed her mouth and kissed me hard and whispered in my ear.

"Oh, Danny, you my dear are delicious, I love you completely."

Bett that was daring and very erotic and very nice, thank you my love. Bett lovingly held my cock in her hands as I slowly went soft and kissed me passionately.

The Octo were still out of it. So, I entered Bett with my mind. She immediately gasped and squeezed me hard in her hands, until I was fully erect again. My eyes closed, as Bett started to reach orgasm, she moaned deeply in my ear, again and again. She was tugging on my cock fast and I started to climax again, hilariously Betty caught it in a big wine glass. A thousand Octo suddenly cheered us. We opened our eyes and they were all wide awake staring at me ejaculating into the wine glass. They were all shaking in bliss and orgasming with us.

Oh, shit, Betty. Stop. Uh!

No, Danny, keep going they love it as much as we do, they are all in rapture. Bett, lifted another glass and put the full one on the table. She kept going so I just closed my eyes. An Octo took the glass and raised it in the air for all to see then took a sip and passed it around. They were all cheering me on. Bett kept me going as I was still inside her mind. She was moaning continuously as I filled another glass. The Octo took the full glass and passed it around as I slowly filled another glass. Bett's hands were a total blur on my steaming hot strong shaft. My body was heaving and my penis was huge. The Octo were falling all over the place, writhing around on the floor in utter ecstasy. The sexual commotion went on for another six minutes.

Outside the horny room a thousand craft with Shiny were all buzzing too, shining brightly. Finally, Bett slowed down and so did I. As the last few drops fell in the glass it was swiftly taken and passed around. The whole city was cheering us in joyful glee. I sat up awkwardly and held Bett in my arms tightly. I whispered in her mind.

What the fuck did we just do in front of them, I can't believe we did that, with an audience, how embarrassing.

Oh, no Danny, you are wrong, look at them, have a look around they are so happy for us and themselves, I feel honor and respect and joy coming from them, surely you feel that too. Danny stand up on the table with me and raise your arms in the air, cheering, come on let's do this please. Reluctantly I joined Betty as we climbed up on the table and lifted our arms high. Betty made my golden rod fully erect again; we jumped up and down loudly cheered with them.

The Octo went absolutely ballistic. The whole city went wild, a million tentacles raised in the air pumping in time with us, the sound was crazy and loud. Bett looked at me and winked smiling gorgeously, she took hold of my hand as we jumped. Europa shook with joy. We jumped down off the table and ran to the two Octo we knew, and embraced them. They wrapped us up in their long-wet tentacles and they felt incredible. Betty reached over and took my hand as the four of us suddenly climaxed together.

We weren't expecting any of this but just went with it. We had no choice really as I had tiny suckers all over me as did Bett. They lifted us gently off the ground singing loudly and shook us in an alien rhythm that felt exhilarating; we trembled in their arms until they gently released us. Bett and I fell gently to the floor on our backs panting and looking at each other in bewilderment. *Holy fuck Bett, Octo Love?*

I know crazy right! That was amazing. What now?

The Octo gently lifted us above their heads and carried us through the city as the crowds roared around us. They took us to a spa like pool and lowered us into the warm bubbly water. Their warbling voices said in our minds. *We leave you in peace to recover. What you did, sharing yourselves with us all, brings us the highest honor in our history Old Ones. Our civilization is in beautiful shock. We thank you and we are forever in your debt. Filling the glasses for us to share you, was an amazing gift that we will never forget. Our entire fleet shared your orgasmic experience too. Rest now as we prepare for another feast in honor of your gift. We will return in four hours, there is wine here, please relax.'*

"Thank you, Octo." They left. Betty swam over to me and hugged me as we rested our heads on the soft edge of the warm pool.

"Danny that was crazy, I never would have done that before, in front of others. In front of aliens, you are incredible babe. I had to keep tugging on you when they started drinking. I could tell they thought you were doing it for them."

"I was Betty." I winked at her. "How many glasses Bett?"

"It was twelve Danny, twelve impossible wine glasses, that is more than you have ever done."

"Feel these Bett, my balls. Shit, they are full again, and heavy." Bett squeezed them gently.

Bett gently sat on my legs just below my groin kissing me. The tip of my soft floating penis was just touching her clitoris. "I really enjoyed giving you head back there," she whispered.

"Well, I enjoyed you doing it to me." Bett moved forward, so my knob was pressed against her sex lips and she took hold of my soft head with her folds.

"How do you control your muscles like that Bett? Hmm," I started to harden.

"The awakening," she whispered. And then squeezed again. She moved forward, forcing me inside her just a little.

"Hmm." she moaned, as she moved off and quickly back on and then further on me, very slowly taking me all in. Gripping me gently but firmly.

"Uh, Bett, they said relax."

"Oh, Danny but I am," she clenched me tightly, *oh*, she slowly lifted and fell back; repeating it tenderly while bringing me to climax, I groaned as I came in her. Bett threw her head back and let go as her whole body shook, moaning loudly.

Oh, yes Danny. She trembled for a few minutes and gently slid off me. She held my face gently in her hands and kissed me.

"I feel so good now, hmm. I like your beard, Danny; you look so handsome, do you want some wine?"

"Sure, why not?" We sat back in the luxurious bubbles, sipping the wine. We did feel totally relaxed. We closed our eyes for a while and slept. The Octo soon returned and we dried off standing under a vent of warm air and followed them. The feast that we were about to consume was under one of the domes in the gardens, with the bright luminescent oceans gloriously above us and the entire population was present.

Please sit here. We sat and all the Octo sat too. The vista before us looked impressive. We sat at one endless table that wove its way through the gardens and there was different food on each plate for the first fifty plates and then it was repeated. Our chairs were on a conveyor that very slowly moved from one plate to the next and our glasses were held in the armrests of the chairs. Seated this way we had different Octo passing us in the opposite direction so they all got a chance to see us up close. They had built this seating arrangement for us. As before there were many live dishes that crawled or wiggled but it was all amazing food. The Octo all said hello as we passed and our friends sat either side of us chatting away continuously. The wine warmed our bellies and fuzzed our heads. After two hours we had arrived back at our starting point, where many Octo lay on the soft grass sleeping. Bett and I excused ourselves and carefully stood and staggered over to the edge of the pool and sat down. We were full and quite drunk, but not like last time. The ground beneath us was spongy and soft and as we lay down it molded to our bodies. I lay on my back with Betty curled up next to me, her head on my chest and her hand gently holding my cock. We peacefully fell asleep.

I woke after an hour or so and Bett was moaning quietly. We were wrapped up with the two Octo on either side of us. I glanced down and realized Bett still had a hold of my now fully erect penis, but it was also wrapped in a tentacle. I was gently being milked into a tube that went into a large wine container. *Bett wake up.* I said in her mind. Bett woke up and freaked out.

"Hey guys this is not cool, what are you doing to Danny, let go of him!" The tentacle pulled away.

Sorry, we were trying to help. It was going everywhere as you slept so we put this on you to catch it. It would be a shame to waste his gift. We meant you no harm. We apologize, honestly you were ejaculating in your sleep; I was holding on, so it went in the tube.

Danny, they are telling the truth, I can feel it, it is my fault. I was dreaming of you at the dinner table, coming in the wine glasses. Oh, I'm so sorry. "Please leave us Octo; we do not hold anything against you." They took the container and left.

Bett, it's okay, I'm fine, perhaps next party don't fall asleep holding on to me.

Sorry Danny I will be more careful. We dived into the pond and swam around for a bit, to refresh ourselves.

Danny how long do we stay here I feel we need to get back to earth and see how Jilly and Ra is doing and the rest of the planet.

Yes, I agree, come on then we'll tell them we need to go. We can always come back. Our friends were nearby. We explained our reasons and thanked them profusely for their hospitality.

Let us walk with you to Shiny. We are the grateful ones, what you both shared was enlightening and beautiful for all Octo kind. We will talk of these days for centuries. Go in peace and good will, we will check in with you soon. We wait for your return. Thank you for your wine, it was delicious Danny.

"Oh, yeah, err that is okay. See you soon." We floated up to Shiny. She opened and we entered her and Shiny shivered as we gulped in her jelly.

Welcome back, are we headed home?

Yes, Shiny, take us slowly through the oceans of Europa first.

Okay Danny, thank you for bringing me home for a while.

That's alright. Shiny lifted into the air and dove into the lake and followed the tube to the ocean. There was so much fluorescent life here, it was astounding. The water was alive, big fish, tiny fish, crustaceans, octopus, snakelike creatures and huge jellyfish.

Okay, the fissure is up ahead, hang on to each other, this will get rough again. Bett pulled me close and kissed me as she reached down and grabbed me.

Okay? She asked silently.

Of course, baby. Kissing and squeezing me until I was hard, she slid onto me just as our ride got rough. *Whoa!* This was rougher going out than coming in. Bett was squeezing me tightly as she rode me, quickly bringing us both to climax. Shiny sped up and the ride became smoother. We shot out of Europa like a bullet.

Whew, I thought you would never stop Bett.

I'm not finished with you just yet. Betty winked at me, but I was still hard, so I took hold of her sexy hips and started thrusting while Bett moaned loudly.

Oh, come on then Danny', she grabbed my bum and pulled me in with each thrust. I sped up for her.

Danny! We climaxed together again loudly.

Uh! We moaned in unison. I slowed down and kissed Betty and she smiled blissfully and licked my nose.

Coming up on Mars lovers.

Hey Shiny, take us down through the trench, please.

Okay, down into Valles Marineris it is. She swooped down and into the largest canyon in the solar system and took us to the bottom. We went twenty-three thousand feet deep down and flew the full two and a half thousand mile length of the impressive trench. We swooped along the walls sideways and upside down. It was an unreal experience, with Bett still squeezing and clenching me erotically the whole way.

Shiny can we see Olympus Mons too please?

Will do Danny! We looked out and ahead and could see it reaching up seventy two thousand feet into the Martian sky. Shiny skimmed expertly across the surface, less than ten feet off the ground. It was so exhilarating. Bett caught her breath and started slowly gyrating on me. I looked at her and she grinned and winked. *Okay,* I followed her sensual movements and before long we were climaxing again in Shiny. We were holding each other tightly, moaning and shaking with Bett biting her lip in joy as I moaned deeply. We both felt amazing and Shiny vibrated and glowed brightly as she sped up, reaching the summit and then straight on into space. She shrieked with glee. Our brown, blue marble was dead ahead.

Shiny when we get to Earth, can we please fly just below the clouds, over all the major strike sites, how long have we been gone?

Yes, will do, Danny, two days gone, seventeen since impact. ETA in five minutes. I looked down at Bett, *sorry baby*, and gently pulled out of her; she gave me one last squeeze, and grinned wickedly at me.

11

As the Dust Settles

Shiny zipped down into the Earth's atmosphere where the clouds were still thick and black with soot and ash. Steamy rain fell heavy all around us, evaporating as soon as it hit the ground. Plant life around the globe was slowly dying from lack of sunlight and the constant high heat. Shiny lit up the first impact crater in Texas.

The temperature right here is still around three hundred. The ground would melt shoes and burn feet for a hundred miles around. Sulphur and carbon dioxide are thick in the air and it is almost unbreathable. Everything around has nearly three feet of soot, ash and dirt over it. I detect no life of any kind for at least two thousand miles around, unless they are deep underground, which is possible.

Thanks, Shiny take us up to Yellowstone Caldera please.

Okay. To the northwest we go. Shiny lifted and turned off her lights. We could still see fires burning below us, especially the cities where gas leaks had erupted, causing major explosions. All the petrol stations had burnt to the ground, everywhere. We reached Wyoming where every town and every city was wiped out completely from the shock wave, the same for Idaho and Montana.

There is life nearby in Colorado, Cheyanne Mountain. There are thousands underground. That facility is huge; I estimate five or six thousand. It is hard to judge as they are deep underground, but they are there. It is controlled by the military. There are more in Denver too; there is a facility under the airport where there are three thousand souls. The air above ground all around here is toxic and definitely not breathable as it's full of Sulphur. Yellowstone Caldera was a bubbling mass of lava; a huge mountain had formed around it, with hardened lava flows in every direction. Pretty much hell on earth, but people had survived here. Across America were all manner of bunkers, some would survive and others not. Many preppers were not prepared for an event like this.

Okay Shiny, a quick trip down the west coast to LA.

South it is. Coming up on The San Fernando Valley, now. Err, Danny, the whole San Andreas Fault has separated from the mainland. California or what is left is now an island. All the way to San Francisco, is all such a mess. LA is destroyed underwater, as is Santa Barbara, Monterey and Santa Cruz.

Oh, shit, this is heartbreaking. Shiny, over to Europe please.

Yes Danny, Strasbourg, France it is. We arrived in minutes. The second impact on the outskirts of Strasbourg was devastating; trees and buildings for a thousand miles were either vaporized or flattened. The remainder burnt to the ground. The mighty Rhine River was clogged with decomposing bodies, as hundreds of thousands jumped in trying to avoid the searing heat. Every head was burnt to a crisp but not their bodies. Bett buried her head in my neck. This was too much. The Black Forest was blacker than night and dying too.

I am detecting life with a few thousand souls scattered. There are many old shelters here, some are used wisely and others people have run to with no supplies. We can help these people, with the help of the Ishta.

How Shiny, what can they do?

Their craft have those tractor beams of light, they can shift things if we can get food from supermarkets and distribution centers out into the open, they can bring it to them. Drop it outside the shelters.

Shiny that is brilliant, we can use our telepathy to shift long life cans and whatever else outside so the Ishta can shift it. Shiny, Bett and I could lift pallets of cans together by ourselves. Imagine pallets of tuna and baked beans just outside the shelters or even shipping containers full of food. We can start now. Shiny, find us a port with shipping containers please. They are likely to be strewn across the countryside.

I'll head towards Le Havre because there used to be a big port there, and I'll look about twenty to a hundred miles inland. Lights on, let's start searching.

Bett, see if we can use our minds to find them, picture them in your head.

Danny, great idea, I can see a clutter of them already, ten miles that way. Shiny slowed as we approached, her light intensifying spreading out.

Here, thousands of them. Wow. Look at all the ships too. Can you tell which have food?

Yes Shiny, over here, stop here. Bett what do you see, canned food?

Yes, Danny there is a few thousand containers here, full of food and bottled water. How many can we lift together?

How about we try and lift a hundred of them. Focus Betty.

Danny, wait, come here first, we will be stronger if we are together. She was right of course, so I took her in my arms and embraced her as she held on to me, making me hard. She glided on and started gyrating and squeezing me. I held her hips and pumped in and out of her gorgeous body. Suddenly we climaxed intensely together as a hundred shipping containers gradually lifted and stacked themselves neatly in the air.

Let's go Shiny. We will drop ten mixed containers at the entrance of each bunker that we come to.

Okay Danny, this is great, arriving at the first drop zone now. The entrance is below us, just there.

Bett let ten down gently. Ten shipping containers full of food silently landed next to the bunker.

Danny, I will tell them with my mind, there is food outside for them when it is safe to leave. But if we tell them now they may try to exit too early. We will need to return later.

Good idea Bett. Next one Shiny. She zipped off to the next site. We repeated our drop–offs until we had no more containers.

Again? I asked. Betty gripped my rod and nodded and winked, kissing me passionately.

Danny, that is a yes to everything, more containers and more humping. She slowly started rocking back and forth as we lifted another hundred containers. We spent the next seven days continuously shifting containers of food. We didn't need the Ishta to help us, we had underestimated ourselves again.

Hey, you two, you have been coupled for nearly three hundred and twelve hours, with only a few outages. That is thirteen days, how do you both feel? We have shifted eighteen thousand five hundred containers and shared over eleven thousand orgasms together, have you had enough yet?

Holy shit! Are you serious? That is crazy. I'm sorry Bett, you poor thing you must be worn out. I gently pulled out of her. She sighed and smiled at me

Oh Danny, my beautiful man, I am tired but not from you or this. She yanked on my still stiff cock and winked. *I'm tired of keeping my eyes open in this jelly that is all.*

Okay Shiny take us back to camp please.

Yes, Danny, back to our home by the lake and Jilly.

I took Betty's hand and held it as we flew over the northern top half of Australia. There was now a huge inland sea, covering tens of thousands of miles from Western Australia into the Northern Territory, South Australia and Queensland. We could see many small islands. It was snowing softly, the white contrasting dramatically with the blackened ash of the islands. We silently flew into Queensland.

Bett, we helped Conner hear Shiny when we flew together, he still has her jelly inside him, we might be able to talk telepathically to him, if we can get close enough. Elouise too.

Danny, you're right! That is fantastic; I just want to say hi to him. Why did you say Elouise too, she hasn't been in Shiny.

But she has Conner's DNA inside her and therefore Shiny's jelly too.

Ha, yes of course Danny. Okay Shiny, please take us to the Faraday camera mounted on the Ra exit in the cemetery. What is Ra time please?

Yes Betty, ETA is two minutes, Ra time is eight o'clock at night twenty-four days since impact. If you wish me to light up brightly you will need to join up.

Danny, I can't talk to them with you pumping away at me. Dad will know and Elouise will lose her shit.

Ha! You are right, Shiny stop here for a bit so we can recharge you before we arrive. I pulled Betty into my arms and she gently took hold of me. As my fingers slipped gently inside her, she immediately moaned as an orgasm took hold. She spread her legs widely as I eased my hard cock inside her, holding her rounded hips. I thrust over and over as my tension grew and she could feel this was going to be a big one and so did Shiny. I groaned loudly as I came explosively inside her. Bett screamed in delight, heaving, her body alive with tremors. She whistled and screamed in two octaves. I kept coming into her, wave after wave. We finally relaxed, and I slowed down and pulled out of her as gently as possible as I was still orgasming. Bett realized and held me tightly watching me and smiling at my huge golden penis throbbing in her hand, pumping until finally I stopped. Betty and Shiny moaned loudly as a final orgasm went through them.

Whew, Danny you are fucking incredible. You and your huge gold swirling cock. Come here and kiss me baby. She held my face in her hands and kissed me tenderly.

Oh, Betty, you feel so amazing. Shall we talk to them now, are you calm enough.

Yes, barely, come on then Shiny, to the cemetery please. Shiny swooped down and stopped just in front of the camera and lit up brightly changing colors dramatically.

Dad, can you hear me? Hello, form words in your head so we can hear you or speak and think of us as you speak. We are outside, can you hear me?

∞

Conner and Elouise had just made love again, the third time this evening. Elouise was on fire and could not get enough. "Elouise, did you say something?" Pete sent a text '*Shiny is at the cemetery camera.*'

"No Conner that is Betty's voice. Where is she?" Conner stood up and went to his monitors on the wall. An alert from control, *Shiny is outside.* He stood there naked flicking through the cameras. Elouise jumped out of the bed totally naked and stood next to Conner. Her heaving warm breasts pushed up against his back as she wrapped her arms around him.

"Shiny is here, outside with them, Bett can you hear me?"

Yes Daddy, I can hear you clearly, how are you both?

"Bett how is this possible? I'm not telepathic, am I?"

"Can you hear me too?" Elouise asked.

Hi Conner, and Elouise, Danny here. You both have Shiny's jelly inside you allowing us to talk like this. Elouise, you have Shiny's jelly from Conner's sperm. We are all linked now. Elouise blushed and squirted some of Conner's cum out in a spasm.

Oh, Daddy it is so good to hear you, we have been so busy; sorry we didn't come back sooner.

"It is good to hear you Bett and Danny. Shiny's jelly is very special, it healed my bullet wound completely within half an hour; a nine-milli-meter straight through my shoulder. Rita was running away and fired a warning shot and I got in the way. I'm fine though, real fine." He looked down; Elouise had reached around and was massaging his cock slowly and kissing his ear as she stood behind him.

Good lord, Rita shot you! Bett exclaimed. *Is she okay? Did she lose the plot or something?*

"Yes, just a bit confused, she is okay now." Elouise replied.

"What have you seen?" Conner was curious and slowly getting an erection.

Oh Daddy, not now, but it is not good; we will show you in Shiny when things clear up a bit, we have so much to tell you. There are other survivors scattered around and we have spent the last seven days shifting hundreds of massive shipping containers filled with canned food and water and delivered them outside their bunkers, some people don't have enough or any food at all. We still have a lot more to do.

"That's fantastic Bett, how long before you can come inside for a visit?"

We will come in for a few hours tomorrow; we haven't slept in thirteen days, so we really need to rest. If you open the hangar briefly, with the airlock closed, we can fly straight in with Shiny. We will need a shower and some towels and clothes, okay?

"Yes, Bett we look forward to seeing you both that will be great, I will have some towels waiting. There are showers in the hangar. Thank you for dropping by now, we understand that you are busy. Uh, see you both real soon..." Elouise slid down on her knees behind Conner spun him around and pushed him back onto the keyboard as she took him eagerly with her mouth. We all said our goodbyes and left. We felt better than a few days ago, we would see Conner's dream; The House of *Ra* in full swing, and we looked forward to it. We were tired but happy none the less. Strange or not, we knew billions had died but there was more to this world, and we knew it. I looked over to Betty at the same instant she looked at me. Her smile was brilliant and knowing. Our love and trust was overwhelming at times, we were so in tune with each other.

Oh Danny, let's go home...

Yes, I agree, let's go home Shiny.

Home is where the heart is. Home it is, Bett. Shiny lifted from the cemetery, up and away, to our lake. *Jilly we are back wake up little fish.*

Come in Shiny, I await you all, Hello my babes!

Hello Jilly. We greeted her with enthusiasm.

Hello babes, how did you go?

Oh, Jilly it is very sad, so many are dead; a lot, we as a species are devastated, humanity has a huge task ahead of it. Thank you Shiny, what we did today is only the start. We will need to spend the next few months doing the same, finding food and delivering it around. Hopefully it will aid the survivors when they exit their bunkers.

Bett I'm sure it will. Everything takes time. The planet needs to heal itself, and that will take years. Your race needs to learn humility, grace and thankfulness. They were killing each other right up until impact. Rest now my friends, get some sleep and close your tired eyes. Goodbye for now.

Thank you, Shiny you show your wisdom well, you are spot on. Good night. We exited Shiny and threw up into the lake. Jilly sat on the shore waving frantically. Bett called the shower gel and grabbed it out of the air as we dived in and washed ourselves. The cool lake enticingly refreshing after so long in the jelly. We whooped and hollered and splashed around enjoying the jelly-less freedom and the fresh air in our lungs. Bett lifted us out of the lake as our towels flew to us, swirling around our bodies, drying us in seconds. I lifted logs and kindling onto the firepit and lit it. Jilly poured us some shots. A big rug came from the tent and wrapped around us as we gently landed on the couch.

Jilly raced over and jumped up on Bett.

"Bett, please drop the rug so I can hug you properly." Betty lowered the rug exposing her breasts and Jilly dived into them, stretching her arms as wide as they would go.

"Oh, babes I am so happy you are both back. Danny, please lean into us." Jilly had tiny sparks of excitement jumping off her to Bett and me. I dropped the rug too and leant in and scratched Jilly gently on the back. She immediately squirmed and let out a moan of delight. "Oh Danny, that is nice, thank you for coming back to me. You are both so golden now, way more than before." We both looked down at each other and even in the light of the bubble we could tell the difference, we were a deep golden tan that shimmered and moved under our skin, like Shiny's hull. "Bett..."

"I know Danny, we look amazing and the color is moving, glistening, sparkling from the inside. Can you pull the rug down further I need to see you?" Jilly looked down at me too.

"Oh, come on girls, it is the same old me."

"Danny, no, that is unreal, it sparkles, swirls and glows inside you."

"Bett, look at your boobs they are incredible." Even Betty's nipples and areola were swirling with sparkles. "Betty, your womb..." There were two small flashes of golden sparks under her skin; the twins were letting us know they were with us.

"Oh Danny..." Bett started to cry.

"Oh, no Bett, they are beautiful, don't cry baby."

"No Bett, you are fabulous, look at you and at them they are amazing little babies in there, and they are both of you two. This is wonderful." Jilly smiled up at her. Bett started bawling but it was from joy and utter happiness. I knew, because I had tears rolling down my face too. My beautiful Bett and my little bright sparks. I wrapped my arms around Bett, the twins and Jilly and held them all tight.

"I absolutely love you all" I spluttered.

"Oh Danny, we know, thank you darling."

Jilly hopped down. "This calls for music, dancing, JD's and horny, okay?" We looked at her and smiled.

"Okay Jilly, but only for a while, we are a bit tired. Cheers Jilly!"

"CHEERS!" We joined Bett in her toast. Jilly was our catalyst to everything, her humor and innocence so refreshing and joyful. Bett put some tunes on loudly and the air filled with 'Finally' by CeCe Peniston. Bett filled two big glasses of Sinatra and a shot for Jilly and stood up and started doing her best disco dancing. Jilly's eyes were wide with wonder, *what is this?* She thought and copied Bett's every move.

"Oh, I like this beat!" Betty lifted Jilly into the air next to her and they danced their seventies disco dance, perfectly, then; 'You Should Be Dancing' by the Bee Gees came on and Betty knew all the John Travolta moves from the 'Saturday Night Fever' movie and Jilly copied her perfectly. I had a smile a mile wide. I could not have been happier watching them. Bett showed no signs of tiredness, and I didn't feel it either. I sat back chuffing on my stogie, smiling at them and every time Bett turned in my direction, she caught my eye or was staring at my long flaccid golden cock. She glowed golden and her skin glistened and swirled. Jilly loved the disco dancing. She was so happy to be dancing with Betty. I kept her glass full, and she kept going back to it, euphoric with joy. Glancing at me quickly, winking and smiling before returning to her dancing. Jilly was a joy to watch. Her moves matched Bett's and Travolta's perfectly. She had the full soundtrack running.

As the songs slowed, I stood and floated to Bett and took her hand and my other went to her naked back. I pulled her in. Her breasts were against me, exciting me; I swayed her from side to side and pulled my love in for a kiss. She gasped and met my lips and shivered in my arms. 'More Than a Woman' by the Bee Gees came on. Bett was lost in me, smiling and breathing in the cool night air deeply, very close to orgasming. We swayed and moved together dancing as one. Jilly had sat down to watch us, blissfully memorizing our every move to relay to generations of Saved Ones.

"Babes, you fill me with love. I watch you full of joy and bliss. You make me very excited; I must join with Shiny now, she understands my horniness. Please enjoy each other, I will go now, I love you my babes." Jilly waltzed off and disappeared into the deep lake. Bett looked into my eyes.

"Danny, oh, this is perfect, your golden body excites me, my battery is fully charged, and I haven't slept yet but please cum inside me. We are not in Shiny now and I want to feel your warmth pump into me. I need you; you excite me so much that I can hardly breathe. Danny..." She slipped her hand down onto me and grasped me firmly. "Oh, baby, you are beautiful, this, in my hand is perfection, kiss me my love." I kissed her with everything I had. "Oh, Danny, she gasped, come here." She lifted off the ground and straddled me. She stuffed my golden rod into her golden pussy and I thrust into the core of her luscious body.

"Oh yes", we groaned together.

12

Golden Ones

"Oh, shit!" We explosively orgasmed together, almost immediately. My hot cum filling her as she wished it would. We were so in tune with each other and so in love. But in reality, so very, very tired. "Uh, my Danny, thank you darling you feel so good inside me, but we do need to sleep soon..."

"Oh, Bett, I know. Come to bed baby, you need to rest." I lifted us to the tent, and we dropped onto the mattresses gently. Our hearts were still pounding loudly in our chests. Bett curled up on me breathing the night air in sync we fell asleep in minutes. Ten hours of solid deep sleep followed. With no dreams just total rest.

♥

Bett was on me, gripping my cock in her warm moist love muscles until I was rock hard and fully awake. "Oh, hello my love, you feel amazing as usual."

"Hello, my darling, how do you do that? Get me inside you without waking me." I smiled up at her.

"That was a great sleep, I feel fantastic and you feel amazing inside me, and that is my little secret, so just enjoy me. Jilly is sitting by the fire outside. How about having a quickie, seeing that you're so hard?"

"I'm okay with that Bett." I took hold of her luscious inviting nipples and licked and caressed them gently; she squeezed down on me hard and shuddered. Lifting I pushed further into her, moving deftly around inside of her. She trembled and shook as she started to climax, her fingernails dug deeply into my chest. Bett pushed my chest down hard and I climaxed in a rush, moaning and heaving as I let go. Bett cried out and held me down firmly as she contracted on me repeatedly; biting down on her bottom lip until it bled as she grinned at me wickedly. Jilly smiled to herself, wishing she was with one of her kind but filled with love for Betty and me. She could feel our passion as could Shiny, Elle, and half of Ra.

∞

Elouise looked up at Conner from his groin where she had just taken him by surprise as he woke up. She moved up his body and gently sat down on him and leaned down kissing him on the neck. She slowly brought herself to climax on him. *Oh, Conner is a sexy man*, she thought, mid-fifties and great in bed. He was perfect for her. But Elle's biggest problem was Danny; she could not get him out of her head. Her lustful thoughts betraying her love to Conner. *Why am I like this? Conner is so good for me*, she reflected. *But Danny*, he has an aura of sexiness and *arousal*, it was undeniable and made her feel alive and horny. She couldn't wait to see him today, oh and Bett.

Ω

Betty looked at Danny and thought to herself how good this man makes her feel, so alive and horny. "Come on my man, we should go and talk with Jilly before we head off to Ra." We stood and went out to Jilly as I sent a few logs to the pit.

"Hello, my sexy babes, your loving makes me happy, and I am so glad for you too. I sense your excitement, the thrill of your love. You share your joy. Your family has not seen you like this all golden and swirling, they will love your skin, I am sure. Do you return after the visit to them or are you working on saving people?"

"Jilly, thank you, we will stay with them for a few hours and then we need to get to work shifting food to help survivors, this is until the planet settles down and people come out of hiding. Then our duty will change. We will need to shift huge amounts of people away from the cold zones or they will perish. Outside the bubble will become very cold for a long time. But we will always return to you. You are special. I, no, we love you, Jilly."

"Oh, my Bett, I thank you, I knew you would fall for me eventually. I love you both and I am so grateful to have won the lottery to join this team. Together with Shiny we are invincible."

"Yes, Jilly, we are the invincible team, that is true. Danny, do you want some eggs and bacon? This is the last of it. We might not get any more."

"Absolutely Bett, don't let it go to waste."

"Good, I've started cooking in Horus, probably five or six minutes ago. Remember when you said I should be on MasterChef? Imagine now, I would kill it without raising a finger."

"Oh, yeah, too bad there will never be TV ever again Betty..."

"But we can still watch re-runs of Friends in *Ra*."

"That is true; the world will be so disconnected now."

"No, Danny, they have us, we can tell them there are others and we can unite the few, and spread hope."

"You are so right, optimism is everything. We can guide them and lead them on a path to salvation and growth."

"Yes Danny, that is our journey, we have this."

"You are so smart, both of you. And so decisive, your decisions are perfect. You understand the process of civilization and your world needs you right now. You need to show your strength to Conner and *Ra* today. Go and talk with them and share your love. I will eat now." Jilly skipped away and dived into the lake.

"Shiny? Are you awake?"

I am always nearly awake.

"Can you take us to The House of Ra, now, please?"

Yes, of course, Bett. Shiny rose out of our lake majestically as we lifted into the air and entered her. She shivered as we gulped her jelly and gagged.

≤≥

Shiny zipped up and was at the hangar in seconds. She started strobing brightly. But the door was already opening. "They are here Elle, let's wait for them down by the hangar."

"Okay, Conner I'll be right with you, I just need to go to the bathroom and I'll meet you down there in a minute." Conner nodded and left the bedroom. Elouise went to the monitors and switched on the hanger bay camera just as Shiny came to a stop. She opened and Bett and Danny floated out, throwing up the jelly and gently landing on the ground. Elouise zoomed in close on Danny's body. She gasped and took three photos with her phone. "*Oh my!*" She said to herself, shivering. She turned the monitor off and raced out to wait with Conner.

≥≤

"Thanks, Shiny." Bett and I walked over and picked up the plush towels and walked to the showers. Conner had a selection of clothes laid out for us in the hangar bathroom.

"Oh, Danny how good does this shower feel?"

"Yes, I know, I could stay in here for ages, the last shower I had was on our wedding day." Bett had already turned hers off.

"Come on Danny. Let's get going." Bett picked a simple flowery dress with thin straps that showed off her golden body. I grabbed some loose linen pants and a button up Hawaiian shirt only doing up a few buttons.

"Open Ra," Bett said to the airlock door. The door slid open. Conner and Elouise stood up from the couch smiling and advanced with arms wide.

"Welcome back to *Ra*." Conner enveloped Betty, wrapping her in his arms and lifting her off the ground. Elouise came straight at me and hugged me tightly, planting a big wet kiss on my cheek, "Great to see you, Danny." She stepped back and her eyes went wide in astonishment. "Oh my god, what has happened to you two?" Conner's eyes were wide in wonder too as he came to me and hugged me before he stepped back as well. Elouise had hugged Bett and was examining her shoulders while Conner pulled my shirt open. "Danny, can you take off your shirt please?" I took it off. "Wow, is this from Shiny? How does it move and swirl like that, can I put my hand on your back?"

"Sure, go ahead." Conner placed his hand on my shoulder blade.

"Elle, come here, do this, sorry Danny, your skin is vibrating ever so slightly, do you feel that, Elouise?" Bett came over too and rested her hand on my chest. Elouise had her hand on my bicep. Elouise turned away from Conner and bit her lip as she let out a husky moan under her breath.

"Hmm, yes Conner, I can feel it too. Bett, can I touch you too, please?" I was looking at Betty and she was totally bemused by all the touching. Conner was peering closely at my skin. "The vibrations are in time with the movement."

"It's the same with Bett." Elouise had one hand on each of us. "Bett feels slightly different to Danny, you are faster Bett."

Did you ever notice this, Bett? I said in her mind.

No Danny, but they are correct.

"Do you want to see something really cool?" Betty grabbed a towel and wrapped it up under her dress to cover her knickers. Then lifted her dress to expose her belly, she darkened the room with her mind. "Look, it's them, the twins." Two sparkling lights flickered in time with their heartbeats.

"Oh wow! Bett, how miraculous." Conner said. Elouise's eyes were wide in wonder again.

"How beautiful that is, Bett. Your bodies are incredible, they always were, but now look at you, this is so freaky but in a good way." Elouise said, shaking her head in utter fascination.

"Shiny said it was a side-effect from staying inside her for so long, we will be like this always now." Conner was shaking his head as Bett dropped her dress and pulled off the towel. Elle finally removed her hands from us.

"Come on guys let's have a drink and chat, we will go to the bar at our place." Conner took Elle's hand and led the way. I could put my shirt on at last. We followed them through Ra, making our way to their quarters. We said a friendly hello as people stopped in their tracks when they saw us. We sat at Conners bar on high comfy stools as Conner poured out some Sinatra 100. "Conner, you were shot, how are you now?" I looked at him.

"Thanks for asking Danny, I have a sexy scar but that is about it. I felt like I was hit by Tyson when it struck me, but after that, Shiny's jelly fixed me right up. Our doctors were so confused." Conner thought it was hilarious. Elle put her hand on his shoulder and squeezed it in admiration of her man.

Danny how much do we tell them, destruction, death, havoc?

Only the good stuff, not the feast with Octo drinking my sperm. Follow my lead.

"Well, we saw the meteor hit. We were right there above the impact on Dallas, we had a whole fleet of over a thousand craft. The Octo with their craft like Shiny helped us to make a huge vortex above the impact. We pulled up as much debris, fire and smoke into space as we could and shifted thousands of tons of rock. We then shifted to the next big hit near Strasbourg in France, moving to India and then China." I told them. "The Ishta and Lloyds had massive triangular craft that used beams of light to pull away many smaller meteors."

"They helped you as well? That is amazing." Conner was shaking his head in surprise at all of this.

"Daddy, before they left, they told us something fantastic. They named their new planet. "They called it, Connerelle Rage. You now have a planet named after you both by an alien race. How cool is that?" Conners face; his jaw dropped; he was genuinely dumbfounded while Elouise kissed him and hugged him tightly.

"What? True? That is incredible, where is this planet?" Elle embraced him lovingly and kissed him again while patting his knee.

"There is a massive, constructed ring sitting on the far side of Mercury that is the entrance to a wormhole that leads to their solar system. It was made by Martians a million years ago. I know that seems a lot. But I haven't even got to the volcanoes yet." Conner looked at me and then to Bett, who was nodding slowly, his head was shaking in bewilderment. "Yellowstone blew it's top, followed by another fifty-one volcanoes all erupting around the globe. We sent it all into space with a lot of help, hopefully this will shorten the coming ice age dramatically. The Earth now has rings, much like Saturn only smaller mostly made up of all the debris and ice. The poles have shifted too, North Magnetic Pole sits off the Western Australian coast and South Pole is in the middle of Russia."

"That could lead to bad solar radiation hitting the earth from the sun." Conner interrupted.

"Yes, correct Conner, Shiny thinks it will swap back soon stabilizing our Magnetic field once more. It is pitch black out there, clouds cover the planet, and it is snowing on the inland sea in the Northern Territory."

Conner skolled his glass and poured another. "Damn Danny, that is a lot. Life in here is so subtle, insulated; I can't wait to see our planet, and what has become of it." He looked at me and raised his glass. "Danny and Bett, you are our champions, here's cheers." We raised our glasses and skolled. "Bett, you seem to be holding back, is everything okay, you haven't said much the whole time."

"Daddy, Shiny is special, very special, she runs on our love... We needed to recharge her, to give her more power..."

"I'm not sure I get you; how can you recharge her?"

Danny I'm telling all.

Okay, whatever, go for it.

"Dad, we needed to make love in her in order to go faster or to light up sights, we had to stay coupled for over two hundred hours, which sounds ridiculous, but Shiny's jelly is very special as you know."

"Two hundred hours? What, that is impossible?" Elouise was bright red, fully flushed. Conner was lost in thought.

"How does that recharge her? What?" He looked to us.

"Our orgasms shared, power her somehow. She is us too, she shares our DNA and orgasms with us. The three of us went to Europa for a feast with The Octo."

No Bett don't go there.

Trust me, Danny.

"They treated us as kings, they adored Danny's err, um penis. For them he was adorable and massive; they have very small genitals. So, he was the alpha and was worshipped..."

"Oh Bett, you and Danny had to stand naked in front of them?" Conner asked.

"Dad, there were thousands cheering Danny's erect penis."

"Bett, did you really need to say that?" I was now a little uncomfortable.

"Sorry Danny but that is part of our journey." Bett gave me a gorgeous smile and winked.

"E-erect?" Elle stammered.

Go on then Bett. Tell them everything. I looked at her, daring her.

"Danny and I jumped up on the tables and jumped with them, pumping our fists and they went totally crazy. I made Danny hard with my mind, and they went absolutely insane when it stood up. Hundreds of thousands of tentacles were in the air, pumping and cheering."

I bet, thought Elouise. She was so aroused and leaking on her chair.

"You can arouse each other with your minds?" Elouise was aroused, just asking that.

"It is crazy what we can do with our minds. Elle," Betty admitted. Elle was staring into my soul.

"Danny. How did you feel with all those aliens looking at your erect penis, was that intimidating?"

"Only at first Conner, after I just went with it. Who cares, I don't know them, I am so used to being naked anyway." Elle sighed and chewed on the inside of her cheek harder than intended and drew blood. She was on the edge and barely in control. We all took a sip of our drinks.

"The Containers?" Conner said.

"Yes, we had the idea to distribute some food around. Ten shipping containers to each bunker and more to bunkers with more people. We are going to continue delivering when we leave here today. This is just the start. We will need to shift people away from the cold zones to more temperate zones as soon as temperatures drop. Another ice Age is coming…"

"How Danny, how do you shift a heap of people?" Conner stared at me.

"Cruise ships. They are strewn everywhere on dry land. We will just lift the ships with our minds all filled with survivors, and then fly them to more temperate zones. We will know where once the Poles settle." Conners head was trying to comprehend all we had shared with him.

"Wow! Danny, you guys came up with all this, you amaze me with your ingenuity and your ideas show wisdom way beyond my simple mind. Has the landscape changed much? You mentioned an inland sea in The Northern Territory."

"The coastlines are dramatically different; many coastal cities are totally wiped out or partially submerged. Japan is just Mt Fuji volcano island now."

"Oh, no, really? Japan's population was one hundred and twenty-something million." Conner looked on in disbelief.

"Indonesia and the Philippines have disappeared underwater and Hawaii's five volcanoes have destroyed all life there. It is a molten mess of rock and lava."

"Oh, how sad, this is awful." Elouise had tears rolling down her cheeks. Bett jumped up and embraced her.

"Let it out Elouise, it is horrible but we are still alive and that is what matters the most. We will survive this." Bett hugged her. Conner took my hands in his and leaned forward.

"Danny, thank you for looking after her we were so worried about the two of you. What you have done is amazing, let's have a cigar and some more Jack. Elle, cheer up please and stay positive. Think of all the wonderous things these two have seen and done. What was Europa like?"

"Oh Daddy, it was beautiful, the oceans are alive and glowing bright with fluorescent sea creatures of all sizes; from massive whale like creatures and huge crabs, glowing sea-snakes and crazy strobing jellyfish. The Octo crystal city was huge and stunningly beautiful. It was filled with crystal domes so you could see the fabulous opalescent oceans. Their seafood was absolutely delicious, and we became very drunk on their wine, made from seaweed grapes."

"Yeah, their food was unreal, some of it was still alive. The Octo would eat and drink until they fell asleep on the ground. We fell asleep at the table and woke up with our lunch crawling all over us." I said. Betty laughed remembering the jelly fish.

"Danny woke up with a little jellyfish sucking on his knob, making him fully erect!" She blurted out. Conner burst out laughing, hysterically. "I ripped it off and ate it; it was a delicious little purple sucker." Conner was laughing hard. Elle shuddered, hiding her orgasm with laughter. I looked at Bett.

That did it Bett, she's lost it.

Oops. She's picturing your beautiful penis in her head, with a jellyfish on it and she wants to finish you off. Ha, poor dear.

"Please excuse me for a second; I must go to the bathroom." She raced out; Conner had no idea she was coming in her panties. Elouise moaned deeply as she entered the toilet, quickly removing her wet undies and stuffing them in the clothes basket, she shuddered and shook as it kept going. She sat on the toilet ejaculating, with her glazed eyes looking up at the ceiling. *Oh fuck, calm down Elle* she told herself. She finally stopped and took some deep breaths. She flushed the toilet and washed her face and then reapplied some makeup. She headed straight to the kitchen and pulled the cheese platter from the fridge and headed back to the bar.

"Oh, thank you Elle, I had forgotten about that." Conner smiled at her warmly. She sat back down and adjusted her hem.

"Yes, please grab some cheese guys." She smiled at us both, her eyes giving away the pleasure that she was feeling inside, her heart was racing.

"Oh, yum thanks Elle." I shoved some cheese in my mouth and winked at her.

Danny, don't tease her, you Ratbag, she'll lose it again.

Sorry Bett, I couldn't help myself. Elouise had seen the wink and wondered if I knew she had just had an orgasm. *God he is such a sexy guy and now he has a huge golden penis. Stop thinking of it Elle, or they will know.* She thought. But we could hear her loud and clear.

Danny, can you make her think of something other than your cock? I changed the subject.

"On our flight back from Europa, we dropped down into the Valles Marineris on Mars, it was incredible. Shiny took us to the bottom, and flew its whole length, and then ten feet above the surface really fast to the top of Olympus Mons, it was so exhilarating."

"Just the thought of being able to do that kind of thing, that is fantastical. I would love to do that." Conner was shaking his head again. "Unbelievable." He poured some more Sinatra. "When will it be safe to venture outside Danny?"

"That is tough. Here in Taxi, the air will be okay very soon maybe in a week or so, but it will be very unpleasant. Your clothes will be instantly black, the soot and dust are very fine. It covers everything and just walking through it would create clouds around you. We have not seen one soul on the surface. Once the clouds clear, things will improve, but it will get very cold soon too. We saw snow only two hundred miles from here."

"Well, good thing we don't need to go anywhere, everything we need is right here. How did Sydney and Melbourne look?"

"Yes Daddy, they are a tragic mess. Hardly any buildings left standing in one piece. The tidal waves and earthquakes have destroyed most cities around the globe. Sydney and Melbourne are both awash in ten to thirty feet of water. The Sydney Harbour Bridge was taken out by a cruise ship and the once spectacular Opera House is all but gone."

"Wow, and we barely had any quakes here." Conner spoke.

"The east coast is less than one hundred miles from here. You owe me a fifty Conner. I smiled at him.

"Look, there it is waiting for you. Spend it how you wish." The two fifties were sitting where we left them. I picked them up and lit my cigar with them. Conner smiled; the irony not lost on him. I dropped the burning money into the ashtray.

"Thanks for the light Conner." I raised my hand for a fist bump. He obliged. Money is dead now, it's just paper. A worthless commodity as it always was just a way to make the wealthy richer. Conner knew what I was doing.

"Danny, you are very smart, I really like you. Thank you, my golden son."

13

Hectic Daze

We talked about other cities we had seen; and the devastation everywhere. Elouise had calmed down and we felt like we needed to get a move on. "Thanks for the cheese and JDs we should probably get going. Our task this week is to find and shift more containers of food and start stockpiling cruise ships and cargo ships to shift people. I want to see if we can do anything with the clouds and maybe try and disperse them somehow. We need to let the sun in that would make a huge difference." I took Betty's hand and stood up. They all stood.

"Thank you both for coming today; we totally understand your urgency. You seem very focused and sure of your plan; we wish you success and a safe journey. You are both our heroes, actually heroes of our planet and we love you very much." Conner wrapped his arms around Betty, and I did the same to Elouise. Kissing her on the cheek, she held on to me tightly, every inch of her body against mine. She was trembling, "Take care Danny."

"I will Elle, you too." I pulled away and grabbed Conner. We man hugged tightly.

"You got this Danny; I am so proud of you and Bett. What you are doing is more than I ever imagined. Well done and keep it up. I look forward to seeing you both as soon as you can and stay for a feed next time. Please." Elle was hugging Bett tight and whispering in her ear.

"Bett, darling please take care of yourselves. You are so lucky to have him. Danny is special, a true alfa male. He commands attention, which

I know you give him. Good luck with your adventures; I know luck has nothing to do with it, just stay safe honey."

"Oh, thank you, so much Elle, you are too kind. Believe me, Danny is very special, and he has a huge heart, he is everything to me. Our love brings everyone together."

"It sure does Bett, and we love it, keep at it Bett." Elle kissed her and went into Conner's arms. We all walked quietly to the hangar.

"See you soon." We said in unison. We walked into the hangar and Bett closed the door.

"Close Ra." We waved to them as the door slid shut. We took off our clothes. "Hi, Shiny, ready to get to work?"

I sure am containers first?

Yes, and let's find some survivors that might need some food. We floated into her gulping her jelly.

How about we have a look at Darwin, Alice Springs, Perth, Adelaide and Tasmania, Shiny?

No problem, Darwin is first. The door of the hangar opened and Shiny slipped out and up into the dark cloudy skies. *We're coming up on Darwin in a few minutes.*

Thanks, Shiny, how many people lived here?

Last count was about one hundred and forty-four thousand. Now I'm sensing only a few thousand scattered around, there are some smaller caves here too. None of these have facilities required for survival. There are some ships here with containers spread around. Danny these are no good, oh wait, there's some food here; about twenty full containers. We can take these. We shifted them and left them near the spots with survivors.

Let's have a look at Alice Springs.

Okay Danny, around thirty-three thousand were living here last year, don't hold your breath, I can't sense any life maybe only a few thousand animals, reptiles mostly. Alice Springs was hit by a bus sized meteor, the shock wave flattened everything. They had no chance of survival. Okay Shiny, Perth. Please.

Yes Danny, Perth it is, do you think you and Bett could join up as my lights are dimming. Hey we are coming up on Coober Pedy, most of the buildings are gone, erased but there are about a thousand survivors here in the underground 'Dugouts.' We can get some containers from Alice Springs and drop them here.

Okay let's do that Shiny. Bett snuggled up to me and her hand took a hold of me and gently made me stiff. I kissed her and ran my hands over her beautiful body. She shivered and moved in front of me as I slowly entered her. She was trembling as I thrust in '*Oh!*' She loudly exhaled and started to climax while gripping down on me and bringing me home.

Go Danny, Hmmm, yes Baby. Shiny started to shiver too as she was lost in her emotions. We dropped down twenty containers in Coober Pedy and headed to Perth.

Perth had nearly two point nine million souls in twenty-five. Perth is or was here. But I do sense people, thousands still alive. We can help them; Freemantle should have plenty of containers. She sped down to Fremantle and we searched for shipping containers. We soon found some and distributed them equally.

Adelaide was somewhat saved from the tidal waves as Kangaroo Island stood in the way likely breaking its momentum but was still awash with water. Minor meteor strikes and the earthquakes destroyed most of the city buildings but there were quite a few thousand survivors here but too widely spread to really assist with food. We moved a few containers to higher spots where we thought could help. *Down to Tasmania, please Shiny.*

Tasmania it is Danny. Shiny barreled up and away from South Australia and we were soon over the Bass Strait. Tasmania was relatively intact, still with much damage to many buildings but no impacts or tidal wave damage. Their rugged forests were dying and everything that wasn't covered in snow was black from soot. Hobart and Launceston were awash with sea water and it looked bitterly cold outside. *We may have to start shifting survivors further north or they will freeze to death.*

The next two weeks were spent traversing the globe, searching for food and life. We shifted about five hundred cruise ships, taking them to areas with survivors that we felt may need to be shifted due to the coming ice age. Shiny informed us that we had shifted thirty thousand shipping containers in the last two hectic weeks. *Let's go home Shiny, floor it!*

Whoopie! Shiny sped up and zipped flat out through the clouds. The clouds were parting and dispersing as we fired through them.

Shiny lights on please. She glowed brightly. *Brighter please, behind us. Danny, what's up?*

Look at the clouds; they are dispersing at this speed. Shiny please go around the globe a few times as fast as you can.

Some help please guys. Bett had already started on me, hardening me. I held her hips and thrust in and she reciprocated by grabbing my butt and pulling me in hard.

Whoa, Bett.

Oh, Danny, yes! She started shaking as the first wave hit her. Her nails were digging into my butt and I came immediately with brute force. Betty gasped and bit me hard on the neck sucking really hard. I kept going as she felt so good. Shiny sped up nearly going fifteen thousand miles an hour. We were causing chaotic lightening, fierce thunderstorms and heavy rain and snow as we zipped through the clouds. We were vaporizing them as we went. Before long Shiny said.

That is three times, keep going? It is certainly dispersing the cover, another forty or fifty revolutions will remove one percent of the clouds.

Okay Shiny, are you up for this Bett?

Sure baby, keep going, oh, I am in heaven, oh, right now. I kept pumping my love into her. The crazy continued orgasms that were not natural kept going. Shiny was throbbing in time with us, shooting through the atmosphere. With each revolution we noticed a slight difference on the day side, with a little more sunlight shining through. Bett was heaving in orgasmic glory.

Oh, babe. Hmm!

Uh Bett, perfect, oh, you feel amazing. Her eyes were on me, staring me down with lust and love. Her mind was vivid with words and full of sexual desire. I thought if Elle can feel her now, she would be fucking Conner's brains out, and she probably was.

∞

Elle was fucking Conner's brains out as hard as she could. She felt so alive and amazing, full of joyous desire. Elle was full of Conners joyous cock. He was good, and she liked his moves. But he was not a Danny. She would casually think of him fucking Bett as Conner was pumping away in her and immediately climax. There was something about Danny's aura something so wild and off the scales. *How do I feel him? In me? Oh, Conner. Yes. Yes, do me Danny, oh my, my Conner, I mean. Oh.* Elouise said to herself.

Ω

Yes, Danny, oh, do me baby. Betty moaned in my mind.

Danny that is one percent at this rate it will take about eight solid months to disperse the majority of the cloud cover. What do you want to do?

Please take us home now, this is a good thing, this will make a huge difference.

It certainly will, home for some rest my beautiful people. Bett and I slowed and stopped completely. She looked at me and groaned loudly as a final orgasm surged through her. She grinned widely and gave me one of her wicked winks. I could sense her tiredness. It had everything to do with our eyes in the jelly. We needed water to wash in and fresh air to breathe in again and we needed our little Jilly to laugh with us.

Shiny came up on Taxi, and slowed, dropping us down to our little bubble paradise.

Hi, Jilly, we are home.

Hi, Shiny, Bett and Danny, come on in my babes. Shiny swooped in and dropped down to our lake. We floated out and immediately threw up the jelly.

Thanks, Shiny see you later.

Goodnight my lovers. Shiny moved out to the middle of the lake and submerged. We dove into the freezing water, both of us screaming as we surfaced, "Shit. Ah. Oh my god!" We both said together. Bett swam over and wrapped herself around me her teeth chattering. "D, D, Dan, Ny this is free, zing. Come here." She kissed me passionately and called over the shower gel. We swam to shallow water and quickly washed ourselves and lit the fire. We lifted out of the freezing water as our towels flew to meet us and quickly dried us. Our Rug came to us before we reached the couch and wrapped us up warmly. We dropped onto the soft couch as two bottles of water and two whiskeys floated in front of us.

"Where is Jilly?" I was slightly worried, but the answer became clear as the lake started to glow and throb. Bett instantly took my flaccid cock in her hand and was stroking my shaft. "Oh Danny, Jilly has missed Shiny, just go with it." She pulled the rug down and went down on me. My hand went in-between her warm legs, and I found her clit. She moaned as I tenderly rubbed her. Her delicious wet mouth took me and engulfed me as her tongue swirled around my engorged tip. She gulped me down and climaxed at the same instant as myself. We were warm, comfortable and content and our lake was full of light.

∞

The House of *Ra* was fully lit in orgasms too. Elouise and Conner on top of each other in reverse, they let go at the same instant as Danny, Bett, Shiny and Jilly. Another seventy couples did exactly the same. As did half the remaining adult population of the world. The survivors lit with love and lust for each other in a sexy unison. These were hectic days and any opportunity to love each other was appreciated by all.

14

The Swirling Clouds

Bett looked up at me smiling as I finished blowing my load into her, my cum was leaking from the corners of her delectable mouth. She was so wet in my hands as she lifted her head, skolled her drink and wiped her mouth and then poured two more. She rested her head on my chest with her hand held firmly around my throbbing shaft. "Oh Danny, this is unreal, this in my hands. You my love, my perfect gold baby," she licked my dripping head again. I shivered as she thrust her tongue into my mouth and swung her legs over me, pushing me down and groaning as I fully entered her. I pushed up fast and let go again as she crushed down on me and screamed out my name. She climaxed and ejaculated all over me. We moaned and trembled for ages as we came together. It felt so good to be out of Shiny's jelly, no matter how much we loved being in her.

∞

Conner had just let go of his load into Elle as she screamed in ecstasy. "Oh. *Fuck* Conner, yes, my love." Her orgasms had been super intense, whilst thinking of Danny, but loving Conner.

"Hmm, Conner, you are my golden love. Just absolute perfection." Jilly left Shiny and everyone calmed down for the night.

Ω

"Danny, are you ready for bed my love?"

"Oh, yes, baby. I am stuffed." Jilly came out of the lake and jumped up on the rug, just as we were about to go to bed.

"Hey, you're not going to bed, it's nearly morning and we haven't had JDs together yet"

"Okay, Jilly just one. Did you miss Shiny?" Bett poured some more Jack Daniels.

"I'm missing her now, she makes me so excited when I am inside her, I use my little suckers on her and my sparks go everywhere making everyone go crazy."

"Jilly, you can spare us the details, we don't need to know everything, but whatever it is certainly turns us on somehow."

"I could show you or do it to you, if you like." We looked at each other then back to Jilly who was smiling up at us.

"No. Thank you; we will just stick with each other. Shiny is different, we fly in her. She needs our coupling to fly faster, she uses our energy. Okay?"

"That's alright, I understand, I am not offended at all. Shiny likes what I do to her, she makes me climax when I do it. That makes me horny-happy. Jilly will let you sleep, and I will stay out of Shiny tonight so you can all rest."

"Thank you, babe, you are very thoughtful, goodnight." We said together.

"Goodnight, you will feel us in the morning." Jilly hopped down and skipped off into the lake. Bett lifted us both and our rug into the tent and laid us on the mattresses gently.

"Look Danny it is snowing outside the bubble." I looked out and could dimly make out the snow falling on the blackened ground and on the bubble.

"Now the fun starts. It will be a very long winter. Bett we should concentrate on the clouds, maybe we could ask The Octo for some help. The more craft at different levels might be able to disperse the clouds quicker. We'll call them down tomorrow. Goodnight gorgeous." Bett kissed me on my nose, and wrapped her hand softly around my drooping rod and closed her eyes. Smiling, I cupped her lovely full breast and closed my eyes too. We slept without moving a muscle for ten hours.

"Wake up Danny" Bett whispered in my ear. I opened my eyes, her face right in front of me, her bright green eyes smiling deep into my soul. Her lips were moist and ready to kiss. We were still wrapped in the rug but floating a few feet up in the tent. Her grip was on me, confirming she had managed to get me inside her without awakening me again.

"Ooh, you ratbag, how did you do that without me knowing?" Bett was grinning widely as she planted her lips on mine, her tongue going in for the kill. She was massaging me smoothly with her love muscles. We were both ready to explode. Bett felt me and tightened her grip, moaning. "Oh." Her body started heaving and shaking as we climaxed in ecstasy together. "Oh, fuck!" Betty screamed. I pushed in deep against her g-spot and she screamed in erotic pleasure again. I kept going and we were absorbing each other's fluids, thank goodness. Otherwise, the rug would have been soaking wet.

∞

"Oh Fuck!" Elle screamed as Conner pushed in harder. *Oh Danny!* It felt as if they were both fucking her at the same time, she was completely losing it, uncontrolled orgasms, one after another. Conner couldn't keep up and pulled out falling down next to her. "No, please." Elouise grabbed Conners's hand and shoved his fingers and hers inside her. Arching her back on the bed, blow by blow, she thrust in. Moaning loudly as Conner watched her in fascination, her love muscles clamping on his fingers tightly. Her moves were slowly making him hard again.

She felt it throbbing against her hip so she pushed Conner hard onto his back and immediately climbed on, pushing down forcefully. Her full breasts swinging wildly as she rocked on him, her wetness flowing all over Conners groin. Her hands were on his chest holding him down. Luckily Conners eyes were closed because if he had opened them, he would have seen a dark fur covered woman with huge tits, cow ears and horns. Hathors had entered Elouise and were using her body to see and feel Danny.

Ω

I could sense something; *Bett?* We slowed down. Betty's eyes locked on mine.

What is it, Danny? Oh! I feel it too. They are using Elle. The Hathors have her, oh shit.

Oh, shit, she thinks it is me she is fucking, Bett what can we do?

Shiny is Jilly with you? Please stop and come to us.

Yes Bett, we are coming, is everything alright?

We just need to talk with you right now. I gently pulled out of Bett. We put dressing gowns on for the first time as it was cool, and my cock was still going down.

They can't see or feel you now and they have left Elle's body, she is an exhausted wreck.

Bett she will need more of Shiny's jelly, how can we give her some? Take her up in Shiny? Dad will want to see the earth. Shiny will need charging and we are not doing that in front of them. Can they take Shiny by themselves? Even if only for a few hours, that will be enough to infuse her.

You're right, and with the jelly inside her they shouldn't be able to enter her ever again. Let's talk to Shiny. We floated out. Shiny and Jilly sat at the edge of the lake.

Hey, Shiny, Jilly, sorry to interrupt; please close your minds this is only for us. The Hathors entered Elouise's body just now while we were all doing it. They were using her to find me, see me and feel me through her mind.

"That is not nice, Hathors are evil." Jilly stated.

Is she okay? What can we do? Do you have a plan? Shiny asked.

I think your broadcasting is allowing them access to her. Elle only has a small amount of your jelly, if she had more like us and Conner, they wouldn't be able to do it.

That is correct Danny. We can all take her for a flight.

Conner wants to see the earth, so you will need recharging at least once or twice. We cannot do that in front of them, or they in front of us. Can you take the two of them without us for a zip around the globe; show them the big cities in ruins, impacts and Yellowstone. The full tour quickly, and then maybe take them into space. Go for as long as necessary for Elle.

Yes, Danny it will be my honor. When?

Let's go, she needs that jelly now. See you soon Jilly take care.

"I will, see you soon." Jilly ran to the water, and dived in. We floated up into Shiny. Gulping and gagging. Shiny closed and lifted us. The dome above us was pure white. We burst through a thick layer of snow.

Lights Shiny please. She lit up the ground and it was pure white as far as we could see. But there were a few breaks in the clouds, with the sun streaming in. The glistening snow looked beautiful across the dead landscape. We arrived at the hangar in under a minute. Shiny flashing bright as alarms went off inside. The hangar door swung open, and we slipped in. *Thanks, Shiny.* She opened and we exited and threw up her precious jelly. We walked forward grabbing the towels and went quickly to the showers. Once we were dry, we threw on some clean clothes. Bett uttered the words.

"Open Ra." The door magically slid open. Conner and a disheveled Elouise stood in front of us. Bett told them everything, "Get your gear off and get inside, and if Shiny requests coupling you need to oblige or you will see nothing. Her jelly needs to be inside you Elle to help you heal, it is a good thing, trust us. Embrace each other as Shiny thrives on loving." Conner looked at us as if we were crazy. "Dad just do it, you need to see the Earth, and Elle needs more of Shiny's jelly. Please trust us."

"Oh, Bett and Danny, we do, but how do we get inside Shiny?"

"Bett and I will lift you, clothes off and wait, okay?"

"Yes Danny, thank you. Elouise is scared."

"Just love her Conner, you will see."

15

Elouise

Elouise had a brilliant career; she was driven by success and thrived on challenge. Always striving to be on top, with so many failed ventures and bed hopping to reach her goals but never really succeeding. She had lost two children in childbirth due to complications and one she did not know who the father was. The other was a failed marriage which after only three years felt doomed from the start. Some fucking banker, boring as batshit, trying to sell his crap to companies who couldn't care less. The executives just after a free lunch and booze. It was all a big boring fucking life, sell, sell, sell. She was required to meet with the ladies for coffees, cake and gossip. Boring. But she pushed back because she was smarter than him. He had no idea what she did behind his back. Elle wanted more excitement in her life and while he went away on his interstate trips, she entertained powerful men who could give her access to wealth and happiness.

Elle was never happy, not with herself or those around her at that time. Her marriage was falling apart after the miscarriage, he blamed her but she knew it was him. Then she met Conner Rage at a chance meeting. He was mysterious, with many secrets, also powerful, rich and filled with so much pain in his eyes, poor man. Conner's eyes met hers, they locked, and her heart skipped a beat. '*Oh.*' *Who is this man? He has my full attention.*' Conner looked at her lustfully.

'*Oh, she is beautiful and everything I love about a woman, and she has noticed me. Too bad she is married to that fucking dickhead!*' Conner thought.

Elouise struggled over the next few years with a messy divorce; he was such a pain in the ass. She was smart and took seventy percent of his worth with the help of some good lawyers she had to fuck. He went bankrupt in two years. Elouise was free. She had all but forgotten Conner until a chance meeting regarding some obscure taxidermy contract with a company called Medi-Corps. Conner was a leading player in this deal and she was more than impressed with his skills. He asked her out to dinner like a gentleman. She accepted without remorse. And she anticipated sex later with him excitingly.

Conner had no such expectations; Conner wanted the deal that was all. This company seemed like a big deal, hundreds of millions of dollars. Elle was a part of it. But not the part he had in mind. Conner thought she was beautiful but out of reach, not knowing she was now free and searching for love. He was centered solely on the deal.

To Elouise, Conner was her goal not her client. She did everything to get his attention. She bought new clothes and made sure she attended every meeting, which was so unlike her. But he still didn't see her. He was so focused on the deal. Medi-Corps meant everything to him. Elouise moved closer to Conner, just in case he became available. She needed to seal the deal that was her job. Medi-Corps never exposed their bosses. If she could sleep with just one of them, she knew she would seal the deal. This company was desperate to acquire the study skins; the skins of people that Conner and Taxi-plus had treated with their special water. Elouise held all the cards and also knew chess. Conner was a player; she dealt her cards and moved her pawns. Conner followed her moves closely, surrounding her with his knight and castle.

Elouise had nowhere to go except into Conner's arms. That was exactly where she wanted to be, and where he wanted her to be. The deal was closed and Elouise would become a millionaire, she had snared a billionaire in the process. Conner and Taxi-Plus was hers. The thing she didn't understand was that she loved Conner and loved him deeply. More than the worth of all the money and that was a good thing, as it all would soon become worthless. Love would be the only thing that mattered to most in the new world.

Then she met Daniel and Betty and this changed everything, but oh she still loved Conner dearly. But for some reason Elle became infatuated with Danny. Every time, Conner was inside her she was imagining it was Danny. She knew that this was unhealthy and no good, but she had never climaxed like this before. Danny intensified everything. His golden skin and huge cock was what she wanted to suck on. With no strings attached. But Conner would probably kill them both somehow if he ever found out she had done that. Every time he was near her; she creamed her undies involuntary and good lord when she had an orgasm in front of them how embarrassing. Bett had said he had an erection because *a jellyfish was sucking his knob.* Elle had imagined finishing Danny off at the feast table with her mouth. That is what made her come.

Then there was that last session with Conner. She had no control whatsoever. No idea what had come over her, she was nearly hurting Conner because she was so rough. But she felt powerful, not in a good way, almost evil. And right now she hated herself for that. *How can I possibly fuck Conner again and now Bett and Danny are telling us to do it in Shiny. No way.*

≈≈≈≈

Elle and Conner stood naked in front of Shiny. Danny lifted them gently up to the opening. "Don't be afraid Elle, she is fantastic, you will see." But Elle was trying to pull away. 'No Conner, please I am scared.'

Breathe deeply Elle, come in please. Swallow my jelly it will save you. Come. They floated in and Elle had her mouth firmly closed, until she could hold her breath no more and started drowning in the jelly. Her eyes were wide with fear.

Relax darling, you're okay. Conner squeezed her hand and kissed her on the lips. She opened her mouth and kissed him with her tongue in the jelly. She was instantly aroused.

Are we ready to go? Feel free to join at any time. It helps me fly.

Okay Shiny, take us out, please. Can we go into space briefly? I would love Elle to experience that.

Absolutely Conner. Conner and Elle were lying prone, hand in hand as Shiny effortlessly lifted out of the hangar and up into the murky sky.

Look Elle it's snowing! They rose through the cloud cover into full sunshine. Elle was exhilarated.

Oh, Conner how beautiful. Shiny zipped up through the atmosphere and into space. Conner and Elle laid there surrounded by stars, below was the murky cloud covered earth, with a few tiny gaps in the clouds. Elle turned her attention to Conner; his muscular body had a golden glistening sheen on it like Danny. She moved closer and ran her hand down his chest to his groin and took hold of him, gently squeezing and pulling. She was making him hard. Conner held her breast and pulled her into his embrace. Elle spread her legs and guided him inside her. *This feels amazing; she thought.* Shiny shuddered as Elle immediately started to climax while tightening on Conner's cock bringing him to climax too. He started pumping wildly into her as she moaned loudly in the jelly. Conner could not stop. Shiny was buzzing now, zooming around the globe, intensifying their orgasms. Wave after wave went through them both until finally Conner slowed and they both stopped orgasming. Conner went to pull out but Elle would not let him and held on tight. *Okay then Elle. I'm happy to stay right here.*

You are amazing Conner, that was incredible. They turned their attention back outside where Shiny had dropped back through the clouds and was floating above the remains of New York City lighting it up brightly. *Oh my god! I know they said it was bad, but when you actually see it for yourself it is shocking.* Conner was shaking his head. *Can we see the first impact, please Shiny?*

Yes Conner, Dallas Texas it is. Shiny lifted with lights off and raced across the ruined countryside. They quickly arrived at the desolation that used to be Dallas. There was some light filtering through the clouds. They could clearly see the massive impact crater, over a hundred miles wide and at least two miles deep. The molten rock was mostly resolidified, with some pockets still glowing red. Any city buildings nearby had turned to dust, vaporized by the compression wave. The surrounds for thousands of miles were totally barren, just bare dirt covered in soot. It looked as barren as the moon. It was as if humanity had been wiped from existence.

Conner and Elle could not say a word as this was way too shocking.

'Yellowstone Caldera please Shiny.'

Okay Conner, Yellowstone. They lifted away, in utter horror. *We will be arriving at Yellowstone in a few minutes.* The first thing Conner noticed was the new huge volcano that had formed where the caldera had been. Shiny floated directly above the molten lake that stretched on for twenty miles around them and slowly lifted higher. They could see the lava had flowed in every direction for hundreds of miles.

Shiny took them around the globe sightseeing to all the horrific destruction. Elle started squeezing Conner again, making him hard. He took hold of her hips smiling at her. Slowly he moved in and out to her delight. *His cock feels amazing, different in this jelly.* She thought. *Oh. Yes Conner, slowly. Oh.* Elle was trying to hold back but he felt so good, she suddenly gasped and climaxed, shuddering and shaking, pressing down on him. Conner came forcefully, moaning with pure lust, grunting like an animal and breathing heavily. Shiny lit up and shook them both, vibrating in time with Conner, making him go harder and faster thrusting in. Elle was impressed, she was having spasms one after another non-stop and she loved it.

See the containers lined up, that is Danny and Bett's work. They shifted thirty thousand containers full of food. And here are all the cruise ships lined up in case we need to move people.

Wow! Oh, look at that, those two are brilliant, don't you think Elle, Oh.

Oh fuck, yes, oh, great.' They are oh, Dan. Elle was way too into this fuck to be able to talk. Shiny's vibrations were intensifying everything. Conner had no idea how he could still be hard. He had stopped coming but kept pumping into Elle because she had his ass in her hands firmly pulling him in over and over. Her face was pure utter ecstasy and she had never felt so erotic in her life. *I got to get me one of these.* She thought, referring to Shiny.

Last stop Sydney, then home. They looked down at the remains of what was once Sydney. What a mess. It already looked like an old pile of ruins, covered in ash and black soot. It was a jumbled pile of dirty rocks, some of which was awash with sea water that had huge waves crashing against the debris. Shiny lifted and headed towards Queensland. Elle had finally stopped with her multiple orgasms. But she felt incredible as her whole-body buzzed, she let Conner pull out, kissing him passionately as he did. *Whew!* Conner thought. *What a woman. I was not expecting that level of sexual intensity.* Shiny slowed as they approached *"Shiny real slow over Taxi please and lights please."* Shiny slowed and lit up the remains of Taxi. They looked on, what a sad sight. Almost every building was in ruins from the fires. All glass shattered and gone with at least thirty inches of black soot covering everything and then covered in a layer of patchy snow. Gerties was a miserable pile of rubble, and at the crematorium the gas bottles had exploded tearing the building in half. It was a smoldering wreck. Elle hugged Conner feeling his dismay. *Thanks, Shiny, to the hangar please. Thank you for helping Elle and showing us everything and also for sharing yourself. You are uniquely astounding, your compassion and love is overwhelming and very infectious.*

Yes Conner, Shiny you are fabulous! Thank you for everything, I have loved coming on this ride with you and Conner. Your jelly is extremely invigorating and erotic.

That was totally my pleasure folks. I thoroughly enjoyed your company; you are welcome to come with me anytime. Thank you both. I am open now. I can float you out.

16

Around We Go

Bett and Danny watched Shiny leave with Conner and Elle inside on the monitors. "What now darling? A hot shower, some food and maybe some drinks at the tavern." We decided to share a shower as they were so big.

"That sounds great Danny, oh, I hope this helps Elle, she is very intense and so in tune with us somehow."

"Yes, you are right Bett. She makes me uncomfortable with her thoughts sometimes."

"Oh Danny, don't worry, I find it amusing that she is obsessed with your cock as much as I am, but she loves dad, I am one hundred percent sure of that."

"Yes, I know that, but it still freaks me a little."

"Well, I think you should flop it out in front of her accidentally one day. Once she sees it, she will know what it looks like and won't be thinking about it all the time." Bett winked at me in the shower and dropped to her knees ogling my penis with wide eyes. She stood back up with a huge, gorgeous smile across her face. Bett turned around and dropped the soap in front of her on purpose and started backing up on me. She stopped directly in front of my penis and raised her hand snapping her finger. I had an instant erection. She lined me up perfectly and pushed her pussy back onto me. I took her hips in my hands and deeply thrust in. She propped her hands against the opposite wall and pushed back moaning loudly.

"You cheeky ratbag Betty! Uh."

"Oh, fuck, yes." She cried. She felt so good. Her whole body was trembling already. She pushed me hard up against the wall and wriggled her sweet ass around on me and I stood my ground as she fucked me hard. She moaned and started climaxing loudly and again she pushed back. I blew my load and heaved forward, trembling as I came. My knees were so weak, but she had me pinned against the wall, gyrating around on me fast. Betty screamed out in erotic pleasure clamping down on me with each orgasm. My cum was going all over the shower floor. She kept going in utter ecstatic bliss. I reached around her and pulled her up. Her nipples were between my fingers and her back was on my chest as I moved one hand down her body until I found her slippery clit. She moaned in my ear "Oh Danny." I was pumping from behind and rubbing her clit whilst lifting her off the ground. Her whole body was trembling and twitching with her toes barely resting on my feet. I finally stopped ejaculating and eased her down. She fell forward and off of me instantly turning and planting the sexiest open kiss on my lips. Her tongue darting halfway down my throat with her arms were wrapping tightly around me. My semi hard cock pushed to one side. "Fuck! Oh, fuck that was incredible Danny. God and what you did at the end just then. Fuck you can do that to me every day. I fucking love you Danny. Are you hungry, because I'm fucking starving?"

We finally washed ourselves properly then stepped out and dried ourselves. We dressed quickly in our favorite and comfortable boho clothes and headed off to the Tavern with our bodies buzzing.

There were two popular places in The House of *Ra*; one was the library, the other the Tavern. So, when we entered it was full of people and very noisy. Everyone was surprised to see us again but happy we had returned. Rita, Candy and Rose were behind the bar. We ordered two Vodka Martinis for a change. Rita needed to know about outside. "Here are your Martinis, how are you both going? You look amazing all golden and swirling, can I touch you, Bett? Hope you don't mind." Her hand was on Betty's arm in a flash. "Oh, you tingle, are you like this all the time?"

"Pretty much, Cheers!" Bett said loudly.

"CHEERS!" The whole Tavern joined in. We raised our glasses and clinked them.

"To Elouise." We said together and took a hefty sip. Rita spun around just catching our toast.

"Elouise? Is everything okay, where is she?" Rita asked.

It's okay Danny. "Rita, Elle and Dad are in Shiny checking Taxi and some other places. I'm sure he will let everyone know what it is like. Please don't ask us now, what it is like, we came to wind down, and order some food. Any recommendations?'

"Our wood fired pizzas are a knockout, we have the Bett and Danny Special and it is finished with gold leaf in your honor." I nearly lost it, choking on my Martini.

"You're not serious? Are you? You are serious." I looked at Bett, she was pissing herself laughing.

"Rita, what else? Tell us please." Bett was in near hysterics now.

"Well, one of our more popular one's is Danny's Extra-Large Golden Salami that only comes in one size." Rita said with a deadpan face. "And Danny's Extra Thick Pepperoni, deep pan, drizzled in cheese sauce." There was a hint of a smile now, but we had both lost it. "Also not to forget; Bett's Golden Seafood." Now she was grinning. "There's one more; Shiny's Jelly Supreme, which has a seafood jelly scattered and salmon caviar. Oops I forgot Danny's Hawaiian Nights, ham, pineapple with full Salami sticks and full red chillis scattered over it. They are all delicious, trust me." We slowly calmed down, shaking our heads in bewilderment.

"So, tell me Rita, who named these Pizza's?" I winked at her; she bit her lip and caught her breath. Rita looked around for support but there was none.

"It was all the girls in the Bar. Candy, Rose, me and Elle. We do half and half too."

"Okay, that is so funny, can we get a half Danny Hawaiian Nights and half Bett's Golden Seafood. Thanks Rita and a couple of shots of Tequila and two Coronas in glasses, thank you." Betty ordered.

"Perfect combination, beer, shots of Tequila and pizza. You know me baby. Do all the girls know about me you know, my err, cock, Bett?'"

"Yes, I think so Danny. Don't forget you have a golden swirling cock that is erotic just thinking about it. Elle must have told them, now all of Ra knows. Do you even care?" She looked at me. I shrugged.

"Nah, I don't care, do you? Knowing these girls are talking about me and my gold-member."

Betty grinned widely, she was so cute and sexy when she did that.

"I'm the lucky one, you are mine and I am yours, always have been, always will. Simple perfection. Danny I couldn't give a rat's ass who talks about us. It is all good anyway. Especially if it makes everyone horny, share the love that's what we are here for, repopulation of the masses." Bett had said that last bit a little too loud and Rita caught it as she returned with our shots.

"Bett, I'm sorry but, what?" Candy brought our Corona's and stayed, "This is Candy, guys, and this here is Rose, come and say hi to the celebrities Rose." She bought over the bottle of Tequila and some more shot glasses. "Just a couple of shots together before your pizza comes out. Then we'll leave you in peace. Okay?" Rita almost pleaded.

"Sure, girls why not?" Rose poured some more shots out. "Okay, here's to survival. Cheers!" Bett toasted. We all lifted our glasses and said it together.

"CHEERS!" The whole tavern joined in as we skolled. Rose immediately poured five more.

"Here's to funky pizza names." I said raising my glass and winking at them. They looked worried. "I love it. Cheers girls!" Instant relief flashed across their faces.

"CHEERS!' The tavern bellowed. We skolled the second drink and then the third, then the fourth. Rose poured the fifth. Bett looked at me and winked. *Watch this, Danny. We'll get the bottle to ourselves, one more wink.* "Here's to Danny's extra-large golden cock. Cheers!" I lifted my glass unfazed and winked at them. All three lost it, they immediately orgasmed as their eyes widened and Candy dropped her glass. Rose dropped down behind the bar, and Rita tried to excuse herself awkwardly running away.

Oh, Bett that was a bit much. Now they will never talk to us. Shazza appeared from the kitchen with our Pizza.

"Here you go, they all took off in a big hurry, moaning and carrying on, gastro, I reckon. You right for drinks?"

"Thanks, Shazza, looks delicious, another bottle of Tequila and two more Coronas would be great."

"No problem, be right back." Shazza returned in thirty seconds flat. 'Here you go.

"Thank you, Shaz." She raced off busy now with no offsiders maybe someone else would jump behind the bar or they would just help themselves. We got stuck into the pizza and I was proud to have pizza named after me, *who gives a shit?*

I do baby. Those girls will be talking about you for years, immediately after you winked, they all saw you, and pictured this (she squeezed me) in their heads, clear as day.

How do you do that?

Bett, you know I don't do anything, don't you?

Of course, baby. You have something else. Something very special. An aura maybe. An erotic aura. Or sexy pheromones that seduce women naturally. It makes them horny. I know you affect me like that. Fuck this pizza is next level!

Sure is, just like you. You changed me I was never a sex idol before you came along. I was just a failed writer.

Oh, sex idol now, are we? Yes, you are. Not me Danny, our awakening changed us both, improved us, modified us, changed our sexual drive, and then the Hathors did that to you. Bett pointed to my larger-than-life groin under the table. We had nearly finished the pizza and the second bottle of Tequila.

Shiny and Jilly have changed us too Bett, we are now gold, don't forget, thanks to the jelly. Oh, I wonder how Conner and Elle are getting along, they will return soon.

Let's get a bottle of Jack and go wait by the hangar Danny.

"Okay Bett, good idea. I liked both halves, how about you?" We took a bottle of Jack and walked out.

"Yes, Danny both delicious, and I can't wait to have Danny's extra-large golden salami in my mouth later and somewhere else." Bett winked at me.

"Bett, do you think all the girls say stuff like that?" I looked at her as I took a swig straight from the bottle.

"Danny, dah! That is why they did it. They can all get off eating pizza." Betty laughed and took a swig as we walked to the couch by the hangar.

Bett turned on the monitor, using the joystick to move around and zoom in. "Danny, maybe Elle saw you on here and zoomed in. Look how close and clear. When we left Shiny, she could have filled the screen with your cock."

"I am going to zoom in on her ass." Just then the hangar door swung open. I took a swig. Shiny swooped in and stopped. She opened and they floated out. Betty turned off the screen. "Oh, Bett really?"

"Danny you can look, I honestly don't mind, I know you love me, but I don't want to see my dad naked." She moved away and took a swig from the bottle. I turned the monitor back on and zoomed in on her just as she threw up the jelly. She stood up straight and slowly walked towards the towels, deliberately looking up at the camera smiling. She was looking directly at me proudly. Her body was stunning for her age. Her tits were full, firm and natural and she was tall and slim with nice hips.

"She is quite beautiful, Bett. Perfect for Conner." Bett took another swig.

"Are you done? Or do you want me to suck you off while you watch her big boobs? I will if you want."

"No Bett, I'm fine. You were right she watched me just like this, took a screenshot or recorded it. But yeah, she did, I can feel it." Bett passed me the bottle and hugged me; she trusted my love for her completely.

"Danny, who cares, the girls saw you perfectly today, in their minds, wait until they share that with Elle. Don't be hard on her because I understand her struggle to snare my dad. That would have been extremely hard; she is a fighter and a chess player, just like him. Let's hope this has helped her." We finished off the Jack while we waited for them to shower.

The door to the hangar slid open. They stood there, arm in arm in dressing gowns. We ran forward into their open arms. Conner with Bett. Elle with me. Elle embraced me lovingly, kissing me on the cheek and lips. "Oh my, Danny, I can't thank you enough. That was life changing, I need to totally reassess my life. You are amazing, you have changed me for the better and my love for Conner has gone through the roof thanks to you. I love you." She had tears running down her face. I was lost and I did not expect this welcome.

"I am so happy for you and Conner, he is madly in love with you, embrace that. Roll in joy darling." She stepped back, looking into my eyes lovingly, but not sexually. She had found the balance and was finally happy with herself.

"Oh Danny, you are so special, Bett is perfect for you, thank you for today." She went straight to Betty and embraced her. Conner came over and pulled me in for a big man hug. He then stepped back.

"Danny today was magical, Shiny took us everywhere, but the best part was the love Elle and I shared; it was next level. This experience opened new doors for us. Thank you for thinking of us, this has changed us. There is a lot to digest, and I need to tell the people of Taxi, of *Ra* about our Earth. The only thing that will save her is love. You already know that; I know that now. Your love for Bett is beautiful, do not be afraid to share it around, the only way we will survive as a species is on love. Shiny showed us your love for mankind. You have done so much already. It is beyond comprehension; your ideas are incredible. I wish you had worked for me years ago, but now is what is important. Thank you, son." He hugged and kissed me on both cheeks.

"Conner, Elle, we need to shift clouds as we are trying to disperse them to let the sun in. We will be asking our friends to assist. We need to go; I hope you understand every day is important."

"Hey, what you are doing is beyond words, get going." We moved towards the door and I looked back at them.

"Conner, look after Elle, she needs you. Take care both of you." Elle pulled Conner in close as the door closed. Our clothes fell away just before the door closed. Elle saw my bare butt for a few seconds and her heart raced.

"Come on Conner let's fuck some more." She pulled her gown open showing him her gorgeous naked body and pushed up against him; hugging him then closed her gown quickly as they entered Ra. Conner was instantly excited.

We entered Shiny, gulping her jelly and gagging, she shivered and welcomed us.

Glad to have you back inside me, you feel so nice.

Shiny time to shift some clouds, can you connect to the Octo? Shiny backed out of the hangar and lifted swiftly into the dark sky. The Octo's wobbly voices greeted us.

Yes Danny, hope you are good, we waited for you. How can we help?

We need a little help; I have discovered we can disperse clouds by flying extremely fast through the atmosphere; if you could assist us, we could expedite our efforts. What do you think?

This sounds like a worthy endeavor; we will assist you. We will arrive in thirty minutes. Shiny lifted into the cloud zone and sped up. Bett slid her hand down and gently took me in her hand, slowly gripping me. I turned to her and kissed her, my fingers finding her clitoris. She moaned and started tugging on me, making me hard. She shifted and mounted me gently. My heart was racing madly. Shiny sped up. Bett sped up; my heart sped up. We were racing through the atmosphere as we all climaxed together dramatically. We made love as we hurtled through the clouds while Bett grinned at me with eyes closed in orgasmic ecstasy.

The Octo soon joined us. I asked them to do the same at different levels in different directions; we soon had five hundred craft zipping through Earth's atmosphere. We were all travelling at over fifteen thousand miles an hour. The clouds swirled around us as we circled the globe. We were causing worldwide thunderstorms with dirty ash and dust filled rain. Betty and I were hard at it as we buzzed through the atmosphere, keeping our love hot. The Octo shared in our orgasms blissfully speeding up in time with us.

But this was hard work. Only one month in and we were all exhausted. Flying super-fast and working hard to keep Shiny fast. Bett and I started falling asleep inside Shiny. That was a first and Shiny knew we needed a break.

Danny and Bett you need to rest, you have done so much but you are so exhausted you are falling asleep. It is time for rest, outside of me by the lake. We have been at it for a month. You cannot keep going. We all need down time. Please. Listen. The Octo will change ships and keep going for they understand your conviction, and will back you up, your plan is working. It takes time. I will take you home my loves.

♋

Shiny, swooped into our camp, '*Jilly they are sound asleep, worn out completely I can shift them to their bedding. Please hold the tent flap aside for me. I need to sleep too, I am done.* "Shiny, you are the best, drop them in their bed and I will cover them and watch them. You also get some rest babe. Thank you. We are the A team." Shiny floated us out, making sure we emptied our lungs. She could not wash her jelly off but wrapped us in rugs and took Bett and I into our tent dropping us gently on the mattresses. Jilly came over to check on us. *They will survive but I will sit here watching them the whole night through.* She said to herself. She propped herself up near Betty and watched us both closely for the next fifteen hours as we slept.

When we eventually woke, we were stuck together.

Bett, we need to wash, I am stuck to you and my lips are stuck together too. Are you okay?

I'm fine, but totally stuck. Hi Jilly, we are stuck and need to wash this jelly off. How long have you been sitting there?

"I have been watching you for fifteen hours, you looked so peaceful, you must have been very tired."

Yes Jilly, please go and eat something we will need to soak in the lake for a while. Jilly nodded and ran off to the lake. Bett lifted us both into the air, including the rug that was stuck to us. It was like we were in a cocoon, and we had melted together. Betty lowered us into the shallows and made water squirt us in the mouth and face. Slowly the jelly started dissolving. Betty winked at me and forced a smile which quickly widened. "That's better." She leant forward and gave me a sexy wet kiss. I could feel her legs trying to pull apart. Her hand still firmly stuck to my dick. *Figures,* I thought.

"What does Danny?" She slowly peeled the rug off us.

"That your hand would be stuck there." She laughed and squeezed me firmly trying to move her stuck hand up and down.

"I can still make you hard like this." She smiled and kissed me as my cock stiffened; I could move one arm so I massaged her breast and nipple and slid my hand down to her still stuck pussy.

"Oh, wow, there is a lot of jelly here, Bett." I gently worked my fingers through it, pulling and pushing it off until I reached her clitoris. She started vibrating and moaning. The jelly started dissolving faster and Bett spread her legs and peeled her breast off my chest. "This is the weirdest feeling, Bett." Her hand was free to slide up and down my shaft.

"That is the last of it, I think. Danny, I need to have a swim before we do anything else, sorry for making you hard already. Come on." She let go and took off like a rocket. I swam after her and soon caught up. We did the freestyle followed by the breaststroke and then the backstroke. Bett was looking at me. My cock was still hard and standing straight up.

"Come into the shallows my extra-large gold salami." Betty took my hand and led me into the shallows. First, she kissed me openly on the lips, with her hand sliding down my body and holding my shaft. She moved down and wrapped her mouth around my crown and sucked on me slowly, watching me. Her tongue sliding all over my engorged head, she felt amazing. Before I could cum, she slid around and sat on me. She was my golden goddess.

"Fuck that was good, oh Danny, mmm, you gorgeous man. Feel my chest, grab my boobs, I'm trembling." I held her stunning breasts. She was vibrating non-stop, like a washing machine on spin cycle.

"Oh, Danny my pussy has started too, *oh, shit!*" She wrapped her arms around me tightly. I climaxed immediately again, and I was pumping into her uncontrollably, she was crying out in bliss, ejaculating all over me and my cum was flowing out of her but she couldn't stop vibrating. We were a dripping mess shaking and moaning together. The lake was lighting up the whole bubble brightly and a whirlpool appeared near us with Shiny at its center. Bett was making my cock go in and out at an incredible rate with her muscles.

Oh Dan-Ney. Oh!

Bett, baby, slow down, oh! Shiny tell Jilly to stop please, oh, now Shiny.

The lake dimmed, and the whirlpool slowed. Betty slowed and my cock slowed it was like everything was in slow motion suddenly. Bett released me and floated back as my cock was still pumping out semen every few seconds. Bett could not take her eyes off it. She came over and put her arm around me solemnly still with her eyes on my pulsing cock. "Danny... That is amazing, look, are you alright? Sorry if I broke you. I want to hold it while it is still going, okay?"

"No, wait baby, I am slowing down now. You can hold it but no playing, okay?' She reached down and gently held me as I slowly came to a stop. "Bett darling, how are you?" She took her eyes off my cock and stared into mine as she opened her mouth slightly and ran her tongue over her lips and pressed them on mine. Her tongue was gently exploring my mouth. She let out a quiet moan and moved back. In the huskiest, sexiest voice ever she whispered in my ear.

"I am fucking in love with you baby, I feel so fucking good right now. And I am never letting go of you. That was insane, not even humanly possible. I need another kiss, come here." She wrapped her other hand around the back of my head and kissed me passionately. "Hmm," she moaned. Bett dropped us down slowly into the cold lake. "Thank you, for letting me hold you." She let go and called for the gel and we quickly washed and flew out the lake. I shifted logs onto the firepit and lit it. Our towels were swiftly swirling around drying us efficiently. Two drinks hung in the air waiting for us to settle. Bett put on 'These days' by Powder Finger loudly and stood next to the fire as I settled on the couch. She swayed slowly in time to the apt lyrics. Jilly came out of the lake quietly and moved next to Bett and copied her moves exactly. She was smiling at me as they danced in unison. They were so beautiful to watch.

Bett broadly smiled at Jilly's dancing and lifted her into the air next to her. What a dance team, I thought as I toked on my stogie watching them. 'Khe Sahn' by Cold Chisel came on. Bett lip synced to the whole song. I was so impressed. But Jilly copied Bett perfectly, making the performance a thousand times better. Our lake was blinking in unison to the music. Shiny was in her element enjoying our feelings. 'The Nips are Getting Bigger,' by Mental as Anything, came on. We were all bopping along and singing. Then Drapht's song, 'Rapunzel' came on and Betty went crazy and Jilly followed her every move. These two were enthralling to watch. I was amused and aroused. Amused by Jilly and aroused by Bett.

'My Happiness' by Powder Finger came on. I lifted into the air and took Bett into my arms and did a slow rock waltz in the air with her. We were swaying and dipping and she was totally with me, enthralled in a blissful dance. We finished the song, only just and she looked into my eyes.

"Oh Danny... You are a heartbreaker." She kissed me. Jilly sat down watching our every move.

"No Bett, I will never break your heart. You are my everything." Jilly sat back skolling her JD, watching.

"Danny, I love you so much. But I worry sometimes about the lure of other women, and there are so many, you are the one man that all women currently alive seem to want. I see your innocence, but I see your lure. Danny you are irresistible to most women right now." "Please Bett. Do not do this. Last thing I care about is other women. We are the Old Ones. Our love is endless, through time."

"Danny, thousands of women want you and your golden cock right now why don't you give it to them."

"Bett, yeah, right. What? What are you talking about? No Baby, that is crazy. Sorry."

"Danny listen, enter them all once, at the same time. Linger and pull out. That will let them experience your cock. They can keep that experience forever and use when they are with their partners if they want. But it will stop all the gossip about what it really feels like." I was totally dumbfounded.

"Honestly Bett that is crazy. It will make things ten times worse. Instead of a once in they will want the real deal. That's not going to happen. They will be knocking on our door lining up. What you are basically telling me to do is mind fuck a thousand women at once, that is as bad as the Hathors. I want no part of it." Jilly shifted her gaze from me to Bett, taking in every word.

"Who? Oh, *shit!* You are totally right. I'm sorry. I've fucked up my thinking badly. Forgive me Danny. What if you show them all? Like at the bar."

"Bett, flashers are arrested for being perverts. What happened at the bar is different, they wanted to see me, I didn't show them on purpose."

"Exactly, what we wanted, but now I think it was likely me, not you who projected that image into their minds unconsciously. As we knew that is what they wanted to see."

"Bett, okay so, now you are the pervert, sharing my cock around with other women and you said we." I shook my head not fully comprehending what Bett wanted.

Bett, are the Hathors playing with us? Somehow, they are in you, in the background. Pulling strings, I am sure. Have they compromised Shiny's ability to hide us? Bett looked at me, lost in thought.

"Hathors, what is that?"

Shh, Bett, use your mind, close off to them. She looked confused.

Who is them, Danny?

∞

17

Hathors Return.

Stop, Hathor sisters. He senses us. Daniel is sharp. This is not working. Allow Betty's memory of us or he will know for sure. It is early enough to save our plan. We will exact our revenge on our children, and they will live on forever with regret as we do. We can outwit them; they are mere children. We need to work on Betty's anger now. Elouise's desire for Danny should soon consume her. Conner's rage will be deadly. Elouise's death can wait while we feed on all their lustful anger. Ra will be in a frenzy of sex and murderous revenge. Anarchy will take over. It worked in Buenos Aires and the Cheyenne Mountain bunkers we will make it work here.

Ω

"Betty?" *Bett, are you okay? You know who the Hathors are, right?*

Yes, of course, Danny, what do you mean?

Bett, you just asked me who are the Hathors? You wanted me to show my cock to all women. Or even enter them all with my mind, all of them.

Danny, no you're kidding right? Why would I want that? Betty was frowning at me as if I was a bit crazy.

Bett, we need to be very careful. I don't understand how they did that.

"What's going on, Bett and Danny, why aren't you talking?" We were so focused on each other we had totally forgotten that Jilly was sitting cross legged on the ground with her JD. She looked at us full of innocence.

"Sorry Jilly we had stuff to work out in our minds."

"You were talking about the Hathors and then you just sat there staring at each other. Don't close your mind to us, I mean me." We both looked at Jilly.

"Us?" I asked. She shrugged but said nothing. "Jilly, you said, us, then corrected yourself." She was clearly uncomfortable but just looked from me to Betty innocently. *Shiny block your mind please.*

Done Danny what's up?

It's Jilly, I think she is compromised by Hathors, can you tell? They were affecting Bett too.

I think you are correct it could be her broadcasting ability that they are tapping into. My jelly might not hide her from them. I'll think of something, just be careful around her. We should return to our work in the atmosphere. She won't affect Bett there.

Shiny, we can't go there just yet, we need to go and visit Ra. We have been away for a month. Bett will want to catch up with her dad. Jilly was watching me closely.

"Danny and Bett, I'm going to eat now, see you later." Jilly raced off and dived into the lake. She seemed normal. We sat on the couch with Bett's head on my shoulder.

"Danny we should go to Ra soon. Dad said to stay for a meal this time." Bett shivered next to me and suddenly wrapped one hand around my head, pulling me in for a kiss, her other hand in my lap gently making me hard as the lake started to glow. I was instantly aroused as her inquisitive tongue probed my mouth. Bett swung her leg over me and gently mounted me. She moved gently around until I was fully inside her with the tip of my cock hard up against her core as she sighed deeply. Her muscles tensed and released me as she grinned widely. She was in total control. My hands were firmly holding her strong hips; slowly gyrating. My tension was building every second. I reached down between her legs with my thumb finding her clit and gently massaged. Bett's eyes widened and she gasped and sped up her gyrations.

Whoa! Betty threw her head back shuddering violently, bringing us both to climax together. I groaned loudly as I came inside her. She silently lifted us into the air and kept gyrating as we floated near the fire in utter rapture.

∞

Elouise was shaking wildly and Conner was exhausted, unsure of how many times they had fucked. They had gone from the kitchen to the lounge, the bed and then the shower. Elle was insatiable but satisfied and Conner had been a lustful animal. She watched him as he sat on the shower floor panting like a dog. He was smiling at her washing herself. *Did I call him Danny?* She said to herself. Maybe in the heat of the moment. *Fuck I hope not.* She shook her breasts at him and blew him a kiss. He gave her one of his sexy winks that she loved so much. Ever since her trip in Shiny she had grown to love Conner even more.

Ω

Danny and Bett had been gone for a month and Danny had been pushed to the back of her consciousness. But he had returned last night she was sure of it; she had felt it was Danny behind her pumping into her, playing with her clit a while ago. That big golden dick of his. *I need to find those photos of it.* She also could have sworn that Conner had cow horns and ears just for a few seconds when she opened her eyes after an intense orgasm. It was by far the weirdest thing she had ever seen. But the absurd vision was gone, just like that. *I need to lay off his bourbon.* She thought.

Conner was watching his stunning goddess as she showered without his cock in her. He was trying hard to catch his breath. *I need to hit the gym more.* He thought, *fuck, she's incredible.* Even when *I'm done*, she doesn't stop, using *our fingers to keep going.* He had never had a woman like her, and he was nearly fifty-five. The weird thing was that a few times he thought that Elle had let out a moo. Yes, just like a cow and had called him Danny too, but she was so full on he could hardly blame her. Her moaning and growling was next level intense and her cunt so tight and full of muscle for her age. His ass was cold, he needed to move but this fucking view he had of her beautiful body, was insane. His eyes were at pussy level and he just couldn't take his eyes off her.

She loved Conner watching her and he knew it. He got to his feet, and she immediately pulled him in for another French kiss.

Careful my Hathor sisters, we need to be subtle. They are not like Bett and Danny, who know us, we can still enter both of them. That damn jelly makes it difficult as long as they don't get any more jelly in their bodies, we can use Jillyish to aid us. Do not let them see us in them. She saw your horns and that is unacceptable, Celaeno. Sterope and Maia you will soon get your turn in them. Electra you did well to make her say Danny. We need more of this. Daniel and Betty will soon regret killing our beautiful Pleione. Her rotting flesh will remain to remind us of the cost of our weakness. Their little stones will never penetrate our fortress again. Sisters our next target must be Europa, now we know that is where they are. The Octo slimebags need to be destroyed; they have messed with us too much. A fleet of Grays will be dispatched.

But Alcyone, they are deep in the oceans. The Grays craft cannot enter deep water.

Sister, Electra, I have a plan to stop their interference. Listen up...

Ω

The lake had dimmed. We knew Jilly had been responsible for that episode of; 'Everybody join the Fuck Party'. Her ability to encourage sex seemed innocent enough but I was slowly having my doubts and thought there may be some bovine influence in the background. They are devious cows. Bett had fallen asleep; our sex had been hectic today. She had been on fire and she had put everything she had into pleasing me and I knew it. I felt her, and she was incredible. Her every move planned, her smiles so alluring and her muscles, well I'll just say delectable; but they were way more than mere words.

If I could draw a diagram of what she does to me with them, it would need a huge legend to explain all the details. She will always control me, of that, I am sure. But her control of me only reinforces my decisions of what needs to be done to help our planet survive. When we make love, our world follows us, unknowingly, but willingly. Survivors choose to survive. We know our children will teach those who crawl out the rubble in fifty years, children themselves born after the impact, with no knowledge of agriculture or farming. No ideas about structure and society. They will need to learn of the dangers from the stars and the date of this impact, so they can prepare for the next. Bett stirred and cut off my rambling mind, I had been completely lost in our futures past.

Danny, what? Prepare for the next? Danger from the stars... I didn't catch you. Another impact? When?

Oh Bett, I was just thinking about resets, it happened before, happened now and likely will happen again. By the time the survivors and our earth are ready to plant food and crops, it will be the children or the children of the children who survived. They will have no idea. This will be a very hard task.

Danny, it is doable, you and I, we got this, we have Shiny to get us around and we have Jilly; who is always willing to help us. Our biggest problem is the Hathors. They are still around, being shifty and sneaking up their pawns, trying to checkmate us. We need my dad in on their game, he is THE player. And he is diabolical. We talked in our minds.

Bett you are right, we need to outwit them; they are coming for us, make no mistake about that. We need to show Conner all our moves and tell him how we think Hathors will counter attack so he can try and work it out from there. He will need to know everything. Can we block him from them?

Danny we can try, that is all we can ever do.

"Shiny, we need to leave for *Ra* as soon as possible."

I am ready to go, right now. I'm coming up to the surface now. Shiny rose from the surface dripping water and moved to within a few feet of us. We floated up and entered her. Her jelly, suffocating us as we swallowed, filling our lungs with her jelly. Shiny shivered joyfully.

Let's go. She lifted effortlessly and within seconds we waited outside the hangar doors. Pete opened the huge door. Shiny slid in and waited for the door to close before opening for us. We floated out and threw up like usual. We showered quickly and dressed minimally.

"Open Ra" Bett commanded. The door slid open, and Conner and Elouise stood there waiting. We ran forward and hugged them both. Elle was as loving as always and Conner stoic but welcoming. We walked forward into *Ra*.

"Come on you two, we have some serious food waiting for you," the door to the hangar closed.

"I hope you are hungry." Conner turned to me. "JD or something different, Danny?"

"Jack Daniels is fine Conner, thanks. Conner, I hate to get serious so quick, but I hope you are willing for a game of chess tonight." He looked at me and grinned, I knew he loved chess.

"You're on Danny, what's up?"

"Conner, Elle I need you both to focus on us, only us and block your thoughts from anyone else, you can do this." We walked to Conner's lair.

Bett they are closed. This is good. Tell them.

Daddy, we killed a Hathor, one of the seven. She was evil, taunting, using our bodies and stealing Danny's DNA. The other Hathors knew and didn't stop her. We warned them but they still allowed her lust to take over me. Conner listened intently. I took over from Bett.

The Hathors feed on negative emotions and lust. They take over their subjects, influencing their actions. They guide their actions for their own gratification. Evil Pleione had Bett and now also Elouise in her grip. Manipulating them for her own sexual gratification. But legends can't be denied; Subaru and the Aboriginal Dreamtime had only six sisters. The other ran away or was banished or chased away by the hunter Orion. The Hathors had lost their sister to us. The legend is fulfilled and the circle complete. Dad, past, present and future all collide and are all present right now. We need your help to defeat The Hathors. We need your A-game in this chess tournament. The stakes are very high. Checkmate could be fatal. It could be any of us as they are looking for revenge. Conner was so engrossed; he was staring at Bett and analyzing every word.

"Betty are they physical beings or something else? Where are they, where do they live?"

Okay daddy, we saw them, their true form. The moon is a construct, a prison built to contain them, arriving here unintentionally hundreds of thousands of years ago. They were mighty when banished; over ten feet tall, now they are mere shadows of their former selves. Small creatures, less than three feet high, they have lost their might. Their strength now lies in their technology as they are so advanced. They are shape shifters who can fool you when they take you over unknowingly. They entered me and basically terrified Danny, taking his DNA to clone him. They use a species called The Grays to do their bidding here on Earth. Bett said in our minds.

Yes, Conner, be wary, they will try to use you and Elle to destroy us, or you. They will appear as beautiful women mixed with cow attributes. They will attack when you are most vulnerable, when you are making love. Be wary." Conner looked to Elle.

"How will we know? What can we do?"

Conner that is your move. You are part of their sick game now, no doubt they would have built up their defenses so we can't kill any more of them the same way, but there must be another way. We need you to help us get them into checkmate, okay?

"Danny and Bett, I will do my best to help but you know how crazy this sounds? I am lost right now and need to stuff my face with roast beef, it will help me think. Come on let's eat and mull this over."

Elle had been silent the whole-time watching, listening. She was confused, was it Danny or the Hathors who were influencing her, but she was too embarrassed to ask anything. She didn't want to know because she had been enjoying the best sex she had ever had. Elouise did not want it to stop. She stood up gracefully and went towards the dining room. "Come on then dears let's eat." Rita and Elle had prepared their lunch a short time ago and kept it warm in a Bain-Marie which sat at one end of the huge table.

Elle lifted the lid as they walked in. Roast beef aroma greeted them as they took their plates. The roast beef had been cooked and carved up beautifully. They helped themselves to a variety of roast vegetables and gravy.

"These smells are amazing; did you do this Elle?" I asked.

"I had plenty of help from Rita; she is an excellent chef, more like I helped her." She smiled as I heaped the food on my plate. Conner sat and proudly poured out four glasses of his best Grange Hermitage. We sat and ate in silence for a while, before Conner announced;

"Danny, The Hathors can't leave their prison, which likely means we can't enter it either. They use their minds to control, to feed on humanity.

We have two choices; we can block their minds completely or use their minds against themselves. Shiny's jelly aids in blocking them. They can't see you when you are in her, we may be able to use that to our advantage. They still think of you as their children, their protégés, this could also be a weakness. They are weak you are strong; this is all in our favor. Jilly is helping the Hathors unwittingly from her bubble, can Shiny's jelly re-enforce her bubble somehow?"

"That is a great start Conner; I will ask Shiny as soon as we leave. You know we are going to try and disperse more of the cloud cover, when we leave here. The Octo are still up there. They are good allies to have and the Ishta too. We should take the Ishta up on their feast offer when we return, that will be interesting considering they don't eat food. And we will be eating with aliens covered in skins from Taxi-Plus, on a planet called Connerelle Rage!"

"Yes Danny, that is all a bit weird, isn't it? I never could have imagined anything so bizarre to be quite honest."

"Any of this a year ago is beyond belief even your Taxidermy town Conner or my beautiful wife Betty. I never thought I could be so happy in love. Why do we have to be called The Old Ones? I would have preferred The Young Ones..." Bett laughed loudly, nodding.

"I agree totally!" We all laughed together.

"This food was seriously delicious, thank you Elle, Conner and Rita." I sat back quite full and sipped my special wine. "This wine is perfect too, thanks Conner." Bett swiftly cleared the table using her mind. Conner and Elle looked on in wonder.

"I will never get used to seeing that." Elle said shaking her head. "Who would like some apple pie and ice cream for dessert?" Without waiting for an answer Elle placed the warm pie on the table, and quickly cut it into generous slices before any of us could even blink. She dished them up with a large scoop of homemade vanilla ice cream and passed them around. The pie was perfect, with just the right amount of cinnamon. The apple was firm and tart and the pastry sweet and flaky. We all agreed it was excellent.

"Bett, when the Hathors entered your body, did you realize at all?"

"No Daddy, even when Danny let me see and feel me from his point of view. It was like I didn't exist, and I had no idea what was happening. Poor Danny had a woman-cow on him, not me, squirting milk all over him. It was terrifying from Danny's point of view. She was making him ejaculate against his will and laughing at his weakness." Elle's eyes were wide.

"Bett, how did you see that? Did Danny share his memory or something?"

"Yes Elle, I saw and felt everything he did, it was an incredible experience, even more intimate once the Hathors had left, I knew immediately how much Danny truly loves me." Elle was chewing her bottom lip again; I could feel she was imagining being inside my mind. Elle in me, feeling my huge throbbing golden cock ejaculating all over herself. Betty rolled her eyes so only I could see. *Yeah, I know Bett.*

"Oh, Bett, that does sound very interesting, Conner how would you like me in your mind?"

"Elle, er no, not sure how that would go dear. I have a lot of dark thoughts. Not about you obviously darling." Conner stood and retrieved his cigar box. "Cigars anyone?"

"Yes, thanks Conner. Bett and I will share." We lit up and Conner took out his Sinatra and poured three, still ignorant to Bett's obviously bulging pregnant stomach.

"Danny, humanities survival is about love, isn't it? That is what I get from you and Bett. If we as a whole race can't learn to love each other, we will end up where we started, shooting each other for bloody TV's and booze."

"Yes, that's right Conner, this time will be different, future generations will all use telepathy and telekinesis. There will be no lies, deceit or control of the masses. Controlled media is a thing of the past. Fossil fuel technology will have passed like the dinosaurs. New means of transport that runs on mind power. Look at Shiny who lives on our love, she is our blueprint for the future. Humans who can fly like us in a world without pollution with our oceans clean and definitely no plastics, ever again. The Hathors took control while humans were weak and ignorant. There will be others who will view this planet as a walk over. We will need to be alert and ready. No other race will control us like the Hathors have.

Conner, we don't need to kill all the Hathors, we just need to stop them. Stop their ability to influence somehow, checkmate."

Conner understood completely. Checkmate in Chess, you make the King helpless, he can't move, he is not captured nor is he killed. He is rendered useless; this was their task to win the game.

"Okay Danny, we are with you. Good luck in our skies, we will be thinking of you." Elle was picturing Danny flying naked in space all alone with his huge erect golden cock searching for her wet pussy amongst the stars. She nearly wet herself again. Bett stood and went straight to Elle, hugging her and saying goodbye. In her mind she said to Elle innocently. *Danny's huge golden cock will soon be caressing my pussy so dream of that darling.* Elle visibly winced as Bett had clearly heard her thoughts.

I'm so sorry Bett, I can't help it, Danny seriously overwhelms me. You must know I love Conner.

Elle, it is okay, I know the effect he has on all women. His attraction is insatiable and undeniable and I would share him if I knew how but it is not possible. I know you love dad. Relax. Bett kissed Elle on the lips softly. "I love you Elle." Elle blushed as a tear rolled down her cheek.

"Oh, thank you, Bett; you beautiful, lovely woman. I love you too, take care up there." Conner had stepped back from saying goodbye to me and grabbed Betty around the waist and pulled her in as Elle came to me with arms wide.

"Daniel, my beautiful man, come here." She wrapped her arms around me tightly and squeezed me. Her head buried in my neck as she was breathing deeply, remembering my scent for later. "Oh, Danny, please take care, trust Conner, he will work out something with the Hathors. I love your, oops I mean you; I love you, Danny." She pulled back and looked into my eyes with a hint of lust and kissed me on the lips. She lingered slightly longer than I expected and let out a tiny gasp before pulling back trembling.

Conner took her hand and led us all towards the hangar. Bett was smiling up at me gorgeously, content in knowing that I would soon be inside her once more. She winked her wicked wink and squeezed my member with her mind. *Oh, you Ratbag!* I said in her mind. She giggled softly as we walked. Conner turned back to us, squeezing Elle's hand and said with a big smile.

"I can hear you giggling Bett, and I reckon you can't wait to get naked with Danny and go flying together, that is my guess, because I would be the same if it were Elle and I going up there. Enjoy yourselves and don't stay away so long." He winked at us as he opened the hangar door. A quick wave as the door slowly slid shut and we stepped out of our clothes.

Are you ready to shift some clouds Shiny?

I sure am Danny; jump in you two let's do this. Shiny shivered as we entered her, gulping and gagging as we swallowed her jelly. We took up our positions laying prone and holding hands as Shiny slipped out of the hangar and up into the dark skies

I am in communication with the other Octo craft and they are relaying their courses. There are also five Ishta craft that have joined in, including Ishta and the Lloyds. They are all happy we are up here with them. Your Octo friends are on their way too. It has been sixty-two days since impact and approximately twenty three percent of cloud cover has been dispersed. Temperature has risen by one-degree worldwide. That may not sound much but it will make a huge difference overall to the length of the ice age. In the slightly warmer zones, the most prevalent plant life is mushrooms. They have taken over as dominant species as they don't require sunlight. They are helping to break down all the dead trees, plants and corpses and aiding in turning the soil fertile once again.

The Magnetic Poles have swung back and stabilized, with solar radiation returning to normal levels as the Earth's Magnetic field is protecting us again. The North magnetic pole sits just off the Russian Coast and the South Magnetic Pole now sits a thousand miles east of Tasmania.

Bett pulled me in for a jelly kiss knowing Shiny would need help to get up to fifteen thousand miles an hour. I kissed her passionately and pushed my whole body against hers. My long flaccid cock was against her gorgeous thigh. She sighed and immediately took me in her hand rubbing the tip of my slowly hardening cock against her already wet clit. She spread her legs and guided me inside as I was now rock hard. I eased in as she grabbed my butt cheeks and slammed me home.

"Oh Danny." Bett whispered as I nudged into her G-spot, all her muscles tightening on me at once. I took hold of her gorgeous butt cheeks and rhythmically tapped into her she panted with pleasure and sucked on my neck. She was trembling and her passion was rising. She was very close to climax. Shiny started to glow bright with each thrust. Bett pulled me in hard each time then suddenly locked onto me tightly and exploded on me in a rush. "Argh! Oh! Oh shit!" And that was it, I let go in a frenzy. I felt like a freight train, powerfully pumping into Bett as she moaned in blissful ragged sobs of joy. "Oh! Fuck. Yes Danny!" She cried out in time with her orgasms. Shiny zipped along at fifteen thousand miles an hour, shivering and shaking in time with us. The Octo ships lit up as did the Ishta and Lloyds.

∞

Earth's atmosphere was alight in orgasmic rapture as we buzzed through the clouds, five hundred and six brightly glowing craft zooming around at fifteen thousand miles an hour. Some human life had ventured out of their shelters by now and in wonder had found rows of large shipping containers filled with food nearby. This would be their salvation. Where had they come from with all the desolation everywhere? Some looked to the skies and could see the strange unearthly glow streaking through the clouds in every direction. But all they felt was love and security that someone or something was looking after them all. Was it God, Allah, Krishna?

After two weeks of going at it strong we had finally calmed down and caught our breath. Our fuck–fest was wearing us out already. Betty was still firm on my crotch. We felt the Ishta's presence.

Bettdanny, your loving brings us much joy, you make our lights shine bright, like it did a millennium ago. Thank you. We are ready for your visit to Connerelle Rage when you are. We will be honored by your atten-dance and that of Connerelle. We have dispersed the clouds by twenty-five percent. It is likely now your planet will not enter a deep ice age as predicted and will stabilize after only a few hundred years. That is much better than a thousand freezing years of darkness. Even now your sun shines through the broken clouds.

Thank you, Ishta. Your loyalty to us is honorable, your aid invaluable, and Earth thanks you too. We will gladly join you as will Connerelle. We will have a break soon and then contact you when we are all ready to visit. They can come with us in Shiny, if that is easier for you. Just give Shiny the co-ordinates of Connerelle. Thank you for your generosity and help.

We will leave now to rest, call us when you are ready. We look forward to your company soon. Their ships disappeared in a blink and then they were gone. The Octo's warbled voices greeted us.

Danny and Bett, you were exceptional again, we thrive on your love. You need to return to Europa; we have an honor to share with you. Our Octo have been circling Earth for fifty- two Earth days now and we are happy to continue as we know it hurts the remaining Hathors plans. They are planning something. We are sure. Their Grays are involved somehow so be prepared to assist as we may need your telepathic skills. Hathors are after us now too, please stay alert.

Our Octo friends, we have your backs, we will watch them closely. We will gladly return to Europa when it is safe for all to do so. Hathors are up to no good right now, that is for sure.

We agree Danny. Good luck. Talk soon Old Ones.

Shiny, keep your mind closed, take us to the Moon, just above the Hathors lair. I need to see them.

Okay Danny, silent mode engaged, Moon it is. We lifted out of the atmosphere and soon sat mere feet above the Hathors dark crater silently. Listening and watching. Above us, oblivious of us, hundreds of Grays craft had gathered. A small armada, but what were they up to? *Bett what do you feel? Can you see the Hathors? Can you hear them?*

Yes Danny, wait, they are talking now, listen.

∞

Sisters, our time is now, we strike Europa tonight. They are tired and week. The Grays will jam their fissure with their craft. There will be no escape; they will be trapped in their moon just like they did to us. Get the rest of the Grays fleet here now.

∞

Quick Shiny take us to Europa. Ishta, Lloyds please hear us, we need as many craft as possible right now at Europa. Octo, Hathors are sending the Grays to block the fissure with their ships.

Bettdanny, we are on our way, that is a suicide mission. Gray ships can block the fissure but will not survive in the water. We will enter the fissure before them and pull them deep into the oceans with our tractor beams. The Octo and sea creatures can finish them off. Bettdanny block the Hathors don't let them see what we are doing they must all commit to this. Hathors will lose the Grays forever.

The Octo's warbling voice joined in.

Danny and Bett go back to the moon, stay there and block the Hathors minds, shield our work. With Ishta's help we will drown them all in our oceans and then our giant enzyme crabs can devour them all.

18

The Battle to save Europa

Okay to go back Danny?

Yes, yes, go back Shiny; quickly and silently. Hathors must not know we are there, same spot please. Bett, darling concentrate on them, listen to the Hathors so when they deploy the Grays, we can move our knight in and block their vision. They must think their plan is working, okay?

Yes Danny, I understand. I hear them and they are nearly ready. The Ishta and Lloyds are in place as are the Octo fleet. We got this. Ready Danny, listen to them.

∞

Fools, they are sleeping. Sisters now is our time to rule again. They expect nothing; their ice-covered moon will soon become their very own tomb. Just like the tomb they put us in. The Grays sacrifice is a worthy price for victory over those cursed jellyfish. Once they are all in place, we will rupture their Ion Drives fusing the hulls into one solid immovable plug. It will take them eons to escape. It will give us time to strengthen. Celaone will recruit a human to be Hathor seven. She will replace our sister Pleione. The remaining Grays will build her a fortress under Taygete's guidance for she is our brilliant engineer. It will be a mighty fortress on Earth to enslave the survivors. We will feed once more.

Bett squeezed me '*Danny, this is bad, we must stop them, they cannot be allowed to succeed.*

Betty, we need to let them see that some of the Grays are falling through the plug, so that they keep sending more to plug the vent. We need Hathors to lose their fleet completely. We must picture the vent with the Grays partially blocking it. Some Grays falling through and the others wedged tight. That is what the Hathors must see. Okay?

Yes, Danny and the Grays too, they must see the same. But that will be hard to project from here.

Bett and Danny, The Octo craft and the Octo can do that on Europa. I can relay your plan and projections to them now, if you wish.

Please do Shiny that will be a great help. Shiny sat a few feet above the surface of the moon in the shadows at Hathors crater's edge. She was totally invisible to the Hathors inside the Moon and the growing fleet of Grays covering the sky above us. *How many up there now Shiny? How long will it take them to reach Europa?*

I estimate there are currently eight hundred craft with more arriving constantly. Their craft are fast, but not as fast as me. I believe they will take at least four to five hours to reach Europa.

Shiny, please tell the Octo and Ishta the Hathors are going to overload the Grays Ion Drives and fuse their hulls together forming a plug in the fissure. That means they can do that if they get wind of what we are up to. How quick can the Enzyme Crabs destroy the Grays craft, and will that neutralize their Ion Drives?

Danny, I am unsure, I will ask them. Those crabs are huge, I have seen one dissolve its prey in minutes, very terrifying... Just a second. They are answering me now. There is thirty Ishta; Lloyd Ships with tractor beams waiting in ambush, each can pull down ten at a time. Gray ships are not made for the water pressure deep in Europa's oceans. The Octo will blind them and disorient them, dropping them onto the Enzyme Crab colony below the fissure. There are thousands of huge crabs living there and they will devour the fleet as soon as it arrives. By the time Hathors realize, it will be too late. The Octo will fool the Grays to keep entering the fissure even if the Hathors tell them to stop. They say you must do your best to fool the Hathors into believing their plan is working.

Yes, okay Shiny, that is excellent. We will do our best. Bett?

Yes Danny, we will do everything we possibly can. I am totally with you.

The Octo have told me; they are working on widening another smaller fissure on the other side of their moon. Just in case this fails. It is wide enough to go through now but pretty rough, due to out-gassing. They should be done by the time the Grays arrive. Shiny explained.

Bett and I searched through the Moon's crust until we could see the pathetic creatures that called themselves The Mighty Hathors. They sat in their little control room with their beady eyes glued to the monitors. They were in constant contact with their slave race of Grays. The Grays had no idea they were to be sacrificed. They would blindly follow the Hathors to the center of the sun if asked to. They were mere shells, much like the skins from Taxi-Plus engineered to carry light beings like the Ishta through space. The Hathors had commandeered their race and controlled them with ease. The Hathors were ready to entomb their enemy slime Octo. Their movements became frantic for such weak little creatures that were too powerless to see flaws in their plan.

∞

SISTERS! *Our time to shine has arrived. Send the fleet to Europa while there is still no movement. Plug their secret base and trap them forever. Pathetic animals, no more sophisticated than octopus or jellyfish, they are mere sacks of water. Go onward Grays to victory. Hold back twenty craft here in reserve. Our children, the Old Ones will soon have no protection from the Octo, and then we can exact our revenge for the killing of our sister Pleione. They must live with regret as we do.*

The fissure on Europa should only take about half the fleet or a little more to fill and as soon as it is blocked; Taygeta you flick the switch and fuse them in place permanently.

Ω

We watched carefully as the Gray craft lifted as one, silently and swiftly disappearing into the darkness of space. *They are on their way Octo, ETA;*

four hours. Stay vigilant Bett there are twenty Gray ships left behind. If Taygeta flicks the switch, they need to overload too and fuse together. Can we do that with our minds?

Yes, Danny, by that time our ruse will be over with the Hathors and we will need to concentrate on those twenty craft ensuring they receive the signal too. It will be doable. Shiny had been quiet for a while.

You two need to be in tune with each other, you are coupled but you need to elevate your heart rates, carefully and quietly to be stronger in me. I can stay hidden as long as you do not get carried away. Understood? It felt like Shiny was smiling at us, daring us to do it so close to the Hathors and I was immediately aroused. Bett felt me and responded with her muscles tensing and relaxing. Her arms were around me tightly and her legs wrapped around my thighs, holding me still. My hands were gripping her tight bum cheeks. Delicately she parted her lips and gave me a long slow French kiss. One hand was on the back of my head, forcing my eager mouth on hers as she started to climax. Her body felt so alive and full of desire. She was writhing on top of me bringing me to a heightened state of euphoria. My cock was slowly pumping into her as I cried out in gratification. Betty moaned as a second orgasm went through her and Shiny shivered quietly just above the crater's surface.

Hmm. Fuck! Danny. I'm ready for anything now. Bett whispered in my mind, nibbling on my ear and quietly trembling in my arms. I slowly stopped and let out a deep sigh in the jelly. Whew. *Bett, you are incredible. Thank you for being so fucking amazing.* I whispered back in her mind.

You nearly made me lose it, far too intense for a quiet fuck if you ask me! Bett and I laughed quietly at Shiny's remark. But she was right we needed to be very careful considering how close our enemy was.

The hours ticked away until finally Shiny announced.

Grays are coming up on Europa now, ETA ten minutes. Everyone is in place and ready. Bett and Danny, it is time for you to do your thing. Concentrate and it will work, you have got this.

Betty gripped my cock firmly and instantaneously straddled me. I sunk into her core as we focused our minds together and overpowered the Hathors minds with our visions. '*Europa lay below us. Our target the Fissure is right there. Proceed Grays let's block this fissure for our masters.*

Fifty yards in and stop; all stop, bunch up, more, send in more, some are falling in. Keep coming, we are at forty percent, now fifty percent.'

The Hathors could only see what we let them see; they were happy with the Grays progress and expected a few would fall below the choke point. They kept sending them in. It was nearly seventy five percent filled now.

'*Good, good, Sisters it is working, we are still the masters of this solar system. Look we can soon fuse them, be ready on the switch Taygeta.'*

But in reality, everything was very different. The first Grays in the fissure disappeared immediately pulled down by the Ishta. The Octo craft were guiding them; pushing them towards the Enzyme Crab colony, which pounced on the intruders dissolving them in minutes. The Grays had no idea either; they thought they were filling up the fissure too, so they kept coming. We could hear the Hathors clearly.

'*Sisters, the stupid Grays keep falling in and yet it is nearly closed. It must be fully blocked. Send them all in. We are on the edge of victory, stay ready Taygeta. The Octo will soon be trapped. Nearly a thousand are in, it looks like it's ninety eight percent closed.'*

The last of the Grays craft descended into the fissure and were destroyed. *Show them the fissure is now full Bett, quick.*

'*Sister Taygeta, it is full, throw the switch and fuse them together now! Victory is ours!'*

We watched as Taygeta threw the switch and we looked up to see the last twenty Gray ships light up brightly. Arcs of electricity were flying between them, pulling them together into a solid mass. The Grays onboard were dead. The burning mass crashed into the Hathors Crater less than one hundred feet from us. *Shiny up, floor it.* We zipped straight up before the crashing Grays shock wave hit us.

∞

Hathors Den shook wildly. Electra fell out of her chair and struggled to return to her seat. Alcyone looked around in disbelief; what had just happened, what was that explosion and what hit the Moon?

Sister Taygeta, what was that, what have you done? Taygeta was looking frantically from screen to screen, screaming in frustration. None of it made any sense, where are the Gray ships? One minute they were all in the fissure, next minute there was no record of any of them. They were all gone. Not one Gray left within two hundred thousand million miles of the Solar System. She hesitated with her results; she had no idea what had happened. Alcyone would be furious.

Sister Alcyone, they are all lost. The Grays have disappeared, they are destroyed, gone. The last twenty crashed into the moon as one, fused together, dead and useless. They were not even targeted with the signal, this is impossible.

Sister Taygeta, now we are done for we have no slaves, no followers. I feel weaker than I have ever felt before. We have been deceived; our children are behind this, of that, I am sure. Alcyone slumped back in her chair and reached across. The six Hathor sisters felt defeated and humiliated as they sat holding hands; staring at the one large monitor pointed towards the Earth watching the dirty cloudy ball slowly rotate.

Ω

Shiny, Europa please. Step on it!

Yippee! Shiny exclaimed as we sped away from the moon. Bett clamped down on me and kissed me warmly. We passed Mars and Jupiter soon loomed ahead.

You are a hero, my love. The Octo will go ballistic; I could go another feast though. Bett pushed down hard on me forcing my head into her G-spot, moaning loudly as it excited her, pulling back and pushing down hard again. I let her have her way with me because she was in total control. She sat up straight on me as I reached down and rubbed her clit gently but firmly. Her smile widened gorgeously as she shut her eyes, trembling and wincing in pleasure. Her whole body tensed and she cried out as we came together with our bodies heaving as one. Shiny squealed.

Oh, we are at Europa, and you are still climaxing... Oh shit, figures, but we weren't stopping for anything. Shiny was now sitting on the podium with two thousand Octo surrounding us as I finished Bett off. Shiny was vibrating in time with my ejaculations. The Octo were writhing around in bliss cheering and orgasming too. I stopped and pulled out slowly, kissed Betty tenderly and we floated out throwing up jelly as we went. The Octo went crazy because my gold cock was still hard and dripping with juices and jelly. They all pointed and cheered. Bett and I fist bumped in the air in time with their crazy music. Our Octo friends came up to us and slowly quietened the crowd. In their wobbly voices they said;

Our Heroes have returned. If not for Betty and Daniel, the Hathors would have trapped us here making our life very hard for a long time. They, along with the Ishta have saved us. The Octo motioned off to one side, where we could make out six beings that took the shape of Grays but were pure energy. We could tell they were smiling at us. They were clapping with sparks flying off their silent hands. We knew it was Ishta and Lloyds and two more.

Bettdanny it is Ishta, Lloyds and Shins we can survive in Europa without our skins. Octo have taken in one hundred thousand of us like this. The remainder of our survivors are on Connerelle wearing the skins. The Octo, Ishta and Humans have forged a strong allegiance against the tyrants Hathor. They have nothing, except you two now. Your love will change them eventually. This we know. The Octo have an announcement for you.

Danny and Bett, please come and wash the jelly from yourselves in the pools and come with us to the Feast Gardens. They led us along the paths first to the pools for a quick wash, then onto the domed gardens. Directly in front of us were two towering structures covered in gigantic golden sheets. These were new. *Please sit here at this new table, constructed in your honor.* The table sat between the two massive sheet covered things. I was getting nervous now and looked to Bett. She winked at me and smiled; she could see through the covers, I could not. *Please help your-selves to our Seaweed Grape wine, we know you love it.* Here we go, I thought, I probably need this, and quickly skolled the first glass and then the second. The buzz crept in. Our Octo stood together as one.

Today, we are once again blessed with the company of our heroes. Daniel and Betty. Today they aided in saving us along with the Ishta's without either we would be lost. Please raise your mugs for a toast. Here is to our champions. 'HERE, HERE! OUR CHAMPIONS.' We all skolled. Today we *unveil two commissioned artworks erected in Betty and Daniel's honor. Betty if you could please stand and cut this string when I say. Octavious Illatious designed and created this first artwork in their honor. Okay Betty.*

Betty cut the string as the sheet fell to ground. The Octo erupted in cheer and some gasped with delight. I looked up. Betty and I stood there, arm in arm; fists raised, fully naked, with my big golden cock exaggerated and standing to attention and it throbbed lightly. I had to admit it was a very close likeness. Bett's body was perfectly reproduced and so was mine. Our golden skin swirling as it did on us. They had not missed a thing. I raised my glass to show my appreciation and the Octo went crazy.

Danny, please stand and cut this string when I ask. Octavious Illatious also won the right to construct this work of art due to his workmanship and accuracy. This piece is titled, 'The Toast' Danny please cut. I cut the string and the huge golden sheets fell. I gasped when I saw it. The Octo applauded like crazy. Bett stood up and kissed me grabbing my penis and made me get a hard on instantly. They went absolutely ballistic. Standing above me was a twenty-foot reproduction of my golden cock and balls, pumping my cum into a massive wine glass with the golden skin swirling around. Even the huge stream of cum looked real. The whole thing moved as if it was alive. It freaked me out. Bett could feel my extreme discomfort.

Oh, Danny Relax, check it out, that is you and it is amazing. I wish the girls at Ra could fucking see this. Shit that would be the end of them. Hah! I walked over and touched it. It shivered as if it was living.

"What the fuck, is it alive? Bett feel it." Betty placed her hand on it. The golden patterns under the skin swirled to her touch and the whole cock quivered. Betty shrieked with delight. "Oh. Wow! This is amazing." The Octo were beaming with pleasure and pride.

Isn't it beautiful? We are glad you like it. It is Bio-engineered, but not sentient, it has no mind.

Thank fuck for that! I said in Bett's mind. She winked at me and smiled. Betty patted it and rubbed it up and down, hugging it. The flow of cum pumped faster. "Ha-ha, look at that!" I shook my head in utter disbelief. Bett shook her head too.

"I wonder if I can break this one?" She rubbed it harder, embracing it in her arms. The flow of cum rose higher in the air but still landed squarely in the wine glass. The Octo went ballistic again. "Very clever. Danny they will probably expect another performance. It is the honorable thing to do." She smiled at me.

That is correct Bett, but we don't expect it. If you want to, that is different. We have modified your chairs to accommodate your offerings. That is for after the feast not before. This time we sit here and our Octo folk travel past us. Our different dishes come up out of these trapdoors. Push the empty here, a new dish comes up here, simple. This is your chair Danny please sit down it is safe. This is yours Bett, it too is safe. As we sat; the seat of the chair trembled, enveloping our bums and molding to our thighs. It was very comfortable. My chair had a large retractable hose with an unusual fitting attached at the front. I looked at Bett and her chair had a large retractable appendage that appeared to be a copy of my cock.

"What do you have there Betty?" She wrapped her hand around it and smirked, winking at me and looking at my chair.

"Well, this is an interesting development. This is stiffening and vibrating as I squeeze it. I can only imagine what that is going to do to you."

Please do not be concerned, we use these all the time. These two are modified for you. You may or may not want to try it, we do not mind either way. Please stay seated while the presentation is on thank you.

There was suddenly a fanfare of music and an amazing laser light show. Our two Octo stood and announced; *Today will go down in history as the day our Heroes saved us from the evil Hathors clutches. Betty, Danny, Ishta, Lloyds and Shins, we thank you from the bottom of all our hearts for our salvation. Watch this screen and see the Grays get destroyed by the Enzyme Crab Colony.* We all looked up to the massive screen. The Grays disc shaped saucers were immediately pulled under and guided to the huge terrifying crabs. The crabs ripped into the craft, dissolving them. The crabs went into a feeding frenzy. Whatever their craft were made of mattered little. They ate it all. The Octo cheered loudly. Ishta, Lloyds and Shins were waving their arms around. Bett and I lifted our arms and waved them around too. It certainly was a spectacle watching them strip the Grays saucers. The last craft was destroyed, and the crabs settled down. The screen went dark and the cheering died down.

Let the feast begin. Enjoy! The conveyors started up and our food appeared in front of us, with bowls of live food again. Yum. We started throwing down the crunchy little strawberry crabs and the purple passionfruit jellyfish. We swallowed the seaweed grape wine in mouthfuls.

"Hello, hi, pleased to meet you. Hi." The Octo filed past and we happily greeted them all. The food was incredible, like the last time. The oyster type shellfish were just delightful and so tasty, like eating the oceans. They had a condiment like chili from their oceans that made your mouth hum, buzz and tingle, with heat and freshness. It was so damned good. Next dish that came out was Enzyme Crab Steaks, these had been treated in their own watered-down enzymes, super tender and super sweet meat that melted in our mouths. Bottles of a distilled whisky made from ocean algae appeared on our table. It was bright green, fiery and a delicious whisky. Bett and I were slowly getting quite drunk again, but in a good way. We could not believe the Ishta, Lloyds and Shins were so chatty and friendly. They did not eat but had power pack type apparatus in front of them that they seemed to be charging on and almost getting high. They were laughing with us and having a ball; they were so different from how we knew them to be.

The Octo feast was epic; it went on for about five solid hours of eating and drinking. Some of the food bought out was designed to wake you up again and give you a second wind. The Octo were so full of love for us. They worshipped Bett and me in a nice way. They kept telling us to try our seats when we had finished eating. Slowly the conveyor chairs were emptying as the Octo crashed out on the grass. The Ishta and friends stood, said goodbye and flashed away like lightening disappearing. We were alone on our table. I glanced at Bett and she had a very wicked look on her face.

"Come, on Dan – Ney, try ya cheer, chair." She had hold of her attachment and it was twitching in her hand. "Oh Dan – Nay I'm' doin it. Putid on ya cock a doodle." She sat back, and spread her legs and brought the 'cock' attachment up to her clit. As it got closer it stiffened and started to vibrate and suddenly slid inside Bett. Her eyes widened with pleasure and she moaned loudly. "Off. Oh! Oh, fuck Danny. Hmmm." She gripped her armrests and pushed her feet up on the edge of the table, legs wide apart and eyes closed. She was going off in my head. '*Oh, fuck yes Danny, try it. Oh!*'

I took my hose and bought it up close to my flaccid rod. Suddenly all these little tentacles appeared around the opening of the hose as if alive. They tickled my head exciting me, making me stiff. Suddenly it surged onto my cock. The little tentacles were seductively wrapping around my balls and massaging them. The feeling was unlike anything I had ever experienced. I closed my eyes in euphoria. Bett's hand reached out and held my left hand, gripping me tightly. We orgasmed together instantly and so intensely. Bett opened her eyes and watched my cock moving erotically within the hose. She was in complete ecstasy, groaning and moaning watching my huge cock pump cum into their collector that measured out little glasses for the Octo. The shot glasses started to line up on the conveyor. I sat back and let it flow. I was making it as quick as they took it. It felt great, very sensual not painful at all, just satisfying. Bett couldn't take her eyes off me. I eventually slowed and pulled the hose off exhausted. Bett pulled her replica of me out and calmed down. We smiled at each other and fell asleep.

"Danny, Danny, wake up babe." I slowly opened my eyes groggily and looked around. The Octo had started up again. When they realized we were awake a cheer went up and hundreds of shot glasses were raised in an honorable toast. Shit, really. We raised our Algae whisky and they raised shots of me. This is getting too weird for me.

Damn Bett these guys are freaky with their cum drinking. I'm not doing this every time we are here.' Bett looked at me seriously.

Danny, their culture is so different to ours. What you have shared is more precious to them than life itself. They are lost in honor and loyalty with your gift. They are aliens, Danny. Don't forget that.

I'm still not doing this every time we come here.

Okay Danny, fair enough, but they are seriously over the moon right now.

Bett, okay, that machine felt great, but I could not help but think of the Hathors milking me; everyone it seems wants a piece of me including the women of Ra.

Yes, they all do, relax baby. I got you babe. The Octo next to us stood.

That concludes our feast in honor of The Old Ones. We thank you all and thank The Old Ones for their help against The Hathors, and Danny's gift of his wine. His love for us is genuine and unselfish. Thank you to the Ishta, Lloyds and Shins we are glad you can stay here with us on Europa. Our love to you all. Goodnight. He motioned for us to stand and take a bow. We did and all the Octo praised us and waved their tentacles. We hugged our Octo and nodded to the Ishta clan and bid them farewell. They walked with us to Shiny. We thanked them once more and entered Shiny. Europa was filled with so much love.

19

A long Cold Winter

*H*ello *Bett and Danny, would you like to go home now?*
Yes, please Shiny, how long have we been away from camp this time?

We have been gone eighteen days all up. Bett and I looked at each other and shook our heads, the time was flying fast.

Shiny, is there any way you can infuse your jelly into Jilly's bubble to block Jilly from the Hathors? Jilly is our weak link right now. The Hathors must be completely shut off. What do you think?

Danny if I stop with my opening up against the bubble. I should be able to mix my jelly with it; we can try on the way in, okay? I nodded, hopefully that will work.

Once my jelly has dispersed it will replicate and multiply.

Bett snuggled into me, her hand sliding down my chest to my groin, grasping me firmly and kissing me on my neck. I looked into her big green eyes. She had a glint of wickedness as she winked at me. I smiled back at her as I took her soft nipple between my fingers; she was instantly hard. She smoothly moved around onto my cock and pushed herself up on me.

"Uggh! Bett!" She felt so damn good. Her beautiful emerald eyes were locked on mine as she squeezed down and forced my cock deep inside her. She moaned loudly in joy and Shiny trembled with bliss.

"Uh! Danny. Hmm. Yes baby." She trembled as the first orgasm hit in a rush shaking her violently as I came immediately after her. We grunted and moaned in unison. Shiny was speeding along vibrating in time with us. We slowed down and relaxed. Bett firmly clasped on me as we passed by Mars in under a minute. Our moon came and went and we slowed down as we approached the Earth. Her cloud cover was very slowly dispersing as more sun was touching the earth. The cloud cover sat now at about seventy per percent. This was better than it had ever been since impact some eighty- seven days ago.

Shiny, go slow above our containers please.

Yes Danny, slow it is. There are people on the surface. They can't open them. They have no tools.

Please stop Shiny.' Bett said with concern. '*Danny, I need to open them all and let them know there is food inside.* We slowly descended and spent another two weeks informing the survivors telepathically of the containers full of food just outside their bunkers. Bett and I used our minds to rip all the big padlocks off the containers to make it easier for them to access. Some survivors waved to us knowing we were helping them, just not knowing who or what we were. We tried to let them know we were their friends. More than seventy percent of the globe was covered in snow and ice. Some areas in the northern hemisphere were already a few hundred feet deep and thickening quickly. Any survivors of the impact in these areas were frozen solid.

We decided to help as many as we could and started shifting people with the cruise ships. Sometimes we would exit Shiny in her golden jelly suits, so that we could talk to people and explain what we were doing in person to help them. They were so grateful, knowing that we cared enough to help complete strangers survive. We would gently place the ships for easy access so the people could board. We shifted containers to the decks of these ships and lifted them all to more temperate zones just south of the Equator. This took another two long weeks, but we managed to move around one hundred thousand people who would have had little chance of survival had we not intervened. Most groups we tried to huddle together to create a sense of community and belonging making sure they had ample food supplies. We eventually headed home totally exhausted; our eyes hurt so much from staying open for so long.

"Bett, we need to return to these survivors later and make sure they are still okay with enough food and supplies as things can change quickly."

"Yes Danny, we will check on them all."

Jilly we are back and very exhausted. I wish to charge your bubble with my jelly.

Hooray, Shiny. I have missed you all. I'm not sure what you are charging but I trust you Shiny. Please proceed.

Shiny entered Jilly's bubble and stopped at the threshold. Her opening lined up against the bubble. Shiny pumped her jelly out, and it was full of our DNA too. We watched as our jelly mixed with Jilly's bubble as it took on a slightly golden hue. We had no idea if we had succeeded in blocking Hathors influence on Jilly. Only time would tell.

Shiny swooped in over our lake; we had now been gone thirty-seven days. We had not meant to be gone this long but this had been a nightmare with Europa under attack and the survivors needing our help. Shiny stopped above our lake. *Thanks, Shiny.* We floated out and threw up the jelly before dropping into the cold water. It was a complete shock to our bodies as it was absolutely freezing. We caught our breath and quickly swam around to warm up as the shower gel came out to us. We quickly washed the jelly off, and our towels flew out as the firepit stoked itself with logs and little sparks and embers went flying.

"Fuck, Danny, I'm going to sleep well tonight." Bett said as she dropped onto the couch by the raging fire. A glass of whiskey hung in front of us both as we collected ourselves.

"Oh, Bett, hell yeah. I'm stuffed."

"Hey babes I missed you this time. My hibernation was off somehow. I kept waking up worried about you." Jilly had jumped up and sat between us on the couch, looking up innocently. "You were gone for a while..."

"Sorry Jilly we had so much to do, come have a JD with us, we missed you too love. Hopefully we can stay longer this time and maybe take you to *Ra* with us if you like."

"Oh, I would like to see that, I have had no contact with anyone other than you two and Shiny. Ra would be a whole other story of experiences to pass on to my people. That would be a very special story. Thank you, I have been busy with my bubble. I can collapse it now, like a blanket kind of. So, if I leave it will still protect our camp without me here. The animals and everything will be safe. When I return, I blow it up like a bubble again. I just need to eat a lot."

"Jilly that is great news. But at *Ra*, you watch and learn, okay not talking so much, these people will be in awe of you."

"Yes. Yes, Jilly gets it. I will be the star of the show. So behave and be a princess."

"Perfect Jilly, behave and be a princess. Tonight, we rest, and sleep, tomorrow The House of *Ra*. Okay?"

"Yes, okay Bett, just a couple of JD's tonight, together. It is cold out there, isn't it?"

"Yes Jilly, the cold has killed many, they freeze to death."

"But you have saved many, Bett and Danny. I feel it and know it."

"Not enough, Jilly. It is hard to save them all."

"But you can't save them all. That is not your job. You have done more than any species thought possible. In this timeline you have been the saviors of humanity. I love you both and I'm glad you are back with me. The people at Ra will not want to eat me, will they?" She asked.

"Oh, no Jilly. But they will be very curious. You do look different to a fish, or a frog and they will struggle with your intelligence. They have no idea of your species, even though you have been here longer than us. Some may ask some awkward questions, so be gentle with your answers. They have the opportunity to learn from you as much as you can learn from them."

"That is beautiful Bett, thank you. I never would have thought of that aspect of learning. The Old Ones are truly wise. Can we hear a few tunes?"

"Of course, Jilly." Bett put on Luke Coombes, 'Beautiful Crazy'. Jilly looked up at us with a little tear in her eyes, shaking her head.

"You guys have the best lyrics to your songs. Life is brighter for lyrics like this; love is so much more worthwhile with songs of joy." 'Wagon Wheel' by Old Crow Medicine Show came on next. Jilly was tapping her foot and loved this song too. Then the Mavericks, 'Back in Your Arms again' came on. Jilly couldn't help herself as she jumped up and started moving to the beat. Bett who was fairly exhausted also stood and danced with Jilly. Why, because dancing is good for the soul. We all loved the tunes and enjoyed the dancing. Bett's golden body in the fire light was so enticing with her beautiful pregnant stomach glowing, and her breasts enlarged with pregnancy. Her nipples and areolas were massive. My cock was so hard watching her. She looked over at me and knew how much I wanted her. Jilly had noticed my stiff cock too. She was wide eyed in astonishment.

"Good night, I go now, see you in the morning." She called to me and swiftly jumped up on Bett and gave her a little kiss on the cheek and whispered something in her ear. Then she jumped down and skipped off into the water humming. Bett turned and faced me. Hands on her hips head to one side, smiling gorgeously from ear to ear. She held out her hand to me and beckoned me to move closer to her.

"Come here my darling. Jilly told me not to let your cock go to waste, it wants me, she said." "How did she know that?" I stood just out of Bett's reach with my hands on my hips, my golden rod pointing straight at her, throbbing and dripping. Bett stared at it longingly, smiling.

"Look at it, it does want something." Bett said as she lifted me into the air in front of her and immediately took me in her inviting mouth. Her hands were grabbing at my butt cheeks pulling me in. Bett gagged as it went in too deep and pulled back. One hand grabbed my shaft as she ran her tongue around my sensitive knob and sucked hard on it. I lasted about twenty seconds. She let my cum go all over her heaving breasts as she quickly moved up my body and pushed my pulsing cock into her hot wet cunt. She wrapped her legs around mine and rammed me into her. Moaning loudly as I went all the way in. Her whole body tensed and then she cried out in bliss as she came in a rush. Her mouth latched onto mine as my cum dripped from the side of her mouth and her tongue went deep.

Oh. Fuck! Bett, yes! I nearly screamed in her mind.

Fucking, fill me, Danny! Harder baby. Oh, fuck! She cried out in my head. She came again, nearly biting my tongue off. We spun around in the air near the fire, our motion fluid and crazy. We moved so fast that anyone watching would have been confused at what they were seeing. I came again almost violently, thrusting in and continually groaning with pleasure. Betty cried out as a third orgasm hit her. Her body was shaking hard then slowed down. She was completely exhausted.

I pulled out and my cock was still pumping out cum. Bett was watching me in awe as I floated over to the lake and dropped into the freezing water. I screamed like a baby as the water reached my hot balls. I went fully under and spun around a few times. I lifted out of the water and looked down at my dick. It was only semi hard now and dripping the last drops of cum. Bett plunged into the lake headfirst, but I still heard her scream under the water.

"Shit, this is cold." She sputtered as she lifted out of the water, her golden body gleaming with huge golden goosebumps. Our towels flew over and buzzed around our bodies in a frenzy. We floated into our tent with two bourbons following us and gently dropped onto the mattresses and pulled the rug over us. We toasted our tiredness and how good our bodies felt after that fantastic fuck and freezing water. Our glasses floated away empty. Bett curled up next to me grasping my penis gently. She kissed me tenderly and we fell sound asleep.

Ω

I suddenly opened my eyes, but I was still asleep. I was lying on a grassy field. Bett was waking up beside me. What am I wearing, some kind of uniform and Bett was dressed as a farmer's girl. 'Bett, where or when are we?'

'I don't know Danny. We made love on the grass here before we fell asleep, your cum is leaking out of me. You're in an Australian army uniform and I am French, I think. We are in a war, but which one?

'This uniform seems to be very old fashioned maybe from the First World War.'

'Can you hear that?'

'It's a plane, look there. It's a Biplane, no two, shooting at each other. Quick Bett run for those trees.' These bodies were nowhere near as fit as ours and the trees were further away than I thought. We were running uphill too. The English plane burst into flames and screamed past us. The burning pilot was crying out in agony. He crashed into the trees we were headed for, exploding into a huge ball of fire. We changed direction but the German pilot had spotted us. He flew in low behind us, lining us up in his

machinegun sights. I pushed Betty to the side as the ground beneath us erupted with hot lead. A bullet tore into my knee, and I crashed into the dirt in agony. Betty immediately picked herself up and raced over.

'No Bett, leave me, run, run. Please go he's coming back. Betty no.'

'I can't leave you Danny.' Bett cradled my head in her arms and looked up at the Biplane and raised her middle finger. 'Fuck you, Schwein Hund!' She yelled at him as his bullets ripped us to shreds.

≤≥≤≥≤≥

We both woke up with a start. I looked at Bett and she had a tear rolling down her cheek.

"Well, that was interesting, first time we've died together. I like your attitude, Bett. But you could have got away."

"No Danny, I wasn't going to leave you, so we were together in the First World War. I wonder why we saw that part of our lives. That is the first dream we have had in ages. How long do you think we slept for?"

'You slept for about thirteen hours; I thought you were never going to wake up. Jilly was sitting cross legged on a big pillow at the end of the bed. "Are we going to Ra now?"

"Good morning, Jilly."

"It's not morning Bett, it is nearly dinnertime. The sun is nearly setting."

"Oh, my bad. We should have a quick wash first, okay? You can freeze your balls off again Danny. Come on race you in." Bett was up in a flash and sprinted in. I was about ten feet behind. Bett dived in and started swimming. I soon caught up and our strokes fell into rhythm as we did five quick laps and stopped.

"Hey we can have a proper wash in *Ra's* showers when we wash the jelly off."

"Yes, of course Danny. Let's go then. Shiny, can we go to *Ra* please?" The lake stirred as Shiny slowly lifted and came over.

Good afternoon guys, hope you had a good sleep. Let's go. Jilly swam over eagerly, and we all floated into Shiny, gulping and gagging as Shiny shivered.

"Watch the bubble as we leave." Jilly said holding Bett's hand. Shiny lifted slowly and passed through the bubble. It looked as if someone had let the air out of it as it slowly deflated, resting on the trees and tent and Horus. It floated about fifteen feet above the ground and lake. It looked like a flat beach ball. "Yay, it worked. Let's go to Ra now, Jilly is very excited." Shiny silently lifted us into the sky. There was snow all over everything, with the sun setting behind the hills and broken cloud cover. It looked beautiful. Betty winked at me.

"Danny, you are beautiful in this light."

"Thank you, Bett, so are you my sweet." Shiny was soon at *Ra*'s hangar door. The heavy steel and concrete door slid open after twenty seconds. We zoomed in. Shiny opened and we all flew out and threw up.

"Jilly come through into the showers to wash off the jelly. I will turn it on for you, just cold water, okay." Jilly stood motionless under the water, too scared to move.

"It's like standing in the rain. It feels nice." Bett and I quickly washed and dressed.

"Jilly is a princess, okay? Come and sit on my shoulder as we walk in to say hello to Conner and Elle, my parents." Jilly clambered up on Bett and sat quietly on her shoulder, eyes wide in expectation. "Open *Ra*." Bett commanded. The door slid open, and Conner and Elle stood there. "Dad, Elle we have a special guest we would love you to meet. This here is Jillyish Fish, we call her Jilly." Their eyes became wide with surprise but looked friendly. They stepped forward and Conner extended his hand. Jilly took hold of his index finger and shook it briskly.

"Hello Conner, I am Jilly, I am pleased to meet you." Elle stepped forward and extended her long index finger with bright red fingernails. Jilly hesitated; she had never seen painted nails before. "Hello Elle, I am Jilly, and I am pleased to meet you too, I like your colored fingertips, they are very pretty."

"Why thank you Jilly, you are lovely. So sweet."

"Hop down please Jilly so I can hug my Daddy." Jilly hopped down and stood back as Conner embraced Betty warmly.

"Thanks for coming back, Bett, we have missed you both." Meanwhile Elle had me in the tightest of hugs and was pushing up against every part of me, making sure everything was still there.

"Oh, Danny so good to feel you again." She kissed me firmly on the lips. "Your beard is amazing, and your hair is so long now. Good lord, look at your swirling golden skin too. My goodness, look at his beard and skin Conner" She stepped back finally and Conner came over and gave me a big hug.

"Great to see you, Danny. You look tremendous, can't wait for your stories. Tonight, we are having a big Greek barbeque with all the extras, hope you are hungry."

"That sounds great Conner. I don't remember the last meal we have had; oh, yes a feast on Europa a few weeks ago, apart from that, I think it was here." Bett was nodding at me.

"Yes, that's right Danny, when was that?" Conner was looking at us in disbelief.

"Bett that is crazy two meals in thirty-nine days, how can you not eat for that long?"

"I think we should start with a drink Dad; do you have some fresh fish for Jilly to eat later tonight?" Conner smiled at Jilly.

"I'm sure we can find something for you Jilly. Would you like to sit on my shoulder as we walk through *Ra*? I can show you things as we go." Jilly looked at Bett and quickly clambered up onto Conner's shoulder proudly.

"Thank you, Conner you are too kind." Conner took Elle's hand and led us into Ra. He pointed at things showing Jilly everything and what she didn't understand she would ask for more information. Jilly loved the zoo area with all the animals. She had never seen any animals like this in person; this was a sensory overload for her. She was so engrossed. Conner then came to the big underground lakes.

"Does Jilly want to have a swim before dinner? You might even find a fish or two in there."

"Thank you, yes Conner I would like to swim in the underground pools." Jilly hopped down and skipped into the lake, disappearing under the water. Conner looked at us, shaking his head.

"What a delightful and wondrous little being she is. Can we adopt her?" We grinned.

"She is on a mission. She won the lottery to join us on our adventures. She must record everything she learns for future generations of Saved Ones. She stays with us until we are gone." Conner was dumbfounded.

"Gone, gone where?"

"Dead. She stays until we are dead and then rejoins her people to tell them all of our stories. She is super intelligent just naïve about humans, but she is a fast learner who loves a shot of JD." Conner looked at me, as the water splashed behind him. He spun around. Jilly had two small fish hanging out of her mouth, grinning widely.

"Hmm, your fish are nice, thanks!" Jilly took one in each hand and chewed on them as we walked to Conner's quarters.

"Take a seat please." We sat in the big leather chairs and Jilly hopped up into Bett's lap. Conner went to the bar and poured out three glasses of whiskey and one-shot glass. He passed the shot to Jilly who smiled and nodded in thanks. He passed ours to us and poured a non- alcoholic wine for Elle. He sat down and looked at us sternly. "Cheers!" He said joyfully. We raised our glasses in unison.

"CHEERS!" We all said.

"Now, please explain thirty-nine days with only one feed in between. Can we get you something right now?"

"No Conner the whiskey is great, thanks. We left you that day to clear the clouds. We did this for two weeks straight at fifteen thousand miles an hour." I went on with the whole story of the suspected plan by the Hathors, using the Grays to block the fissure on Europa and then our counter plan to destroy the Grays. I spoke about our success and the following feast featuring the twenty-foot effigy of my golden cock pumping cum into a huge wine glass. Elle was biting down on her lip again, squirting in her panties and squirming in her seat. Breathing hard, thinking; *even they appreciate it*. I could sense the tiny shake of Bett's head; she had sensed Elle as well as me. I purposefully left out the erotic chairs, skipping instead to our return to Earth, knowing people were freezing to death and unable to open the containers.

"We shifted over one hundred thousand people using the cruise ships by shifting them to more temperate zones with shelter and containers full of food. This all took another few weeks. Sorry we were gone for so long; we had no idea we would be gone all that time. Even Jilly had missed us." Jilly sat there engrossed as she had not heard half of what we had done in space or on Earth. "Shiny's jelly kept us going all that time and our love for each other. That played a huge part in all of this."

"Yes. Your love is the answer. Rita and Davo have been busy since you arrived, cooking up our feast. It started out as a Moussaka for Elle and I and now has grown to a barbeque feast. You are all incredible; Jilly you and Shiny included, simply amazing. We love you all; maybe we should go and eat right now." Conner picked up his land line and said a few things into it. "Let's go to the dining table." He stood and we all followed. He had organized a special chair with a few extra pillows for Jilly. We all sat at the cozy, hospitable dinner table. Jilly's face was full of excitement, looking around in anticipation.

Conner poured the Grange for us and another shot of JD for Jilly. Rita and Davo came into the room pushing a wooden trolley full of food. Rita held a large silver platter covered with a big cloche. She smiled at us and said a quiet hello and walked confidently to Jilly.

"Hello little one, you must be Jilly. I'm Rita, this is for you." She raised the cloche, revealing a wonderful selection of fresh raw fish.

"*Oh*, thank you Rita, this looks delicious, *pleased to meet you*." Jilly beamed up at Rita. Bett jumped up and gave Rita a hug and a big kiss on the cheek and lips.

"So nice to see you, lovely."

"Oh, you too, Bett. You look fabulous all golden and sparkling and your belly is gorgeous too." She hugged and kissed Bett so full of love. I stood up and shook Davo's hand vigorously. "Good to see you mate." I said honestly. He was looking me up and down, shaking his head in astonishment.

"Jeeze, Danny you look so different now, like bloody He-Man on steroids, are you spending all your time in the gym?" I looked at Bett, who was trying to keep a straight face.

"Er, yeah you could say that just healthy living mate." He moved back to the trolley and started placing trays of Lamb-racks, Eye Fillets, Keftedes, Moussaka, Pita bread, Greek Roast potatoes and Greek salads. Rita rushed over and kissed and hugged me tight.

"Hi-ya handsome, good to see you too, you look great and so very sexy."

"Here you go folks, get stuck into this lot. Please help yourselves. Hope we can catch up for a beer later in the tavern if you have any spare time." Davo nodded to us, and he left with Rita.

"Jilly you can start eating, just mind your manners princess."

"Yes, yes, thank you Bett. Jilly is a princess." Jilly picked up a fish and as delicately as possible bit off its head and crunched down on it. She looked around watching and listening to everything with wide eyes. I loaded up my plate, Bett did the same and sat back and tucked in. I hadn't had a proper Greek feast in years; this was more than making up for it.

"Delicious Conner and Elouise, thank you for this spread, it is so good." I really meant it. Bett was nodding, her mouth too full to speak. Finally, she took a breather.

"Oh yes, this is fantastic, I haven't had a Greek meal forever. I just love the garlic, oregano and lemon combination in their cooking, especially on the lamb. Yum!" Conner and Elle both agreed. Conner wiped his mouth with his napkin and took a sip of wine.

"I do hope plenty of diverse nationalities survived. I would hate to think we could lose some cultures and cooking styles forever." I thought about what he said.

"Yes, I agree Conner. But now they won't be Greeks or Italians, Germans or Chinese. They will just be survivors in a new world. The cultures that slowly develop will take centuries to form any kind of identity. Much of the old-world history will be lost for good. It will have a lot to do with how severe this ice Age is and how long it lasts. And how many survive it." Conner was looking at me thoughtfully, nodding in agreement.

"How very true Danny. The new world will be very different, won't it? Settlements will be more like little villages, with some people becoming like savages again so they can survive. It will be survival of the strongest. Chinese Take Away is lost forever. Cheers to The New World." He raised his glass. We all did.

"The New World!" We all said, even Jilly who had quietly finished off all her fish.

"My mother was Greek, my father Irish. Good combination, don't you think?" Elle asked us with a smile. "I took my mother's looks and my father's height. Mum was only five-foot four, whereas dad was over six-foot tall."

"Your mum must have been gorgeous; to give you that face, you remind me of Sofia Loren or Gina Lollobrigida, one of those beautiful movie stars." Bett said admiringly. Elle blushed.

"You are too kind. But yes, she was beautiful. By a twist of fate my dad backed over her in the driveway and killed her in a tragic accident. I was nineteen. Dad never recovered from that and became a drunken shell of a man who died later from kidney failure." We were all staring at her, in shock. "I'm all good with it now so don't feel sorry for me, please. It was an accident, devastating at the time. But these things make you stronger and I doubt I would have met Conner if I had not been as strong as I am now."

"Elouise, you are correct my dear. All of us here at this table have been influenced by personal tragedy and it has defined who we have become today. Our planet has suffered a huge catastrophe, and all its survivors will have lost family and friends. This will heavily influence the future of this planet but hopefully in a good way." We had all finished eating, so Bett and I cleared the table neatly placing all the plates and cutlery onto the wooden trolley and wheeled it out to the kitchen. Rita came straight out with some dessert.

"Desserts are served. Kataifi and Baklava, enjoy." Jilly was looking on excitedly.

"Can I try some desserts?" Jilly asked.

"Yes Jilly, just a little to try first in case you don't like it, it is very sweet." Bett cut off two small slices and placed them in front of Jilly. She wrinkled up her cute face comically, sniffing the food in front of her. "You might want to use a spoon on this one, the Kataifi, it is made using yogurt, which is fermented milk." Too late, Jilly's little hand went straight through the soft cake with it all squeezing out between her tiny fingers. She pushed her hand into her mouth and sucked it off clean in an instant.

"Yum, I love this one!" She gently picked up the Baklava and took a big bite; it stuck firmly to her mouth and she struggled to chew on it. It took her forever to swallow it. She was making little grunting sounds, and we had no idea whether she liked it or hated it. She finally cleared her throat. "Hmm, this is nice and sweet, just very sticky and crunchy. Hmm, can I have a little more of the first one please?" Betty cut her another slice. She popped the cake and her gooey hand in her mouth and sucked it away. "Yum! Thank you, I must get the recipe to make for the others when I get home."

Elle was shaking her head, totally enthralled in Jilly.

"Do you miss your home, Jilly?" She asked.

"Oh yes, but I love being with Danny and Bett and Shiny, I wouldn't change a thing. I love *Ra* and you and Conner. Can I see the animals you have here again after?"

"Yes, you can Jilly, Danny told us you are making a record of your adventures for your people, how are you recording it all, do you have some kind of recording device?" Conner asked.

"Of course, it's my head. I remember everything perfectly. It's what you call a photographic memory. Anything I see, I can draw exactly; years later, even hundreds of years later. If you show me that recipe, I will remember it forever. All your conversations are locked in here eternally. I can retell my people all of it, word for word. When the sailing boat sank into our realm it had books on it which we saved. One book was a first edition 1851 Moby Dick by Herman Melville. I can recite the whole book word for word to you if you wish."

"That is not necessary but what an incredible ability to possess."

"Thank you Conner but we can all do this. All the Saved Ones, I am not special."

"Oh, but you are Jilly. You are here with us now. None of the other Saved Ones will experience what you have. We feel blessed to be in your company, we have never had an experience like this either. We thank you for just being with us. To us you are very special." There was hardly a dry eye around the table. Bett grabbed my hand and squeezed it tight as a tear rolled down her cheek. Elle was the same. Jilly was looking at each of us.

"Why are you all sad?' Jilly asked. Bett spoke up.

"Jilly we're not sad, we are happy; these are tears of joy, thanks to you and your company here, now. We are grateful for your friendship and your innocence. You saved our camp, our lake. You make us want to come back to you each time we are away. Jilly, Danny and I, love you very much." Jilly launched herself at Bett's chest landing squarely between her breasts and stretched her little arms wide. One hand on each nipple as she hugged Bett as tight as she could squeezing her bosoms against her. Then she flew onto me. Clasping her arms around my neck she buried herself into my beard.

"I knew you would love me eventually." She cried out with glee. I smiled at Bett and patted our little Jilly on the back. Conner and Elle looked at us with love in their eyes. I could feel it.

"What now, you up for the tavern? We can stop back at the farm on the way, take our drinks and cigars as we walk, come on guys." Conner stood and handed out the cigars and drinks. Jilly jumped up on Elle to her surprise and sat on her shoulder. Her eyes were wide with excitement. Elle stood carefully and passed Jilly her JD. Conner looked at Elle with Jilly sitting there on her shoulder and smiled, *she will make a good mother to my children*, he thought.

We walked back to the farm. Jilly was beside herself; she adored this part of *Ra*. She had seen kangaroos and wildlife around our camp that she had allowed to enter her bubble. But here there were cows, lambs, horses, rabbits, dogs, cats, llama, deer, pigs, and many birds including ducks and chickens. Jilly was amazed at the diversity of the animals as they all looked so different, just like all the fish in the oceans. She was clamped on tight to Elle, asking questions the whole time. Which ones do you eat? Which ones are smart, can any communicate with you? Elle and Conner had all the answers for her. We slowly walked on to the tavern. It was pumping and the noise was full of life. We had not experienced this since our wedding or the last day outside. Jilly jumped across to Bett slightly out of fear and apprehension.

"Don't worry sweetie, it is okay, they are loud because they are happy, and some have had a few drinks and are very relaxed. We talk loudly when we have had a few drinks." Dave came over and thrust a beer into my hand.

"Glad you could make it, good to see you." He was slightly drunk and disappeared in a flash. We made our way to the bar, where Rita had reserved four seats for us and a nice small cushion for Jilly on the bar. Rose and Lola said hello and fetched a bottle of Sinatra Century, and a bottle of Patron Tequila. This was all placed in front of us along with some shot glasses and whiskey glasses. A few of the people in the bar were noticing Jilly and telling the people near them to check out the thing on the bar. Jilly raised her full shot glass in the air.

"Cheers!" She said as loud as she could. Everyone in the tavern raised their glasses.

"*CHEERS!*" The whole tavern replied in unison. Jilly nearly spat her drink out. She looked at us, blinking.

"Everybody said it! They all joined my toast." We all smiled at her.

"That is a Taxi Dermy tradition and now a *Ra* Tavern tradition. If someone says that, then we all do." Conner explained. Jilly liked it and nodded. Her eyes were wandering over all the taxidermy animals around the walls. She thought it was a strange thing to do, stuff dead animals but she kept her mouth shut she didn't want to upset the good vibe she felt with all these loud people. *It is okay Jilly, not everyone likes taxidermy.* Bett said into Jilly's head and winked at her. Jilly winked back.

Meanwhile Elle was staring down at my groin again, trying to imagine my cock hard, pushing against my pants so she could see it. Bett knew instantly and made me hard. There it was plain as day for Elle to see, halfway down my thigh. I looked daggers at Bett. She released me and made it go down. Too late, Elle was standing.

"I'm off to, to the ladies' room, be, be right back, back." She was wetting her panties uncontrollably. Lucky it was dark and the toilet close by. She had her very moist knickers off in a flash as she sat on the toilet moaning as the orgasm took over. *Oh, my god. That looks bigger than I thought; did I make it hard, just thinking about it? Oh! Oh! Fuck!* She finally slowed down and let out a big sigh shaking. Whew! That was so intense.

You're a devil, you ratbag! Poor Elle couldn't help herself. I said in Bett's mind.

Danny, look the other way when she comes back and talk to Jilly. She is close to losing it a second time. Whatever you do, don't wink at her. Bett was teasing me. If I winked at Elle, she would see my cock in her head like the girls had, perhaps I should wink, and at the girls. *I'm doing it.* I teased her. But instead, I slid my cock inside Bett's damp pussy in my mind, pulled it out and slid it into her parted mouth, leaving it in for a bit so she sucked on it. Bett's eyes opened wide in surprise as she nearly came too.

In the toilet just as Elle was about to come back out, she felt Danny's huge golden cock slip inside her, pull out and then straight into her eager mouth. *Oh! God! There it is in my mouth at last. Oh!* She wrapped her hand around my huge golden shaft and ran her tongue around my irresistible head. But I pulled out. She collapsed on the floor as another orgasm racked her body. Conner was chatting to Jilly about her society.

Danny, Elle saw and felt you too when you did that to me. We need to be way more careful. Shit, she is on the floor, I need to go and help her.

Oops, sorry. I didn't mean to do that. Send Rose or Lola in there with your mind. Lola suddenly had the urge to go and pee and raced into the toilet finding Elle sitting against a wall, shaking and moaning. She raced over and took her hand. Elle opened her eyes, grateful it was Lola and not Bett who had found her as she slowly calmed and caught her breath. Lola had seen this behavior before.

"Did you see him in your mind?" Lola asked. Elle nodded. *Fuck it was in my mouth and my wet cunt.* She thought to herself she even tasted it and herself on it.

"We did too Elle, Rose, Candy and Rita, we all saw it, and immediately came right in front of him. We had to run and hide."

"What, when was this, how did I miss out on that?"

"It was here at the Tavern when you and Conner checked on the Earth in Shiny. They had ordered pizza, and we had some shots together. Bett made a toast to it; I won't say the word. But he raised his glass as if it was normal and winked. That did it, we all lost it. It went on and on."

"Was it erect?" This was important to Elle. She wanted that experience to herself.

"Yes it was right in front of our eyes. Elle did you see it erect?" Elle nodded and Lola gasped.

"Bett, can you check on Elle? She has been gone for ages." Conner asked.

"It's okay dad, she's catching up with Lola in the toilets, as women do, I can sense them. She is fine." Bett side glanced at me *She didn't spill that you were inside her. Thank goodness, if that ever got out Danny, Daddy would cut it off.* I winced and took a slug of JD.

"Come on Elle let's get you tidy before Conner sends in a search party." Lola tidied Elle's hair with her fingers. Elle applied some lipstick and perfume.

"Thanks Lola, you're a champ." They exited the toilet and hugged each other and said goodbye. Conner caught it all, *women, so open with their emotions.* He thought.

"Welcome back Elle, that was a long pee." Elle leant in and kissed Conner on the cheek. "Sorry darling, I hadn't seen her for ages and we had a lot of catching up to do. Sorry Bett, Danny and Jilly." She sat back down and skolled her drink and poured out some shots of tequila for everyone, including Jilly. She was being very mindful of not looking at my lap. Jilly looked at the clear liquid in her glass and took a whiff. She frowned, unsure of whether she wanted to try it or not. Conner stood and went behind the bar, grabbing the salt and lemon wedges.

"Jilly this is a new family tradition of tequila shots at the bar. You can try it or not it is up to you. Lick the salt on the back of your hand, skoll the drink and then suck on the lemon. You then wait for the next one." Jilly looked at Bett and then me, watching us put salt on our hands. She took some salt and a lemon wedge. Conner raised his glass.

"Here's to our beautiful Jilly, cheers!" We licked the salt; Jilly pulled a face, skolled our tequila and sucked on the lemon. Jilly did it all and put her glass down grinning widely.

"CHEERS!" the tavern joined in.

"Can I do a toast?"

"Of course, you can Jilly." Conner poured out five more. We prepared the salt and lemon.

"Here's to my beautiful new friends Elle and Conner. Cheers!" We all smiled and did our shot.

"CHEERS!" The tavern echoed. Elle leant forward and gave Jilly a kiss on the cheek.

"Thank you, Jilly you are very sweet. Do you like tequila?"

"Yes, I do, I have another toast" Elle poured out five more.

"Here's to Danny's big heart and Bett's compassion: they are working very hard to save this planet, I love them dearly. Cheers!"

"CHEERS!" The tavern was getting louder. Jilly began to sway a little.

"Are you okay Jilly? You seem a little unsteady." I looked her in the eye.

"I'm good, this tequila is the weird thing but it is relaxing me. I want to dance soon with you both naked by the fire. Dancing and whirling and twirling in the air with your golden bodies." Elle was suddenly captivated by Jilly's words instantly turned on and wet. She chewed on her bottom lip. She wished she could dance in the air naked by the fire with Danny.

Shh, Jilly that is for us, okay? Bett said into Jilly's head.

"Okay, Bett, sorry." Jilly said out loud.

"It is okay Jilly. Any more toasts anyone?"

"I have one." Elle announced. *Uh, oh.* I thought, *here we go.* Elle poured out five more. "Here's to free love, dancing naked by the fire and owning our bodies. Cheers!" Okay that wasn't so bad. But Elle was close to letting go again.

"CHEERS!" The tavern joined in. We all skolled our drinks. Then Jilly fell back hard on her pillow. Her innocent eyes confused staring up at the ceiling.

"I'm so done with this weird shit. My head is swimming around in circles."

"No more tequila for Jilly. Have some water, here." She opened her acidic mouth. I poured some tap water in her mouth and on her face.

"A little more please, and some on my body too." I poured the cold water into her mouth and on her face and body. She sat straight up, blinking and smiling. The Tequila had dehydrated her, making her very dizzy.

"That is much better, I'm okay now one more for Jilly, please." Conner poured five more.

"My turn for a toast, here's to my lovely Elouise, who I love for all the right reasons and who makes me extremely happy, I thank you for loving me. Cheers!" We all raised our glasses as did the entire tavern.

"CHEERS!" We all joined in. Elle put her glass down and grabbed Conner and kissed him so passionately that we all looked away. It was a get a room type kiss.

Hey babe, time to go, Elle wants to fuck Conner and Conner wants to fuck Elle, I want to fuck you and Jilly wants Shiny. What do you want? Instantly in my mind Bett had my cock in her mouth, sucking hard, squeezing my balls. She looked up at me innocently. *Damn girl, please wait.* I thought. She smiled and stopped to wink at me. *Jilly are you ready to go home? How long will the bubble take to inflate?* Jilly looked at me.

Yes Danny, this has been great, but I would like to go to camp now. The bubble I can reconnect on the way back and have it nearly full by the time we arrive. She replied telepathically.

"Hey Conner, Elle, we are headed home, little Jilly is tired, and we need to rest too. Tonight has been absolutely great. The food and company was amazing. Thank you. We will come more often now things are settling down. But we still have much to do around the planet; we need to check on our relocated survivors and any others we may have missed. There is always someone to save." Conner looked proudly at us. Two unlikely heroes who have done more for the survival of Earth than anyone. He shook his head in wonder. This was his daughter and her partner doing this.

"Look, Daniel, Betty, I am stunned by you both. You are incredible human beings; you have sacrificed so much time to help others and I am so blown away. Your hearts are huge, and your influence on all of us is beautiful. You have amazing friends." He patted Jilly on the back, and she grinned at Conner lovingly. "You are always welcome in The House of *Ra*. You know that. Thank you all for coming tonight, especially you Jilly." She jumped up and wrapped her little arms around Conners neck. He pulled back in surprise. Then he put his hand on her back and fondly embraced her. "Thank you, Jilly." She squished her face into his neck squirming in a show of genuine affection before launching herself at Elle's chest. She grabbed each nipple with arms outstretched and pulled them in on her. Elle was delighted and surprised with how nice Jilly felt squeezing her tits like this. She placed her hand on Jilly's back and nearly climaxed. *Oh, so much loving tonight.* She thought. Look out Conner. But Conner was watching Elle's face and couldn't wait to have his cock in her mouth and wet pussy. All their emotions and thoughts filled our heads.

We all stood up and walked slowly to the hangar. Jilly jumped from Conner to Elle's shoulders as we walked and they loved it. Our goodbye hugs were quick, but Elle nearly lost it in my arms, only because she thrust her leg in between mine somehow as we hugged so she could feel my lovely cock on her again. She kissed me and her tongue licked my lip as she moved back. Her eyes fluttered at me as the door closed and we dropped our clothes and entered Shiny. She shivered as we gulped in her jelly.

20

Jilly's Gift

Welcome back friends. Are we ready to go back to camp?

Yes, please Shiny, home please. I looked across at Bett who was staring at my cock again; she looked up at my eyes and giggled and winked. She was horny as hell. Jilly had her eyes closed and appeared to be counting or calculating something, working on the bubble no doubt. Bett silently slid down and took my head in her mouth and went to work. I was instantly hard and ready to blow. Jilly opened her eyes and saw what we were doing so she went to Shiny's shell and started running all over the inside of her hull. This caused Shiny to vibrate. I pulled Bett up and kissed her passionately as I made love to her delectable pussy, gyrating into her magical G-spot. She was caught off guard and nearly lost it completely. Bett grabbed my butt tightly and pulled me in again and again. Jilly was a glowing blur with sparks flying everywhere. She was moving that fast and Shiny was lit up like the sun in every color vibrating and pulsing in time with Bett and I.

"*Oh! Fuck Betty! Oh!*" I released myself into her, and she cried out in bliss as the first orgasm hit her. It flowed through her body in waves as Shiny moaned and shook. Jilly stopped and was stuck to Shiny's hull, shaking and heaving with her eyes closed, tiny sparks of energy emanating from her. Her crazy energy was jumping across to us. Jilly's skin was fluorescent and glowing brightly with all kinds of green and purple streaks. She was smiling ever so broadly with eyes still firmly shut. We had Jilly's sparks of pent-up energy flying into us and out of us. Bett eased up and I slowly stopped coming, I could see my cock was glowing brightly inside Betty.

∞

Elle lay next to Conner totally exhausted. As soon as the hangar door had shut Elle had pulled Conner into the showers and locked the door. Her hands fumbled with his fly as she went down on her knees in front of him. Conner pulled it out for her and thrust it into her mouth. She moaned as it hit the back of her throat and she sucked hard, squeezing his balls. In and out it went until Conner let go. She pulled him down on the ground and pulled her dress up and off. Her panties were already gone, and she slipped her bra off quickly. She pulled his stiff cock into her, and he moaned loudly as he entered her. She had him stone hard as she started rocking on him. He fervently ran his thumb down to her soft clit and rubbed as he started to come again. Elle's pulse raced as she looked down at him with her sexy pout. She could not believe how lucky she was to have such a virile man.

Shiny had flown up above the clouds instead of going straight home. The cloud cover was still at about seventy percent, and the planet was very cold. Snow covered most of the mountains. Humanity was huddled away underground barely clinging to life. Just south of the equator were some areas void of snow, but still cold with temperatures not above ten or fifteen degrees on any day. Below zero at night, here and there a volcano still spewed out smoke and Hawaii was still smoldering, covered in lava flows. Shiny flew down low again. The Australian coastline was vastly different as the sea had swallowed all the coastal cities and advanced inland fifty to one hundred miles. Shiny came up on Taxi and it looked surreal covered in a layer of snow. "Looks like Queensland will be having a white Christmas this year." I stated the obvious as we arrived at the snow-covered bubble which was nearly fully inflated.

Shiny came to a stop just above the lake and opened. Jilly left first. We followed, threw up and dropped into the freezing cold lake.

"Come on Danny, let's swim. Ten laps." Betty took off; I followed and fell into rhythm with her. The fresh water was waking us up and making us feel invigorated. I was busy preparing the firepit as we swam, and Bett poured some whiskey. We startled some kangaroos that had moved in while we were gone. They jumped away at the sight of flying logs. Jilly was catching fish and eating them as she went. It was about two am in the morning, but time was irrelevant to us, it was meaningless.

As we walked slowly from the lake, I looked across at my golden goddess. Her perfect pregnant body was so fit and gorgeous and her breasts were large and full. Her hair was long and glistening gold and her body swirling golden patterns. The beautiful mound in her stomach reminded me of our responsibility to this planet's survival.

Bett's eyes were on me. *Danny is my true alfa male.* She thought quietly to herself. *His body now chiseled and perfect. Oh god! That cock of his. Golden perfection, look at it swing as he walks, he has no idea how much he turns women on.* She started picturing Danny in all types of sexual positions, trying to work out which one she wanted first. *That was my fault Elle experienced him, I wanted her to. I wanted to share him. Why? I don't even know. It was only in her mind. But that is as real as anything.* She thought, hiding her thoughts from Danny. *Elle had him in her mouth, why did I want that? Danny should be shared. I hope it doesn't spoil what she has with my dad.* She hadn't seen that Elle and Conner's love making had practically mirrored her and Danny's.

Our towels swiftly dried us, and our woolly rug came out to us as we sat on the soft couch. We clinked glasses and took a swig, the whiskey warming our insides. Bett leant on me; my arm around her shoulder and the fire giving off warmth with a red glow to everything. Our bodies were warming each other, tingling and vibrating ever so lightly.

"Danny, can you feel that?" Bett looked up at me.

"Yes baby, you feel so amazing." I said to her. She shifted her hand under the rug and rested it on my cock lightly going up and down its length.

"So do you baby. This is like electricity, tingling under my fingers." She pulled the rug away so she could see it. "Danny look, there are tiny sparks, between my fingers and your cock. Oh, that feels crazy good." Bett's fingers were hovering just above my hardening cock and tiny sparks were flying in-between us.

"What is this? This is new, this is Jilly's energy. I am glowing too, looks like my cock is glowing." Bett pulled the rug over her head to block the light and moved her hand away.

"Danny come under the rug with me." I pulled the rug over my head too. Sure enough, my cock and balls were glowing gold and swirling. As Bett moved her hand closer a sudden intense burst of radiant energy leapt between us. She wrapped her hand around me, and I gleamed brighter, swirling faster.

"Oh wow! Danny what is going on?" We pulled the rug down to our knees exposing my golden glowing, swirling and sparking phallus to the world. Just at that moment Jilly hopped up onto Betty's knee.

"Oh, Danny. Oh, you have some of my energy. I didn't think of that, but when I saw Bett with that in her mouth I couldn't help myself." She pointed at my golden shimmering cock.

"Jilly what did you do?"

"I had sex with Shiny, but you were in her jelly too; so when I gave my energy to Shiny when I came, you both took it too. I had not expected that. I glow and spark when I get excited. My energy created the bubble, along with my toolbox. You had better watch out when you orgasm." Jilly looked so innocent, smiling up at us, looking from Bett to me and back.

"What exactly does that mean, Jilly?" I looked at Bett who was busy studying my erect sparking, glowing, swirling golden penis in her hand.

"Bett? Are you even listening?" She looked at up at me surprised.

"Yes, sorry Danny, er what? I can't take my eyes off it. It is irresistible." Jilly was smiling but hadn't answered me.

"Jilly? Watch out for what?"

"Well, I'm not sure with human physiology, but it won't be a bad thing it will be a good thing. No harm to you or anyone else. Just a few sparks. I think I should go now, I'm sorry for making that irresistible. Bye." She pointed at my cock and quickly jumped down and skipped off to the lake. Bett had let go and had her hands a few inches on either side of my cock measuring how far the sparks would fly. My cock felt amazing when she was doing this.

"Okay Bett, spread em." I pulled her leg towards me she opened her beautiful legs. I slowly moved my hand near her and watched as tiny sparks flashed from my fingertips to her clit. Her eyes glazed in awe as she exhaled loudly.

I slowly lifted us off the couch and moved in front of her and she immediately climbed onto me. We both intertwined in utter pleasure as our bodies lit up and we climaxed with intense power almost immediately, lighting up the whole campsite. Shiny shone bright in the lake and the whole bubble shook as we came together. "*Oh, Fuck!*" Betty screamed in bliss. "*Look at us!*" Our golden light was lighting up outside the bubble all the way to The House of *Ra*.

Ω

Pete sat at the monitors unsure of what he was recording.

"Conner, check this out." he clicked on the intercom. Conner looked at the monitor in front of him but couldn't catch his breath to reply. Elle was leaning forward over his desk as he had just fucked her for a second time standing behind her. She was worn out but deliriously happy. The whole time she thought only of Danny's golden cock inside her, surging golden electricity through her body. She was happy and fulfilled and she loved Conner but wanted Danny. She too saw the golden glow in the sky on the monitor, lighting up the clouds and knew it was Danny. *What a fuck. What a cock.* She said to herself as Conner pulled out.

∞

I wasn't quite finished with Bett, and neither was she with me. She closed in on my open mouth as tingling sparks flew between our moist lips. She thrust her tongue in as she came a third time her whole-body arching and glowing bright as she tightened involuntarily on me. I immediately climaxed again as she cried out in ecstasy. Shiny was off the scale as the lake produced huge waves across its surface and was glowing gold just like us. Bett and I were floating high in the bubble, that we hadn't even noticed. We dropped down near the fire once more. Betty was so exhausted her eyes were closed and she was smiling but she was deep asleep. I gently floated us to the tent and released us onto the mattress.

Our warm rug flew in and snugly covered us. Bett quietly moaned as tiny sparks flew between us. I closed my weary eyes and fell fast asleep.

Ω

We suddenly opened our eyes. Where are we now? I sat up and looked around. Bett is lying next to me, not pregnant but stunningly beautiful as always, this is a different time again but when exactly. Bett smiled as I stood up, above her. I was golden and glowing and full of flickering sparks. She sat up.

Danny?

I don't know baby. I was lost. I'm sure it is our future. But it seems like a distant future. Way ahead. My mind is in turmoil. I perceived a huge city, not a cement city. One made of thought. It is beyond description. A living breathing city full of beautiful souls who are all connected telepathically. We are human but evolved. Ten thousand years have passed. Bett stood and took my hand. Our glittering sparks awakened the golden city. Our minds join and we share our love. We were separate entities but entwined with love. Ours is a peaceful world connected to a million others across the galaxy with time once more irrelevant. Our bodies are melting together in our minds as one and our world sighs with our bliss. All species suddenly united as two people feel love in the real world. Not in Sims or other revelations. Our love goes beyond boundaries; uniting all. We bow down humble and free. Our light is for all to feel.

∞ ∞ ∞

"Bett, babe wake up." She opened her big beautiful emerald eyes and smiled at me gorgeously. Her hands had tiny sparks as they slipped all over my chest, feeling my abs and down to my taut stomach and groin.

"Good morning my beautiful man." She moved under the rug and sat up on my thighs, running her fingers through my pubic hair, she laid my cock to one side so she could play with my balls. She lifted my still flaccid cock and bought it up close to her golden folds. It started glowing as tiny sparks flew between us. We watched enthralled with our own bodies. I hardened and glowed brighter as it stood nearly straight up. I ran my fingertips around her areolas with glittering sparks flying to her erect nipples. She shuddered and shivered with ecstasy, close to orgasming. Now I shivered. She gently lifted up and lowered herself onto me slowly. Bett moaned as she slowly started to gyrate on me lifting and dropping and trying ever so hard not to come. I was close too and she knew it. She leant forward and licked my lips. "Oh, Danny, I love you so much. Oh! Hmm!" She whispered. "*Oh, fuck yes!*" she cried out. I lost control and blew my load, lifting us into the air as we spun around sensually. I vigorously pumped into Bett; her hair standing on end with it sparking and glowing. I thrust in hard again as she scratched my back with her fingernails until I bled and bit my neck as a second orgasm took her. We flew out of the tent and up through the bubble into the cold air, then above the clouds into the warm morning sunshine.

"Oh, Bett stop, baby please stop." She slowly let go of me and watched me in utter joy as I floated in front of her in all my glory. All my muscles were taut and tight with my golden glowing semi stiff cock swaying this way and that in the breeze. She glided back into my arms and kissed me hard and hugged me tightly in an affectionate embrace.

"It's time for a cold swim Danny-boy. That was perfection. You are still pretty stiff but I'll fix that in the water." We zoomed down through the snow-covered dome and into the freezing lake. "Catch me, Danny." She tore off and I swam after her, but she slowed right down wanting me to catch her. She stopped in front of me and pushed back, reaching down and positioning me inside her. My hand slipped down to her clit as I started pumping into her from behind. We were both insatiable and could not get enough of each other. We both came hard and fast. Bett lifted us out of the water with her arms in the air like a ballerina as I kept making crazy love to her. Her body moved against me like a dance as she continually moaned. We both felt so alive and amazing. I kissed her sweet neck and shoulders and she pushed back hard squeezing my cock and came again, and I did too. I slowed down as we both knew we were done. Bett sighed loudly with great satisfaction and dived into the icy water. I followed her in. We swam around for a while as I lit the fire and Bett had our towels waiting for us as we stepped onto the shore.

Unlike Betty and Daniel, Conner and Elouise couldn't fly but they sure could fuck like rabbits. From the moment she had seen Danny's cock and somehow felt it in her mouth, she just wanted to fuck Conner; anywhere, anytime and anyway possible. She had stopped wearing panties and often stopped wearing her bra, opting for dresses she could drop off her shoulders and fall to the floor She served Conner's breakfast or dinner naked, so he knew exactly what dessert he was having next. He loved all the extra attention and sex. The sneaky sex too, like, when he was talking to Pete on the monitor and Elle was sucking him under the table or playing with herself off camera as he had a meeting; even pulling him into side rooms around *Ra* for a quickie. Conner had told Elle they were going to fly in Shiny to the Ishta's new planet. They would be naked with Bett and Danny in space. How could she do that? She knew she wouldn't be able to control herself as soon as she saw him, even if he was blurry. Christ just thinking about that made her horny.

Ω

Bett was thinking exactly the same thing too.

"Danny, if Elle is in Shiny with us, she won't stay in control. What will dad say or do? It will be embarrassing for all of us if Elle is suddenly having an orgasm. How long does it take to get there? We can't possibly block her the whole way, can we?"

"I don't have the answers, Bett. You are right though. She will likely lose it before we even get inside Shiny. We even find it hard not to fuck when we are in Shiny."

Hello Danny and Bett. The Octo were here. *Do you mind if we come into your bubble?*

"Hello Octo, please come on through." We stood and went over to the lake. Their craft came through the bubble silently and stopped just above the lake. The Octo jumped into the water and swam around joyfully before coming over to us. They stood in front of us smiling. *Hello friends, good to see you again so soon. We have some things to tell you. We have recommenced shifting clouds today with five hundred craft up there right now. We plan to carry on working for another thirty days. We should clear another ten percent bringing cover to sixty percent. Hathors are playing up across the globe. They can't see or feel you so they are messing with other survivors, ones they can easily influence. We can sense great turmoil in some bunkers. They are killing each other thanks to Hathors. They are feeding off their anguish. Hathors have summonsed The Grays from Zita Reticula to come to their aid. They will arrive in two hundred years. So, we need to act soon. Shut them down for good. We sense they can grow strong from what they are doing right now. They are devious and have future plans for you. They rely on you for their survival. As soon as we made Shiny for you, their power diminished. Shiny is vital to your survival against them, please look after her. Be wary of them always, they will use friends or family against you. They have had control of Conner and Elle before. If anyone around you dies, they will grow and become strong on your grief. Your love is very powerful, that is your strength. Do not let lust consume you. It feels good but it can also make you weak to them.*

"You are true friends to warn us of this. We thought they had faded away after the Grays were destroyed. We had no idea they were still destroying lives and feeding off human anguish. We will think of something. We fooled them before. We can do it again."

We sense turmoil over your trip to Connerelle Rage, do not concern yourselves, we are going too. We will take Conner and Elouise, they can orgasm with us as much as they like, we will enjoy that.' Bett and I looked at each other with relief. But they had not met the Octo yet, how would that go?

"What do you think Danny, will Elle be okay with that?"

"Bett, I can help her, if you don't mind, sharing me."

"Danny, you have been in her mouth and other places in her mind there is nothing you could do with her that would upset me, except actually fucking her. Just be careful of dad, it needs to be about him. Okay?"

"Bett, I got you. I love you."

I know that, Danny. I love you too"

"I would never compromise Conner either; just make her want him, covering any fear of The Octo. Okay?"

"That is fine Danny."

"She will see me again Bett, or feel me, but she won't freak out about The Octo."

"Danny, just make it quick and short, you are going to owe me for this."

"Bett, I got you babe. This will be safer than having her join us in Shiny."

"Yes Danny, I agree."

21

'Connerelle Rage'

W*hat do you think, can we take them?*
"Yes, Octo, we will make it work, you will fly into the hangar at The House of *Ra* and wait in your craft for them to enter. We will be there waiting with them in Shiny. I will smother Elle with thoughts of love and lust for Conner, so she is at ease with your appearance. Conner will be fine. He loves anything to do with off world beings like you. So just be relaxed and be yourselves."

Danny that is all we can ever be. We will look after them as soon as they are ready to leave. I looked to Betty. She was watching me intently.

"Babe, I've got this, I've got you Bett. Let's go Octo. Shiny, we need to go, are you good?"

Yes Danny, Ra, and then wormhole at Mercury then onto Connerelle Rage. We flew to *Ra*'s hangar with The Octo craft following right behind Shiny.

Bett had already told Conner telepathically of our arrival and that they would travel with our Octo friends. Conner was looking forward to meeting the Octo, but Elle was apprehensive and frightened. We entered the hangar and the outer door shut. Shiny stayed high and the Octo went down low and opened. Conner and Elle came in and took off their bath robes. Conner took Elle's hand and moved towards the craft. Elle froze and stood her ground. Bett looked at me and nodded. Then she quickly moved down my body stopping in front of my cock and started slowly pulling on it, watching it closely. All I did was let Elle see what Bett was seeing. Elle moved forward as if in a trance, her breathing was heavy and she looked straight at Shiny. Elle was picturing my gold cock in front of her face slowly becoming fully erect and throbbing.

They entered the craft gulping and gagging. The Octo were floating above them.

Hello Conner and Elle, we are The Octo, please be comfortable and feel free to couple if you desire as your love helps power this craft. We will fly to Mercury, enter the gate and then a quick passage through the wormhole and come out in the Connerelle solar system. Bett took me in her mouth and licked my golden cock with her tongue. Elle shook and grabbed Conner pulling him towards her. She reached down and took hold of his cock and started pulling, taking him by surprise just as he greeted The Octo.

"Hello Octo, pleased to uh, oh, meet oh, Elle! You." He looked at Elle and realized she was in the grips of an orgasm already. He moved around and pushed inside her pussy with his now hard cock. She moaned loudly as he suddenly came inside her. The Octo watched them joyfully and entwined themselves in each other. We hadn't even left the hangar as I came in Bett's mouth, she moved and climbed onto me and started gyrating fast.

Fuck, yes Danny! She cried out in my mind as she started to come. Our two craft glowed bright as we lifted into space. Shiny was moaning too. Bett's muscle squeezed me tight making me come a second time even harder. *That's it Danny, oh yes baby!*

∞

Elle's second orgasm was a result of Danny's second. She looked down and watched as his big golden glowing cock was going in and out of her and she was mesmerized. *That's it Danny, oh yes baby!* She said in her mind, squeezing Conner hard and making him cum a second time. I could hear her clearly in my mind.

We have arrived at the stargate, watch this. Shiny slowed down and lined us up in the center of the ring. As we approached, the stars inside the ring began to swirl around and disappear as a whirlpool of light enveloped Shiny. *Whoopee!* Shiny shrieked as we zipped along in a tunnel of light. I looked behind and could see The Octo were not far behind us.

Elle looked into Conner's eyes. She could feel his love for her, she kissed him passionately. *He is a good man.* She thought and hugged him tightly, squeezing his cock at the same time. *Fuck, Elle is full of surprises I didn't expect this ride would play out like this.* He thought to himself. *Her muscles are so tight on my cock, fuck she feels good. Fucking in a wormhole with octopi next to us is a first.* His mind was racing as fast as his heart.

Ω

Danny, Elle coped okay, she got stuck into dad as soon as they entered. She saw your cock again from my point of view. That is okay, it took her mind off everything else. Your cock is too nice to keep entirely to myself. I suppose that is what the wife of a porn star would say. She winked at me and squeezed my cock tight.

Ha-ha, a porn star, thanks Bett. Do you like watching my gold cock go in and out of you?

Oh yes Danny, I just love looking at it anytime. She relaxed and slid off me. Taking my cock in her hand she moved so she could see it better. She smiled and seductively winked at me.

Suddenly we shot out of the wormhole into normal space and all the stars reappeared. Space here looked quite different with a huge pink nebula that seemed to fill half of what we could see.

"*Oh, wow. How beautiful!*" Bett's eyes were wide with wonder. "*Your cock looks even more beautiful in this light.*" She started slowly going up and down its length with her hand. Elle gasped in wonder too as she could clearly see Danny's huge cock right in front of her, swirling and glowing gold and pink.

"*What an amazing sight!*" She exclaimed loudly in Conner's mind. He nodded.

"*It sure is beautiful Elle.*" He answered. Elle started trembling and tightened on Conner's cock. Conner realized she was about to have another orgasm, so he started pumping into her.

Oh! It is so fucking big and beautiful. Oh. Oh fuck! Conner and Elle came at the same time as Betty and I. I had slipped my fingers slowly down into Bett as she kept playing with me until I came right in front of her face. We were both amazed that nothing was coming out of me in the jelly like last time. Elle watched as I exploded right in front of her face in the jelly, and she moaned loudly. She could see the golden swirls on my pulsing shaft. My head swollen and fanned out as I kept coming with sparks flying from it. Elle couldn't take her eyes off this wondrous sight. She even moved her head forward trying to get it into in her open mouth. Her thoughts were suddenly disrupted by the Octo's warbling voice.

Connerelle Rage, ahead. We will be landing in a few minutes. As you exit, the jelly will form a protective suit around you, leaving your head bare. If you need to use the toilet any waste will be absorbed back into your body. The suit will last for about three hours. If more time is needed just come back in and out again. Please look at their beautiful planet below us. Their new city is ahead.

We heard all of that information too in Shiny. Bett released me as we looked down at this amazing city. It appeared to be made of ethereal crystals. We came to an open area where there were thousands of skins standing around waiting for us. They all looked up as we approached. We could hear them cheering in our heads as we landed. Shiny opened and we exited slowly so the suits could form on us. We threw up. The shiny golden suits were so skintight and slightly see-through. Unfortunately for me this made my cock and balls look even bigger. I looked at Bett and whistled, she looked like a stunning space girl.

"Wow Betty, you look fantastic in that."

"You look damn good yourself Danny, err there is no hiding that in a suit like this" I looked down.

"I will have to hold my hands in front."

"They won't cover that, Danny. Don't worry about it." I looked at her and shrugged.

"I'm not." We glanced over at Conner and Elle who stood there somewhat awkwardly looking at themselves. They came over to us. Conner grinned like a little boy.

"Look at us, bloody gold spacemen. What a flight, that wormhole was incredible." Conner suddenly noticed my cock and balls bulging in my suit. *Oh my god, he is huge.* Elle stood back a little shy in her suit, but she looked beautiful. Her curvy body was very sexy in that suit.

"What do you think Elle? You look fabulous." Bett complimented her. She blushed. *Danny, dad thinks you're huge. I'm trying to make him think he was mistaken.*

'Bettdanny, Connerelle, Octo welcome to Connerelle Rage. We are honored to have you all here. Please let us show you around our new city called Dannystarr.' They named their city after me how sweet, and they can speak out loud now. No sunglasses, tiny stars in their eyes and all dressed in jumpsuits. Conner spoke up.

"Thank you, Ishta, Lloyds and Shins it is our honor also to be invited here. We are all so grateful for the aid you gave with our planet. Danny has told us of your amazing deeds. I am glad you have put our skins to good use. I'm sorry I know your names, but I do not know what you call your race."

'Conner, we are humans, were humans. We left the Earth for the stars some twenty thousand years ago. We merged with AI and became pure energy beings. We refer to our race now as The Starborns.'

"You say you left Earth twenty thousand years ago but we had no civilizations that advanced then, we only had hunters and gatherers." Conner replied. "How could you possibly travel in space?"

'Conner your planet has many secrets that remain hidden to the current civilization. We are not the only children of the Earth that live out here in space. We know of dozens who have evolved into different species all together. Some of the visitors to Earth are also children of the Earth.'

Elle was staring at my bum; I could feel her lustful eyes on me. Conner was nodding.

"Wow that is fascinating, we have no idea really; we are like kids who haven't been taught the truth at school."

'Connerelle some of the secrets were hidden on purpose. Hathors have hidden so much from you on purpose so they can control you as a species and that is why we left. They still try to control us out here. Their minds combine and she becomes all powerful. You Bettdanny are the first to have killed one. We will do anything to help you stop their control of others. They are weak, together we are stronger and together we must act. I spoke up.

"We agree, we stopped them at Europa, they had no idea until they lost. I want to confront her face to face; all of us together."

'That would be very dangerous. In person their mind is very strong. They fool you with their weak bodies. Do not forget they are ancient and once ruled a thousand worlds. Even if we could enter their prison, it would be hard to know if it is really them in front of us. We should consider all options, and plan well. Please follow us as we show you around.'

Your city is glorious. Do you grow these crystals or mine them? The Octo asked. Conner and I were in front next to Ishta and the Octo. Bett and Elle were following us with Lloyds and Shins. Now Bett and Elle were both watching my bum as I walked. After all I looked practically naked in the suit; they could see all my muscles flexing as I walked. Bett glanced at Elle who blushed and Bett winked at her and shrugged. Then she went back to watching me. So did Elle.

'We grow them using the rocks of this planet. Our machines can shape them into any shape we desire. These crystals enable us to remove our skins if we wish while we are inside the buildings. Here are some of our machines, you would call them robots.' They were much like robots on earth but way more streamlined and sophisticated.

'This is our quiet room; citizens can enter to relax from thought waves. Our telepathy is highly advanced and can be overwhelming at times so the crystals in these walls simply cancel out our thought waves. It is very relaxing to shut off for a while.'

"Is this how you sleep?" I asked.

'Yes, it is. We can also power down while we are in here. It is very relaxing. This leads to our power generators which run off thermal energy of this planet.' Conner looked at him.

"That powers *Ra* too, it is very efficient."

'Yes, that is correct, and it has unlimited supply. Here is our feast hall' We entered a huge empty room that had one long table big enough for the twelve of us.

'Please understand, our citizens are not being rude, but we cannot eat more than once a day. It is not food but a charge of energy, if we have too much it has the same effect as being drunk on alcohol. We all fasted today and rested so we can feast with you. All food and beverage we serve you today has been certified safe for all of you, so please enjoy. It is the best our planet has to offer. We must remove our garments to eat, we hope you don't mind.' They moved off to one side and exited the skins through the eye sockets in a flash of light. The skins fell to the ground like rag dolls. Elle stepped back in shock. It was time to do my thing. I casually turned so Elle could see my groin clearly. She instantly forgot how terrified she was from seeing that. Her eyes fixed on my cock under my skin-tight suit. I carefully turned so Conner couldn't see and Elle could only just see it. Conner was busy looking at the Starborns to even notice where Elle was looking and Elle moved so she could see me better. *Oh god, he may as well be naked.* She thought to herself. Bett heard Elle's silent thought and glanced over. *Watch this, Danny.* I looked at Bett and shook my head. Too late. She used her mind and gently squeezed both of Elle's soft nipples. They were instantly rock hard and poking through her suit and they were big and obvious.

Oh, shit Bett, really? Elle moved her hand up to her hair as if to adjust it and tried to push her nipples in with her forearms. It didn't work.

'Please take a seat, your food is on its way.' We moved to the table.

She cannot sit next to me Bett. Betty moved in between us and sat down quickly; I sat next to her and The Octo next to me. Elle was next to Bett and then Conner and the Starborns.

Once again, we feast together old friend. The Octo said in his warbled voice.

"Yes, my friend, is there much wildlife on this planet, or fish?"

We have no idea Danny, this is our first visit too and here comes the food. A row of mechanical men arrived with large trays and placed them on the table.

'Please enjoy friends; our machines have prepared all of this. They caught the fish and the animals; the plant life has been cultivated on our farms. These are genuine Wagyu beef steaks; all those stories of cows being beamed up by spacecraft were true, it was us. We have full farms of Earth animals. The liquid is whiskey and grape wine here.' I was sure the Ishta were smiling when he mentioned the cows being beamed up. The Octo's tentacles were moving in every direction without getting in anyone's way. Bett and I loaded up. There was one bowl of live food; it was the little jellyfish and crustaceans from Europa. Yum.

"Conner, you must try the live food, you won't be disappointed." Conner reached out and took a little crab and inspected it before crunching down. His face lit up as he nodded at me and grabbed a jellyfish, inspected it and popped it in his mouth.

"Delicious Danny, the flavor and textures are astounding. Is this the little jellyfish you had sucking on your knob?" *Uh, oh. Don't get her wound up Conner.* I thought. Bett looked at Elle quickly; she was squirming in her seat with her mouth full of Wagyu beef. She was moaning with pleasure. Conner looked at her. *Is she coming?* He thought. She was doing her best to cover it. Bett and I knew she was.

"Is the steak that good Elle?" He patted her on the knee. She was shaking slightly as she nodded.

"Hmm, yes, it, mmm, it is delicious." Elle could barely talk. Betty piped up.

"Yes daddy, one of those tasty little suckers was going to town on Danny's knob. Put one on your finger, see how hard they suck.'

Damn it, Bett. Lucky, she has that suit on, she is squirting like mad. Conner had one on his finger and put one on the back of Elle's hand. Elle squealed but not from that. Bett had pictured the jellyfish on my cock. Elle squealed again seeing it on Danny's huge golden cock. She immediately put her lips around the Jellyfish and sucked it off her hand. Conner was laughing hard at Elle; he had no idea. She moaned; it was delicious so was her orgasm. I took a steak, and it was glorious. I looked at Conner who was about to put a slice in his mouth. I nodded my approval pointing to my steak. His eyes went wide with pleasure. He finished chewing and swallowed.

"Fuck, this steak is incredible." He said nodding, looking at me.

"Ishta this is the best steak I have ever eaten; I think we all agree it is beautiful meat and it is perfectly cooked. How do you teach them to cook so well?" I asked Ista.

'Simple, they watched every cooking show on your TV programs that have been beaming out into space for seventy years. They memorized everything they watched.' Conner looked at them, lost in thought.

"Is that how you learnt English so well?"

'Connerelle, we learnt all languages perfectly. You are a strange variant of humans who have no universal language for the Earth. Every language on your planet is a variation of your original one language that you lost. It is another means for Hathors to control you. Language, diverse culture, and religion segregate you, so you are not united as one. Easier for them to control and easier to pit you against each other in wars so they can feed.'

I glanced at Elle; she had calmed down but was now looking at my groin, trying to see my cock. I spread my legs and scratched my shaft. That nearly did it again. Bett looked at me.

You're the fucking ratbag Mr. Starr. You want her to come again? I can do that for you.

No, Bett, leave her, she is already excited again.

So, you are teasing her then? Bett leaned forward blocking Elle's view; in case Conner saw her. We had all been eating and chatting for nearly three hours and had finished our desserts which were fantastic. I looked at Elle; one of her nipples was poking out of her suit. I frowned, what? I looked down at myself, my cock had put a tear in my suit and it was nearly ready to fall out. Bett could feel my rising anxiety and looked down at me then saw Elle's nipples.

"Excuse me, dad we need to get back to the ships to renew our suits, they are dissolving." Bett said with alarm. Conner looked down and he had a small tear as well near his groin. Then he noticed Elle's nipples. Not wanting to embarrass her, he said nothing. He stood up covering his rip.

"Our suits are falling apart we need to leave, sorry, your hospitality has been exceptional Starborns. Thank you so much." The Starborns re-entered their skins in a flash. Elle saw the rip exposing my cock. Conner pulled her forward his cock was nearly hanging out now but she hadn't noticed him. My cock was entirely swinging free as both of Bett's nipples were free. Conner walked faster as Elle's breasts were now fully exposed. They remained walking in front of us so we couldn't see. But we knew anyway. Elle's butt crack split apart and Bett and I struggled not to laugh. I looked down and my suit had all but fully dissolved and Bett had a few strands still covering her crotch. Elle glanced back at me and saw my cock swinging free. Her heart raced.

'Thank you all for coming here; we have really enjoyed your company. Thank you Connerelle for all the skins. Thank you, Octo, for taking in our people. Thank you Bettdanny for your brilliant plans against Hathors, and thank you for reducing their control by taking one out completely. We are glad you are with us against them. Thank you. Let us know your next plan Bettdanny. We are here for you. You are all welcome anytime on Connerelle Rage. We will talk soon.'

We thanked them profusely. We arrived at our craft where The Octo entered first followed by Conner who didn't say a thing for he was too embarrassed. Elle stopped and turned to us; she was not shy at all sharing her naked beauty with us.

"Thank you, you beautiful people. I love you both, see you soon." She entered the jelly and gagged. She had grown some more. She grabbed Conner's hand and squeezed it tight. She moved closer and kissed him, her voluptuous breasts pushed up against him, her tongue enticing Conner. He was getting hard again but she was looking outside at us, totally naked saying goodbye as she was ready to let go.

"Come on Bett, let's go." We turned to Ishta, Lloyds and Shins, fully naked we waved goodbye to them. They waved back. We entered Shiny and immediately gagged. Will we ever get over that sense of drowning? She shivered.

Good to have you inside me once again, Danny and Bett. Home to camp or Ra?' I looked at Bett, she shrugged.

Home to camp please Shiny, take us low over this planet first please, we have a lot to think about. Conner and Elle will need some time too. Bett snuggled up to me. We looked down as Shiny lifted and flew around Connerelle Rage. It was a beautiful planet young in its development but very stable. Shiny lifted above the atmosphere heading off to the stargate. Bett looked at me.

Danny, Elle is stunningly beautiful, her body perfect. I could turn for her.

Is this a test Bett? She is beautiful, baby, but I have you. It is fun messing with her; she has a hair trigger that sets off with no abandon. Honestly, I love that, but she is enjoying herself now more than ever. She has a beautiful soul and Conner is madly and blindly in love with her. Her obsession with me is harmless, you can see that. She loves Conner and I love you.

Oh, Danny you are perfect, aren't you? That is the response I wanted to hear. Bett took hold of me and kissed me passionately. My hands moved all over her body, exploring everything, she felt electric as we made love as we neared the wormhole.

Ω

Before entering the jelly, Elle looked back at Bett and Danny, she felt she had to. They stood there so perfect, so naked. Their golden glistening bodies were in perfect proportion. Betty was gorgeous, curvy, full breasts with a little pregnant stomach and sexy snatch. She could turn for her if Danny and Conner didn't exist. Her simple goodbye was much more than that. She knew he was naked. She had to see him again for herself. Not in her mind. Danny did not disappoint. His cock was huge, golden and so enticingly erotic. She took one last look before entering the Octo craft. Gulping, gagging and grabbing Conner's cock as she entered. He gasped in surprise.

"Come here big boy." She whispered sexily in his ear. He obliged pulling her into him, running his hands all over her stunning body. The Octo were instantly aroused too. Elle was in her happy place. Fantasizing about Danny and pushing Conner's cock inside her as she looked out at Danny's huge cock as he said goodbye to the Ishta.

We soon arrived at the stargate, Conner, Elle and the Octo entered first, then we followed. We entered the wormhole with Betty pushing up tight against me and moaning deeply. My body went into absolutely overdrive. My hands grasped her hips and I loved her in Shiny's jelly. She responded by grabbing my cheeks and pulling me in hard. She was always in control and she knew it. She sat up on me and then looked down to watch my golden rod flash brightly as she moved sensually back and forth. We just couldn't get enough of each other. We moaned in unison in the jelly as Shiny shone brightly spinning through the wormhole.

Ω

We could feel Conner and Elle's sexual excitement as they made torrid love in the wormhole both insatiable and off the charts. These Octo craft intensified sexual desire tenfold especially while hurtling through space and they thrived on it too.

22

Finding Our Way Ahead.

Ω

We shot out of the wormhole next to Mercury right behind the Octo craft. Bett tensed on me and started to vibrate our exhausted bodies in time with Shiny. My body started shaking too. Finally, we slowed as our familiar stars reappeared in the sky. We followed The Octo down to the surface of the Earth. Queensland's weird coastline was below us. We silently dropped down through the atmosphere. They went left at Taxi; we went right and came to our snow-covered bubble.

"Stop here, please Shiny." She stopped above the bubble.

"Bett look down, what does this look like?"

"Oh, Danny it looks like the biggest ice-cream I have ever seen."

"That is exactly what I thought, too. Okay Shiny, take us in." She dropped down above our lake.

"Thanks, Shiny, awesome as always. We have more work to do tomorrow." We exited and threw up the jelly that had filled our lungs and dove into our cold lake. Shiny slipped beneath the waves and Bett summoned the shower gel. We swam around for a while, warming and relaxing our bodies and then we washed. We floated up as our towels zipped around us, efficiently drying our skin. As we floated to the couch, I stoked the fire and soon had it burning well. Jilly was watching us from the couch. "Hi Jilly."

"Hi Danny, hello Bett good to see you. I love watching you fly." She smiled as we landed next to her.

"Hello Jilly, good to see you too." Jilly jumped onto Bett's knee and tightly hugged her. As Jilly's little hands neared Bett's breasts sparks flew from Jilly's fingers to Bett's nipples. Jilly pulled back forgetting she had charged us with her energy in Shiny.

'Oops, sorry Bett.'

"Oh, come here Jilly, that doesn't hurt, it feels good." Bett pulled Jilly in against her chest, the tiny sparks covered Jilly and they both glowed. Tiny arcs of energy were jumping between Bett's leg and mine where they were close. Our bodies glowed brightly and shimmered in a dazzling golden hue as we felt an electric buzz surging through us. It was erotic and soothing and highly addictive. My cock soon stood straight up and lit up brightly.

"Oh, Jilly perhaps you should jump down now, you are making us both highly aroused all of a sudden."

'Oops, I'm sorry Bett. This was the first time my kind has shared our energy with humans. We, together, are unique.' She jumped down onto the sand blinking rapidly and smiling up at us innocently.

"Yes Jilly, we are certainly that. Whew, I need a drink. Would you like one?" I said staring at my sparkling glowing semi hard cock.

'Absolutely Danny, what we shared before was different to anything I have felt before. My little hearts still beat fast and my body is buzzing.' Bett patted Jilly on the back, smiling at her and looked back to me her eyes drifting down in fascination at my still glowing member.

"Jeese Danny, that rod of yours, lit up so brightly just then and the swirls are so pronounced. You must be full of her electricity it nearly filled the bubble with light." She leant down and licked it like a lollypop smiling up at me as I sighed.

"Bett, I think all of *Ra* saw that glow." I answered, trying to relax.

∞

"Conner, that golden light just filled the screens again." John informed Conner on the intercom. Conner acknowledged by a double click just as Elle rolled off him utterly exhausted. She had climaxed so intensely; she was buzzing with excitement and had enjoyed Conner immensely.

I Skolled my JD and poured another. Jilly was carefully watching me, still unsure if everything was okay with me. "Relax Jilly, I'm good. We were taken by surprise by your sparking energy gift that's all. Your energy is wild. We don't understand it, but it feels great." Bett nodded. Her eyes were glassy and distant she was ready for bed.

"Jilly I'm going to take Bett to bed now; she is really tired, okay?"

'Yes, that is okay, I need to eat and then sleep too. Goodnight Danny and Bett.' Jilly jumped up and skipped off to the lake. I lifted Bett off the couch and we floated into our tent and landed softly on the mattresses. I pulled the rug up and Bett nestled in to me. We were soon asleep.

Ω

A new dawn greeted my eyes as I awoke. I stood and went to the tent flap. The pyramids of Giza were right outside our tent, the power flowing from these behemoths was incredible. The forest outside was wet with rain. The Lioness's power was evident everywhere with the Sphinx off to my left. Her huge lion head was looking up towards Leo in the night sky. I looked down at Bett who was slowly stirring from her sleep. She moaned and looked up at me.

'Oh Danny, come back to bed. I looked to the sky;, too late Bett, it was filled with hundreds of flying craft that I did not recognize. Round flat saucer shaped craft. Our time was limited.

'Bett, watch out, this is not good. They are here for us. We are dead.' Giza was doomed; a forest to a desert in mere days. Destruction from the skies was overwhelming. North Africa will be transformed in weeks. A ten thousand year civilization lost beneath the consuming sands. Hathors were way too strong. Bett and I burned to a crisp. Our lives lost in that timeline. The pyramid's power destroyed. Hathors menacingly laughed.

'Oh, our pathetic children, you will never realize your full potential. Thank you for the sexual entertainment and your food. See you next life.

∞

Oh, but we finally had realized though. I stirred and Bett had moved against me, her electric body, awakening me. *Hathors, you have no real power now. We are strong against you. I hope you are ready for our retribution. You will be ours. Your rule on Earth is over and it is soon time for solitary confinement.* I looked across at Bett; was that dream really set twenty thousand years ago? I believed it. *Show that to mainstream archaeology.* I thought.

"What Danny, show what? Did we die again in another time? I couldn't wake up fully. I only had glimpses of that life." Bett was barely awake. I pulled her tenderly towards me.

"Bett, our deaths have not been in vain. We have grown more powerful than that Hathor bitch. Our love is stronger than ever before. Bett, I think we have the answers to contain their control."

"Danny, what are you talking about? What have you worked out?"

"Bett, the future, our future lies in our past. We need to see more; our past holds the answers to our future. Our dreams hold the truth. We can defeat her, but we will need to die a thousand times to piece it together. The clues are there I know it Bett and what about Isis, who is that? She seems very important, lurking in the back of my mind."

"Danny, darling, I can't do that, live through a thousand deaths. One or two are bad enough. Danny. Danny?"

"Bett, I'm sorry, but we probably already have. I get it babe, I feel you. The answers are there, we can find them eventually. In the meantime, we have a whole lot more to do for humanity. Our duty is not over yet. Today we need to check on survivors and see if we have missed anything. Tomorrow, we disperse clouds for weeks possibly. But we do need to explore our past to work out Hathors weakness. She needs to fear us now. She or they are still killing us, people we are trying to save. We need to find them and save them from her. Fuck her. I will confront her if I need to. I don't want to, but I will. You okay with that Bett?"

"Oh, Danny, I trust your decisions completely. Do you want to go now? I'm ready, I don't care for eating. Let's do our stuff Danny."

"Shiny, are you ready?" Our lake glowed as Shiny lifted from the depths; she sat ten feet above the water and came to the shore majestically. *I'm totally ready for anything you can throw at me. Let's do this.* She sounded like me. Good, let's do this together. Bett and I lifted out of the tent and entered Shiny, gulping, gagging, nearly drowning but soon accepting the gift of her special jelly. Shiny shivered in appreciation. She always loved us inside her. We held hands and looked down as our lake shrunk beneath us.

"Shiny, slow around Australia, let's see how our survivors are doing there."

Danny. The bunkers here are not sophisticated, many are stocked for only a few months and are nearly out of supplies. They are small and dispersed. The Aussies never expected this to really happen. We could set up a few containers in areas with more bunkers so they can access them.

"Okay Shiny let's do that; anything we can do is better than nothing." The next eighteen hours we shifted containers all over Australia to areas we thought could benefit. We planted the thought of the containers nearby so they would look. We made sure they were open and given with our love. We felt their appreciation. They had no idea who we were, we told them we were Queenslanders, they felt our love and we knew they did. Some of the outback towns fared much better than the big cities. Big old pubs with huge basements that locals sheltered in for the first few weeks They had raided the local shopping centers, stripping them clear of food. We arrived with ten full containers of food for them.

Initially they had raised rifles towards Shiny. We flooded their minds with love and hope.

We are your friends. We have food and drinks for you. We are here to help. Bett would say this into their minds.

"But who are you? Where are you from?" They would yell up at Shiny.

We are Betty and Daniel; we live in North Queensland near Charters Towers. We have been gifted this craft to assist all we can. These containers are full of food. Please enjoy and stay safe. We will return to make sure you are okay and meet you in person one day. Please help each other get through this.' This routine was repeated over and over.

Shiny, please take us to the ship community; we will stop for some more containers on the way. Bett was looking at me as she moved steadily closer. Her hand was gliding down my leg to my cock and her lips were begging to be kissed. I obliged and kissed her hard, my tongue going in deep. She gasped and squeezed me tight, making me stiff.

Yes Danny, Ship City. Oh Bett, your passion is so intense. You both feel incredible. Bett slid around me, upside down in the jelly, and pushed my cock inside her. She moaned loudly, pulling me in with her muscles and long legs wrapping around me. *Oh, she is flying.* We lasted about fifteen seconds before coming intensely together. Bett hugged me tight, her head buried in my bearded neck.

I love you so much Danny. Bett pulled back and looked me in the eyes.

I know baby, I love you too. She smiled and moaned, her muscles contracting on my cock as she came again. She pushed onto me, driving me deep. I let go a second time, grabbing her hips.

Betty baby! Shiny shivered as her own orgasm took over as she glowed brightly and shook all over.

Uh, food containers up ahead. That was amazing. Oh. Bett and I sifted through the piled-up containers, finding thirty. We silently and effortlessly lifted them. Shiny headed to the ships that we had relocated over two thousand miles away. We came up to the ships that we had arranged in circles. Three circles of ten cruise liners arranged in a huge triangle. We came in low and slow, announcing our presence telepathically.

Hello friends we have more food and water for you. Please share it wisely amongst all. We can bring more as required but this will not last so you need to start preparing the ground for crop. We can provide the seed. Find any animals you can for meat, but they are scarce. We can get some rabbits for you to breed and possibly chickens. We can help but you need to work out how to provide for yourselves. Please stay united. We want you all to survive. We will do everything in our power to help you. Our love goes out to you. You are all so strong. We cannot stay, we are sorry but there are many we still need to help. We must go now. We carefully placed the containers in equal spacing around the settlement. Our minds were full of love, appreciation and wonder reflected from them.

∞

Shiny lifted slowly glowing brightly. The people were cheering us and waving as we left. For them it was a blessing. They had been saved by these unknown benefactors who cared for them. They were a couple of Aussie's in a spaceship. It made no sense, but nothing did anymore. They knew they would have frozen to death where they were. Now there was a feeling of community. People helping each other and they had someone looking out for them. That was the best part; the uniting factor. All they felt was love it was beautiful and warming. This community was made up of all nationalities that learned to communicate through necessity. Their benefactors had bought much needed food and safe drinking water. They had bought camping gear and rugs and batteries and a container full of tools for farming. They started digging and turning soil and preparing it for the promised seed.

Mushrooms were everywhere and when cooked correctly tasted like meat. They made soups and stir fries, sautéed them and they were healthy. Most of the survivors lived off mushrooms mixed with canned food, noodles or pasta. The survivors started to send out hunting parties not to kill but capture for breeding any animal they could find. They were sparsely spread but they found some water buffalo, deer, wild turkeys and lizards. One day they came upon a cave full of goats that they rounded up and took back to the cruise ship settlement. This was a great start.

When they came to a building still standing, they would search for clothing or anything useful. Often taking everything they could carry. Buildings still standing were a rarity though. Often the contents of buildings were burnt or water damaged. On occasion they would find bodies, lots of bodies huddled together these poor souls were looking for salvation but found nothing but death. It was tragic but the survivors moved on. These bodies were shells, left over from humanity that had left. They would be absorbed back into the earth along with everything valued from the twenty first century the third Millennium. All the high rise buildings were out of bounds as they were deemed unsafe and avoided.

But this was a new dawn, a new horizon waited. Survivors were full of optimism. Thanks to Bett and Danny. Love and peace surrounded the globe and the Hathors were furious. They searched for disarray and angst but struggled to find it. Love was consuming the planet. Betty and Daniel remained invisible thanks to Shiny. Hathors became more frustrated and they struggled to feed. The lives they destroyed in the bunkers provided little nourishment without Pleione's help.

23

Hathors Deceptive Plan.

∞

*M*y sisters, we need a plan. Our children have deceived us. They killed Pleione and destroyed our Gray fleet. They hide in the Octo craft zipping around undetected. How is this possible? If we are not careful, they will destroy us. Their power now is beyond ours. We understand that now but cannot let on to them how strong they are. They will end our bond which will kill us. We cannot allow that. Sisters we must stay united and strong our children cannot take control of us.

We need to follow a different path, one of empathy and retribution. Try to fool them into trusting us, sharing their love with us again. Meanwhile we must take over a friend from Ra maybe one of the bar girls to woo Danny. We have to anger Betty or turn Conner against Danny. Then bring Elouise into a threesome as Conner's rage will consume him. If he kills Danny then Betty's pain will be unfathomable. Our strength will grow unbounded. If he kills Elouise our strength will double and Betty will hate Danny and Conner and this will destroy her. It is a win, win scenario. We need to talk to them. We need to show how devastated we are, how vulnerable and defenseless we are. With all their love around it should be easy to fool them. Find me a girl to seduce Danny and enhance her if we can without the Grays. Betty will feel betrayed. Elouise is full of that shit jelly that inhibits us and Jilly is protected now too so we need to infiltrate them another way. We cannot wallow in sadness of loss and our own failure.

That will be our downfall. Danny and Bett should not be so strong. We need to work that out, how are they doing what they are doing? They seem to be showing their love and sexual joy to the whole planet but not to us, how is this possible? WE designed them, they are our protégé. Yet they seem to outsmart us over and over.

Sisters, hear me now. If we are not together, we will lose. I don't even know what that means we have never truly lost before. There are shadows on the horizon that are impenetrable to me. This is also a first. Our future is hidden from all of us. GIVE ME FUCKING ANSWERS!

ΩΩΩ

Shiny, please take us to the edge of the frozen zones. We must search for any survivors that we can help.

Okay Danny, I'm headed north towards the ice. Shiny swiftly headed away from the Cruise Community. We passed through thunderstorms and pouring rain, and then snowstorms where we couldn't see a thing. We searched and searched with our minds until we found a bunker with around two hundred people, barely clinging to life.

Quick Shiny we need to get back to our empty ships and food containers. She zipped back to the ships where we found a smaller one. We loaded it up with food and lifted it into the air. Taking it high to avoid the storms we raced back to the bunker. We lowered the ship gently next to the opening and we built a ramp quickly out of rocks, so they could enter easily. Betty called to them telepathically.

Friends we are here to save you, please get aboard the cruise ship. We will transport you to a warmer climate. Somewhere that is safe with other people. Please gather your possessions. Do not be afraid. We are Betty and Daniel we are from Queensland. Please we will look after you. The doors to the bunker opened slowly and three men came out with automatic rifles. They immediately saw the ship and then saw Shiny as she floated ten feet off the ground.

"Fucking aliens trying to abduct us!" They all fired at us. Bett and I ducked instinctively. Shiny glowed brightly as she absorbed the bullets. They fired again.

Shiny, take us out of range. She lifted straight up. *Listen folks, I am Daniel; I live in North Queensland, Australia. We have been given this craft as a gift to help humanity, if you get on the ship, we can fly you south to below the equator where it is warmer. Have a look at all the food we have left for you on board this ship. We will leave you for a few hours to decide. There are other survivors we will take you to them. We have others to help. We will come back later.'* Shiny swooped down slowly and headed west. The three men lowered their guns and looked at each other in bewilderment.

"Who the fuck is Daniel, anyway? Let's check out the food they talked about."

Danny, I sense some more survivors. There are only ten in a backyard bunker. It is solid and strong, but we could shift the whole thing. Just need to get them to trust us. Can you feel them, it is two families, they will listen. Should we get in the suits to meet them in person?

Yes Bett, that is a good idea. Let's suit up first and then let them know we are here.

Take us down please Shiny, suits please, not on our faces. How cold is it out there?

Okay, Danny it is 28 Fahrenheit. It is cold but bearable, invigorating. Good luck. Shiny opened and we exited slowly, the suits forming on us as we left. We threw up and wiped the jelly from our faces. The suits kept our feet warm on the cold ground. Bett called out to them.

Hello, please listen. I am talking telepathically to you. We are friends of humanity and we have been rounding up survivors and shifting them to warmer climates. If you stay here, you will not survive the long winter. The ice sheet will cover this whole area in the coming months. I am Bett and Danny is with me please trust us. Come out we are outside we have technology to shift your whole bunker safely to a community of over a hundred thousand survivors. You can feel I am telling the truth.' We knocked on the door; the bunker entrance was a steel panel on the fake rear section of their garage. We could hear bolts being undone. We stepped back about six feet with our palms open, smiling, oozing our love. The panel slid open; two men stood in the doorway hands on their side arms.

"Hi, I'm Bett, this is Danny. That is our craft called Shiny."

"Are, are you aliens?" The first man asked trembling.

"Oh, no we are Aussies from North Queensland." I stepped forward and spoke gently.

"Please believe us, we just want to save you, we have shifted a hundred thousand people already and we can save your families. We can lift your whole bunker; it is very strong. You just sit inside and hold on. The trip will only take twenty minutes. The start will be a bit shaky as we lift you but once we are in the air it will be fine, what do you think?"

"I think you are crazy enough to be telling the truth, pretty fancy suits you have there. Martha, come out here meet the spaceman and woman. Why are your faces gold if you are Aussies?" His hand stayed on his gun. Martha poked her head around the corner and let out a gasp.

"Hello Martha. That is a long story to tell, but this flying machine makes our skin gold after a while, some friendly aliens landed in our camp before the impact of the comet and gave it to us to help people. We have been doing just that for the last seventy-one days." Bett piped up.

"We will take you where it is warmer, there are nice people there. They have their own food and supplies and they have started farming already." Another head poked out.

"Come on out Alice, these folks are genuine, have a look at their beautiful suits and gold skin. My name is Robert, and this is my wife, Martha. This here is Benjamin and his wife Alice we have three children each inside.' He held out his hand to me. I shook it firmly, then Benjamin's. Martha and Alice shook Betty's hand. "Pleased to meet you two. I thought we were done for. How long is this big freeze going to last?"

"We are not sure, could be a couple of hundred years. Everything north of here is under thick ice sheets that are moving south. What would you like us to do, shift you or leave you alone?" They all talked at once in a little huddle, all nodding. They had agreed.

"Yes please, Danny and Betty take us to somewhere safe. If our bunker is sitting above ground, how will we get out?'

"We can mound some dirt up at the doorway, make a ramp for you, it will only take a few minutes. Please go back inside, shut the door and turn on your torches and hang on tight while we shift you.'

"What, now? Don't you have to prepare or something?"

"No, we are good to go, lift off in two minutes, okay?" They all nodded and went inside. We floated into Shiny; our suits being absorbed as we entered. Shiny had heard everything.

Cruise Ship Community Danny. She lifted to twenty feet and sat there. Bett was making me hard and moved around ready to mount me; she pushed me in as we snapped all the steel foundation rods and loosened the soil with vibrations. We cut all wires and pipes. I held Bett's hips as I pounded into her. We started to climax immediately as we lifted the whole bunker gently into the air. Our strength comes from within our love.

Let's go Shiny, we got it. Shiny was vibrating in time with us and Bett winked at me and smiled in erotic bliss. We flew the bunker across the skies and placed it gently near the ships. The locals looked on in wonder. We quickly shifted soil making a solid ramp up to the door and then we left to find another bunker.

We ended up shifting eighty bunkers and it was time consuming taking us three solid weeks. We were exhausted and needed to close our eyes.

Home please Shiny. Oh, I nearly forgot those other dudes with the automatic guns, take us there first. Shit, I said a few hours to them, it has been three weeks. Hope they are okay. As we arrived, we could tell something was amiss. There were dead bodies everywhere. *Bett, anything? Is anyone alive?*

Danny, I can't feel anyone. This was a massacre. They must have killed each other over the food. Lucky, we didn't relocate this lot. Danny look there one of the containers has bags of cocaine lying all over the ground in front. Did we cause this?

No Bett. How could we have known that was hidden inside? They didn't have to use it; they could have destroyed it instead. Not all people are good people. Your dad gave me a gun; I didn't go on a shooting spree, did I? Come on Shiny let's go. We lifted the container and the loose cocaine and all of their guns into a clearing and set it all on fire destroying it completely.

Okay Danny, let's go home. Bett was right though; lucky we didn't shift this lot.

∞

What are they doing now sisters? Moving people, really? They are too nice for their own good. This group here, they left them. They were shooting at Bett and Danny. Ha ha, good. Why didn't they go with our children? They didn't trust them? They are drug cartels and their families. Too bad they didn't go to the ship place, there would have been anarchy.

Quick Taygeta, there is cocaine there in that container, show them. Take over that bitch there and fuck her husband's friend. Let them get caught. Now sit back and feed on the fun. Bett and Danny can't stop this mayhem. They are all high as fuck, shooting and fucking each other. Hmm this is very satisfying and tasty.

Ω

Jilly we are back! Shiny called as we arrived. There was no answer. The bubble was up so *Jilly was here. Jilly we are here, where are you? Jilly? Jilly?* Shiny was frantic so Bett and I searched for her.

There on the couch, but she is not good, unresponsive, quick, land Shiny. Shiny zoomed in and landed next to the camp and we swiftly flew out and threw up, not wasting time washing. *Look a liter of Jack is empty next to her, but her skin looks terrible, I think she is dehydrated and stuck in hibernation. I can't tell if she is breathing or even alive.* Bett gently lifted her and carried her to the lake. Bett's hand was sparking up as she carried her. We walked out and dunked her in the cold water holding her little head and mouth just out. Bett kissed her. *Come on little one.* She begged and kissed her again. Suddenly Jilly flipped over in Bett's hand and she nearly dropped her. Jilly opened her bloodshot eyes, unsure of where she was.

'What's-up...?'

"Jilly, are you drunk? Did you drink a whole liter of Jack?" We looked down at her little face.

'Nope. Not me, that is too much. How am I out here? I was napping over there by the bottle.' She was okay, just very hungover and dehydrated. Bett did not want her swimming off just yet.

"Jilly, that is not good, that is way too much to drink; how long have you been lying by the bottle?"

'Ever since you left on that day...'

"Oh, Jilly, that was weeks ago, you were all dried up, how come you didn't die?"

'Oh, dah, that is how I hibernate, I dry out and shut down, nearly dead.'

"Well, you scared us, how are you still drunk?"

"I must have fallen asleep after the drinks. It is still in me. Sorry.'

"Look it is okay, you are older than us, I can't tell you what to do. But too much alcohol is not good for anyone."

'Okay, Jilly gets it. Not too much.' Bett released Jilly and she swam around joyfully.

Please excuse us Jilly we need to wash this jelly off. Jilly swam off in search of fish as Bett grabbed the gel that was hanging in front of her. I dived in and swam around relieved that all was well with our little friend.

∞

Sisters, I found her, the one who will fuck Danny's brains out. Her name is Rita, she already wants him. She has a jealous boyfriend. Perfect. Her mind is easily controlled too. It will be easy to make her appear as Betty. Elouise is protected by the Octo jelly, but we don't need to take her mind. We can just make her look like Betty to Danny, and she will do the rest not knowing it is real, she will think she is dreaming. When Conner walks in on them, we will feed, when Betty finds out about them both, the shit will hit the fan and we will engorge ourselves. Sisters this is perfect. Timing is everything, now we must wait for circumstance to fall in our hands. Our children will feed us generously. As six we can still be full Hathor. Celaeno, start now on Rita, meld with her and become her. Our time for Pleione's revenge starts now.

Ω

Bett washed herself and then dived in. I did the same and then followed her out to the camp. Our fire was going strong; the towels dried us as we briskly walked. Two whiskeys hung above the couch as we arrived.

"Danny, we need to see dad again, make sure everything is okay in Ra, maybe tomorrow?"

"Yes Bett, that is fine, I am up for that. Are you as tired as I am?"

"Oh Danny, my eyes are so tired, staying open in the jelly for so long. I need to close them." I looked into her eyes and they kept getting greener and her skin more intensely swirling golden.

"Bett, we need to sleep darling, come with me." I lifted us into the tent and laid us on the mattress. Bett curled up to me naturally and fell asleep instantly. I followed her in deep sleep soon after.

∞

Rita rolled off from Charlie, exhausted. Their sex had been so intense lately. She was insatiable and every time she thought of Danny while Charlie was pumping away, she would climax instantly. *That's not cheating, is it?* She thought. She leaned over and kissed Chuck.

"Goodnight darling." He moaned and rolled away snoring his head off. *Oh, great now I must listen to that all night.* She curled up facing away from him. As she drifted off to sleep, Chuck's snoring became cows mooing in a big grassy field. They all gathered around Rita watching her face and body slowly change into Betty. Rita lay motionless but she was a perfect copy of Betty.

∞

Look at her Alcyone, she is perfect, and she is so easy to control watch this. Betty quietly got out of bed and went to the bathroom and stood in front of the mirror naked. She put her hands on her hips, tilted her head and winked.

Perfect Celaeno, you are amazing she looks exactly like Betty, say something.

"*Come here Danny you Ratbag!*"

Oh, Celaeno she is perfection. Tomorrow Betty needs to go into the toilet before her shower with Danny. Rita will be waiting. Now change her back and let her go.

- - -

Betty's features rapidly transformed back into Rita. Rita stood for a moment wondering why she had come to the bathroom; she had a pee and went back to bed.

∞

Now how can you change Elouise, Celaeno? She has that damn jelly inside her.

Alcyone, I don't need to control her, just influence her appearance and put her in a trance, like she is sleeping she will do the rest. I'll show you.

- - -

Elle was having a swim by herself; she often did this to keep fit. She stopped in the water with her feet touching the ground. One hand slid down to her moist folds; Danny seemed to be floating in front of her. Her face and body slowly morphed; her features became that of Betty. She moaned as Danny moved closer with his huge golden cock pushing up on her sweet spot. Betty slid onto him and came immediately moaning loudly into the water. Betty lifted her head out of the water and shook her head becoming Elouise once more. Her body shuddered as a second orgasm shook her.

∞

I have no idea how you did that Celaeno, but that will fool Danny long enough. Perfect the stage is set for a fuck fest shoot-out. Thank you, sister for being so ingenious.

- - -

I opened my eyes and Bett's face was inches away, smiling gorgeously at me while squeezing my cock gently. She winked at me. I winked back; I had one hand cupping her breast and the other sliding down slowly to Bett's warm sanctuary. I sensually flicked her lightly a few times as I gently slid my fingers inside her. Her eyes widened and went cross eyed briefly as she moaned and shuddered and gripped hard on my cock. She moved around and tried to shove my cock in with my fingers but there was no room. I pulled my fingers away and thrust in. She came immediately. Her fingers dug deeply into my bum cheeks. I came explosively in a rush as we moaned and groaned together gradually slowing down and stopping.

"Oh Danny, you are fucking amazing. I love you baby." She slid off me and stood up. "Danny, I need a swim." She sprinted off and I jumped up, my cock still semi hard and raced after her. Bett was powering away swimming fast. I pushed myself; she was thirty feet away. We reached the other side and Bett was only ten feet in front.

"Wow! Danny you were super-fast then, come here." She wrapped her legs and arms around me and kissed me passionately. "You are the best baby." She reached down and pushed me inside her. She felt so fucking good. "Okay now swim back." I looked at her.

"Swim back, but don't drown me."

"Okay then, I got you." I rolled onto my back and kicked off. Kicking my legs furiously and swinging my arms back widely so I didn't hit Bett. She screamed in delight and came shuddering. I nearly lost it but held on. I swam faster and faster and Betty was lost in orgasmic override. Each kick of my legs would set her off. She had one orgasm after another in time with my fast kicking. She felt just incredible. We reached the shore just barely as I was totally spent. Our orgasms had been off the charts; I could hardly stand up, let alone breathe.

"Uh, oh, sorry. I won't be asking you to uh, swim me across the lake for a long while. That was exhausting but fabulous, my huge golden super-cock man." She panted, grinned widely and kissed me passionately. I hadn't said a word. Panting hard, I shook my head, looking into her eyes.

"Oh, baby. You are the ratbag. I love you gorgeous girl. We should go and dry off and get to *Ra* in time for lunch. Agreed?"

"Yes Danny, let's get a move on. We floated out of the lake our towels dried us as we went. Jilly was waiting for us at the fire pit. She was shaking her head at us.

'What was that all about? So many orgasms, both of you. The House of Ra couldn't keep up if they tried. I am exhausted just watching you. The lake is full of you Danny; I will swim in it to make me stronger like you. I go now to swim and eat a lot of fish, see you later.'

"Yes, see you later. We are going to Ra for a little while but will be home in a few hours. See you." We had a quick couple of drinks and called Shiny.

Good morning lovers, talk about going off, you both had me in rapture too. Ra now?

Yes Shiny let's go. We floated in and gagged as we entered. Shiny shivered and lifted us through the soot and snow-covered bubble.

∞∞

The hangar showers and toilets were locked from the inside and no one from *Ra* could enter. But two women were locked in there. Rita sat naked on a toilet next to her clothes. Elouise sat in a naked trance on a bench next to the pile of clothes left for Bett and Danny near the showers. Her mind was blank, apart from Danny's huge golden cock. Neither of them knew the other was there. Conner was busy with his engineers; they were having issues with a generator. He would be there for a while.

Shiny zoomed into the airfield. The huge hangar door swung open as Rita transformed into Betty perfectly. We floated out and threw up. Hand in hand we walked along the hall. Suddenly Betty heard Rita in her head calling to her from the toilets faintly.

"Hang on a second Danny, be right back." I leant against the wall and waited. Betty entered the ladies' toilets but there was no one there but she noticed two cubicles were closed.

"Hello?" She called softly and pushed the first door open. There were some clothes on the floor. She leant down to pick them up as an arm stealthily slipped around her neck swiftly and silently in an expert choke hold. Bett was unconscious in mere seconds. Rita checked Betty's pulse;

she would have about twenty minutes. Rita rubbed Betty's jelly all over her body and hair and quickly walked out with her finger on her lips.

I smiled as I saw her, *what is she up to?* Betty grabbed my cock and got on her knees and started sucking on my knob.

"Whoa! Bett, oh, we haven't even showered yet, uh." She looked up at me and shrugged, I was nearly there almost instantly, *fuck she is good!* She stopped and pulled me down pushing me onto my back on the cold corridor floor and sat down slowly but firmly, moaning as she pushed me all the way in. She started trembling so I grabbed her hips and thrust up hard as she buried her head in my neck and rocked fast, speeding me up. I closed my eyes about to blow. Bett knew it and sat up pushing down hard, her hands on my shoulders. Her tight fanny squeezing my cock hard as we both climaxed together.

"Fuck yes Danny, do it baby. Ugg." She came again in seconds. That didn't sound like Betty at all. I opened my eyes. Hathors big round eyes stared down at me, mocking me and laughing as I suddenly came again. Her big cow ears were furiously flapping as she rocked on me, her pussy squeezing the life out of my cock and her huge fur covered tits swinging madly.

"Hathor, leave Bett, leave her now!" I demanded as she took my semen. She hysterically laughed.

"Oh yes fuck me hard Danny! You're a great fuck! Uh, uh."

"Bett wake up, baby come back to me." Then I remembered that last time I kissed her to bring her back. Reluctantly I reached behind her head and pulled her down and kissed her as passionately as I could. She immediately changed; she slowed down, her movement becoming more erotic and sensual. My Bett was coming back to me. Now she really kissed me and fucked me like she loved me. I closed my eyes as we shared more strong orgasms together erotically. After a minute of continued orgasm, Bett said.

"Oh, Danny you are fucking amazing. Your cock is crazy and so gorgeous, oh yeah, thank you. I didn't expect oh, you to be this incredible." She whispered huskily in my ear. That didn't sound like Bett either. She sped up riding me. I opened my eyes as Rita squeezed down firmly on me. I moaned and came dramatically. I couldn't help but push up into

Rita as she sped up rocking faster. I gripped her hips tight and pumped into her. "Oh yes, Danny fuck me baby!"

Oh, uh Rita how? Why? Uhm. Uh. "Oh, fuck Rita!" I couldn't stop myself; she felt so good. We went on and on as she was consumed in another orgasm, shaking and trembling uncontrollably. One more orgasmic heave then she pulled back and my cum shot all over her chest. She grinned and rolled off me in a totally exhausted mess. She closed her eyes and fell instantly asleep.

"*What the actual fuck? Where is Betty? How did you get me like that Rita?*" I could hear the shower running just down the hall, I stood and ran to the showers totally confused. Betty was standing there washing her long hair staring at my hard cock and smiling gorgeously.

"Danny, get over here baby. It's okay." She placed her hand over my mouth to stop me from saying anything. Then she swiftly covered me in bubbles and rinsed me in a flash and pushed me gently up against the wall, kissing me with her tongue going deep. Her hand was tugging firmly on my stiff cock. She turned the shower off and dropped down taking me in her mouth and sucked like crazy.

"Oh, Bett, no baby stop, I need to tell you, oh... Rita..." But she felt so good. She looked up at me with my cock in her mouth and winked. I fucking lost it and ejaculated. She gagged and pulled away as she dragged me down on to the wet tiles and then swiftly climbed on top and pushed me deep inside her luscious inviting entry. She moaned as I hit her g-spot and climaxed immediately. I grabbed her beautiful firm breasts and squeezed sensually with my thumbs on her nipples. She started gyrating faster and faster. I climaxed a second time explosively as she cried out in utter ecstasy. She fell forward and started kissing me sensually in between her moans. Bett's wet body on mine was driving me wild. She pushed down on me as another orgasm racked her sexy body. I exploded a third time like crazy. She sat back up but it was Elouise, this time, not Betty. *Oh shit!* I came again instantly; this one went on and on. She cried out and shook like an obsessed woman engulfed in erotic bliss. She lifted her arms in the air and swayed erotically with her voluptuous breasts swaying in time as she stared into my soul. We climaxed repeatedly. Elouise leant forward and thrust her tongue eagerly into my mouth;

passionately I kissed her back. Suddenly she lifted off and sat with my balls hard up against her clit and my throbbing ejaculating cock in her hands.

"Oh, fuck me Danny. I want you all over me, uh." I opened my eyes but I couldn't stop and I pumped out even harder. My semen was going all over her. I winced with guilt at how amazing Elle felt. She was pushing my balls into her pussy with one hand, fucking my balls with her juicy folds and sucking and licking my tip at the same time. My cum was oozing out of her mouth and running down her chin and slender neck. *This was fucking insane.* Her eyes were locked on mine in utter ecstasy and pure lust.

∞∞

Eventually the real Betty woke up on the toilet floor. *What the fuck, who knocked me out so easily.* She pushed open the door to the corridor. Rita was laying naked in the missionary position. Knees up and legs apart, practically covered in cum and sound asleep. A pool of it was in between her legs. *Oh my god Danny, what have you done?* Betty suddenly heard loud moaning coming from the showers and she quickly raced around the corner just as Elle released my cock. She was covered in cum from head to toe, heaving hard from all of her orgasms. Elle sat back on the shower floor staring at my still stiff cock that stood straight up next to her.

"DANNY! What the actual Fuck? What have you done?" I looked up as Elle started rubbing my cum all over her body and sucking on her fingers. Her eyes were fixated on my stiff cock. *What the fuck just happened? Oh, shit I'm in huge trouble now. What have I done? I let Elouise fuck me and it was amazing...*

Bett ran into the showers. I looked up at her with total confusion on my face. Bett turned on the showers and started quickly washing the cum off Elle.

"Fuck Danny, good job. Elle darling, can you hear me. Elle, snap out of it. Elle!" Bett slapped her twice hard across her face. Elle's eyes focused on Bett squatting naked next to her. She looked at her sticky hands covered in semen and put a hand on her pussy, it was buzzing and dripping wet. She looked over at me, my golden cock still semi hard and dripping. Realization dawned on her and the gravity of what had just happened. She looked at Betty and started to cry uncontrollably.

"Oh, Bett, I am so sorry, I don't even know how that happened. I'm so sorry. Danny I'm sorry. Why was I even in here?"

"Danny! Get the fuck up, get yourself washed and get the fuck out of here please. What a fucking mess! Elle, honey, you need to stand. Let me wash all this off you. Let's get moving. Fuck Danny, how much? Elle can you squat we need to get Danny's cum out of you. Please excuse me." Elle squatted and Bett slid two fingers into her dribbling pussy as a mass of cum flowed out. Elle shuddered. Bett removed her fingers and held Elle tight as she moaned and ejaculated, flushing out most of Danny's cum. "It's okay Elle, I've got you." Bett washed Elle's hair and body thoroughly. I washed quickly and dried myself, threw some clothes on and walked out towards the tavern without saying a word.

* * * *

"Elle, here is your dress; you know it wasn't your fault, don't you. Hathors are responsible for this, I am sure. Where is Conner?"

"He, he was busy with the engineers. Bett. Thank you. I love you." She held Betty's face in her hands and kissed her on the lips.

"That is okay Elle; we will be good as long as Conner doesn't find out. He cannot know, he would kill Danny over this, or you, do you under-stand? It could really break him. Elle, please go to the lakes and have a swim I will meet you there later. Go!" Elle left in a daze and Bett raced around to Rita. "Rita wake up. Rita wake up!" Betty shook her hard, she stirred. "Rita, come on, you need to shower. Come on I'll help you." Rita was confused. What had happened, her pussy felt soaked.

"Is that cum all over me? Danny did that. He fucked me hard and I fucked him hard Bett, oh he's a great fuck you know. His golden cock is massive, fuck he knows how to use that! We had orgasm after orgasm and did it over and over! The best part was he knew it was me and kept going"

"Rita that is enough, please shut up." She pushed Rita into the shower and started washing her. "Rita, I need you to squat down, I need to get his cum out of you, okay?" Bett turned off the shower and they squatted; Bett slid two fingers into Rita's wet pussy and a mass of cum flowed out. Rita grabbed Bett's hand and pushed it further into her. One hand behind Bett's head forcing her mouth onto hers as her own fingers entered Betty's cunt. They both moaned. Bett struggled and tried to pull away. Hathor held her firm, her fingers moving fast, thumb on her clit and fingers at her g-spot. Betty moaned as she and Hathor climaxed together. Bett could not remove her fingers; Rita's muscles were so tight. Hathors tongue felt huge, as it swirled around in Bett's mouth.

"Come on Bett, you know you want this..." Betty remembered Danny kissing Hathor with passion to release the grip she had on her. She changed tactics and relaxed as she started moving her fingers sensually inside Hathor and kissing her passionately. They both moaned together. It was working. Hathor slowly relaxed and suddenly it was Rita kissing Betty with real passion now and Bett couldn't hold back. They climaxed together tumultuously on the floor. Rita spun around and pushed her pussy into Bett's face as she started to lick Betty's clit. Betty could taste Danny inside her and it drove her wild, she tasted so good. They came again, ejaculating over each other. Bett could hardly breathe. They were both groaning in utter erotic ecstasy fully engaged in each other on the warm shower tiles.

I looked down at the two women as they heaved and moaned on the shower floor; I kind of wished I had stayed for this as I slowly hardened.

"Come on ladies, that is enough, time to get washed up. You're lucky no one else walked in on you. I'll see you in the tavern Betty." I turned and left a wide-eyed Betty and a shocked Rita. They rolled off each other shaking their heads and stood up, then quickly showered without saying a word. They were totally lost in their own thoughts. Finally dressing they opened the door together to leave. Rita turned and kissed Betty passionately on the lips as they wrapped tongues briefly. Then as Rita ran off, she let out a soft moo. Bett stood there, staring after her. *Hell of a life, this one.* She thought.

It sure is Bett. I replied from the tavern skolling a shot of Sinatra.
The End... Of that moment.

By S.J. Rose

The Old Ones Saga

1. A Town Called TAXI.

2. TAXI, The House of RA.

3. TAXI, The Dawn of Isis.

www.ingramcontent.com/pod-product-compliance
Lightning Source LLC
Chambersburg PA
CBHW031200020726
47499CB00002B/427